ALFRED A. KNOPF
1915 · 100 YEARS · 2015

ALSO BY ORHAN PAMUK

The Innocence of Objects

The Naïve and the Sentimental Novelist

The Museum of Innocence

Other Colors

Istanbul

Snow

My Name Is Red

The New Life

The Black Book

The White Castle

Silent House

A Strangeness in My Mind

Being the Adventures and Dreams of Mevlut Karataş, a Seller of Boza, and of His Friends, and Also a Portrait of Life in Istanbul Between 1969 and 2012 from Many Different Points of View

A Strangeness in My Mind

Orhan Pamuk

Translated from the Turkish by Ekin Oklap

ALFRED A. KNOPF
New York Toronto
2015

THIS IS A BORZOI BOOK
PUBLISHED BY ALFRED A. KNOPF
AND ALFRED A. KNOPF CANADA

 Published in the United States by Alfred A. Knopf, a division of Penguin Random House LLC, New York, and in Canada by Alfred A. Knopf Canada, a division of Penguin Random House Ltd., Toronto. Originally published in Turkey as *Kafamda Bir Tuhaflik* by Yapı Kredi Yayinlari, Istanbul, in 2013. Copyright © 2013 by Orhan Pamuk. This translation originally published in hardcover in Great Britain by Faber and Faber Ltd, London, in 2015.

www.aaknopf.com
www.penguinrandomhouse.ca

Knopf, Borzoi Books, and the colophon are registered trademarks of Penguin Random House LLC. Knopf Canada and colophon are registered trademarks of Penguin Random House Ltd.

Library of Congress Cataloging-in-Publication Data
Pamuk, Orhan, [date] [Kafamda bir tuhaflik. English]
A strangeness in my mind : being the adventures and dreams of Mevlut Karataş, a seller of boza, and of his friends, and also a portrait of life in Istanbul between 1969 and 2012 from many different points of view : a novel / Orhan Pamuk.—
First edition. pages cm
ISBN 978-0-307-70029-2 eBook ISBN 978-1-101-87583-4
1. Street vendors—Turkey—Istanbul—Fiction. 2. Istanbul (Turkey)—Social life and customs—Fiction. 3. Istanbul (Turkey)—Social conditions—Fiction. I. Title.
PL248.P34K3513 2015 894'.3533—dc23 2015006769

Library and Archives Canada Cataloguing in Publication
Pamuk, Orhan, [date] [Kafamda bir tuhaflik. English]
A strangeness in my mind / Orhan Pamuk ; translated from the Turkish by Ekin Oklap.
Translation of: Kafamda bir tuhaflik. Issued in print and electronic formats.
ISBN 978-0-307-36126-4 eBook ISBN 978-0-307-36128-8
1. Street vendors—Turkey—Istanbul—Fiction. 2. Istanbul (Turkey)—Social life and customs—Fiction. 3. Istanbul (Turkey)—Social conditions—Fiction. I. Oklap, Ekin, translator. II. Title.
III. Title: Kafamda bir tuhaflik. English.
PL248.P34K3513 2015 894'.3533 C2015-903373-X

Photograph on page 585 by Ara Güler
Jacket art by Orhan Pamuk
Jacket design by Chip Kidd

Manufactured in the United States of America
First American Edition

For Aslı

I had melancholy thoughts . . .
a strangeness in my mind,
A feeling that I was not for that hour,
Nor for that place.

—William Wordsworth, *The Prelude*

The first man who, having fenced off a plot of land, thought of saying "This is mine" and found people simple enough to believe him was the real founder of civil society.

— Jean-Jacques Rousseau, *Discourse on the Origin and Foundations of Inequality Among Men*

The gulf between the private and public views of our countrymen is evidence of the power of the state.

—Celâl Salik, *Milliyet*

Contents

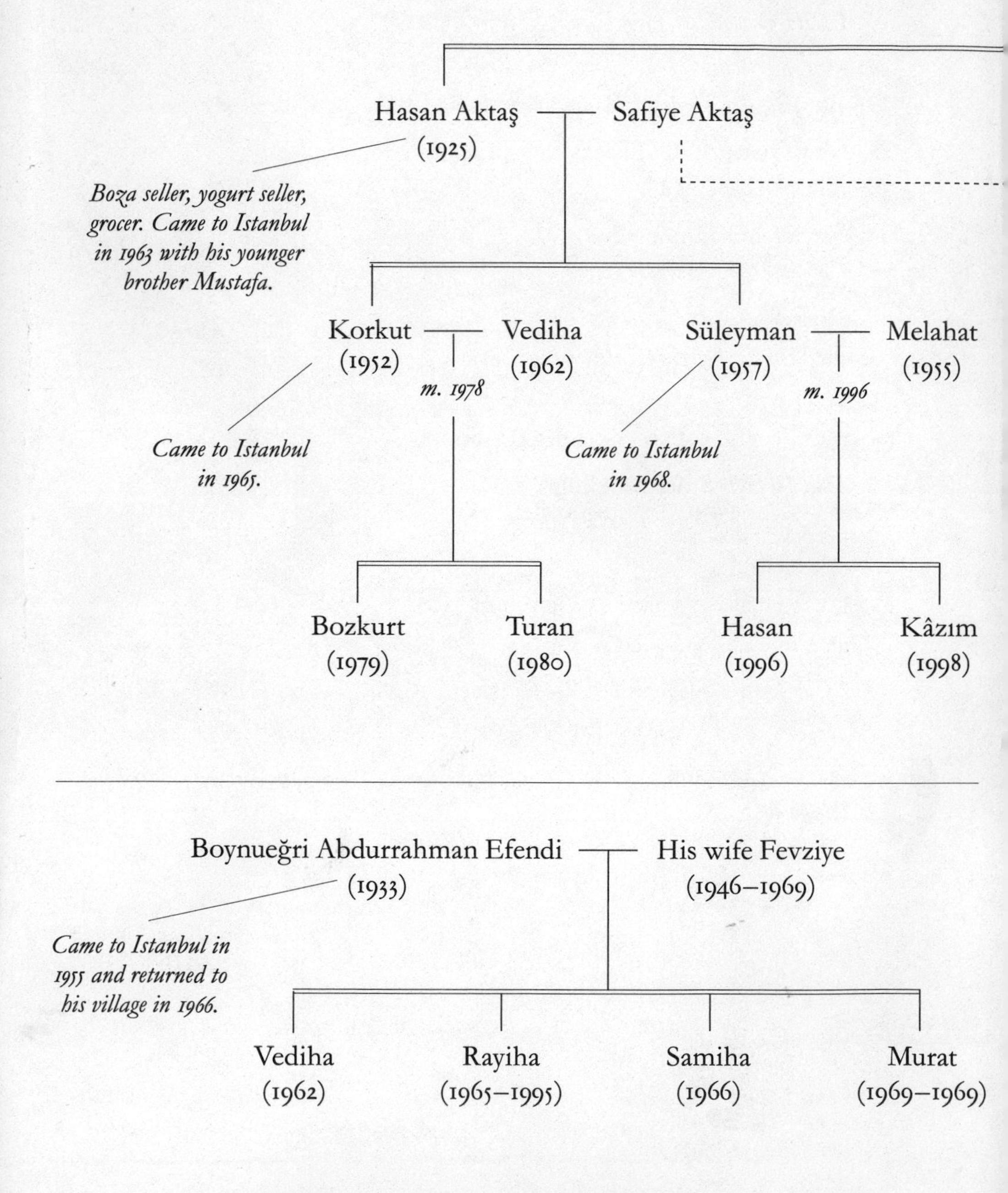

Hasan Aktaş
(1925)
Safiye Aktaş
Boza seller, yogurt seller, grocer. Came to Istanbul in 1963 with his younger brother Mustafa.
Korkut
(1952)
Vediha
(1962)
m. 1978
Süleyman
(1957)
Melahat
(1955)
m. 1996
Came to Istanbul in 1965.
Came to Istanbul in 1968.
Bozkurt
(1979)
Turan
(1980)
Hasan
(1996)
Kâzım
(1998)
Boynueğri Abdurrahman Efendi
(1933)
His wife Fevziye
(1946–1969)
Came to Istanbul in 1955 and returned to his village in 1966.
Vediha
(1962)
Rayiha
(1965–1995)
Samiha
(1966)
Murat
(1969–1969)

Mevlut and Rayiha

Elopement Is a Tricky Business

THIS IS the story of the life and daydreams of Mevlut Karataş, a seller of boza and yogurt. Born in 1957 on the western edge of Asia, in a poor village overlooking a hazy lake in Central Anatolia, he came to Istanbul at the age of twelve, living there, in the capital of the world, for the rest of his life. When he was twenty-five, he returned to the province of his birth, where he eloped with a village girl, a rather strange affair that determined the rest of his days: returning with her to Istanbul, he got married and had two daughters; he took a number of jobs without pause, selling his yogurt, ice cream, and rice in the street and waiting tables. But every evening, without fail, he would wander the streets of Istanbul, selling boza and dreaming strange dreams.

Our hero Mevlut was tall, of strong yet delicate build, and good-looking. He had a boyish face, light brown hair, and alert, clever eyes, a combination that roused many a tender feeling among women. This boyishness, which Mevlut carried well into his forties, and its effect on women were two of his essential features, and it will be worth my reminding readers of them now and again to help to explain some aspects of the story. As for Mevlut's optimism and goodwill—which some would call naïveté—of these, there will be no need for reminding, as they will be clear to see throughout. Had my readers actually met Mevlut, as I have, they would agree with the women who found him boyishly handsome and know that I am not exaggerating for effect. In fact, let me take this opportunity to point out that there are no exaggerations anywhere in this book, which is based entirely on a true story; I will narrate some strange events that have come and gone and limit my part to ordering them in such a fashion as to allow my readers to follow and understand them more easily.

So I will start in the middle, from the day in June 1982 when Mevlut eloped with a girl from the village of Gümüşdere (linked to the Beyşehir district of Konya and neighboring his own village). It was at the wedding of his uncle's eldest son, Korkut, celebrated in Mecidiyeköy, Istanbul, in 1978, that Mevlut had first caught sight of the girl who would later agree to run away with him. He could scarcely believe that this girl, then only thirteen—a child still—could possibly reciprocate his feelings. She was the little sister of his cousin Korkut's wife, and she had never even seen Istanbul before that day. Afterward, Mevlut would write her love letters for three years. The girl never replied, but Korkut's younger brother Süleyman, who delivered Mevlut's letters, gave Mevlut hope and encouraged him to persevere.

Now, Süleyman was helping his cousin Mevlut again, this time to take the girl away. Driving his Ford van, Süleyman returned with Mevlut to the village of his childhood. The two cousins had hatched a plan to run away with the girl without being detected. According to the plan, Süleyman would wait in the van at a spot about an hour away from Gümüşdere. Everyone would assume the two lovebirds had gone off to Beyşehir, but Süleyman would drive them north over the mountains and drop them off at the Akşehir train station.

Mevlut had gone over the plan many times in his head and twice made secret reconnaissance expeditions to crucial locations like the cold fountain, the narrow creek, the wooded hill, and the back garden of the girl's home. Half an hour before the appointed time, he stopped off at the village cemetery, which was on the way. He turned toward the tombstones and prayed to God for everything to go smoothly. He was loath to admit it, but he didn't quite trust Süleyman. What if his cousin failed to bring the van to the appointed spot near the fountain? Mevlut tried not to think about it too much; no good could come of these fears now.

He was wearing the dress trousers and blue shirt he'd bought from a shop in Beyoğlu when he was back in middle school and selling yogurt with his father. His shoes were from the state-owned Sümerbank factory; he'd bought them before doing his military service.

At nightfall, Mevlut approached the crumbling wall around the white house of Crooked-Necked Abdurrahman, the girl's father. The window at the back was dark. Mevlut was ten minutes early and anxious to get going. He thought of the old days when people trying to elope got entangled in blood feuds and wound up shot, or when, running away in the dead of night, they lost their way and ended up getting caught. He thought of how embarrassing it was for the boys when girls changed their minds and decided not to run away after all, and he stood up with some trepidation. He told himself that God would protect him.

The dogs barked. The window lit up for a moment and then went dark again. Mevlut's heart began to race. He walked toward the house. He heard a rustling among the trees, and then the girl calling out to him in a whisper:

"Mev-lut!"

It was a voice full of love, the voice of someone who had read the letters he'd sent during his military service, a trusting voice. Mevlut remembered those letters now, hundreds of them, each written with genuine love and desire; he remembered how he had devoted his entire being to winning over that beautiful girl, and the scenes of happiness he'd conjured in his mind. Now, at last, he'd managed to get the girl. He couldn't see much, but in that magical night, he drew like a sleepwalker toward the sound of her voice.

They found each other in the darkness. They held hands without even thinking about it and began to run. But they hadn't gone ten steps when the dogs started barking again, and, startled, Mevlut lost his bearings. He tried to find his way on instinct, but his head was a muddle. In the night, the trees were like walls of concrete looming in and out of view; they dodged them all as in a dream.

When they reached the end of the footpath, Mevlut made for the hill ahead, as planned. At one point, the narrow, winding path through the rocks and up the hill was so steep that it seemed to reach all the way to the clouded pitch-black sky. They walked hand in hand for about half an hour, climbing without rest until they reached the peak. There, they could see the lights of Gümüşdere and, farther back, the village of Cennetpınar, where Mevlut had been born and raised. Mevlut had taken a circuitous path away from Gümüşdere, partly to avoid leading any pursuers back to his own village, and partly on instinct, in order to thwart any treacherous scheme of Süleyman's.

The dogs kept barking as if possessed. Mevlut realized that he was, by now, a stranger to his village, that none of the dogs recognized him anymore. Presently, he heard the sound of a gunshot coming from the direction of Gümüşdere. They checked themselves and continued to walk at the same pace, but when the dogs, who'd gone quiet for a moment, started barking again, they broke into a run down the hill. The leaves and branches scraped their faces, and nettles stuck to their clothes. Mevlut couldn't see anything in the darkness and feared that they might trip and fall over a rock at any moment, but nothing of the sort happened. He was afraid of the dogs, but he knew that God was looking out for him and Rayiha and that they would have a very happy life in Istanbul.

They reached the road to Akşehir, out of breath. Mevlut was sure they were on time. All that remained now was for Süleyman to turn up with the van, and then nobody could take Rayiha away from him. Mevlut had begun every letter invoking this girl's lovely face and her unforgettable eyes, inscribing her beautiful name, Rayiha, with lavish care and desperate abandon at the head of each missive. Now he was so happy at the thought of those feelings that he couldn't help but quicken his step.

In that darkness, he could scarcely see the face of the girl he was eloping with. He thought he might at least take hold of her and kiss her, but Rayiha gently rebuffed his attempts with the bundle she was carrying. Mevlut liked that. He decided that it would be better not to touch the person he was to spend the rest of his life with until they were married.

Hand in hand, they crossed the little bridge over the river Sarp. Rayiha's hand in his was light and delicate as a bird. A cool breeze carried the scent of thyme and bay leaves over the murmuring water.

The night sky lit up with a purple hue; then came the sound of thunder. Mevlut worried about getting caught in the rain before the long train ride ahead, but he did not speed up his pace.

Ten minutes later, they saw the taillights of Süleyman's van beside the gurgling fountain. Mevlut felt himself drowning in happiness. He felt bad for having doubted Süleyman. It had started raining, and they broke into a joyful run, but they were both exhausted, and the lights of the van were farther away than either of them had judged. By the time they reached the van, they were soaked through.

Rayiha took her bundle and sat in the back of the van, engulfed in darkness. Mevlut and Süleyman had planned it that way, in case word got out that Rayiha had run away and the gendarmes started searching vehicles on the roads. It was also to make sure that Rayiha wouldn't recognize Süleyman.

Once they were seated up front, Mevlut turned to his accomplice and said, "Süleyman, as long as I live, I will be grateful for this, for your friendship and loyalty!" He couldn't stop himself from embracing his cousin with all his strength.

When Süleyman failed to reciprocate his enthusiasm, Mevlut blamed himself: he must have broken Süleyman's heart with his suspicions.

"You have to swear you won't tell anyone that I helped you," said Süleyman.

Mevlut swore.

"She hasn't closed the back door properly," said Süleyman. Mevlut got out and walked toward the back in the darkness. As he was shutting the door on the girl, there was a flash of lightning, and for a moment, the sky, the mountains, the rocks, the trees—everything around him—lit up like a distant memory. For the first time, Mevlut got a proper look at the face of the woman he was to spend a lifetime with.

He would remember the utter strangeness of that moment for the rest of his life.

Once they had started moving, Süleyman took a towel out of the glove compartment and handed it to Mevlut: "Dry yourself." Mevlut sniffed at the towel to make sure it wasn't dirty and then passed it to the girl in the back of the van.

A while later, Süleyman said to him "You're still wet, and there aren't any other towels."

The rain peppered the roof, the windshield wipers wailed, but Mevlut knew they were crossing into a place of endless silence. The forest, dimly lit by the van's pale orange headlights, was thick with darkness. Mevlut had heard how wolves, jackals, and bears met with the spirits of the underworld after midnight; many times at night, on the streets of Istanbul, he had come face-to-face with the shadows of mythical creatures and demons. This was the darkness in which horn-tailed devils, big-footed giants, and horned Cyclopes roamed, looking for all the hopeless sinners and those who had lost their way, whom they would catch and take down to the underworld.

"Cat got your tongue?" Süleyman joked.

Mevlut recognized that the strange silence he was entering would stay with him for years to come.

As he tried to work out how he had fallen into this trap life had set for him, he kept thinking, It's because the dogs barked and I got lost in the dark, and even though he knew his reasoning made no sense, he held fast to it, because at least it was of some comfort.

"Is something the matter?" said Süleyman.

"Nothing."

As the van slowed down to take the turns in the narrow, muddy road, and the headlights lit up the rocks, the ghostly trees, the indistinct shadows, and all the mysterious things around them, Mevlut beheld these wonders with the look of a man who knows he will never forget them for as long as he lives. They followed the tiny road, sometimes snaking up a hill, then back down again, stealing through the darkness of a village sunk in the mud. They would be met by barking dogs every time they crossed a village, only to be plunged once again into a silence so deep that Mevlut wasn't sure whether the strangeness was in his mind or in the world. In the darkness, he saw the shadows of mythical birds. He saw words written in incomprehensible scripts, and the ruins of the demon armies that had traversed these remote lands hundreds of years ago. He saw the shadows of people who had been turned to stone for their sins.

"No regrets, right?" said Süleyman. "There's nothing to be afraid of. I doubt anyone is following us. I'm sure they all knew the girl was going to run away, except maybe her crooked-necked father, and he'll be easy to deal with. You'll see, they'll all come around in a month or two, and then before the summer's over, you two can come back to get everyone's blessing. Just don't tell anyone I helped you."

As they turned a sharp corner on a steep incline, the van's back tires got stuck in the mud. For a moment, Mevlut imagined that it could all be over, that Rayiha would go back to her village and he would go back to his home in Istanbul, without any further trouble.

But then the van started moving again.

An hour later, one or two lonely buildings and the narrow lanes of the town of Akşehir appeared in the headlights. The train station was on the outskirts, at the other side of town.

"Whatever happens, don't get separated," said Süleyman as he dropped them off at Akşehir railway station. He glanced back at the girl waiting with her bundle in the darkness. "I shouldn't get out, I don't want her to recognize me. I've got a hand in this, too, now. You must make Rayiha happy, Mevlut, got it? She's your wife now; the die is cast. You should lie low for a while when you get to Istanbul."

Mevlut and Rayiha watched as Süleyman drove away until they could no longer see the van's red taillights. They walked into the old train station building without holding hands.

Inside the brightly lit train station, gleaming under fluorescent lights, Mevlut looked once again at the face of the girl he had run away with, a closer look this time, enough to confirm what he had glimpsed but not quite believed while shutting the back door of the van; he looked away.

This was not the girl he had seen at the wedding of his uncle's elder son Korkut in Istanbul. This was her older sister. They had shown him the pretty sister at the wedding, and then given him the ugly sister instead. Mevlut realized he'd been tricked. He was ashamed and couldn't even look at the girl whose name may well not have been Rayiha.

Who had played this trick on him, and how? Walking toward the ticket counter at the train station, he heard the distant echoes of his own footsteps as if they belonged to someone else. For the rest of his life, old train stations would always remind Mevlut of these moments.

In a daze, he bought two tickets for Istanbul.

The man at the counter had said, "It'll be here soon," but there was no sign of the train. They sat on the corner of a bench in a tiny waiting room crowded with baskets, parcels, suitcases, and tired passengers and did not say a single word to each other.

Mevlut recalled that Rayiha did have an older sister—or, rather, the pretty girl he thought of as Rayiha, because the real Rayiha had to be this girl. That's how Süleyman had referred to her earlier. Mevlut had sent love letters addressed to Rayiha but with someone else, a different face, in mind. He didn't even know the name of the pretty sister he had always pictured. He had no clear understanding of how he had been tricked, no memory of how he'd arrived at this moment, and so the strangeness in his mind became a part of the trap he had fallen into.

As they sat on the bench, he looked only at Rayiha's hand. This was the hand he had lovingly held such a short while ago; it was this hand, as he had written in his love letters, that he had yearned to hold, this well-formed, pretty hand. It rested quietly on her lap, and every now and then it carefully smoothed the creases on her skirt and on the cloth wrapped around her possessions.

Mevlut got up and went to the station café. As he walked back toward Rayiha with two stale buns, he observed her covered head and her face once more from afar. This definitely wasn't the beautiful girl he had seen at Korkut's wedding, a wedding he had attended even though his father had told him not to. Once more, Mevlut was sure he had never even seen this girl, the real Rayiha, before. How had they come to this moment? Did Rayiha realize that his letters had actually been intended for her sister?

"Would you like a bun?"

Rayiha held out her delicate hand and took it. In her face, Mevlut saw gratitude—not the excitement of runaway lovers.

With Mevlut sitting next to her, Rayiha labored over her bun as if committing a crime. He ate the other stale bun, not with any relish but only because he wasn't sure what else to do.

They sat without talking. Mevlut felt like a boy waiting for the end of the school day, finding that time just would not pass. His mind kept working unbidden, trying to figure out what mistake he had made to find himself here.

His thoughts returned repeatedly to the wedding where he'd first seen the pretty sister to whom he had written all those letters; his late father, Mustafa Efendi, telling him not to go to that wedding; and how he had snuck away from the village and gone to Istanbul anyway. Could that one act really have caused all of this? Like the headlights of the van that had brought them here, his thoughts roamed over a half-lit landscape, the gloomy memories and shadows of his twenty-five years, trying to shed some light on the present situation.

The train did not arrive. Mevlut got up and went to the café again, but now it was closed. Two horse-drawn cabs were waiting to take passengers to town. One of the coachmen was smoking a cigarette in the boundless silence that reigned. Mevlut walked up to an ancient plane tree next to the station building.

In the pale light from the station he could make out the sign under the tree.

THE FOUNDER OF OUR REPUBLIC
MUSTAFA KEMAL ATATÜRK
DRANK COFFEE UNDER THE SHADE
OF THIS ANCIENT PLANE TREE
WHEN HE CAME TO AKŞEHIR IN THE YEAR 1922.

Mevlut remembered Akşehir from his history lessons. He had learned about the important role this village had played in Turkish history, but at that moment he couldn't remember any of it, and he blamed himself. He just hadn't worked hard enough in school to be the kind of student that his teachers would have wanted. Maybe that was his biggest flaw. But, he thought with some optimism, he was only twenty-five and had plenty of time to improve himself.

On his way back to their bench, he looked at Rayiha one more time. No, he couldn't remember seeing her at all at the wedding four years ago.

The rusty Istanbul train groaned its way into the station four hours late, and they managed to find an empty carriage. There was no one in their compartment, but still Mevlut sat next to Rayiha rather than across from her. Every time they went over a switch or a worn stretch of railroad, the train shook, and Mevlut's upper arm brushed against Rayiha's. Even this seemed strange to Mevlut.

He went to the toilet and listened to the click-clacking sound coming through the hole in the floor, just the way he used to do as a child. When he returned to his seat, the girl had fallen asleep. How could she sleep so peacefully on the night she had run away from home? "Rayiha, Rayiha!" he whispered in her ear. The girl woke up as naturally as only someone whose name was really Rayiha could have done and smiled at him sweetly. Mevlut sat next to her without a word.

They did not speak as they looked out the carriage window, like a couple who had been married for years and had nothing left to say to each other. Every now and then they saw the streetlamps of a little hamlet or the taillights of a car on an isolated road and the green and red lights of railroad signals, but mostly the world outside was pitch black, and they could see nothing but their own reflections in the windowpane.

Two hours later, at dawn, Mevlut saw that there were tears in Rayiha's eyes. The compartment was still empty, and the train was making its noisy way down a purple-hued landscape with cliffs at every corner.

"Do you want to go back home?" Mevlut asked her. "Have you changed your mind?"

She cried even harder. Mevlut put his arm around her shoulders awkwardly, but then, because it was so uncomfortable, he pulled his arm back. Rayiha cried for a long time. Mevlut felt guilt and remorse.

"You don't love me," she said at length.

"Why do you say that?"

"Your letters were so loving, but you tricked me. Was it really you who wrote them?"

"I wrote them all myself," said Mevlut.

Rayiha kept crying.

An hour later, when the train stopped at Afyonkarahisar station,

Mevlut jumped off the carriage and bought some bread, two triangles of cream cheese, and a pack of biscuits. A boy was selling tea from a tray. They bought some to have with their breakfast while the train made its way alongside the river Aksu. Mevlut was happy to watch Rayiha as she looked out of the carriage window at the towns they passed, the poplars, the tractors, the horse carts, the kids playing football, and the rivers flowing under steel bridges. Everything was interesting; the whole world was new.

Between Alayurt and Uluköy stations, Rayiha fell asleep with her head on Mevlut's shoulder. Mevlut couldn't deny that this made him happy, nor that it made him feel a sense of responsibility. Two gendarmes and an old man came to sit in their compartment. Mevlut saw transmission towers, trucks on the asphalt roads, and new concrete bridges and read them as signs that the country was growing and developing. He did not like the political slogans he saw scrawled on factory walls and around poor neighborhoods.

Mevlut fell asleep, surprised that he was about to fall asleep.

They woke up together when the train stopped at Eskişehir and panicked for a moment, thinking the gendarmes had caught them, but then they relaxed and smiled at each other.

Rayiha had a very genuine smile. It was hard to believe that she might be hiding anything or to suspect her of scheming in some way. She had an open, decent face, full of light. Mevlut knew deep down that she must have colluded with those who had tricked him, but when he looked at her face, he couldn't help but think that she had to be innocent in all of this.

As the train moved closer to Istanbul, they talked about the huge factories they passed along the way and the flames that poured out of the tall chimneys of the Izmit oil refinery, and they wondered what corner of the world the big freight ships they spotted might be headed for. Like her sisters, Rayiha had gone to elementary school, and she could name the distant countries across the sea without too much trouble. Mevlut felt proud of her.

Rayiha had already been to Istanbul once for her elder sister's wedding. But still she humbly asked, "Is this Istanbul now?"

"Kartal counts as Istanbul, I suppose," said Mevlut, with the confidence of familiarity. "But there's still a ways to go." He pointed out the Princes' Islands ahead of them and vowed to take her there one day.

Not once during Rayiha's brief life would they ever do this.

PART II

Wednesday, 30 March 1994

Asians . . . once let them feast and drink their fill of boza at a wedding or a funeral, and out will come their knives.

—Lermontov, *A Hero of Our Time*

Mevlut, Every Winter Evening for the Last Twenty-Five Years

Leave the Boza Seller Alone

IN MARCH 1994, twelve years after Mevlut and Rayiha eloped to Istanbul, Mevlut was selling boza on a very dark night when he came face-to-face with a basket lowered down quickly but quietly from above.

"Boza seller, boza seller, boza for two, please!" a child's voice called.

The basket had fallen through the night to Mevlut like an angel. He was amazed to see it, because in Istanbul the custom of buying goods from street vendors by means of a basket tied to a rope and dropped down from an upper-story window had all but disappeared. It took him back to his middle-school days, twenty-five years ago, when he used to help his father sell yogurt and boza. Into the enameled pot in the basket, Mevlut poured more boza than the children upstairs had asked for—not just enough for two glasses, but almost a kilo's worth. He felt good, as if he'd been touched by an angel. In the past few years, his thoughts and daydreams had frequently turned to spiritual questions.

Before we go any further, and to make sure that our story is properly understood, perhaps I should explain for foreign readers who've never heard of it before, and for future generations of Turkish readers who will, I fear, forget all about it within the next twenty to thirty years, that boza is a traditional Asian beverage made of fermented wheat, with a thick consistency, a pleasant aroma, a dark yellowish color, and a low alcohol content. This story is already full of strange things, and I wouldn't want people to think it entirely peculiar.

Boza is quick to spoil and turn sour in the heat, so in the old days, when the Ottomans ruled, it was sold mainly in shops and during the winter. By the time the Republic of Turkey was founded in 1923, the boza shops in Istanbul had long closed down, pushed out by German breweries. But the street vendors who sold this traditional drink never left. After the 1950s, boza selling became the preserve of those like Mevlut, who walked the poor and neglected cobblestone streets on winter evenings crying "Bozaaa," reminding us of centuries past, and the good old days that have come and gone.

Sensing some impatience from the children up on the fifth floor, Mevlut pocketed the paper money they'd left in the basket and set the change in coins next to the pot. He gave the basket a gentle pull, just as he used to do as a child when he and his father would sell their wares on the street, and off it went.

The wicker basket made a quick ascent, giving the children some trouble as it swayed from side to side in the cold wind, bumping against the windowsills and the gutters on the floors below the children's window. When it got to the fifth floor, it hovered for a moment, like a happy seagull gliding on the perfect current. Then, like a mysterious and forbidden thing, it disappeared into the night, and Mevlut went on his way.

"Booo-zaaaaa," he called out into the half-lit street. "Goooood boozaaaaa."

Using a basket to buy things off the street was a custom from the days when buildings in Istanbul had no elevators or automatic doorbells and were rarely more than five or six stories high. Back in 1969, when Mevlut first started working with his father, housewives who preferred to stay indoors would use the basket for purchasing not just boza but their daily yogurt, too, and even various items from the grocer's boy. As they did not have telephones in their homes, they would tie a little bell to the bottom of the basket to alert the grocer or a passing vendor that they needed something. The vendor would, in turn, ring the bell and rock the basket to signal that the yogurt or the boza had been safely placed inside. Mevlut had always enjoyed watching these baskets make their way back up: some of them would sway in the breeze, bumping into windows, branches, electrical and telephone cables, and the laundry lines stretched between buildings, and the bell would respond to each collision with a pleasant chime. Regular customers would put their account ledger in the basket, too, so that Mevlut could add the day's yogurt to their tab before sending the basket back up. Mevlut's father could not read or write, and before his son joined him from the village, he used to enter purchases into these ledgers with tally marks (one stroke was one kilo, half a stroke a half a kilo, and so on). He would swell with pride at the sight of his boy writing down numbers as well as more detailed notes, like "Yogurt with cream; Monday–Friday," for some clients.

But Istanbul had changed so much over the past twenty-five years that these memories now seemed like fairy tales to Mevlut. Most of the streets had been paved with cobblestones when he first arrived in the city, but now they were asphalt. The three-story buildings, surrounded by their own gardens, which had made up most of the city, had been razed to the ground and replaced with taller apartment blocks in which those who lived on the upper floors couldn't possibly hear the call of a vendor passing in the street below. In place of radios, there were now television sets that were left on all evening, drowning out the boza seller's voice. The quiet, browbeaten folk in gray and drab clothes who used to populate the streets had been replaced by rowdy, energetic, and more assertive crowds. Mevlut had experienced these changes in daily increments, not as a sudden shock, and so, unlike some others, he did not bemoan the transformation. Rather, he tried to keep pace with these momentous changes and always chose neighborhoods where he knew he was guaranteed a friendly reception.

A place like Beyoğlu, for example! The most populous neighborhood and the one closest to his house. Fifteen years ago, toward the end of the 1970s, when the area's ramshackle cabaret bars and nightclubs and half-hidden brothels were still in business, Mevlut was able to make sales in the backstreets until as late as midnight. The women who sang and worked as hostesses in stove-heated basement nightclubs;

their devoted fans; the middle-aged mustachioed men who came from rural Anatolia to shop in Istanbul and, at the end of a long day, liked to buy drinks for the hostesses; Istanbul's newest miserable arrivals and the Arab and Pakistani tourists who were thrilled to be sitting at a table in a nightclub with a few women; the waiters, the bouncers, and the doormen—they all bought boza from Mevlut even at the midnight hour. But in the last decade or so, the demon of change had cast its spell over the neighborhood as it had over the whole city, and the fabric of that past had been torn asunder, causing those denizens to leave and the clubs playing Ottoman and European-style Turkish and continental music to shut down, giving way to noisy new establishments serving Adana and shish kebabs cooked over an open grill and washed down with *rakı*. The young crowds who liked to go dancing had no interest in boza, so Mevlut no longer went anywhere near İstiklal Avenue.

Every night for twenty-five years, around eight thirty, when the evening news broadcast was drawing to a close, Mevlut got ready to leave his rented home in Tarlabaşı. He wore the brown sweater his wife had knit, his woolen skullcap, and the blue apron that made such an impression on customers, picked up the jug containing the boza sweetened and flavored with special spices by his wife or his daughters, made an experienced guess as to how much it weighed (sometimes, on cold nights, he would say that they hadn't prepared enough), put on his dark coat, and said good-bye to those at home. When his daughters were little, he used to tell them not to wait up for him, but these days he just told them "I won't be long" while their eyes remained firmly fixed on the TV.

The first thing he would do when he stepped outside into the cold was to shoulder the thick oak-wood yoke he'd been using for twenty-five years to carry his load, a plastic jug full of boza tied at each end; like a soldier about to step onto the battlefield he would check his ammunition one last time, his belt pouches and the inner pockets of his jacket full of little bags of roasted chickpeas and cinnamon (prepared at home either by his wife, his increasingly irritable and impatient daughters, or by Mevlut himself), and finally he would set out on his night's endless walk.

"Gooood booozaaaa . . ."

He would quickly reach the upper neighborhoods and then, once he got to Taksim, he would head toward whatever location he'd picked for that day, making steady sales with only a half-hour cigarette break.

It had been nine thirty when the basket fell to Mevlut like an angel that night, and he'd been in Pangaltı. By ten thirty, he was in the backstreets of Gümüşsuyu, on a dark lane leading up to the little mosque, when he saw a pack of street dogs he'd first noticed some weeks ago. Stray dogs never bothered street vendors, so until recently Mevlut hadn't been afraid of them. But now he felt his heart quicken with a strange impulse, and he began to worry. He knew that street dogs attacked at the smell of fear. He tried to think about something else.

He tried to think of his girls laughing as they watched TV; the cypress trees in the cemetery; the home to which he'd soon return and where he'd be chatting with his wife; his Holy Guide who said that you should keep your heart pure; the angel he'd seen in a dream the other night. But this wasn't enough to banish his fear of the dogs.

"Woof! Woof!" barked one approaching him.

There was a second behind the first. It was difficult to see them in the darkness; they were a muddy-brown color. In the distance, Mevlut saw a black one.

The three dogs and a fourth one he couldn't see all started barking at the same time. Mevlut was gripped by a kind of fear he'd experienced only once or twice as a street vendor, and then only as a child. He couldn't remember any of the verses and prayers that were meant to repel dogs. He did not move a muscle. But the dogs continued to bark.

Mevlut looked around for an open door through which to escape, a doorstep on which to take refuge. Should he use the stick across his back as a weapon?

A window opened. "Shoo!" someone yelled. "Leave the boza seller alone! Shoo, shoo!"

The dogs were startled into silence, and then they walked away.

Mevlut felt much gratitude toward this figure at the third-floor window.

"You can't show them your fear, boza seller," said the man. "They're mean bastards, these dogs, they can tell when someone's afraid. Got it?"

"Thanks," said Mevlut, ready to continue on his way.

"Well, come on up and let us buy some of this boza, then." Mevlut wasn't too happy with the man's patronizing manner, but he went to the door anyway.

It opened with a *bzzzz* from the buzzer. Inside the building, there was a smell of butane, frying oil, and paint. Mevlut took his time climbing the stairs to the third floor. Once he got to the apartment, they invited him inside just like kindly people used to do in the old days, rather than keeping him waiting at the door:

"Come on in, boza seller, you must be cold."

There were several rows of shoes lined up outside the door. As he bent down to untie his laces, he remembered his old friend Ferhat. "There are three types of buildings in Istanbul," he used to say: (1) those full of devout families where people say their daily prayers and leave their shoes outside, (2) rich and Westernized homes where you can go in with your shoes on, (3) new high-rise blocks where you can find a mix of both sorts.

This particular building was situated in a wealthy neighborhood. People here did not take their shoes off and leave them at the door before going in. But for some reason Mevlut felt as if he were in one of those new, big apartment blocks mixing the traditionally religious with others more Westernized. In any case, on those rare occasions nowadays when he was invited into living rooms or kitchens, he was always respectful enough to remove his shoes at the door, regardless of whether he was at an ordinary home or a wealthier family's apartment. "Don't worry about your shoes, boza seller!" they would sometimes call to him from inside, but he would ignore them.

There was a strong smell of *rakı* in this apartment. He could hear the cheerful chatter of people already drunk before dinner was even over. A mixed group of six or seven men and women sat at a table that took up almost the entire length of a sitting room, drinking and laughing at the television, which was, as in all homes, turned up too high.

The table went quiet once they realized Mevlut was in the kitchen.

There was a man in the kitchen who was completely drunk. "Go on, give us a little boza, boza seller," he said. This wasn't the man Mevlut had seen at the window. "Did you bring any roasted chickpeas and cinnamon?"

"I did!"

Mevlut knew better than to ask this lot how many kilos they wanted.

"How many of you are there?"

"How many of you are there?" the drunken man called to the living room in a mocking tone. There was much laughter and argument in response, and the group at the table took some time to count.

"Boza seller, I don't want any if it's sour," Mevlut heard a woman say from the dinner table.

"My boza is sweet," Mevlut answered.

"Then don't give me any," said a male voice. "Good boza is sour boza."

They started arguing among themselves.

"Come here, boza seller," another drunken voice called out.

Mevlut went from the kitchen to the living room, feeling poor and out of place. For a moment, everything was still and silent. Everyone at the dining table was smiling at him, giving him curious looks. It was probably the novelty of seeing a living relic of the past that had now fallen out of fashion. In the past few years, Mevlut had grown used to getting this sort of look.

"Boza seller, should proper boza be sweet or sour?" said a man with a mustache.

The three women all had dyed-blond hair. Mevlut noticed that the man who had opened the window earlier and rescued Mevlut from the dogs was sitting at one end of the table across from two of the women. "Boza can be both sweet and sour," said Mevlut. This was an answer he'd memorized over twenty-five years.

"Boza seller, can you make a living from this?"

"I do, thank God."

"So there's good money in this work, eh? How long have you been doing it?"

"I've been doing this for twenty-five years. Earlier I also used to sell yogurt in the mornings."

"If you've been doing this for twenty-five years, and if it's good money, then you must be rich by now, right?"

"I cannot say that I am," said Mevlut.

"Why?"

"All the relatives that came with me from the village are rich now, but I guess it just wasn't meant to be for me."

"Why not?"

"Because I'm honest," said Mevlut. "I can't lie or sell spoiled food or cheat anyone just to buy a house or give my daughter a proper wedding . . ."

"Are you a religious man?"

Mevlut knew by now that this question carried political connotations in the wealthier households. The Islamist party, which was supported mainly by the poor, had won the municipal elections three days ago. Mevlut, too, had voted for its candidate—who had unexpectedly been elected mayor of Istanbul—because he was religious and had gone to the Piyale Paşa school in Kasımpaşa, which Mevlut's daughters were now attending.

"I'm a salesman," Mevlut replied cunningly. "How could a salesman possibly be religious?"

"Why shouldn't he be?"

"I'm always working. If you're out on the streets all the time, there's no way you can pray five times a day . . ."

"And what do you do in the mornings?"

"I've done all sorts of things . . . I've sold rice with chickpeas, I've worked as a waiter, I've sold ice cream, I've been a manager . . . I can do anything."

"A manager of what?"

"The Binbom Café. It was in Beyoğlu, but it shut down. Did you know it?"

"And now what do you do in the mornings?" said the man from the window.

"These days I'm free."

"Do you have a wife, a family?" asked a blond lady with a sweet face.

"I do. We have two beautiful girls. They're like angels, thank God."

"You'll send them to school, right? Will you make them cover their heads when they get older?"

"Does your wife wear a headscarf?"

"We're just poor village people from the countryside," said Mevlut. "We're attached to our traditions."

"Is that why you sell boza?"

"Most of my people came to Istanbul to sell yogurt and boza, but actually it's not something we really knew in my village."

"So you first discovered boza in the city?"

"Yes."

"And where did you learn to call out like a proper boza seller?"

"You have a lovely voice, like a muezzin."

"It's the emotion in the seller's voice that really sells the boza," said Mevlut.

"But boza seller, don't you get scared at night on the streets, or at least bored?"

"The Almighty God will always look after the poor boza seller. I always think nice things when I'm out."

"Even when you're in a dark and empty street, even when you walk past cemeteries and prowling dogs, when you see demons and fairies?"

Mevlut did not reply.

"What's your name?"

"Mevlut Karataş."

"Go on then, Mr. Mevlut, show us how you say 'bozaaaa.'"

This wasn't the first table of drunk people Mevlut had faced. When he'd first started working as a street vendor, plenty of drunk people would ask him whether there was electricity in his village (there hadn't been when he'd first come to Istanbul, but now, in 1994, there was) and whether he'd ever been to school, followed by questions like "How did you feel when you first got on an elevator?" "When was the first time you went to the cinema?" In those early years, Mevlut would come up with amusing answers to endear himself to the customers who let him into their living rooms; he had no qualms about making himself seem more innocently ignorant and less streetwise than he was, and his friendly regulars did not need to ask twice to hear his rendition of the "Boozaaaa" call he usually reserved for the streets.

But those were the old days. Nowadays, Mevlut felt a resentment he couldn't explain. Had it not been for his gratitude to the man who had rescued him from the dogs, he would have ended the conversation there, given them their boza, and left.

"So how many people would like boza?" he asked.

"Oh, haven't you given them boza in the kitchen yet? And here we were thinking you'd sorted that out already!"

"Where do you get this boza from?"

"I make it myself."

"No, really? I thought all the boza sellers just bought it ready-made."

"There's a factory now in Eskişehir; it's been there for five years," said Mevlut. "But I buy the raw boza from the oldest and the best place, the Vefa Boza Shop. Then I mix it up with my own ingredients and turn it into something you can drink."

"So you add sugar to it at home?"

"By nature, boza is both sweet and sour."

"Oh, come on now! Boza is meant to be sour. It's the fermentation process that makes it sour, it's the alcohol, just like with wine."

"There's alcohol in boza?" asked one of the women, with eyebrows raised.

"Darling, you don't know anything, do you?" said one of the men. "Boza was the drink of choice under the Ottomans, when alcohol and wine were banned. When Murad the Fourth went around in disguise at night, he didn't have just the taverns and coffee shops shut down but the boza shops, too."

"Why did he ban the coffee shops?"

This sparked one of those drunken discussions Mevlut had witnessed many times in bars and at the tables of seasoned drinkers. And for a moment, they forgot about him.

"Boza seller, you tell us, is there alcohol in boza?"

"There is no alcohol in boza," said Mevlut, knowing full well that this was not true. His father, too, used to lie about it.

"Come on now, boza seller . . . There is some alcohol in boza, though maybe not much. I suppose that's how all those religious types got away with getting drunk during the Ottoman era. 'Of course there's no alcohol in boza,' they would say, and then happily down ten glasses and get absolutely sloshed. But after the Republic was founded and Atatürk made *rakı* and wine legal, there was no point to boza anymore; that was the end of it right there, seventy years ago."

"Maybe boza will make a comeback if some of the religious bans are reinstated . . . ," said a drunk man with a thin nose, shooting a challenging glance at Mevlut. "What do you think about the election results?"

"No," said Mevlut, without batting an eye. "There is no alcohol in boza. Otherwise, I wouldn't be selling it."

"See, the man's not like you, he cares about his beliefs," said one of the other men.

"You speak for yourself. I'm religious, but I also like my *rakı,*" said the one with the thin nose. "Boza seller, are you saying there's no alcohol in boza because you're afraid?"

"I'm not afraid of anyone but God," said Mevlut.

"Oooh, there's your answer, eh?"

"But don't you worry about street dogs and robbers at night?"

"No one would harm a poor boza seller," said Mevlut, smiling. This, too, was another of his practiced responses. "Bandits and robbers don't bother boza sellers. I've been doing this job for twenty-five years. I've never been mugged. Everyone respects a boza seller."

"Why?"

"Because boza has been around for a long time, passed down to us from our ancestors. There can't be more than forty boza sellers out on the streets of Istanbul tonight. There are very few people like you who will actually buy boza. Most are happy just to listen to the boza seller's call and remember the past. And that affection makes the boza seller happy, it's what keeps us going."

"Are you religious?"

"Yes, I am a God-fearing man," said Mevlut, knowing that these words would scare them a bit.

"And do you love Atatürk, too?"

"His Excellency Field Marshal Mustafa Kemal Pasha passed through Akşehir, near where I come from, in the year 1922," Mevlut informed them. "Then he set up the Republic in Ankara, and then he went to Istanbul, where he stayed at the Park Hotel in Taksim . . . One day he was standing at the window of his room when he noticed that the usual joy and bustle seemed to be missing from the city. He asked his assistant about it, who told him, Your Excellency, we've banned street vendors from entering the city, because they don't have those in Europe and we thought you'd get angry. But it was precisely this which made Atatürk angry. Street vendors are the songbirds of the streets, they are the life and soul of Istanbul, he said. Under no circumstances must they ever be banned. From that day on, street vendors were free to roam the streets of Istanbul."

"Hurrah for Atatürk!" said one of the women.

Some of the other diners cheered in response. Mevlut joined in.

"All right, fine, but what will become of Atatürk, of secularism, if the Islamist parties take power? Will Turkey become like Iran?"

"Don't you worry about that; the army won't let them do that. They'll organize a coup, close the party down, and lock them all up. Isn't that so, boza seller?"

"All I do is sell boza," said Mevlut. "I don't get involved in high politics. I leave that to my betters."

Even though they were all drunk, they heard the sting in Mevlut's remark.

"I'm just like you, boza seller. The only things I'm afraid of are God and my mother-in-law."

"Boza seller, do you have a mother-in-law?"

"I never got to meet her, unfortunately," said Mevlut.

"How did you get married?"

"We fell in love and ran away together. Not everyone can say that."

"How did you meet?"

"We saw each other at a relative's wedding, and it was love at first sight. I wrote her letters for three years."

"Well, well, boza seller, aren't you full of surprises!"

"And what does your wife do now?"

"She does some needlework from home. Not everyone can do the things she does, either."

"Boza seller, if we drink your boza, will we get even more drunk than we already are?"

"My boza won't get you drunk," said Mevlut. "There are eight of you, I'll give you two kilos."

He went back to the kitchen, but it took a while to assemble the boza, the roasted chickpeas, and the cinnamon and for him to get his money. He put his shoes back on with an alacrity from the days when he used to have customers waiting in line for him and he had to hurry all the time.

"Boza seller, it's wet and muddy outside, be careful," they called from the living room. "Don't let anyone mug you, don't let the dogs tear you apart!"

"Boza seller, come back again!" said one of the women.

Mevlut knew full well that they weren't really going to want boza again, that they had only called him in because they'd heard his voice and wanted to be entertained while they were drunk. The cold air outside felt good.

"Booo-zaaaa."

In twenty-five years, he'd seen so many homes like this one, so many people and families, he'd heard these questions thousands of times. Toward the end of the 1970s, in the dark backstreets of Beyoğlu and Dolapdere, moving among the nightclub entertainers, the gamblers, the thugs, the pimps, and the prostitutes, he'd come across many groups of drunk diners. He became well versed in the art of not getting too involved with the drunks, of dealing with them "without catching anyone's eye," as some of the wily types in military service used to say, and getting back out on the street without wasting too much time.

Twenty-five years ago, almost everyone invited him inside, into the kitchen, where they asked him whether he was cold, did he go to school in the mornings, and would he like a cup of tea? Some invited him into the living room, and even to take a seat at their table. Those were the good old days when he was so busy hurrying off to deliver orders he couldn't pause to properly enjoy people's hospitality and affection. Mevlut knew he'd been particularly sensitive to it that night because it had been a long time since anyone had shown so much interest in him. It had been a strange crowd, too; back in the old days it was rare to find men and women having *rakı* and making drunken conversation in a proper family home with a kitchen and all the rest. His friend Ferhat used to tease him, only half jokingly: "Why would anyone want your three-proof boza when they can all get drunk together as a family on the state's forty-five-proof Tekel brand *rakı*? There's no future in this business, Mevlut, let it go for God's sake! This country no longer needs your boza to get drunk."

He took one of the side streets that led down to Fındıklı, where he dropped off half a kilo to a regular customer, and on his way out of the building he saw two suspicious shadows in a doorway. If he gave these "suspects" too much thought, they would know (as in a dream) that he was thinking about them, and then they might try to harm him. But he couldn't help it; the shadows had seized his attention.

When he turned around instinctively to check whether any dogs were following, he was sure, for a second, that the shadows were tailing him. But he couldn't quite believe it. He rang his bell twice with vigor, and twice halfheartedly, but with urgency. "Bo-zaa," he shouted. He decided to avoid Taksim, taking a shortcut home down the steps to the hollow between the hills, and then back up to Cihangir.

As he was making his way down the stairs, one of the shadows called out, "Hey, boza seller, hang on a minute."

Mevlut pretended not to hear. He gingerly ran down a few steps, with his pole balanced across his back. But when he got beyond the light of the streetlamps, he had to slow down.

"Hey, boza seller, I said wait! We won't bite, we just want some boza."

Mevlut stopped, feeling a little ashamed for being afraid. A fig tree blocked the light from one of the streetlamps, so the landing at the bottom of the stairway was particularly dark. It was the same spot where he used to park his three-wheeled ice-cream cart in the evenings that summer when he eloped with Rayiha.

"How much is your boza?" said one of them, coming down the stairs with the air of a bully.

Now, the three of them were standing under the fig tree, in the darkness. People who craved a glass of boza did tend to ask how much it cost first, but they usually did so in a soft, even sheepish way, politely rather than aggressively. Something was not quite right here. Mevlut quoted half his normal price.

"That's a bit expensive," said the beefier of the two men. "All right, give us two glasses. I bet you make loads of money."

Mevlut lowered his jugs and took out a large plastic cup from his apron pocket. He filled it with boza. He handed it over to the younger, smaller man.

"Here you are."

"Thank you."

As he filled the second cup, he felt almost guilty about the awkward silence that had set in. The bigger man sensed his embarrassment.

"You're in a hurry, boza seller, is there that much work?"

"No, no," said Mevlut. "Business is slow. Boza is over, we don't do nearly as well as we used to. No one buys boza anymore. I wasn't going to come out at all today, but someone's ill at home, and we need the extra money for some hot soup."

"How much do you make in a day?"

"You know what they say, never ask a woman her age, nor a man his salary," said Mevlut. "But you asked, so I'll tell you," he said, now handing the silhouette of the bigger man his glass of boza. "When sales are good, we make enough to live on for a day. But on a slow day like today, we go home hungry."

"You don't look like you're hungry. Where are you from?"

"Beyşehir."

"Where on earth is that?"

Mevlut didn't reply.

"How long have you lived in Istanbul?"

"Must be around twenty-five years now."

"You've been here for twenty-five years and you still say you're from Beyşehir?"

"No . . . it's just that you asked."

"You must have made some good money in all that time."

"What money? Look at me, I'm still working at midnight. Where are you from?"

The men didn't reply, and Mevlut was afraid. "Would you like some cinnamon on top?" he asked.

"Go on then. How much is the cinnamon?"

Mevlut took his brass cinnamon shaker out from his apron. "The chickpeas and the cinnamon are on me," he said as he shook some cinnamon over the two cups. He took two bags of roasted chickpeas from his pocket. Instead of just handing them over to the customers as he would usually do, he tore the bags open and sprinkled the chickpeas onto the cups in the dark of night, like a helpful waiter.

"Boza goes best with roasted chickpeas," he said.

The men looked at each other and drained their cups.

"Well, then, do us a favor on this bad day," said the older and bulkier of the two men once he had finished his drink.

Mevlut knew what was coming and tried to preempt it.

"If you don't have any money on you right now, you can pay me some other time, my friend. If us poor fellows in this big city don't help each other out in times of need, then who will? Let this one be on me, if it pleases you." He moved to lift the stick back across his shoulders as if to go on his way.

"Not so fast, boza seller," said the well-built man. "We said do us a favor today, didn't we? Give us your money."

"But I don't have any money on me," said Mevlut. "Just some small change from one or two glasses for a couple of customers, that's all. And I need that to buy medicine for our patient at home, and I don't—"

Suddenly, the smaller man drew a switchblade from his pocket. He pressed the button, and the blade snapped open in the silence. He rested the point of the knife on Mevlut's stomach. Meanwhile, the bigger man had gone behind Mevlut's back and pinned his arms. Mevlut went quiet.

The smaller man pressed the switchblade against Mevlut's stomach with one hand, and with the other hand he did a fast but thorough search of the pockets on Mevlut's apron, and every fold of his jacket. He quickly pocketed everything he could find: banknotes and coins. Mevlut could see that he was very young and very ugly.

"Look away, boza seller," said the bigger, stronger man when he noticed Mevlut looking at the boy's face. "Now then, you've got plenty of money, don't you? No wonder you were trying to run away from us."

"That's enough now," said Mevlut, shaking himself loose.

"Enough?" said the man behind him. "I don't think so. Not

enough. You come here twenty-five years ago, you loot the city, and when it's finally our turn, then what, you decide to close up shop? We get there late, so now it's our fault?"

"Not at all, not at all, it's nobody's fault," said Mevlut.

"What do you have in Istanbul? A house, an apartment, what?"

"I haven't got a single thing to my name," Mevlut lied. "Nothing at all."

"Why? Are you stupid or what?"

"It just wasn't meant to be."

"Hey, everyone who came to Istanbul twenty-five years ago has a house in one of those slums by now. They've got buildings sprouting on their land."

Mevlut twitched irritably, but this only resulted in the knife being jabbed into his stomach a little harder ("Oh God!" said Mevlut) and in his being searched once again from head to toe.

"Tell us, are you actually stupid or are you just playing dumb?"

Mevlut made no response. The man behind him expertly twisted Mevlut's left arm and brought his hand behind his back in a smooth motion. "What do we have here! It's not houses or land that you like to spend your money on. You prefer wristwatches, don't you, my friend from Beyşehir? Now I see how it is."

The Swiss watch that Mevlut had received twelve years ago as a wedding gift was off his wrist in an instant.

"What kind of person robs a boza seller?" Mevlut asked.

"There's a first time for everything," said the man holding his arms back. "Be quiet now and don't look back."

Mevlut watched in silence as the two, one old and one young, walked away. In that moment, he realized they had to be father and son. Mevlut and his late father had never been partners in crime like these two. His father was always blaming him for something. Mevlut went down the steps. He found himself on one of the side streets that led to Kazancı Hill. It was quiet; there wasn't a soul around. What would Rayiha say when he got home? Would he be able to rest without telling someone what he'd been through?

He imagined for a moment that the robbery was a dream and that everything was as it always had been. He was not going to tell Rayiha that he'd been mugged. Because he hadn't been mugged. Wallowing in this delusion for a few seconds made him feel better. He rang his bell.

"Booozaaaa," he called, out of habit, and realized immediately that there was no sound coming out of his throat.

Back in the good old days, when something happened on the streets to upset him, whenever he felt humiliated and heartbroken, he could count on Rayiha to cheer him up when he got back home.

For the first time in his twenty-five years as a boza seller, Mevlut rushed home without calling "Boo-zaaa," even though he still had some boza left.

When he walked into his one-bedroom house, he deduced from the quiet that his two daughters had both gone to sleep.

Rayiha was sitting on the edge of the bed, doing some needlework in front of the television with the volume turned down, as she did every night while waiting for Mevlut to return.

"I'm going to stop selling boza now," he said.

"Where's this coming from?" said Rayiha. "You can't stop selling boza. But you're right, you need to get another job. My embroidery isn't enough."

"I'm telling you, I've had enough of boza."

"I hear Ferhat makes a lot of money at the electricity board," said Rayiha. "He'll find you a job if you give him a call."

"I'd rather die than call Ferhat," said Mevlut.

PART III

September 1968–June 1982

I was hated by my father from the cradle.

—Stendhal, *The Red and the Black*

I

Mevlut in the Village

If This World Could Speak, What Would It Say?

IN ORDER TO UNDERSTAND Mevlut's decision, his devotion to Rayiha, and his fear of dogs, we must look back at his childhood. He was born in 1957 in the village of Cennetpınar in the Beyşehir district of Konya and never set foot outside the village until he turned twelve. In the autumn of 1968, having finished primary school, he expected to join his father at work in Istanbul while also continuing his studies, just like all the other children in his position, but it turned out his father didn't want him there, so he had to remain in the village, where he became a shepherd for a while. For the rest of his life, Mevlut would wonder why his father had insisted that he should stay in the village that year; he would never find a satisfactory explanation. His friends, his uncle's sons Korkut and Süleyman, had already left for Istanbul, so this was to prove a sad and lonely winter for Mevlut. He had just under a dozen sheep that he escorted up and down the river. He spent his days gazing at the pale lake in the distance, the buses and the trucks driving by, the birds and the poplar trees.

Sometimes, he noticed the leaves on a poplar quivering in the breeze and thought that the tree was sending him a message. Some leaves showed him their darker surface while others their dried, paler side, until, suddenly, a gentle wind would come along, turning the dark leaves over to show their yellow underside and revealing the darker face of the yellowed leaves.

His favorite pastime was to collect twigs, dry them, and use them to build bonfires. Once the fire really got going, Mevlut's dog Kâmil would bounce around it a couple of times, and when he saw Mevlut sitting down to warm his hands over the flames, the dog, too, would sit down nearby and stare into the fire, motionless, just like Mevlut.

All the dogs in the village recognized Mevlut, they never barked at him even when he crept out in the middle of the darkest, quietest night, and this made him feel that this village was a place where he truly belonged. The local dogs barked only at those who came from outside the village, anyone who was a threat or a foreigner. But sometimes a dog would bark at someone local, like Mevlut's cousin Süleyman, who was his best friend. "You must be having some pretty nasty thoughts, Süleyman!" the others would tease.

Süleyman. Actually, the village dogs never barked at me. We've moved to Istanbul now, and I'm sad that Mevlut had to stay behind in the village, I miss him . . . But the dogs in the village treated me the same way they treated Mevlut. I just thought I should make that clear.

Every now and then, Mevlut and his dog Kâmil climbed one of the hills, leaving the herd to graze down below. From his vantage point looking over the fields stretched out beneath him, Mevlut would yearn to live, to be happy, to be someone in the universe. There were times when he would dream of his father coming on a bus to take him away to Istanbul. The plains below, where the animals grazed, ended in a steep rock face at a bend in the stream. Sometimes you could spot the smoke from a fire at the opposite edge of the plain. Mevlut knew that the fire must have been lit by shepherd boys from the neighboring village of Gümüşdere, who, like him, hadn't been able to go to Istanbul to continue their studies. From atop Mevlut and Kâmil's hill you could see, when it was windy and the sky was clear, and especially in the mornings, the little houses of Gümüşdere and the sweet little white mosque with its slender minaret.

Abdurrahman Efendi. I will take the liberty to quickly interrupt here, as I actually live in the abovementioned village of Gümüşdere. In the 1950s, most of us who lived in Cennetpınar, Gümüşdere, and the three neighboring villages were all very poor. During winter, we would become indebted to the grocer and could just barely make it through to spring. Come springtime, some of the men would go to Istanbul to work on construction sites. Some of us couldn't even afford the bus ticket to Istanbul, so the Blind Grocer would buy it for us and write it down at the very top of his account book. Back in 1954, a tall, wide-shouldered giant from our village of Gümüşdere, a man named Yusuf, went to Istanbul to work as a builder. Then he became, *by pure coincidence,* a yogurt seller and made a lot of money selling yogurt street by street. He first brought over his brothers and his cousins to help him in Istanbul, where they all lived in bachelors' apartments. Until then, the people of Gümüşdere hadn't known the first thing about yogurt. But soon, most of us were going to Istanbul to pursue this opportunity. I first went there when I was twenty-two, after completing my compulsory military service. (Owing to various disciplinary mishaps, this took me four years; I kept getting caught trying to run away, I got beaten up a lot and spent a great deal of time in jail, but let it be known that no one loves our army and our honorable officers more than I do!) At the time, our soldiers hadn't yet decided to hang the prime minister Adnan Menderes; he was still driving around Istanbul in his Cadillac, and whenever he came across any remaining historic homes and mansions, he had them demolished to make way for wide avenues. Business was good for street vendors plying their trade among the rubble, but I just couldn't manage that whole yogurt-selling thing. Our people here tend to be tough and strong, big boned and with wide shoulders. But me, I'm a bit on the skinny side, as you will see for yourself should we ever meet one day, God willing. I got crushed under that wooden pole all day, with a thirty-kilo tray of yogurt tied at each end. To top it all, like most yogurt sellers I also went out in the evenings to try to make a little more money by selling boza. You can try all you want to cushion the weight of the pole, but a novice yogurt seller will inevitably get calluses on his neck and shoulders. At the beginning, I was pleased to see that I wasn't getting any, because my skin is as smooth as velvet, but then I realized that the damned stick was doing much worse; it was damaging my spine, so off I went to the hospital. I spent about a month in hospital queues before the doctor told me I had to stop shouldering loads immediately. But obviously I had to earn a living, so instead of giving up the stick, I gave up the doctor. And that's how my neck began to get crooked, and I came to be known among friends no longer as Little Miss Abdy but as Crooked-Necked Abdurrahman, which was rather heartbreaking. In Istanbul I avoided those who came from my village, but I used to see this Mevlut's hot-tempered dad, Mustafa, and his uncle Hasan all the time, selling yogurt on the streets. That was also when I got hooked on *rakı,* which helped me forget about my neck. After a while I gave up on my dreams of buying a house, a little place in some slum, some real-estate property. I stopped trying to save more money and just tried to enjoy myself instead. I bought some land in Gümüşdere with the money I'd made in Istanbul, and I married the poorest orphan girl in the village. The lesson I learned during my time in the city is that in order to make it there, you need to have at least three sons that you can bring over from the village to slave away for you. I thought I'd have three strapping boys before going back to Istanbul, and this time I'd be able to build myself a home on the first empty hill I came across and go on to conquer the city from there. But I ended up with no sons and three daughters. So two years ago I came back to the village for good, and I love my girls very much. Let me introduce them to you now:

Vediha. I wanted my first strapping boy to be serious and hardworking and had decided to call him Vedii. Unfortunately, I had a daughter. So I called her Vediha, the female version of Vedii.

Rayiha. She loves to sit on her father's lap and has a lovely smell, too, as her name suggests.

Samiha. She's a clever little thing, always crying and complaining; she's not even three yet and already thundering about the house.

41

Mevlut would sit down in Cennetpınar in the evenings with his mother, Atiye, and his two older sisters, who both doted on him, to write to their father, Mustafa Efendi, in Istanbul, asking for shoes, batteries, plastic clothes pegs, and soap, among other things. Their father was illiterate, so he rarely replied, ignoring most of their requests or else claiming, "You could buy those things cheaper from the blind village grocer." Mevlut's mother could sometimes be heard complaining in response: "We didn't ask you to bring these things because the Blind Grocer doesn't have them, Mustafa, but because we haven't got them at home!" The letters Mevlut wrote to his father ended up instilling in the boy a particular understanding of what it meant to ask for something in writing. There were three elements to consider when WRITING A LETTER TO ASK SOMETHING OF SOMEONE WHO IS FAR AWAY:

1. What you truly want, which you can never really know anyway
2. What you are prepared to say openly, which usually helps you gain a slightly better understanding of what you truly want
3. The letter itself, which though imbued with the essence of items 1 and 2 is really an enchanted text with a much-greater significance

Mustafa Efendi. When I came back from Istanbul at the end of May, I brought the girls their flowery purple and green dress fabrics; for their mother, a pair of closed slippers and the Pe-Re-Ja–brand cologne Mevlut had written down in his letter; and for Mevlut, the toy he'd asked for. I was a bit hurt by his halfhearted thanks for the present. "He wanted a water pistol like the village headman's son . . . ," said his mother while his sisters smirked. The next day, I went to the Blind Grocer with Mevlut, and we went through each item on our account. Every now and then I lost my temper: "What the hell is this Çamlıca gum?" I'd bellow, but Mevlut kept his eyes down, as he was the one who had been buying it. "No more gum for this one!" I told the Blind Grocer. "Mevlut should go to school in Istanbul next winter anyway!" said the Blind Grocer, that know-it-all. "He's got a good head for numbers and sums. Maybe he'll be the one to finally go to college from our village."

The news that Mevlut's father had fallen out with Uncle Hasan in Istanbul over the past winter quickly reached the village . . . Last December, during the coldest days of the month, Uncle Hasan and his two sons, Korkut and Süleyman, had left the house they lived in with Mevlut's father in Kültepe and moved into a new one they had all built together on Duttepe, the hill opposite Kültepe, leaving Mevlut's father behind. Uncle Hasan's wife, Safiye, who was both Mevlut's maternal aunt and his paternal uncle's wife, had quickly followed, coming from the village into this new home in Istanbul to look after her husband and sons. These developments meant that Mevlut could now join his father in the autumn so that Mustafa Efendi would not be left alone in Istanbul.

Süleyman. My father and Uncle Mustafa are brothers, but our surnames are different. When Atatürk decreed that everyone should take a surname, the census officer from Beyşehir came to our village on the back of a donkey, toting his reams of records, to write down the surnames everyone had chosen for themselves. On the last day of the whole operation, it was our grandfather's turn. He was a very devout and pious man who had never gone anywhere farther than Beyşehir. He took his time thinking and finally went for "Aktaş." His two sons were arguing in their father's presence as usual. "Put me down as Karataş," demanded Uncle Mustafa, who was a little boy at the time, but neither my grandfather nor the census officer paid him any heed. Still, my uncle Mustafa is very stubborn and prickly, and many years later, before Mevlut was enrolled in middle school, he went down to the judge to have his surname changed, and from then on they became Karataş, "Blackstone," while we remained Aktaş, "Whitestone." My cousin Mevlut Karataş is really looking forward to starting school in Istanbul this autumn. But of the kids from around our village who have been sent to Istanbul on this pretext, not a single one has graduated from high school yet. There are almost a hundred villages and towns around where we come from, and so far only one boy has ever made it to college. That bespectacled mousy creature eventually went off to America, and no one has ever heard from him again. Many years later, someone saw his picture in the newspapers, but because he had changed his name, no one was even sure whether this was our bespectacled rodent or not. If you ask me, that bastard must have converted to Christianity by now.

One evening toward the end of that summer, Mevlut's father brought out a rusty saw Mevlut remembered from his childhood. He led his son to the old oak tree. Slowly and deliberately, they sawed off a branch that was about as thick as an arm. It was a long and slightly curved branch. Using a bread knife and then a pocketknife, Mevlut's father trimmed the twigs off one by one.

"This will be the pole you use when you work as a street vendor!" he said. He took some matches from the kitchen and asked Mevlut to light a fire. He charred and blackened the knots on the rod, turning it slowly over the fire until it had dried up. "It's not enough to do it once. You have to leave it out in the sunshine all through the summer and dry it over the fire again. Eventually, it will become as hard as stone and as smooth as silk. Go on, have a look and see if it sits well on your shoulders."

Mevlut placed the stick across his shoulders. He felt its toughness and warmth with a shiver.

At the end of summer, they went to Istanbul, taking a small sack of homemade soup powder, some dried red chilies, bags of bulgur and flatbread, and baskets of walnuts. His father would give the bulgur and walnuts as gifts to the doormen in some of the more prestigious buildings so that they would treat him well and let him take the elevator. They also took a broken flashlight that was to be fixed in Istanbul, a kettle that his father particularly liked and would bring back with him to the village, some straw mats for the dirt floor at home, and other paraphernalia. Plastic bags and baskets bursting with their belongings kept popping out of the corners into which they'd stuffed them during their one-and-a-half-day train ride. Mevlut immersed himself in the world he could see beyond the carriage window, even as he thought of the mother and the sisters he was already missing, and had to jump up every so often to chase after the hard-boiled eggs that kept falling out of their bags and rolling into the middle of the carriage.

The world beyond the train window contained more people, wheat fields, poplars, oxen, bridges, donkeys, houses, mosques, tractors, signs, letters, stars, and transmission towers than Mevlut had seen in the first twelve years of his life. The transmission towers looked as if they were coming straight at him, which sometimes made his head spin until he fell asleep with his head on his father's shoulder, and woke up to find that the yellow fields and the sunny abundance of wheat had been replaced by purplish rocks all around, so that later, in his dreams, he would see Istanbul as a city built out of these purple rocks.

Then his eyes would fall upon a green river and green trees, and he would feel his soul changing color. If this world could speak, what would it say? Sometimes, it seemed to Mevlut that the train wasn't moving at all but that an entire universe was filing past the window. Each time they passed a station, he would get excited and shout the name out to his father—"Hamam . . . İhsaniye . . . Döğer . . ."—and when the thick blue cigarette smoke in the compartment made his eyes water, he went outside to the toilet, stumbling like a drunk before he could force the door open with some difficulty, and watched the railroad tracks and the gravel go by under the toilet hole. The clacking of the train's wheels could scarcely be heard through the hole. On the way back to his seat, Mevlut would first walk through to the very end of the train, looking into each compartment to observe the traveling multitudes, the women sleeping, the children crying, the people playing cards, eating spiced sausages that made entire compartments smell of garlic, and performing their daily prayers.

"What are you up to, why are you always going to the toilet?" his father asked. "Is the water running?"

"It isn't."

Children selling snacks would board the train at some stations, and while eating the wrap his mother had dutifully packed for him, Mevlut would examine the raisins, roasted chickpeas, biscuits, bread, cheese, almonds, and chewing gum these children sold before the train pulled into the next town. Sometimes shepherds would spot the train from afar and run down after it with their dogs, and as the train sped past, these boys would yell for "newspaprrrrsss" with which to roll cigarettes filled with smuggled tobacco, and hearing this Mevlut would feel a strange sense of superiority. When the Istanbul train stopped in the middle of the grasslands, Mevlut would remember just how quiet a place the world really was. In that quiet time, during those waits that felt like they might never end, Mevlut would look out the window to see women picking tomatoes from a small garden of a village house, hens walking along the train tracks, two donkeys scratching each other next to an electric water pump, and, just a bit farther, a bearded man dozing on the heath.

"When are we going to move?" he asked during one of these interminable stops.

"Be patient, son, Istanbul isn't going anywhere."

"Oooh, look, we're moving again!"

"It's not us, it's just the train next to us," said his father, laughing.

In the village school that Mevlut had attended for five years, a map of Turkey, with a flag on it and a portrait of Atatürk, used to hang right behind where the teacher stood, and throughout the journey, Mevlut tried to keep track of where they might be on that map. He fell asleep before the train entered Izmit and didn't wake up again until they arrived in Istanbul's Haydarpaşa station.

The many bundles, bags, and baskets they were carrying were so heavy that it took them a full hour to make their way down the stairs of Haydarpaşa train station and catch a ferry to Karaköy. That was the first time Mevlut saw the sea, in the evening twilight. The sea was as dark as dreams and as deep as sleep. There was a sweet smell of seaweed in the cool breeze. The European side of the city was sparkling with lights. It wasn't his first sight of the sea but of these lights that Mevlut would never forget for the rest of his life. Once they got to the other side, the local buses wouldn't let them on with all their luggage, so they walked for four hours all the way home to the edge of Zincirlikuyu.

2

Home

The Hills at the End of the City

HOME WAS a *gecekondu,* a slum house. This was the word Mevlut's father used to refer to this place whenever he got angry about its crudeness and poverty, but on those rare occasions when he wasn't angry, he preferred to use the word "home," with a tenderness akin to what Mevlut felt toward the house. This tenderness fostered the illusion that the place might hold traces of the eternal home that would one day be theirs in this world, but it was difficult to truly believe this. The *gecekondu* consisted of a single fairly large room. There was also a toilet next to it, which was a hole in the ground. At night, the sound of dogs fighting and howling in distant neighborhoods could be heard through the small unglazed window in the toilet.

When they arrived that first night, a man and a woman were already in the house, and Mevlut thought for a moment that they'd walked into the wrong building. Eventually it became clear that they were the lodgers Mevlut's father had taken in for the summer. Mevlut's father started arguing with them, but then he gave up and made a bed in another dark corner of the room, where father and son ended up sleeping side by side.

When Mevlut woke up toward noon the next day, there was no one home. He thought of how his father, his uncle, and eventually his cousins, too, had all lived in this house together only recently. Thinking back on the stories Korkut and Süleyman had told him over the summer, Mevlut tried to picture them in this room, but the place felt eerily abandoned. There was an old table, four chairs, two beds (one with bedsprings and one without), two cupboards, two windows, and a stove. After six winters working in this city, this was the extent of his father's possessions. After arguing with his father last year, Mevlut's uncle and cousins had moved out to a different house, taking their beds, their furniture, and the rest of their belongings. Mevlut couldn't find a single thing that had been theirs. Looking inside a cupboard, he was pleased to see one or two things his father had brought over from the village, the woolen socks his mother had knit for him, his long johns, and a pair of scissors—now rusty—that Mevlut had once seen his sisters using back home.

The house had a dirt floor. Mevlut saw that, before leaving for the day, his father had laid out one of the straw mats they had carried from the village. His uncle and cousins must have taken the old one with them when they left last year.

The rough old table on which his father had left a fresh loaf of bread that morning was of hardwood and plywood both. Mevlut would put empty matchboxes and wooden shims under its one short leg to keep it steady, but every now and then the table would wobble, spilling soup or tea over them and making his father angry. He got angry about lots of things. Many times during the years they would spend together in this house after 1969 his father vowed to "fix the table," but he never did.

Even when they were in a rush, sitting down and having dinner with his father in the evening made Mevlut happy, especially during his first few years in Istanbul. But because they soon had to go out to sell boza—either his father on his own or with Mevlut by his side—these dinners were nowhere near as fun as the lively, joyful meals they used to have back in the village, sitting on the floor, with his sisters and his mother. In his father's gestures, Mevlut could always sense an eagerness to get to work as soon as possible. No sooner had he swallowed his last morsel than Mustafa Efendi would light up a cigarette, and before even half finishing it, he would say, "Let's go."

When he got back from school and before setting out again to sell boza, Mevlut liked to make soup, either on the stove or, if it wasn't lit, on their little butane cooktop. Into a pot of boiling water, he would throw a spoonful of margarine and whatever was left in the fridge, such as carrots, celery, and potatoes, as well as a handful of the chilies and bulgur they'd brought from the village, and then he would stand back and listen to the pot bubbling away as he watched the infernal tumult inside. The little bits of potato and carrot whirled around madly like creatures burning in the fires of hell—you could almost hear them wailing in agony from inside the pot—and then there would be sudden unexpected surges, as in volcanic craters, and the carrots and celery would rise up close to Mevlut's nose. He loved watching the potatoes turn yellow as they cooked and the carrots give their color off to the soup, and listening to the changing sounds the soup made as it bubbled away. He likened the ceaseless motion in the pot to the orbits of the planets, which he had learned about in geography class at his new school, the Atatürk Boys' Secondary School, and this made him think that he, too, was spinning around in this universe, just like these little particles in the soup. The hot steam from the pot smelled good, and it was nice to warm himself over it.

"The soup is delicious, my boy!" his father said every time. "I wonder if we should make you a cook's apprentice?" On evenings when he didn't go out to sell boza with his father but stayed at home to do his homework, as soon as his father had gone Mevlut would clear the table, take out his geography textbook, and start to memorize all of the city and country names, getting lost in sleepy daydreams as he looked at pictures of the Eiffel Tower and the Buddhist temples in China. On days when he went to school in the morning and helped his father carry around the heavy yogurt trays in the afternoon, he collapsed on the bed and fell asleep as soon as they'd had their dinner. His father would wake him before going out again.

"Put your pajamas on and get under the blanket before you go to sleep, son. Otherwise you'll freeze when the stove goes off."

"Wait for me, Dad, I'm coming, too," Mevlut would say without really waking up, as if talking in his sleep.

When he was left alone in the house at night, and set his mind to his geography homework, try as he might Mevlut could never ignore altogether the noise of the wind howling through the window, the relentless scurrying about of mice and of imps, the sounds outside of footsteps and of wailing dogs. These city dogs were more restless, more desperate, than the dogs back in the village. There were frequent power cuts so Mevlut couldn't even do his homework, and in the darkness the flames and the crackling from the stove seemed bigger and louder, and he became convinced that there was an eye watching him closely from the shadows in a corner of the room. If he took his eyes off his geography book, the owner of the eye would realize that Mevlut had seen it and would certainly pounce on him, so there were times when Mevlut couldn't even bring himself to get up and go to bed, and slept with his head resting on his books.

"Why didn't you turn off the stove and get into bed, son?" his father would say when he came back in the middle of the night feeling tired and irritable.

The streets were freezing cold, so his father didn't mind that the house was warm, but at the same time he didn't like to see so much wood used up in the stove. As he was reluctant to admit to this, he would say, at most, "Turn off the stove if you're going to sleep."

His father either got their firewood from Uncle Hasan's little shop or else chopped it himself with a neighbor's ax. Before winter arrived, Mevlut's father taught him how to light the stove using dry twigs and bits of newspaper, and where to find these sticks and scraps in the nearby hills.

In the first months after they'd arrived in the city, on returning from his yogurt rounds, Mevlut's father would take him farther up Kültepe, the hill on which they lived. Their house was at the edge of the city, on the lower part of a balding, muddy hill dotted with mulberry trees, and with a fig tree here and there. At the bottom, the hill was bound by traces of a narrow little creek, which wended its way around and through the other hills, from Ortaköy to the Bosphorus. The women of the families who had migrated here in the midfifties from impoverished villages around Ordu, Gümüşhane, Kastamonu, and Erzincan used to grow corn and wash their laundry all along the creek, just as they had done back home, and in summer their children would swim in its shallow waters. Back then, the creek was known by its old Ottoman name Buzludere, "Icy Creek," but the waste generated over fifteen years by more than eighty thousand Anatolian migrant settlers on the surrounding hills, and by a multitude of factories, small and large, soon caused the river to be known as Bokludere, "Dung Creek." By the time Mevlut arrived in Istanbul, neither name was used anymore, as the river had long been forgotten, absorbed by the growing city and mostly buried under layers of concrete from its source to its mouth.

At the top of Kültepe, "Ash Hill," Mevlut's father showed him the remains of an old waste-incineration plant whose ashes had given the hill its name. From here, you could see the slums that were rapidly taking over the surrounding hills (Duttepe, Kuştepe, Esentepe, Gültepe, Harmantepe, Seyrantepe, Oktepe, et cetera), the city's biggest cemetery (Zincirlikuyu), factories of all shapes and sizes, garages, workshops, depots, medicine and lightbulb manufacturers, and, in the distance, the ghostly silhouette of the city with its tall buildings and its minarets. The city itself and its neighborhoods—where Mevlut and his father sold yogurt in the mornings and boza in the evenings, and where Mevlut went to school—were only mysterious smudges on the horizon.

Farther out still, you could see the blue hills on the Asian side of the city. The Bosphorus was nestled between these hills, and although invisible from Kültepe, whenever Mevlut climbed up the hill during his first months in the city, he always thought he could glimpse its blue waters between the mountains. Atop each hill that sloped down to the sea was one of those enormous transmission towers carrying a key power line into the city. The wind made strange noises when it blew against these gigantic steel constructions, and on humid days, the buzz of the cables scared Mevlut and his friends. On the barbed wire surrounding the tower was a picture of a skull warning DANGER OF DEATH, the sign pockmarked with bullet holes.

When he first used to come up here to gather sticks and paper, Mevlut would look out at the view below and assume that the danger came not from the electricity but from the city itself. People said that it was forbidden and bad luck to get too close to the enormous towers, but most of the neighborhood got its electricity from illicit cables expertly hooked into this main line.

Mustafa Efendi. So that he would understand the hardship we've endured, I told my son how all the hills around here, except for ours and Duttepe, still lacked power. I told him that when his uncle and I first came here six years ago, there was no electricity anywhere, no water supply or any sewage drains either. I showed him those places on the other hills where Ottoman sultans used to hunt and where soldiers took their target practice, the greenhouses where the Albanians grew strawberries and flowers, the dairy farm run by those who lived in Kâğıthane, and the white graveyard, where the bodies of soldiers who died in the typhus epidemic during the Balkan War of 1912 were covered with lime; I told him just so he wouldn't be fooled by the bright lights of Istanbul into thinking that life was somehow easy. I didn't want to crush his spirit entirely, though, so I also showed him the Atatürk Boys' Secondary School, where we would soon have him enrolled, the dirt field laid out for the Duttepe football team, the Derya Cinema with its feeble projector, which had just opened this summer among the mulberry trees, and the site of the Duttepe Mosque, which had been under construction for four years now, sponsored by the baker and contractor Hadji Hamit Vural and his men, all from Rize, with their matching oversize chins to prove it. On the slopes to the right of the mosque, I pointed out the house his uncle Hasan had finished building last year on the plot we had marked out together four years ago with a wall of whitewashed stones. "When your uncle and I arrived here six years ago, all of these hills were empty!" I said. I explained that for the poor souls who'd come here from far away the priority was to find a job and settle down in the city, and in order to get to the city ahead of everyone else in the mornings, they all tried to build their homes as close as possible to the roads at the foot of the hills, so that you could almost see the neighborhoods growing from the bottom of each hill toward the top.

3

The Enterprising Individual Who Builds a House on Empty Land

Oh, My Boy, Istanbul Is a Little Scary, Isn't It?

LYING IN BED at night during his first months in Istanbul, Mevlut would listen closely to the sounds of the city drifting in from afar. He would wake up with a start on some quiet nights to the faint sound of dogs barking in the distance, and when he realized that his father wasn't back yet, he would bury his head under the blanket and try to go back to sleep. When it seemed that Mevlut's nighttime fear of dogs was getting out of hand, his father took him to a holy man in a wooden house in Kasımpaşa who said a few prayers and breathed a blessing over Mevlut. Mevlut would remember it all many years later.

He discovered in a dream one night that the vice principal of Atatürk Boys' Secondary School, the so-called Skeleton, looked just like the skull on the DANGER OF DEATH sign on the electric transmission tower. (Mevlut and his father had met Skeleton when they had gone to present Mevlut's primary-school certificate from the village so that they could enroll him.) Mevlut didn't dare look up from his math homework lest he should come face-to-face with the demon that he believed was always watching him from the darkness outside the window. That was why sometimes, when he wanted to go to sleep, he couldn't even work up the courage to get up and go to bed.

Mevlut got to know Kültepe, Duttepe, and the neighborhoods of the surrounding hills through Süleyman, who had become very familiar with the whole area in the year he'd already spent there. Mevlut saw many *gecekondu* homes, some of whose foundations had only just been laid, some with the walls only half built, and others awaiting the finishing touches. Most of them were occupied by men only. The majority of those who had come to Kültepe and Duttepe from Konya, Kastamonu, and Gümüşhane these past five years had either left their wives and children behind, as Mevlut's father had done, or were single men with no prospects for marriage, no gainful employment, or any property whatsoever back in their village. They left their doors open sometimes, and Mevlut would see as many as six or seven single men in one room, all sleeping like logs, and in those moments he could really feel the sullen presence of the dogs that lurked about. The dogs must have been able to detect the thick smell of stale breath, sweat, and sleeping bodies. Unmarried men were aggressive, unfriendly, and always scowling, so Mevlut was mostly afraid of them.

On the main road in the center of Duttepe down below, where bus routes would one day terminate, there was a grocer whom Mevlut's father called a swindler; a shop that sold sacks of cement, used car doors, old tiles, stovepipes, scraps of tin, and plastic tarpaulins; and a coffeehouse where unemployed men loitered all day. Uncle Hasan also had a little shop in the middle of the road that led up the hill. In his free time, Mevlut used to go there and make paper bags out of old newspapers with his cousins Korkut and Süleyman.

Süleyman. Mevlut wasted a year back in the village because of my uncle Mustafa's temper, so he ended up in the year behind me at Atatürk Boys' Secondary School. When he first arrived in Istanbul my cousin was a fish out of water, and whenever I saw him standing all alone in the school yard during recess, I made sure to keep him company. We are all very fond of Mevlut and don't let his father's behavior affect how we treat him. One night before the start of the school year they came to our house in Duttepe. As soon as he saw my mother, Mevlut gave her a hug that showed how much he missed his own mother and his sisters.

"Oh, my boy, Istanbul is a little scary, isn't it?" said my mom, hugging him back. "But don't be afraid, we're always here for you, see?" She kissed his hair as his own mother used to do. "Now tell me, am I going to be your Safiye Yenge here in Istanbul, or will it be Safiye Teyze?"

My mom was both Mevlut's uncle's wife—his *yenge*—and his mother's older sister, his *teyze*. During the summer, when Mevlut was likely to be influenced by our fathers' constant bickering, he tended to call her Yenge, but during winter, when Uncle Mustafa was in Istanbul, Mevlut called my mom Teyze with all the sweetness and charm he had in common with his mother and sisters.

"You're always Teyze to me," said Mevlut now, with feeling.

"Your father won't like that!" said my mom.

"Safiye, please look after him as much as you can," said Uncle Mustafa. "He's like an orphan here, he cries every night."

Mevlut was embarrassed.

"We're sending him to school," Uncle Mustafa went on. "But it's a bit pricey, what with all the textbooks and exercise books and so on. And he needs a blazer."

"What's your school number?" asked my brother Korkut.

"Ten nineteen."

My brother went to the next room to rummage in the trunk and brought back the old school blazer we had both used in the past. He beat the dust off and smoothed down the creases and helped Mevlut into it like a tailor waiting on a customer.

"It really suits you, ten nineteen," said Korkut.

"I'll say! No need at all for a new blazer, I think," said Uncle Mustafa.

"It's a bit big for you, but it's better that way," said Korkut. "A tight blazer can give you trouble during a fight."

"Mevlut isn't going to school to get into fights," said Uncle Mustafa.

"If he can help it," said Korkut. "Sometimes you get these donkey-faced monsters for teachers who pick on you so much that it's hard to stop yourself."

Korkut. I didn't like the way Uncle Mustafa said "Mevlut doesn't get into fights"; I could tell he was patronizing me. I stopped going to school three years ago, back when Uncle Mustafa and my father were still living in the house they built together in Kültepe. On one of my last days of school, to make sure I would never be tempted to go back, I gave that donkey-faced show-off of a chemistry teacher Fevzi the lesson he deserved: two slaps and three punches in front of the entire class. He had it coming ever since the year before when he asked me what $Pb_2(SO_4)$ was, and I said, "Pebbles," and he started mocking me, as if he could bring me down in front of everyone; he also made me fail the year for no reason. It may well have "Atatürk" in the name, but I have no respect for a school where you can go to class and beat your teacher up at will.

Süleyman. "The blazer's got a hole in the lining of the left pocket, but don't get it sewn up," I told a bewildered Mevlut. "You can hide cheat notes in there," I said. "This blazer wasn't of much benefit in school, but it really comes in handy when you're out selling boza in the evenings. No one can resist a boy out on the cold streets at night in his school uniform. 'Don't tell me you're still a schoolboy, son?' they say, and then they start stuffing your pockets with chocolates, woolen socks, and money. When you get home, all you have to do is turn your pockets inside out, and it's all yours. Whatever you do, make sure you don't tell them you've left school. Tell them you want to be a doctor."

"Mevlut isn't going to leave school anyway!" said his father. "He really is going to be a doctor. Aren't you?"

Mevlut realized that their kindness was tinged with pity, and he couldn't fully enjoy its fruits. The house in Duttepe, into which his uncle's family had moved last year, having built it with the help of his father, was a lot cleaner and brighter than the *gecekondu* Mevlut and his father occupied in Kültepe. His aunt and uncle, who used to eat on the floor back in the village, now sat at a table covered with a flowery plastic tablecloth. Their floor was not of dirt; it was of cement. The house smelled of cologne, and the clean, ironed curtains made Mevlut wish he belonged there. They already had three rooms, and Mevlut could tell that the Aktaş family, who had sold everything they had in the village—including their cattle, their house, and their garden—would live a happy life here, an outcome, Mevlut felt ashamed and resentful to admit, his father hadn't yet managed, nor even seemed inclined to try for.

Mustafa Efendi. I know you go to see your uncle's family in secret, I would tell Mevlut, you go to your uncle Hasan's shop to fold up newspapers, you sit and eat at their table, you play with Süleyman, but don't forget that they cheated us, I would warn him. It is a terrible feeling for a man to know that his son would rather be in the company of the crooks who tried to trick his father and take what was rightfully his! And don't get so agitated about that blazer. It's yours by rights! Don't you ever forget that if you stay close to the same people who so shamelessly grabbed the land your father helped them claim, they will lose all respect for you, do you understand, Mevlut?

Six years ago and three years after the military coup of 27 May 1960, while Mevlut was back in the village learning how to read and write, his father and his uncle Hasan came to Istanbul to find a job and start earning some money, and they moved into a rented house in Duttepe. Mevlut's father and uncle lived together there for two years, but when the landlord raised the rent, they left and went across to Kültepe (which was only just beginning to fill up), where they hauled hollow bricks, cement, and sheets of scrap metal to build the house where Mevlut and his father now lived. His father and Uncle Hasan got on very well in those early days in Istanbul. They learned the secrets of the yogurt trade together, and at the beginning—as they would later laughingly recall—these two towering men would go out together on their sales rounds. Eventually, they learned to split up to cover more ground, but in order to prevent either from getting jealous of how much the other brought in, they always pooled their daily earnings. Their natural closeness was also helped by the fact that their wives back in the village were sisters. Mevlut smiled when he recalled how happy his mother and his aunt were whenever they went to the village post office to pick up their money order. In those years, Mevlut's father and Uncle Hasan used to spend Sundays idling in the parks and teahouses and on the beaches of Istanbul; they would shave twice a week sharing a shaver and razor; and when they came back to the village at the start of summer, they would bring their wives and kids the same presents.

In 1965, the year they moved into the unregistered house they had built in Kültepe, the two brothers claimed two empty lots, one in Kültepe itself and the other in Duttepe, with the help of Uncle Hasan's eldest son Korkut, who had just joined them from the village. The 1965 elections were approaching, and there was a sense of leniency in the air, with rumors that the Justice Party would declare an amnesty on unregistered property after the elections, and with this in mind they set out to build a new house on the land in Duttepe.

In those days, no one in either Duttepe or Kültepe formally held title to their land. The enterprising individual who built a house on an empty lot would plant a few poplars and willow trees and lay the first few bricks of a wall to mark out his property, after which he would go to the neighborhood councilman and pay him something to draw up a document certifying that said individual had built the house in question and planted those trees himself. Just like the genuine title deeds issued by the State Land Registry, these documents included a crude plan of the house, which the councilman himself would draw with a pencil and ruler. He would jot down some additional notations in his childish scrawl—the adjacent plots belonging to this or that person, a nearby fountain, the location of the wall (which in fact might have consisted of no more than a rock or two here and there), and the poplar trees—and if you gave him some extra money, he would add a couple of words to widen the imaginary boundaries of the plot, before finally affixing his seal underneath it all.

In reality, the land belonged to the national Treasury or to the forestry department, so the documents provided by the councilman did not guarantee ownership at all. A house built on unregistered land could be knocked down by the authorities at any moment. Sleeping for the first time in the homes they'd built with their own hands, people would often have nightmares about this potential disaster. But the value of the councilman's document would prove itself when the government decided, as it tended to do every decade or so in election years, to issue title deeds for homes built overnight—for these deeds would be handed out in conformity with the documents drawn up by the local councilman. Furthermore, anyone who was able to procure a document from the councilman certifying ownership of a plot of land could then sell that plot to someone else. During periods when the flow of unemployed and homeless immigrants to the city was particularly heavy, the price of these documents would rise, with the increasingly valuable plots quickly split up and parceled out, and the political influence of the councilman, needless to say, also climbing in proportion to the influx of migrants.

Through all this feverish activity, the authorities could still send the gendarmes to a hastily built home and knock it down whenever they felt like it or found it politically expedient to do so. The key was to finish building the house and start living in it as soon as possible. If a house had occupants, it could not be demolished without a warrant, and this could take a long time to obtain. As soon as they had the chance, anyone who claimed a plot of land on a hill would, provided they had any sense, recruit their friends and family to help them put up four walls overnight and then move in immediately so that the demolition crews couldn't touch them the next day. Mevlut liked to hear the stories of mothers and their children who had their first night's sleep in Istanbul with the stars as their blankets and the sky as their ceiling, in homes with no real roof yet, and with even the walls and the windows not yet finished. Legend has it that the term *gecekondu*—"placed overnight"—was coined by a mason from Erzincan who in one night built about a dozen homes ready for people to move into; when he died at a ripe old age, thousands paid their respects at his grave in Duttepe cemetery.

The construction project undertaken by Mevlut's father and uncle had also been inspired by the preelectoral mood of permissiveness, but it was abandoned when that same mood caused a sharp increase in the price of construction materials and scrap metal. Rumors of a coming amnesty on unregistered property had sparked a frenzy of unlicensed building on state-owned land and forests. Even those who'd never before thought about building an illegal home went off to a hill somewhere at the edge of the city and, with the help of the local councilman, bought some land from whatever organization controlled the area (gangs, really, some of which carried sticks, others armed with pistols, and others still with political affiliations) and built homes in the most isolated and absurdly remote locations. As for buildings in the city center, many had floors added on to them around this time without permits. The wide expanses of empty land on which Istanbul was spread quickly turned into one vast construction site. The newspapers of the homeowning bourgeoisie decried the unplanned urban sprawl, while the rest of the city basked in the joy of home building. The small factories that produced the substandard hollow bricks used to build the *gecekondu* homes, and the shops that sold other construction materials, were all working overtime, and you could see horse carts, vans, and minibuses carrying bricks, cement, sand, timber, metal, and glass around the dusty neighborhood roads and up the hill paths at all hours of the day, gleefully ringing their bells and blowing their horns. "I hammered away for days to build your uncle Hasan's house," Mevlut's father would say to him whenever there was a religious holiday and father and son went to Duttepe to visit their relatives. "I just want to be sure you remember that. Not that I would want you to make enemies of your uncle and your cousins."

Süleyman. That's not true: Mevlut knows that the real reason why construction on the Kültepe house had to stop was that Uncle Mustafa kept sending all the money he made in Istanbul back to the village. As for what happened last year, my brother and I really wanted to work with Uncle Mustafa on the house, but my father understandably had had enough of my uncle's mood swings, of his constantly picking fights and treating his own nephews so badly.

Mevlut would become very upset whenever his father told him that his cousins Korkut and Süleyman "would stab him in the back one day." He couldn't even enjoy going to see the Aktaş family for holidays and other special occasions, like the day the Duttepe football team made its debut or when the Vural family invited everyone to celebrate the construction of the mosque. He'd always relished those visits because he knew his aunt Safiye would feed him pastries, that he would get to see Süleyman and catch a glimpse of Korkut, and of course he'd enjoy the comforts of a clean and tidy home. At the same time he dreaded those barbed exchanges between his father and his uncle Hasan, which always filled him with a sense of impending doom.

The first few times they went to visit the Aktaş family, Mevlut's father would take a good long look at the windows of the three-room house, and declare "this bit should have been painted green, the wall on that side needs replastering," to remind Mevlut of the injustice they'd suffered and to ensure that everyone knew of the claim that Mustafa Efendi and his son Mevlut had on this house.

Later, Mevlut would overhear his father telling Uncle Hasan: "As soon as you get hold of some money, you'll sink it all into some swamp or something!" "What, like this one?" his uncle Hasan would reply. "They're already offering me one and a half times the initial value, but I won't sell." Instead of gently fizzling out, these arguments would typically escalate. Before Mevlut even got a chance to eat his stewed fruit and orange after dinner, his father would rise from the table and take hold of his hand, saying: "Come on, son, we're leaving!" Once they were out in the dark night, he would add: "Didn't I say that we shouldn't have come at all? That's it, we're never coming again."

On the way back from Uncle Hasan's in Duttepe to their own place in Kültepe, Mevlut would see the city lights sparkling from afar, the velvety night, and the neon lamps of Istanbul. Sometimes, as he walked with his little hand in his father's bigger one, a single star in the starry dark blue sky would catch Mevlut's eye, and even as his father kept grumbling and muttering to himself, Mevlut imagined that they were walking toward it. Sometimes, you couldn't see the city at all, but the pale orange-hued lights from the tens of thousands of tiny homes in the surrounding hills made the now-familiar landscape more resplendent than it really was. And sometimes, the lights from the nearby hills would disappear in the mist, and from within the thickening fog, Mevlut would hear the sound of dogs barking.

4

Mevlut Begins to Work as a Street Vendor

It's Not Your Job to Act Superior

I'M SHAVING in honor of your first day of work, my boy," his father said one morning just as Mevlut was waking up. "Lesson one: if you're selling yogurt, and especially if you're selling boza, you need to look neat. Some customers will look at your hands and your fingernails. Some of them will look at your shoes, trousers, and shirt. If you're going inside a house, take your shoes off immediately, and make sure your socks don't have holes in them and your feet don't smell. But you're a good lad, you've got a kind heart, and you always smell all nice and clean, don't you?"

By clumsily imitating his father, Mevlut soon worked out how to hang yogurt trays on opposite ends of his pole so that the two sides balanced, how to slide slats between the trays to keep them separate, and how to cover each stack with a wooden lid.

The yogurt did not seem so heavy at first, because his father had taken some of his load, but as they advanced on the dirt road linking Kültepe to the city, Mevlut realized that a yogurt seller was essentially a porter. They would walk for half an hour along the dusty way full of trucks, horse carts, and buses. When they reached the paved road, he would concentrate on reading billboards, the headlines on newspapers displayed in grocery stores, and signs affixed to utility poles advertising circumcision services and cram schools. As they advanced farther into the city, they would see old wooden mansions that hadn't yet burned down, military barracks dating back to the Ottoman era, dented shared taxis decorated with checkered livery, minivans blowing their musical horns and raising a cloud of dust in their wake, columns of soldiers marching by, kids playing football on the cobblestones, mothers pushing baby carriages, shopwindows teeming with shoes and boots in all colors, and policemen angrily blowing their whistles as they directed the traffic with their oversize white gloves.

Some cars, like the 1956 Dodge with its enormous and perfectly circular headlights, looked like old men staring with their eyes wide open; the radiator grille on the 1957 Plymouth suggested a man with his thick upper lip topped by a handlebar mustache; other cars (the 1961 Opel Rekord, for instance) looked like spiteful women whose mouths had turned to stone in the middle of an evil cackle, so that now you could see their countless tiny teeth. Mevlut likened the long-nosed trucks to big wolf dogs, and the Skoda-model public-transport buses, which huffed and puffed as they went, to bears walking on all fours.

There were enormous billboards that look up one whole side of a six- or seven-story building with images of beautiful women using Tamek tomato ketchup or Lux soap; the women, like those in European movies or in Mevlut's schoolbooks, did not wear headscarves, and they would smile down at him until his father turned away from the square and into a shaded lane on the right, calling, "Yogurt sellerrr." In the narrow street, Mevlut felt as if everyone was watching them. His father would call out again without ever slowing his pace, swinging his bell along the way (and though he never turned to look at his son, Mevlut could tell from his father's determined expression that he was nonetheless thinking of him), and soon a window would open somewhere on an upper story. "Over here, yogurt seller, come on upstairs," a man or a middle-aged lady in a headscarf would call out. Father and son would go inside and make their way up the stairs, through the vapors of frying oil, until they reached the door.

Mevlut became attuned to the lives in the thousands of kitchens he would see during his career as a street vendor, of the countless housewives, middle-aged women, children, little old ladies, grandpas, pensioners, housekeepers, the adopted and the orphaned that he would meet:

"Welcome, Mustafa Efendi, half a kilo right here, please." "Ah, Mustafa Efendi! We've missed you! What have you been up to in that village all summer?" "Your yogurt better not be sour, yogurt seller. Go on then, put some in here. Your scales are honest, aren't they?" "Who's this beautiful boy, Mustafa Efendi, is it your son? God bless him!" "Oh dear, yogurt seller, I think they must have called you upstairs by mistake, we've got some yogurt from the shop already, there's a huge bowl of it in the fridge." "No one's home, please make a note and we'll pay you next time." "No cream, Mustafa Efendi, the kids don't like it." "Mustafa, once my youngest daughter is all grown up, shall we marry her off to your boy here?" "What's the holdup, yogurt seller? It's taken you all day to climb two flights of stairs." "Are you going to put it in the bowl, yogurt seller, or shall I give you this plate?" "It was cheaper the other day, yogurt seller . . ." "The building manager says street vendors aren't allowed on the elevator, yogurt seller. Got it?" "Where do you get your yogurt from?" "Mustafa Efendi, make sure you pull the door shut behind you as you leave the building, our doorman's run off." "Mustafa Efendi, you will not drag this boy around on the streets with you like a porter, you will send him to school, okay? Otherwise I'm not buying your yogurt anymore." "Yogurt seller, please drop off half a kilo every two days. Just send the boy upstairs." "Don't be scared, son, the dog doesn't bite. All he wants is to have a sniff, see, he likes you." "Have a seat, Mustafa, the wife and kids are out, no one's home, there's some rice with tomato sauce, I'll heat it up for you if you'd like?" "Yogurt seller, we could barely hear you over the radio, shout a little louder next time when you go past, okay?" "These shoes don't fit my boy anymore. Try them on, son." "Mustafa Efendi, don't let this boy grow up like an orphan. Bring his mother over from the village to look after you both."

Mustafa Efendi. "God bless you, ma'am," I'd say on my way out of the house, bowing all the way to the floor. "May God bless all that you touch, sister," I would say so that Mevlut would learn that if you want to survive in this jungle, you have to make certain compromises, so that he would understand that if you want to be rich, you must be prepared to grovel. "Thank you, sir," I would say with an elaborate show of obeisance. "Mevlut will wear these gloves all through winter. May God bless you. Go on, son, kiss the man's hand . . ." But Mevlut wouldn't kiss it; he would just stare straight ahead. Once we were back out in the street, I'd tell him "Look, son, you mustn't be proud, you mustn't turn your nose up at a bowl of soup or a pair of socks. This is our reward for the service we provide. We bring the world's best yogurt all the way to their doorstep. And they give us something in return. That's all it is." A month would pass, and this time he might start sulking because a nice lady tried to give him a woolen skullcap, until, fearing my reaction, he would make as if to kiss her hand, only to be unable at the last moment to make himself do it. "Now listen here, it's not your job to act superior," I'd say. "When I tell you to kiss the customer's hand, you have to kiss the customer's hand. This one's not just any old customer, she's a kindly old lady. Not everyone is as nice as she is. There's scum in this city who will buy yogurt on credit, then move houses without warning and just disappear without paying up. If you act all haughty when a good person tries to show you some kindness, you will never be rich. You should see how your uncle sucks up to Hadji Hamit Vural. Don't let rich people make you feel ashamed. The only difference between us and them is that they got to Istanbul first and started making money before we did."

Every weekday between five past eight in the morning until one o'clock in the afternoon, Mevlut was at Atatürk Boys' Secondary School. When the last bell rang, he'd run off to join his father on the yogurt rounds, emerging through the crowd of street vendors amassed outside the school gates and the boys who'd been unable to settle their scores inside the classrooms and were now taking their blazers off for a fistfight. Mevlut would drop off his schoolbag full of books and notebooks at Fidan Restaurant, where his father was waiting for him, and the two would head out to sell yogurt side by side until dusk.

There were other places like Fidan dotting the city where his father made regular deliveries two or three times a week. Occasionally he would fall out with the proprietors, who were always trying to push his prices down, causing him to drop one restaurant and pick up another instead. Delivering to these places was a lot of hard work for not much profit, but his father couldn't give them up entirely because he depended on their kitchens, their massive fridges, and their terraces or back gardens as storage spaces for his trays of yogurt and jugs of boza. These were alcohol-free restaurants that catered to local shopkeepers, serving home-cooked food, *döner* kebabs, and fruit stews, the owners and headwaiters all on good terms with Mevlut's father. Sometimes, they would show father and son to a table at the back, give them a helping of meat and vegetable stew or rice with chickpeas, a bit of bread, and some yogurt, and sit down with them to chat. Mevlut was fascinated by these conversations: a man who sold raffle tickets and Marlboros, a retired policeman who knew everything that went on in Beyoğlu, and the apprentice at the photography studio next door might also join them at the table, and they would talk about the rising prices, sports betting, how the police were cracking down on those who sold cigarettes and foreign liquor on the black market, the latest political intrigues in Ankara, and the inspections being carried out by the municipal police on the streets of Istanbul. Listening to the stories of these mustachioed chain-smokers, Mevlut felt as if he were entering the secret world of the city. He heard how a carpenters' neighborhood on the back edge of Tarlabaşı was gradually being settled by a branch of a Kurdish clan from Ağrı; how the authorities wanted to clear out the bookstalls that had taken over Taksim Square because of their links with left-wing organizations; how the gang that controlled the car-parking racket on the lower streets had entered into a full-blown turf war, complete with clubs and chains, against the gang of Black Sea coast immigrants that operated in Tarlabaşı.

Whenever they came across street fights, car crashes, pickpockets, or incidents of sexual harassment, people shouted, threats were made, curses were flung and knives pulled, and Mevlut's father left the scene as fast as possible.

Mustafa Efendi. Watch out or they'll call you in as a witness, I'd tell Mevlut. Once you're in their books, you're done for. Even worse: if you give them your address, they'll send you a court summons. If you don't show up, the police will come knocking at your door. They won't just ask you why you didn't appear in court, they'll ask you what you do, how much tax you pay, where you're registered, how much you make, and are you left wing or right wing.

Mevlut did not always understand why his father would suddenly turn into a side street and sink into a long silence only moments after having shouted "Yogurt seller" with all his might; why he pretended not to hear a customer who stood at a window calling out "Yogurt seller, yogurt seller, hey, I'm talking to you"; why he greeted and embraced the Erzurum lot so warmly but then called them bastards behind their backs; or why he might give a customer two kilos of yogurt for half the usual price. There were times, too, when with many customers still left to visit, many more homes waiting for them to pass by, his father would walk into a coffeehouse, leaving his pole and his precious cargo of yogurt outside the door, and slump into a chair with a cup of tea, just sitting there without moving a muscle. This, Mevlut could understand.

Mustafa Efendi. The yogurt seller spends his day walking. Neither the city buses nor those run by private companies will pick up a passenger carrying yogurt trays, and the yogurt seller can't afford a taxi either. So you walk thirty kilometers every day carrying thirty, maybe forty kilos on your back. Our job is mostly heavy lifting.

Two or three times a week, Mevlut's father would walk from Duttepe to Eminönü. This took two hours. A truckload of yogurt from a Thracian dairy farm was delivered to an empty lot near Sirkeci train station in Eminönü. The unloading of the truck, the pushing and shoving among the yogurt sellers and restaurant managers waiting to pick up their supply, the sorting out of payments and returns of the empty aluminum trays to the warehouse among the buckets of olives and cheese (Mevlut loved the smell of this place), the settling of accounts—it would all be over in a flurry, just like the recurring commotions on Galata Bridge, the whistling of ferries and trains and the grunting of buses. As this organized chaos unfolded, Mevlut's father asked him to keep track of their transactions. It was such a simple job that Mevlut suspected his illiterate father of bringing him along only to introduce him to the business and make sure the people there knew who he was.

As soon as they were done stocking up, his father would shoulder just under sixty kilos of yogurt with determination, walking nonstop for forty minutes before, dripping with sweat, he would drop off a portion of his cargo at a restaurant at the back of Beyoğlu and the rest at a different one in Pangaltı, then return to Sirkeci to collect the second load, dropping it off either at one of those two places or at a third, these spots serving as bases from which he would "distribute" his yogurt to various neighborhoods, to streets and homes that he knew like the back of his hand. In early October, once the temperature dropped, Mustafa Efendi would start going through the same steps twice a week with the boza. To his pole he would tie the jugs of raw boza filled at the Vefa Boza Shop, dropping them off at one of the restaurants where he had friendly relations, and later taking them home to be sweetened with sugar and flavored with spices, ready for him to sell out on the streets from seven o'clock every evening. To save time, sometimes Mevlut and his father would mix the sugar and spices into the raw boza in the kitchens and back gardens of these restaurants. Mevlut was in awe of the way his father was always able to keep track of where exactly he had left the empty, half-empty, and full yogurt trays and boza jugs and how he could always work out which route would allow them to make the most sales while walking the shortest distance.

Mustafa Efendi was on first-name terms with many of his customers; he could remember their yogurt preferences (with cream or without) and how they liked their boza (sour or fresh). When, one day, they got caught in the rain and took shelter in a musty teahouse along the way, Mevlut was amazed that his father knew both the owner and the owner's son; just as he was when they were walking down the street one day, lost in thought, and they crossed paths with a junk dealer on a horse cart who embraced his father like a long-lost friend; or when his father showed himself so hand in glove with the local constable only later to call him "a piece of shit." Considering all the streets, buildings, and apartments they saw—so many doors, doorbells, garden gates, staircases, and elevators—how could his father possibly remember how everything worked, how to open and close things, which buttons to push, how each gate bolted shut? Mustafa Efendi was always giving his son tips: "This is the Jewish cemetery. You walk by quietly." "Someone from Gümüşdere village works as a janitor in this bank; he's a good man, just something to bear in mind." "Don't cross here, try farther up where the metal guardrails stop; the traffic's less dangerous, and you won't have to wait as long!"

"Let me show you something," his father would say as they groped their way around a dark, dank stairwell in a block of apartments. "Ah, there it is! Go on, open it." In the semidarkness, Mevlut would find a little compartment beside the door to an apartment and open it carefully, as if lifting the lid off Aladdin's magic lamp. In the shadows inside there would be a bowl with a sheet of paper ripped from a school notebook. "Read what it says!" Mevlut would hold the note under the pale light of the stairwell lamp, handling it delicately, like some sort of treasure map, and he would read out in a whisper: "Half a kilo, with cream."

Seeing how his son looked up to him as a man of wisdom who could speak the special language of the city, and how the boy couldn't wait to learn the secrets of the city himself, was enough to put a proud spring in Mevlut's father's step. "You'll learn it all soon enough . . . You will see everything without being seen. You will hear everything but pretend that you haven't . . . You will walk for ten hours a day but feel like you haven't walked at all. Are you tired, son, shall we sit down for a bit?"

"Yes, let's sit down."

They hadn't been in the city even two months before it got cold enough to start selling boza in the evenings, and Mevlut began to feel the strain. After going to school in the mornings and walking fifteen kilometers in four hours to sell yogurt with his father in the afternoons, he would fall asleep as soon as they got home. Sometimes, when they stopped to rest in diners and teahouses, he would put his head down on the table for a quick nap, but his father would tell him to wake up, as this was the kind of thing you would expect to see in one of those disreputable twenty-four-hour coffeehouses, and it might not go down so well with the manager.

Mevlut's father would wake him in the evenings, too, before he left to sell boza. ("Dad, I have a history test tomorrow, I have to study," Mevlut might say.) Once or twice when he couldn't get up in the morning, Mevlut told his father, "There's no school today," and his father was happy that they could go out together to sell yogurt that day and make a little more money. Some evenings, his father couldn't bear to wake him, and he would pick up the jugs of boza himself and walk out pulling the door softly shut in his wake. Later, when Mevlut woke up all alone in the house, he would hear the familiar strange noises coming from outside, and he would feel remorseful, not just because he was afraid, but also because he missed his father's companionship and the feeling of his hand inside his father's. With all these thoughts weighing on his mind, he couldn't even study, which only made him feel guiltier.

5

Atatürk Boys' Secondary School

A Good Education Removes the Barriers Between Rich and Poor

PERCHING ON a low, flat expanse at one end of the road linking Duttepe and the hills behind it to Istanbul, Duttepe Atatürk Boys' Secondary School was situated in such a way that mothers hanging laundry up in their gardens, old ladies rolling out dough with their rolling pins, and unemployed men sitting in teahouses playing *rummikub* and card games in the neighborhoods along Dung Creek and in the profusion of *gecekondu* homes on the surrounding hills could all see the school's orange building, its bust of Atatürk, and its students doing endless gym exercises (in their trousers, long-sleeved shirts, and rubber-soled shoes) in the big school yard, like so many colorful flecks in the distance, under the supervision of Blind Kerim, teacher of religion as well as gym. Every forty-five minutes, hundreds of students would pour out into the yard, released by a bell that wasn't heard in the faraway hills, until another silent signal caused them all to disappear just as quickly. But every Monday morning, all twelve hundred students, both the middle school and the high school, would gather around the bust of Atatürk, their collective interpretation of the national anthem echoing mightily off the hills and heard in thousands of nearby homes.

The national anthem ("The Independence March") was always preceded by an address from the principal, Mr. Fazıl, who would climb to the top of the stairs at the entrance of the school building to give a lecture on Atatürk, love of country, the nation, and the unforgettable military victories of the past (he was partial to engagements of bloody conquest, like the Battle of Mohács) and to encourage the students to follow Atatürk's example. From the crowd, the school's older, more rebellious elements called out derisive comments, which Mevlut initially struggled to understand, while other miscreants interrupted with strange if not downright rude heckles, so the vice principal, Skeleton, stood careful watch beside Mr. Fazıl, like a policeman. This strict surveillance meant that it would not be until a year and a half later, when he was fourteen and had begun to question the protocols of the school, that Mevlut finally got to know those serial dissenters, who farted impertinently even when surrounded by a large group and who were respected and admired by both the religious, right-wing students and the nationalist, left-wing students (the right-wing students being invariably religious, and the left-wing students invariably nationalist).

According to the principal, it was a depressing sign of the school's and the nation's prospects that twelve hundred students were unable to sing the national anthem together and in unison. The sight of them all singing to their own beat and, worse, of a number of "hopeless degenerates" who didn't bother to sing at all drove Mr. Fazıl insane. Sometimes, by the time one side of the school yard had finished singing, the other side wouldn't even be halfway through, so the principal, who yearned for them all to work together "like the fingers of a closed fist," made the twelve hundred students sing the anthem over and over again, come rain or shine, until they got it right, while some of the boys, stubborn and determined to make mischief, flubbed the rhythm on purpose, causing fits of laughter and fights between the patriotic kids suffering the cold and the sneering, cynical defeatists.

Mevlut watched these fights from a distance, laughing at the boys' insolent jokes while biting the insides of his plump cheeks to avoid detection by Skeleton. But then, slowly, the national flag would be raised, with its star and crescent moon, and Mevlut's eyes would fill with guilty tears as he sang the anthem with genuine emotion. For the rest of his life, the sight of a Turkish flag being raised—even in movies—was enough to leave him misty eyed.

As the principal demanded, Mevlut wanted very much "to think of nothing else but his country, like Atatürk." But in order to do this, he'd have to get through three years of middle school and three years of high school. No one from Mevlut's family or from his entire village had ever performed such a feat, so this idea became ingrained in Mevlut's mind from the very first days of school, assuming the same mythical contours as the flag, the country, and Atatürk—beautiful to imagine but difficult to reach. Most of the boys who came to the school from the new poor neighborhoods also helped their fathers in their work as street vendors or worked with local shopkeepers or were perhaps waiting in line to start an apprenticeship with a baker, an auto mechanic, a welder—knowing all along that they would drop out of school as soon as they got a little older.

Principal Fazıl was chiefly concerned with maintaining discipline, which required a proper harmony and order between, on the one hand, the children of respectable families, who in class always sat in the front rows, and, on the other hand, the throngs of poorer boys. He had developed his own brand of thinking on this subject and shared it every Monday during the flag-raising ceremony, distilled as a slogan: "A good education removes the barriers between rich and poor!" Mevlut wasn't quite sure whether Principal Fazıl meant to say to his poorer students, "If you study hard and finish school, you, too, will be rich," or whether he meant, "If you study hard and finish school, no one will notice how poor you are."

In order to show the rest of the country what Atatürk Boys' Secondary School had to offer, the principal wanted the school's team to make a good showing at Istanbul Radio's Quiz Competition for Secondary Schools. So he fielded a team of middle-class children from the better neighborhoods (the lazy and the resentful called them nerds) and spent most of his time having them memorize the birth and death dates of Ottoman sultans. At the flag-raising ceremonies, with the whole student body there, the principal bad-mouthed those who'd dropped out to work as repairmen and welders' apprentices, cursing them as weak and worthless traitors to the cause of enlightenment and science; he also told off those like Mevlut, who went to school in the morning and sold yogurt in the afternoon; and he tried to lead those who'd become more concerned with getting ahead than with school back onto the right path, shouting: "Turkey will not be saved by cooked rice peddlers, hawkers, and kebab vendors, but by science!" Einstein, too, had grown up poor, and he'd even failed physics once, but he had never thought of giving up school to make a living—to his own benefit and that of his nation.

Skeleton. In truth, our Duttepe Atatürk Boys' Secondary School was originally founded to serve the neighborhoods on the hills in and around Mecidiyeköy, to make sure that the children of civil servants, lawyers, and doctors, who lived there in modern and European-looking cooperative housing, received a proper state education. Sadly, over the past ten years the school has been overrun by hordes of Anatolian children, who live in the new neighborhoods that have sprung up illegally on the once-empty hills, making it almost impossible to run this lovely school properly. Even though many skip class to work as street vendors, or take a job and drop out, and a significant number of boys are expelled for stealing, battery, or threatening teachers, our classrooms remain overcrowded. There can be, I regret to say, as many as fifty-five students taking lessons in one of our modern classrooms built with thirty students in mind, three students may have to squeeze onto desks designed for two, and during recess, the boys cannot run or walk or play without crashing into one another like bumper cars. Every time the bell rings or a fight breaks out or there is any kind of sudden rush, there follows a stampede in which some students get crushed and the weaker ones faint, and there is nothing we can do but take them to the staff room, where we try to revive them with cologne. With all the overcrowding, it is of course more effective to have students learn by rote rather than try to explain things to them. Rote learning doesn't just develop children's memory, it teaches them to respect their elders. This is also the reasoning behind the education ministry's textbooks. There are five regions in Turkey. A cow's stomach has four parts. There were five reasons that the Ottoman State entered a period of decline.

For one and a half school years, between sixth and seventh grade, Mevlut worried constantly about where to sit in the classroom. The inner turmoil he endured while grappling with this question was as intense as the ancient philosophers' worries over how to live a moral life. Within a month of starting school, Mevlut already knew that if he wanted to become "a scientist Atatürk would be proud of," as the principal liked to say, he would have to befriend the boys from good families and nice neighborhoods, whose notebooks, neckties, and homework were always in good order. Out of the two-thirds of the student body who, like Mevlut, lived in a poor neighborhood, he had yet to meet anyone who did well in school. Once or twice in the school yard, he'd bumped into boys from other classes who took school seriously because they, too, had heard it said, "This one's really clever, he should be sent to school," but in the apocalyptically overcrowded school, he had never managed to communicate with these lost and lonely souls who, like the quiz team, were belittled by the rest as nerds. This was partly because the nerds themselves regarded Mevlut with some suspicion, as he, too, was from a poor neighborhood. He rightly suspected that their rosy worldview was fatally flawed: deep down, he felt that these "clever" boys, who thought they would become rich one day if only they could learn the sixth-grade geography textbook by heart, were, in fact, fools, and the last thing he wanted was to be anything like them.

Mevlut felt better when he got to make friends with and sit next to some of the wealthier boys, who took the front-row seat in class and always kept up with their homework. In order to be allowed to sit near the front, Mevlut had to maintain constant eye contact with the teachers; when they began a sentence and left it hanging—the logic being that the students might learn something by completing the thought—Mevlut tried to be the first to finish the sentence. When the teacher asked a question, even when he didn't know the answer Mevlut always raised his hand with the optimistic manner of someone who did.

But these children among whom Mevlut strove to fit in, who lived in proper apartment blocks in the nicer neighborhoods, could also be strange and break your heart at any time. In his first year of middle school, Mevlut earned the privilege of sitting in the front row next to "the Groom," but one day when they were outside in the snowy school yard the Groom was nearly trampled by swarms of boys playing football (with a ball made out of crumpled old newspapers bound in string, proper footballs being forbidden on school grounds), hurtling about, shouting, fighting, pushing and shoving in the dirt, and gambling (the wager being collectible footballer stickers, tiny pencils, or cigarettes split in three). In a fit of pique, the Groom turned to Mevlut and said, "This school has been taken over by peasants! My dad is going to transfer me."

The Groom. They gave me this nickname during the first month of school because I take a lot of care over my tie and blazer, and some mornings I splash on some of my father's aftershave (he's a women's doctor) before coming to class. The smell of aftershave is like a breath of fresh air in a classroom that stinks of dirt, stale breath, and sweat, and on days when I don't wear it, people ask me, "Hey, Groom, no wedding today?" Contrary to what some people think, I'm no pushover. Once some clown was trying to mock me, leaning into my neck pretending he wanted to smell my aftershave, as if I were some sort of queer, so I gave him an uppercut that sent him flying, and that won the respect of all the back-row bullies. The only reason I'm here is because my father's too cheap to pay for private school.

This is the sort of thing Mevlut and I were discussing in class one day when the biology teacher, Massive Melahat, said: "Ten nineteen, Mevlut Karataş, you're talking too much, go to the back!"

"We weren't talking, ma'am!" I said—not because I'm the brave white hat Mevlut thinks I am, but because I knew I was safe; Melahat wouldn't dare send someone like me, a boy from a good family, all the way to the back rows.

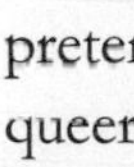

Mevlut wasn't too worried. He'd been sent to the back before, but his good behavior, his innocent, boyish face, and his readiness to raise his hand meant that he would always manage to creep back to the front. Teachers looking for ways to lower the noise level would sometimes move everyone around. On these occasions, the sweet-faced Mevlut would look into the teacher's eyes with such fervent enthusiasm and deference that he would manage to get himself moved right to the front—but only until some misfortune forced him back.

Another time, the brave Groom tried again to protest the busty biology teacher Melahat's decision to send Mevlut to the back rows yet again. "Please, ma'am, why not let him sit at the front; he loves your lessons."

"Don't you see he's as tall as a tree?" was the cruel Melahat's response. "Those at the back can't see the board because of him."

Mevlut was in fact older than most of the other boys in his class, because his father had needlessly kept him behind in the village for a whole year. Having to return to the back rows was always mortifying, and he soon came to imagine that there must be some sort of mysterious link between the size of his body and his newly acquired habit of masturbation. The back rows would greet Mevlut's return to their ranks with applause and chants of "Mevlut, coming home!"

The back rows were the domain of the delinquents, the lazy, the stupid, the ones conditioned into hopelessness, the bulky thugs, the older boys, and those about to be kicked out of school anyway. Many who had been pushed to the back ended up finding a job and dropping out, but you would also find boys who aged there year after year as their search for employment proved fruitless. Some chose to sit there from the very beginning, knowing they were guilty from the outset or too stupid, too old, or too big for the front rows. But others, Mevlut among them, refused to accept that the back rows were their ugly fate and only grasped the painful truth after many empty efforts and much heartbreak, like some poor people who only realize at the end of their lives that they will never be rich. Most teachers, such as Ramses the history teacher (who really did look like a mummy), knew firsthand the futility of trying to teach anything to the back rows. Still others, like the young and timid English teacher Miss Nazlı—looking into her eyes from a front-row seat was pure bliss, and Mevlut fell slowly and unwittingly in love—were so afraid of antagonizing the back rows or of quarreling with any of the students there that they barely even glanced in that direction.

Not a single teacher, not even the principal, who was sometimes able to scare all twelve hundred boys into submission, would willingly challenge the back rows. For such tensions could escalate into out-and-out feuds, with not just the back rows but the entire class turning on the teacher. A particularly delicate matter likely to provoke everyone was when teachers mocked the students from the poor neighborhoods, their accents, their looks, their ignorance, and the pimples that blossomed daily on their faces like bright red hydrangeas. There were boys who would not stop making jokes, and whose stories were a lot more interesting than anything the teachers could come up with, and the teachers would try to silence and subdue them with the humiliating thwack of a ruler. There was a period when the young chemistry teacher, Show-Off Fevzi, whom everyone hated, was pelted with rice-grain bullets blown through empty ballpoint-pen tubes every time he turned toward the board to write down the formula for some lead oxide. His crime was to have mocked the accent and clothes of a student from the east (no one called them Kurds in those days), whom he had wanted to intimidate.

The back-row louts were always interrupting, purely for the pleasure of bullying a teacher they thought too meek, or perhaps simply because they felt like it:

"We've had enough of your rambling, ma'am, we're really bored! Will you tell us about your trip to Europe?"

"Sir, did you really take a train on your own all the way to Spain?"

Like those people who will sit at open-air summer cinemas and talk throughout the show, the back rows provided a noisy running commentary on the goings-on at any given moment; they told their jokes and anecdotes, laughing so hard at their own wit that a teacher asking a question and the student in the front row trying to answer it often couldn't hear each other. Whenever he was exiled to the back, Mevlut could barely keep up with the lesson. But his idea of perfect happiness was to be within earshot of the jokes from the back and able to listen to Miss Nazlı at the same time.

6

Middle School and Politics

There's No School Tomorrow

Mustafa Efendi. The next autumn, Mevlut was already in seventh grade, and still he was embarrassed about having to shout "Yogurt seller!" on the streets, but at least he was now used to carrying the yogurt trays and boza jugs on a stick across his shoulders. In the afternoons, I would send him off on his own to carry empty trays from, say, a restaurant in the back alleys of Beyoğlu to the warehouse in Sirkeci, and then back to Beyoğlu again with fresh trays or a jug of raw boza from the Vefa shop to drop off at Rasim's place, which stank of fried oil and onions, before returning to Kültepe. "Any more of this and we'll finally have the first professor to come out of our village, by God!" I'd say if he happened to be up, sitting there all alone doing his schoolwork when I got back home. If he'd worked hard, he'd say "Dad, will you sit down with me for a minute?" and then, with his eyes turned toward the ceiling, he would begin to recite the facts he'd learned by heart. When he got stuck, he would turn his eyes back down to look at my face. "You won't find the answers here, son, I don't even know how to read," I'd say. In his second year of middle school, he wasn't tired of school yet, nor of working as a street vendor. Some evenings he'd say, "I'll come out with you to sell boza, there's no school tomorrow!" and I wouldn't object. Other times he'd tell me, "I've got homework, I'll go straight home after school."

Like most students at Atatürk Boys' Secondary School, Mevlut kept his after-school life a closely guarded secret; even the other boys who worked as street vendors didn't know what he did after the last class. Sometimes he'd spot another student out on the street selling yogurt with his father, but he would always pretend not to have seen him, and when they met in class the next day, he would act as if nothing had happened. He would, however, keep a close watch on how the boy did in school, whether it showed that he worked as a street vendor, and he would wonder what the other boy would grow up to be, how his life would turn out. There was a kid from Höyük who did his rounds on a horse cart, pulling the horse along by its harness and collecting old newspapers, empty bottles, and scrap metal with his father. Mevlut first noticed him when they crossed paths in Tarlabaşı toward the end of the year. Later, he realized that this boy, who used to sit in class staring out the window with a dreamy expression, had disappeared four months into seventh grade, never to come back to school, though not once had anybody even mentioned him or the fact of his absence. In that moment, Mevlut also understood that his mind would soon forget all about this boy's existence, just as it had that of all his other friends who had found a job or an apprenticeship and dropped out.

The young English teacher Miss Nazlı had a fair complexion, big green eyes, and an apron with printed green leaves. Mevlut realized that she came from another world, and he wanted to become class president just so he could be closer to her. Class presidents could employ kicks, slaps, and threats in order to subdue any delinquent who refused to listen and whom the teachers were too scared to punish themselves with a swipe of the ruler. This help was essential for teachers like Miss Nazlı, who would otherwise be defenseless against the clamor and indiscipline of the classroom, and many a volunteer from the back rows leaped at the chance to offer his services to female teachers by patrolling the other rows for disobedient scamps, ready to dole out a slap on the neck or a twist of the ear. To ensure that Miss Nazlı took note of their gallantry, these volunteers would preface any blow to the miscreant with a loud cry of "Oi! Pay attention to the lesson!" Or: "Stop being disrespectful to the teacher!" If Mevlut sensed that Miss Nazlı appreciated this assistance, even though she barely ever looked at the back rows, he would be gripped by a jealous fury. If only one day she should choose him as class president, Mevlut would not resort to brute force to silence the mob; the lazy good-for-nothings and the troublemakers would listen to him because he was from the poor neighborhoods. Unfortunately, owing to extracurricular political developments, Mevlut never got to realize his political dreams.

In March 1971, there was a military coup, and the long-standing prime minister Demirel stepped down, fearing for his life. Revolutionary groups were robbing banks and kidnapping foreign diplomats for ransom; the government kept declaring martial law and imposing curfews; the military police were searching people's homes. Every wall in the city was plastered with photos of the most wanted; booksellers were banned from the streets. All of this was bad news for street vendors. Mevlut's father railed against "those who have caused this anarchy." Yet even after thousands had been locked up and tortured, things still didn't go back to normal for street sellers and anyone working on the black market.

The army whitewashed all of Istanbul's pavements, anything that seemed dirty or untidy (the whole city pretty much qualified), the trunks of huge plane trees, and walls dating back to the Ottoman era, turning the whole place into an army cantonment. Shared taxis were banned from stopping where they pleased to let passengers board or alight, and street vendors were barred from big squares and avenues, those nice parks where the water fountains actually worked, and from the ferries and trains. With journalists in tow, the police targeted famous gangsters, raiding their semisecret gambling dens and brothels and disrupting their trade in cigarettes and liquor smuggled in from Europe.

After the coup, Skeleton relieved any left-wing teachers of administrative roles and, in so doing, eliminated any chance of Miss Nazlı's choosing Mevlut as class president. At times she wouldn't even turn up for class, and it was rumored that her husband was wanted by the police. Everyone was affected by the radio and TV proclamations concerning order, discipline, and cleanliness. The school painted over the political slogans, the obscenities, and the assortment of illustrated filthy stories about the teachers (including a caricature of Skeleton and Massive Melahat copulating) that had previously adorned walls, toilet stalls, and assorted nooks around the campus. The hotheads who stood up to the teachers, the rabble-rousers who kept shouting political slogans, miring every lesson in propaganda and ideology, were ultimately subdued. To ensure that everyone now sang the national anthem in unison during the flag-raising ceremony, the principal and Skeleton placed one of those loudspeakers found in mosque minarets on either side of the bust of Atatürk, though the effect was only to add a new metallic voice to the tone-deaf choir. Besides, the loudspeakers were so loud that many of those who'd actually been trying to sing the anthem simply gave up. Ramses the history teacher now spent more time than ever on blood-soaked military triumphs, teaching that the color of the Turkish flag represented the color of blood and that the blood of the Turkish people was no ordinary blood.

Mohini. My real name is Ali Yalnız. "Mohini" is the fine name of the elephant that the Indian prime minister Pandit Nehru gave as a gift to Turkish children in the year 1950. To earn the nickname "Mohini" in Istanbul's high schools, it wasn't enough just to look and act like an elephant, big and heavy, older looking than you were, and ambling along unsteadily as I did. You also had to be poor and sensitive. As the prophet Abraham also said, elephants are very sensitive animals. For our school, the most horrifying political consequence of the 1971 military coup was that, after waging a heroic resistance against Skeleton and the other teachers, we were all forced to cut our long hair short. Many tears were shed over this catastrophe, not just by the rock- and pop-fan sons of doctors and civil servants, but also by kids who came from poor neighborhoods but had nice hair. The principal and Skeleton had been threatening some kind of action for ages during the Monday flag-raising ceremony, saying it was inappropriate for boys to wear their hair like women, just to imitate some degenerate European pop stars. But it wasn't until soldiers came into the school after the coup that those tyrants got their wish. They say that the army captain who arrived by jeep that day had come to coordinate our relief efforts for the victims of the earthquake in eastern Turkey. But the opportunistic Skeleton took the chance to call in Duttepe's best barber as well. Regrettably, I also panicked at the sight of the soldiers and allowed my hair to be cut. Afterward, I looked even uglier and hated myself even more for bowing to authority so passively, shuffling obediently into the barber's chair.

Skeleton had sensed Mevlut's presidential ambitions, and after the coup, he entrusted this model student with the task of assisting Mohini during the long recess. Mevlut was pleased, as this was an opportunity to be out in the empty corridors during class and to stand out from the crowd. Every day just before the long recess at 11:10, he and Mohini left the classroom and made their way through dark, dank corridors and stairwells, down to the basement. There, Mohini's first stop was the high-school boys' toilet next to the coal cellar (where Mevlut wouldn't even dream of following), a foul, stinking pit, with a thick blue fog of cigarette smoke hanging over it, where he would go begging the older boys for cigarette stubs, and if he was lucky enough to get one, he would smoke it on the spot while Mevlut waited patiently at the door; "This is my sedative right here," Mohini would say with a knowing look. Then they would go wait in line in the school kitchen for Mohini to be given a jug, which he would carry on his back all the way upstairs, though it was almost as big as he was, and finally place it gently over the classroom stove.

This big ugly jug held the smelly and scalding hot milk prepared down in the stinking kitchens from powdered milk that UNICEF distributed for free to schools in developing countries. Concentrating on his task like a good housewife, Mohini poured the milk into plastic cups of all sizes, which the students brought in from home, while the teacher on recess duty took out a blue box holding another UNICEF beneficence, the dreaded fish-oil capsules. He presented one of these carefully to each student, as some precious gemstone, before patrolling the rows to make sure that they were actually swallowing both malodorous kindnesses. Most of the boys threw the pills out the window toward the corner of the school yard where all the trash accumulated, which was also the designated gambling spot, or they would crush them on the floor for the simple pleasure of stinking up the classroom. Others loaded them into their hollowed ballpoint tubes and shot them at the blackboard. Wave after wave of fish-oil bombardment had left the blackboards of Duttepe Atatürk Boys' Secondary School with a slippery sheen and an unpleasant aroma that made visitors queasy. When one of these projectiles hit the portrait of Atatürk in classroom 9C upstairs, an alarmed Skeleton called in inspectors from the municipal police as well as the board of education to investigate, though the easygoing president of the board, who'd seen plenty over the years, ably defused the situation by explaining to the officers enforcing martial law that no insult to the founder of the Republic or any government dignitaries had been intended by anyone. At the time, any attempts to politicize the powdered-milk and fish-oil rituals would fail, but years later there would be many histories and memoirs written on the subject, with the Islamists, the nationalists, and the leftists united in claiming that the state, under pressure from Western powers, had conspired to force-feed them those reeking, poisonous pellets throughout their childhood.

In literature class, Mevlut loved reading Yahya Kemal's verses about the Ottoman raiders rejoicing on their way to conquering the Balkans, sword in hand. When the teacher didn't show up, they passed the hour by singing songs, and even the back rows' most mischievous elements would temporarily assume a guise of cherubic innocence, and as he watched the rain falling outside (the thought of his father, out there selling yogurt, briefly crossing his mind), Mevlut felt as if he could have sat there singing in that cozy classroom forever and that, though he was far from his mother and his sisters, city life had much to recommend it over village life.

Within a few weeks of the military coup, the reign of martial law, curfews, and house searches had led to thousands of arrests, until eventually, as usual, the restrictions were relaxed, the street vendors felt comfortable coming out again, and so the roasted chickpeas, sesame rolls, gum-paste sweets, and cotton candy reappeared with their respective sellers by the gates of Atatürk Boys' Secondary School on the same spots they'd occupied before. On one of those hot days of spring, Mevlut, normally a stickler for the rules, felt momentarily envious of a boy roughly his age who was among those breaking the ban on hawking. The boy, whose face looked familiar, was carrying a cardboard box that said KISMET. Inside the box, Mevlut could see a large plastic football and some other toy prizes that looked rather interesting: miniature plastic soldiers, chewing gum, combs, collectible football stickers, handheld mirrors, and marbles.

"Don't you know we're not allowed to buy anything from street vendors?" he said, trying to look stern. "What's that you're selling?"

"God loves some people more. Those people end up rich. He loves some people a little less, and those people stay poor. You take a pin and scratch off one of these colored circles, and underneath you'll find your gift and your fortune."

"Did you make this yourself?" asked Mevlut. "Where do you get the prizes from?"

"They sell the whole game as a set, including the prizes, for thirty-two liras. There are one hundred holes, so if you go around letting people scratch them for sixty cents apiece, by the end you'll have made sixty liras. There's a lot of business to be done in the parks on the weekends. Want to have a go right now and find out if you're going to be rich, or if you're going to wind up as that poor wretch everyone looks down on? Go on, scratch one and have a look . . . I won't charge you."

"I'm not going to be poor, you'll see."

With a flourish, the boy produced a pin, which Mevlut took without hesitation. There were still many holes left to scratch on the box. He picked one carefully and scratched away.

"Tough luck! It's empty," said the boy.

"Let me see that," said Mevlut, losing his temper. Under the colored aluminum foil he'd scratched away, he could see nothing—not a single word nor any gift. "Now what?"

"If it comes up empty, we give people one of these," said the boy, handing Mevlut a piece of a wafer bar the size of a matchbox. "Maybe you've got no luck, but you know what they say: lucky at cards, unlucky at love. The key is to win when you lose. Got it?"

"Got it," said Mevlut. "What's your name and your registration number?"

"Three seventy-five, Ferhat Yılmaz. Are you going to report me to Skeleton?"

Mevlut waved his hand as if to say "obviously not," and Ferhat made an "obviously not" face of his own, and they both knew straightaway that they would be the best of friends.

The first thing about Ferhat that struck Mevlut was that, though they were the same age, Ferhat was already well versed in the language and chemistry of the streets, the location of all the shops in town, and everyone's secrets. Ferhat said that the cooperative running the school was crawling with crooks, that the history teacher Ramses was an idiot, and that most of the others were a bunch of jerks whose only thought was getting through the day in one piece so that they could collect their salaries at the end of the month.

One chilly day, Skeleton took the small army he had carefully assembled out of the school's janitors and cleaners, the kitchen staff who prepared the powdered milk, and the guardian of the coal cellar and led an attack on the street vendors who camped outside the school walls. Mevlut and the others watched from the foot of the wall as the battle unfolded. Everyone was rooting for the street vendors, but power was on the side of the government and the school. A roasted-chickpea-and-sunflower-seed seller exchanged blows with Abdülvahap, who looked after the coal cellar. Skeleton threatened to call the police and the military command center. The whole scene etched itself into Mevlut's memory as a demonstration of the state and the school administration's general attitude toward street vendors.

The news that Miss Nazlı had left the school proved devastating for Mevlut. He felt empty and lost as he realized just how much time he spent thinking about her. He skipped school for three days and later explained his absence by saying his father was very sick. More and more, he enjoyed Ferhat's jokes, his ready wit, and his optimism. They skipped school together and took to the streets selling Kısmet in Beşiktaş and Maçka Park. Ferhat taught him plenty of jokes and bits of wisdom involving one's "intentions" and "kismet"—fate—insights that he later repeated to any yogurt and boza customers who had a soft spot for him. He began to tell his evening boza customers: "If you don't make your intentions clear, you will never find your kismet here."

Another of Ferhat's achievements was his exchange of letters with some teenage girls in Europe. The girls were real. Ferhat even had photos in his pocket to prove it. He got their addresses from the section "Young People Looking for Pen Pals" in *Milliyet* newspaper's youth magazine *Hey,* which the Groom would bring into class. *Hey,* which claimed to be Turkey's first youth magazine, published the addresses of European girls only—never Turkish ones, as this would have offended conservative families. Ferhat had someone else write his letters for him, without ever revealing who this person was, and he never told the girls that he was a street vendor. Mevlut always wondered what he would put in a letter to a European girl, but he never worked it out. In class, the boys pored over the photos Ferhat had received from the European girls and either fell in love or tried to prove that the girls weren't real, while some particularly jealous types ruined the photos by scribbling all over them.

One day, Mevlut read a magazine in the school library that would have a profound influence on his future career as a street vendor. The library at Atatürk Boys' Secondary School was a place where students were made to sit still and behave when a teacher failed to show up for class. Whenever unsupervised kids were brought in, the librarian, Aysel, gave them copies of old magazines donated by the retired doctors and lawyers who lived in the upper neighborhoods nearby.

On Mevlut's last visit to the library, Aysel went through her customary routine of handing out twenty- to thirty-year-old, discolored back issues of magazines like *The Great Atatürk, Archaeology and Art, Mind and Matter, Our Beautiful Turkey, Medical World,* and *Knowledge Trove.* Once she had made sure that there was one magazine for every two students to look at, she launched into her brief and famous speech about reading, to which Mevlut turned his full attention.

ONE MUST NEVER TALK WHEN READING was the famous and endlessly mocked first line and refrain of her speech. "You must read inside your head, without making a sound. Otherwise you will learn nothing from the writing on the page. When you get to the bottom of the page you are reading, do not turn the page straightaway, but wait until you are sure that your classmate has also finished reading the page. Once you have done that, you may turn the page, but without moistening your fingertips or creasing the paper. Do not write on the pages. Do not scribble, do not add any mustaches, glasses, or beards to the illustrations. A magazine is not just for looking at the pictures; you must read the text, too. Read the writing on every page first before you look at the pictures. When you have finished your magazine, raise your hand quietly, and I will come and give you a new one. But you will not have time to read a whole magazine anyway." Librarian Aysel went quiet for a second and looked around to see whether her words had had any effect on Mevlut's class, and then, like an Ottoman general ordering his impatient troops to attack and pillage, she pronounced her immortal last line:

"Now you may read."

There was a murmur and the rustle of curious boys leafing through old, yellowed pages. Mevlut and Mohini had been given the June 1952 issue (only twenty years old) of Turkey's first parapsychology magazine, *Mind and Matter,* to share. They were gently turning pages, without wetting the tips of their fingers, when they came face-to-face with the picture of a dog.

The title of the article was "Can Dogs Read People's Minds?" The first time Mevlut read through the piece, he didn't really understand much of it, but oddly, his heart started racing. He asked Mohini if he'd let him read it one more time before they turned the page. Years later, it wasn't the ideas or the concepts explored in the piece that Mevlut would remember most vividly but the way he had felt as he was reading it. While reading the piece, he had sensed the way everything in the universe was connected. He had also realized that street dogs watched him at night from cemeteries and empty lots even more than he had ever known. The dog in the picture wasn't one of those cute little European lapdogs you usually found in magazines but one of the mud-brown curs you saw on the streets of Istanbul; perhaps that was also why the article had made such an impression.

When they got their final report cards in the first week of June, Mevlut saw that he'd flunked English and had to take a makeup exam.

"Don't tell your dad, he'll kill you," said Ferhat.

Mevlut agreed, but he also knew that his father would demand to see his middle-school diploma with his own eyes. He'd heard there was a chance that Miss Nazlı, who now worked at a different school in Istanbul, might come back to proctor the makeup exams. Mevlut spent that summer in the village cramming for the English exam so that he could finish middle school. The Cennetpınar primary school didn't have an English-to-Turkish dictionary, and there was no one in the village who could help him. In July, he started to take lessons from the son of a man who had emigrated to Germany and had just come back to Gümüşdere village with a Ford Taunus and a TV set. Mevlut had to walk three hours each way just so that he could sit down with a book in the shade of a tree and practice his English for an hour with this boy, who went to a German middle school and spoke both Turkish and English with a German accent.

Abdurrahman Efendi. The story of our dear, lucky Mevlut, who took English lessons from the son of that man who went to work in Germany, has once again brought him to our humble village of Gümüşdere, so I hope you will let me offer a quick update on the dark fate that has befallen the rest of us. When I first had the honor of meeting you in 1968, I had no idea how lucky I was, having my three beautiful daughters and their silent angel of a mother! After my third daughter, Samiha, was born, I tempted fate again. I just couldn't get the thought of a son out of my head, and we couldn't keep from trying for a fourth child. Indeed I had a son, whom I named Murat as soon as he was born. But not an hour after his birth, the Lord called him and his mother, too, covered as she was in blood, and so from one minute to the next, Murat, my heart's desire, and my wife were both taken, gone to live with the angels in heaven, leaving me a widowed father of three orphaned girls. At first, my three daughters would get into their late mother's bed next to me, sniffing in the last whiffs of her scent as they cried through the night. Ever since they were babies, I've pampered them like the daughters of the Chinese emperor. I bought them dresses from Beyşehir and Istanbul. To those cheapskates who say that I have squandered my money on drink, I would like to say that a man whose neck has gone crooked from selling yogurt on the streets can only entrust his future to his three beautiful daughters, each more precious than any earthly treasure. Now my little angels are old enough that they can speak for themselves better than I can. The eldest, Vediha, is ten, while Samiha, the youngest, is six.

Vediha. Why is it that the teacher looks at me the most during class? Why can't I bring myself to tell anyone that I want to go to Istanbul to look at the sea and the ships? Why do I always have to be the one to clear the table, make the beds, and cook for my father? Why does it make me angry when I see my sisters talking and giggling together?

Rayiha. I've never seen the sea in my life. There are clouds that look like things. I want to grow up to be as old as my mom and get married as soon as possible. I don't like sunchokes. Sometimes, I like to think that my departed little brother, Murat, and my mom are watching over us. I like to cry myself to sleep. Why does everyone call me "clever girl"? When the two boys look at their book under the plane tree, Samiha and I watch them from far away.

Samiha. There are two men under the pine tree. I am holding Rayiha's hand. I never let go. Then we went home.

In late August, Mevlut and his father returned to Istanbul earlier than usual so that they would be on time for Mevlut's makeup exam. At the end of summer, the house in Kültepe smelled of damp and earth, just as it had when Mevlut had first walked into it three years ago.

Three days later, he was in the biggest classroom in all of Atatürk Boys' Secondary School taking his exam, but there was no sign of Miss Nazlı. Mevlut's heart broke. But still he did his best, answering the questions well. Two weeks later, when high school had begun, he went to Skeleton's office.

"Well done, ten nineteen, here's your middle-school diploma!"

All day long, Mevlut kept taking it out of his bag to have another look, and that evening he showed it to his father.

"Now you can become a policeman or a watchman," said his father.

Mevlut would miss those years for the rest of his life. In middle school, he had learned that being Turkish was the best thing in the world and that city life was so much better than village life. They had sung in class all together, and after all the fighting and intimidation, even the very worst bullies and troublemakers sang with joyful innocence all over their faces; Mevlut would think back on that and smile.

7

The Elyazar Cinema

A Matter of Life and Death

One Sunday morning in November 1972, Mevlut and his father were planning their yogurt distribution routes for the week when it became clear to Mevlut that they would no longer be going out to sell yogurt together. The yogurt companies were growing and had started delivering their truckloads straight to shops and street vendors in Taksim and Şişli. The art of a good yogurt seller no longer lay in lugging around sixty kilos of product from Eminönü to Beyoğlu and Şişli, but in stocking up wherever the trucks dropped it off and distributing it as quickly as possible among the surrounding streets and homes. Mevlut and his father realized that their overall income would increase if they split up and followed different routes. Twice a week, one of them would also bring some boza home to sweeten with sugar, but that, too, they now sold separately, in different neighborhoods.

This new state of affairs filled Mevlut with a sense of freedom, but it was to prove a fleeting illusion. Getting along with the restaurant owners, the increasingly demanding housewives, the doormen, and the people at the places where he parked his yogurt trays and boza jugs took a lot more time and effort than he'd anticipated, and he often found himself skipping school.

Back when he used to stick to his father's side, keeping accounts and adding weights to their scale, they'd had a customer called Tahir—Uncle Tahir to his friends—who hailed from the town of Torul. Now that he was working alone, Mevlut secretly relished the challenge of haggling with Uncle Tahir over the price of a kilo; it made him feel a lot more important than he ever did sitting in chemistry class staring blankly at the chalkboard. Two strong and capable young men from the village of İmrenler, nicknamed the Concrete Brothers, had begun to monopolize the diners and cafés in the Beyoğlu-Taksim area. To make sure he didn't lose some long-standing customers from the streets of Feriköy and Harbiye, which he'd taken over from his father, Mevlut lowered his prices and made new friends. There was the boy from Erzincan whom Mevlut had gone to school with, who also lived in Duttepe and had just started working in a grilled-meatball restaurant that used up vast quantities of the yogurt drink *ayran;* meanwhile, Ferhat knew the Alevi Kurds from Maraş who owned the convenience store next door to that restaurant. In all this, Mevlut had begun to feel as if he'd grown up in the city.

At school, he had graduated to the basement toilet favored by the smokers and had begun to carry Bafra cigarettes to gain the acceptance of the regulars. They knew he earned his own money and had just started smoking, so he was expected to be the one always to have a pack at hand to distribute among the scroungers. Now that he was in high school, Mevlut realized that in middle school he had made too much of this same pack of braggarts who kept failing every year even though they had nothing to do but go to school, who worked no outside jobs, and passed the day trading gossip. The world out on the streets was in fact much bigger and more real than the world inside the school.

Anything he made working on the street was still passed straight on to his father, at least in theory. He did, actually, spend some on cigarettes, movies, sports gambling, and lottery tickets. He had no qualms hiding these expenses from his father, though he did feel guilty about the Elyazar Cinema.

The building that housed the Elyazar Cinema, in one of the small lanes between Galatasaray and Tünel, was built for an Armenian theater company (and used to be called the Odeon) in 1909, in the climate of freedom that reigned after the deposition of Abdul Hamid II; after the foundation of the Republic, it became a cinema (the Majestic) favored by the Greek community and Istanbul's upper middle class; later, it took the name Elyazar, and for the past two years, like all of the cinemas in Beyoğlu, it had been screening adult films. In the dark (amid a strange confluence of human breath and eucalyptus), Mevlut would pick a seat off to one side, out of the way of the unemployed from the lower neighborhoods, the desolate old men and the hopeless loners, and there, hiding even from himself, shrinking and squirming in his seat, he would try to figure out the plot of the movie—not that it mattered.

Inserting sex clips into Turkish movies would be embarrassing for the half-famous film actors who lived in the area, so the Elyazar Cinema did not show any of those early Turkish blue films, in which the male actors (some of them very well known) appeared in their underpants. Most of the films shown were imports. Mevlut didn't like how, in Italian films, the lustful female lead, her voice dubbed into Turkish, was made to seem so absurdly naïve and foolish. In German films, it made Mevlut uncomfortable to hear the protagonists cracking jokes throughout those "sex scenes" he'd waited for so eagerly, as if sex were something to be taken lightly. In French films, he would be amazed, if not furious, to see women jumping into bed with someone with practically no excuse. These women's lines, and those of the men who tried to seduce them all, were always dubbed by the same handful of Turkish voice actors, so that sometimes it seemed to Mevlut that he was watching the same film over and over again. The scenes that the audience had come to see were never at the beginning. Thus, at the age of fifteen, Mevlut learned that sex was a kind of miracle that always kept you waiting.

The crowd that stood smoking and milling about in the lobby would hurry inside before the sex scenes began. "It's starting!" the ushers would announce to these eager voyeurs just as the crucial scene approached. Mevlut couldn't believe how comfortable with it they all seemed to be. As soon as he got his ticket, he would make his way through the crowd with his eyes fixed firmly on his shoes ("Have my laces come undone?"), never looking up.

When the erotic scenes began, the whole cinema would fall silent. Mevlut would feel his heart racing; slightly dizzy and sweating profusely, he would struggle to control himself. The "indecent" scenes were in fact cut from other films and spliced into these features at random, so Mevlut knew that the incredible things he was witnessing in that moment had nothing to do with the plot he had been trying to figure out just before. But his mind would still make connections between the sex scenes and the rest of the film, and if he allowed himself to believe for a second that the naked women whose lewd acts had just left him openmouthed were the same women in the house or at the office during the rest of the film, everything was somehow even more arousing, and as the front of his pants bulged, Mevlut would hunch over in growing shame. In all those times during high school when he went to the Elyazar Cinema on his own, he never put his hand in his pocket to play with himself, unlike some of the other patrons. It was said that there were elderly queers who came to this kind of place for the sole purpose of waiting for someone to undo his pants and jerk off to the film, whereupon they would pounce on his private parts. Mevlut himself had been accosted by these perverts—"So tell me, son, how old are you?" "Still a kid, aren't you?"—but he'd played dumb, pretending he couldn't hear. For the price of a single ticket you could spend the whole day in the Elyazar Cinema, watching the same two films over and over, and so sometimes Mevlut found it hard to leave.

Ferhat. In springtime, when the amusement parks and garden cafés opened, and the teahouses, children's parks, bridges, and pavements on the Bosphorus began to fill up, Mevlut started to come with me to sell Kısmet on weekends. We really went at it for a couple of years and made a lot of money. We would go up to Mahmutpaşa together to buy the sets, and on the way back down the hill we'd already be making sales to kids out shopping with their parents; we would go on to the Spice Bazaar, Eminönü Square, and by the time we got over the bridge into Karaköy, we would be pleasantly surprised to find that half our colored circles had been scratched off by those trying their luck.

Mevlut could spot customers from afar before they even rose from their seats at the teahouse, and he approached everyone, young or old, with the same winning optimism and a surprising new pitch every time. "You know why you should try your luck? Because your socks and our gift comb are the same color," he would say to some dopey kid who didn't even know what color his socks were. "See, it said MIRROR under the twenty-seventh circle in Ferhat's box, but my twenty-seventh circle hasn't been scratched yet," he would point out to a shrewd boy with spectacles who knew the game a bit and was hesitant to play. Some spring days, we would do such brisk business on the piers, the ferries, and in the parks that we'd run out of circles and head back to Kültepe. We went to the Bosphorus Bridge when it was opened in 1973, before it was closed to pedestrians following a bunch of suicides, and made good money over three sunny afternoons, but then it was "No vendors allowed," and we couldn't go back. "This is not a harmless game, this is gambling!" bearded old men would say as they turned us away from mosque courtyards; the same cinemas that were happy to let us see their sex films now told us "You're too young to come in here"; and many times we were turned away from bars and nightclubs with the old "No vendors allowed."

When they received their report cards in the first week of June, Mevlut learned that he had flunked the first year of high school completely. Under a section of the yellow card headed "Evaluation," there was a handwritten note that said: "He has failed this year outright." Mevlut read this sentence ten times. He had skipped too many classes, missed so many exams, and he'd even neglected to win over those teachers who would have pitied him for being a miserable yogurt seller and let him pass. Because he'd failed three classes, there was no point in studying over the summer. Ferhat hadn't failed even one, Mevlut was disappointed to learn, but he had so many plans for his summer in Istanbul that he wasn't even that upset.

"You've taken up smoking, too, haven't you?" said his father when he found out that night.

"No, Father, I don't smoke," said Mevlut, with a pack of Bafras in his pocket.

"You smoke like a chimney, you jerk off all day like some horny soldier, and, to top it off, you're lying to your father."

"I'm not lying."

"Damn you," said his father, and he gave him a slap. Then he left, slamming the door behind him. Mevlut threw himself onto the bed.

He couldn't get up for a long time. But he didn't cry either. What really stung wasn't that he'd failed the year, or that his father had slapped him . . . What had really broken his heart was how offhandedly his father had referred to Mevlut's big secret, his habit of self-abuse, and called him a liar. He'd had no idea anyone knew what he was up to. This heartbreak set off such an explosion of anger inside him that he knew immediately he would not be going back to the village at all that summer. He alone would decide what would become of his life. He was going to do great things one day.

When his father prepared to head back to the village at the beginning of July, Mevlut explained once more that he did not want to lose their regular customers in Pangaltı and Feriköy. He was still handing over the money he earned, but things had changed. Mustafa Efendi used to say that they were saving money for the house they would build in the village, while Mevlut used to give his father a report of where he'd earned whatever he was handing over on a given day. Now, he no longer bothered; he just gave his father some money every few days, as if paying some sort of tax. And his father no longer spoke of a house they would build in the village. Mevlut understood that his father was now resigned to the fact that his son would never return to the village, that he would spend the rest of his life in Istanbul, like Korkut and Süleyman. In those moments when he felt most alone in the world, Mevlut would resent how his father could just never find a way to get rich in the city, or stop thinking about going back to the village one day. He wondered if his father could sense that this was how Mevlut felt.

The summer of 1973 was one of the happiest Mevlut had ever known. He made quite a bit of money with Ferhat, selling Kısmet on the city streets in the afternoons and evenings. He used some of it to buy German twenty-mark notes from a jeweler in Harbiye (Ferhat knew the man), and he stashed them under the foot of his mattress. This was how Mevlut first began to hide some of his earnings from his father. Most mornings, he stuck to Kültepe, rarely leaving the house since he no longer had to share it and often jerking off even as he vowed it would be the last time. Playing with himself at home made him feel guilty, but this never turned into miserable feelings of inadequacy, as it would in later years, since he didn't for now have a girlfriend, or a wife to sleep with. No one could blame a sixteen-year-old high-school kid for not having a lover. Besides, even if they were to marry him off at that moment, Mevlut wasn't entirely sure what he was meant to do with a girl.

Süleyman. One very hot day at the beginning of July, I thought I'd drop in to see Mevlut. I knocked on his door a few times, but no one answered. He couldn't have gone out to sell yogurt at ten in the morning? I did a lap around the house, rapping on the windows. I picked up a stone and tapped on the glass. The dusty garden was a mess; the house was a wreck.

I ran back around when the door opened. "What happened? Where were you?"

"I fell asleep!" said Mevlut. But he looked exhausted, like he hadn't slept at all.

Thinking for a second that he had someone else in there, I felt strangely jealous. I stepped inside that tiny, stuffy room that reeked of sweat. The same table, the one bed, still just those same two shabby pieces of furniture . . .

"Mevlut, my father says we should go up to his shop. There's a job. He said come and bring Mevlut."

"What's the job?"

"Nothing we can't handle, I'm sure. Come on, let's get going."

But Mevlut stayed put. Maybe he'd become more withdrawn after flunking so royally. When I realized he wasn't going to come, I got testy with him. "You should take a break from jerking off all the time, or you'll go blind and lose your memory, you know?" I said.

He turned around and went back inside, slamming the door behind him, and after that he didn't visit us in Duttepe for quite a while. Eventually, I had to go get him myself when my mother insisted. Those jerks who sit in the back at Duttepe Atatürk Boys' Secondary School like to make fun of the younger kids: "Nice bags under your eyes, and your hands are shaking, and look, even the pimples are out in force. Have you been up all night jerking off again, you pervert?" they'll say, throwing in a slap or two for good measure. I know that some of the workers and followers that Hadji Hamit Vural boards near us at the *gecekondu* house for bachelors get so addicted to jerking off that they have to give up their jobs; they lose all their strength and end up being sent back to the village. I wonder if Mevlut knows, if he understands, that this is a matter of life and death. Doesn't his friend Ferhat tell him that even Alevis are forbidden to jerk off? Maliki Sunnis aren't allowed under any circumstances. At least Hanafi Sunnis like us can do it in some cases, but only to avoid a bigger sin, like adultery. Islam is a religion based on tolerance and logic, not punishment. You're even allowed to eat pork if you're starving. Masturbation is frowned on when it's purely for pleasure, but knowing Mevlut, to that he would just say, "Is there some way that doesn't involve pleasure, Süleyman?"—and go right back to his sinful ways. Can someone like Mevlut, so quick to go off the rails, ever succeed in Istanbul?

8

The Height of Duttepe Mosque

People Actually Live There?

Mevlut felt more at ease selling Kısmet out on the streets with Ferhat than he ever did at the Aktaş house talking with Süleyman. With Ferhat, he could discuss anything that crossed his mind; Ferhat would say something just as funny and wise in return, and they would have a good laugh. He did visit the Aktaş family when he got scared of being alone on summer evenings, but Süleyman and Korkut would sneer at everything he said and use it against him, so he would say as little as possible. "Stop bothering my darling Mevlut, you rascals, leave him alone," Aunt Safiye would say. Mevlut never let himself forget that if he was to survive in the city, he had to make sure to get along with his uncle Hasan and also with Süleyman and Korkut. After four years in Istanbul, his dreams now were of setting up a business of his own, so he wouldn't have to depend on anyone, relatives or otherwise. He was going to do it with Ferhat. "If it wasn't for you, I would never have thought of coming all the way here," said Ferhat one day as they counted the day's earnings. They had taken a train (dodging the conductor's call for tickets while they made their sales) from Sirkeci to the Veliefendi Race Course, where among all those people who'd come to bet on the horses, they had sold out of their colored circles in just two hours. This was also how they came up with the idea of going to football stadiums for the opening ceremonies that clubs organized for the start of the season, going to summer sports tournaments, and setting up shop at the Sports and Exhibition Hall when there was a basketball game on. Whenever they made money off some new idea, their thoughts would turn immediately to the business they were going to set up together one day. Their biggest dream was to run a restaurant in Beyoğlu, or at the very least a café. Every time Mevlut came up with a new moneymaking scheme, Ferhat would say "You've got a real capitalist instinct!" and Mevlut would feel proud of himself, even though he knew it wasn't meant as a compliment.

The summer of 1973 saw the opening of a second summer cinema in Duttepe. The movies were projected onto the side of an old two-story *gecekondu* building. Mevlut would go there occasionally, with his box of Kısmet, and run into Süleyman or Ferhat, all of them looking for a way to sneak in without paying. But when the Derya had first opened, Mevlut used to go regularly, even buying a ticket. He would make a healthy profit while watching Türkân Şoray on the big screen, but he soon grew indifferent to the place. Those in the neighborhood all knew him and couldn't feign much awe at his pronouncements on fate and fortune.

In November, once the Duttepe Mosque, with its machine-loomed carpets, had opened its doors to the public, the old men of the neighborhood began accusing Mevlut of encouraging gambling, so he took his box elsewhere. The God-fearing elders and pensioners of Duttepe had given up their little makeshift prayer rooms in favor of the new mosque, to which they flocked five times a day. Friday prayers were conducted for a devout and enthusiastic crowd worthy of Judgment Day.

The formal inauguration of the mosque took place on the morning of the Feast of the Sacrifice in 1974. Having bathed, laid out his clean clothes, and ironed his white school shirt the night before, Mevlut woke up early with his father. The mosque and the raised arcades outside were already full half an hour before the scheduled time, with thousands of men swarming in from the surrounding hills. Mevlut and his father had trouble squeezing through, but Mustafa Efendi was determined to witness this historic moment from a front-row seat. They managed to elbow their way to the front, saying, "Sorry, brother, we've got a message to pass on."

Mustafa Efendi. We were praying in the front, with Hadji Hamit Vural, the man who built the mosque, sitting just two rows ahead of us. That man and the lackeys he brings in from his village act like they own this neighborhood, but I thanked God for him that morning, and I thought to myself, God bless you. The murmur that rose from those gathered, their joyful whispering, it all cheered me up in an instant. Sharing in one another's fervor as we prayed together, feeling the presence of that quiet but earnest army of believers that had emerged through the darkness to come here, I felt as good as if I'd spent weeks reading the Koran. "God is greaaat," I said reverently, and then again "Gooood is great" to a different melody. "Dear God," the imam said in his affecting sermon, "please look after this nation, this congregation, and all of those who are busy at work, day and night, come rain or shine." He said, "Dear God, please watch over those who come here from the distant villages of our dear Anatolia and work as street vendors to earn their daily bread," and also "Help them succeed and forgive their sins." My eyes were tearing up as the preacher continued—"Dear God, bless our government with authority, our army with strength, and our policemen with patience"—and I said "Amen!" along with everyone else. After the sermon, while all the men in the congregation were wishing one another a happy holiday, I threw ten liras into the collection box. I grabbed Mevlut's arm and took him over to kiss Hadji Hamit Vural's hand. His uncle Hasan, Süleyman, and Korkut were already in the queue waiting to do the same. Mevlut greeted his cousins first and then paid his respects to his uncle Hasan, who gave him fifty liras. There was a whole host of Hadji Hamit Vural's men hanging about and so many people waiting to see him that half an hour passed before our turn came. We ended up keeping Safiye Yenge waiting, back home in Duttepe, where she was busy making us filled pastries. It was a rather nice holiday lunch, after all. But I couldn't stop myself from saying, if only once: "I'm not the only one who has a right to this house, Mevlut does, too." Hasan pretended not to hear. The kids had finished their food by then, and they ran out to the garden, expecting their father and uncle to hunker down for one of their usual property disputes, but we managed to get through at least that holiday without any arguments.

Hadji Hamit Vural. The mosque made everyone happy in the end. All the wretched and lost souls of Duttepe and Kültepe stood in line on that holy day to kiss my hand (though it would have been good to see the Alevis, too). I gave each of them a crisp new one-hundred-lira note from the bundles we'd picked up at the bank just for the Feast of the Sacrifice. With tears in my eyes, I thanked Almighty God for blessing me with such a day. My late father used to wander the mountains near the city of Rize in the 1930s, going from village to village on the back of a donkey selling all sorts of bits and bobs he would buy from the city. I was just about to take over from him when the Second World War broke out and I was drafted into the army. They took us to the Dardanelles. We never went to war, but we spent four years guarding the strait and the military outposts. The quartermaster, a man from Samsun, said to me, "Hamit, it would be a waste to send you back to your village, you're too bright. Come to Istanbul, I'll find you a job." May he rest in peace. It was thanks to him that I got to be a grocer's apprentice in Feriköy after the war, back when these apprenticeships didn't yet exist and home deliveries were unheard of. I would buy a basketful of bread from the baker and take it around on the back of a donkey, until eventually I realized that I could do this job myself and opened a grocery store in Kasımpaşa next to the Piyale Paşa Primary School, after which I went and built up some empty lots and sold them off at a profit. I opened a little bakery in Kağıthane. There was plenty of labor in the city back then, though not much experience. You can't really trust any old villager.

I began bringing men over from our own village, starting with my relatives. There were some huts in Duttepe back then, and that's where I put up those young men—all of them very well behaved and always respectful—and before long we were taking over more empty land, and business was booming, thank God. But all of these unmarried men, how were they going to remember to say their daily prayers and be thankful to God, so that they would feel at peace and do their jobs properly? On my first pilgrimage to Mecca, I prayed to God and to our Blessed Prophet and racked my brains for a solution. I thought I might as well do it myself and started putting some money aside from the bakery and the construction projects to buy steel and cement. We went to the mayor and asked for some land; we went to our wealthy neighbors and asked for donations. Some were generous, God bless their souls, but others said, What, in Duttepe? People actually live there? And so I made a promise to myself that I would build a mosque at the top of Duttepe, so tall that it would be visible from the mayor's residence in Nişantaşı and from any apartment block in Taksim, so they could see for themselves all of the people who did indeed live in the hills of Duttepe (Mulberry), Kültepe (Ash), Gültepe (Rose), Harmantepe (Harvest).

After the foundations were laid and covered up, I stood there at the door every Friday at prayers, collecting donations. The poor would say, "Let the rich pay for it!" The rich would say, "He buys the cement from his own shop," and give nothing. So I gave everything out of my own pocket. Whenever we had two or three idle builders on one of our construction sites, or some leftover steel, I sent them all to the mosque. The ill-wishers said, "Hadji Hamit, your dome is too big and too ambitious; when the wooden supports come off God will bring the whole thing down on your head, and then you'll understand how proud you've been." I stood right under the dome when the supports came off. It did not fall. I gave thanks to God. I climbed to the top of the dome and cried. My head spun. It was like being an ant on top of a great ball: all you can see at first from the top of the dome is a circle around you, but then you discover a whole universe at your feet. From up there, when you can't see where the dome ends, the line between death and the universe blurs, and it frightens you. Still, there were dissenters who would go down to the city and come back saying, "We couldn't see your dome, where is it?" So I poured all my energy into the minarets. Three years went by, and they said, "Do you think you're some sort of sultan, building two minarets with three balconies?" Every time I walked up the narrow staircase with the master builder, we would go a little higher, and up at the top I would get dizzy and black out. They said to me, "Duttepe is no more than a village; who ever heard of a village mosque with two minarets with three balconies each?"

So I said, If Duttepe is a village, then let the Hadji Hamit Vural Duttepe Mosque be the greatest village mosque in Turkey. They didn't even know what to say. Another year went by, and now they all came knocking on my door, eating my salt, and telling me how well the mosque had turned out, and all the while begging for votes in the elections: "Duttepe isn't a village, Duttepe is part of Istanbul, we've upgraded you to a municipality now, so you'd better let us have your votes," they said, "Hadji Hamit, tell your men to vote for us." Yes, it's true that these were my men. But that's why they will never trust you, they will vote for whomever I tell them to vote for . . .

9

Neriman

What Makes the City a City

One early evening in March 1974, Mevlut had just stashed his yogurt paraphernalia in a cupboard under the stairs at a friend's and was on his way from Pangaltı to Şişli, when, outside the Site Cinema, he saw an attractive woman who looked vaguely familiar, and without really thinking about it, he began to follow her. Mevlut knew there were some—his classmates and other boys of Mevlut's age in Duttepe, for instance—who got a kick out of following women on the street. He never took these stalkers' stories seriously, either because they were coarse and he disapproved or because they seemed completely improbable ("This chick kept turning around like she wanted me to follow her"). He did, however, keep a close eye on his own feelings when he followed the woman that day. He was enjoying it, and worried that he might do it again.

She went into an apartment block in the backstreets of Osmanbey. Mevlut recalled delivering yogurt to this building, and perhaps this was how he'd seen her face before, but he had no regular customers in there. He made no effort to find out on what floor or in which apartment the woman lived. Still, he would pass by the spot where he'd first noticed her whenever he had the chance. He saw her again in the distance around noon on a day when he was carrying a relatively light load, and he ended up following her with the pole across his back all the way to Elmadağ, where she walked into the office of British Airways.

That was where the woman worked. Mevlut decided to call her Neriman. Neriman was a brave and righteous woman who had sacrificed her life to defend her honor and chastity in a TV film.

Clearly, Neriman wasn't English. Her job was to find customers for the English airline in Turkey. Sometimes she could be found at a table on the ground floor, selling tickets to those who walked in. Mevlut liked that she took her job seriously. But some days she wasn't there at all. When Mevlut couldn't see her in the office, he felt sad, and he didn't like waiting for her either. Sometimes he felt there was a special sin, a secret he shared with Neriman. He had already discovered that his guilt only seemed to strengthen her pull on him.

Neriman was quite tall. Mevlut could pick out her chestnut hair even when it was nothing but a tiny blur in the distant crowd. Neriman didn't walk particularly fast, but she was as lively and determined as a high-school girl. Mevlut guessed she must be about ten years older than he was. Even when she walked way ahead of him, Mevlut could still guess what went on in Neriman's mind. She's going to turn right now, he would think to himself, and that's what Neriman would do, turning into a side street to get to her house in Osmanbey. Mevlut felt strangely empowered knowing where she lived, where she worked, that she had bought a lighter from a corner shop (which meant she was a smoker), that she didn't wear those black shoes every day, and that she slowed down every time she walked past Ace Cinema to look at the movie posters and stills.

Three months after their first meeting, Mevlut began to wish that Neriman would find out that he was following her and all the things he knew about her. During those three months, Mevlut had followed Neriman on the streets only seven times. It wasn't a huge number, but of course Neriman wouldn't be happy if she found out; perhaps she would even think he was some sort of pervert. Mevlut could accept that such a reaction would not be unwarranted. If someone in the village were to follow his sisters as he followed Neriman, he would want to beat the bastard up.

But Istanbul was not a village. In the city, that guy you thought was stalking that woman he didn't know could turn out to be someone like Mevlut, who carried important thoughts in his head and was destined to make it big someday. In a city, you can be alone in a crowd, and in fact what makes the city a city is that it lets you hide the strangeness in your mind inside its teeming multitudes.

As Neriman walked among the crowd, there were two reasons that Mevlut sometimes liked to slow his pace and let the distance between them grow:

1. Being able to spot the chestnut dot that was Neriman in a crowd and always knowing how to predict her movements, no matter how far she was, gave Mevlut the impression that they shared a very special spiritual intimacy.
2. All the buildings, stores, shopwindows, people, advertisements, and movie posters that came between them seemed like pieces of the life he shared with Neriman. As the number of steps between them multiplied, it was as if they also had more memories to share.

In his head, he would picture her being harassed on the street or dropping her handkerchief or a pickpocket trying to grab her dark blue bag. He would rush to the scene immediately to save her or at least present her with the handkerchief she'd dropped. All the bystanders would say what a gallant young man he was, while Neriman would thank him and catch on to his interest in her.

Once, a young man selling American cigarettes on the street (most of these youths were from Adana) went a little too far in trying to get Neriman's attention. She turned around and said something. (Mevlut imagined it might be "Leave me alone!") But the pushy young man would not give up. Mevlut sped up. Suddenly Neriman turned back, gave the youth some money, and quickly grabbed a pack of red Marlboros and put it in her pocket.

Mevlut thought he could say something like "You better watch it next time" when he walked past the man, acting like he was Neriman's protector. But it wasn't worth the trouble with these brutes. He wasn't sure he liked seeing Neriman buying contraband cigarettes on the street anyway.

At the start of summer, when he was finally done with the first year of high school, Mevlut was following Neriman when he witnessed an incident that would weigh on his mind for months. Two men standing on the pavement in Osmanbey called out to her. Neriman went on her way, pretending she hadn't heard them, and they began to follow her. Mevlut was just about to catch up with them when . . . Neriman turned and looked at the men, smiled in recognition, and started to chat with them animatedly, waving her arms about with the joy of running into long-lost friends. When the two men left Neriman and walked past Mevlut, talking and chuckling, he tried to eavesdrop on their conversation but couldn't hear them say anything bad about Neriman. All he heard was something like "It's harder in the second period," but he wasn't sure he'd heard properly, nor whether they were even talking about Neriman. Who were these two men? As they crossed paths, he felt the urge to tell them, "Gentlemen, I know that lady better than you do."

Sometimes he would be cross with Neriman because they hadn't met in so long, and he would start looking for another Neriman among the women on the street. He found a few likely candidates here and there when he was out walking without his yogurt vendor's shoulder pole and followed them all the way home. One time he jumped on a bus at the Ömer Hayyam stop and went all the way to Laleli on the other side of the Golden Horn. He liked that these new women took him away to other neighborhoods, and he enjoyed finding out about their lives and daydreaming about them, but he could never seem to get attached to any of them. His fantasies weren't so different from the things he'd heard from his classmates and other wasters who went around stalking women. Mevlut hadn't jerked off to Neriman even once. His affection and respect for her were founded on the purity of his feelings for her.

He didn't go to school much that year. Unless they were twisted enough to want to make enemies of their students, teachers would not want to fail a student twice for the same year, because that would get the kid kicked out of school. Trusting in this principle, Mevlut arranged for his name to be left out during roll calls and otherwise ignored school entirely. He passed the year and decided to sell Kısmet with Ferhat over the summer. Mevlut was even happier once his father went to the village and he had the house to himself, and meanwhile he was making lots of money with Ferhat.

One morning, Süleyman came knocking on the door, and this time Mevlut answered straightaway. "There's a war on," said his cousin. "We're conquering Cyprus." Mevlut followed him to his uncle's house in Duttepe. Everyone was hunched around the television watching military marches, and every time the TV showed a tank or an airplane, Korkut would jump in to say what model it was, C-160 or M47. Then they showed the same picture of Prime Minister Ecevit over and over again, saying "May God bless this endeavor, for our nation, for all Cypriots, and for humanity." Korkut used to call Ecevit a Communist, but all was forgiven now. Whenever President Makarios of Cyprus or one of the Greek generals came up on the screen, they would swear at him and dissolve into giggles. They walked down to the Duttepe bus stop and went into the coffeehouses. Everywhere you looked people were happy and excited, watching the same images of fighter planes, tanks, and flags, Atatürk and the army generals. Regular announcements on TV kept urging anyone who had dodged their compulsory military service to report to the draft office immediately, and Korkut never failed to say, "I was going to go anyway."

The country was, as ever, already under martial law, but now there were also new blackout regulations for Istanbul. Uncle Hasan was worried about blackout patrols and possible fines, so Mevlut and Süleyman helped him dim the lights in his shop. They cut up some cheap, thick dark blue paper into pieces roughly the size of a glass of water, which they then carefully slipped over the naked bulbs like little hats. Can you see it from outside? Pull the curtain; the Greek planes might not see this, but the patrols will, they snickered. That night, Mevlut felt like a real Turk from Central Asia, like the ones in the history books.

But as soon as he got back to Kültepe, his mood changed. Greece is a lot smaller than Turkey, and it would never attack us, and even if it did, it wouldn't bomb Kültepe, he reasoned as he started now to think about his place in the universe. He hadn't lit any lamps at home. Just as when he had first moved to Istanbul, he couldn't see the masses living on the other hills, but he could sense their presence in the darkness.

The same hills that had been half empty five years ago had filled up with houses now, and even on the empty hills farther out you could see the first transmission towers and mosque minarets. All those places and all of Istanbul were dark now, and Mevlut could see the stars in the summer sky. He lay down on the dirt and watched them for a long time, thinking of Neriman. Had she also blacked out the lamps in her home as he had? Mevlut felt that his feet would be taking him to Neriman's streets again, more than they ever had before.

10

The Consequences of Sticking Communist Posters on Mosques

God Save the Turks

Mevlut could see that tensions between Duttepe and Kültepe were on the rise, and he was aware of a number of disputes escalating into all-out blood feuds, but he never anticipated the fierce war that would erupt between the two hills like something out of the movies. After all, at first sight there wasn't much setting the two hills apart, nothing that could conceivably lead to such deep-seated enmity and bloody battle:

- On both hills, the first *gecekondu* homes had been built in the mid-fifties, out of hollow bricks, mud, and tin. These homes had been occupied by migrant settlers from the poor villages of Anatolia.
- Half of the male population on both hills slept in the same blue-striped pajamas (though with some minor variation in the width of the stripes) while the other half wore no pajamas at all and slept in a shirt, sweater vest, or pullover and under that an old undershirt, sleeveless or long sleeved depending on the season.
- Ninety-seven percent of the women on both hills covered their heads when they went out on the streets, just as their mothers used to do. They had all been born to village life, but now that they were in the city, they discovered that the "street" here was something else entirely, and so even in the summer they wore a

loose-fitting coat of faded dark blue or brown whenever they went out.

- Most people on both hills thought of their house not as their home for life but rather as a refuge in which to rest their weary heads until they got rich and returned to the village or as a place to stay while they waited for their chance to move into an apartment in the city.
- With astonishing consistency, the people of Kültepe and Duttepe all saw the same figures in their dreams at regular intervals:

Boys: the female primary-school teacher
Girls: Atatürk
Men: the Holy Prophet Muhammad
Women: a tall, anonymous Western film star
Old men: an angel drinking milk
Old women: a young postman bringing good news

- Afterward, they would revel in the thought of having been entrusted with an important message, seeing themselves as extraordinary individuals, though they rarely shared the contents of these dreams with anyone else.
- Electricity came in 1966, tap water in 1970, and asphalt roads in 1973 to both Kültepe and Duttepe within days of each other, so that neither had cause to resent the other for having been favored.
- By the mid-1970s, every other house in Kültepe and Duttepe had a black-and-white television set with a grainy picture (father-and-son teams would constantly be at work on their homemade TV aerials to improve it), and during important broadcasts, such as football matches, the Eurovision song contest, and Turkish movies, families with no television went to their neighbors', and on both hills it was for the women to serve tea to the assembled audience.
- Both hills got their bread from Hadji Hamit Vural's bakery.
- The five most commonly eaten foods on both hills were, in order: (1) underweight bread, (2) tomatoes (in summer and autumn), (3) potatoes, (4) onions, and (5) oranges.

Yet there were those who argued that these data were as deceptive as Hadji Hamit's underweight bread, because the future of a society was not determined by the traits its members shared but rested entirely on their differences. Some fundamental differences had cropped up between Duttepe and Kültepe over the course of twenty years:

- The top of Duttepe was now dominated by Hadji Hamit Vural's mosque. On hot summer days when the light filtered through its fine high windows, the mosque would be nice and cool inside; you would feel grateful to God for having created such a place and wrestle all your rebellious thoughts into submission. As for Kültepe, it was still topped by the giant, rusty transmission tower, with its sign picturing a skull, which Mevlut had seen on his first day in Istanbul.
- Ninety-nine percent of the people of Duttepe and Kültepe fasted, in theory, during the month of Ramadan. But in Kültepe, those who did so in practice were no more than seventy percent, because Kültepe was home to a high proportion of Alevis—Alawites—who had come in the 1960s from in and around Bingöl, Dersim, Sivas, and Erzincan. The Alevis of Kültepe did not use the mosque in Duttepe.
- There were many more Kurds in Kültepe than in Duttepe, but even the Kurds themselves didn't like this term being bandied about too freely, so the knowledge of their presence remained, for the time being, strictly within the bounds of people's private thoughts, lying dormant in a corner of their minds like a secret language spoken only at home.
- One of the back tables at the Motherland Coffeehouse in Duttepe had been taken over by young nationalists, the "Idealists" who called themselves Grey Wolves after an ancient Turkic myth. Their ideals involved liberating the Turks of Central Asia (in Samarkand, Tashkent, Bukhara, Xinjiang) from the hegemony of the Russian and Chinese Communist governments. They were ready to do anything, even to kill, for this cause.
- One of the back tables at the Homeland Coffeehouse in Kültepe had been taken over by young men who called themselves leftist-

socialists. Their vision involved creating a free society modeled on Russia or China. They were ready to do anything, even to die, for this cause.

After scraping through sophomore year on his second try, Mevlut stopped going to class entirely. He didn't even show up for exams. His father was aware of the situation, and Mevlut no longer even bothered claiming there was an exam tomorrow and pretending to study.

One night, he felt like a cigarette. He left the house on a whim to go over to Ferhat's place. A young man was standing with Ferhat in the back garden, pouring something into a bucket and stirring. "Caustic soda," explained Ferhat. "If you add flour to it, it'll turn into glue. We're going to put some posters up. Come along, if you want." He turned to the other young man. "Ali, meet Mevlut. Mevlut's a good guy, he's one of us."

Mevlut shook hands with the tall Ali, who offered him a cigarette; it was a Bafra. Mevlut decided to join them. He thought to himself that he was embarking on this dangerous mission because he was a truly valiant young man.

Slowly, they made their way through the alleys, under cover of darkness. Whenever he saw an appropriate spot, Ferhat would stop, put down his bucket, and with the brush spread the sticky, corrosive liquid evenly over the chosen surface or wall. While he was at it, Ali would unroll one of the posters he was carrying under his arm, plastering it over the wet surface in a quick and practiced motion. As Ali ran his hands over the poster to ensure that it stuck, Ferhat would use the brush for a quick sweep over the poster, taking special care over the corners.

Mevlut was the lookout. They all held their breath when a family on its way back from watching TV at the neighbors' almost walked right into them, the mother and father laughing at their son's saying, "I don't want to go to bed yet!"

This poster work was not so different from going out to sell things on the street at night. First you mixed certain liquids and powders at home like a wizard, and then you headed out into the darkness. But while, as a street vendor, you went out of your way to be heard, calling out or ringing your bell, when you were putting posters up you had to keep as quiet as the night itself.

They went a roundabout way in order to avoid the coffeehouses, the shopping street, and Hadji Hamit's bakery down below. Once they got to Duttepe, Ferhat lowered his voice to a whisper, and Mevlut felt like a guerrilla fighter sneaking into enemy territory. Now Ferhat was lookout while Mevlut carried the bucket and brushed glue over the walls. It started to rain, the streets emptied out, and Mevlut caught an eerie scent of death.

The sound of distant gunfire came echoing through the nearby hills. They stopped where they were, exchanging glances. For the first time that night, Mevlut read the writing on their posters, giving it his full attention: HÜSEYIN ALKAN'S KILLERS WILL BE BROUGHT TO JUSTICE. There was a sort of decorative border underneath, made out of hammer-and-sickle signs and red flags. Mevlut wasn't sure who Hüseyin Alkan was, but he knew he must have been an Alevi like Ferhat and Ali, just as he knew that Alevis preferred to be called leftists, and he felt a sort of guilt mixed with a sense of superiority about not being one of them himself.

As the rain got heavier, the streets grew quieter and the dogs stopped barking. They sheltered under the overhang of a building while Ferhat whispered an explanation: Hüseyin Alkan had been on his way back from the coffeehouse two weeks ago when he was shot dead by the Grey Wolves of Duttepe. They got to the street where his uncle Hasan lived. There was the house he'd been to hundreds of times since he'd come to Istanbul, and where he'd spent many happy hours in the company of Süleyman, Korkut, and Aunt Safiye; seeing it now through the eyes of an angry, poster-wielding left-wing militant, he saw his father's point. His uncle and his cousins, the entire Aktaş family, had built this house with Mevlut's father and then wrenched it away from him without a second thought.

There was no one around. Mevlut slathered glue over the most prominent spot at the back of the house. Ali put two posters up. The dog in the garden recognized Mevlut's scent, so he only wagged his tail. They stuck posters onto the back and side walls of the house, too.

"That's enough, they'll see us," muttered Ferhat. Mevlut's fury had scared him. The liberating thrill of the forbidden had gone to Mevlut's head. The caustic soda was burning the tips of his fingers and the back of his hands, and he was getting wet in the rain, but none of that bothered him. They went all the way up to the top of the hill, putting up posters on all the empty streets along the way.

The wall of the Hadji Hamit Vural Mosque that gave onto the square said POST NO BILLS in massive letters. But the warning was covered over with advertisements for soap and laundry powders, posters of ultranationalist associations and the Grey Wolves that said GOD SAVE THE TURKS, and signs announcing Koran classes. Mevlut spread glue over all this with great gusto, and soon they had covered the whole wall with their own posters. There was no one around, so they even did the walls of the mosque courtyard from the inside.

They heard a noise. It was just a door slamming in the breeze, but at first they mistook it for gunfire and started running. Mevlut could feel the liquid in the bucket dousing him, but he ran anyway. They got out of Duttepe, but they were so embarrassed for being scared that they kept working away on the other hills until they ran out of posters. By the end of the night, their hands burned and in places were even bleeding from the caustic soda.

Süleyman. As my brother always says: an Alevi who dares to put Communist posters up on a mosque must be ready to meet his maker. Alevis are a harmless, quiet, hardworking lot at heart, but some scoundrels in Kültepe are trying to sow the seeds of discord between us with the backing of the Communists. These Marxist-Leninists first targeted the bachelors that the Vurals brought in from villages near their hometown of Rize, trying to recruit them to the cause of communism and trade unions. Obviously the bachelors from Rize hadn't come to Istanbul for such nonsense but to make a living; they had no intention of ending up in some labor camp in Siberia or Manchuria. They are a sensible bunch, and they rejected the advances of these godless Alevi Communists. Meanwhile, the Vurals reported the Communist Alevis to the police. That's how all these plainclothes policemen and government agents ended up in our coffeehouses, smoking cigarettes (like all government workers, their brand is Yeni Harman) and watching TV all day. Of course, what lies beneath all this is some old land in Duttepe that the heretical Alevi Kurds claimed years ago and that the Vurals later seized and started building on. That old land in Duttepe, and the land in Kültepe that has houses all over it now, the whole lot of it belongs to them, they say! Is that so? If you don't have a title deed, my friend, the neighborhood councilman's word is law. Incidentally, the councilman—Rıza from Rize—is on our side. In any case, if you truly believed you were in the right, your conscience would be clear, and if your conscience were clear, you wouldn't be sneaking around our streets in the middle of the night putting up Communist propaganda and promoting godlessness on the walls of a mosque, would you?

Korkut. When I came from the village to join my father here twelve years ago, Duttepe was half empty, and the other hills were even emptier. The people who ended up taking advantage of all that land weren't just folk like us who had no roof over their heads and no other place in Istanbul to call home, but even people who had proper jobs and lives down in the city. New factories and workshops were cropping up daily, like the drug-manufacturing plant on the main road and the lightbulb factory, and they all needed free, empty lots to build dormitories for their cheap labor, so whenever anyone turned up and took over some of the vacant public land, no one objected. The news quickly spread that there was land here for the taking, and quite a few office clerks, teachers, and even shop owners who were based in the city center were shrewd enough to come to our hills and grab some land, thinking they might make a profit off it someday. But how are you going to take ownership of the land if you don't have a title deed to prove it's yours? The safest way is to build a house on it, preferably when the authorities are looking the other way, and move in overnight, but if that's not possible, then you have to at least be prepared to pick up a gun and stand guard over your plot. Or you find an armed guard for your land. In that case you must also treat that guard as a friend, share your meals with him and keep him company, so that he will put his heart into looking after your land, and when the time comes for the government to start handing out title deeds, no one else can come along and use your man to tell the government "Actually, sir, this land is mine and I have witnesses to prove it." Our esteemed Hadji Hamit Vural of Rize really knew what he was doing. Those young men he brought over from his village, he gave them jobs on his construction sites and in his bakeries, he fed them (though technically, I suppose they were baking their own bread), and he deployed them like soldiers to stand guard over his construction sites and his land. But it takes more than just a bunch of Rızas from the Rize countryside to make an army. To make sure they learned the ropes properly, we gave our friends from the village free membership in our club and in the Altaylı Karate and Taekwondo School, so that they would understand what it means to be a Turk, where Central Asia, the cradle of the Turkic races, is located, who Bruce Lee is, and the significance of the blue belt. We picked appropriate, clean family films and held educational screenings in our clubhouse in Mecidiyeköy, all to keep these boys who broke their backs every day in bakeries and on construction sites out of the clutches of Beyoğlu's nightclub whores and also of the pro-Moscow leftist organizations. There were boys who really believed in our cause, tearing up whenever they looked at the map that showed all the Turks in Central Asia that had yet to be freed, and I made sure to recruit these first-rate fellows for the club. As a result of our efforts, the political influence and the patriotic militia of the Grey Wolves in Mecidiyeköy grew bigger and stronger and naturally spread to the other hills. By the time the Communists realized they'd lost their hold over our hill, it was too late. The first to notice was the father of that sneak Ferhat, whom Mevlut loves to hang out with. That greedy miser didn't waste a minute building his house here and moving the entire family over from Karaköy, just so that he could stake a better claim on the land. Then he started bringing his Kurdish-Alevi comrades over from their village near Bingöl so that they could help him keep an eye on all the other land he'd taken over in Kültepe. This Hüseyin Alkan who got killed was also from that village, but I have no idea who killed him. Whenever one of these Communist troublemakers gets killed, his friends all march together at his funeral, shouting political slogans and putting up posters, and once the funeral is over, they like to go on a little glass-breaking rampage. (Secretly, they all love a good funeral, because it lets them indulge their destructive impulses.) But once they realize that it could be their turn next, they come to their senses and either just slink off quietly or renounce communism altogether. That is how you freely spread your beliefs.

Ferhat. Hüseyin, who gave his life for our cause, was a really nice person. It was my dad who brought him over from the village and put him in one of the houses we built in Kültepe. I'm sure it must have been one of Vural's thugs who shot him in the back of the neck that night. It didn't help that the police closed their investigation by blaming us. I have a feeling the Grey Wolves are going to attack Kültepe soon, backed by the Vurals, and try to get rid of us once and for all, but I can't tell Mevlut (he's thick enough to pass it along to the Vural camp). I can't even mention it to our guys. Half the Alevi youth is pro-Moscow, and the other half are Maoists, and they beat each other up so often over their differences, there's really no point warning them of the danger of losing Kültepe. The sad truth is that I don't really believe in the struggle I'm supposed to believe in. I'm hoping to take the leap and set up my own business soon. I also really want to go to college. But like most Alevis, I'm left-wing and secular and hate the Grey Wolves and the counterinsurgents out to kill us. Even though I know we are never going to win, I still go to the funerals; I raise my fist and shout slogans along with everyone else. My dad sees the danger in all this and sometimes he says, "I wonder if we should sell the house and move out of Kültepe," but he can't bring himself to do it because he's the one who brought everyone here in the first place.

Korkut. I could tell by the number of posters stuck to our house that this wasn't just the work of a political organization; it had to be someone who knows us personally. When Uncle Mustafa came by two days later and mentioned that Mevlut was never home, especially at night, and that he barely went to school anymore, that's when I really got suspicious. Uncle Mustafa was checking to see whether Süleyman would let anything slip, about him and Mevlut getting in trouble together. But I just knew it was that bastard Ferhat who was corrupting Mevlut. I told Süleyman to trick Mevlut into coming over for roast chicken two days later.

Aunt Safiye. Both my sons want to be friends with Mevlut, especially Süleyman, but they can't stop themselves from winding him up. Mevlut's father hasn't managed to save enough money to sort out their house back in the village, and they don't have enough to improve the one-room shack in Kültepe either. Sometimes I think I should go over to Kültepe for a day and bring a woman's touch to that pigsty they've been living in all these years, but then I fear I just couldn't bear it. Because of his father's insistence on leaving the rest of the family behind in the village, Mevlut has been like an orphan in Istanbul all his life since primary school. At first, when they'd just moved here, he used to come to me whenever he missed his mum. I would sit him on my lap, stroke his hair, kiss his cheeks, and tell him how clever he was. Korkut and Süleyman were jealous, but I didn't care. He still has that innocent look about him, and I've got the same urge to sit him on my knees again and cuddle him a bit, I can tell he still needs it, even though he's so grown up now, his face is covered in pimples, and he's shy with Korkut and Süleyman. I've stopped asking him about school—it only takes one look at him to understand the confusion inside his head. As soon as he came in that evening, I took him to the kitchen and kissed him on the cheeks before Korkut and Süleyman saw us. "You've grown so tall, but stand up straight, don't be ashamed of your height," I said. "That's not it, Auntie, it's the stick I use to carry the yogurt, it's bending my back, but I'm going to give it up soon," he said . . . The way he wolfed that chicken down at dinner, I fell to pieces. Korkut talked about how the Communists would try to sweet-talk kindhearted innocents over to their side, but Mevlut kept quiet. "Stop trying to scare the poor orphan, you rascals," I told Korkut and Süleyman in the kitchen.

"Stay out of this, Mom, we've got our reasons," said Korkut.

"Nonsense, you just like taunting him . . . Who could possibly suspect my darling Mevlut? I am sure he has nothing to do with these evil people."

"Mevlut is going to come out with us tonight to write on the walls and prove he's not working with the Maoists," said Korkut as he returned to the table. "Isn't that so, Mevlut?"

There were three of them again, and again one of them was carrying a large bucket, but this time it was full of black paint rather than glue. Whenever they found a suitable place, Korkut would write on the wall with his brush. Mevlut would hold the paint bucket for him while trying to guess what Korkut was writing. GOD SAVE THE TURKS, one slogan he already knew, was his favorite. He'd seen it all over the city. He liked it because it seemed a harmless plea, and it was a reminder of what he'd learned in history class: that he was part of one big Turkish family spanning the whole world. Some of the other slogans, though, were rather sinister. When Korkut wrote DUTTEPE IS WHERE COMMUNISTS COME TO DIE, Mevlut sensed that it referred to Ferhat and his friends and hoped that these sentiments would not get beyond mere posturing.

A stray remark from Süleyman ("My brother's got the shooting iron") on lookout duty alerted Mevlut to the fact that they were carrying a gun. If there was enough room on the wall, sometimes Korkut would write GODLESS before COMMUNIST. He usually failed to anticipate how many words and letters he needed, and some letters would end up small and crooked, which finally was what bothered Mevlut the most. (When the letters listing a street vendor's wares on his cart or his sesame roll trolley were all squished up, Mevlut could tell the man had no future.) Eventually Mevlut could no longer refrain from pointing out to Korkut that he'd made the letter *C* too big. "You try it, then!" said Korkut, forcing the brush on him. Deep into the night, Mevlut covered up ads for circumcision services, walls that said DON'T BE A LITTER LOUT, and the Maoist posters he'd put up four nights before, with the slogan GOD SAVE THE TURKS!

They walked through the dark, thick forest of *gecekondu* homes, walls, gardens, shops, and suspicious dogs. Every time he stopped to write GOD SAVE THE TURKS, Mevlut could feel the depth of the surrounding darkness in which these words were a beacon, a signature appended onto the boundless night, transforming the neighborhood. That night, he discovered many things about Duttepe and Kültepe that he had previously overlooked while loafing around with Ferhat and Süleyman in the evenings: every inch of the neighborhood fountains was covered in political slogans and posters; the people who hung around smoking outside coffeehouses were actually armed watchmen; at night, everyone—families, passersby—fled the streets and took refuge in their own private world; in this night, pure and everlasting, like an old fairy tale, being Turkish felt infinitely better than being poor.

11

The War Between Duttepe and Kültepe

We Don't Take Sides

One night toward the end of April, a round of gunfire from a passing taxi hit the people playing cards and watching television in the Homeland Coffeehouse at the entrance to Kültepe. Five hundred meters away, in their house on the other side of the hill, Mevlut and his father were having lentil soup in what was, for them, an uncharacteristically friendly atmosphere. They exchanged a look while they waited for the machine gun's report to die down. When Mevlut got too close to the window, his father yelled, "Come back here!" Presently, they heard the metallic clatter of the machine gun again, now farther away, and so they went back to their soup.

"See?" said his father with a meaningful expression, as if this were proof of what he'd been saying all along.

The attack had targeted two coffeehouses, both frequented by leftists and Alevis. Two people had been killed in the coffeehouse at Kültepe and another in Oktepe, and almost twenty had been injured. The next day, Marxist groups calling themselves armed vanguards and the Alevi relatives of the victims rose up in protest. Mevlut joined Ferhat among the crowds, shouting out a slogan every now and then and marching through the neighborhood, though not in the front row. He didn't clench his fist quite as forcefully as others in the crowd, nor did he know enough of the words to keep up with their chants, but he was certainly angry . . . There were no plainclothes policemen around, nor any of Hadji Hamit Vural's men. As a result, it took just two days for all the streets and walls in Kültepe and Duttepe to be covered in Marxist and Maoist slogans. Amid the excitement of the protests, new posters were printed in the city, and fresh slogans were coined for the resistance movement.

On the third day, when the victims' funeral was meant to take place, an army of mustachioed policemen wielding black batons arrived in a fleet of blue buses. There were also growing numbers of photojournalists who were assailed by children gesticulating wildly for their pictures to be taken, too. When the funeral procession reached Duttepe, the angry young men broke off from the rest of the crowd and, as expected, began to march.

Mevlut didn't join them this time. His uncle Hasan's house gave onto the mosque courtyard, and he could see his uncle, Korkut, Süleyman, and some of Vural's men smoking and looking out the windows at the crowds down below. Mevlut wasn't cowed by their presence, nor was he worried that they might punish or shun him. All the same, he felt awkward clenching his fist and shouting slogans when he knew they were watching. There was something pretentious about politics when it was taken to extremes.

A scuffle broke out when the police outside the mosque tried to block the advance of the marching funeral crowds. Some youths within the crowd threw stones, one shattering the window of a shop displaying posters of the Grey Wolves. The Fatih Real Estate Agency, run by Hadji Hamit's family, and the small contractors' offices next door were soon also damaged. Apart from desks, televisions, and typewriters, there wasn't much of value in these places, where the Grey Wolves controlling Duttepe liked to come and pass the time watching TV and smoking cigarettes. But as a result of the attacks, the war of the Grey Wolves against the Marxists, or the right-wing idealists against the left-wing materialists, or Konya against Bingöl, was brought vividly to the whole neighborhood's attention.

These rough and vicious early battles went on for more than three days, with Mevlut and other curious observers watching from a distance. He saw helmeted men drawing their batons and charging the crowd, shouting "Allah! Allah!" like Janissaries. He watched from a sheltered spot as tanklike armored vehicles shot water at the demonstrators. In the midst of all this, he would still go down to the city to drop some yogurt off with his loyal regulars in Feriköy and Şişli, and in the evenings he would go out selling boza. On one of these nights, he hid his student ID from the police, who had set up a security cordon between Duttepe and Kültepe, and deducing from the way he looked that he was only a poor street vendor, they let him through without trouble.

Filled with anger and a sense of solidarity, he went back to class. In just three days, the atmosphere at the school had become heavily politicized. Leftist students would raise their hands and brashly interrupt classes to give political lectures. Mevlut enjoyed the sense of freedom but did not himself say a single word.

Skeleton had instructed the teachers to make sure that the students who interrupted lessons about the Ottoman conquests and Atatürk's reforms with diatribes against capitalism and American imperialism ("Yesterday, one of our comrades was shot," they would begin) were silenced and their registration numbers noted down, but the teachers, who mostly wanted to stay out of trouble, didn't much cooperate. Even the biology teacher, Massive Melahat, the most combative of them all, tried to humor those who interrupted her to condemn "the systematic exploitation" and to accuse her of trying to gloss over the class struggle by teaching them about tadpoles. Melahat had explained how difficult her life was, that she'd been working for thirty-two years and was really just hanging on until she reached retirement age, which moved Mevlut and made him quietly hope that the agitators would leave her alone. The older, bigger students in the back rows had interpreted the political crisis as an invitation to torment the weak; the know-it-alls, the richer kids, and the obsequious front-row nerds had all been bullied into obedience; the right-wing nationalist students had gone quiet, and some were avoiding school altogether. Whenever there was news from the students' neighborhoods about a fresh skirmish, police raids, and torture, the militants would take to the corridors, striding up and down every floor of Atatürk Boys' Secondary School shouting slogans ("Down with fascism," "Independence for Turkey," "Free education"), and snatch the roll-call sheet from the class president and set it on fire with a cigarette. Then they'd either join the fray in Duttepe and Kültepe or go off to the cinema (provided they had enough money or knew someone at the box office to let them in).

This atmosphere of liberty and rebellion lasted only a week. Two months before, the unpopular physics teacher Fehmi had humiliated a student from Diyarbakır by imitating his provincial Turkish accent while the rest of the class, including Mevlut, looked on in anguish and fury. Now that students were bursting into his classroom demanding a formal apology, and others were announcing a student strike just as they were doing in the universities, Skeleton and the principal called in the police. The blue-uniformed policemen and the newly arrived undercover agents who guarded both entrances began to check IDs at the door, again just as they were doing in the universities. There was the same postapocalyptic atmosphere that usually follows earthquakes or big fires, and Mevlut couldn't deny that he was enjoying it. He attended the classroom meetings, but whenever tensions escalated into brawls, he would stand to one side until they were over, and when a new student strike was announced, he would avoid school altogether and go out selling yogurt instead.

A week after the arrival of the police at school, a third-year high-school student from the Aktaş family's street blocked Mevlut's path to tell him that Korkut would be expecting him that night. Mevlut made his way to his uncle's house in the late-night gloom, getting searched several times and having to present his ID to the police and to the lookouts that the various right- and left-wing crews had posted on the streets, and when he reached his destination he saw one of the school's new "undercover" students eating bean stew at the same table where Mevlut had eaten roast chicken two months ago. His name was Tarık. Mevlut quickly figured out that Aunt Safiye didn't like him but that Korkut trusted him and held him in high regard. Korkut told Mevlut to stay away from Ferhat "and all the other Communists." As always, the Russians were after warm water ports, and in order to weaken Turkey, which was thwarting their dreams of empire, they were trying to pit Sunnis against Alevis, Turks against Kurds, and the rich against the poor by inflaming our destitute Kurd and Alevi compatriots against us. Thus it was strategically crucial that the Kurds and Alevis from Bingöl and Tunceli be driven out of Kültepe and all the other hills.

"Give Uncle Mustafa my regards," said Korkut, with the bearing of Atatürk inspecting military maps before a final siege. "Make sure you stay indoors on Thursday. There is a danger the wheat might burn with the chaff." Noticing Mevlut's quizzical look, Süleyman revised his brother's pronouncement: "There's going to be an attack," he said, seeming all the while pleased to be in the know about everything before it happened.

That night, Mevlut could barely sleep for the sound of gunfire.

The next day, he found out that the rumors had spread, and everyone at Atatürk Secondary, including the middle-school kids and even Mohini, knew that terrible things were going to happen on Thursday. The coffeehouses in Kültepe and on other hills with a large population of Alevis had been attacked again during the night, and two more people had been killed. Most coffeehouses and shops had lowered their shutters, and some didn't open at all for the day. Mevlut heard reports that the doors of Alevi homes were going to be marked with crosses during the night, in preparation for Thursday's raids. He wanted to get away from it all, just to go to the cinema and be left alone to masturbate in peace, but he also wanted to be there and witness everything.

The funeral processions on Wednesday were led by slogan-chanting left-wing organizations, and the crowds attacked the Vural bakery. When the police failed to intervene, the bakery workers from Rize defended themselves as best they could with blocks of firewood and peels before escaping through the back door and leaving all those delicious loaves of fresh bread behind. In the evening, Mevlut heard that the Alevis had targeted mosques, that the Grey Wolves' offices in Mecidiyeköy had been bombed, and that people had been drinking alcohol in mosques, but he found all this too far-fetched to believe.

"Let's go sell our boza in the city tonight," said his father. "No one will bother a poor boza seller and his son, anyway. We don't take sides." They picked up their poles and their jugs and left the house, but the police surrounding the neighborhood weren't letting anyone through. When Mevlut spotted the flashing blue lights in the distance, along with ambulances and fire engines, his heart beat faster. He basked in the attention; it made him, and everyone else in the neighborhood, feel important. Five years ago, the whole neighborhood could have come tumbling down, and still no police or firefighters, let alone any journalists, would have turned up. When they got back home, they stared in vain at the black-and-white TV. Of course there was no mention of any of this on the news. The TV (which they'd finally managed to save up for) was showing a panel discussion on the conquest of Istanbul. As ever, his father started complaining about "the anarchists" who caused trouble "and robbed poor street vendors of their livelihood," distributing his curses evenly on the left and right.

At midnight, they were woken by the sound of running in the streets, people screaming and shouting slogans. They did not know who was out there. His father checked the bolt on the door and barricaded it with the table with the short leg, which Mevlut did his homework on in the evenings. They saw flames shooting up from the other side of Kültepe, their light hitting the low, dark clouds above, and the sky kindled with a strange brightness; the light that reflected back down onto the streets flickered as the flames quivered in the wind, and it was as if the whole world were quaking along with the shadows. They heard gunshots. Mevlut spotted a second fire. "Don't stand so close to the window," said his father.

"Dad, I heard they're putting marks on the homes that need to be raided, shall we check?"

"Why? We're not Alevis!"

"They might have put one by mistake," said Mevlut, thinking that perhaps he should have been more careful showing his face around the neighborhood in the company of Ferhat and the other leftists. But he hid this worry from his father.

In a quiet moment, when the street was calmer and the shouts had died down, they opened the door to check. There was no mark. Mevlut wanted to inspect the walls, too, just to make sure. "Get back inside!" his father shouted. The white slum house in which Mevlut and his father had spent years together now looked like an orange ghost in the night. Father and son shut the door tight, but they didn't sleep until dawn, when the sounds of gunfire ceased.

Korkut. To be honest, I didn't believe that the Alevis had put a bomb in the mosque either, but lies spread fast. The patient, quiet, devout people of Duttepe had seen "with their own eyes" the Communist propaganda that had appeared on mosques and even in the farthest neighborhoods, and their anger was a force to be reckoned with. You can't just come here from downtown in Karaköy, or maybe even from outside of Istanbul, from Sivas or Bingöl, and think you can take this land away from the people who actually live in Duttepe! Last night we saw who really owns these houses, who actually lives in them. It's hard to stop a young nationalist whose faith has been insulted. Many homes were damaged.

Ferhat. The police did nothing, and if they did, it was only to join in the raids. Groups with scarves wrapped around their faces started to break into homes, vandalize property, and loot Alevi shops. Three houses, four shops, and the grocery store run by a family from Dersim were all burned to the ground. They retreated when our people started shooting at them from the roofs. But we think they'll be back after sunrise.

"Come on, let's go down to the city," said Mevlut's father in the morning.

"I'm staying," said Mevlut.

"But, son, these people will never stop fighting, they'll never tire of hacking away at each other—politics is just an excuse . . . Let's just sell our yogurt and our boza. Please don't get involved. Stay away from the Alevis, the leftists, the Kurds, and that Ferhat. We don't want to get kicked out, too, while they're busy rooting them out."

Mevlut gave him his word that he would not set foot outside. He said he would sit and look after the house, but once his father had gone, he found it impossible to stay at home. He filled his pockets with pumpkin seeds, grabbed a small kitchen knife, and rushed off to the higher neighborhoods like a curious child running to the movies.

The streets were busy, and he saw men armed with sticks. He also saw girls chewing gum as they walked back from the grocery store with armfuls of bread and women scrubbing their laundry in the garden, as if nothing had happened. Those God-fearing citizens who hailed from Konya, Giresun, and Tokat did not support the Alevis, but neither did they wish to fight them.

"Don't walk through there, mister," said a little boy to a distracted Mevlut.

"They can shoot all the way here from Duttepe," said the boy's friend.

Looking as if he was trying to avoid some invisible rainfall, Mevlut worked out where the bullets were likely to hit and crossed to the other side of the street in a single move. The kids followed his movements closely, but they also laughed at him.

"Why aren't you in school?" said Mevlut.

"School's closed!" they shouted gleefully.

At the doorway of a house that had burned down, he saw a woman crying; she was bringing out a woven basket and a wet mattress, just like the kind Mevlut and his father had at home. A tall, thin young man and another who was decidedly chubbier stopped Mevlut as he was making his way up a steep slope, but they let him pass when an onlooker confirmed that Mevlut was from Kültepe.

The upper sections of the slope of Kültepe that faced Duttepe had been transformed into a military outpost. Slabs of concrete, steel doors, tin cans filled up with earth, rocks, tiles, and hollow bricks had been used to build crenellated fortifications that sometimes ran right up to people's homes, only to emerge and fork out from the other side. The walls of Kültepe's oldest houses were not bulletproof. Yet Mevlut had seen people shooting at the other hill even from these buildings.

Bullets were expensive, and people didn't shoot too frequently. There would often be long spells of silence, and Mevlut and many others would use these unofficial cease-fires to move around the hill. Toward midday, he found Ferhat near the peak, standing on the roof of a new concrete building right next to the transmission tower that carried electricity into the city.

"The police will be here soon," said Ferhat. "We don't stand a chance. The fascists and the police have more weapons, and they have more people. And the press is on their side."

This was Ferhat's private view. In front of everyone else, he would say, "We will never let these sons of bitches in!" and would act as if he was about to start shooting any moment, even though he didn't have a gun.

"Tomorrow the newspapers won't talk about the massacre of Alevis in Kültepe," said Ferhat. "They'll write that the political uprisings were quashed and that the Communists set themselves on fire and committed suicide out of spite."

"If it's not going to end well, then why are we even fighting?" said Mevlut.

"Should we just hold our hands up and surrender?"

Mevlut was confused. He saw that Kültepe and the slopes of Duttepe were bursting with houses, streets, and walls and that, in the eight years he'd been in Istanbul, extra floors had been added to many rickety houses, some homes that had originally been built out of mud had been razed to the ground and rebuilt using hollow bricks or even concrete, houses and shops had been painted over, gardens had flourished and trees grown tall, and the slopes of both hills had been covered with ads for cigarettes, Coca-Cola, and soap. Some of these were even illuminated at night.

"The leftists and the rightists should each send their leader to the square down near the Vural bakery to fight it out honorably," said Mevlut, only half in jest. "Whoever wins the battle can win the war."

There was something reminiscent of old fairy tales in the fortifications that arose on both hills like castle bastions and in the way the warriors on each side were standing guard.

"Which side would you support in a fight like that, Mevlut?"

"I'd support the socialists," said Mevlut. "I'm against capitalism."

"But aren't we supposed to set up shop in the future and become capitalists ourselves?" said Ferhat with a smile.

"I like how the Communists look out for the poor," said Mevlut. "But why don't they believe in God?"

When the yellow helicopter that had been hovering over Kültepe and Duttepe since ten o'clock in the morning returned, the people on both sides of the face-off between the hills went quiet. Everyone positioned at the top of the two hills could see the headphones on the soldier inside the helicopter's clear cockpit. To see that a helicopter had been sent filled Ferhat and Mevlut with pride, just as it did everyone else on both hills. Kültepe was bedecked with red-and-yellow flags bearing the hammer and sickle, banners made out of cloth were suspended between buildings, and groups of youths hiding behind scarves over their mouths shouted slogans at the helicopter flying above.

The exchange of bullets lasted all day, but there were few injuries, and no one died. Just before sundown, the robotic sound of police loudspeakers informed everyone that a curfew had been imposed on both hills. It also announced that homes in Kültepe would be searched for weapons. A few armed stalwarts stayed on the fortifications preparing to fight the police, but Mevlut and Ferhat were unarmed, and they both went home.

When his father returned from a day spent selling yogurt without running into any trouble on his way back, Mevlut was amazed. Father and son sat down at the table, talking over their lentil soup.

Late at night, there was a power cut in Kültepe, and armored vehicles entered the dark neighborhoods with floodlights blazing, like clumsy but malevolent crabs. Marching behind them like Janissaries after chariots were policemen armed with guns and batons who rushed up the slopes and fanned out into the neighborhoods. There was the sound of heavy gunfire for a time, and then everything sank into a nervous silence. When Mevlut looked out of the window into the pitch-black night, he saw masked informants leading the soldiers to the homes that needed to be raided.

In the morning, their doorbell rang. Two soldiers were looking for weapons. Mevlut's father explained that this was a yogurt seller's house and that they had nothing to do with politics, and he welcomed them inside with a respectful bow, sitting them down at the table and offering some tea. The soldiers were both potato nosed, but they weren't related. One of them was from Kayseri, the other from Tokat. They sat there for about half an hour, discussing the sad events they were witnessing and the danger that innocent bystanders might get caught up in the fray, and whether the Kayseri football team had any chance of getting promoted this season. Mustafa Efendi asked them how long they had to go until they were discharged and whether their commander was nice or beat them for no reason.

While they had their tea, all the weapons, leftist literature, posters, and banners in Kültepe were confiscated. The vast majority of local university students and angry protesters were taken into custody. Most of them had barely slept for days, and as they were herded onto buses, they were subjected to a first round of beatings, followed by more systematic tortures: bastinadoes, electric shocks, and the like. Once their wounds had healed, their heads were shaved and they were photographed for the newspapers standing beside weapons, posters, and books. Their trials went on for years; in some cases, the prosecutors demanded the death penalty, while in others they asked for a life sentence. Some of these protesters spent ten years in jail, some only five, one or two broke out of prison, and others were acquitted. Some got involved in prison riots and hunger strikes, ending up blind or paralyzed as a result.

Atatürk Boys' Secondary School had been closed down, and its reopening was delayed by the political tensions that followed the death of thirty-four left-wing demonstrators on International Workers' Day in Taksim Square as well as a spate of political assassinations all over Istanbul. Mevlut grew even more distant from his classes. He was selling yogurt late into the evening on streets covered with political slogans, and at night he gave most of his earnings over to his father. When school opened again, he really didn't feel like going back. No longer was he just the eldest in his class, he was now older than anyone else in all of the back rows.

When their report cards were issued in June 1977, Mevlut learned that he had failed to graduate from high school. He spent that summer in uncertainty and fear of loneliness. Ferhat and his family were leaving Kültepe, along with some other Alevis. Back in winter, before all this political upheaval, Ferhat and Mevlut had made plans to start their business—as street vendors—in July. But now Ferhat, busy with the logistics of the move and his Alevi relatives, was no longer so eager. In the middle of July, Mevlut returned to the village. He spent a lot of time with his mother, ignoring her talk of "getting you married." He hadn't done his compulsory military service yet, and he had no money, so marriage would mean a return to the village.

At the end of that summer, just before the start of the new term, he stopped by the school. It was a hot September morning, but the old school building was, as ever, cool and shaded. He told Skeleton that he wanted to postpone his registration for a year.

Skeleton had come to respect this student he had known for eight years. "Why would you do that; just grit your teeth for another year and you'll be done with school," he said, with surprising warmth. "We'll all give you a hand, you're the oldest student here . . ."

"I'm going to go to cram school next year to prepare for the university admissions exams," said Mevlut. "This year, I'm going to work to save some money for cram school. I'll finish high school next year." He'd thought out every detail of this scenario on the train to Istanbul. "It's possible."

"Possible, yes, but by then you'll be twenty-two," said Skeleton, ever the heartless bureaucrat. "Never in this school's history have we graduated anyone at the age of twenty-two." But he saw the resignation on Mevlut's face. "Well, good luck, then . . . I'll defer your registration for a year. But first you're going to need a document from the city health department."

Mevlut didn't even ask what document he needed. The moment he set foot outside, his heart told him that this would be his last visit to the school building. His mind, meanwhile, warned him not to get too sentimental about the smells of UNICEF milk that still drifted up from the kitchens; of the coal cellar that was no longer in use; of the basement toilet, which he'd been scared even to look at when he was a middle-school kid and where he'd spent his high-school years smoking scrounged cigarettes with all the other boys. He walked down the stairs without a single glance back at the staff room and library doors. Whenever he'd been to school recently, he had always thought, Why do I even bother coming, I'm never going to graduate anyway! Now, as he walked past the Atatürk statue for the last time, he told himself, I could have made it if I'd really wanted to.

He did not tell his father that he wasn't going to school. He even hid the truth from himself. Since he didn't go to the health department to get the document he needed in order maintain the illusion that he might really go back to school, his true and private thoughts on the matter gradually adapted to the more official version of the facts. There were even times when he genuinely believed that he was saving money to go to cram school next year.

Other times, as soon as he was done delivering yogurt to a gradually shrinking roster of regular customers, he would drop off his stick, his scales, and his trays with someone he knew and run out into the city streets, to wherever his legs happened to take him.

He loved it as a place where all manner of wonderful things seemed to be going on at the same time, no matter where he looked. Mostly, these things tended to happen around Şişli, Harbiye, Taksim, and Beyoğlu. He would hop on a bus in the morning with no ticket, going as far into these neighborhoods as he could without getting caught, and then, with no load on his shoulders, he would walk freely into those same streets he couldn't enter when he had yogurt to carry, savoring the joy of getting lost in the commotion and the noise of the city, looking in the shopwindows on his way. He liked the mannequin displays of women in long skirts next to cheerful children in two-piece suits, and he always looked closely at the trunkless mannequin legs in hosiers' shops. He might get caught up in a fantasy his mind had invented on the spot and spend ten minutes following a woman with light brown hair walking on the other side of the road, until an impulse would lead him toward the first restaurant he came across, and he would enter it, asking for the first high-school classmate that popped into his head: "Is he around?" Sometimes they would put him off with a brusque "We don't need a dishwasher!" before he could even get a word in. Back on the street, Neriman would cross his mind for a moment, but then he would follow his imagination again and start walking in the opposite direction, toward the backstreets of the Tünel area, or he might pay a visit to the Rüya Cinema, where he would linger in the narrow lobby looking at the posters and movie stills, until he could see whether Ferhat's distant relative was there, checking tickets at the door.

All the happiness and beauty that life had to offer only revealed themselves when his mind drifted off into fantasies of a world far removed from his own. His guilt would flare up like a gentle ache in a corner of his soul whenever he went to the cinema and got caught up daydreaming. He would blame himself for wasting time, for missing the subtitles, for focusing only on the beautiful women in the film or on odd details that weren't that important to the plot. Whenever he got an erection at the cinema, sometimes for good reason and sometimes for no reason at all, he would hunch over in his seat and work out that if he got home two hours before his father did in the evening, he would have plenty of time to masturbate without any worry of getting caught.

Sometimes, instead of going to the cinema, he would visit the barbershop in Tarlabaşı where Mohini worked as an apprentice, or drop by a coffeehouse favored by Alevis and left-wing chauffeurs to have a chat with the cashier boy he knew through Ferhat, watch people playing *rummikub* while keeping an eye on the television. He knew that he was just killing time, doing nothing at all, and heading down the wrong path anyway because of having dropped out of high school, but the truth was so painful that he preferred the comfort of other thoughts: he would start a business with Ferhat, they would be street vendors but different from all the others (he imagined stacking yogurt trays on a wheeled vehicle with a bell that chimed with every movement), or they could open a small tobacco store in the empty shop he'd just passed or maybe even a convenience store in place of that struggling shop that sold dress shirts and did dry cleaning . . . One day, he was going to make so much money that everyone would be amazed.

Even so, he could see for himself that it was getting harder to make a living by selling yogurt door to door, and families were growing accustomed to serving yogurt on their dinner tables in the same glass container the grocer sold it in.

"Mevlut, my boy, you know the only reason we still buy farm yogurt is so we can see your face every now and then," said a kindly old lady. No one asked when he would finish high school anymore.

Mustafa Efendi. If they'd stopped at the glass bowls that came out in the 1960s, we would have found a way to deal with it. Those first bowls were thick and heavy and looked like clay pots, the deposit costs were high, and if they cracked or you chipped a corner somewhere, the store would refuse to refund the deposit for the empty container. Housewives would put these empty pots to good use: as cat-food bowls, ashtrays, storage jars for used cooking oil, bath bowls, and soap dishes. Having used the pots for all sorts of kitchen and household needs, people might suddenly think that they should return them to the shop and get their deposit back, and that's how any one family's makeshift bin or slimy dog bowl would get a quick rinse from a hose in some workshop in Kağıthane before landing on some other Istanbul family's lovely, radiant dinner table, touted as the cleanest, healthiest new type of yogurt bowl. Sometimes, instead of using a clean plate as usual, customers would put one of these empty bowls on my scale pans so I could weigh my yogurt into it, and then I just couldn't resist saying something. "Ma'am, you have to believe me when I say I'm telling you all this for your own good," I'd begin. "But you should know that the hospitals in Çapa use these bowls to store urine, and on Heybeliada they use them as spittoons in the TB sanatorium . . ."

Eventually they brought out a lighter, cheaper version of these glass bowls. With this kind, there was no deposit for the grocer to refund, and they said, Just give them a rinse and use them as tumblers, and they even make nice gifts for housewives. They buried the cost in the price of the yogurt, of course. Still, thanks to my strong shoulders and to original Silivri yogurt, we were somehow keeping up, but only until the big dairy companies designed a fancy sticker with a picture of a cow on it and stuck it on their glass bowls, spelling out their brand name in great big letters, and advertising on the TV. Then they sent their Ford minivans, each sporting a picture of the same cow, down the narrow, winding streets to supply the grocery stores, and that destroyed our livelihoods. Thank goodness we still have boza to sell in the evenings and keep us going. If only Mevlut would stop messing around and start working a little harder, and hand over all the money he makes to his father, we'd have something to send back to the village for the winter.

12

How to Marry a Girl from the Village

My Daughter Is Not for Sale

Korkut. Six months after the war and all the fires last year, most of the Alevis in the neighborhood were gone. Some of them moved to other hills farther away, like Oktepe, while others went to live in the Ghaazi Quarter at the far outskirts of the city. I wish them all the best. Let's hope they don't start troubling our police and our gendarmes over there, too. If you find yourself on the path of a six-lane motorway built to modern international standards, speeding toward your unregistered chicken coop of a house at eighty kilometers an hour, you can claim all you want that "Revolution is the only solution!" but you'd only be fooling yourself.

Once that whole tangle of leftists was gone, the value of the deeds issued by the councilman increased overnight. Armed gangs and profiteers cropped up trying to claim new land. The same people who wouldn't give old Hamit Vural a penny when he said, Let's buy new carpets for the mosque, who said behind his back that he should pay for them himself, since he drove the Bingöl and Elazığ Alevis out and took their land, were themselves quick to snatch up land and title deeds according to the new development plans. Mr. Hamit also embarked on some new construction projects in Kültepe. He opened a new bread factory in Harmantepe and spared no expense building a dormitory with televisions, a prayer room, and a karate school for the bachelors he brought over from the village. When I got back from military service, I started working as an assistant on the construction site for this dormitory, and I managed the on-site supply store. On Saturdays, Mr. Hadji Hamit would share a meal of *ayran,* meat, rice, and salad with all these unmarried, patriotic young men in the dormitory cafeteria. I would like to thank him here for having so generously helped me to get married.

Abdurrahman Efendi. I am struggling to find a suitable match for my eldest daughter, Vediha, who is already sixteen. Normally it is best for the women to sort these things out among themselves while they're washing their laundry or out at the public baths or the market, or while visiting each other, but my orphan girls have no mother and no aunts to speak of, so it's all been left up to your humble servant. When people found out that I took a bus all the way to Istanbul just for this purpose, they said all I was after was a rich husband for my beautiful darling Vediha and that I would take her whole bride price and spend it on *rakı.* The reason that they would envy a cripple like me and talk behind my back is simple: despite my crooked neck, I'm still a jolly fellow who takes joy in his daughters, lives life to the fullest, and can also enjoy an occasional drink. It's just a jealous lie that I used to get drunk and beat my late wife, or that I only went to Istanbul so I could forget my crooked neck and throw some money at the girls in Beyoğlu. In Istanbul, I dropped by the coffeehouses where the yogurt sellers are usually found early in the day and saw some old friends who are still working, still selling yogurt in the morning and boza in the evening. Not that you can just come straight out and say, "I'm looking for a husband for my daughter!" You have to start with some small talk and let friendship do the rest, and if you end up in a bar at night, one bottle will lead to the next, and before you know it, everyone's talking more freely. I may have boasted drunkenly about my darling Vediha during one of these conversations, passing around a photo we took at the Billur Photography Studio in Akşehir.

Uncle Hasan. Every now and then I looked at the photograph of the girl from Gümüşdere in my pocket. Very pretty. I showed it to Safiye in the kitchen one day. "What do you think, Safiye?" I said. "Might she be right for Korkut? She's our Crooked-Necked Abdurrahman's daughter. Her father came to Istanbul, all the way to my shop. We talked for a while. He used to be a hardworking man, but it turns out he wasn't strong enough; he got crushed under that stick and had to go back to the village. Clearly he's out of money. But Abdurrahman Efendi is a wily old fox."

Aunt Safiye. My little Korkut is getting worn out from all this building work, the dormitory, that car, being a driver, and with his karate, too, and we would love to get him married, but he's so tough, God bless him, and so proud as well. If I were to say to him, You've turned twenty-six, let me go to the village and find you a girl, he'd say, No, I'll find one myself in the city. If I were to say, All right, do it yourself, look around in Istanbul for a girl you want to marry, he would just say that he wants a girl who is pure and obedient, and you don't find any of those here in this city. So I took the photograph of Crooked-Necked Abdurrahman's pretty daughter and stuck it somewhere by the radio. When he gets home, my beloved Korkut is too tired to do anything but watch TV and listen to the horse races on the radio.

Korkut. Nobody knows that I bet on the horse races, not even my mother. I don't do it for the money; I just do it for fun. One night four years ago, we added a room to the house. I sit alone in that room listening to the horse races live on the radio. This time, while I was staring at the ceiling, a ray of light seemed to shine on the radio, and I felt that the girl in the photograph set there was looking at me, and that the way she was looking at me would be a consolation to me for the rest of my life. I was filled with gladness.

"Mom, who's this girl whose picture is by the radio?" I asked in passing. "She's from back home, from Gümüşdere!" she said. "Isn't she an angel? Shall I arrange a match for you two?" "I don't want a village girl," I said. "Especially not the kind who gives out her photograph left and right." "It's not like that," said my mom. "I heard her crooked-necked father refuses to show her picture to anyone, they say he's jealous of his daughter and turns suitors away at the door. Your father pressed him for a picture because he knew that this shy girl was meant to be such a beauty."

I believed this lie. Perhaps you know for sure that it was a lie, and you're laughing at how easily I let myself be taken in. I'll tell you one thing, though: people who make fun of everything can never truly fall in love, nor truly believe in God. That's because they're too proud. But just like believing in God, falling in love is such a sacred feeling that it leaves you with no room for any other passions.

Her name was Vediha. "I can't get this girl out of my head," I told my mother a week later. "I'll go back to the village to watch her in secret and speak to her father."

Abdurrahman Efendi. The suitor is just a hothead. He took me to a bar. Vediha is my daughter, my treasure, my bouquet of flowers, these people would never understand, they've scrounged up a little money here in Istanbul and now they're getting above themselves. Some karate-chopping upstart makes a little money sucking up to Mr. Hadji Hamit from Rize and he's driving a Ford so now he thinks he can have my daughter? I said several times MY DAUGHTER IS NOT FOR SALE. They were frowning at the next table when they heard me, but then they smiled as if it were a joke.

Vediha. I'm sixteen years old, I'm not a child anymore, and I know (as everyone does) that my father wants to marry me off, though I pretend I have no idea. Sometimes I dream that an evil man is following me . . . I finished Gümüşdere Primary School three years ago. If I'd gone to Istanbul, I would have graduated from high school by now, but there's no middle school in our village, so no girl has ever gone that far.

Samiha. I'm twelve and just in my last year of primary school. Sometimes my sister Vediha picks me up after school. A man started following us one day on the way back home. We walked on in silence, and doing like my sister, I didn't turn around to look. Instead of going straight home, we headed for the grocer's, though we didn't go in. We walked down dark streets, past houses with no windows, under the shivering plane tree, and through the neighborhood behind our house, and we got home late. But the man kept following us. My sister never even smiled. "He's an idiot!" I said, fuming, as I stepped inside. "All boys are idiots."

Rayiha. I'm thirteen years old, and I finished primary school last year. Vediha has plenty of suitors. The latest, supposedly, is from Istanbul. That's what they're saying, but really he's the son of a yogurt seller from Cennetpınar. Vediha loves going to Istanbul, but I don't want her to like this man, because then she'll get married and leave. Once Vediha is married, it'll be my turn next. I still have three years to go, but once I'm her age, I won't have anyone running after me the way she has now—and even if I did, who cares, it's not like I want any of them. Everyone always says, "You're so clever, Rayiha." Looking out the window with my crooked-necked father, I can see Vediha and Samiha coming home from school.

Korkut. I couldn't take my adoring eyes off my beloved as she walked her little sister home from school. It was my first glimpse of her, and it filled my heart with a love far deeper than I had felt just seeing her photograph. Her straight back, her slender arms, were all so perfect, and I thanked the Lord for that. I knew that I would be unhappy if I didn't get to marry her. So I got more and more worked up thinking about how that sly Crooked Neck would drive a hard bargain, until I rued the day I'd fallen in love.

Abdurrahman Efendi. At the suitor's insistence, we met again in Beyşehir. I thought to myself, If you're so in love, then money should be no object. The fate and fortune of my darling Vediha, of all my daughters, are in my hands, so I was leery even as I went to the restaurant, and before I'd even had my first drink, I said once again, "I'm really sorry, young man, I understand you very well, but MY BEAUTIFUL DAUGHTER IS ABSOLUTELY NOT FOR SALE."

Korkut. That pigheaded Abdurrahman Efendi had already spouted a whole list of demands before he'd even finished his first drink. I wouldn't be able to afford it even with my father and Süleyman's help, even if we all pulled together, took out a loan, sold our house in Duttepe and the land we'd fenced off in Kültepe.

Süleyman. Back in Istanbul, my brother decided that the only hope of solving his romantic woes was to call upon Mr. Hadji Hamit, so we decided to put on a karate exhibition match for his first visit to the dormitory. The clean-shaven workers fought well in their spotless training uniforms. Mr. Hamit had us sit on either side of him during dinner. The venerable gentleman had been to Mecca two times—twice a hadji!—he had huge holdings of land and property, many men at his command, and he had founded our mosque, so that every time I looked at his white beard, I felt lucky to be sitting so close to him. He treated us like his own sons. He asked after our father. ("Why isn't Hasan here?" he said, remembering Dad's name.) He inquired about the condition of our house and about the latest room we'd built and the half floor we'd added with its own external staircase, and he even asked where that land was that my father and Uncle Mustafa had claimed and gone to register with the neighborhood councilman. He knew everything: he knew where all the land was, whose plot was next to or across from anyone else's, he knew about the houses that had been built or left half finished, when people were arguing over a plot they owned jointly, he kept track of which buildings and shops had been built over the past year, down to the last wall and chimney, he knew exactly which street was the last street on any given hill to have electricity and running water, and he knew what route the ring road was going to take.

Hadji Hamit Vural. "Young man, I hear you're lovesick and in a lot of pain, is it true?" I asked, and he turned his eyes away in shame: he was embarrassed not about being head over heels but about his friends discovering his hopeless romance and his being unable to sort it out by himself. I turned to his fat little brother. "God willing, we shall find a solution to your brother's heartache," I said. "But he has made a mistake that you must avoid. Tell me, what's your name? All right, then, Süleyman, my son, if you're going to love a girl as deeply as your brother here . . . you've got to make sure to start loving her after you're married. If you're in a rush, then maybe wait until you're engaged, or perhaps until you've got an informal agreement . . . At least wait until the bride price has been decided. But if you fall in love before all that, like your brother, and you sit down to discuss the price with the girl's father, then those cunning, crafty fathers will ask you for the moon. There are two kinds of love in our land. The first kind is when you fall in love with someone because you don't know them at all. In fact, most couples would never fall in love if they got to know each other even a little bit before getting married. This is why our Blessed Prophet Muhammad did not think it was appropriate for there to be any contact between the boy and the girl before marriage. There is also the kind that happens when two people get married and fall in love after that, when they have a whole life to share between them, and that can only happen when you marry someone you don't know."

Süleyman. I said, "Sir, I would never fall in love with a girl I didn't know." "Did you say a girl you do know, or a girl you don't know?" asked the radiant Mr. Hadji Hamit. "Leave the knowing to one side; the best kind of love is the love you feel for someone you haven't even seen. Blind people know how to fall in love, you know." Mr. Hamit laughed. Then his men laughed, too, though they didn't really get it. Before we left, my brother and I kissed Mr. Hadji Hamit's blessed hand with deference. My brother punched me hard on the shoulder when we were alone, saying, "We'll see what kind of wife you find in this city."

13

Mevlut's Mustache

The Owner of Unregistered Land

NOT UNTIL much later, in May 1978, in a letter his elder sister had written to their father in Istanbul, did Mevlut discover that Korkut was about to marry a girl from the neighboring village of Gümüşdere. His sister had been writing her father for almost fifteen years, sometimes regularly, sometimes when the mood struck her. Mevlut would read the letters to his father in the same focused, serious voice he used to read out the newspaper. On finding out that the reason for Korkut's visit was a girl from Gümüşdere, they both felt strangely jealous, and downright angry. Why hadn't Korkut mentioned anything? Two days later, when father and son went over to visit the Aktaş family and learned all the details, it occurred to Mevlut that his life in Istanbul would be so much easier if only he, too, could count on a patron and protector as powerful as Hadji Hamit Vural.

Mustafa Efendi. Two weeks after our visit to the Aktaş family, during which we found out that Korkut was getting married with Hadji Hamit Vural's support, I was at my older brother Hasan's grocery store, chatting about trivial matters, when he suddenly put on a serious face and announced that it had been decided: the new ring road would pass through Kültepe, and the cadastral surveyors would therefore no longer be coming to that side of the hill (and even if they did, they would have no choice but to set those plots aside for the road, no matter how much you tried to bribe them), meaning that no one would be able to have the land around there registered officially in his name, and the government would be paying no one a single penny of compensation for the land it expropriated to build its six-lane highway.

"I realized our plot in Kültepe was going to go for nothing," he said, "so I sold it to Hadji Hamit Vural, who is collecting all the land on that side of the hill. He's a generous man, God bless him, and he paid me handsomely!"

"What! You mean you sold my land without even asking me?"

"It's not your land, Mustafa. It's *our* land. I went to claim it, and you gave me a hand. The councilman did things properly and wrote both our names under the date and signature on the piece of paper he gave us, just as he did with everyone else. He gave the document to *me,* and you didn't seem to mind him doing that. But that piece of paper was going to be worthless in another year. Forget about a house, no one's going to start anything on that side of the hill, because they know it'll just get demolished. You must have noticed that not a single wall has been going up."

"How much did you sell it for?"

He was saying "Now, why don't you calm down a little and stop using that tone with your older brother . . ." when a woman walked into the shop and asked for some rice. I stormed out angrily while he was busy with his plastic scoop, putting rice from a sack into a paper bag. I could have killed him! I have nothing in this world except for my slum house and half of that land! I didn't tell anyone. Not even Mevlut. The next day, I went back to the shop. Hasan was folding old newspapers into paper bags. "How much did you sell it for?" Again, he didn't say. I could no longer sleep at night. A week later, when the shop was empty, he suddenly told me how much the land had gone for. What? He said I would get half, of course. But it was such a pittance that all I could say was: I DO NOT ACCEPT THAT SUM. "Well, I don't exactly have it anymore," said my brother, "we're arranging Korkut's wedding, aren't we!" "Excuse me? Are you saying you're marrying off your son with the money from my land?" "I told you poor Korkut is smitten!" he said. "Don't get so mad, it'll be Mevlut's turn soon, Crooked Neck's daughter has two sisters. Let's get one married off to Mevlut. What's that poor boy going to do?" "Don't you worry about Mevlut," I said. "He's going to finish high school first and then do his military service. Anyway, if there was a suitable girl, you'd take her for your Süleyman."

It was from Süleyman that Mevlut found out that the unregistered land his father and his uncle had claimed in Kültepe thirteen years ago had been sold. According to Süleyman, there was no such thing as "the owner of unregistered land" anyway. No one had built a home there, or even planted a single tree, and it would be impossible to stop the government's six-lane road with a piece of paper obtained from a neighborhood councilman years ago. When his father brought the topic up two weeks later, Mevlut acted as if it were news to him. He understood his father's fury, and he resented the Aktaş family for having sold their shared property without even asking, and when he considered that, on top of this, they had been so much more successful in Istanbul than Mevlut and his father had, he felt increasingly angry, as if he'd suffered a personal injustice. But he also knew that he couldn't afford to cut his ties with his uncle and cousins, that without them he would be left all alone in the city.

"Now listen here, if you ever go to your uncle's place again without my permission, if you meet up with Korkut and Süleyman again, it'll have to be over my dead body," said his father. "Understood?"

"Understood," said Mevlut. "I swear I won't."

But as his oath kept him away from his aunt's kitchen and stopped him from spending time with Süleyman, he regretted it almost immediately. Ferhat wasn't around either, as he had left Kültepe with his family last year after high school. So after his father had gone back to the village, Mevlut spent part of the month of June wandering around teahouses and children's playgrounds alone with his box of Kısmet. But the money he earned in a day was only slightly more than what he spent, and he found he couldn't make even a quarter of what he used to pull in working with Ferhat.

At the beginning of July in 1978, Mevlut took a bus back to the village. At first, it was fun being with his mother and sisters as well as his father. But the whole village was busy preparing for Korkut's wedding, and Mevlut found it unsettling. He walked around the hills with his aging dog, his old friend Kâmil. He remembered the smell of grass drying in the sun, the scent of acorns and cold streams weaving through the rocks. But he just couldn't shake off the feeling of missing out on all the things happening in Istanbul and on the opportunity to get rich.

One afternoon he dug out the two banknotes he had hidden in a corner of the garden under the plane tree. He told his mother he was going back to Istanbul. "Your father won't like it!" she said, but he ignored her. "There's lots of work to do!" he said. He managed to take the minibus down to Beyşehir that day without running into his father. In town, he ate minced meat and eggplant at the cheap diner across from the Eşrefoğlu Mosque while he waited for the bus. At night, as the bus made its steady way toward Istanbul, he sensed that his life and his future were now entirely in his own hands, that he was a grown man standing on his own, and he was thrilled at the endless possibilities that lay ahead.

In Istanbul, he realized that his month away had already cost him some customers. It never used to be that way. Of course some families would always just draw their curtains shut and stay out of sight, while others would leave for the summer. (Some yogurt sellers followed their customers all the way to their summerhouses on the Princes' Islands, in Erenköy, and in Suadiye.) Still, sales never used to suffer this much during the summer, because the cafés would buy yogurt to make *ayran*. But in that summer of 1978, Mevlut grasped the truth that selling yogurt on the streets was a dying craft. The number of yogurt vendors was obviously dwindling fast among both the hardworking, apron-clad men of his father's generation and the eager young strivers of Mevlut's, who were always looking for something else to do.

The increasing hardship of the yogurt seller's life had turned his father into a man full of nothing but anger and hostility, but it did not affect Mevlut in the same way. Even on his lowest, loneliest days, he never lost the smile that his customers found so refreshing. The aunties and the doormen's wives in the tall new apartment blocks with their NO STREET VENDORS signs, and the old shrews who usually took so much pleasure in pointing out "Street vendors are not allowed on the elevator," always took pains to explain to Mevlut exactly how to open the elevator doors and what buttons he was supposed to press. There were many maids and doormen's daughters who admired his boyish good looks from kitchens, stairwells, and apartment doors, though he had no idea how to go about even talking to them. To hide his ignorance even from himself, he became convinced that this was the way to "be respectful." He had seen men his age in the movies who had no trouble at all talking to girls, and he would have liked to be more like them. But in truth, he wasn't too fond of foreign films, in which you never quite knew who were the good guys and who were the bad guys. But whenever he touched himself, he still mostly fantasized about the foreign women from the movies and the Turkish magazines. He liked to indulge in these fantasies dispassionately as he lay in bed with the morning sun warming his half-naked body.

He liked being at home all by himself. It meant he was his own master, if only until his father came back. He tried moving the wobbly table with the short leg somewhere else, he stood on a chair and fixed that end of the curtain that drooped on its rail, he put the cutlery and the pots and pans he didn't use back into the cupboard. He swept the floor and cleaned everything much more often than when his father was around. Still, he couldn't ignore the thought that this one-room house was even smellier and messier than usual. Savoring his solitude and his own ripe smell, he felt himself captive to the same urge that had always drawn his father toward a moody loneliness, the very same feeling that roiled his own blood. He was now twenty-one years old.

He stopped by the coffeehouses in Kültepe and Duttepe. He felt like hanging out with the familiar faces from the neighborhood and the youths who loafed around watching TV, so he went a few times to the place where day laborers congregated in the mornings. At eight o'clock every morning, they would gather in an empty lot at the entrance to Mecidiyeköy, offering their labor. They were mostly unskilled workers who, having been put to work somewhere immediately upon arriving from the village, had then been let go to save their employers the insurance costs; now they would take any job they could get while they stayed with their relatives on one of the nearby hills. Young men living the shame of unemployment and foolish hotheads who couldn't hold any job, they all came here in the morning to smoke their cigarettes as they waited for the foremen who came with their vans from all over the city. Among the young men who whiled away the hours in the coffee-houses, there were some who occasionally went out to the ends of the city for day jobs and boasted about the money they made, but it took Mevlut only half a day to make as much.

At the end of one of those days, when he felt particularly alone and demoralized, he left his trays, his stick, and all of his other equipment at a restaurant and went to look for Ferhat. It took Mevlut two hours, packed like a sardine in a red public-transport bus that reeked of sweat, to get to Gaziosmanpaşa on the outskirts of the city. Out of curiosity, he looked inside the fridges that served as window displays for convenience stores, and he saw that the yogurt companies had conquered these neighborhoods, too. In a grocery store in a backstreet, he saw a fridge with yogurt in a tray, ready to be sold by the kilo.

He got on a minibus, and by the time he reached the Ghaazi Quarter outside the city, it was already getting dark. He walked to the mosque at the other end of the neighborhood, on a road that consisted entirely of an almost-vertical slope. The forest behind the hill was supposed to be an unspoiled, verdant marker of Istanbul's outer limits, but it seemed the city's newest migrants had been nibbling away at bits of the woodland, undeterred by all the barbed-wire fencing. The neighborhood was covered in revolutionary slogans, hammer-and-sickle signs, and red-star stencils; the whole place seemed much poorer to Mevlut than Kültepe or Duttepe. In a daze, but with a vague fear always at the back of his mind, he wandered the streets, in and out of the most crowded coffeehouses, hoping to see the familiar face of one of the Alevis who had been forced out of Kültepe. He asked around for Ferhat but found nothing, nor did he see anyone he knew. The streets of the Ghaazi Quarter after dark, without even a lamppost to illuminate them, seemed to him more dismal than any distant Anatolian town.

He got back home and masturbated all night. He would do it once and then, after he'd ejaculated and wound down, the shame and guilt would set in, and he would swear: never again. Some time would pass before he would begin to worry about breaking his oath, and therefore committing a sin. It would seem to him only prudent to do it quickly once more, to get it out of his system at last, and then renounce the wicked habit until the end of his days. That's how he would end up masturbating again two hours later.

Sometimes his mind went places he really wished it wouldn't. He questioned the existence of God, he thought about the most obscene words he knew, and sometimes he visualized an explosion, like something from the movies, which would shatter the whole world into pieces. Was it really him thinking all these horrifying thoughts?

Ever since he'd stopped going to school, he'd been shaving only once a week. He could sense the darkness inside him looking for an excuse to manifest itself. Then he didn't shave at all for two weeks. He decided to start again when his stubbly face began to scare some of his loyal customers, who valued cleanliness as much as a layer of cream on their yogurt. Inside the house, it was no longer as dark as it used to be. (He couldn't remember why it used to be that way.) But he still went outside with his shaving mirror as his father did. Once he had shaved off his beard, he finally accepted the truth he had been dimly aware of for some time. Wiping the foam from his face and his neck, he looked in the mirror: yes, he had a mustache now.

Mevlut didn't like himself too much with a mustache. He didn't think he looked "nice." That baby-faced boy everyone thought was so cute had disappeared, replaced by one of the millions of men he saw out on the streets every day. All those customers who thought he was so charming, the old ladies who still asked whether he was in school, and the housemaids who gave him longing looks from under their headscarves, would they still like him now? His mustache took the shape of everyone else's, even though he hadn't touched it at all. It was heartbreaking to think that he was no longer the person his aunt used to cuddle on her lap; he realized that this was the start of something from which there could be no turning back, but at the same time he felt a greater strength in this new self.

Whenever he masturbated, there was something at the back of his mind that he had always forbidden himself to think about but that now, sadly, he could no longer keep back there: he was twenty-one years old and he had never slept with a woman. A pretty girl with a headscarf and good morals, the kind he would like for a wife, would never sleep with him before they got married; and he would never want to marry a woman willing to have sex with him before the wedding.

His priority wasn't marriage anyway, but finding a kind woman he could hold and kiss, a woman he could have sex with. In his mind, he saw all these things as being separate from marriage, but apart from marriage, he found himself unable to obtain sexual contact. He could have tried to start something with one of the girls who showed some interest (they might go to the park or to the cinema, or have a soft drink somewhere), made her believe he intended to marry her (this would probably be the hard part), and then slept with her. But only a selfish brute would do that sort of thing, not Mevlut. Not to mention that he might end up getting shot by the tearful girl's older brothers or her father. The only girls who would sleep with a boy casually and without their families finding out were those who didn't wear headscarves, and Mevlut knew that no girl born and bred in the city would ever be interested in him (no matter how rakish he looked with a mustache). The last resort was to go to one of the brothels in Karaköy. Mevlut never did.

One night toward the end of summer, a day after he'd happened to walk past Uncle Hasan's shop, Mevlut heard a knock at his door and was really pleased to see Süleyman standing outside. He embraced his cousin warmly and noticed that Süleyman had also grown a mustache.

Süleyman. Mevlut called me his brother and gave me such a big hug that I ended up with tears in my eyes. We laughed about how we'd both grown mustaches unbeknownst to each other.

"You've styled yours like the leftists!" I said.

"What?"

"Oh come on, you know what I'm talking about, it's the leftists who cut the tips into triangles like that. Did you copy Ferhat?"

"I didn't copy anyone. I just cut it the way I felt like, I wasn't going for any particular shape . . . Anyway, that means you've cut yours like a Grey Wolf."

We took the mirror from the shelf and examined each other's facial hair.

"Mevlut, don't come to the wedding in the village," I said, "but there's going to be a wedding reception for Korkut two weeks from now at the Şahika Wedding Hall in Mecidiyeköy, and you're coming to that. Uncle Mustafa is being difficult, he's tearing the family apart, but you don't need to be like him. Look at how the Kurds and the Alevis always watch out for each other. They band together and build each other houses, nonstop. When one of them finds work somewhere, the first thing he does is bring over anyone from the clan still left in his village."

"Isn't that how the rest of us got here, though?" said Mevlut. "You lot are turning a profit, but no matter how hard we work, my father and I still can't seem to save enough to enjoy any of the opportunities Istanbul has to offer. And now our land is gone."

"We haven't forgotten your share in the land, Mevlut. Hadji Hamit Vural is a just, generous man. Otherwise my brother Korkut would never have been able to find the money he needed to get married. Crooked-Necked Abdurrahman Efendi has another two beautiful daughters. We'll take the older one of the two for you; I hear she's very pretty. Otherwise, who is going to find you a wife, look after you, and protect you? Being alone in this big city is unbearable."

"I'll find myself a girl to marry, I don't need anyone's help," Mevlut said stubbornly.

14

Mevlut Falls in Love

Only God Could Have Ordained This Chance Encounter

At the end of August, Mevlut went to Korkut and Vediha's wedding party. Even he wasn't exactly sure why he'd changed his mind. The morning of the wedding, he wore a suit he had bought at a discount from a tailor his father knew. He also put on the faded blue tie his father wore on religious holidays and whenever he had to go to a government office. With some money he'd put aside, he bought twenty German marks from a jeweler in Şişli.

The Şahika Wedding Hall was on the sloping road from Duttepe to Mecidiyeköy. It was often used by municipal authorities and labor unions for circumcision parties or to host the wedding receptions of foremen as well as laborers, typically with the support of their employers. During those summers when they had worked together as street vendors, Mevlut and Ferhat had snuck inside two or three times toward the end of a party to cadge a free lemonade and a few biscuits; and yet this place, which he had so often passed, had not left much of an impression on Mevlut. When he walked downstairs into the hall, the place was so packed, the little orchestra was so loud, the subterranean atmosphere so hot and stuffy that, for a moment, Mevlut had trouble breathing.

Süleyman. Me, my brother, and all the rest of us were so happy when we saw that Mevlut had come. My brother, looking sharp in his off-white cream suit and a purple dress shirt, could not have been nicer to Mevlut, introducing him to everyone before bringing him over to our table, where all the young men were sitting. "Don't be fooled by this baby face," he said. "He's the toughest guy in our family."

"Well, my dear Mevlut, now that you've got a mustache, plain lemonade just won't cut it," I said. I showed him the bottle under the table and filled his glass up with vodka. "Have you ever had genuine Russian Communist vodka?" "I haven't even tried Turkish vodka yet," said Mevlut. "If this stuff is even stronger than *rakı,* it'll go straight to my head." "It won't, it'll just make you relax, and maybe you'll even find the courage to look around and see if anyone catches your eye." "I do look around!" said Mevlut. But he didn't. When the first sip of vodka and lemonade touched his tongue, he recoiled as if he'd been burned, but then he pulled himself together. "Süleyman, I wanted to pin a twenty-mark note on Korkut, but I'm not sure it's enough?" "Where on earth do you find these marks, if the police catch you they'll lock you up," I said, just to scare him. "Everyone does it, though. You're a fool if you keep your savings in Turkish liras; with all this inflation it'll be worth half as much by the end of the day," he said. I turned to the rest of the table. "Mevlut here might look all innocent," I said. "But he's the craftiest, most tightfisted street vendor I've ever seen. For a scrooge like you to pin twenty marks on the groom . . . it's a big deal . . . But enough with this yogurt business, Mevlut. Our fathers were yogurt sellers, too, but we've all got different jobs now." "I plan to set up my own business one day, don't you worry. Then you're all going to wonder why you didn't come up with it yourselves." "Go on, then, tell us what you're going to do." "Mevlut, you should come and be my business partner!" said Hidayet the Boxer. (This was his nickname because he had a nose like a boxer's and because, once he knew he would be kicked out of school anyway, he knocked out the chemistry teacher Show-Off Fevzi with a single punch, just like my brother.) "I haven't got some grocery store or kebab joint like this bunch. I've got a real shop, it sells building materials," said Hidayet. "It's not even yours, it's your brother-in-law's," I said. "We can all manage that much." "Guys, the girls are looking this way." "Where?" "The girls at the bride's table." "Hey, don't all stare like that," I said. "Those girls are my family now."

"We're not," said Hidayet the Boxer, still staring. "Those girls are too young anyway. We're not child molesters." "Careful, guys, Hadji Hamit is here." "So what?" "Are we supposed to stand up and sing the national anthem?" "Hide the vodka, don't even try to have it with your lemonade, he doesn't miss a trick. He hates this sort of thing, and he'll make us pay for it later."

Mevlut was looking at the girls sitting with the bride at the far table when Hadji Hamit Vural came in with his men. All heads turned as soon as he walked in, and he was immediately surrounded by people wanting to kiss his hand.

Mevlut would also have liked to marry a pretty girl like Vediha once he turned twenty-five. This would only be possible after making lots of money and gaining the protection of someone like Hadji Hamit. He understood that, for this to happen, he would have to go and do his military service, work very hard, and leave the yogurt to find a proper occupation or run a shop.

Eventually, emboldened by the alcohol, the rising noise levels, and the increasingly lively atmosphere inside the hall, he started staring at the bride's table directly. He also felt that God was with him and that his fortunes might be about to lift.

Many years later, Mevlut would still be able to replay those moments—the conversation around him and what he saw at the table where the pretty girls sat (occasionally obscured by people standing in his line of sight)—like scenes from a movie. But it was a movie in which the dialogue and the photography were not always entirely clear:

"They're not that young, you know," said a voice at the table. "They're all old enough to get married."

"Even the one with the blue headscarf?" "Guys, please don't look straight at them like that," said Süleyman. "Half these girls are going back to the village, the other half will stay in the city." "We don't even know where they live . . ." "Some of them live in Gültepe, some in Kuştepe." "You're definitely taking us there . . ." "Which one would you want to write letters to?" "None of them," said an honest young man Mevlut didn't know. "They're sitting so far that I can't even tell them apart." "All the more reason to write them letters, since they're so far away."

"Our Vediha's ID card says she's sixteen, but actually she's seventeen," said Süleyman. "Her sisters are fifteen and sixteen. Crooked-Necked Abdurrahman Efendi had them registered late, so they would have more time to sit at home and entertain their father."

"What's that youngest one called?"

"Yes, she's the prettiest."

"Her sister's nothing special."

"One of them is Samiha; the other one is Rayiha," said Süleyman.

Mevlut flushed with surprise at his own quickening heartbeat.

"The other three girls are also from their village . . ." "The one with the blue headscarf isn't bad at all . . ." "None of these girls is younger than fourteen." "They're children," said the Boxer. "If I were their father, I wouldn't let them wear headscarves yet."

"In our village, you put on your headscarf once you're done with primary school," said Mevlut, unable to contain his excitement.

"The youngest finished primary school this year."

"Which one's that, the one with the white headscarf?" asked Mevlut.

"She's the pretty one, the younger one."

"I would never get married to a village girl," said Hidayet the Boxer.

"And a city girl would never get married to you."

"Why?" said Hidayet, somewhat offended. "How many city girls do you even know?"

"Loooads."

"You do realize, don't you, that customers who come into your shop don't count as girls you know?"

Mevlut ate some sweet biscuits with another glass of vodka and lemonade, which smelled like mothballs. When it was time to give the bride and groom their gifts and jewelry, he was able to take a good long look at the incredible beauty of Korkut's wife, Vediha Yenge. Her younger sister Rayiha, sitting at the girls' table, was just as beautiful; as he kept looking at that busy table, staring at Rayiha, he noticed a desire stirring inside him as strong as the will to live, but at the same time he felt ashamed and afraid that he would turn out to be a failure.

Mevlut pinned his twenty marks onto Korkut's lapel with a safety pin Süleyman had given him, but he couldn't bring himself to look up at his sister-in-law's beautiful face, and his own shyness embarrassed him.

On the way back to the table, he took an unplanned detour: he went up to congratulate Abdurrahman Efendi, sitting with the other Gümüşdere villagers. He was now very close to the girls' table, but he didn't look in that direction. Abdurrahman Efendi was dressed up in a white dress shirt with a high collar to hide his crooked neck, as well as a tasteful jacket. By now he was used to the antics of young street vendors and yogurt sellers who were dazzled by his daughters. Like a sultan, he held his hand out to Mevlut, who gamely kissed it. Had his beautiful daughter been watching this exchange?

For a second, Mevlut lost concentration and glanced at the girls' table. His heart started beating madly; he was afraid, but he was happy, too. At the same time, he felt a little disappointed. There were now a couple of empty chairs at the table. In truth, Mevlut hadn't been able to get a proper look at any of the girls from where he had been sitting. So as he was walking back he kept his eyes on their table, trying to figure out who exactly was missing, when . . .

They almost crashed into each other. She was the prettiest among the girls. She must have been the youngest, too; there was a childlike quality to her.

They looked into each other's eyes for a moment. She had a very honest, open face, and girlish dark eyes. She walked off to her father's table.

Even in his confusion, Mevlut could see the hand of fate—kismet—at work. Only God could have ordained this chance encounter. He was having trouble thinking straight, and he kept looking toward the crooked-necked father's table, trying to catch another glimpse of her, but there were too many people. He had already walked off too far. But though he couldn't see her face, he felt her in his soul every time she moved, every time the blue blur of her headscarf fluttered in the distance. All he wanted to do was to tell everyone about that pretty girl, their miraculous meeting, and the moment her dark eyes looked into his.

At some point before the party started winding down, Süleyman mentioned that "Abdurrahman Efendi and his daughters Samiha and Rayiha are staying with us for another week before they return to the village."

Over the next few days, Mevlut thought constantly about the girl with the dark eyes and the childlike face and about what Süleyman had said. Why had he mentioned this to Mevlut? What would happen if Mevlut revived his old habits and went over to knock on the Aktaş door out of the blue? Would he get to see that girl again? Had she also noticed Mevlut? He definitely needed an excuse to visit them, otherwise Süleyman would realize that he had come to see her, and he might hide her away from him. He might even make fun of Mevlut, or put a stop to it all by saying that she was still a child. If Mevlut admitted his infatuation to Süleyman, Süleyman would probably say that he was in love with her, too—that he'd fallen in love with her first, in fact—and not let Mevlut anywhere near her. Mevlut spent the whole week selling yogurt and failing to find a reasonable excuse to visit the Aktaş family, no matter how hard he looked for one.

When the migrating storks had come back over Istanbul on their way to Europe, August had come to an end, and the first two weeks of September had passed, Mevlut did not go to school, nor did he exchange any of the German marks he kept hidden under his mattress to pay for one of the cram schools he had said a year ago that he would be attending now. He hadn't even gone to the city health department to get the document Skeleton had told him to get last year in order to defer his school enrollment. All this meant that his academic career, which for all practical purposes had ended two years ago, could no longer survive even as a dream. The gendarmes from the draft office were bound to turn up at his village soon.

Mevlut didn't think his father would be willing to lie to them in order to delay his son's military service. Rather, he would probably say "Let him do his service, he can get married afterward!" Of course his father didn't even have enough money to find a wife for his son. But Mevlut wanted to marry this girl he had found, and as soon as possible. He had made a mistake, he had been weak, he should have come up with an excuse to go over to the Aktaş home and see Vediha's sisters, whose names all rhymed. In those moments when he most regretted the way he'd handled the matter, he comforted himself with some impeccable logic: if he had gone over there and seen Rayiha, she might have shown no interest in him at all, leaving Mevlut heartbroken and empty-handed. But even just thinking about Rayiha as he walked the streets with his yogurt seller's yoke across his shoulders was enough to lighten his burden.

Süleyman. My brother got me a job in Hadji Hamit Vural's building-supply business three months ago. Now I'm the one who gets to drive around in the company Ford van. The other day, at around ten in the morning, I bought a pack of cigarettes from a grocery in Mecidiyeköy run by some folk from Malatya (I don't buy cigarettes from our family shop, because my dad doesn't approve of me smoking), and I was just about to pull out when who should knock on the right-hand-side window: Mevlut! He had his stick across his back and was off to the city to sell yogurt, poor guy. "Jump in!" I said. He put his stick and his trays in the back and quickly hopped in. I gave him a cigarette and lit it with the car lighter. Mevlut had never seen me at the wheel before; he could hardly believe his eyes. Here we were, gliding along at sixty—I could see him marveling at the speedometer, too—along the same potholed street on which he'd normally be carrying thirty kilos of yogurt on his back at maybe four kilometers an hour. We talked about this and that, but he seemed to be somewhere else, and finally he asked about Abdurrahman Efendi and his daughters.

"They've gone back to the village," I said.

"What were Vediha's sisters called?"

"Why do you ask?"

"No reason . . ."

"Don't be annoyed, Mevlut, Vediha is my brother's wife now. And the girls are my brother's sisters-in-law . . . They're part of the family now . . ."

"Am I not part of the family, too?"

"Of course you are . . . That's why you're going to tell me everything."

"I will . . . but you have to swear you won't tell anyone else."

"I swear to God, and I swear on my country and on my flag that I will keep your secret."

"I'm in love with Rayiha," said Mevlut. "The one with the dark eyes, the youngest one, that one's Rayiha, isn't she? We met when I was going over to her father's table. Did you see us? We almost ran into each other. I looked right into her eyes from up close. At first I thought I'd forget. But I can't."

"What can't you forget?"

"Her eyes . . . The way she looked at me . . . Did you see how our paths crossed at the wedding?"

"Yeah."

"Do you think it was just a coincidence?"

"Sounds like you've fallen for Rayiha, my friend. We're going to have to pretend I know nothing about this."

"Isn't she beautiful, though? If I were to write her a letter, would you give it to her?"

"But they're not in Duttepe anymore. I told you they went back to the village . . ." Mevlut looked so sad that I said, "I'll do what I can for you. But what if we get caught?" He gave me such an imploring look that it melted my heart. I said, "All right, fine, let's see what we can do."

Once we got to Harbiye, he took his stick and his trays and cheerfully hopped off. Believe me, it breaks my heart to think there's still someone in our family who has to sell yogurt on the streets.

15

Mevlut Leaves Home

If You Saw Her on the Street Tomorrow, Would You Recognize Her?

Mustafa Efendi. When I heard that Mevlut had gone to Korkut's wedding in Istanbul, I couldn't believe my ears. For my own son to do this to our family! I'm on my way to Istanbul now, my head keeps bumping against the cold window every time the bus rocks, and I keep wishing I had never gone to that city in the first place, that I'd never ventured outside the village at all.

One evening at the start of October 1978, just before the weather turned cold and the boza season began, Mevlut walked into the house to find his father sitting in the dark. The lights were on in most of the other houses, so it hadn't occurred to Mevlut that there could be anyone inside. When it was clear there was, at first he put his fear down to the thought that this might be a thief. But then his racing heart reminded him that he was afraid because his father knew he had gone to the wedding. It would have been impossible for the news not to reach Mustafa Efendi, since everyone who had gone to the wedding—and indeed the whole village—was more or less related. His father was probably even angrier knowing that Mevlut was aware of this, that he had gone to the wedding knowing full well that his father would find out.

It had been two months since they'd last seen each other. Father and son hadn't spent this much time apart since Mevlut had first come to Istanbul nine years ago. But despite all his father's moods and their countless little arguments, or perhaps because of them, Mevlut felt that they had become friends—companions, even. But he'd also had enough of his father's punishing silences and furious outbursts.

"Come here!"

Mevlut approached, half expecting his father to slap him. But he didn't. Instead, he gestured to the table. Only then in the half darkness did Mevlut spot his bundles of German twenty-mark notes. How had his father found them inside the mattress?

"Who gave you these?"

"I earned it myself."

"How did you make all this money?" His father put all his savings into a bank account and stood by as an eighty percent inflation rate against the thirty-three percent interest paid by the bank ground his money into dust. And still, unable to admit that his small holdings were disappearing into thin air, he refused to learn how to invest in foreign currency.

"It's not that much," said Mevlut. "Just one thousand six hundred eighty marks. Some of it is from last year. I saved it all up by selling yogurt."

"And you hid the money from me. Are you lying to me? Have you been getting involved in anything you shouldn't be getting involved in?"

"I swear I—"

"I remember your swearing on my life that you wouldn't go to that wedding."

Mevlut bowed his head and sensed that his father was about to slap him. "I'm twenty-one now, you shouldn't hit me anymore."

"Why shouldn't I?" said his father. He slapped Mevlut.

Mevlut lifted his elbows to protect his face, so the slap hit his arm instead. His father got hurt and, losing his temper, gave Mevlut two quick punches to the shoulder, with single-minded force. "Get out of my house, you wretch!" he yelled.

Mevlut took two steps backward in shock, reeling from the pain of the second blow. He fell backward onto the bed and curled up into a ball just as he used to do as a child. He turned his back to his father, shaking a little. His father thought he was crying, and Mevlut didn't disabuse him of that thought.

Mevlut wanted to take his things and leave immediately (he played out the scene in his head and imagined that his father would regret the things he'd said and try to stop him from leaving), but he was also scared of setting out on a path from which there was no turning back. If he was going to leave this house, he shouldn't do it right now, in anger, but wait until he'd regained his composure in the morning. Now, Rayiha was the only bright spot left in his life. He needed to be alone somewhere and think about the letter he was going to write to her.

Mevlut remained motionless where he lay on the bed. If he got up, he thought, he might get into another fight with his father. If that happened and he ended up on the receiving end of more slaps and punches, it would be impossible for him not to leave the house.

From the bed, Mevlut could hear his father pacing in the single room that constituted their house, pouring himself some water and a glass of *rakı,* and lighting a cigarette. Throughout the nine years he had spent here, and especially while still in middle school, as he drifted in and out of sleep Mevlut had always found it reassuring and comforting to hear the little sounds of his father's presence, his muttering to himself, inhaling and exhaling, the persistent cough he suffered when selling boza in wintertime, even the way he snored at night. He no longer felt the same way about his father.

Mevlut fell asleep in his clothes. When he was younger, he'd always liked drifting off to sleep on the bed in his clothes whenever his father beat him and made him cry, and in later years, too, whenever he came home exhausted after a day spent working, and still had his homework to do.

When he woke up in the morning, his father wasn't home. Mevlut put his socks, shirts, shaving kit, pajamas, sweater vest, and slippers into the little suitcase he carried whenever he went back to the village. He was surprised to see that it was still half empty after he'd put in all of the things he wanted to take. He wrapped up the bundles of German marks on the table in some newspaper, putting them inside a plastic bag that said LIFE, and placed them in the suitcase. As he walked out of the house, he felt neither fear nor guilt in his heart—only freedom.

He went straight to the Ghaazi Quarter to see Ferhat. This time, unlike his first visit to the neighborhood a year ago, he had only to ask a couple of people before quickly finding Ferhat's place.

Ferhat. Mevlut never managed to finish high school, but I did, thank God. I didn't do very well in the university placement exams, though. After we moved here, I briefly looked after the parking garage of a candy factory where some of my relatives worked in the accounts department, but there was a hooligan from Ordu there who bullied me. At some point I also got involved in a political organization with some of my friends from the neighborhood. It wasn't really my thing. I felt guilty knowing that but still staying with them, out of respect and fear. It's a good thing Mevlut came along with some money. We could both tell that the Ghaazi Quarter was no good for us, just like Kültepe. We thought that if we managed to get a foothold in the city center before we had to go off on military service, maybe somewhere near Karaköy and Taksim, there would be more work for us to do and more money to earn, and instead of wasting so much time on roads and buses, we would be among the throngs on the city pavements, where there is business to be done.

Karlıova Restaurant was a small, old Greek tavern off Nevizade Street, at the Tarlabaşı end of Beyoğlu. The original owner left the city in 1964 when Prime Minister Ismet Pasha kicked the Greeks out of Istanbul overnight, and the restaurant was taken over by a waiter from Bingöl named Kadri Karlıovalı, who served stews during the day to the tailors, jewelers, and shopkeepers of Beyoğlu and *rakı* and meze by night to middle-class drinkers out to enjoy themselves or on their way to the cinema; now, after fifteen years, he was on the brink of bankruptcy. The restaurant wasn't just in trouble because the sex films had taken over the cinemas and the political terror had taken over the streets, so that the middle-class crowds were scared away from

Beyoğlu. The irascible, penny-pinching Karlıovalı had accused a very young dishwasher of stealing and threatened to fire both the boy and a middle-aged waiter who had spoken up in his defense, leading four other already disgruntled employees to pick up and leave in solidarity. The owner used to buy yogurt from Mevlut's father, and Ferhat's family knew him as well, so the two friends decided to help this weary old man to sort things out at the restaurant before they went to do their military service. They had sensed an opportunity.

They moved into an old apartment the owner had set aside to board his dishwashers and busboys (who were all still children) and for the young waiters; now, with all the staff having gone, the place was almost completely empty. The apartment was in a three-story Greek building in Tarlabaşı built eighty years ago as a single-family house. But after the events of the sixth and seventh of September 1955, when nearby Greek Orthodox churches were burned down and Jewish, Greek, and Armenian shops were looted, the social fabric of the neighborhood had begun to fray, and the building, following the same trend, was split into several apartments separated by drywall. The landlord, who held official title to the building, now lived in Athens and couldn't come to Istanbul too easily, so the rents were collected by a man from Sürmene, whom Mevlut never saw.

Two other dishwashers, aged fourteen and sixteen, both from the southeastern town of Mardin and both with primary-school diplomas, shared a bunk bed in one room of the apartment. Mevlut and Ferhat got rid of the other bunk beds, and each picked one of the other rooms, which they decorated according to their tastes with whatever they could find lying around. This was the first time in his life that Mevlut had ever lived apart from his family, or even had a room of his own. He bought a rickety old coffee table from a junk shop in Çukurcuma and took a chair from the restaurant, with the owner's permission. After the restaurant closed at around midnight, they would set up a *rakı* table with the dishwasher boys (cheese, Coca-Cola, roasted chickpeas, ice, and plenty of cigarettes) and spend a good two or three hours merrily drinking. The boys told them that the argument at the restaurant hadn't really been started by a dishwasher stealing something but by the discovery of the relationship between the owner and that dishwasher boy, over which the waiters who slept on the bunk beds in the apartment had risen up in furious protest. They asked the dishwasher boys to repeat the story several times, and pretty soon, they began to nurture a secret resentment against their elderly boss from Bingöl.

The two boys from Mardin had their hearts set on selling stuffed mussels. All the stuffed-mussel vendors in Istanbul and Turkey were from Mardin. The boys kept going on about how Mardin had cornered the stuffed-mussel business even though it was an inland city, and clearly this must mean people from Mardin were all exceptionally cunning and clever.

"Oh, come on, kid, all the sesame roll vendors are from Tokat, but I've never heard anyone say this was proof that people from Tokat are so brilliant!" Ferhat would say whenever he got fed up with the boys' exuberant devotion to Mardin. "But you can't compare stuffed mussels with sesame rolls," the boys would reply. "All bakers are from Rize, and they're always boasting about it, too," Mevlut would say, just to give another example. These two boys, who were six or seven years younger than Mevlut, had come to Istanbul straight after primary school, and they had a rowdy liveliness that captivated Mevlut no less than their dubious stories and gossip about the restaurant owner and the older waiters; Mevlut often found himself swallowing anything they told him about the streets, Istanbul, and Turkey:

The journalist Celâl Salik was so harsh in his criticisms of the government because of the conflict between America and Russia and because the owner of his newspaper *Milliyet* was a Jew . . . The fat man next to the Ağa Mosque who sold soap bubbles to kids, and was known to all of Istanbul by the way he said "flying balloon," was of course a plainclothes policeman, but his main purpose was to act as a cover for two more undercovers at the other end of the street, one disguised as a shoeshine and the other as a pan-fried liver vendor . . . Whenever customers at the Sultan's Pudding Place next to the Palace Cinema left any chicken-topped rice or chicken soup on their plates, the waiters wouldn't throw away the leftovers but rather just collect them in metal bowls, rinse them in hot water, and then serve them back to customers as fresh soup, rice toppings, or shredded-chicken blancmange . . . The

Sürmene gang, who managed the houses officially registered to Greek families who'd run away to Athens, tended to rent most of them out to brothel keepers, who had very good relations with the Beyoğlu police station anyway . . . The CIA was going to fly Ayatollah Khomeini to Tehran on a private jet to clamp down on the popular unrest that had just begun over there . . . There was going to be a military coup soon and General Tayyar Pasha would be declared president of the Republic.

"What a load of nonsense," said Ferhat one night.

"No, no, one of our people from Mardin was at the brothel at number sixty-six Sıraselviler Street when the general came in, and that's how I heard."

"Our Tayyar Pasha is a big shot now, he's the commander of the Istanbul detachment, why should he even need to go to a brothel? The pimps would be happy to bring the most perfect example of the kind of woman he wants right to his doorstep."

"Maybe the pasha is scared of his wife, because our friend from Mardin saw him with his very own eyes at number sixty-six . . . You don't believe us, you turn your nose up at people from Mardin, but if you were to go there one day, breathe its air, drink its water, and let us look after you, you would never want to leave again."

Ferhat would lose his patience sometimes and say, "If Mardin is such a wonderful place, why did you come all the way to Istanbul?" at which the dishwasher boys would laugh as if he'd made a joke.

"We're from a village near Mardin, actually. We didn't even pass through the city on our way here," one of them earnestly confessed. "No one except people from Mardin will help us out, here in Istanbul . . . so I suppose this is our way of saying thanks."

Sometimes Ferhat would start berating these sweet dishwasher boys: "You're Kurds, but still you have no class consciousness to speak of," he would scold them. "Now go to your room and sleep," he'd say, and off they would go.

Ferhat. If you've been following this story closely, you will have understood by now that it is difficult to get mad at Mevlut, but I did. His father came to the restaurant one day when he wasn't there, and when I asked what had happened, Mustafa Efendi told me that Mevlut had gone to Korkut's wedding. When I found out he'd been mingling with those Vurals, who have the blood of so many of our young men on their hands, I didn't think I could get over it. I didn't want to argue with him in front of all the waiters and the customers, so I dashed home before he arrived. When he got home and I saw the innocent look on his face, half my anger evaporated. "I hear you pinned some money on Korkut at his wedding," I said.

"Oh, I see, my father must have come by the restaurant," said Mevlut, looking up from the boza he was mixing for the evening. "Did the old man look troubled? Why do you suppose he wanted you to know that I went to that wedding?"

"He's all alone now. He wants you to come back home."

"He wants me to fight with you and end up alone and friendless in Istanbul, just like him. Should I go?"

"Don't go."

"Whenever there's politics involved, everything somehow ends up being my fault," said Mevlut. "I can't get my head around it right now. I've fallen for someone. I think about her all the time."

"Who?"

After a brief silence, Mevlut said: "I'll tell you in the evening."

But Mevlut had to work all day before he could meet up with Ferhat again at the apartment and talk over a glass of *rakı* in the evening. On a typical winter's day in 1979, Mevlut would first go to Tepebaşı to pick up the raw boza that the Vefa Boza Shop's vans had been delivering direct to the vendors' neighborhoods for the past two years; then he'd head back home to add sugar and prepare the mixture he would sell in the evening, all the while thinking about the letter he was going to write to Rayiha; and then from noon until three he would be at the Karlıova Restaurant, waiting tables. From three to six o'clock, he delivered yogurt with cream to his best customers and to three restaurants like the Karlıova before going home to nap for a bit while thinking about Rayiha and his letter, and then heading back to the Karlıova Restaurant at seven.

After a three-hour shift at the Karlıova Restaurant, having worked right up until the time when all the drunks, the hotheads, and the generally disagreeable would start picking fights, Mevlut would take off his waiter's apron and go out into the cold and dark streets to sell boza. He didn't mind the extra work at the end of the day because he knew that his boza-loving customers were expecting him.

While the demand for yogurt sellers' services was mostly declining, there was a growing interest in buying boza from nighttime street vendors. The frequent skirmishes between nationalist and Communist militants had something to do with it. Families now too scared to go outside, even on a Saturday, preferred an evening spent gazing out the window at the boza seller on the pavement, waiting for him to arrive, listening to the feeling in his voice, and drinking his boza as they remembered the good old days. Selling yogurt was tough now, but longtime street vendors from Beyşehir were still making good money thanks to boza. Mevlut had heard from the Vefa Boza Shop itself that boza sellers had begun to appear in neighborhoods like Balat, Kasımpaşa, and Gaziosmanpaşa, where they had rarely ventured before. At night, the city was left to poster-plastering armed gangs, stray dogs, foragers rummaging through trash cans, and of course to boza sellers; after a day in the ceaseless din of the restaurant and in the hubbub of Beyoğlu, walking down a dark and silent sloping street in the back of Feriköy felt to Mevlut like a homecoming, a return to a familiar universe. Sometimes the bare branches on a tree would twitch when there was no wind, and the political slogans covering every inch of a dried-up marble fountain, of which not even the tap remained intact, would seem to him at once familiar and as eerie as the hoot of an owl in the cemetery behind the little mosque. "Bozaaa," Mevlut would cry out toward the eternal past. Sometimes, when he happened to look into a little house through a pair of open curtains, he would dream about living in just such a place with Rayiha someday and picture all the happiness that lay ahead.

Ferhat. "This girl—did you say her name was Rayiha?—if she's really only fourteen as you say, then she's too young," I said.

"But we're not getting married right away," said Mevlut. "First I'm going to do my military service . . . By the time I'm back, she'll be old enough."

"Why should a girl you don't even know, and a pretty one, too, wait until you're back from the army?"

"I've thought about that, and I have two answers," said Mevlut. "First, I don't believe it was just luck that made us look into each other's eyes at the wedding. She must have wanted it, too. Why else would she pick the moment I was standing there to walk from her table to her father's? Even if it was really just a coincidence, I'm sure Rayiha must also think that the way our eyes met had a special significance."

"How did you look into each other's eyes?"

"You know how you meet someone's gaze and you know you're going to spend the rest of your life with them . . ."

"You should write that down," I said. "How did she look at you?"

"She didn't lower her eyes in shame the way girls usually do when they see a boy . . . She looked straight and proud into my eyes."

"How did you look at her? Show me."

Mevlut pretended I was Rayiha and gave me such a fervent, heartfelt look that I was moved.

"Ferhat, you'd write a better letter than I ever could. Even the European girls used to be impressed with your letters."

"Fine, but first you have to tell me what you see in this girl. What is it about her that you love?"

"Don't call Rayiha 'this girl.' I love everything about her."

"Okay, so tell me one of these things . . ."

"Her dark eyes . . . We were very close when we looked at each other."

"I'll put that in . . . What else . . . Do you know anything else about her?"

"I don't know anything else about her because we're not married yet . . . ," said Mevlut, smiling.

"If you saw her on the street tomorrow, would you recognize her?"

"Not from afar. But I would recognize her eyes immediately. Everyone knows how pretty she is anyway."

"If everyone knows how pretty this girl is, then"—I was going to say, They won't let you have her, but instead all I said was—"you're in trouble."

"I would do anything for her."

"Yet here I am writing your letter for you."

"Will you be nice and write this letter for me?"

"I'll write it. But you know one letter's not going to be enough."

"Shall I bring pen and paper?"

"Wait, let's talk first and figure out what we're going to say."

We had to cut our conversation short when the dishwasher kids from Mardin walked in.

16

How to Write a Love Letter

Your Eyes Are Like Ensorcelled Arrows

IT TOOK THEM a long time to write that first letter. They started in February 1979, when the famous *Milliyet* columnist Celâl Salik was shot dead on the street in Nişantaşı, and Ayatollah Khomeini flew into Tehran as the Shah of Iran fled his country. The dishwasher boys from Mardin had long predicted these events, and emboldened by their prescience, they joined Mevlut and Ferhat's evening confabulations on the love letter.

It was only Mevlut's inveterate optimism that allowed everyone to contribute so freely. He smiled and didn't mind too much when they teased him about his feelings. Even when they purposely made useless suggestions—"You should send her a lollipop" or "Don't say that you're a waiter, tell her you work in the catering industry" or "Write about how your uncle took your land"—he took it in stride, smiling benevolently before returning to the solemn task at hand.

Following months of endless debate, they decided that these letters should be based not on Mevlut's notions about women but rather on what he knew about Rayiha in particular. Since the only aspect of Rayiha known to Mevlut was her eyes, logic dictated that they should be the focus of the letters.

"I walk down the dark streets at night, and suddenly I see those eyes before me," said Mevlut one evening. Ferhat thought this was a very good sentence, so he included it in their draft version, changing "those eyes" to "your eyes." At first he had suggested that they shouldn't write about walking down the streets at night, as this might give away the fact that Mevlut was a boza seller, but Mevlut had ignored him. After all, Rayiha was going to find that out eventually.

After much deliberation, Ferhat wrote down the second sentence: "Your eyes are like ensorcelled arrows that pierce my heart and take me captive." "Ensorcelled" seemed too pretentious a word, but one of the boys from Mardin allowed that "people use it where we come from," which thereby validated the choice. It had taken them two weeks to agree on these two sentences. Mevlut would recite them to himself while out in the evening selling boza, wondering impatiently what the third sentence should be.

"I am your prisoner, I can think of nothing else but you ever since your eyes worked their way into my heart." Mevlut and Ferhat both agreed at once on the importance of this sentence, which would help Rayiha understand why the look they had shared had ensnared Mevlut.

On one of the evenings devoted to the third poetic sentence, Mahmut, the more confident and hopeful of the two dishwashers from Mardin, asked Mevlut: "Do you really think about this girl all day?" When Mevlut didn't immediately respond, Mahmut explained apologetically: "After all, what can you think about a girl you've only seen for a second?"

"That's the point, you dimwit!" said Ferhat, losing his temper a little in defending Mevlut. "He thinks about her eyes . . ."

"Please don't take this the wrong way, I fully support and respect my brother Mevlut's feelings. But it seems to me—and please forgive me for saying it—that you can fall more deeply in love with a girl once you truly get to know her."

"What do you mean?" said Ferhat.

"We know this guy from Mardin who works up in the Eczacıbaşı medicine factory. There's this girl his age he sees every day on the packaging line. She wears the same blue apron as all the other girls in the department. Our friend from Mardin and this girl spend eight hours a day facing each other, and the job demands they do some talking, too. Our guy starts off with these strange feelings, his body feels funny, he ends up in the infirmary. At the beginning, he doesn't even realize he's fallen in love with this girl. I guess you could say he couldn't accept it. Apparently there was nothing special about the girl, not her eyes nor any other part. But he fell madly in love with her just because he saw her and talked to her every day. Can you believe it?"

"What happened next?" asked Mevlut.

"They married the girl off to someone else. When our friend went back to Mardin, he killed himself."

For a moment, Mevlut worried he might meet with the same fate. How much had Rayiha really intended to make eye contact with him? On nights when he didn't drink any *rakı,* Mevlut had the honesty to admit that there had been an element of chance in their encounter. But in those moments when he felt most profoundly in love, he would claim that such an exalted emotion was only possible because God had willed it so. As for Ferhat, he was strongly of the opinion that Mevlut's letter should imply that some part of Rayiha had wanted them to share that brief glance. So they ended up with the following sentence: "You must have meant your ruthless deeds, or else you would not have barred my path with your meaningful looks and like a bandit stolen my heart away."

It was easy enough to refer to Rayiha in the main body of the letter, but they had some trouble figuring out how Mevlut should address her at the start. Ferhat came in one evening with a book called *Examples of Beautiful Love Letters and How to Write Them.* To make sure they took it seriously, he read a selection of possible forms of address out loud, but Mevlut always found reason to object. He couldn't address Rayiha as "Ma'am." Both "Dear Ma'am" and "Little Lady" sounded equally strange. (Still, the word "little" definitely worked.) As for things like "My beloved," "My beauty," "My heart's companion," "My angel," or "My one and only," Mevlut found them too forward. (The book was full of counsel against assuming too much familiarity in the early letters.) That night, Mevlut took the book from Ferhat and began to read it very closely. "Lingering Lady, "Demon Damsel," and "Miss Mystery" were among some of the openers he liked, but he worried they might be misinterpreted. Weeks went by, and they had almost finished all nineteen sentences of their letter before they finally agreed that "Languid Eyes" would be a decent form of address.

When he saw how the book had inspired Mevlut, Ferhat went to look for others. He went to rummage the storerooms of the old bookshops on Babıali Street, the ones that regularly sent books to the countryside on popular topics ranging from folk poetry to the life stories of famous wrestlers, Islam and sex, what to do on your wedding night, the tale of Layla and Majnun, and the Islamic interpretation of dreams, and he emerged with six more guides to writing love letters. Mevlut examined the pictures of blue-eyed women, fair haired and light skinned with red lipstick and red nail polish, and flanked by men in ties, and he found these couples who graced the covers of these paperbacks reminiscent of American movies; he would cut the folded pages open carefully with a kitchen knife, breathing in their pleasant scent, and whenever he had some time alone before going out to sell yogurt in the mornings or after coming back from selling boza at night, he would pore over the sample letters and the authors' advice to the lovelorn and smitten.

The books were organized the same way: the letters were categorized according to various occasions that lovers might face, such as the first encounter, an exchange of glances, a chance meeting, a rendezvous, moments of happiness, longing, and arguments. As he rifled through to the end of each book in search of appropriate phrases and expressions he could use, Mevlut found that all love stories progressed through the same stages. He and Rayiha had only just begun. Some of the books also included typical responses from the girls. Mevlut pictured all sorts of people—suffering from lovesickness, playing hard to get, dealing with heartbreak—and as he discovered these lives unfolding like the pages of a novel, he considered his own situation compared with theirs.

He became interested in the subject of love stories that went badly and ended in a breakup. These books taught Mevlut that "when a romance did not end in marriage," the two parties could ask each other for their love letters to be returned.

"If things end badly with Rayiha, God forbid, and she asks me to return her letters, then I will," he resolved one night after his second glass of *rakı*. "But I would never ask her to return mine; Rayiha can keep them until the day the world ends."

The Western couple on one cover looked like movie stars in the throes of a heated and highly emotional argument, with a bundle of letters bound with pink ribbon resting on a table in the foreground. Mevlut vowed to write Rayiha enough letters for such a bundle, two hundred at least. He realized that the paper he chose for his letters, the way they smelled, the envelope they came in, and of course any gifts he might send along with his missives would be key in winning her over. They talked about these things until the sun came up. They spent many sleepless nights throughout that melancholy autumn studying which perfume bought from which store would be best to spray on their letters, carrying out tests with some of the cheaper scents.

They had just about decided that the most meaningful gift that could accompany the letter was a nazar amulet, to protect against the evil eye, when an altogether different sort of letter arrived to trouble Mevlut. It came in a rough government-issue manila envelope and had passed through a number of hands before Süleyman finally brought it to Mevlut one evening, by which time many people already knew its contents. Now that he no longer had any ties with the Atatürk Secondary School, the authorities had gone looking for him in the village to register him for mandatory military service.

When the Beyoğlu police station had sent its plainclothes policeman to the restaurant to ask for Mevlut, he was busy with Ferhat in Sultanhamam and the Grand Bazaar looking for an eye bead and a handkerchief for Rayiha, and even though the restaurant workers were taken by surprise, they still had the wherewithal to say what people in Istanbul usually did in these circumstances: "Oh, him? He's gone back to the village!"

"It'll take about two months for them to send gendarmes to the village and find out you're not there either," said Kadri the Kurd. "Anyone your age who's trying to dodge the draft is either an upper-class rich kid who can't live without his creature comforts or someone who's worked out some get-rich-quick scheme at the age of twenty and can't give it up just when the dough's started rolling in. How old are you, Mevlut?"

"Twenty-two."

"Well, you're a big boy now. Go and do your military service. This restaurant's sliding. It's not like you two are making that much money here. Are you scared of the beatings? Don't be, there might be a few smacks now and then, but the army is a just place. They won't beat a sweet-faced boy too much if you do as they say."

Mevlut decided he would do his military service right away. He went down to the Beyoğlu draft office in Dolmabahçe and was showing his letter to the officer there when another officer whose rank he wasn't sure of told him off for standing at attention in the wrong spot. This scared Mevlut, but he didn't panic. Back out on the street, he sensed that life would go back to normal as soon as he finished his military service.

His father, he thought, would welcome his decision to get it done without further delay. He went to Kültepe to see him. They kissed and made up. Emptied as it had been, home seemed even more desolate and miserable than he remembered. Still, in that moment, Mevlut became aware of just how attached he was to this room where he'd spent ten years of his life. He opened the kitchen cupboard; the heavy old pot on the shelf, the rusty candlestick, and the blunt cutlery pulled on his heartstrings. In the wet night, the dried-up caulk in the window frame looking out to Duttepe smelled like an ancient memory. But he was wary of spending the night here with his father.

"Do you still go over to your uncle's place?" his father said.

"No, I never see them," said Mevlut, aware that his father knew this wasn't true. There was a time when he would never have been able to blurt out such an obvious lie about such a delicate matter but instead would have devised an answer that wouldn't hurt his father's feelings too much while also being technically true. At the door, he did as he would normally do only on religious holidays: he respectfully kissed his father's hand.

"The army might make a man out of you yet!" said Mustafa Efendi as he was seeing off his son.

Why such a derisive, dispiriting remark right at the very end of their meeting? The combined effect of his father's words and the smoke from lignite coal fires made Mevlut's eyes water as he made his way down to the Kültepe bus stop.

Three weeks later, he went to the draft office in Beşiktaş and found out that he was to undergo his basic training in Burdur. He forgot for a moment where Burdur was and panicked.

"Don't worry, there are four buses from Istanbul to Burdur every evening from the Harem bus terminal on the Asian side," said the quieter of the two boys from Mardin that night, and he began to list all the companies that provided this service. "Gazanfer Bilge is the best of the lot," he said, continuing, "Isn't it nice? You're off to join the army, but you've got your lover in your heart and her eyes on your mind. Military service is a breeze when you've got a girl to write letters to . . . How do I know? There's this friend of ours from Mardin . . ."

17

Mevlut's Army Days

Do You Think You're at Home?

IN ALMOST TWO YEARS of military service, Mevlut learned so much about how to go undetected in provincial towns, among other men, and within large groups that he ended up believing the old saying that only the army could make "men" out of boys and started spouting his own version: "You're not a real man until you've done your military service." The military taught him the physicality and fragility of his own body and manhood.

Before he became a man, Mevlut never used to distinguish his body from his mind and soul, thinking of all three together as "me." But in the army he would discover that he was not necessarily the sole master of his own body and that, in fact, it might be worth surrendering it to his commanders if to do so at least allowed him to save his soul and keep his thoughts and dreams to himself. During the infamous first physical that created exemptions for hapless fellows who didn't even know that their health was poor (tubercular street vendors, nearsighted laborers, and half-deaf quilters) and for rich guys shrewd enough to bribe the doctors, one elderly physician, noticing Mevlut's embarrassment, told him gently, "Go on, son, take your clothes off. This is the military, we're all men here."

Trusting the kind doctor, Mevlut did so, thinking he'd be examined straightaway, but instead they put him in a queue with a whole host of down-and-outs, standing in their underwear, carrying their things, since no one was allowed to leave anything anywhere lest it be stolen. Like worshippers entering a mosque, the men in the queue had also taken off their shoes, and they were holding them, sole to sole, with their shirts and trousers neatly folded on top and, on top of the clothes, the medical forms the doctors were supposed to stamp and sign.

After two hours of standing in the cold corridor in a queue that wouldn't budge, Mevlut found out that the doctor hadn't arrived yet. It wasn't even clear what sort of checkup this was going to be; some said it was an eye test, so that anyone able to feign shortsightedness convincingly could hope to weasel out of serving; others announced menacingly that when the doctor arrived, he wouldn't be checking their eyes but their asses so that all the queers would be weeded out. Terrorized at the prospect of anyone running his eye or, worse still, his finger over that most intimate place and, by some mistake, being singled out as a queer (this second worry would recur throughout his army days), Mevlut forgot his own nudity and started to talk to the other undressed men in the queue. Most, he discovered, had likewise come originally from a village and were now living in poorer city neighborhoods, and every single one, down to the dumbest wretch of them all, proudly declared that he had someone "pulling strings" for him. He thought of Hadji Hamit Vural, who had no idea Mevlut had even been conscripted, and soon he, too, was boasting of some pretty solid backing that would allow him to coast through military service.

This was how from the start he learned that, by frequent mention of friends in high places, he could protect himself from the cruelty and spite of other recruits. He was just telling one guy, who also happened to have a mustache (Good thing I let mine grow, Mevlut kept thinking), that Hadji Hamit Vural knew absolutely everyone, and what a fair and generous philanthropist he was, when a commander yelled at them all to "Be quiet!" They trembled into submission. "This isn't the beauty parlor, ladies. No more tittering. Have some dignity. This is the army. Giggling is for girls."

As he drifted in and out of sleep on the bus to Burdur, Mevlut kept thinking back to that moment in the hospital. Some of the men had used their shoes and clothes to cover their nakedness as the commander walked past, while others who had seemed to cower before him couldn't contain their laughter as soon as he was gone. Mevlut felt he could get along with both types, but if this was what the whole army was like, he feared he might end up left out and lonely.

But until boot camp was over and he had sworn his oath of enlistment, he didn't even have a spare moment to worry about loneliness and belonging. His unit would go on long runs every day, singing folk songs as they went. They had to tackle obstacle courses, perform gymnastics like those Blind Kerim used to teach in high school, and learn how to salute properly by practicing hundreds of times a day on other soldiers, real or imagined.

Before reporting for military service, Mevlut had long imagined the beatings doled out by officers, but after just three days on the army base, they'd become a routine, unremarkable sight. Some fool got slapped for wearing his cap the wrong way even after the sergeant had warned them about it many times; another idiot failed to keep his fingers straight when he saluted, and down came a smack on him; someone else fidgeted for the thousandth time during a drill, got an earful of humiliating insults from the commander, and was told to drop to the floor and do a hundred push-ups while the rest of the squad laughed at him.

They were having tea one afternoon when Emre Şaşmaz from Antalya said, "Man, I can't believe how many stupid, ignorant people there are in this country." He had a shop that sold car parts, and Mevlut respected him because he seemed like a serious guy. "I still don't understand how they can be so dumb. Even a beating doesn't straighten them out."

"I think the real question is whether they get beaten up all the time because they're so dumb, or if they're so dumb because they get beaten up all the time," pronounced Ahmet, who had a haberdashery in Ankara. Mevlut, who'd ended up by chance in the same squad as these two distinguished characters, figured you at least had to own a shop before you could make sweeping statements about stupid people. The unhinged captain of the fourth company had it in for a private from Diyarbakır (in the army, you weren't allowed to use the words "Kurd" or "Alevi") and treated him so viciously that the poor fellow hanged himself with his own belt while in solitary confinement. Mevlut resented the two shopkeepers for their relative indifference to this suicide and for calling the private an idiot for having taken the commander so seriously. Like most privates, Mevlut also thought about suicide every now and then, but he, again like most, was able to laugh it off. One day shortly thereafter, the two shopkeepers, Emre and Ahmet, were walking out of the canteen in high spirits when they had the misfortune of catching the lieutenant colonel in a bad mood. Mevlut watched from afar with quiet satisfaction as the colonel gave them two slaps each on their clean-shaven cheeks for holding their caps wrong.

"As soon as I've finished my military service, I'm going to find that asshole colonel and stuff him back down the hole he crawled out of," said Ahmet from Ankara as they drank their tea that evening.

"I don't really care, man, there's no logic in the army anyway," said Emre from Antalya.

Mevlut respected Emre for being flexible and confident enough to put the slap out of his mind, though the view that there is no logic in the army was not his own but a favorite slogan among the commanders. If anyone dared to question the logic of an order, they'd shout: "I can withdraw your pass for two weekends in a row just because I feel like it or make you crawl through the mud and wish you'd never been born." They would always make good on their promises.

A few days later, on receiving his first slap, Mevlut realized that a beating wasn't as bad as he had thought. His squad had been sent out to clean up some trash, for lack of anything better to do, and they had picked up all the matchsticks, cigarette butts, and dried leaves they could find. They had just scattered for a cigarette break when an enormous commander (Mevlut still hadn't learned how to tell rank by the insignia on the collars) appeared out of nowhere, yelling "What the hell is this?" He got the squad to line up and then gave each of the ten privates a smack with his huge hand. It certainly stung, but Mevlut was relieved to suffer the thing he had so feared—his first beating—without too much damage. The tall Nazmi from Nazilli had been the first in line, so he'd really felt the force of the blow, and afterward he looked like he could have killed someone. Mevlut tried to be comforting. "Don't worry about it, my friend," he said. "Look at me, I don't mind, it's over already."

"You don't mind because he didn't hit you as hard," said Nazmi in anger. "Your face is as pretty as a girl's, that's why."

Mevlut thought he might be right.

Someone else said, "The army doesn't care if you're pretty or plain, handsome or ugly. They'll beat you all the same."

"Don't kid yourselves, guys. If you're from Eastern Anatolia, if you've got dark skin and that darkness in your eyes, you will get beaten up more."

Mevlut didn't join this debate. He had managed to preserve his pride by reasoning that the slap hadn't been brought on by any mistake of his.

Two days later, he was walking around with his shirt unbuttoned, lost in thought (how long had it been since Süleyman had delivered the letter? he wondered), when a lieutenant spotted him in this "undisciplined" state. He gave Mevlut two quick slaps with the palm of his hand, and then the back, calling him an idiot, too. "Do you think you're at home or something? What's your unit?" He went on his way without even waiting for Mevlut's answer.

Mevlut would receive plenty more slaps and blows in his twenty months of military service, but this would always be the one that hurt the most—because the lieutenant was right. Yes, he had indeed been busy thinking about Rayiha, and in that moment he hadn't given a thought to the tilt of his cap, his salute, or the way he walked.

That night, Mevlut got into bed before everyone else, pulling the covers over his head and musing bleakly about his life. He would have liked to be at the house in Tarlabaşı with Ferhat and the kids from Mardin right now, but ultimately that wasn't really home. It was as if the lieutenant had meant exactly this when he'd said, "Do you think you're at home?" The only place he could think of as home was the house in Kültepe, where he imagined his father would have fallen asleep in front of the television just then, but that place wasn't even registered in their name yet.

In the mornings, he would open at random to a page from the letter-writing handbooks he kept hidden under the sweaters at the bottom of his cupboard and hide behind the closet skimming through them so he might have something to keep his mind busy for the rest of the day, during pointless drills and interminable hikes where he would use what he had learned to mentally compose future letters to Rayiha. He would memorize the words, like those political prisoners who sit in cells with no pen or paper and write poetry in their heads, and whenever he had a weekend pass, he would write it all down and post the results off to Duttepe. Happiness was sitting down at a forgotten desk in the intercity bus terminal writing letters to Rayiha, instead of going to the coffeehouses and the cinemas frequented by the other privates, and sometimes Mevlut felt like a poet.

At the end of the four-month boot camp, he had learned how to use a G3 infantry rifle, how to report to an officer (slightly better than everyone else), how to salute, how to stand at attention, how to obey orders (just as well as everyone else), how to scrape by, and how to lie and be two-faced (not as well as everyone else) when circumstances called for it.

There were some things he had trouble with, but he couldn't decide whether to blame his own incompetence or his moral reservations. "Now listen here, I'm off, but I'll be back in half an hour, and you will keep going during that time," the commander would say. "Understood?"

"Yes, sir, understood!" the whole unit would shout.

But as soon as the commander disappeared around the corner of the yellow headquarters building, half the unit would stretch out on the floor and start smoking and prattling away. Of those still standing, half would now continue the drill, but only until they were sure the commander wasn't suddenly coming back, while the other half (Mevlut among them) would only pretend to continue. There were a very few who kept faith with the drill and were pushed around and ridiculed by all the others, until they were forced to stop, so in the end no one actually carried on as ordered. Was all this really necessary?

In the third month of military service, Mevlut worked up the courage to put this philosophical and ethical question to the two shopkeepers over tea one evening.

"Mevlut, you really are an innocent, aren't you?" said the one from Antalya.

"Either that or you're pretending to be and tricking us all," said the one from Ankara.

If I had a shop like they do, even a small one, I would have definitely finished high school and gone to college, and then I'd be doing my military service as an officer, thought Mevlut. He no longer had any respect for these shopkeepers, but he knew that if he broke with them now, he'd still be playing the "sweet-faced dumb kid who fetches the tea" for any new friends he might make. He would still be using his cap to pick up the kettle with the broken handle, as everyone else did.

In the lottery that decided where he would end up next, he drew the tank brigade stationed in Kars. Some guys were lucky enough to draw cities in the western part of the country, and even bases in Istanbul. These lots were rumored to be rigged. But Mevlut felt neither envy nor resentment, nor did he worry about having to spend sixteen months on the Russian border, in Turkey's coldest and poorest city.

He got to Kars in a day, changing buses in Ankara, without even paying a visit to Istanbul first. In July 1980, Kars was an impoverished city of fifty thousand. As he made his way, suitcase in hand, from the bus station to the army barracks in the center of town, he noticed that the streets were covered in left-wing slogans, and he recognized some of the tags from those he had seen on the walls in Kültepe.

Mevlut found the army base calm and peaceful. The soldiers stationed in the city, with the exception of those attached to the secret services, did not get involved in the political fighting. Sometimes the gendarmes searched for leftist militants hiding out in farmers' villages and on dairy farms that specialized in cheese, but those gendarmes were based elsewhere.

During musters one morning, less than a month after he'd arrived in the city, he told the commander that he worked as a waiter in civilian life. After that, he started working in the officers' mess. This meant he no longer had to stand on guard duty in the cold or deal with senseless and arbitrary orders from the more irksome commanders. He now had plenty of time to sit at the little desk in the barracks or at one of the tables in the mess and write to Rayiha when no one was looking, filling up page after page while the radio played Anatolian folk songs and the singer Emel Sayın's interpretation of the classic Nihavend-style song "That First Look That Fills the Heart Can Never Be Forgotten," composed by Erol Sayan. Most of the privates who were assigned to work in headquarters or in the barracks, trying to look busy while they worked as "clerks," "painters," or "repairmen," carried small transistor radios in hidden pockets. Mevlut wrote many love letters that year under the influence of his evolving musical tastes, drawing a range of expressions from Anatolian folk songs to describe Rayiha's "coy glances," "languid looks," "doelike, ink-black, dreaming, teasing, piercing eyes," and "enchanting gaze."

The more he wrote, the more he felt as if he'd known Rayiha since way back when they were both children, that they had a shared spiritual history. He was creating an intimacy between them with every word and every sentence he wrote down, and he sensed that all the things he was imagining now would one day come true.

Toward the end of summer, he was arguing with a cook in the kitchens about an eggplant stew that had been served too cold and angered the major, when someone took his arm and pulled him to one side. For one alarming moment, Mevlut thought it was a giant.

"Oh my God! Mohini!"

They hugged and kissed each other's cheeks.

"They say people lose weight in the military, they end up skin and bones, but you've become fat."

"I'm a waiter at the officers' club," said Mevlut. "The scraps are pretty good."

"I'm at the club's hairdresser."

Mohini had come to Kars two weeks before. After he had failed high school, his father had sent him to be a hairdresser's apprentice, and so it was decided that this was what he would do for a living. Dyeing the hair of the officers' wives blond was easy, as far as army assignments went. Yet Mohini was full of complaints, as Mevlut learned when they spent their off-duty day together at the teahouse across from the Asia Hotel, watching football.

Mohini. Actually, my job at the hairdresser's wasn't too difficult. My only worry was how to pay each woman attention exactly according to her husband's rank; I had to make sure that I saved the best hairstyle for the base commander Turgut Pasha's tubby little wife, paying her all the best compliments; the bony wife of Turgut Pasha's second-in-command got a tiny bit less; and finally there were the lieutenant colonels' wives, though even there I had to make sure to respect the order of seniority, and the whole thing was bringing me to a state of nervous collapse. One day, I told Mevlut, a young officer's pretty wife had come in, and I let slip a compliment on her dark hair, and you should have seen how they all sneered, not least Turgut Pasha's wife, and the horrible way they treated me.

The lieutenant colonel's prudent wife would say, "What color did you dye Turgut Pasha's wife's hair? Make sure mine isn't lighter than hers." I heard everything—who was free for a game of rummy, whose turn it was to host the others, where they would gather to watch their soap operas, and what kind of cookies were being bought from which bakery. Sometimes I sang songs and performed magic tricks at their children's birthday parties, I did the shopping for those ladies who didn't like to step outside the grounds of the base, and I helped a commander's daughter with her math homework.

"What the hell do you know about math, Mohini!" said Mevlut, interrupting rather rudely. "Or are you fucking the pasha's daughter?"

"Shame on you, Mevlut . . . I see the army's fouled both your mouth and your soul. All those privates who find some cushy job at an officer's house near headquarters, or end up working as servants and footmen in a colonel's home, getting yelled at every day, they all like to say 'I'm screwing the colonel's daughter' as soon as they get back to their barracks at night, just to save what little is left of their dignity. Don't tell me you believe those stories? Besides, Turgut Pasha doesn't deserve such treatment. He is an honest military man, and he's always shielding me from his wife's malice and her moods. Are we clear?"

Since joining the military, these were the most sincere words Mevlut had heard a private utter, and he felt ashamed. "The colonel is a good man, after all," he said. "I'm sorry. Come here and let me give you a hug so you won't be mad."

The moment he'd said these words, he saw the truth he'd been hiding even from himself: since Mevlut had last seen him in high school,

Mohini had become more effeminate, revealing the existence of a secret homosexual he harbored inside of him. Was he even aware of it? Should Mevlut pretend he hadn't noticed? They stood still for a moment, staring at each other wordlessly.

Turgut Pasha found out soon enough that the private who did his wife's hair and the private who worked in the restaurant had been schoolmates. So Mevlut started going over to the pasha's house for special assignments. He might be asked to paint the kitchen cupboards or to play horses and coachmen with the children (Kars still had horse-drawn carriages as taxis). The pasha had informed the captain of his company and the manager of the officers' club that Mevlut would occasionally be needed at the pasha's house to help organize parties, and this had the immediate effect of promoting him to "pasha's favorite," which everyone knew was the highest rank a private could reach. Mevlut took pleasure in watching word of his new standing spread among his unit first, and then to the rest of the garrison. Those who used to greet him with "What's up, baby face," who would ambush him with a goosing and treat him like a queer, were the first to back off. The lieutenants began to treat Mevlut with a certain regard, too, like some rich kid who'd ended up in Kars by mistake. Others asked him if he could please try to find out from the pasha's wife the secret date of the upcoming exercises on the Russian border. No one ever even flicked his ear again.

18

The Military Coup

The Cemetery of the Industrial Quarter

THE MILITARY OPERATION whose secret date everyone wanted to know did not take place after all, because another military coup occurred on the night of 12 September. Mevlut realized that there was something extraordinary going on when he saw that the streets outside the base were deserted. The army had declared martial law and curfews throughout the country. He spent the day watching General Evren Pasha's proclamations on TV. The total emptiness of the streets of Kars, which had so recently been full of villagers, shopkeepers, unemployed men, frightened citizens, and undercover policemen, seemed to Mevlut like a projection of his own strange mind. In the evening, Turgut Pasha gathered all base personnel together and explained that blinkered, selfish politicians who only cared about clinging to their seats had brought the country to the brink of collapse, but those bad days were over now, the Turkish army, the sole and true guardians of the nation, would not allow the country to go to the dogs, and they would punish all the terrorists and the seditious politicians. He talked at length about the flag, how it took its color from the blood of martyrs, and about Atatürk.

A week later, when it was announced on TV that Turgut Pasha would become mayor of Kars, Mevlut and Mohini started coming and going between the base and city hall, ten minutes away. The pasha spent his mornings at the base, planning operations against the Communists in light of the intelligence from his informants and the secret services, and after lunch he took his jeep to the city hall, then situated in an old Russian building. Sometimes he walked, flanked by his bodyguards, listening happily to grateful shopkeepers who told him what a good thing the coup had been, and letting people kiss his hand if they wanted to, and any letters that he received, he read himself as soon as he got back to headquarters. It was one of the pasha's responsibilities, as mayor, base commander, and the man in charge of enforcing martial law in the district, to investigate any illegalities and allegations of corruption reported to him by post and to refer any suspects to the army prosecutor. Like the pasha, the prosecutor acted on the logic "They'll be acquitted if they're innocent!" and he was therefore quick to lock people up to intimidate them.

The military treated wealthy offenders relatively gently. Those who had committed political crimes, though, and Communists who were often labeled "terrorists" had the soles of their feet whipped. When the wind was blowing in the right direction, the cries of youths picked up during raids on impoverished neighborhoods and tortured for information could be heard all the way to the base, and Mevlut would cast his eyes down in guilt as he made his way toward the officers' club.

During musters one morning early in the new year, the new lieutenant called out Mevlut's name. Mevlut stood up and shouted, "Mevlut Karataş, Konya, at your orders." He saluted and stood to attention.

"Come over here, Konya," said the lieutenant.

This guy must not have heard I've got the pasha's backing, thought Mevlut. He had never been to the city of Konya in his life, but that was the district to which Beyşehir belonged, so, as was the custom, everyone here called him Konya, which was rather irritating, though he didn't show it on this occasion.

"My condolences, Konya, your father's passed away in Istanbul," said the new lieutenant. "Go back to your unit and get the captain to give you some leave."

Mevlut got a week off. At the terminal, he had a glass of *rakı* while he waited for the bus to Istanbul. As the bus shuddered and swayed from side to side, an inexplicable heaviness dragged his eyelids shut, and in his dreams his father told him off for being late to the funeral, and numerous other failings.

His father had died in his sleep. The neighbors had discovered him after two days. The empty bed was in a mess, as if his father had left the house in a hurry. To Mevlut's soldierly eyes, the place looked unkempt and pitiful. But he also found that unique scent he had never smelled anywhere else: the smell of his father, of Mevlut's own body, of breath, dust, the stove, twenty years' worth of soup dinners, dirty laundry, old furniture—the smell of their very lives. Mevlut had imagined he would remain in the room for hours, weeping and mourning his father, but the sorrow was so overwhelming that he threw himself out the door.

Mustafa Efendi's funeral took place at Hadji Hamit Vural's mosque in Duttepe two hours after Mevlut got to Kültepe, during the afternoon prayers. Mevlut had brought his civilian clothes, but he wasn't wearing them yet. Those who tried to comfort him with sympathetic looks smiled to see him dressed like a private on a day pass.

Mevlut carried the coffin on his shoulder to the grave site. He threw spades of earth over his father's body. He thought he was about to cry, his foot slipped and he almost fell into the grave. There were around forty people at the funeral. Süleyman hugged him, and they sat down on another grave. From the tombstones around him, Mevlut could tell that the Cemetery of the Industrial Quarter was a burial ground for migrants. It was growing fast, as it was where those who had settled the surrounding hills were buried when they died; and as Mevlut read the inscriptions around him distractedly, he realized that not a single person there had been born in Istanbul. Nearly all of them were originally from Sivas, Erzincan, Erzurum, and Gümüşhane.

There was an engraver at the gates with whom he agreed on a midsize headstone without even haggling. Borrowing from the inscriptions he had just been reading, he wrote something down on a piece of paper and gave it to the engraver: MUSTAFA KARATAŞ (1927–81). CENNETPINAR, BEYŞEHIR. YOGURT AND BOZA SELLER. MAY HE REST IN PEACE.

He could tell that his army uniform made him look both sweet and somewhat distinguished. Back in the neighborhood, they headed out to Duttepe's shopping district and went into shops and coffeehouses.

Mevlut realized how attached he was to Kültepe, Duttepe, and all these people who were embracing him. But to his surprise, he also seemed to harbor against them a rage close to hatred—even against his uncle and cousins. He had to struggle to hold back a torrent of obscenities he felt like spewing on them all, just like the kind you might hear in the army.

At dinnertime, his aunt remarked to everyone at the table how good Mevlut looked in his uniform. How unfortunate that his mother hadn't been able to make the trip from the village and see her son like this. In the few minutes he was left alone with Süleyman in the kitchen, Mevlut still didn't ask after Rayiha, even though he was dying to know. He ate his chicken and potatoes in silence, watching TV with everyone else.

He thought about writing Rayiha a letter that night on the shaky table at home. But as soon as he was back in Kültepe and inside the house, this place seemed to him so desolate that he lay down on the bed and started crying. He wept for a very long time, unsure of whether it was on account of his father or of his own loneliness. He fell asleep in his uniform.

In the morning, he took it off and wore the civilian clothes he'd put in his suitcase almost a year ago. He went to the Karlıova Restaurant in Beyoğlu. They weren't particularly welcoming. Ferhat had left for his military service after Mevlut, and most of the waiters were new; any old ones still there were preoccupied with customers. So Mevlut ended up leaving without getting the chance to savor the "Return to Karlıova" fantasy that had so often helped him pass the time on guard duty.

He went to the Elyazar Cinema ten minutes away. When he walked in this time, he felt no shame at the sight of the other men in the lobby. He walked through this crowd of men with his head held high and looking straight at them.

Once he sat down, he was pleased to have broken free of everyone's gaze, happy to be left alone in the dark with the wanton women on the screen to become nothing more than another pair of leering eyes. He noticed immediately that the way the men in the military swore and the barrenness of their souls had changed the way he himself saw the women on-screen. He felt more vulgar but also more normal now. Whenever anyone made a loud, obscene joke about the movie, or answered an actor's line with some innuendo, he laughed along with everyone else. When the lights came on between movies, Mevlut looked around and figured out that any men with really short hair must be soldiers in their day clothes, on leave as he was. He watched all three features from start to finish. He left at the sex and grape-eating scene, which he remembered from when he had first walked in halfway through the same German movie. He went home and masturbated until nightfall.

That night, worn out by guilt and loneliness, he went over to his uncle's house in Duttepe.

"Don't worry, everything's fine," said Süleyman when they were alone. "Rayiha loves your letters. Where did you learn to write such good letters? Will you help me write one, too, someday?"

"Is Rayiha going to reply to me?"

"She'd like to, but she won't . . . Her father wouldn't tolerate it. I got to see for myself how much they love their father the last time they were here, before the coup. They stayed in that new room we've just added."

Süleyman opened the door to the room where Crooked-Necked Abdurrahman and his two daughters had stayed for a week when they'd last come from the village, switched on the lights, and gave Mevlut the tour, like a museum guide. Mevlut saw there were two beds in the room.

Süleyman understood what Mevlut was wondering about. "Their father slept in this bed, and the girls slept together in the other bed the first night, but they didn't really fit. So we made Rayiha a bed on the floor."

Mevlut shot a timid glance at the spot where Rayiha's bed had been laid out. The floor in Süleyman's house was tiled and carpeted.

He was pleased to find out that Vediha knew about the letters. She didn't act too familiar or let on that she knew everything and had even helped deliver his letters, but she smiled at Mevlut sweetly every time she saw him. Mevlut interpreted this as a sign that she was on his side, and he was delighted.

Vediha Yenge really was amazingly beautiful. Mevlut played a little with her son Bozkurt (named after the legendary Grey Wolf that saved the Turks), who'd been born when Mevlut was working at the Karlıova

Restaurant, and with her younger son, Turan, who arrived when Mevlut was in the military. Vediha had become even more radiant after the birth of her second child, more mature and attractive. Mevlut was moved by the tenderness she showed toward her two sons and was pleased when he sensed that she had a soft spot for him, too, or at least a sort of sisterly affection. He kept thinking how Rayiha was just as beautiful as Vediha, if not more so.

He spent most of his time in Istanbul writing new letters to Rayiha. Having been away for a year, he already felt estranged from the city. Istanbul had changed after the military coup. The political slogans had been wiped off the walls again, street vendors had been driven off the main roads and squares, the brothels in Beyoğlu had been shut down, and the delinquents who sold bootleg whiskey and American cigarettes on the streets had been rounded up. Even the traffic was better. You couldn't stop wherever you wanted anymore. Mevlut thought some of the changes were good, but in a strange way, he felt like an outsider. Maybe it's because I don't have a job, he thought.

"I'm going to ask you something, but please don't take it the wrong way," he told Süleyman the next evening. His father was gone now, so he could easily go over to his uncle's every night.

"I never misunderstand you, Mevlut," said Süleyman. "You're the one who's always misunderstood my understanding."

"Can you get me her photograph?"

"Rayiha's? No."

"Why?"

"She's the sister of my brother's wife."

"If I had her photograph, I'd write her better letters."

"Believe me, Mevlut, they couldn't get any better."

Süleyman helped him rent out the house in Kültepe to an acquaintance of the Vurals. He decided he could do without a contract when Süleyman said, "There's no need, we know the guy, and you don't want to pay taxes." In any case, he wasn't the only one who was entitled to a share of revenue from the house (which was still not registered in anyone's name); his mother and sisters in the village also had a claim. He decided he didn't want to get too involved in these matters.

He was putting his father's clothes and shirts into a suitcase before renting the place out, when he caught a trace of his father's smell and went to curl up on the bed. This time he didn't cry. He felt angry and resentful toward the world. He also understood that when his military service was over, he was not coming back to Kültepe or this house. Yet when it came time to return to Kars, something jarred deep inside of him and rebelled at the thought. He did not want to wear his uniform, nor did he want to complete the remainder of his military service. He hated his commanders and all those army thugs. Alarmingly, he could now see why some people deserted. He put on his uniform and set off.

In his last few months in Kars, Mevlut wrote Rayiha forty-seven letters. He had plenty of time: he had been assigned to the detachment the base commander had taken with him to the town hall, where he managed the canteen and the small tearoom, acting as Turgut Pasha's personal waiter when the pasha was there. But the pasha was too suspicious and picky to eat in the town hall, so it wasn't a very difficult job: Mevlut brewed the pasha's tea himself, prepared his coffee with one sugar and double foam, and personally served him water and soft drinks. The pasha bought a cookie from the bakery once, and another time he took a pastry from the canteen, and put both items in front of Mevlut, telling him what to look out for.

"Go on, have a taste . . . we don't want city hall poisoning us."

He wanted to write to Rayiha about his army days, but in the end he knew his letters would be read before they went out, so he confined himself to the usual poetic flights, invoking yet more piercing eyes and ensorcelled looks. Mevlut would keep composing letters until the last day of his military service, which never seemed to come, and when it finally did arrive, never seemed to pass.

19

Mevlut and Rayiha

Elopement Is a Tricky Business

MEVLUT FINISHED his military service on 17 March 1982 and took the first bus back to Istanbul. He rented a second-floor apartment with linoleum floors in an old Greek house in Tarlabaşı, two streets down from the Karlıova Restaurant's dormitory, and he began working as a waiter in a nondescript restaurant. From a flea market in Çukurcuma he bought a table (one that didn't wobble) and four chairs (two of which matched), and from junk dealers who sold their wares door to door he selected a worn old bed with an enormous wooden headboard carved with birds and leaves. He furnished this room dreaming all the while about the happy home he would one day share with Rayiha.

At his uncle's house one evening at the start of April, Mevlut saw Abdurrahman Efendi. He was nestled at one end of the table with a bib around his neck, sipping his *rakı* and enjoying his grandsons, Bozkurt and Turan. Mevlut realized he must have come from the village on his own, without his daughters. Uncle Hasan wasn't home; for the last few years, he had been leaving the house every night for evening prayers before going to his grocery store to watch TV and wait for customers. Mevlut greeted his future father-in-law respectfully. Abdurrahman returned the greeting but hadn't really registered Mevlut's presence.

Korkut and Abdurrahman Efendi were soon engaged in a vehement discussion of bankers. Mevlut heard them mention a number of names—the Pilgrim Banker, Banker Ali. With inflation at one hundred percent, your money would soon be worth less than the paper it was printed on—unless you took it out of the banks, which paid so little in the way of interest, and gave it over to these new bankers, most of whom seemed like they'd only just landed in the city and wouldn't have looked out of place manning a village shop. They all promised very high annual interest rates, but could they really be trusted?

Finishing his third drink, Abdurrahman Efendi was boasting of how each of his daughters was a beauty and how he had made sure they all got a proper education back in the village. "Enough, Dad," said Vediha as she went to put her sons to bed; Abdurrahman Efendi went with them.

"Go wait for me at the coffeehouse," said Süleyman once they'd been left alone at the table.

Mevlut's heart hammered in his chest.

"What's all this about?" said Aunt Safiye. "Do whatever you want, but don't get involved in politics. We should really be getting you two married off."

From the TV at the coffeehouse Mevlut learned that Argentina and England were at war. Süleyman came in to find him admiring the English aircraft carriers and warships.

"Abdurrahman Efendi has come to Istanbul to take his money from one banker and give it to another who's even worse . . . We can't figure out whether any of it is true, or even if he's really got any money. He's also been talking about some 'good news,'" said Süleyman.

"What good news?"

"Rayiha's got a suitor," said Süleyman. "One of these redneck bankers. Apparently he used to have a tea stall. It's serious. That greedy Crooked Neck might well just hand his daughter over to the banker. He won't listen to anyone. You need to run away with Rayiha, Mevlut."

"Really? Oh, Süleyman, please help me run away with her."

"Do you think running away with a girl is easy?" said Süleyman. "One little mistake, and before you know it, someone gets shot, there's a blood feud, and then people kill one another over it for years for no good reason, and proudly say it's all about honor. Are you willing to take the risk?"

"I have no choice," said Mevlut.

"You don't," said Süleyman. "But you don't want anyone to think you're just cheap, either. What can you offer this girl when there are so many rich men ready to spend a fortune on her?"

They met again in the same place five days later, and while Süleyman watched the English taking over the Falklands, Mevlut produced a piece of paper from his pocket.

"Go on, take a look," he crowed. "You can have it."

"What's this?" said Süleyman. "Oh, it's the papers for your house. Let's have a look. It's got my father's name on it, too. They had claimed the land together. Why did you bring it? Don't be so eager to give this away just to show off. You're going to need it if you want your share when they hand out title deeds for that side of Kültepe one day."

"Give it to Crooked-Necked Abdurrahman . . . ," said Mevlut. "Tell her father no one can love his daughter like I do."

"I will, but put that back in your pocket," said Süleyman.

"It's not just talk, I mean it," said Mevlut.

The first thing Mevlut did the next morning when he woke up from his *rakı* hangover was to check inside his jacket pocket. He couldn't decide whether to be glad or disappointed that he still had the piece of paper his father and his uncle Hasan had obtained from the local councilman fifteen years ago.

"You should be grateful that you have Vediha Yenge and the rest of us," said Süleyman ten days later. "She's gone all the way to the village for you. Now let's see if you'll get your way. Bring me another *rakı,* will you?"

Vediha took her two sons—three-year-old Bozkurt and two-year-old Turan—along with her to the village. Mevlut thought they would be back almost immediately, as the kids would quickly tire of a muddy village dwelling where the lights went out all the time and the water never ran, but he was wrong. Restless, he would go over to Duttepe twice a week, thinking Vediha Yenge must surely be back by now, but he would find no one but Aunt Safiye sitting alone in the gloomy house.

"Who would have thought it was that daughter-in-law of mine who was breathing life into this house," said Aunt Safiye to Mevlut who was visiting late one night. "Ever since Vediha's been gone, there's been a few nights when Korkut hasn't come home. Süleyman is out, too. I made lentil soup, shall I warm some up for you? We can watch television. Did you hear, Kastelli ran away, and all the bankers have gone bust. You haven't given these bankers any of your money, have you?"

"I don't have any money, Aunt Safiye."

"Don't worry . . . Don't spend your life stressing about money, you're bound to get your big break someday. Money doesn't make happiness. Look at how much Korkut earns, and still he and Vediha are at each other's throats every day . . . I feel sorry for Bozkurt and Turan, they've known nothing but arguments and fights all their life. Never mind . . . Hopefully this thing of yours will work out, God willing."

"What thing?" said Mevlut, his heart speeding up as he turned away from the television, but Aunt Safiye said no more.

"I have some good news," said Süleyman three days later. "Vediha Yenge is back from the village. Rayiha loves you very much, my dear Mevlut. It's all thanks to your letters. She definitely doesn't want the banker her father means for her to marry. The banker himself is officially bankrupt, but he bought gold and American dollars with his customers' money and buried it all away somewhere. Once all this media attention dies down and the newspapers move on to the next story, he's going to dig up the money from whatever garden he's buried it in and live the good life with Rayiha while the greedy blockheads who gave him their cash have to deal with the courts. He's promised the Crooked Neck a bundle. If her father gives his consent, he's going to marry Rayiha in a civil ceremony and go to Germany until the storm blows over. Apparently that crook of a ruined banker—and former tea vendor—is hiding out learning German and wants Rayiha to learn enough herself to be able buy meat from the halal butcher in Germany."

"That bastard," said Mevlut. "If I don't get to elope with Rayiha, I'll kill him."

"You won't need to kill anyone. I'm going to take the van and we're going to go to the village and take her away," said Süleyman. "I'll sort everything out for you."

Mevlut hugged and kissed his cousin. That night, he was too exhilarated to sleep.

When they met again, Süleyman had planned everything: after

Thursday's evening prayers, Rayiha was going to take her belongings and come out to her back garden.

"Let's get going," said Mevlut.

"Sit back down, will you. It's no more than a day's drive by van."

"It might rain, it's flood season . . . And we have to make preparations in Beyşehir."

"There's no need for any preparations. As soon as it gets dark, you'll find the girl in the Crooked Neck's back garden as if you'd put her there yourself. I'll drive you both to Akşehir and drop you off at the train station. You and Rayiha will take the train, and I'll come back on my own so her father doesn't suspect me."

Just hearing Süleyman say "you and Rayiha" was enough to send Mevlut into raptures. He'd already taken a week off work, and extended his leave for another week, claiming "family matters." When he asked for yet another week of unpaid leave, his boss grumbled. So Mevlut told him not to expect him back.

He could find another job in an ordinary restaurant like that anytime. He had also been thinking of entering the ice-cream business. He had met an ice-cream vendor who wanted to rent out his three-wheeled ice-cream cart and ice-cream churn from the month of Ramadan onward.

He tidied up the house a little and tried to put himself in Rayiha's shoes to imagine what she would see when she walked through the door, what sorts of things she would notice. Should he buy a bedspread now or let her choose one? Every time he imagined Rayiha inside the house, he thought of how she would see him walking around in his underwear, and he both craved that intimacy and shied away from the thought.

Süleyman. I fooled them all—my brother, my mother, Vediha, and everyone else—telling them I was going to take the van and disappear for a couple of days. On the eve of our departure, our would-be groom was jumping for joy; I took him to one side to have a word.

"Now listen very carefully, my dear Mevlut, because I'm talking to you not as your best friend and your cousin right now but as a member of the girl's family. Rayiha isn't even eighteen yet. If her father loses it, if he decides 'I can't forgive someone who's run away with my daughter' and sends the gendarmes after you, you're going to have to hide until she turns eighteen, and you won't be able to marry her until then. Now I want you to give me your word of honor that, when the time comes, you are absolutely going to marry her."

"You have my word," said Mevlut. "I'm going to marry her in a religious ceremony, too."

In the van the next morning, on our way to the village, Mevlut was in a great mood, joking around, looking at every passing factory and bridge, telling me "Faster, floor it!" and generally just babbling away. Then, he went quiet.

"What's wrong, scared of running away with a girl all of a sudden? We're just coming into Afyon. If we spend the night in the van, the police will get suspicious and they might take us to the police station, so I think we'd better go to that motel over there, all right? It's on me."

On the ground floor of the Nezahat Hotel, there was a restaurant that served alcohol. I was just draining my second drink as I sat there listening to Mevlut still going on about the tortures he saw in the military, when I finally snapped.

"Look, I'm Turkish and I won't hear a word said against my army, got it?" I said. "Maybe all these tortures and beatings and locking up a hundred thousand people is a bit much, but I'm happy with the coup. I'm sure you'd agree that the whole country's calmed right down, not just Istanbul, the streets are spotless, there's no more arguing about left or right, no more assassinations, the traffic's flowing smooth ever since the army put their foot down, the brothels have been shut down, and all the prostitutes, the Communists, the Marlboro sellers, the black-market traders, the mafia thugs, bootleggers, pimps, and street vendors have been swept away. Now don't get all offended; there just isn't any future for street vendors in this country, and you better accept it, my dear Mevlut. A man forks out a fortune on rent to open his nice fruit-and-vegetable shop in the best spot in the city, and along you come and sit on the pavement right on his doorstep to sell your potatoes and tomatoes from the village . . . Is that fair? The army's just regulating things a little. If only he'd lived a little longer, Atatürk wouldn't have stopped at the fez and the skullcap, he would have also banned street vendors all over the country, starting from Istanbul. I'm told they don't have these things in Europe."

"On the contrary," said Mevlut. "When Atatürk was visiting from Ankara one day, he thought the streets of Istanbul were too quiet and—"

"Anyway, if the army were to stop using the stick for one moment, our people would either take the Communists' bait or run to the Islamists. There's also those Kurds who want to split this country up. Do you still see that Ferhat? What's he up to?"

"I don't know."

"He's a real scumbag."

"He's my friend."

"Fine then, I'm not taking you to Beyşehir, good luck eloping now."

"Oh come on, Süleyman, don't be that way," said Mevlut, suddenly desperate.

"Here I am, serving you a real beauty on a silver platter. She's all packed up and waiting for you in the garden. On top of that, I'm putting you in my van and personally driving you seven hundred kilometers to the village. I'm paying for the gas. Even the hotel you're sleeping in tonight and the *rakı* you drink is on me. And still you won't say 'You're right, Süleyman, Ferhat is a bastard,' not even once. You won't even pretend. You never say 'You're a good guy, Süleyman.' If you think you're so smart, if you still think you're so much better than me the way you did when we were kids, then why come begging for our help?"

"Forgive me, Süleyman."

"Say it again."

"Forgive me, Süleyman."

"I will forgive you, but first I need to hear what your excuse is."

"My excuse is that I'm afraid, Süleyman."

"But there's nothing to be afraid of. When they realize Rayiha's run away . . . they're obviously going to head toward our village. You two are going to climb the hill. They might even fire a couple of rounds just for show. Don't be scared, I'll be waiting for you with the van on the other side. Rayiha will sit in the back so she doesn't see me and recognize me. She did see the van once back in Istanbul, but she's a girl, they can't tell cars apart. You won't say a word about me, of course. What you should worry about is what you'll do once you've run away and gotten back to Istanbul and you're alone in the same room with her. You haven't slept with a woman yet, have you, Mevlut?"

"I'm not worried about all that, Süleyman, I'm scared she'll change her mind and decide she doesn't want to run off with me after all."

First thing the next morning, we scouted out the Akşehir train station. From there, we sidled up to our village through muddy mountain roads, but even though Mevlut wanted to see his mother, he worried all our plans would unravel if he drew too much attention to himself, so we didn't even say hello. We took the roundabout route to Gümüşdere village and snuck up to Crooked-Necked Abdurrahman Efendi's house, right up to the garden with the crumbling wall. We went back. I drove the van farther on and pulled over.

"There's not long to go before sunset and the evening prayers," I said. "There's nothing to be afraid of. Good luck, Mevlut."

"God bless you, Süleyman," he said. "Pray for me."

I got out of the van with him. We embraced . . . I was almost welling up myself, looking fondly at his back as he walked down the dirt path to the village, and in my heart I wished him a happy life. I drove to our meeting point thinking that he was soon going to realize his fate was different from what he had expected, and I wondered what he would do when he found out. If I didn't truly want the best for Mevlut, if I really wanted to con him, as some may think, then when he gave me the papers to his house in Kültepe that night in Istanbul when he was drunk on *rakı* and wanted me to arrange a match with Rayiha, I wouldn't have given them back to him, would I? I'm the one who found him a tenant for that house, and it's all that Mevlut's got in this world. I'm not counting his mother and sisters in the village. In theory, they're also my late uncle Mustafa's heirs, but that's none of my business.

When Mevlut was back in middle school and about to take an important exam, he used to feel as if his heart were pumping flames up to his forehead and his face. A much more intense version of that feeling had taken over his entire body now as he walked to the village of Gümüşdere.

He chanced upon the cemetery on the hill just outside the village, walked in among the headstones, sat on the edge of a grave across from a moldy, old, but equally elaborate and mysterious headstone, and thought about his life. "God, please make Rayiha show up, please, God, make Rayiha show up," he repeated. He wanted to pray and implore God, but he couldn't seem to recall any of the prayers he knew. He said to himself, "If Rayiha shows up, I'll learn the Holy Koran by heart and become a hafiz." He prayed with insistence and vigor while feeling like a tiny, helpless speck in God's universe. He'd heard that it could help to repeat prayers beseechingly.

Just after sundown, Mevlut approached the crumbling wall. The window at the back of Abdurrahman Efendi's house was dark. He was ten minutes early. As he waited for the agreed sign, a light switching on and off, he felt that he was at the beginning of his life, just as he had thirteen years ago on the day he had arrived in Istanbul with his father.

The dogs barked and the window lit up and went dark again.

PART IV

June 1982–March 1994

It shocked him to find in the outer world a trace of what he had deemed till then a brutish and individual malady of his own mind.

—James Joyce, *A Portrait of the Artist as a Young Man*

I

Mevlut and Rayiha Get Married

Only Death Can Tear Us Apart

Süleyman. When do you think Mevlut realized that girl he was running away with was not the beautiful Samiha whose eyes he'd stared into at my brother's wedding, but her less beautiful older sister Rayiha? Was it at the moment he met her in the dark of her garden in the village, or did he only see her face later, as they made their way together across rivers and over hills? Did he already know by the time he sat down next to me in the van? That's why I asked him "Is something the matter?" and "Cat got your tongue?" But Mevlut gave nothing away.

When they got off the train and joined the crowds taking the ferry from Haydarpaşa to Karaköy, Mevlut's mind wasn't on weddings and marriage contracts but on the fact that soon he would finally be alone in a room with Rayiha. It was perhaps a bit childish of her to be so interested in the commotion on Galata Bridge and the white smoke from the ferries, but he could think of nothing except how they were shortly going to walk into a house with no one else there.

When Mevlut took out his keys—tucked safe in his pocket like something precious—and unlocked the door to the apartment in Tarlabaşı, he felt as if the house had become a different place in the three days it had taken him to make the round trip to the village: on early June mornings, the apartment would feel almost cool, but it was stiflingly hot now in high summer, and the old linoleum floors, heating up under the sunlight, emitted a smell of cheap plastic mixed with beeswax and hemp. You could hear the din of the people and traffic of Beyoğlu and Tarlabaşı drifting in from outside. Mevlut had always liked that sound.

Rayiha. "Our house is lovely," I said. "But it needs airing." I couldn't manage to turn the handle and open the window, so Mevlut rushed over to show me how to work the bolt. I immediately sensed that once we'd given the house a thorough scrubbing and swept away the cobwebs, it would be cleansed of all of Mevlut's disappointments, his fears, and the demons in his mind. We went out to buy some soap, a plastic bucket, and a mop, and the moment we walked out the door, the tension of being alone inside the house was lifted, and we relaxed. We spent the afternoon window-shopping, looking for things on store shelves from Tarlabaşı to Balıkpazarı, and buying whatever we needed. We bought sponges for the kitchen, scrubbing brushes, and cleaning liquid, and as soon as we got home, we cleaned the house from top to bottom. We got so involved in what we were doing that we forgot to be embarrassed about being alone at home together.

By evening time, I was soaked through with sweat. Mevlut showed me how to light the gas boiler with a match, how to regulate the butane supply, and which one was the hot water tap. We had to stand on a chair to insert a lit match into a black hole in the boiler and turn it on. Mevlut suggested I crack open the little frosted-glass window that opened onto the dark inner courtyard of the building.

"If you leave it open just so, you'll let the dirty air out, and no one will see you . . . ," he whispered. "I'll be gone for an hour."

Rayiha was still in the same outfit she'd been wearing when they had run away from the village, and Mevlut had figured out that she wouldn't be comfortable taking her clothes off and bathing if he was in the house. He sat in a coffeehouse just off İstiklal Avenue. On winter evenings, this place would be full of doormen, lottery-ticket sellers, drivers, and tired street vendors, but now it was empty. He looked at the cup of tea that had been placed in front of him and thought of Rayiha bathing. Where had he gotten the idea that she had fair skin? From looking at her neck! Why had he said "an hour" when he'd left? Time was moving very slowly. He looked at a lonely tea leaf at the bottom of his glass.

Not wanting to go back home before an hour had passed, he had a beer and took the long way back through the backstreets of Tarlabaşı: it pleased him to be a part of these streets where kids cursed at one another as they played football, mothers sat outside small three-story houses with big trays on their laps, picking stones out of rice, and everyone knew everyone else.

Mevlut haggled for watermelons with a man sitting under the shade of a black cloth gazebo in an empty clearing, tapping a number of watermelons with his fingers to try to guess how red they were inside. There was an ant walking on a watermelon. Whenever Mevlut turned the fruit over in his hands, the ant would end up upside down, but it would never fall; it would just run around until it was back on top of the watermelon. He had the vendor weigh the watermelon, taking care not to knock the patient ant off. He walked back into the house without a sound and put the watermelon in the kitchen.

Rayiha. Once I had bathed and put on some fresh, clean clothes, I lay down on the bed with my back to the door and fell asleep without covering my hair.

Mevlut went up to her quietly. For a long time, he looked at Rayiha lying on the bed, knowing that he would never forget this moment. Her body and feet looked delicate and pretty under her clothes. Her shoulders and her arms stirred gently every time she breathed. For a moment, Mevlut felt that she was only pretending to be asleep. He lay down quietly and cautiously on the other side of the double bed, without changing his clothes.

His heart was beating fast. If they started having sex now—and he wasn't even sure how to go about doing that—he would be taking advantage of her trust.

Rayiha had put her trust in Mevlut, she had surrendered her life into his hands, and she had taken off her headscarf and shown him her long, beautiful hair before they were married—before they'd even had sex. As he looked at her long, flowing locks, Mevlut sensed that this trust and surrender would be enough to bind him to Rayiha and understood just how much he was going to love her. He wasn't alone in the world. He watched Rayiha breathing in and out, and his happiness seemed boundless. She had even appreciated his letters.

They fell asleep in their clothes. Late at night, they embraced in the dark, but they did not make love. Mevlut could tell that it must be easier to engage in sexual activities at night. But he would have liked his first time with Rayiha to be in the light of day, when he could look into her eyes. Come morning, however, every time they did look into each other's eyes from up close, they got embarrassed and found other things to keep them busy.

Rayiha. The next morning, I took Mevlut shopping again. I picked a plastic tablecloth that looked like waxcloth, a duvet cover with blue flowers, a plastic breadbasket that looked like it was made of wicker, and a plastic lemon press. Mevlut soon tired of my browsing the stores looking at slippers, teacups, jars, and saltshakers just for fun, without buying anything. We went back home. We sat on the edge of the bed.

"No one knows we're here, right?" I said.

Mevlut's boyish face gave me such a look in response that I said, "There's food on the stove," and ran off to the kitchen. In the afternoon, when the sun warmed up the small apartment, I felt tired and went to lie down on the bed.

When Mevlut went to lie down next to her, they hugged and kissed for the very first time. His desire intensified when he saw the look of childlike guilt on clever Rayiha's face. But every time his desires announced themselves in fleshly form, they were both overcome with embarrassment. Mevlut put his hand inside Rayiha's dress and touched her left breast for a moment, and his head spun.

She pushed him away. He got up, his pride bruised.

"Don't worry, I'm not angry!" he said as he walked out the door with decision. "I'll be back in a minute."

In one of the streets behind the Ağa Mosque, there was a Kurdish scrap-metal dealer who had graduated from a religious institute in Ankara. He charged a small fee to perform quick religious wedding ceremonies for couples who'd already had their civil ceremonies but wanted to be on the safe side; men who had wives back in their villages but had fallen in love with someone else in Istanbul and had no one else to turn to; and conservative teenagers who kept their meetings a secret from their fathers and older brothers, let things get too far, and then couldn't live with the guilt. The scrap dealer claimed he was a Hanafi because only Sunnis of the Hanafi school were allowed to marry young people without their parents' permission.

Mevlut found this man among old radiators, stove lids, and rusty engine parts in the back room of his shop, dozing with his head under a copy of the Istanbul daily *Akşam*.

"Sir, I would like to get married according to the laws of our faith."

"I understand, but what's the rush?" said the learned man. "You're too poor and too young to take a second wife."

"I ran away with a girl!" said Mevlut.

"With her agreement, of course?"

"We're in love."

"The world's full of philanderers who like to kidnap girls and rape them, claiming all the while that it's love. These villains sometimes even manage to persuade the girls' helpless families to let them marry their daughters . . ."

"It's not like that at all," said Mevlut. "We are getting married by mutual consent and hopefully with love."

"Love is a disease," said the scholar. "And marriage is the only cure, you're right. But it is a cure you may regret, for it is like having to take awful quinine for the rest of your life even after your typhoid fever is cured."

"I won't regret it," said Mevlut.

"Then what's the rush? Haven't you consummated yet?"

"Only after we're properly married," said Mevlut.

"Either she's really ugly, or you're a real innocent. What's your name? You're a good-looking lad, sit down and have some tea."

Mevlut drank the tea served by a pale assistant with big green eyes, trying to cut the small talk short, but the man was determined to raise his price by telling him how bad business was. There were still some young men and women who decided to get married after they'd kissed and fondled each other, and then went home to their separate families and did not say a word to their parents at the dinner table, but their numbers, too, were sadly dwindling.

"I don't have much money!" said Mevlut.

"Is that why you ran away with the girl? Good-looking boys like you can turn out to be real rakes sometimes, and as soon as they've quenched their thirst they'll say *talaq* and get rid of the girl. I've known many a lovely but ingenuous girl to kill herself or end up in a brothel over someone like you."

"We're going to have a civil ceremony, too, as soon as she turns eighteen," said Mevlut, feeling guilty.

"All right. I will do a good deed and marry you tomorrow. Where shall I come?"

"Could we just do it here without bringing the girl in?" said Mevlut, looking around at the dusty junk shop.

"I don't charge for the ceremony itself, but I do for the room."

Rayiha. After Mevlut left the house, I went out and bought two kilos of slightly overripe but cheap strawberries from a street vendor, and sugar from the grocery store, and before Mevlut got back, I'd washed the strawberries and started making jam. When he came home, he breathed in the sweet strawberry fumes happily but didn't try to approach me.

In the evening, he took me to see a double feature at the Tulip Cinema. During the break between the first movie starring Hülya Koçyiğit and the second starring Türkân Şoray, the air in the theater so humid that the seats felt wet, he told me that we would be getting married tomorrow, and I cried a bit. I still paid attention to the second movie, though. I was so happy.

Once the movie was over, Mevlut said, "Until your father gives us his blessing or you turn eighteen, let's at least make sure we're married in the eyes of God so no one can split us up . . . I know this scrap-metal dealer. The ceremony will be in his shop. He said there's no need for you to come . . . All you have to do is give someone permission to act on your behalf."

"No, I want to be there for the ceremony," I said with a frown. But then I smiled so Mevlut wouldn't worry.

Back home, Mevlut and Rayiha acted like two strangers forced to share a hotel room in a provincial town, hiding from each other as they changed into their nightgown and pajamas. Avoiding each other's gaze, they switched the lights off and carefully lay down side by side on the bed making sure to leave some space between them, Rayiha with her back to Mevlut again. He felt a mixture of joy and fear, and just as he was thinking this excitement would keep him up all night, he fell asleep.

He woke up in the middle of the night to find that he had buried himself in the thick strawberry scent of Rayiha's skin and the aroma of children's cookies coming from her neck. They'd both been sweating in the heat and fallen prey to ravenous mosquitoes. Their bodies embraced of their own accord. With his eyes on the dark blue sky and the neon lights outside, Mevlut felt briefly as if they were floating away somewhere outside the world, in a childhood place where gravity did not exist, when Rayiha said, "We're not married yet," and pushed him away.

From a waiter he used to know at the Karlıova Restaurant, Mevlut had found out that Ferhat was back from military service. The next morning, one of the two dishwasher boys from Mardin led him to where Ferhat was staying, a second-rate rooming house for bachelors in Tarlabaşı. He was living here with waiters ten years younger than he was, and Kurdish and Alevi kids from Tunceli and Bingöl just out of middle school who'd started working as dishwashers. Mevlut didn't think this stinking, stuffy place was good enough for Ferhat and felt sorry for him, so he was relieved when he learned that Ferhat still spent plenty of time at his parents' house. Mevlut could see that Ferhat was a sort of older brother to the kids in the dormitory, and that there were other things going on here, too—cigarette smuggling, which had become nearly impossible in the aftermath of the coup; trade in a drug that was known as grass; and a feeling of political outrage and solidarity—but he didn't ask too many questions. The things he'd witnessed and experienced in the military, and the stories he'd heard from acquaintances imprisoned and tortured in Diyarbakır, had all left an indelible impression on Ferhat and made him even more political.

"You need to get married," said Mevlut.

"I need to find a city girl and make her fall for me," said Ferhat, "or I need to run away with a girl from the village. I don't have enough money to get married."

"I ran away with a girl," said Mevlut. "So should you. Then we can start a business together, open a shop, and get rich."

Mevlut told Ferhat a rather embellished version of the story of how he'd run away with Rayiha. Neither Süleyman nor his van featured in it. Mevlut said that he had walked hand in hand with his lover through the mud and the mountains for a whole day, all the way to Akşehir train station, while her father chased after them.

"Is Rayiha as beautiful as our letters said she was?" asked an eager Ferhat.

"She's even prettier and smarter," said Mevlut. "But the girl's family, the Vurals, Korkut, Süleyman, they won't give up the chase even in Istanbul."

"Damned fascists," said Ferhat, and agreed straightaway to act as a witness at their wedding.

Rayiha. I wore my floral-print dress with the long skirt and a clean pair of jeans. I also wore the purple headscarf I'd bought in the backstreets of Beyoğlu. We met up with Ferhat in the Black Sea Café on İstiklal Avenue. He was a tall, polite man with a high forehead. He gave us each a glass of sour-cherry juice. "Congratulations, *yenge,* you picked the right man," he said. "He's a bit of a weirdo, but he's got a heart of gold."

Once we'd all gathered at his shop, the scrap-metal dealer found another witness from the grocer's next door. He opened a drawer and took out a frayed notebook covered in Ottoman script. He flipped it open and carefully took down everyone's names and our fathers' names, too. We all knew these records had no official value, yet it was impressive to see this man earnestly writing everything down in Arabic letters.

"How much did you spend on her bride price? How much will you pay if you split up?" asked the scrap-metal dealer.

"What bride price?" said Ferhat. "He ran away with the girl."

"How much will you pay her if you divorce her?"

"Only death can tear us apart," said Mevlut.

The other witness said, "Just put down ten Sultan Reshad gold bullion coins for one, and seven State Mint gold coins for the other."

"That's too much," said Ferhat.

"It seems I shall not be able to perform this ceremony in full respect of Sharia law," said the scrap-metal dealer, going over to the set of scales in the front room of the shop. "Any physical intimacy that might occur without there being a religious union in place is to be considered fornication. Anyway, the girl is too young."

"I'm not too young, I'm seventeen!" I said, showing them the identification card I took from my father's cupboard.

Ferhat took the scrap-metal dealer to one side and put some money in his pocket.

"Now, repeat after me," said the scrap-metal dealer.

Mevlut and I looked into each other's eyes and recited a long series of words in Arabic.

"Dear God! Bless this union!" said the scrap-metal dealer as he concluded the ceremony. "May there be companionship, understanding, and love between these two forsaken souls of yours, and please, O Lord, allow their marriage to stand the test of time, and protect Mevlut and Rayiha from hatred, discord, and separation."

2

Mevlut Sells Ice Cream

The Happiest Days of His Life

As soon as they got home, they made straight for the bed. Now that they were married, they could relax; the thing both had craved so much, been so curious about while never getting to do it, was now a duty everyone expected them to perform. They were shy about seeing each other naked (even with some parts remaining covered) and touching each other's bodies where they burned hottest—on their arms, their chests—but the sense that it was all unavoidable relieved their shame somewhat. "Yes, this is really embarrassing," their eyes were saying. "But unfortunately, it must be done."

Rayiha. I only wish the room had been dark! I didn't like feeling so self-conscious every time we looked into each other's eyes. The faded curtains couldn't block out the bright summer afternoon light. I had to push Mevlut away once or twice when he got too greedy and rough. But part of me liked it when he was forceful, and I just let myself go. I saw Mevlut's thing twice, and it scared me a little. I cradled my pure and handsome Mevlut's head like a baby, so that the huge thing down there wouldn't catch my eye.

Contrary to what they'd always heard from their friends, Mevlut and Rayiha had learned in religion class back in the village that there was nothing lascivious about physical intimacy between husband and wife, but they still felt uncomfortable whenever they looked into each other's eyes. They realized soon enough, however, that their shyness was bound to abate, and that they would come to see sex as a normal human activity, perhaps even a sign of maturity.

"I'm so thirsty," said Mevlut, feeling as if he were about to suffocate.

It was almost as if the whole house—the walls, the windows, and the ceiling—were sweating with them.

"There's a glass by the water pitcher," said Rayiha, burrowing under the bedsheets.

Mevlut could sense from the look in her eyes that she was seeing the world from outside her own body. He felt the same as he poured water into the glass on the table—as if he had stepped outside himself and now existed purely as a soul. Handing his wife her glass of water, he realized that even though there was something obscene and shameless about sex, it also had a divine, spiritual side to it. They stole a few glances at each other's bodies while they were drinking their water, feeling almost resigned, shy, and amazed at what life could be.

Mevlut saw light pouring out into the room from Rayiha's milk-white skin. He briefly considered that he might be responsible for those pink and light purple marks on her body. Once they were back under the covers, they embraced in the comfort of knowing that everything was fine. Tender words tumbled unrehearsed from Mevlut's mouth.

"My darling," he told her. "My sweetheart, you're so lovely . . ."

His mother and sisters used to say these things to him when he was little, but where they would say them in their normal voices, he was whispering them fervently into Rayiha's ear like secrets. He called out to her in the restless voice of a traveler afraid of getting lost in the woods. They made love until morning, falling in and out of sleep, and getting up to drink water in the dark without ever switching the lights on. The best thing about being married was that you could have sex whenever and as often as you wanted.

In the morning, when they saw stains the color of sour cherries on the sheets, Mevlut and Rayiha felt a bit embarrassed, but also pleased—though they hid this satisfaction from each other—for here was the expected proof of Rayiha's virginity. They never spoke of it openly, but all through that summer, whenever they were busy preparing sour-cherry ice cream for Mevlut to sell in the evenings, he would always remember that other smudge of cherry hue.

Rayiha. We both keep the fast during Ramadan—Mevlut started the year he finished primary school and stayed behind in the village, while I began even earlier, when I was just ten years old. When we were little, Samiha and I were napping until it was time to break the fast one day when my sister Vediha felt faint with hunger and keeled over like a minaret in an earthquake, and the trays she was carrying came tumbling down with her. That's how we learned that whenever we felt too weak to stand from all that fasting, we should sit down on the floor immediately. Even when we didn't feel faint, sometimes just for fun we would pretend that the world was spinning and sway backward and forward a little before throwing ourselves on the floor in fits of laughter. Anyone who keeps the fast, even kids, knows that there should not be any physical contact between husbands and wives during fasting hours. But three days after we got married, it was already Ramadan, and Mevlut and I began to question what we thought we knew.

Sir, does a kiss on the hand void the fast? It does not! What about a kiss on the shoulder? Probably not. What about kissing the neck of your lawfully wedded wife? Her cheek? The council for religious affairs says that a chaste kiss is fine as long as you aren't planning to take things any further. The scrap-metal dealer who married us says that even a kiss on the mouth won't void the fast provided there is no transfer of saliva. Mevlut trusted him and thought that, since he was the one who'd married us, he alone could decide the matter. In our faith, things can be interpreted in many different ways. Vediha once told me that on long, hot summer days, boys keeping the fast will disappear into the woods and hide in dried-up riverbeds where they shamelessly play with themselves and justify it by saying that "the imam states you mustn't touch your spouse, not that you mustn't touch yourself . . ." Maybe there isn't anything in the holy book that forbids sex during Ramadan either.

You've probably figured it out by now: during the long, hot days of Ramadan, Mevlut and I couldn't control our urges and started having sex. If it's a sin, let it be on my head. I love my beautiful Mevlut so very much. We weren't doing anyone any harm! Of those who would call us sinners, I'd like to ask one question: when thousands of young people are married off to each other in a hurry just before Ramadan and are having sex for the first time in their lives, what do you think they get up to at home during the long and dizzying hours of fasting?

Hızır had gone back to his village near Sivas for Ramadan, leaving Mevlut his three-wheeled ice-cream cart, some ladles, and a wooden cooler. Every summer, many street vendors like Hızır would arrange for someone to take over their carts and customers so that they wouldn't lose any regulars while they were away in their villages.

Hızır wasn't charging Mevlut much rent for the equipment because he trusted him to be honest and diligent. He had invited Mevlut over to his house on a gloomy backstreet of the Dolapdere neighborhood, where his tiny and rather rotund wife befriended Rayiha immediately and joined her husband in teaching them how to make the ice cream, how to knead the mixture with a continual heartfelt motion until it was the right consistency, and how to add a little citric acid to lemon juice and a little food coloring to sour-cherry juice. Hızır said that ice cream was not only a treat for children but also for adults who thought they were still children. As much as the flavor of the ice cream itself, the key to success lay in the ice-cream vendor's exuberance and sense of humor. Hızır had sat Mevlut down and shown him a map he himself had drawn with great care, marking out which streets Mevlut should pass through and which spots would be most crowded at what times, so he could focus his efforts accordingly. Mevlut memorized the map and would visualize it every evening as he pushed his ice-cream cart from upper Tarlabaşı down to İstiklal Avenue and Sıraselviler.

There was a sign on the little white ice-cream cart that said

HIZIR'S ICE CREAM
Strawberry, Sour Cherry, Lemon, Chocolate, Cream

in red letters. Sometimes Mevlut would run out of a flavor toward the end of the evening, around the time he really began to miss Rayiha. "I don't have any sour cherry," he would tell a customer, who might try to get clever with him: "Then why did you write 'sour cherry' on your cart?" Mevlut's initial urge would be to answer back, "I didn't write it myself, did I?" but then he would think of Rayiha, and, feeling happy, he wouldn't respond at all. He left behind the old bell he had inherited from his father and went out with a jollier and noisier one Hızır had given him, swinging it about until it swayed like a handkerchief fluttering on a clothesline in a storm, and he cried "Ice creeeam" in the melody Hızır himself had taught him. But the kids who would come running after him at the sound of the bell would shout, "Ice-cream man, ice-cream man, you're not Hızır!"

"Hızır's gone to a wedding in the village, I'm his little brother," Mevlut would tell these children who emerged from the darkness like little imps, popping out from street corners, house windows, tree trunks, and mosque courtyards where they played hide-and-seek.

Mevlut was reluctant to leave the cart unattended, and it was difficult for him to enter homes and kitchens, so most families who wanted ice cream would send someone down to the street to fetch it. Big families would send servants carrying huge trays inlaid with silver or mother-of-pearl or use a rope to dangle a basket carrying as many as a dozen narrow-waisted little teacups and a piece of paper with detailed instructions on the flavors desired, and Mevlut soon discovered that filling these orders by the light of a streetlamp was as delicate and difficult a task as a pharmacist's job. Sometimes there would be new customers rounding the corner before he'd finished, and even the children, who buzzed around him like flies on a plate of jam and never stopped talking, would grow impatient and agitated. Sometimes, when there wasn't a soul on the street or around his ice-cream cart—during special nighttime Ramadan prayers, for example—a large family would send down a servant with a tray, and everyone in the house, starting with the children, their uncles watching football on TV, their happy guests, gossipy aunts, spoiled little girls, and finally the shy and irritable little boys, would shout down from the fifth floor for all the world to hear exactly how much sour cherry and how much cream they wanted and which flavor should go inside the cone and which one on top, with an impertinence that surprised even Mevlut. Sometimes people would insist he come upstairs, and he would stand by a crowded family dinner table or by the doors of a rich family's chaotic kitchen, witnessing little children doing joyful cartwheels on the carpet. Some families, hearing the sound of the bell, would conclude that it must be Hızır down there, and the uncles and aunties would lean out the first-floor window, saying, "Hızır Efendi, how are you, you're looking good!" even as they stared straight into Mevlut's face; and far from correcting them, he would answer "Thank you, I have just returned from a wedding in the village . . . Ramadan has been particularly bountiful this year" in a manner designed to please, though always followed by a twinge of guilt.

What he felt most guilty about during Ramadan was his failing to resist temptation with Rayiha during fasting hours. Like her, he was smart enough to know that these were the happiest days of his life, and this happiness was too great for regret to dampen it, so he understood that his guilt sprang from a deeper source: the heart of someone who had been admitted to paradise by accident, without really deserving it.

At around ten thirty, before he was even halfway through the route Hızır had drawn, he would start to miss Rayiha enormously. What was she doing at home right now? Two weeks after the start of Ramadan, in whatever bit of the afternoon remained after making ice cream and having sex, they went to the movies a couple of times in the backstreets of Beyoğlu, to one of those cinemas that showed three comedy films starring people like Kemal Sunal and Fatma Girik, all for the price of a large ice-cream cone. Maybe if Mevlut were to buy her a secondhand television, Rayiha wouldn't get bored waiting for him at home.

His last stop every night was a stairway that looked out on the tens of thousands of lit windows in Istanbul. This was the spot where Mevlut would one day get mugged by the father-and-son duo described at the start of our book, and as he stood here watching the oil tankers crossing the Bosphorus in the dark, and the lit-up Ramadan decorations hanging between minarets, Mevlut would think how lucky he was to have a home in Istanbul and a sweet girl like Rayiha waiting for him to return. He would pick out the brightest looking from among the kids that swooped around him like hungry seagulls tailing a fishing boat and tell him, "Go on, show me how much money you've got in your pockets." This child and a few more like him would each get a cone piled high with ice cream, even though their small change was hardly enough to pay for it, and so, having used up the remaining ice cream in his tub, Mevlut would head home. He would ignore kids who had no money at all and pleaded, "Uncle Hızır, at least give us an empty cone!" or those who mimicked him for a laugh. He knew that the moment he gave a kid free ice cream, he wouldn't be able to sell him or any of the other kids anything the next day.

Rayiha. I would know Mevlut was back by the sound of him pulling the cart into the back garden, and while he was busy chaining the front wheel to the almond tree, I would pick up the tubs ("Not a drop left, well done!" I'd say every time), the rags that needed washing, and the ice-cream scoops, taking them all upstairs. As soon as he stepped into the house, Mevlut would remove his apron and fling it to the floor. Some people handle the money they earn with the same veneration they would show a piece of paper with our Prophet's name on it, holding it aloft like the source of life itself, so it was nice to see Mevlut casting off the apron with its pockets stuffed full of money in his eagerness to return to our bliss. I would kiss him.

On summer mornings, he would go out looking for strawberries, sour cherries, melons, and other ingredients for the ice cream, trying the Albanian fruit seller or else going to Balıkpazarı, and as I put on my shoes and my headscarf, Mevlut would say "Come along!" as if taking me along were his idea. After Ramadan, Mevlut started selling ice cream in the afternoons too.

Whenever I noticed Mevlut growing weary or bored in my presence, I would stand back a little as he caught up with his friends in barbershops, carpenter's workshops, and garages. Sometimes he would say, "Wait over here for a minute, will you," and go into a store, leaving me behind. I could keep myself entertained just by looking through an open door at workers in a factory that made plastic bowls. Mevlut would relax as we moved farther away from home. He would tell me about the awful backstreet cinemas we saw on the way, and another restaurant where he used to work with Ferhat, but he would feel uneasy whenever he spotted a familiar face among the crowds in Taksim and Galatasaray. Was it because he was the villain who'd seduced a woman, and I was the stupid girl who'd fallen for his tricks? "Let's go home now," he'd say, fuming from five steps ahead, and I would run to catch up with him, wondering how he could suddenly be so furious about something so small. (I spent my whole life trying to figure out why Mevlut would lose his temper all of a sudden.) He would soften as soon as we started to sort the fruit, and while we washed and juiced it, he'd plant kisses on my neck and my cheek, telling me he knew where the sweetest cherries and strawberries really were, which made me blush and laugh. The room was never dark no matter how tight we shut the curtains, but we would still pretend that it was and that we couldn't see each other as we MADE LOVE.

3

Mevlut and Rayiha's Wedding

Only Desperate Yogurt Sellers Bother with Boza

Abdurrahman Efendi. It's tough when your daughter elopes: if you're not up in arms the second you find out, firing bullets left and right, you'll have the gossips whispering "Her father knew" behind your back. It was only four years ago that a lovely girl was kidnapped in broad daylight by three armed bandits while she was working the fields. Her father went to the judge and had him send the gendarmes after them, he tortured himself for days wondering what horrible things they must be doing to his daughter, but he still couldn't avoid that slander: "Her father knew." I asked Samiha over and over again to tell me who'd taken Rayiha, I even told her she had a slap coming if she wasn't careful, but she didn't believe me, of course—my daughters know I couldn't even bear to twist their ears—and I didn't get a thing out of her.

To head off any gossip in the village, I went down to the magistrate in Beyşehir. "But you didn't even manage to keep hold of your daughter's identity card," he said. "It's clear to me that the girl ran away because she wanted to. She's under eighteen, though, so I can press charges. I can send the gendarmes after them. But then if your anger fades and you decide to forgive your son-in-law so they can be married properly, you'll still have this court case to deal with. Go and think it over at the coffeehouse for a bit, and if you're still determined to pursue the matter, I'll be here."

On my way to the coffeehouse, I stopped at the Broken Ladle for some lentil soup, and when I overheard the people at the next table talking about an imminent cockfighting match at the Animal Welfare Club, I followed them out of the diner. So I ended up going back to the village before I could decide what to do. A month later, just after Ramadan, there was some news from Vediha: Rayiha was in Istanbul, she was well, she was pregnant, and the man she had run away with was Mevlut, her husband Korkut's cousin. Vediha had seen this fool Mevlut and knew that he was completely penniless. I said, "I will never forgive them," but Vediha could already tell that I would.

Vediha. Rayiha came over to our place one afternoon sometime after the holiday marking the end of Ramadan, but she didn't tell Mevlut. She said that she was very happy with him and that she was pregnant. She hugged me and cried. She told me how lonely she'd been feeling, how scared she was of everything, and how she wanted to live the way we used to do back in the village, with all her sisters and a family buzzing around her, among the trees and the chickens, in other words in a house with a garden like ours in Duttepe—not in some shabby, cramped apartment. What my dear Rayiha really wanted was for our father to stop thinking "There cannot be a wedding for a girl who runs away" and just forgive her, allowing her a civil ceremony and a wedding reception, too. Might I be able to coax everyone gently into agreement, placating Korkut and my father-in-law, Hasan, without hurting my father's feelings, and sorting this all out before the baby in her belly grew too big? "I'll see what I can do," I said. "But first you must swear one more time that you will never tell Dad or anyone else that it was Süleyman and I who delivered Mevlut's letters." Rayiha, who is an optimist by nature, swore without any hesitation. "I'm sure everyone's secretly glad I ran away and got married, because it's Samiha's turn now," she said.

Korkut. I went down to Gümüşdere, and after a brief negotiation, I convinced my weeping crooked-necked father-in-law to "forgive"

Rayiha. I was a bit irritated at first because he was acting as if I'd been involved in the elopement (later I interpreted this tone of his as a sign that Vediha and my brother, Süleyman, must have had a hand in the matter), but really, he was pleased that Rayiha was married—he was just annoyed to have let Mevlut snatch his daughter away for free. To smooth his ruffled feathers, I promised that I would help him repair the broken wall around his garden and that I would tell Mevlut and Rayiha to go to the village to kiss his hand and beg for forgiveness, and later, I sent him two thousand liras with Vediha.

Mevlut became anxious when he found out that Crooked-Necked Abdurrahman would forgive them only on the condition that they went back to the village to pay their respects to him. Such a visit would inevitably entail coming face-to-face with the beautiful Samiha, who had been the intended recipient of all his letters, and he was sure he wouldn't be able to hide his embarrassment when he saw her and his face turned crimson. Mevlut spent the fourteen-hour bus ride from Istanbul to Beyşehir wide awake, brooding over this prospect, while Rayiha slept like a baby beside him. The hardest part was having to hide his unease from Rayiha, who was so glad that everything had been resolved in the best way possible and overjoyed to be seeing her father and sister again. Mevlut feared that even allowing himself to think about it too much would lead Rayiha to sense the truth. In practice this meant that he thought about it even more, which, just as with his fear of dogs, only made things worse. Rayiha could sense that there was something eating away at her husband. They were having a cup of tea at the Mountain View way station, where their bus had stopped for a quick break in the middle of the night, when she finally asked him, "For God's sake, what's the matter?"

"There's a strangeness in my mind," said Mevlut. "No matter what I do, I feel completely alone in this world." "You will never feel that way again now that I'm with you," said Rayiha with maternal feeling. As Rayiha snuggled up to him, Mevlut watched her dreamlike reflection in the window of the teahouse, and he knew that he would never forget this moment.

They spent two days in Cennetpınar, Mevlut's village. His mother made up their best bed for Rayiha and brought out some candied walnut wrap, Mevlut's favorite. She kept kissing her daughter-in-law, showing Mevlut Rayiha's hands, her arms, even her ears, and saying, "Isn't she just lovely?" Mevlut basked in the maternal affection he'd missed ever since moving to Istanbul at the age of twelve, but at the same time he felt a sense of resentment and superiority he couldn't quite explain.

Rayiha. In the fifty days I'd been away from my village, my home, our garden, I'd missed them all so much, even the old village road and the trees and the chickens, that now I felt I had to go off on my own for a while. In the very room in which I'd switched the lights on and off to signal Mevlut the night we ran away, my husband now went like a naughty schoolboy up to my father asking his forgiveness. I will never forget how happy I was to see him kiss my dear father's hand. Afterward, I walked in with a tray and served the coffee, smiling charmingly at everyone, as if they were guests come to look at a potential match for their son, and I was the girl who hadn't managed to find a husband yet. Mevlut was so nervous that he downed his boiling coffee like lemonade, without even blowing on it first, and tears sprang from his eyes. They were talking about mundane things, until Mevlut got upset when he realized that I would be staying behind with my father and Samiha and not coming back to Istanbul until the wedding, just like a real bride.

Mevlut was annoyed that Rayiha hadn't warned him about her plans to stay in the village for a while. He was walking back toward his village in a huff, having instinctively cut his visit short, and deep down, he was very pleased not to have seen Samiha in the house at all. Rayiha had mentioned her sister, but for whatever reason, Samiha hadn't shown her face; he was glad for the temporary reprieve from that humiliation, knowing nonetheless that the matter hadn't been resolved, only postponed until the wedding in Istanbul. Did the fact that Samiha hadn't been home mean that she, too, had hidden away in embarrassment and that she wanted to forget all this?

On the way back to Istanbul the next day, on a bus that swayed in the night like an old spaceship, Mevlut slept deeply. He woke up when it stopped at the Mountain View way station again, sat at the same table where he'd had a cup of tea with Rayiha on their way to the village, and realized now how much he loved her. To spend a single day on his own was enough to understand that in just fifty days his love for Rayiha had already transcended anything he'd seen in the movies or heard of in fairy tales.

Samiha. We're all so pleased that Rayiha has found a husband who loves her and is as cute as a little boy. I've come to Istanbul for the wedding with my father and Rayiha. It's our second visit, and of course we're staying with Vediha again. My sisters and I had a great time with all the other women at the henna ceremony the day before the wedding, and we laughed to the point of tears: Rayiha did an impression of my father telling people off, while Vediha pretended to be Korkut losing his temper in traffic and swearing at everyone around him. I imitated the suitors who came calling for me at home but didn't know what to do with themselves, let alone where to put the box of sweets and the bottle of cologne they'd bought from Affan's Haberdashers across the street from the Eşrefoğlu Mosque in Beyşehir. I was on the spot now that it was my turn to get married, after Rayiha. I didn't like my father standing guard over me, or all the curious eyes watching us whenever someone opened the door to the henna party. I didn't mind seeing my suitors' soulful glances from afar, as if they've already fallen hopelessly in love (or even the way some would stroke their mustaches while they stared), only to turn away pretending they hadn't been looking at all. But there were also those who thought it would be simpler to impress my father and not bother with me, and that made me furious.

Rayiha. Sitting on a chair in that crowd of noisy women, I was wearing the pink dress Mevlut had bought me in Aksaray, which his sisters had decorated with flowers and lace; Vediha had placed a veil over my head, and a gauze you couldn't quite see through hung over my face, but through a gap in the veil, I could watch all the other girls enjoying their songs and games. The henna paste was lit up and waved over my head on a tray bearing coins and candles, and all the girls and women tried to make me feel sad, saying "Poor little Rayiha, you're leaving your childhood home to live with strangers, you're not a little girl anymore, you're a grown woman now, poor dear," but I just couldn't make myself cry. Every time Vediha and Samiha parted my veil to check whether I was weeping yet, I thought I might burst out laughing, and they would have to turn around and announce, "No, she isn't crying yet," which only encouraged the women sitting in a circle around me to resort to all sorts of provocative insinuations—"This one's certainly ready, isn't she! She's not looking back." Worrying that the more envious among them might mention my swollen belly, I thought of my mother's death and the day we buried her, trying my best to squeeze some tears out, but still I couldn't cry.

Ferhat. "Forget it!" I said when Mevlut invited me to his wedding, which got him upset, though I must admit I wouldn't mind seeing the Şahika Wedding Hall again. I've been to so many left-wing gatherings in that big basement room. Socialist political parties and left-wing clubs used to hold their annual conferences and general meetings there. They'd start off with folk songs and "The Internationale," but by the end there'd be fistfights and chairs flying, not because of any nationalists trying to break the meetings up with sticks, but because the rival pro-Soviet and pro-China factions among us could never get their fill of beating each other bloody. When Kültepe's leftists lost the turf wars of 1977, all these places were taken over by state-sponsored right-wing organizations, and we never really set foot there again.

Mevlut hadn't even told Ferhat that the Şahika Wedding Hall was run by one of the Vurals, without whom this party wouldn't be happening. Ferhat found an excuse to needle him anyway.

"You're pretty good at keeping left and right happy, aren't you," he said. "You'd make a good shopkeeper now, with all this bowing and scraping."

"I wouldn't mind being a good shopkeeper," said Mevlut, sitting with Ferhat and offering him some vodka and lemonade underneath the table, before moving on to straight vodka. "One day," he said, hugging his friend, "you and I are going to open the best shop in Turkey."

The moment Mevlut told the marriage officiant "I do," he felt he could put his life in Rayiha's hands and trust in her intelligence. During the reception, he gladly went along with whatever his wife was doing—as he would do throughout their married life—knowing that life would be easier that way and that the child within his soul (not to be confused with the one inside Rayiha's womb) would always be happy. So it was that half an hour later, after having greeted everyone else, he went up to Hadji Hamit Vural, who had taken over a table like a politician surrounded by his bodyguards, to kiss the great man's hand, and then the hands of the men he'd brought with him (all eight of them).

As he sat with Rayiha on two shiny red velvet chairs reserved for the bride and groom and set right in the middle of the wedding hall, Mevlut looked around at the tables for the men (which took up more than half the room) and saw many familiar faces: most were former yogurt sellers of his father's generation, their hunched backs long broken under the weight of the loads they'd carried for years. Ever since the decline of the yogurt business, the poorest and least successful among them had started working various jobs by day while selling boza at night, as Mevlut did. Some had built illegal homes on the outskirts of the city (these dwellings occasionally collapsed and had to be rebuilt from scratch), and as the value of their land had risen, they'd been able to relax at last and retire, or even go back to the village. Some had a place there with a distant view of Lake Beyşehir as well as their house in one of Istanbul's poorer neighborhoods. Those men sat puffing on their Marlboros. But those who'd believed the newspaper ads promoting the Workers' Bank's deposit schemes, and the things they'd learned in primary school, had banked every cent of their earnings over the years, only to see their savings turn to dust in the latest surge of inflation. Those who'd tried to avoid this fate by giving their money to the new self-styled bankers had also lost everything. So now their sons worked as street vendors, too, just like Mevlut, who understood as well as anyone there how men who had withered away selling goods on the street for a quarter century could still have nothing to show for it, like his father, not even a village house with a garden. His mother was sitting with all the other street vendors' wives, tired, aging ladies who'd stayed behind in the village; Mevlut couldn't bear to look their way.

The drums and the woodwinds started playing, and Mevlut joined the other men on the dance floor. While he hopped and skipped about, his eyes followed Rayiha's purple headscarf as she greeted each and every single young woman and middle-aged lady on the women's side of the hall. That was when he spotted Mohini, who had made it back from military service just in time for the wedding. It wouldn't be long before the guests started pinning jewelry on the bride and groom, when a burst of energy surged through the sweltering wedding hall and the crowd lost any semblance of order, drunk on their plain lemonade, the noise, and the stuffy air. "I can't deal with all these fascists unless I'm looking over to where the Vurals are sitting, and drinking to their health," said Ferhat, passing his friend a glass of vodka and lemonade under the table as discreetly as possible. Mevlut thought he'd lost Rayiha for a moment, but then found her again and rushed to her side. She was coming out of the toilets flanked by two girls in headscarves the same color as hers.

"Mevlut, I can see how happy Rayiha is and I'm so glad for the both of you . . . ," said one of the girls. "I'm sorry I never got the chance to say congratulations in the village."

"Didn't you recognize her? That was my little sister, Samiha," said Rayiha once they'd sat back down on their red velvet chairs. "She's really the one with the beautiful eyes. She's so happy here in Istanbul. There are so many suitors that my father and Vediha don't know what to do with all the love letters she's getting."

Süleyman. At first I thought Mevlut had skillfully kept his emotions in check. But then I realized—no, he hadn't even recognized Samiha, the beautiful girl he'd written all those letters to.

Mohini. Mevlut and Rayiha asked me to make a list of the presents they were given and to be a sort of emcee during the gift-giving ceremony. Every time I picked up the microphone and announced a new gift—"The venerable Mr. Vural, businessman and construction magnate from Rize, generous philanthropist and founder of the Duttepe Mosque, presents the groom with a Swiss wristwatch, made in China!"—there would be a ripple of applause, setting off lots of gossip and giggling, and the misers who thought they could get away with a small gift saw they were about to be humiliated in front of everyone and quickly whipped out a bigger banknote.

Süleyman. I couldn't believe my eyes when I saw Ferhat in the crowd. Five years ago, this scumbag and his Moscow-funded gang would have been ready to ambush my brother and his friends on a street corner somewhere; if we'd known Mevlut was going to find some excuse to have him at the wedding—"He's my friend, he's mellowed now!"—you can bet we wouldn't have taken the trouble to deliver his letters, sort out his marriage, and even arrange his wedding reception . . .

But Comrade Ferhat looks rather disheartened. He was once the kind of guy who thought he knew everything, he'd stare you down spinning his prayer beads around like a key chain and acting like some Communist thug right out of prison, but those days are gone. Since the coup two years ago most of his comrades have been rotting away in jail or else tortured to the point that they've come out maimed. The smart ones ran off to Europe to avoid the torture. But since our comrade Ferhat can't speak any other language but Kurdish, he has toned down his politics and stayed put, figuring that he wouldn't get very far with the human rights crowd over there anyway. It's just like my brother says: a clever Communist will forget about ideology as soon as he's married and focus on making money; but a stupid Communist, like Ferhat, unable to make a living because of his ridiculous ideas, will make it his business to find paupers like Mevlut to "advise."

Then there are those types the rest of us guys naturally disapprove of: like the rich guy who falls for a pretty girl and visits her family's mansion to ask for her hand, but when he goes in and sees that she has a prettier and even younger sister, he turns to her father right then and there and tells him that actually he doesn't want the girl he came for but the little one playing hopscotch in the corner. That guy, we can all agree, is a true scumbag; but at least we can understand where he's coming from. How do you even explain someone like Mevlut, who wrote a girl weepy love letters for years and then said nothing when he saw that he'd run away in the dead of night not with the pretty girl he'd fallen for but with her sister?

Rayiha's pure, childlike joy magnified Mevlut's happiness. She seemed genuinely delighted when people pinned banknotes on her, showing none of the feigned amazement Mevlut had seen on other brides. Mohini was trying to amuse the crowd with his gift-by-gift commentary, remarking on the amounts of cash or gold and jewelry being given by various guests ("Fifty American dollars from the youngest of all yogurt-selling grandpas!"), and as at every wedding, the guests were applauding in a spirit halfway between irony and politeness.

While everyone was busy looking elsewhere, Mevlut secretly studied Rayiha. Her hands, her arms, and her ears all seemed beautiful to him, but so did her nose, her mouth, and her face. Rayiha's only flaw right now was that she looked exhausted, but she still showed a friendly warmth that really suited her. She hadn't found anyone to look after her plastic bag stuffed full of gifts, envelopes, and packages, so she'd leaned it against her chair. Her delicate little hand was resting on her lap. Mevlut remembered how he'd held it when they were running away together, and the first time he'd had a good look at it, in the train station in Akşehir. The day they'd run away together already felt like the distant past. In the last three months, they'd had so much sex, grown so close, and talked and laughed so much that Mevlut was amazed to realize there was no one he knew better than he knew Rayiha, and the men showing off their dance moves to the young women in the hall seemed to him like children who knew nothing about life. Mevlut felt he'd known Rayiha for years and slowly began to believe that his letters had been meant for someone like her—perhaps even for Rayiha herself.

4

Rice with Chickpeas

Food Tastes Better When It's Got Some Dirt in It

WHEN THEY GOT HOME, Mevlut and Rayiha were not surprised to find that many of the envelopes people had made such a show of giving them were empty. Trusting neither the banks nor the bankers, Mevlut took most of the money they'd received and bought Rayiha some gold bangles. He also bought a secondhand black-and-white television in Dolapdere, so Rayiha wouldn't get bored while she waited for him at home in the evenings. Sometimes they would hold hands as they watched TV together. Mevlut had started coming home early on Saturday evenings when *Little House on the Prairie* was on and on Sundays when it was time for *Dallas,* as there would be no one left out on the streets to buy his ice cream anyway.

When Hızır came back from the village at the start of October and took back his ice-cream cart, Mevlut was unemployed for a while. Ferhat had gone quiet after the wedding. Even if they happened to run into each other in a Tarlabaşı coffeehouse, they no longer had the conversations they had back in the day, when Ferhat used to tell him about a new business opportunity no one else had thought about, which would make the two of them "lots of money." Mevlut went to the Beyoğlu restaurants where he'd worked in the past and spoke to the headwaiters and restaurant managers who spent their afternoons doing the books, or reading the newspaper and betting on football, but no one could offer him a job with the kind of salary he expected.

There were some new upscale restaurants opening in the city, but those places were looking for people with some form of "hospitality training" who spoke enough English to understand "yes" from "no"—not someone like Mevlut who'd come from the village ready to take any job that came his way and had learned as he went along. In November, he started working in a restaurant somewhere, but after a couple of weeks he'd already given his notice. Some self-important guy wearing a tie had complained that his spicy tomato salad wasn't spicy enough, and Mevlut had snapped at him before remorsefully casting off his uniform. But it wasn't a case of some sad and weary soul acting impulsively: these were the happiest days of his life. He was going to be a father soon, and he was planning to use all the wedding jewelry on a chickpea-rice business that would guarantee his son a future.

A waiter introduced Mevlut to a street vendor from Muş who'd sold rice with chickpeas for years but had recently suffered a stroke. The indisposed street vendor wanted to sell his cart and "his" spot behind the Kabataş pier for car ferries. Mevlut knew from experience that most street vendors hoping to sell their businesses tended to exaggerate their claims to certain spots. Whenever one of them managed to bribe and cajole the neighborhood constable into letting him park his cart somewhere for a few days, he'd forget that the corner wasn't truly his property but belonged to the nation. Even so, after years spent walking the streets with a stick across his back, Mevlut had high hopes and began to entertain dreams of having his own place in Istanbul, like a real shop owner. He knew he was overpaying a little, but he couldn't bring himself to haggle too much with the elderly half-paralyzed street vendor from Muş. Mevlut and Rayiha went to see the man and his stammering son in a poor neighborhood behind Ortaköy, in the rented apartment that they shared with cockroaches, mice, and a pressure cooker, and after two visits, they'd learned the trade. Mevlut went back again one day to collect the cart and push it all the way home. He bought a sack each of rice and chickpeas from a wholesaler in Sirkeci and stacked them between the kitchen and the television.

Rayiha. Just before going to bed, I would give the chickpeas a good soak and set the alarm for three in the morning, so I could get up and see that they'd softened properly before putting them in a pot on low heat. After I took the pot off the stove, Mevlut and I would embrace and go back to sleep with the comforting gurgle of the pot cooling in the background. In the morning, I would fry the rice a little in oil, just the way the man from Muş had taught us, and then leave it to simmer in water for a while. While Mevlut was out buying groceries, I would boil and then panfry the chicken. I'd set some of it aside, removing the bones and skin with my fingers, adding as much thyme and pepper as I liked, perhaps one or two cloves of garlic if I felt so inclined, and I would split the rest of the chicken into four pieces, placing them beside the rice.

Mevlut would come back home from his morning shopping with carrier nets full of fruit or tomatoes, breathe in the delicious smell of Rayiha's cooking, and stroke his wife's arm, her back, and her growing belly. Rayiha's chicken satisfied all of Mevlut's customers—the clerks who wore a shirt and tie or a skirt to their desk jobs at the banks and offices in Fındıklı, the rowdy students from the neighborhood's schools and universities, the builders who worked at the construction sites nearby, and the drivers and passengers killing time as they waited for the ferry. He soon had his regulars—the big, friendly security guard at the local branch of Akbank, who was built like a barrel and always wore sunglasses; Mr. Nedim, who sold ferry tickets in a white uniform from his booth on the pier; the men and women who worked for the insurance company close by, who always seemed to be mocking Mevlut with their smiles—and Mevlut always found some topic of conversation with any customer, perhaps the penalty Fenerbahçe had been denied in their last match or the blind girl who knew all the answers yesterday on the TV quiz show. He won the municipal police over with his charm and lots of free plates piled high with chicken.

As an experienced street vendor who knew that chatting people up was part of the job, Mevlut never discussed politics. Just as in the days when he sold yogurt and boza, it wasn't really the money that he cared about; what made him happy was seeing a customer come back again a few days later (which was rare) just because he'd enjoyed the rice and chicken, and be kind enough to tell him so (which was even rarer).

Most of Mevlut's customers made it plain that the main attraction of his food was that it was cheap and close at hand, and some of them even said so outright. Occasionally, though, customers were kind enough to tell him, "Congratulations, rice vendor, your food's delicious," and this made Mevlut so happy that he would temporarily forget the harsh truth he kept trying to hide from himself as much as from Rayiha: he wasn't clearing much at all from this rice business. If the street vendor from Muş had spent eight years in the same spot only to die in sickness and destitution, perhaps it hadn't been his own fault after all.

Rayiha. Most days, Mevlut would bring back half the chickpeas, chicken thighs, and rice I'd cooked in the morning. These leftover drumsticks, small chicken halves, and bits of skin would have lost their shine by then, the fat around them would be discolored, but I would add them all to the pot again for the next day's batch. I'd also put any leftover rice to simmer some more. It tasted even better after it had been cooked over a gentle flame for a second time. Mevlut wouldn't say we were using leftovers; instead, he would call it seasoning, the way jail-block bosses and rich inmates would take the awful food served in prison and have it cooked again using their secret stash of good olive oil, spices, and pepper. He'd heard about this from a wealthy Kurd from Cizre who'd been in jail and now ran a parking lot. Mevlut would watch me cooking in the kitchen and take great pleasure in reminding me that food always tastes better when it's got some dirt in it—a truth commonly acknowledged by anyone in Istanbul who makes a habit of consuming street food. I didn't like this, and I would tell him there's nothing "dirty" about food that's been cooked again because it didn't get eaten the first time around. But then he told me that those bits of skin that had been in and out of the pan a few times, and the chickpeas that had been boiled so many times that they'd softened into mush, were usually his customers' favorites, and rather than go for the fresher, cleaner chunks of meat, they would pick out giblets that had been cooked a few times over, smothering them in mustard and ketchup before wolfing them down.

In October, Mevlut started selling boza again in the evenings. He'd walk for kilometers every night with all kinds of beautiful images and strange thoughts crossing his mind. During these walks, he discovered that the shadows of the trees in some neighborhoods moved even when there was no breeze at all, stray dogs got braver and cockier where streetlamps were broken or switched off, and the flyers for circumcision ceremonies and cram schools pasted on utility poles and in doorways were all written in rhyming couplets. Hearing the things the city told him at night and reading the language of the streets filled Mevlut with pride. But when he went back to his rice cart in the morning and stood in the cold with his hands in his pockets, the power of his imagination waned, he sensed that the world was hollow and meaningless, and he felt the urge to return to Rayiha as quickly as possible, afraid of the overwhelming loneliness growing inside him. What if she went into early labor while she was at home alone? Yet he would tell himself, Just a little longer, and start walking in restless circles around the big wheels and glass box of his rice cart or just shift his weight from his right foot to his left, glancing at his Swiss watch as he waited.

Rayiha. "He gave you that watch because it was in his interest to do so," I would say whenever I noticed Mevlut looking at Hadji Hamit's gift. "He did it so you'd feel like you owe him, not just you but your uncle and your cousins, too." When Mevlut came back in the afternoon, I'd make him some herbal tea with leaves I picked from the tree in the courtyard of the Armenian church. He would check on the boza I'd already prepared for the evening, switch on the TV to the only program they were showing, a high-school geometry lesson, as he drank his sugary herbal tea, and then sleep through his own coughing fits until it was time for dinner. He spent seven years selling cooked rice, and during that time, I was always the one who prepared the chickpeas and the rice, who bought, boiled, and fried the chicken; I also added the sugar to the boza so it was ready for his evening rounds; and I spent my days washing all the dirty tools, spoons, jugs, and plates that needed washing. When I was pregnant, I also listened closely to the baby in my womb, taking care not to throw up in the rice from the stink of panfried chicken, and treasured the little corner with a cot and pillows for the baby. Mevlut had found a book called *Islamic Names for Your Child* in a junk shop. He would flip through the pages before dinner and read out some names for my consideration during the TV commercials—Nurullah, Abdullah, Sadullah, Fazlallah—and because I didn't want to break his heart, I kept putting off telling him that our baby was a girl.

Vediha, Samiha, and I found out when we went to the Etfal Hospital in Şişli. I left the hospital fretting. "Who cares, for God's sake!" Samiha said. "There are enough men roaming the streets of Istanbul already."

5

Mevlut Becomes a Father

Do Not Get Out of the Van

Samiha. My father and I came to Istanbul for the wedding and ended up staying. Every morning when I wake up in that room in Vediha's place, I look at the shadows of the water pitcher and the bottle of cologne on the table, and I get lost in thought: I had so many suitors in the village that my father thought I'd find an even better match in Istanbul . . . But I have yet to meet anyone here other than Süleyman . . . I don't know what he and Korkut have promised my father. I do know they're the ones who paid for his dentures. He puts them in a glass before he goes to sleep; when I'm in bed waiting for him to wake up, I always feel like taking those false teeth and throwing them out the window. I help Vediha with the housework all morning and do some knitting for the winter, and we watch TV together when the programs start in the afternoon. My father plays with Bozkurt and Turan in the mornings, but they like to pull on his beard and his hair, and he ends up arguing with his grandchildren. Once, my father and I went down to the Bosphorus with Vediha and Süleyman; another time we went to the cinema in Beyoğlu and for some milk pudding afterward.

Süleyman came up to me this morning, spinning his car keys on his finger like a string of prayer beads; he said he needed to cross the Bosphorus around noon to pick up six bags of cement and some steel from Üsküdar, he was going to drive over the Bosphorus Bridge, and I could go with him if I wanted. I asked my sister Vediha. "It's up to you," she said. "But for God's sake be careful!" What did she mean? When we went to the Palace Cinema that time, my father and Vediha had no objections to Süleyman sitting right next to me, so when I felt his hand creeping up like a cautious crab to touch the side of my leg halfway through the movie, I tried to figure out whether it was on purpose or just a coincidence, but I couldn't decide . . . Süleyman was being perfectly polite and considerate as we crossed the Bosphorus Bridge under the midday sun on this bright, freezing cold winter's day. He said, "Samiha, would you like me to switch to the right lane so you can have a better view?" and took the Ford van so close to the edge of the bridge that for a moment, I felt we might fall onto the Russian ship with the red chimney passing by down below.

We crossed the Bosphorus Bridge and drove along this horrible, potholed road on the outskirts of Üsküdar, and that was the end of all the prettiness and the wonderful tourist spots: there were cement factories surrounded by barbed wire; workshops with smashed windows; derelict houses worse than anything we have back in the village; and thousands of rusty metal barrels, so many that I wondered whether they'd rained down from the sky.

We stopped in a flat stretch covered with ramshackle houses. If you ask me, it looked a lot like Duttepe (poor, in other words), only newer and uglier. "This is a branch of Aktaş Construction, we set it up with the Vurals," said Süleyman as he got out of the car, and just as he was about to walk into an ugly building, he turned around and warned me menacingly: "Do not get out of the van!" Naturally, this made me really want to get out of the van. But there wasn't a single woman around, so I stayed where I was, waiting in the front passenger seat.

By the time we got through the traffic on the way back, there wasn't time for lunch, and Süleyman couldn't drop me home either. When we got to the start of Duttepe, he spotted some friends of his and abruptly stopped the car. "Well, we're in the neighborhood now, you shouldn't have too much trouble getting up the hill," he said. "Here, take this and buy my mother some bread on the way!"

I bought the bread and slowly made my way up to the Aktaş house, which was shaping up to be a real house made of concrete, and I started to think about how people say that the trouble with two strangers getting married isn't necessarily that the woman has to marry someone she doesn't know but that she has to learn to love someone she doesn't know . . . But I think it must be easier for a girl to marry someone she doesn't know, because the more you get to know men, the harder it is to love them.

Rayiha. The unnamed baby girl in my belly had grown so big that I was having trouble sitting down. Mevlut was reading names out of his book one evening—"Hamdullah is one who gives thanks to Allah; Uybedullah is Allah's servant; Seyfullah is the sword, the soldier of Allah"—when I decided to interrupt him: "Darling, isn't there anything in that book about girls' names?" He said, "Oh, look, there is, who would have thought?" like a man who finds out one day that his favorite diner has a "family room" on the second floor reserved for women. That man might peep through a crack in the door for a quick, bashful look at the women's section, and in a similar way, Mevlut took a halfhearted glance at the back pages before returning to the boys' names. Luckily, Vediha went and got me two more books from a nice shop in Şişli that sold toys as well. One of the two books had mostly nationalistic names from Central Asia, like Kurtcebe, Alparslan, or Atabeg, while the girls' names lived in separate pages from the boys', just as men and women lived separately in Ottoman palaces. In the *Handbook of Modern Baby Names,* however, the boys and girls sat in mixed groups, as they do in private high schools or at the wedding receptions of rich and Westernized families, but Mevlut laughed at the girls' names—Simge, Suzan, Mine, Irem—and only took the boys' names seriously: Tolga, Hakan, Kılıç.

In spite of all this, I wouldn't want you to think that Mevlut regarded the birth of our daughter Fatma in April as some sort of tragedy, or that he was mean to me because I hadn't been able to give him a son. It was, in fact, the very opposite. Mevlut was so happy to be a father that he kept telling everyone he'd wanted a girl all along, and he really believed it. There was a photographer called Şakir on our street who would take photos of people getting drunk on *rakı* and wine in the bars of Beyoğlu, which he developed in the darkroom in his old-fashioned studio; Mevlut brought him over to our house one day to take a picture of him holding the baby in his arms, looking like a giant as he grinned from ear to ear. Mevlut stuck the photo on his cart and gave out some free rice, telling his customers, "I've had a baby girl." As soon as he came home in the evenings, he would sit Fatma on his lap, bring her left hand right up to his eyes, examine her perfectly formed hands up close like a watchmaker in his shop, and say, "Look, she's got fingernails, too," and then he would compare his fingers and mine with the baby's and kiss us both with tears in his eyes, full of wonder at this miracle of God.

Mevlut was very happy, but there was also a strangeness in his soul of which Rayiha knew nothing. "God bless your beautiful baby!" his customers would say when they saw the photos on his cart (where they got soggy from the steam rising from the rice), and sometimes he wouldn't tell them that the baby was a girl. It took him a long time to admit to himself that the true cause of his unhappiness was that he was jealous of the baby. At first he thought he was getting annoyed about being woken up several times in the middle of the night when Rayiha had to breast-feed Fatma. There was also the problem of the mosquitoes that kept getting under the baby's mosquito net and sucking her blood, a subject of quarrels all summer. Eventually, though, Mevlut noticed that a strange feeling seized him whenever he saw Rayiha cooing to the baby and offering it one of her enormous breasts: it troubled him to see Rayiha looking at the child with the kind of love and adoration he felt should be for him alone. He couldn't tell her, though, and began to resent her, too. Rayiha and the baby had become one, and Mevlut had been made to feel insignificant.

At home, he needed his wife to tell him how important he was all the time. But since Fatma had been born, Rayiha had stopped telling him, "You've done really well today, Mevlut; how clever of you to think of using the leftover fruit syrup to sweeten the boza, Mevlut; all the clerks in the government offices love you, Mevlut!" During Ramadan, no one sold food out on the streets, so Mevlut was at home during the day. He would have liked to have sex with Rayiha all morning to take his mind off his jealousy, but she didn't like doing "those things" in front of the baby. "Last summer you were scared that God would see us, now you're scared that the baby will see us!" Mevlut yelled at her one day. "Now get up and stir the ice cream." Mevlut would delight in watching Rayiha, intoxicated with the joys of maternal and marital love, climb out of bed obediently and stir the ice cream using both hands to grip the long spoon handle, the veins in her graceful neck becoming more defined under the strain, and while he looked at her he would occasionally rock the baby's crib by the bed.

Samiha. It's been a while since we came to Istanbul. We're still at my sister's place in Duttepe, where I can hardly sleep because my father snores so much. Süleyman got me a woven golden bangle. I accepted the gift. My sister is saying there'll be talk if we don't go ahead with the engagement ceremony soon.

Rayiha. Mevlut seemed so jealous of me breast-feeding Fatma that first I got really upset, and then I stopped getting any milk. In November, I got pregnant again because I'd stopped breast-feeding Fatma. What will I do now? I cannot tell Mevlut about the new baby until I'm sure it's a boy. But what if it isn't? I couldn't stand being home on my own; I thought I might go over to Vediha's, and that way I'd see Samiha, too. At the Taksim post office, I found out what had happened and hurried back home in fear.

6

Samiha Runs Away

Blood Will Be Shed over This

Vediha. Samiha showed up at our bedroom door one afternoon wearing her headscarf and carrying her bag. She was shaking like a leaf. "What's going on?" I said.

"I'm in love with someone else, I'm running away with him, the taxi's already here."

"What? Are you crazy? Don't do this!"

She started crying but wouldn't relent.

"Who is it? Where did you find this guy? Look, Süleyman is in love with you, don't put Father and me in this situation," I said. "Who elopes in a taxi anyway?"

My little sister, blinded by her love, was so worked up that she couldn't even speak. She took me by the hand and led me to the room where she and Father were staying. She'd placed Süleyman's gifts in a neat pile on the table—the bangle and the two headscarves, one of them decorated with purple flowers and the other with pictures of gazelles. She gestured toward them as if she'd been struck dumb.

"Samiha, Father will have a fit when he gets home," I said. "You know he's accepted gifts from Süleyman and taken money for the false teeth and a whole load of other things. Do you really want to put our dear father through this?" She looked at her feet and kept quiet. "Father and I would have to live with the shame for the rest of our lives," I said.

"Rayiha ran away, too, but it was all right in the end."

"Rayiha didn't have any other suitors, and she hadn't been promised to anyone," I said. "But you're not like Rayiha, you're beautiful. And Father hadn't taken anyone's money in exchange for Rayiha's hand. Blood will be shed over this."

"I wasn't aware I was promised to anyone," she said. "Why would my father do that, why would he take people's money without asking me first?"

We heard the taxi honking from the street. Samiha was moving toward the door. "If you run away, Korkut is going to beat me for weeks, you know that, don't you, Samiha? He'll cover my arms and legs in bruises, you know that, right?" I said.

Samiha. We hugged each other, and started crying . . . I felt so sorry for my sister, and I was so afraid . . .

Vediha. "Go back to the village first!" I said. "Then you can elope! If you do it now, they'll blame it all on me; they'll think I arranged it. You know they'll kill me, Samiha. Who is this man anyway?"

Samiha. My sister was right. I said, "Let me just send the taxi away." But somehow I picked my bag up on my way out anyway. I was walking through the garden and toward the gate when Vediha, who was watching from the window, saw the bag in my hand and started pleading, "Don't go, Samiha, don't go, my darling sister!" When I walked through the gate and reached the taxi, I didn't know what to say or do. I was just thinking of telling them, "I've changed my mind, my sister's crying," when the taxi door opened and they pulled me inside. I didn't even get the chance to turn around and look at my dear sister one last time.

Vediha. They forced Samiha into the car. I saw it all from the window. Help! I screamed. Hurry up, or they're going to blame me! Those villains are abducting my sister, help!

Süleyman. I woke up from my afternoon nap and saw a car waiting at the back door . . . Bozkurt and Turan were playing in the garden . . . I heard Vediha screaming outside.

Vediha. How far could I possibly run in slippers . . . Stop the taxi, I yelled. Samiha, get out of that car!

Süleyman. I ran after them, but I couldn't catch them! I was so enraged I could have exploded. I went back, jumped into my van, and sped off. By the time I'd passed our shop and reached the bottom of the hill, the black car had already rounded the corner toward Mecidiyeköy. But this is not over yet. Samiha is a virtuous girl, she'll jump out of that taxi any moment now. She's not gone, they haven't taken her yet. She'll come back. Don't think there's anything going on here. Don't write about this, do not BLOW THIS OUT OF ALL PROPORTION by writing about it. Don't ruin a good girl's reputation. I could see the black car farther ahead, but I couldn't catch it. I leaned over to the glove compartment, took out the Kırıkkale gun, and fired two shots into the air. But don't write that down either, because it's not true that she's eloping. People will misunderstand!

Samiha. Actually, they've understood perfectly well. I eloped. I eloped out of my own free will. Everything you've heard is true. I can't believe it either. I'm in love! Love made me do this, and I felt better when I heard the gunshots. Maybe because it meant there was no turning back now? We fired a couple of shots into the sky ourselves, just to make it clear that we weren't unarmed, but once we got to Mecidiyeköy, the guns were put away. It turns out Süleyman was at home at that time of day, and now he's chasing after us in his van, and it's scary, but I know he can't find us in this traffic. I'm so happy now. You saw for yourselves: no one can buy me . . . I've been so furious at them all!

Süleyman. I accelerated as soon as the traffic cleared up. But then—damn it!—a truck came out of nowhere, I swerved to the right, and, well, it was inevitable: I crashed into a wall! I'm feeling a little woozy now. Where am I? Better keep still, try to figure out what's going on. Seems I've hit my head on something. Oh, that's right! Samiha has run away. A bunch of nosy kids were already coming toward the van, enjoying the scene . . . I'd hit my head on the rearview mirror, and my forehead was bleeding, but I reversed the van and then sped off again after them.

Vediha. The children heard the gunshots and rushed joyfully out into the garden as if someone had set off firecrackers. Bozkurt, Turan, I yelled after them, go back inside and shut the door. They didn't listen, so I smacked one and dragged the other inside by the arm. I thought I should call the police. But it was Süleyman who'd fired the shots; would it be wise to call? "What are you doing standing there, you idiots, call your father!" I said. I'd told them not to touch the phone without my permission; otherwise they would have played with it all the time. Bozkurt rang the number and told Korkut, "Dad, Aunt Samiha's run away!"

I started crying, though part of me felt Samiha had done the right thing—just don't tell anyone I said that. It's true, poor Süleyman is hopelessly in love with her. But he is not the smartest guy in the world, or the handsomest. He's already a little overweight. He has these long eyelashes, some girls might love them, but Samiha always found them stupid and girlish. The main problem, though, is that despite being in love with her, Süleyman kept doing all kinds of things he knew would get on Samiha's nerves. Why are men mean to the women they fall in love with? Samiha can't stand the way he struts around, trying to be macho, and he's such a show-off, he thinks everyone wants his advice just because he happens to have some money in his pocket. I say to my little sister good for you, not giving yourself to a man you can't love, but then I wonder if this other guy she's run off with can be trusted.

After all, taking a girl away in a taxi in the middle of the city in broad daylight isn't the brightest idea. We're in Istanbul, not the village; did he really have to come honking at the door like that?

Samiha. Everything I see on our drive through Istanbul just amazes me: the crowds, the people dodging buses as they run to the other side of the road, the girls in skirts, the horse-drawn carts, the parks, the big old apartment buildings; I love it all. Süleyman knew how much I liked driving around the city in his van (he knew because I kept asking him to take me), but he rarely took me, and do you know why? (In fact, I've given it a lot of thought.) Because although he wanted to be close to me, he couldn't respect a girl who got too friendly with a boy before she was married to him. But I'm the kind of girl who only marries the man she loves—is that clear? I didn't think about money, I only followed my heart, and now I'm ready to face the consequences of what I've done.

Süleyman. Before I'd even reached Mecidiyeköy, they'd already passed Şişli. I went back home and parked the van, trying to keep calm. I'd never thought anyone would dare to take my betrothed away in broad daylight, right in the heart of Istanbul, so I still couldn't believe what I'd seen. No one would ever do something this crazy; everyone knows it's the kind of thing that people get killed for.

Samiha. Duttepe is neither "the heart of Istanbul" nor, as you know, did I promise Süleyman anything. It's true that someone might end up getting killed, but that's exactly why we're running so far away, and besides, everyone has to die someday. Istanbul never ends. Now that the coast is clear, we've stopped in a café to enjoy the salty yogurt drink *ayran* from carton bottles. My darling's mustache is all white from it. I'll never tell you his name, and you will never find us, so don't even bother asking.

Süleyman. When I got home, Vediha cleaned the wound on my forehead with a cotton ball. I went out to the garden and fired two shots at the mulberry tree with the Kırıkkale. The strange silence began soon after that. I couldn't stop thinking that Samiha would surely come back home as if nothing had happened. That evening, everyone was in the house. Someone had switched the TV off as if we'd had a death in the family, and I realized that what really pained me was the silence. My brother kept smoking. Crooked-Necked Abdurrahman was drunk; Vediha was crying. I went out into the garden at midnight, and as I looked down from Duttepe to the city lights spread out below, I swore to God that I would avenge what had happened. Samiha is standing at a window somewhere among the millions of lights down there. Knowing that she doesn't love me hurts so much that I'd rather think she was taken against her will, which in turn makes me think of how I want to kill those bastards. Our ancestors used to torture criminals before they executed them—it's in times like these that one truly understands the importance of tradition.

Abdurrahman Efendi. What is it like to be a father whose daughters keep running away? I'm a little embarrassed, but I'm also proud that my daughters don't settle for the husbands someone else picks out for them but bravely go with the men they choose for themselves. Though, if they'd had a mother to confide in, they would have done the right thing, and no one would have run away . . . In a marriage, trust is more important than love, as we all know. I worry about what they'll do to poor Vediha after I go back to the village. But my eldest is smarter than she looks, and perhaps she'll find a way to avoid getting punished for this.

Süleyman. I fell in love with Samiha even more after she ran away. Before she eloped, I loved her because she was beautiful and clever and because everyone admired her. That was understandable. Now, I love her because she left me and ran away. This is even more understandable, but the pain is unbearable. I spend mornings at our shop, daydreaming about her coming back and thinking that if I were to rush home right now I would find her there and we would get married and have a huge wedding reception.

Korkut. I made a few insinuations about how hard it would be to run away with a girl unless you had someone helping you inside the house, but Vediha didn't take the bait. All she did was cry and say, "This city is huge, how was I supposed to know?" One day it was just me and Abdurrahman Efendi in the house. "Some fathers take a man's money and anything else they can get, and then when a better match shows up, they secretly sell their daughter to the richer man and then pretend the girl eloped. Please don't get me wrong, Abdurrahman Efendi, you're a respectable man, but how could Samiha not think about this when she ran away?" I asked. "I'll be the first to make her pay for this," he said. Later, he decided that he was offended by what I'd said and stopped coming home for dinner. That's when I told Vediha: "I don't know which of you helped her, but you will not leave this house until I find out where Samiha went and with whom." "It's fine, you never let me go outside the neighborhood anyway, so now I just won't even bother leaving the house," she said. "Can I at least go out in the garden?"

Süleyman. One night I put Abdurrahman Efendi in the van and drove down to the Bosphorus, telling him we needed to talk. We went to the Tarator Seafood Restaurant in Sarıyer and sat in a corner away from the fish tank. Our fried mussels hadn't arrived yet, and we were already on our second glass of *rakı,* all on an empty stomach, when I said, "Abdurrahman Efendi, you've lived much longer than I have, and I'm sure you will know the answer to my question. What does a man live for?" Abdurrahman Efendi had sensed a while ago that our conversation tonight could potentially head into dangerous territory, so he spent a long time trying to find the most harmless answer he could think of.

"For love, my son!" he said. "What else?" He thought again and said, "For friendship." "And?" "For happiness. For God and country . . ." "A man lives for his honor, Father!" I interrupted.

Abdurrahman Efendi. What I didn't say is that, actually, I live for my daughters. I tried to humor this angry young man because part of me felt he wasn't entirely wrong, but more than that, I felt sorry for him. We had so much to drink that I began to see all my forgotten memories floating around like submarines inside the distant fish tank. Toward the end of the night, I gathered up the courage to say, "Süleyman, my son, I know how hurt and angry you are, and I completely understand. We're hurt and angry, too, because Samiha's actions have put us in a very difficult position. But there's no reason to drag honor and wounded pride into this! Your dignity hasn't been compromised in any way. You weren't married or even engaged to Samiha. Yes, I wish we'd had the two of you tie the knot before you got to know each other. I'm absolutely sure you would have been happy that way. But it's not right for you to turn this into a matter of honor now. Everyone knows that all these big proclamations about honor are really just excuses invented to let people kill each other with a clear conscience. Are you going to kill my daughter?"

Süleyman bristled. "I'm sorry, Father, but shouldn't I at least have the right to go after the bastard who ran away with Samiha and punish him for what he did? That bastard humiliated me, didn't he?" "Don't take things the wrong way." "Do I or do I not have the right?" "Calm down, son." "When you come from the village and toil away for years trying to build a life for yourself in this dump of a city, and then a swindler comes along and tricks and sucks you dry, it's really very difficult to stay calm." "Believe me, son, if it was up to me I would pick Samiha up by the scruff of her neck and bring her home myself. I'm sure she knows she's made a mistake. For all we know, maybe while we've been busy drinking, she's on her way back home with her bag in hand and her tail between her legs." "Who's to say my brother and I would take her back?" "You won't take my daughter back if she returns?" "I have to think about my honor." "But what if no one's laid a finger on her . . ."

We sat there drinking until the bar closed at midnight. I'm not sure how it happened, but at some point Süleyman got up and apologized, respectfully kissing my hand while I promised him that I wouldn't tell anyone what we'd talked about. I even said, "I won't tell Samiha." Süleyman started crying. He said my frown and my gestures reminded him of Samiha. "Fathers resemble their daughters," I said with pride.

"I made a mistake, I kept showing off, I didn't try to be friends with her," said Süleyman. "But she has a sharp tongue on her. It's hard talking to girls; no one ever taught us how to do it properly. I just talked to her as I would talk to a man, only without swearing. It didn't work."

Süleyman went to wash his face before we headed home, and when he came back, he'd really sobered up. On the way home, the traffic police in İstinye pulled us over to search the car, and we had to give them a hefty bribe to let us go.

7

A Second Daughter

It Was as If His Life Were Happening to Someone Else

MEVLUT REMAINED a stranger to these events until much later. He hadn't lost any of his early enthusiasm for his work: he was as optimistic as "the entrepreneur who believes in the idea," beloved hero of books like *How to Be a Successful Businessman.* He was convinced that he could still make more money, if only he installed some brighter lighting inside the glass case of his three-wheeled cart, made deals with the *ayran,* tea, and Coke vendors that kept popping up and disappearing all around him, and tried harder to have truly heartfelt and sincere conversations with his customers. Mevlut did everything he could think of to build a regular clientele in the Kabataş-Fındıklı area. He didn't mind so much when the corporate clerks who had their lunch standing up at his cart ignored his efforts, but he was furious when the smaller businesses he worked with asked him for receipts. He used his network of doormen, janitors, security guards, and tea servers who worked inside company buildings to try to build a rapport with accountants and managers. One night, Rayiha told him that she was pregnant again and that it was going to be another girl.

"How do you know it's a girl? Did the three of you go to the hospital again?"

"Not all three of us, Samiha wasn't there. She eloped with someone else so she wouldn't have to marry Süleyman."

"What?"

Rayiha told him what she knew.

That night, Mevlut was roaming around Feriköy like a sleepwalker, crying "Bozaaa," when his feet led him to a cemetery. The moon was out; the cypress trees and the gravestones alternated between a silver gleam and a thick blackness. Mevlut took a paved road through the middle of the cemetery, feeling as if he'd picked a path in a dream. But the person walking in the cemetery wasn't him, and it was as if his life, too, were happening to someone else.

The farther he walked, the farther downhill the cemetery went, unfurling like a carpet, and Mevlut found himself on an ever-steepening slope. Who was the man Samiha had run away with? Was she going to turn to him one day and tell him, "Mevlut wrote me love letters about my eyes for years, and then he married my sister"? Did Samiha even know about all that?

Rayiha. "Last time you went through all the boys' names, and we ended up having a girl," I told Mevlut as I gave him the handbook of Islamic names. "Maybe if you try reading all the girls' names, we'll have a boy this time. You can check whether any of the girls' names have 'Allah' in them!" "A girl's name can't have 'Allah' in it!" said Mevlut. According to the Koran, the most that girls could hope for was to be named for one of the Prophet Muhammad's wives. "Maybe if we keep eating rice every day, we'll turn Chinese," I teased. Mevlut laughed with me, picked up the baby, and covered her face with kisses. He didn't even notice that his prickly mustache was making Fatma cry until I told him so.

Abdurrahman Efendi. My daughters' late mother was called Fevziye. I suggested the name for their second daughter. You'll be surprised to hear that even though all three of her daughters are in Istanbul now, and two of them rebelled and ran away from home, Fevziye, may she rest in peace, did not have a very adventurous life: she got married to me, the first man who asked for her hand, at the age of fifteen and lived peacefully to the age of twenty-three, without ever setting foot outside

Gümüşdere village. I am on my way back there now, having accepted the painful truth that I've failed yet again to make it in Istanbul, and as I sit on this bus, looking mournfully out the window, I keep thinking how I wish I'd been like Fevziye and never left the village at all.

Vediha. My husband barely talks to me, he never comes home, and he sneers at everything I say. Korkut's and Süleyman's silences and all their subtle insinuations wore my father down until the poor man packed his bags and went back to the village. I cried a lot, secretly. In the space of just a month, my father and Samiha's room has emptied completely. I go in there sometimes to look at my father's bed on one side and Samiha's on the other, and I weep, completely mortified about what happened. Every time I look outside the window, I try to picture where Samiha went and whom she might be with. Good for you, Samiha, I'm glad you ran away.

Süleyman. It's been fifty-one days since Samiha ran away; and still there is no news. The whole time, I've been drinking *rakı* nonstop. Never at the dinner table, though, as I don't want my brother getting angry; I either drink quietly in my room, as if taking a dose of medicine, or out in Beyoğlu. Sometimes I drive around in the van just to get my mind off things.

I go to the market on Thursdays when we need to stock up on nails, paint, or plaster for the shop, and once the van gets sucked into the bustle of shopkeepers and enters that sea of human activity, it can take hours to get out. Every now and then I drive into a random street somewhere on a hill behind Üsküdar, past houses built out of hollow bricks, concrete walls, a mosque, a factory, a square; I keep going and see a bank, a restaurant, a bus stop; but no sign of Samiha. Still, the feeling that she might be around here somewhere grows inside me, and as I sit at the steering wheel, I almost feel as if I'm racing around in my own dream.

Mevlut and Rayiha's second daughter, Fevziye, was born in August 1984, comfortably and without generating any extra hospital bills. Mevlut was so happy that he wrote THE TWO GIRLS' RICE on his cart. Apart from the chaos of two babies crying in unison through the night, chronic lack of sleep, and the meddlesome Vediha, who kept coming over to help out, Mevlut had nothing to complain about.

"Let this rice project go, Mr. Bridegroom, join the family business and give Rayiha a better life," Vediha said one day.

"We're doing very well," said Mevlut. Rayiha looked at her sister as if to say, That's not true, which irked Mevlut, and once Vediha had left, he started grumbling. "Who does she think she is, intruding on our private life like that?" he said, and briefly considered forbidding Rayiha from visiting her sister's home in Duttepe, though he didn't insist, as he knew it wouldn't be right to demand such a thing.

8

Capitalism and Tradition

Mevlut's Blissful Family Life

TOWARD THE END of February 1985, as a long, cold, unpropitious workday drew to a close, Mevlut was gathering his plates and glasses to leave Kabataş and go home when Süleyman pulled up in his van. "Everyone's already brought you gifts and good-luck charms for the new baby, except for me," he said. "Come and sit in the car, let's talk for a bit. How's work? Aren't you cold out there?"

Climbing into the front seat, Mevlut was reminded of how often the doe-eyed Samiha had sat in this very same place before she'd run away and disappeared a year ago, how much time she had spent driving around Istanbul with Süleyman.

"I've been selling cooked rice for two years and in all this time I've never sat in a customer's car," he said. "It's too high up here, it's making me dizzy, I should get down."

"Sit, sit, we have so much to talk about!" said Süleyman, grabbing Mevlut's hand as it made for the door handle. He gave his childhood friend a lovelorn, disheartened look.

Mevlut saw that his cousin's eyes were telling him: "We're even now!" He pitied Süleyman, and in that moment he grasped the truth he'd been trying to ignore for two years: Süleyman had laid the trap that had tricked Mevlut into thinking that the girl with glimmering eyes was called Rayiha, not Samiha. If Süleyman had managed to marry Samiha as planned, they would have gone on pretending that no such trap had been set, and everyone would have been happy . . .

"You and your brother are doing great, Süleyman, but the rest of us just can't seem to find our way to prosperity. I hear the Vurals have already sold more than half the new apartments they're building even though the foundations aren't even finished yet."

"Yes, we're doing all right, thank God," said Süleyman. "But we also want you to do well. My brother feels the same way."

"So what's the job you're offering? Will I end up running a teahouse in the Vurals' offices?"

"Would you like to do that?"

"There's a customer coming," said Mevlut, getting out of the vehicle. There was no customer, but he turned his back on Süleyman's van and busied himself with a portion anyway. He scooped some rice onto a plate, flattening the mound with the back of a spoon. He turned off the butane stove in the three-wheeled cart and was pleased to notice that Süleyman had followed him out of the van.

"Look, if you don't want to talk, that's fine, but let me give the baby her gift," said Süleyman. "At least I'll get to see her."

"If you don't know the way to my place, you'd better follow me," said Mevlut, and he began to push his cart.

"Why don't we load the cart into the back of my van?" said Süleyman.

"Don't underestimate this cart, it's like a restaurant on three wheels. The kitchen unit and the stove are very delicate, and they weigh a ton."

He was climbing Kazancı Hill (which typically took him twenty minutes) toward Taksim, panting behind his cart as he did on his journey home between four and five o'clock every day, when Süleyman caught up with him.

"Mevlut, let's tie it to the bumper, and I'll slowly tow you along."

He seemed sincere and friendly enough, but Mevlut kept going as if he hadn't heard. A few yards later, he pushed his restaurant on wheels to one side of the road and put the brakes on. "Go up to Taksim and wait for me at the Tarlabaşı bus stop."

Süleyman accelerated, disappearing over the hill, and Mevlut began to fret about what he would think when he saw the state of the house and realized how poor they were. In truth, he'd been enjoying Süleyman's solicitude. Somewhere in the back of his mind was the notion that he might be able to use his cousin to get closer to the Vurals and perhaps provide a better life for Rayiha and the kids.

He chained his cart to the tree in the back garden. "Where are you!" he called out to Rayiha, who was taking longer than usual to come down and help him. They met upstairs in the kitchen, his arms loaded with rice cart paraphernalia. "Süleyman's gotten the baby a gift, he's on his way now! For goodness' sake tidy up a little and make this place look decent!" said Mevlut.

"Why?" said Rayiha. "Let him see exactly how we live."

"We're all right," said Mevlut. He was smiling now, cheered by the sight of his daughters. "But we shouldn't give him any reason to talk. It stinks in here, let's get some fresh air in."

"Don't open the window. The girls will catch a cold," said Rayiha. "Should I be ashamed of the way we smell? Doesn't their house in Duttepe smell exactly like this?"

"It doesn't. They've got that huge garden, they've got electricity and running water, it's all like clockwork. But we're much happier here. Is the boza ready? At least put these dishcloths away."

"Sorry, but when you've got two babies to look after, it's a little hard to keep up with the boza, the rice, the chicken, the dishes, the laundry, and everything else that needs doing."

"Korkut and Süleyman want to offer me a job."

"What job is that?"

"We're going to be business partners. We're going to run the Vurals' company teahouse."

"I think the job is an excuse and Süleyman just thinks he can get us to tell him who Samiha ran away with. If they think you're so great, why did it take them so long to come up with this job for you?"

Süleyman. I would have rather spared Mevlut the grief of knowing I'd watched him standing there in Kabataş getting buffeted by the wind as he glumly waited for customers. I knew I wouldn't be able to find parking in Taksim, what with all the traffic, so I parked the van on a side street and watched dejectedly as Mevlut tried and mostly failed to push his rice cart up the hill.

I drove around Tarlabaşı for a bit. The general who became mayor after the coup in 1980 flew into a rage one day and kicked all the carpenters and the mechanics out of the neighborhood, driving them away to the outer edges of the city. He also shut down the bachelor dormitories, where the dishwashers who work in the restaurants of Beyoğlu used to sleep, claiming that these places were breeding grounds for germs. As a result, these streets emptied out. The Vurals came here at the time looking for places to take over on the cheap for development later on, but they gave up when they discovered that most of the buildings in the area are owned by the Greeks who were deported to Athens overnight in 1964. The mafia here is stronger and more vicious than the gangs who run Duttepe. In the last five years, this whole place has been overrun by drifters and castaways, and there are so many poor rural migrants, Kurds, Gypsies, and foreigners who have settled on these streets that the neighborhood is worse than Duttepe was fifteen years ago. Only another coup could clean this place up now.

Once I got to their house, I handed the doll I'd brought for the baby to Rayiha. The single room they lived in was a dizzying mess: diapers, plates, chairs, piles of laundry, sacks of chickpeas, bags of sugar, the butane stove, boxes of baby food, cartons of detergent, pots and pans, milk bottles, plastic cans, mattresses, and duvets had all merged into one big monochrome blur, like clothes spinning inside a washing machine.

"Mevlut, I never believed Vediha Yenge when she told me, but now that I've seen it with my own eyes . . . You know this beautiful, happy family life you've got here with Rayiha Yenge and the girls? It makes me so happy for you that I can't think of anything I'd rather see."

"Why didn't you believe Vediha when she told you?"

"Seeing what you've got here, this blissful family life, it makes me want to get married right away."

"Why didn't you believe her, Süleyman?"

Rayiha served them tea. "No girl seems to be good enough for you, Süleyman," she teased. "Go on, have a seat."

"It's the girls who don't think I'm good enough," I said. I didn't sit.

"My sister tells me, 'All these pretty girls are in love with Süleyman, but Süleyman doesn't like any of them.'"

"Oh, sure, Vediha is so helpful. Does she always come and tell you everything afterward? Who is this pretty girl who's supposed to be in love with me?"

"Vediha means well."

"I know, but seriously, that girl wasn't right for me. She supported the wrong team, Fenerbahçe," I quipped, laughing along with them, and surprised at my own quick wit.

"What about the tall one?"

"Good God, is there anything you don't know? She was too modern, Rayiha, she wasn't right for me."

"Süleyman, if you were to meet a girl you liked who was beautiful and respectable but didn't wear a headscarf, would that be reason enough for you not to marry her?"

"Where on earth are you getting all these ideas from, Rayiha?" Mevlut called from the other side of the room, where he was busy checking the consistency of the boza. "Is it the television?"

"You make me sound like I'm really stuck up and I think no one's good enough for me. But you should know that I almost agreed to marry a maid, the daughter of Kasım from Kastamonu."

Rayiha frowned. "I could be a maid," she said proudly. "What's wrong with that, as long as you've got your dignity?"

"Do you think I'd give you permission for something like that?" said Mevlut.

Rayiha smiled. "At home I'm already the cleaning lady, the maid, the head chef of a three-wheeled restaurant, and the cook in a boza shop." She turned to Mevlut. "Now give me an employment contract and make sure it's notarized, or else I'll go on strike. The law says I can."

"Who cares what the law says or doesn't say? The government can't interfere in our home!" said a defiant Mevlut.

"Rayiha, if you know about all these things, then you must also know that other thing I really want to know," I ventured.

"We have no idea where Samiha went or whom she went with, Süleyman. Don't waste your breath trying to get us to tell you. I heard

Korkut was really horrible to my poor dad just because he thought he knew something . . ."

"Mevlut, let's go to the Canopy Restaurant around the corner and talk for a bit," said Süleyman.

"Don't let Mevlut drink too much, all right? He'll say anything after he's had a glass. He's not like me."

"I know how much to drink!" said Mevlut. He was getting annoyed at the indulgent and overfamiliar tone his wife was using with Süleyman, and she hadn't even covered her head properly. Clearly Rayiha was spending a lot more time than she let on at the house in Duttepe, basking in the comforts over there. "Don't soak any more chickpeas tonight," Mevlut commanded as he was walking out.

"You've brought back all the rice I gave you this morning anyway," Rayiha shot back.

At first Süleyman couldn't remember where he'd parked his van. His face lit up when they found it just a few steps farther on.

"You shouldn't park here, the neighborhood kids will steal the side-view mirrors," said Mevlut. "They'll even take the Ford logo . . . They sell them to the spare-parts dealers up the hill or wear them as necklaces. If it had been a Mercedes, they would have ripped the sign out long ago."

"I doubt this neighborhood has ever seen a Mercedes."

"I wouldn't be so quick to dismiss it, if I were you. All the brightest, most creative Greeks and Assyrians used to live here. Craftsmen are the lifeblood of Istanbul."

The Canopy Restaurant was an old Greek place situated just three streets up toward Beyoğlu, but Mevlut and Rayiha had never been there. It was still early, so the restaurant was empty. They sat down, and Süleyman ordered two *rakı* doubles (without even bothering to ask Mevlut) and some starters (white cheese, fried mussels) and got straight to the point.

"It's time to put our fathers' property dispute behind us. My brother sends his regards . . . We have a serious job opportunity we want to talk to you about."

"What's the job?"

Süleyman responded by raising his glass of *rakı* for a toast. Mevlut reciprocated, but he only had a small sip before putting his glass back down on the table.

"What, you're not drinking?"

"I can't let my boza customers see me drunk. They'll be expecting me soon."

"Not to mention that you have no faith in me, you think if you get drunk I'll make you tell me things, right?" said Süleyman. "And yet, have I ever told anyone your big secret?"

Mevlut's heart thumped in his chest. "What's my big secret supposed to be?"

"My dear Mevlut, it seems you trust me so blindly that you're forgetting things. Believe me, I've forgotten, too, and I haven't told anyone either. But let me refresh your memory so you'll remember that I'm on your side: when you fell in love at Korkut's wedding, did I or did I not offer you my guidance and help?"

"Of course you did . . ."

"I went all the way from Istanbul to Akşehir in my van just so you could elope with the girl, didn't I?"

"I'm grateful, Süleyman . . . I'm so happy now, and it's all because of you."

"Are you actually happy, though? . . . Sometimes our heart wants one thing, but we end up with another instead . . . Yet we still claim that we're happy."

"Why would anyone say they're happy unless they really were?"

"Out of shame . . . and because accepting the truth would make them even more miserable. But none of this applies to you. You're more than happy with Rayiha . . . Now it's your turn to help me find happiness."

"I'll help you the way you helped me."

"Where is Samiha? . . . Do you think she'll come back to me? . . . Tell me the truth, Mevlut."

"Get that girl out of your head," said Mevlut after a brief silence.

"Do things ever get out of our heads just because we tell them to? No, they get stuck even deeper. You and my brother married her sisters, so you're fine. But I failed to get the third sister. Now the more I tell myself I should forget Samiha, the more I think about her. I can't stop thinking about her eyes, the way she walks and talks, how beautiful she is. What can I do? The only other thing I think about is the person who has brought this humiliation upon me."

"Who is that?"

"The son of a bitch who took my Samiha away from me in broad daylight. Who was it? Tell me the truth, Mevlut. I'll have my revenge on that bastard." Süleyman raised his glass as a sort of peace offering, and Mevlut reluctantly downed his own *rakı,* too.

"Aaaah . . . just what we needed," said Süleyman. "Isn't that so?"

"If I didn't have to work tonight, I'd have another . . . ," said Mevlut.

"Mevlut, you've been calling me a nationalist and a pathetic little fascist for years, and now you're the one who is so worried about sin that he's scared of *rakı.* What happened to that Communist friend of yours who got you hooked on wine . . . What was that Kurd called again?"

"Enough of these old stories, Süleyman, tell me about this new job."

"What sort of job would you like?"

"There *is* no job, is there . . . You only came here to try to get me to tell you who took Samiha."

"You know those Arçelik three-wheelers, you should sell your rice from one of those," said Süleyman callously. "You can buy them on monthly installments. Mevlut, if you had some cash to spend, what kind of shop would you open, and where would you put it?"

Mevlut knew he shouldn't take the question seriously, but he couldn't help himself. "I'd open a boza shop in Beyoğlu."

"But is there enough demand for boza?"

"I am sure that anyone who tries boza once is bound to come back for more, as long as it has been prepared and served properly," said Mevlut eagerly. "I'm talking to you as a capitalist, here . . . Boza's got a real future."

"Does Comrade Ferhat give you these capitalist tips?"

"Just because people don't drink that much boza today doesn't mean they won't tomorrow. Have you ever heard that true story about the two footwear entrepreneurs who went to India? One of them said,

'People here walk around barefoot, they won't buy any shoes,' and went back home."

"Don't they have their own capitalists over there?"

"The other one said, 'There's half a billion barefoot people here, it's a huge market.' So he persevered, and eventually he got rich selling shoes in India. Whatever money I lose selling chickpea rice during the day, I more than make up for with my evening boza sales . . ."

"You've become a real capitalist," said Süleyman. "But let me remind you that the reason boza was so popular in Ottoman times was that they used to drink it instead of alcohol. Boza is one thing; shoes for barefoot Indians are another . . . We no longer need to fool ourselves into believing that boza is alcohol-free. Alcohol's legal now anyway."

"No, drinking boza doesn't mean you're fooling yourself. Everyone loves it," said Mevlut, getting agitated. "If you're selling it from a clean shop with a modern look . . . What job is your brother offering me?"

"Korkut can't decide whether he should stay with his old friends from the Grey Wolves or run as a candidate of the Motherland Party," said Süleyman. "Now tell me why you said earlier that I should get Samiha out of my head."

"Because it's done now, she's run away with someone else . . . ," Mevlut mumbled. "There's nothing more painful than love." He sighed.

"You might not want to help me, but there are others who will. Now look at this one here." Süleyman took a battered old black-and-white photograph out of his pocket and handed it to Mevlut.

The photograph showed a woman singing into a microphone, with darkness and too much makeup around her eyes and a world-weary expression. She was dressed conservatively. She wasn't very pretty.

"Süleyman, this woman is at least fifteen years older than we are!"

"Only three or four years older, in fact. If you met her, you'd see she doesn't look a day older than twenty-five. She's a very good person, very understanding. I see her a couple of times a week. You won't tell Rayiha or Vediha, of course, and least of all Korkut. You and I share lots of secrets, don't we?"

"But weren't you meant to settle down with a suitable girl? Isn't Vediha supposed to find you a good girl to marry? Who is this singer woman?"

"I'm still a bachelor, I'm not married yet. Don't get jealous now."

"Why would I be jealous?" said Mevlut. He got up. "It's boza time for me." He'd figured out by then that there wasn't any business to set up with Korkut and that Süleyman had come here purely to pump Mevlut for information about Samiha's whereabouts, just as Rayiha had predicted.

"Come on, sit down, stay at least a few minutes more. How many cups do you think you'll sell tonight?"

"I'm going out with two jugs filled halfway. I'm sure I'll sell out by the end of the evening."

"All right then, I'll buy a whole jug's worth off you. How many cups would that make? You'll give me a discount, of course."

"Why would you do that?"

"I'm buying it off you so you'll stay here with me, keep me company, and not go out freezing on the streets."

"I don't need your charity."

"But I really need your friendship."

"All right then, you can pay me for a third of a jug," said Mevlut, sitting back down. "I won't make a profit off you. That'll cover the costs. Don't tell Rayiha I stayed here drinking with you. What will you do with the boza?"

"What will I do with it?" said Süleyman, pondering an answer. "I don't know . . . I'll give it away to someone . . . or I guess I could just get rid of it."

"Where?"

"What do you mean where? It belongs to me, doesn't it? It can go down the toilet hole."

"Shame on you, Süleyman . . ."

"What's the matter? Aren't you a capitalist? I'm paying you for it."

"Süleyman, you aren't worth a single penny of the money you make here in Istanbul."

"As if boza is holy or something."

"Yes, boza *is* holy."

"Oh, fuck off, boza is just something someone invented so Muslims could drink alcohol; it's booze in disguise—everyone knows that."

"No," said Mevlut, his heart beating fast. "There is no alcohol in boza." He was relieved to feel an expression of utter calm coming over his face.

"Are you joking?"

In the sixteen years he'd spent selling boza, Mevlut had told this lie to two different types of people:

1. Conservative customers who wanted to drink boza and also wanted to believe that they were not committing a sin. The clever ones knew that there was alcohol in boza, but acted as if the mixture that Mevlut sold was a special invention, like sugar-free Coke, and if there was alcohol in it, then Mevlut was a liar, and the sin was his.
2. Secular, Westernized customers who wanted to drink boza and also wanted to enlighten the country bumpkin who sold it to them. The clever ones understood that Mevlut knew there was alcohol in boza, but they wanted to shame the cunning religious peasant who lied to them just to make more money.

"No, I'm not joking. Boza is holy," said Mevlut.

"I'm a Muslim," said Süleyman. "Only things that obey the rules of my faith can be holy."

"Just because something isn't strictly Islamic doesn't mean it can't be holy. Old things we've inherited from our ancestors can be holy, too," said Mevlut. "When I'm out at night on the gloomy, empty streets, I sometimes come across a mossy old wall. A wonderful joy rises up inside me. I walk into the cemetery, and even though I can't read the Arabic script on the gravestones, I still feel as good as I would if I'd prayed."

"Come off it, Mevlut, you're probably scared of the dogs in the cemetery."

"I'm not scared of stray dogs. They know who I am. What did my late father say to people who claimed there was alcohol in boza?"

"What did he say?"

"He'd tell them 'Sir, if there was alcohol in it, I wouldn't be selling it,'" said Mevlut, imitating his father.

"They didn't know that it contained alcohol," said Süleyman. "Anyway, if boza really were as blessed as holy water, people would be drinking it all day and you'd be rich by now."

"It's not like it can only be holy if everyone is drinking it. Very few people actually read the Koran. But in all of Istanbul, there is always at least one person reading it at any given time, and millions of people can feel better just by thinking of that person. It's enough for people to know that boza was our ancestors' favorite drink. That's what the boza seller's call reminds them of, and it makes them feel good to hear it."

"Why do they feel good?"

"I don't know," said Mevlut. "But thank God they do, because that's why they drink boza."

"So that means you're like a symbol of something bigger, Mevlut."

"Yes, exactly," said Mevlut with pride.

"But you're still willing to sell me your boza without a profit. The only thing you don't want is for it to go down the toilet. You're right, wasting food is a sin, so we should distribute it among the poor, but I don't know if people will want to drink something that's got alcohol in it."

"If you're going to start insulting boza after all the years you've spent lecturing me about patriotism and boasting about what a good fascist you are, then you're on the wrong track, Süleyman . . ."

"There you go, the moment they see you succeed, they get jealous and tell you you're wrong."

"I'm not jealous of you. It's clear that you're spending time with the wrong woman, Süleyman . . ."

"You know full well that it makes no difference whether it's the right woman or the wrong woman or any other woman."

"I got married, and thankfully I'm very happy," said Mevlut, rising from his seat. "You find yourself a good girl, too, and get married as soon as possible. Good night."

"I won't get married until I've killed the bastard who took Samiha," Süleyman yelled after him. "You go tell that Kurd."

Mevlut made his way home as if walking in his sleep. Rayiha had brought the boza jugs down. He could have tied them to his stick and gone out. Instead he went up the stairs and into the house.

Rayiha was breast-feeding Fevziye. "Did he make you drink?" she whispered, trying not to startle the baby.

Mevlut could feel the force of the *rakı* inside his head.

"I didn't drink at all. He just kept asking who Samiha had run off with and where did she go. Who's the Kurd he keeps mentioning?"

"What did you say?"

"What could I have said? I don't know anything."

"Samiha ran away with Ferhat!" said Rayiha.

"What? . . . Why didn't you tell me?"

"Süleyman's lost his mind," said Rayiha. "You should hear the things he says back home in Duttepe . . . If he finds out who took Samiha, he'll kill him."

"No way . . . he's all talk," said Mevlut. "He's a loudmouth, but Süleyman wouldn't kill anyone."

"But why are you so tense, what's making you so angry?"

"I'm not tense and I'm not angry," he shouted. He went out, slamming the door behind him. He heard the baby start to cry.

Mevlut was fully aware that it would take countless nights of walking on dark streets before he could even begin to accept what he'd just found out. That night he walked from the backstreets of Feriköy all the way to Kasımpaşa, even though he had no customers there.

At some point during the evening, he lost his way and climbed down several steep roads, and when he came across a small graveyard squeezed between two wooden houses, he went in to have a cigarette among the gravestones. One dating all the way back to Ottoman times, and surmounted by a large sculpted turban, filled him with awe. He had to put Samiha and Ferhat out of his mind. On his long walk that night, he convinced himself that he wouldn't dwell on the news. In any case, whenever he went home and lay down to sleep with Rayiha in his arms, he forgot all his troubles. Besides, the things that troubled him in this world were all just specters of the strangeness in his mind. Even the dogs in the cemetery had been nice to him that night.

9

The Ghaazi Quarter

We're Going to Hide in Here

Samiha. Yes, I eloped with Ferhat. I've kept quiet for two years now, just to make sure no one finds out where we are. But I've got so much to tell.

Süleyman was really in love with me. It's true that love can make a fool of any man. He was acting so strange—especially in the days just before I ran away—and whenever he spoke to me, his mouth would go dry from nervousness. No matter how hard he tried, he could never figure out how to say all the sweet things I would have liked to hear. He used to play pranks on me like a naughty kid taunting his little brother, and even though he liked taking me for drives, every time we got in the van he would still say, "Let's hope no one sees us" or "We're wasting so much gas."

I left behind all the presents Süleyman had given me, though I can't see my father returning his false teeth or any of the other gifts, either . . . he must be so angry at me. To tell the truth, I'm pretty angry too about how they all decided Süleyman was good enough for me without even bothering to ask what I thought.

Ferhat says he first saw me at Rayiha and Mevlut's wedding. I hadn't even noticed him. But he couldn't forget me; that's what he said when he stopped me out in Duttepe one day to declare face-to-face that he was in love and intended to marry me.

So many boys had wanted to marry me but couldn't even work up the courage to come near me, so I liked the boldness of his approach: he told me he was a university student who worked in the restaurant industry (he didn't say he was a waiter). He used to call me at home in Duttepe, though I've no idea where he got our number. If Süleyman and Korkut had found out, they would have beaten him bloody and broken his bones, but Ferhat didn't care, he would call me anyway and try to arrange a meeting. When Vediha was home, I wouldn't pick up. "Hello . . . Hello? Hello, hello!" my sister would say, with one eye on me. "No one's speaking . . . Must be that guy again. Be careful, Samiha, this city is full of perverts looking for a good time." I wouldn't respond. But Vediha understood perfectly well that I would prefer a fun-loving rascal over a fat, lazy rich boy any day.

When my father and Vediha weren't home, I'd be the one to pick up the phone, since Bozkurt and Turan weren't allowed to touch it anyway. Ferhat wouldn't say much. There was a place behind the Ali Sami Yen football stadium where he used to wait for me under a mulberry tree. There were some old stables there where homeless people lived. There was a little shop where Ferhat would buy me a bottle of Fruko orange soda, and we would check under the cap to see whether we'd won anything. I never once asked him how much he made in the restaurant industry, whether he had any savings, or where we would live. That's the way I fall in love.

Once I got into the taxi, we didn't head straight for the Ghaazi Quarter. First we turned back toward Taksim Square, where we figured we could lose Süleyman in the bustle, in case he was still following us; from there we went down to Kabataş, where I admired the simple deep blue of the sea, and as we drove over Galata Bridge I was entranced at the sight of all the ships with their passengers and all those cars around us. At one point, I felt like crying at the thought of being separated from my father and my sister and going to a place I didn't know, but at the same time I felt in my heart that this whole city was now mine and that I was starting a very happy life.

"Ferhat, will you take me out with you? Are we going to go and see things together?" I asked him.

"Whatever you want, my darling," he said. "But we've got to get home first."

"You couldn't have made a better decision, miss, trust me," said his friend, the taxi driver who was helping us. "The guns didn't scare you, did they?"

"She doesn't get scared!" said Ferhat.

We passed Gaziosmanpaşa, formerly known as Taşlıtarla—"Stony Field." As we drove uphill on a dusty dirt road, the world seemed to grow older with every house, chimney, and tree that passed. I saw single-story houses that hadn't even been finished but already looked old; pitifully empty lots; walls built out of hollow bricks, scrap metal, and bits of wood; and dogs that barked at anyone. The roads were unpaved, the gardens were big, the houses few and far between; this place was like a village, yet everything, down to the last door and window, had once been in one of those old Istanbul homes before someone ripped it out and brought it here. People here were always in a hurry, as if this neighborhood were just a temporary place to stay until they could move into the actual Istanbul home they were going to buy one day. I saw women like me wearing skirts over faded blue trousers; old ladies in baggy trousers and headscarves wound tight around their faces; I saw straight, loose trousers that looked like stovepipes, long skirts, and women in overcoats.

The house Ferhat was renting, a single room with two windows, stood halfway up the slope. From the window at the back, you could see a plot of land far away that Ferhat had marked out with stones he had limewashed, so that on summer nights when the moon was big, we could see his plot from our bed, glowing in the dark like a ghost. "The land is calling to us," Ferhat would whisper, and then he'd start telling me about the house we would build there as soon as we'd saved enough. He would ask me how many rooms the house should have and whether the kitchen should face uphill or downhill, and I'd tell him what I thought.

The first night after I'd run away, we got into bed with our clothes still on and did not make love. If I share these intimate details with you, dear readers, it is because I hope that my story might serve as an example to you all. I liked it when Ferhat stroked my hair while I cried in the night. For a week, we slept that way, with our clothes still on and without ever making love. One night I saw a seagull outside the window, and because we were so far from the sea, I thought this had to be a sign of God's forgiveness. Ferhat realized that I was ready to give myself to him now; I could tell from the look in his eyes that he knew.

He had never tried to force me into doing anything I didn't want to do, which made me love and respect him even more. Nevertheless, I told him, "We better have a civil wedding as soon as I turn eighteen, or I'll kill you."

"With a gun or with poison?"

"That's my business," I said.

He kissed me the way they do in the movies. I had never kissed a man on the lips, so I got confused and forgot what I was saying.

"How much longer until you turn eighteen?"

I proudly produced my identity card from my suitcase and worked out that there were seven months and twelve days to go.

"If you're seventeen and still haven't got a husband, you might as well call yourself a spinster," said Ferhat. "Even if we were to make love now, God would feel sorry for you and wouldn't count it as a sin."

"I don't know about that . . . but if God forgives us, it'll be because we have to hide out here, with no one to rely on except each other."

"Not true," said Ferhat. "I have a family; I have relatives and friends all over this hill. We're not alone." At that word—"alone"—I burst into tears. Ferhat stroked my hair to comfort me, just as my father used to do when I was little. I don't know why, but that made me cry even harder.

We made love feeling deeply self-conscious, though I would never have wanted it to happen that way. I was a little lost at first, but I got used to my new life fairly quickly. I wondered what my sisters and my father might be saying about me. Ferhat would leave just before noon, taking a dusty old minibus like the ones we used to have back in the village, all the way to the fully licensed New Bounty Restaurant in Gaziosmanpaşa, where he worked as a waiter. In the mornings he watched university lectures on TV, and I, too, would watch the professor as Ferhat followed the lesson.

"I can't concentrate if you sit right next to me while I'm watching,"

Ferhat would say. But when I didn't sit next to him, he would start to wonder where I'd gone to in our tiny house—was I outside feeding bread crumbs to the chickens?—and he still couldn't concentrate.

I won't tell you how we made love or what I did to make sure I didn't get pregnant until we were married, but whenever I was in the city, I would go to Rayiha and Mevlut's house in Tarlabaşı without informing Ferhat, and I would tell my sister everything. Mevlut was out selling rice from his cart, so he was never home. Vediha came along, too, sometimes. We would play with the children while Rayiha prepared the boza and the chicken, and we'd watch TV as Vediha offered pearls of wisdom to her little sisters.

"Do not trust men," she would say at the beginning of every lesson. I noticed she'd started smoking. "Samiha, you can't get pregnant until you and Ferhat have had a civil wedding. If he won't marry you once you've turned eighteen, don't waste another second on that bastard. You always have your room waiting for you in Duttepe. Rayiha, not a word to Mevlut or Süleyman that the three of us meet up in here. Have a cigarette, dear. It'll calm your nerves. Süleyman's still furious. We can't find him a suitable girl, he doesn't like any of them, he's still stuck on you, and—God help us—he's still charging around saying he'll murder Ferhat."

"Vediha, Samiha, I'm going out for half an hour or so. Look after the babies for a bit, will you?" Rayiha would say. "I haven't left the house in three days."

When I first went to live there, the Ghaazi Quarter looked like a different place every time I saw it. I met a young woman who wore jeans like me and who'd also run away with someone to avoid a marriage she didn't want; she wore her headscarf loose, too. There was a Kurdish woman who loved to talk about how she had come from Malatya and how the police and the gendarmes were after her, and when we'd walk back home together from the fountain carrying our jerricans full of water, she would tell me about the pain in her kidneys, the scorpions in her woodshed, and how even in her dreams she was always walking uphill.

The Ghaazi Quarter was just one steep hillside populated by people of every conceivable city, country, trade (though most were unemployed), race, tribe, and tongue. There was a forest behind the hill, and below the forest was a dam with a green reservoir that supplied water to the whole city. If you made sure to get along with the Alevis, the Kurds, and later with the fanatics of the Tariqi sect and their sheikh, too, your home was unlikely to get demolished, and word of this spread fast so that now all sorts of people lived on this hill. But no one ever said where they were really from. I took Ferhat's advice and gave a different answer every time anyone asked.

Ferhat went to Gaziosmanpaşa every day, avoiding Istanbul for fear of running into Süleyman (of course, he had no idea about my trips to the city, so please don't mention them); he told me he was saving, though he didn't even have a bank account. After he left, I would keep myself busy sweeping the dirt floor (it took a month before I realized that the more I swept the floor, the higher the ceiling got), shifting the tiles and the tin sheets on the roof, which would leak even when it wasn't raining, and trying to block out the wind, which even on calm, cloudless days with no trace of a breeze outside would still find its way through the chipped bricks and uneven stones, upsetting the nervous lizards on our walls. Some nights, instead of the wind blowing we would hear the howling of wolves, and the roof wouldn't leak water but slush and rusty nails. On winter evenings, the seagulls would come to perch and warm their orange feet and backsides on the stovepipe coming out of the window, and when their squawking drowned out the voices of American gangsters and policemen on TV, I would get scared to be home alone and think wistfully of my father, who had returned to the village.

Abdurrahman Efendi. My darling daughter, my beautiful Samiha. I can sense that you've been talking about me all the way from this table in the village coffeehouse where I am dozing in front of the television, I know you're all right and have no complaints about that bastard who ran off with you, and I wish you every happiness, my dear. Forget about money. Marry whoever you want to marry, my child, even an Alevi is fine, just as long as you bring your husband to the village so you can both kiss my hand. I wonder where you are . . . I wonder if my feelings and my words are reaching you in return . . .

Ferhat. As soon as I realized that Samiha was scared of being home alone while I worked late at the New Bounty Restaurant, I told her she could go watch TV in the evenings with our neighbors from the town of Sivas. Haydar was an Alevi who worked as a doorman in a new apartment block in Gaziosmanpaşa, where his wife, Zeliha, scrubbed the stairs five days a week and also helped out a baker's wife on an upper-floor apartment with the cooking and the dishes. Samiha noticed how Haydar and Zeliha always left the house together in the morning and took the bus home together every evening, keeping each other company all day. We were walking up the slope to our house one night, an icy wind from the Black Sea rattling our bones, when Samiha told me that there were other tenants in that building where Haydar's wife worked looking for maids to come in for the day.

Once we got home, I put my foot down. "I'd rather go hungry than have you working as a maid!" I said.

I was holding a rusty old wheel rim, which I added to the pile of old doors, scrap metal, wire, tin drums, bricks, and smooth rocks I was collecting for the house I would build one day on the plot I had marked out with phosphorescent stones.

People in the Ghaazi Quarter had started to help one another build houses out of the doors, chimneys, and hollow bricks they'd amassed when the leftists, Alevis, and Kurds took over the neighborhood six years earlier. Before then, the quarter had been ruled by Nazmi the Laz from the eastern Black Sea coast. In 1972, Nazmi the Laz and two of his men (who also hailed from Rize) opened a shop at the foot of this hill, which was empty back then except for nettles and shrubs. He sold overpriced tiles, hollow bricks, cement, and other construction materials to poor migrants from Eastern Anatolia who came here hoping to build an unlicensed home on an empty patch of public land. He was like a friend to his customers, offering them advice and tea (later, he would open a teahouse next door), and his shop soon became a meeting point for those flocking to Istanbul from every corner of the Anatolian peninsula—especially from Sivas, Kars, and Tokat—migrants yearning for four walls and a ceiling.

Nazmi the Laz would take his famous horse-drawn cart with rubber tires and do the rounds of Istanbul's demolition crews, collecting wooden doors, newel posts, window frames, cracked bits of marble and paving, metal railings, and old roof tiles, which he displayed all around his shops and his teahouse. He would demand exorbitant prices for these rusty, rotten furnishings, just as he did for the cement and the bricks he sold in his shop. But if you were willing to pay and to hire Nazmi's horse cart to deliver the materials to your construction site, you could count on Nazmi and his men to keep an eye on the land you'd seized and the house you were building on it.

Those not prepared to pay Nazmi, or who thought it was shrewder to go elsewhere for the building materials—"I know where I can get it all a lot cheaper," they'd say—were likely to see their ramshackle homes damaged overnight without a witness in sight, if not completely demolished, with the blessing of the Gaziosmanpaşa police. Once the demolition crews and the police were gone, Nazmi the Laz would pay a condolence call on those penny-wise fools weeping over the rubble of their ruined homes: he would say how he was friends with the captain at the Gaziosmanpaşa police station, they played cards together in the coffeehouse every evening, and had he only known this was going to happen, he could have done something.

In fact, Nazmi the Laz had connections in the nationalist party then in power. From around 1978 onward, when those who'd built on government land using the materials bought from Nazmi started to fight over one another's land, Nazmi the Laz set up his so-called office to keep a record of all these transactions, just like an official land registry. He also issued documents resembling proper title deeds to anyone who paid him for the right to claim a plot of empty land. To make these documents look as legitimate as he could, he followed the practice of the state's official deeds by affixing a photograph of the owner (he'd recently installed a small coin-operated photo booth for his clients' convenience) as well as including the name of the previous owner (he was always proud to name himself), and noting the precise location and dimensions of the plot, before finally sealing the whole thing with a red stamp he'd ordered from a stationery shop in Gaziosmanpaşa.

"When the government's giving out land here one day, they're going to look at my records and the title deeds I've been handing out," Nazmi would boast. Sometimes he would address the unemployed men playing *rummikub* in his teahouse with a little speech on how happy he was to serve his countrymen—who'd left the poorest villages of Sivas and come all the way to Istanbul without a single thing to call their own—by turning them into landowners overnight, and to those who asked, "When are we going to get electricity here, Nazmi?" he would say that they were working on it, hinting that in the event the Ghaazi Quarter was declared a municipality, he would stand for local elections under the banner of the ruling party.

One day, a tall, pale man with a dreamy look in his eyes appeared on the empty hills behind the neighborhood, on land that Nazmi had yet to parcel out. His name was Ali. He never came down to Nazmi the Laz's shop and teahouse; he kept to himself, avoiding neighborhood gossip, living alone on that isolated plot at the farthest edge of the city, where he settled down with his cheap bricks, pots and pans, gas lamps, and mattresses. Nazmi the Laz sent two of his truculent mustachioed henchmen to remind Ali that someone owned that land.

"This land belongs neither to Nazmi the Laz, nor to Hamdi the Turk, nor Kadir the Kurd, nor the state," Ali told them. "Everything—the whole universe and this nation, too—belongs to Allah. We are nothing more than His mortal subjects passing through this temporary existence!"

One night, Nazmi the Laz's men showed this reckless Ali just how right he was—with a bullet to his head. They buried him near the reservoir, keeping things neat and tidy so as not to give the city newspapers an excuse to write about their favorite topic: how the people who lived in the poor neighborhoods were polluting the beautiful green waters of the reservoir that served as Istanbul's water supply. But the neighborhood dogs, who spent their winters warring with the wolves that came down looking for food, soon found the body. Instead of seizing Nazmi the Laz's mustachioed men, the police arrested and tortured a family from Sivas who lived in the house closest to the lake. They ignored the many anonymous tips that Nazmi the Laz was behind it all and pressed on, applying their usual expert torture methods to the people from the lake, first whipping their feet and then setting up simple circuits to administer electric shocks.

When a Kurd from Bingöl died of a heart attack under questioning, the whole neighborhood rose up in protest and raided Nazmi the Laz's teahouse. Nazmi was away, enjoying a wedding at his village near Rize. Taken by surprise, his armed men panicked and ran away, doing no more than firing a few futile shots in the air. Leftist, Marxist, and Maoist youths from various neighborhoods and universities around the city heard what was happening in the Ghaazi Quarter and came to lead this "spontaneous uprising of the people."

Ferhat. Within two days, Nazmi the Laz's offices were taken over and university students seized the land registry, and soon the news spread all over Turkey, especially among the Kurds and the Alevis, that anyone who came to the Ghaazi Quarter and announced that they were "poor and left wing" (or "godless," according to the nationalist papers) would be given some land. That's how, six years ago, I got my plot, which is still marked out with phosphorescent rocks. I didn't settle there at the time, because, like everyone else, I believed that Nazmi the Laz would surely return one day to get his revenge and get his land back with the help of the state. Besides, Beyoğlu, where Mevlut and I were working as waiters, was so far from the Ghaazi Quarter that it took half the day just getting there and back by bus.

We are still living in fear of Süleyman's rage. Nobody wanted to get involved to help us make peace with the Aktaş family (I resented Mevlut, Rayiha, and Vediha for this). So Samiha and I ended up having a quiet, simple wedding in the Ghaazi Quarter. No one pinned any gold or hundred-dollar bills on us the way they did on Mevlut and Rayiha. I was sad not to have been able to invite Mevlut, to have had to get married without my best friend there, but at the same time it made me furious to see how close he was with the Aktaş bunch and how he was willing to mingle with fascists just because he imagined he could get something out of it.

10

Getting Rid of City Dust

My God, Where Is All This Filth Coming From?

Samiha. Ferhat is so worried about what people will say that he's skipping the best parts of our story, supposedly because they're "private." We did have a very small wedding, but it was wonderful. We borrowed a white dress for me from the Pure Princess Bridal Shop on the second floor of the blue building in Gaziosmanpaşa. I didn't put a foot wrong all evening and refused to let anything bring me down—not the ugly, envious biddies around me saying "Poor dear, what a waste for such a pretty girl!" or those who kept their mouths shut but looked at me as if to say, You're so beautiful, why marry some penniless waiter? I could never be anyone's slave, harem girl, or prisoner . . . Look at me and you'll know what freedom looks like. That night, Ferhat got so drunk on all the *rakı* he'd been sneaking under the table that I ended up having to get him home. But I held my head up and proudly faced the crowd of jealous women and admiring men (including the unemployed ones who'd only come for the free lemonade and tea biscuits).

Two months later, Haydar and his wife, Zeliha, had talked me into working as a housemaid in Gaziosmanpaşa. Haydar would sometimes have a drink with Ferhat, and he and his wife had come to our wedding. So when they suggested that I start working, they meant well. Ferhat initially resisted the idea, not wanting to be the kind of man who sends the girl he's just eloped with off to work as a maid only two months after marrying her. But one rainy morning, we all took the minibus to Gaziosmanpaşa together. Ferhat came along to meet the doorman at the Civan Apartment, the building where Zeliha and many of her relatives worked. We went down to the basement, where we sat—three women and three men—drinking tea and smoking cigarettes in the doorman's quarters, which were smaller than the room we lived in, lacking even a window. Afterward, Zeliha took me to apartment number 5, where I was supposed to start work. As we walked up the stairs, I felt shy to be entering a stranger's home and scared of being away from Ferhat. We'd been inseparable ever since we'd run off. At first, Ferhat would come with me every morning and spend afternoons smoking downstairs in the doorman's place until I was done, and at four o'clock, when I emerged from apartment number 5 and found him downstairs in that stuffy basement, he would walk me right up to the minibus or else leave me with Zeliha to make sure I got on, before rushing off to make his shift at the Bounty Restaurant. But within three weeks, I had already started making my own way to work in the mornings, and by the time winter came around, I was coming back home alone in the evenings, too.

Ferhat. I'm just going to interrupt for one minute because I wouldn't want you to get the wrong impression: I'm a hardworking man of honor who knows his responsibilities, and if it were up to me, I would never allow my wife to work. But Samiha kept saying how bored she was at home and how much she wanted to work. She cried a lot, too, though she won't tell you that. Besides, Haydar and Zeliha are like family now, and the people at the Civan Apartment are like brothers and sisters to them. When Samiha told me, "I can get there by myself, you stay at home and keep up with your college courses on TV!" I decided to let her. But then I felt even worse every time I couldn't understand the accounting lessons or couldn't post my homework assignments to Ankara on time. There's this mathematics professor on right now who's got so many white hairs sprouting out of his enormous nose and ears that you can make them out on TV. I can barely follow what he's doing with all those numbers he's writing on the blackboard. The only reason I put up with this torture is because Samiha believes—more than I do—that everything will be different once I manage to earn a degree and find a job as a government clerk.

Samiha. My first "employer," the lady in apartment number 5, was a troubled, short-tempered type. "You look nothing alike," she said, eyeing us suspiciously. We'd agreed that I would gain her trust by saying I was a relative of Zeliha's on her father's side. Mrs. Nalan did believe that I meant well, but at first she couldn't quite trust me to get rid of all the dust properly. Until four years ago, she'd done the cleaning herself, as she didn't really have that much money to spare. But then her firstborn son died of cancer while still in middle school, and Mrs. Nalan had been waging a ruthless war on dust and germs ever since.

"Did you wipe under the fridge and inside the white lamp?" she would ask, even when she had just seen me doing exactly that. She worried that the dust would infect her second son with cancer, too, and as it came time for him to get home from school, I would become increasingly agitated, dusting with more determination and running back and forth to the window to shake out the duster, furious as a pilgrim stoning the devil. "Well done, Samiha, well done!" Mrs. Nalan would say to spur me on. She would stand there talking on the phone while pointing out some speck I'd missed. "My God, where is all this filth coming from!" she'd complain. She'd wag her finger at me, and I'd feel as guilty as if I'd brought it all with me from the poor neighborhood I lived in, but even so, I loved her.

Within two months, Mrs. Nalan trusted me to come in three times a week. By now she had started leaving me home alone, armed with soaps, buckets, and rags, while she went out to do her shopping or to play rummy with the same friends she was always on the phone with. Sometimes she'd sneak back in without warning, pretending to have forgotten something, and when she saw me still hard at work cleaning, she'd be pleased and say, "Well done, God bless you!" Sometimes, she would pick up the photo of her dead son that stood on top of the TV next to the china dog and cry as she wiped the silver frame over and over again, so I would set down my dusting cloth and try to console her.

Zeliha came to visit me one day just after Mrs. Nalan had gone out. "Have you gone crazy?" she said when she saw me working as hard as ever; she sat down to watch TV while I worked. From then on, Zeliha started coming over whenever the lady she worked for wasn't home (sometimes Zeliha's lady and Mrs. Nalan would leave together). While I dusted, she would talk about what was happening on TV and rummage through the fridge for a snack, telling me that the spinach wasn't bad, but the yogurt had gone sour (it was the kind that you bought from the grocery store in a glass bowl). When she started looking through Mrs. Nalan's drawers, commenting on her underwear, her bras, her handkerchiefs, as well as other things we weren't even sure what to call, I couldn't resist joining in for a laugh. Among the silk headscarves and foulards right at the back of one drawer, there was a triangular amulet charmed to bring wealth and good fortune. Tucked away in another corner, among old identity cards, tax returns, and photographs, we found a carved wooden box that smelled wonderful, though we had no idea what it was for. Hidden among the medicine bottles and cough syrups in the drawer on Mrs. Nalan's husband's side of the bed, Zeliha found a strange bottle with a liquid the color of tobacco. The bottle was pink, with a picture of an Arab lady with big lips on the label, and our favorite thing about it was the smell (perhaps it was some sort of medicine, or perhaps Zeliha was right that it was poison), but we were too scared to ever pour any of its contents out. A month later, while exploring the secrets of the house on my own (I liked finding pictures of Mrs. Nalan's dead son and his old homework assignments), I noticed that the bottle had disappeared from its usual place.

Two weeks later, Mrs. Nalan said she needed to talk to me. She told me that Zeliha had been fired in deference to her husband's wishes (though I wasn't entirely sure whose husband she was referring to), and regrettably, although she was absolutely sure that I was innocent, this meant I couldn't work there anymore either. I hadn't fully grasped what was going on yet, but when I saw that she was crying, I started crying, too.

"Don't cry, my dear, we've arranged something wonderful for you!" she said with the upbeat tone of a fortune-telling Gypsy saying,

Your future looks very bright! A wealthy, distinguished family in Şişli was looking for a hardworking, honest, and trustworthy maid like me. Mrs. Nalan was going to send me there, and I was to go straightaway without making a fuss.

I didn't mind, but Ferhat wasn't happy with this new job because the house was so far away. I had to wake up even earlier now to catch the first minibus to Gaziosmanpaşa while it was still dark outside. In Gaziosmanpaşa, I had to wait another half hour for the bus to Taksim. This leg of the trip took well over an hour, and the bus was usually so full that everyone waiting to board would elbow one another out of the way to get on first and grab an empty seat. Looking out of the window of the bus, I'd watch the people going to work, the street vendors pushing their carts to their chosen neighborhoods, the boats on the Golden Horn, and—my favorites—all the children going to school. As we drove past I would try to make out the big newspaper headlines in shopwindows, the posters on the walls, and the enormous billboards. I would absentmindedly read the rhyming couplets of wisdom people had stuck on the back of their cars and their trucks, and I would start to feel as if the city were talking to me. It was nice to think that Ferhat had spent his childhood in Karaköy, right in the middle of the city, and when I got home I would ask him to tell me about those days. But he got back late in the evenings, and we saw less and less of each other.

In Taksim, where I had to change buses again, I would buy a sesame roll from one of the men in front of the post office and either eat it on the bus as I looked out the window or put it in my plastic handbag and have it later at the house where I worked, with a cup of tea. Sometimes the lady I worked for would tell me, "Have some breakfast if you haven't eaten already." So I would help myself to cheese and olives from the fridge. But sometimes she wouldn't say anything at all. Around noon, I would start making grilled meatballs for her lunch, and she would tell me, "Throw in three more for you, Samiha." She would take five meatballs on her plate but only eat four; I'd eat her leftover meatball in the kitchen, and so we'd end up having four each.

But Madam (that's what I used to call her—I never used her name) would not sit at the table with me, and I wasn't allowed to eat when she did. She wanted me near enough to hear her when she said, "Where's the salt?" or "Clear this away now," so I would stand in the doorway to the dining room watching her eat, but she wouldn't talk to me. She kept asking me the same question and always forgot the answer: "Where are you from?" When I told her Beyşehir, she would say, "Where's that? I've never been," so eventually I started saying I was from Konya. "Ah, yes, Konya! I'm going to go one day and visit Rumi's grave," she'd reply. When I went to work in two other homes, one in Şişli and the other in Nişantaşı, I said I was from Konya again, and though the people there also immediately mentioned Rumi, they didn't want me performing any daily prayer rituals. Anyway, Zeliha had already taught me to say no if ever anyone asked, "Do you pray?"

I'd started going to these other houses on Madam's recommendation, and the families there didn't like me using the same bathroom as they did. These were old houses with small servants' bathrooms that I would sometimes have to share with a cat or a dog and where I'd also leave my handbag and my coat. Madam had a cat who stole food from the kitchen and never left her lap, and sometimes, when the cat and I were home alone, I'd give it a swipe and confess to Ferhat when I got home in the evening.

There was a period when Madam fell ill, and I had to spend a few nights in Şişli to look after her, because I knew that she would find someone else if I didn't. I was given a small, clean room that shared a wall with the next building; there was no window, but the bedsheets smelled lovely, and I liked it there. I got used to it eventually. The road to and from Şişli could take four to five hours a day, so on some evenings I would stay over at Madam's, serve her breakfast in the morning, and then go to work in a different house. But I was always dying to get back to Ferhat and the Ghaazi Quarter, and a single day away was enough to make me miss our home and all our things. Every now and then I liked to get off work early in the afternoon and wander around the city for a while before getting on the bus or before changing at Taksim, but I also worried that someone from Duttepe might see me on the street and tell Süleyman.

When the ladies I worked for went out during the day, they'd tell me, "Samiha, when you're done, don't waste your time on prayers and TV, go straight home." I worked so hard sometimes that I could have wiped the whole city clean, but then my mind would wander and I'd slow down. Right at the back of the bottom drawer in the wardrobe with all of Sir's shirts and vests, I found a foreign magazine with pictures of men and women in poses so dirty that even just having seen them I felt dirty, too. Inside Madam's medicine cabinet, on the left-hand side, there was a strange box that smelled of almonds, and under the comb inside the box, there was a foreign banknote. I liked leafing through family albums, discovering old photographs of weddings, school days, and summer holidays tucked away in drawers, and seeing what the people I worked for used to be like when they were young.

Every home I worked in would have a pile of dusty old newspapers, empty bottles, and unopened boxes stashed away and forgotten in a corner somewhere, and I would always be told not to touch this pile—almost as if there were something sacred about it. Every house had a corner that I was meant to stay away from, and when no one was home, I would indulge my curiosity and have a look, taking care not to touch any of the fresh banknotes, gold coins, strange-smelling soaps, and decorative boxes they would leave out on purpose just to test me. Madam's son had a collection of plastic toy soldiers that he would deploy in line formation on his bed or on the carpet. As he had one line fight another, I enjoyed watching him get so lost in his game that he forgot everything else, and sometimes when I was alone in the house I would sit down and play with the soldiers myself. Many families bought newspapers just to collect the coupons that came with them, and once a week I'd be tasked with cutting them all out. Once a month, when it was time to collect the enameled teapots, illustrated cookbooks, floral pillowcases, lemon squeezers, and musical pens that you could get if you had enough coupons, they would send me to stand in line for half a day at the nearest newsstand. There was one electric kitchen appliance that Madam—who spent the whole day gossiping on the phone—kept stored away with her winter woolens in a wardrobe that smelled of mothballs, and although, just like the gifts she got with the coupons, she never used it, not even for guests, she still kept this machine carefully stored away because it was, after all, a European import. Sometimes I would look through the receipts, newspaper clippings, and flyers that I might find tucked inside envelopes right at the bottom of a cupboard, or at the girls' dresses and underwear and the writing in their notebooks, and it was as if I were about to find something I'd been seeking for a long time. Sometimes I felt as if those letters and those scribbles were meant for me and that I was in those photographs, too. Or I would feel it was my fault that Madam's son had taken his mother's red lipstick and hidden it in his room, and I became at once deeply attached to and yet somehow resentful of these people who were laying their private world open for me to see.

Sometimes, halfway through the day, I would already begin to miss Ferhat, our home, and the phosphorescent outline of our land we could see from the bed. Two years after I'd started working as a maid, as my overnight stays became more frequent, I began to resent Ferhat for failing to pull me away, once and for all, from these other families' lives that were fast becoming my own, from their cruel sons and spoiled daughters, from the grocers' boys and the doormen's sons who chased after me because I was pretty, and from the tiny servants' room where, if the heating was on, I would wake up in the middle of the night soaked in sweat.

Ferhat. A year after I went to work at the Bounty Restaurant, they started putting me in charge of the cash register. This was partly because of those university courses Samiha was always encouraging me to take—even if they were only correspondence courses and on TV. But in the evenings, when the restaurant was noisy and full, and a pleasant smell of *rakı* and soup hung in the air, the manager's brother would sit at the desk and handle everything himself . . . The owner, whose main restaurant was in Aksaray (ours was a sister branch), had one rule that was repeated to the cooks and dishwashers, and to us waiters and busboys, on a monthly basis: every single plate of french fries, tomato salad, grilled meatballs, and chicken-topped rice, every small beer and shot of *rakı,* every bowl of lentil soup, kidney-bean stew, and leek with lamb, had to be noted down by the cashier before it was served.

With its four big windows (the lace curtains always drawn) on Atatürk Street, and its crowd of eager regulars (teetotaling local shopkeepers having their stews at lunchtime and, in the evening, groups of men sipping *rakı* in moderation), the Bounty Restaurant was a veritable institution, so busy it wasn't easy sometimes to follow the manager's commandment. Even at lunchtime, when I got to sit at the cashier's desk, I couldn't always keep up with where the waiters were taking their plates of chicken-and-vegetable stew, celery roots in olive oil, fava-bean spread, and oven-baked mackerel. The waiters would queue up at my table to have each portion noted down (while impatient customers shouted, "That's mine and it's getting cold!"), until, sometimes, there was no choice but to set the rule aside for a few minutes, letting the waiters deliver their orders first and report them to me later, when things had calmed down a little: "Ferhat, stuffed peppers and fried pastry rolls for table seventeen, two chicken blancmanges for sixteen." But the queuing problem remained, since the waiters would now try to shout over one another instead of waiting their turns: "A salad for number six, two yogurts for number two." Some would call out the order as they hurried past with piles of dishes, and the cashier wouldn't always have time to write it all down, or else he would forget, or, like me, he'd make something up on the spot or just give up entirely, the way I did when I just couldn't follow a class I was watching on TV. The waiters didn't mind at all if some portions went unrecorded; they knew that when customers thought they'd gotten something for free, they'd leave a better tip. As for the manager, his rule had less to do with money than with having some basis to answer drunken customers shouting, "We only ordered one plate of panfried mussels, I tell you!" and arguing over the bill.

I may not have manned the register during the dinner shift, but while I was serving, I got to know all the little tricks of a dishonest waiter. One of the simplest was one that I used myself from time to time: you find an appreciative customer, and you serve him a larger portion of his order (six meatballs instead of four, for example); but you tell him you're only charging him for the smaller portion, and he is so delighted he adds the difference to your tip. In theory, all tips were supposed to be pooled and then split equally among the staff (though the manager himself would first take a cut), but in practice every waiter would hide part of what he received in some trouser pocket or in his white apron. No one ever said anything about it: getting caught would mean getting fired, and in any case, everyone did it, so no waiter would ever question what was in another waiter's apron.

My evening station was near the entrance, and in addition to my tables, another duty of mine was to assist the manager. I wasn't really the headwaiter, but I did help him to supervise. "Go and check on the stews for table four, they're complaining," he would say, and even though it was Hadi from Gümüşhane's table, I'd go into the kitchen myself to look for the cook hiding in the cloud of smoke that rose from the meat and fat on the grill, and then I would go to table number 4 and tell them with a smile and a little joke that their stews were on their way, asking perhaps whether they might like them with garlic or would prefer them plain or otherwise trying to find out what football team they were for and talk about the match-fixing scandals, the corrupt referees, and the penalty we should have had on Sunday.

Whenever that idiot Hadi managed to upset a table, I'd go to the kitchen and grab a plate of fries or a huge pot of sizzling prawns, which were probably meant for some other table, and present it on the house to the table complaining that its order was taking forever or got screwed up. If there was a mixed-grill platter to spare, I might bring it to a table of drunks—"Here is the meat, finally," I'd announce—never mind they'd never ordered it; they were having such a good time discussing politics, football, or the cost of living that they wouldn't notice or care. In the later hours, I would appease quarrelsome diners, subdue tables that broke into song annoying everyone, resolve any disagreements over whether the window should be open or closed, remind the busboys to empty people's ashtrays ("Go check on number ten, kid, get going . . ."), and flush out the waiters and dishwashers smoking in the kitchen, outside, or in the back storeroom, sending them to their stations with just a look.

Sometimes the manager of some law firm or architects' firm would take his clerks out for lunch, women included, or a mother in a headscarf would treat her good-for-nothing sons to some meatballs and *ayran,* and we would sit them at the tables right by the door, reserved for families. Our manager, who had three portraits of Atatürk in civilian clothes up on the wall—one smiling and two looking stern—had a particular fixation with drawing more female customers to the Bounty Restaurant. His idea of success was for a woman to come in with a group of men and be able to have a pleasant evening—especially during the dinner shift, when *rakı* was served—without being subjected to innuendo and arguments all night, and to enjoy herself enough to come again, though in all the Bounty Restaurant's checkered history, this had sadly never happened. The day after any night a woman had visited the restaurant, our furious and despairing boss would do his impression of the male customers from the night before, wide eyed and with their mouths hanging open, and tell us waiters that, next time a woman came in to eat, we shouldn't panic and crowd around her but act instead as if it were perfectly normal for her to be there and shield her from the loud, foulmouthed men at the other tables and their sleazy looks. This last request was the hardest to fulfill.

Late at night, when it seemed the last drunk customers were never going to leave, the manager would tell me, "You can go now, you've got a long way home." I'd spend the journey home thinking of Samiha, feeling guilty, and making up my mind that it wasn't right for her to be working as a maid. I hated waking up in the mornings and realizing she'd already left for work, and I would curse my poverty and my ever having allowed her to work in the first place. In the afternoons, the dishwasher and the two busboys, who all shared an apartment, would laugh as they shelled beans and peeled potatoes while I sat at the table in the corner, trying to follow *Learn Accounting* on the public channel. Even when I could follow the lesson, the homework sheets that came in the post would stump me, and I would get up and walk out of the Bounty to wander around the streets of Taşlıtarla like a sleepwalker, feeling helpless and angry, and dream about hijacking a taxi at gunpoint like in the movies, going to find Samiha at the house where she worked in Şişli, and taking her away to our new home in some distant neighborhood. In my dreams, the house I was going to build on the land framed by the phosphorescent stones, using the money I'd saved up, already had twelve rooms and four doors. But at five o'clock in the evening, when every employee of the Bounty Restaurant, from the dishwasher to the headwaiter, gathered round a big pot in the middle of the long table at the back to eat their fill of meat and potato soup with fresh bread before donning their uniforms and beginning their shifts, I'd get bitter thinking how I was wasting away out here when I should have been running my own business in the city center.

On those evenings when Samiha was expected to come home, my kindly manager, seeing me itching to get out of the Bounty as early as possible, would say, "Take off that apron and go home, Mr. Bridegroom." Samiha had been in the restaurant a few times, so the other waiters, the busboys, and the dishwashers had all seen how beautiful she was; they would laugh and jealously call me Mr. Bridegroom, and as I waited and waited for the bus to the Ghaazi Quarter (there was a new direct bus service to our neighborhood, but it wasn't very regular), I would lament my failure to make the most of my good fortune, until, in my frustration, I began to fear that I was doing something wrong.

When it arrived, the bus to the Ghaazi Quarter was so slow and wasted so much time at each stop that I could barely keep my nervous legs still. At a stop near the end of the route, there would be a voice calling out from the darkness, trying desperately to catch the last bus to the end of the city—"Driver, driver, wait"—so the driver would light a cigarette, and the bus would wait, and in my impatience, I'd have to stand the rest of the way. When I finally got off at the last stop, I'd sprint up the hill to our house, forgetting how tired I was. The silence of the dark night, the pale light from the poor neighborhoods in the distance, and the stinking smoke of lignite fuel that rose from some of the chimneys around me soon became signs that I associated with Samiha waiting for me at home. It was Wednesday, so she had to be home. Maybe she'd already collapsed from exhaustion and gone to sleep, as she often did. She looked so pretty when she was sleepy. Or maybe she'd made me some chamomile tea, and she was watching TV while she waited for me. I'd think about her intelligence and her friendship and start running, believing that if I ran, then Samiha would definitely be home.

If she wasn't home, I would quickly have some *rakı* to calm myself and ease the suffering, and then I would start blaming myself for everything. The next day, I'd get out of work even earlier, just as impatient as ever to be on my way home.

"I'm sorry," Samiha would say when we saw each other. "Madam had guests last night . . . She really wanted me to stay over, and she gave me this!"

I'd take the money from her and put it away. "You're not going to work anymore, you're never leaving this house again," I'd declare. "We'll stay right here, together, until the day the world ends."

The first few times this happened, Samiha said, "How will we eat?" Soon, though, she was laughing about it, telling me, "All right, I won't go to work anymore." But of course she still went to work every morning.

11

Girls Who Refuse to Meet Their Suitors

We Were Just Passing By

Süleyman. Yesterday evening I went to see Uncle Asım in Ümraniye. He is a friend of my father's and a former yogurt seller. He's a wise man, smart enough to have given up yogurt years ago and set up his own grocery store. Now he's retired. Last night he showed me the poplars he planted in his garden and the enormous walnut tree that had been a tiny sapling when he'd first claimed this plot of land twenty years ago. The noise and the light that filtered into the garden from the tube factory next door made everything look strange and wonderful. We were both completely drunk on the *rakı* we'd been sipping all night. His wife was inside, already asleep.

"They're offering me really good money for this land, but I know it'll go higher, I'm already regretting the piece I did sell, it went too cheap," said Uncle Asım. Fifteen years ago, he had a shop in Tophane and a rented apartment on Kazancı Hill. Three times last night, he told me how wise he had been to come here all the way from the city and claim some vacant land for himself on the off chance they'd eventually give him a title deed. Another thing he said three times was that his daughters are all married now, "thank God," and their husbands are all good men—though not quite as good as I am. What he was really trying to say was "Son, why did you come knocking on my door tonight, all the way from across the Bosphorus in Duttepe, when I don't even have a daughter left for you to marry?"

Like everything else, this reminded me of Samiha. It's been two years since she ran away. I swear I'm going to find the scum who took her, that bastard Ferhat, and make him pay for this insult and the humiliation. Even now, there are times when I dream that Samiha's coming back to me, but deep down I know it will never happen, so I stop indulging in the fantasy. If I'm free of these troubles now, I owe it to Melahat and Vediha. Vediha has really applied herself to finding me a wife.

Vediha. As a family, we decided that the best way to help Süleyman get over Samiha was to get him married. One night, he was at home, and he was drunk. "Süleyman," I said, "you and Samiha went out for a while, you really got to know each other, and in the end it didn't work out. Maybe it would make more sense for you to marry a girl you don't know at all, someone you've only ever met once . . . Love can come after marriage." "I guess you're right," he said, cheering up. "So have you got a new girl for me, then?" But then he began to get picky. "I can't marry some village yogurt seller's daughter." "Your brother Korkut and your cousin Mevlut both married a yogurt seller's daughter. What's so terrible about us?" "It's not like that, I don't see you three that way." "How *do* you see us?" "Don't get me wrong . . ." "I'm not, Süleyman. But why do you think we'd marry you off to a village girl?" I asked him in my sternest voice. The truth is, Süleyman needs a strong woman to reprimand him every now and then; he even likes it.

"And I don't want one of those eighteen-year-old high-school graduates either. They find something wrong in everything I say, and all they ever do is argue . . . Besides, these are the same girls who'll insist we have to go out together before we get married, go to the movies maybe, as if we'd met at university instead of being introduced by matchmakers, and even then they're always worried about getting caught by their parents, always trying to tell me what to do . . . It's an uphill battle."

I told Süleyman, Don't worry, Istanbul is teeming with girls who want a good-looking, successful, intelligent man like him.

"But where are they?" he asked me earnestly.

"They're at home with their mothers, Süleyman; they don't go out much. You just listen to my advice, and I promise you I'll show you all the sweetest and the prettiest ones, and then when you've found the most beautiful of them all, the one your heart desires, we'll go and ask for her hand in marriage."

"Thank you, Vediha, but to be honest, I've never really gone for the straitlaced types, who stay at home with their mothers and always do as they're told."

"But if you're looking for a different kind of girl, then how come you never tried to win Samiha over with a sweet word or two?"

"I just couldn't get the hang of it!" he said. "She would make fun of me every time I tried."

"Süleyman, I'll comb every inch of Istanbul if I have to, but I'll find you a girl. But if you like her, you've got to treat her right, understood?"

"All right, but what if she gets spoiled?"

Süleyman. I'd take Vediha in the van, and we would go out to meet eligible girls. People with experience in this sort of thing said we should take my mother along, too, as this would give our delegation an air of formality, but I didn't want to do that. My mother's clothes and her manner are still too close to village ways. Vediha would wear blue jeans under her usual dress, a long, dark blue overcoat I never saw her wear anywhere else, and a headscarf that matched that blue exactly; you might have mistaken her for a lady doctor or judge who happened to be wearing a headscarf. Vediha loved being out of the house so much that as soon as I stepped on the gas and we went flying down the streets of Istanbul, she would practically forget our mission, taking in every inch of the city and talking nonstop, until I had to laugh.

"This bus route is run by a private company, not by the municipality, and that's why it keeps the doors open while it's moving," I'd tell her as I tried to pass the bus crawling ahead of us letting passengers jump on and off.

"Careful we don't run them over, these people are crazy," she'd say, laughing. As we got closer to our destination, I'd grow silent. "Don't worry, Süleyman," she'd say. "She's a nice girl, I like her. But if you don't, then we'll just get up and leave. You can drive your sister around for a bit on your way back."

Vediha was always making new friends, thanks to her warmth and kindness, and through these connections, she would identify the eligible girls, and then the two of us would go to see them at home. Most had either come to Istanbul after finishing primary school in the village (like me), or else they'd gone to a school in a poor city neighborhood that was even worse than the village. Some of them were determined to finish high school; others could barely read and write. Most were too young, but once they reached high-school age, they really didn't want to be still living with their parents in some tiny, rundown, stove-heated house that was always freezing. It was always nice to hear Vediha telling me that all these girls were sick of their parents and looking for a chance to get away from home, but a part of me knew that this wasn't really true of every girl we met.

Vediha. Oh, Süleyman . . . the truth—though I never told him this—is that good girls don't know how to think for themselves, and girls who think for themselves aren't any good. There were other things I never told him, too. If you're looking for a girl like Samiha, a girl with character, you're not going to find her at home with her mother, waiting for a man to marry her. You expect a girl who has her own mind and her own personality to bow down to your every wish? That's not going to happen. You want her to be pure and innocent, but also eager to fulfill all your wild desires (let's not forget that I married his brother)? That's never going to happen either. What you don't realize, poor Süleyman, is that you need a girl who doesn't wear a headscarf—though I assume you wouldn't want a girl like that. But this was a sensitive subject, and I never brought it up. But I kept trying, because the surest way to get permission to leave the house was to tell Korkut I was going out to find Süleyman a wife. Soon enough, Süleyman came to accept the gap between his expectations and reality.

When families want to get their sons and daughters married off, the first place they look is back in the village, among their own relatives, or down the street and around the neighborhood. Only a girl who can't find a husband nearby—usually because everyone knows there's something wrong with her—will ever say she wants to marry a stranger from some other part of town. Some try to dress this up as the beauty of a free spirit. But whenever I heard about one of these freedom-loving girls, I would always try to figure out what she was hiding. Naturally, these girls and their families had their own cause for suspicion (after all, hadn't we also come a long way from home to find a match?), and they would give us a very close look, trying to work out what we had to hide. Anyway, I warned Süleyman, if a girl has got nothing obviously wrong with her but still can't find a husband, it means she's probably setting her sights too high.

Süleyman. There was this high-school girl who lived on the second floor of a new building in the backstreets of Aksaray. Not only was she wearing her school uniform (with her headscarf) when she greeted us, but she also spent the entire time poring over a notebook and math textbook at the dining table. Meanwhile, another girl, a distant relation, took on the role of the polite young woman who entertains the candidate's guests, even though she has her own homework to do.

In a house somewhere behind Bakırköy, we went to see Behice, who during our brief visit got up from her chair five times to go to the window and peek out through the lace curtains at the kids playing football in the street. "Behice likes to look out the window," said her mother, as if to make excuses for this behavior but also imply, as so many mothers did, that this particular quirk was further proof of what an excellent wife her daughter was bound to be.

In a house across from the Piyale Paşa Mosque in Kasımpaşa, two sisters—neither of them the girl we'd come to see—kept whispering and giggling between themselves, or biting their lips trying not to laugh even more. After we left the house, Vediha told me that our quarry—their frowning older sister—had in fact entered like a ghost while we were having our tea and almond biscuits, crossing the room so quietly that I didn't even notice my potential wife come and go, let alone whether she was pretty or not. "A man mustn't marry a girl he wouldn't even notice," Vediha wisely advised on our leisurely way home in the van. "I was wrong about her; she isn't right for you."

Vediha. Some women are born matchmakers, blessed with a God-given gift for making people happy. I'm not one of them. But when Samiha ran away after my father had already taken money from Korkut and Süleyman, I became a quick study, not only out of fear they might blame me for what happened but also because I felt so sorry for silly Süleyman. I also really loved getting out of the house and driving around in the van.

I'd start by saying that my husband had a younger brother who'd already finished his military service. Growing very serious, I would then launch into a somewhat embellished tale of just how clever, good-looking, respectful, and hardworking Süleyman was.

Süleyman asked me to make sure I told people that he came from a "religious" family. The girls' fathers appreciated this, but I'm not sure it was much of a draw for the girls themselves. I would explain that having become wealthy since moving to the city, the family didn't now want a village girl for their son. Sometimes I'd hint that they had enemies in the village, but this could scare some families off. Whenever I met someone new, I'd almost always mention that I was looking for a suitable girl and ask whether they knew any; but since Korkut's patience with my being out of the house was limited, even for this purpose, I didn't exactly have my pick of candidates. And half of those I did find still acted as if there is something embarrassing about an arranged marriage, which is ridiculous considering this is the way everyone gets married eventually.

People would always say they knew a girl who was exactly what I was looking for, but unfortunately she would never agree to an arranged marriage or even to a visit from a potential suitor. We soon realized that when visiting a prospect it was better not to reveal our purpose and just act as if we happened to be in the neighborhood—perhaps our mutual friend so-and-so had recommended we say hello if we were ever in the area. Or maybe we would say Süleyman needed to check on a site he was managing for his construction company . . .

Sometimes the drop-in approach depended on coming along with someone else paying a call at a particular house. This was essentially a form of mutual assistance between matchmakers, not unlike the way property brokers sometimes help each other out. The invited guest would explain our presence with some excuse made up on the spot—but not before having given the entire household a rather exuberant and exaggerated account of who we were. These small, old-fashioned apartments would invariably be packed with a crowd of inquisitive mothers, aunties, sisters, friends, and grandmothers. The expected guest would introduce us as the famous Aktaş family of Konya, owners of a thriving construction business for which Süleyman oversaw many projects; we'd called on her unexpectedly, and she'd decided to bring us along with her. The only one who even remotely believed these lies was Süleyman himself.

Still, no one ever asked, "If you really were just passing by, then why is Süleyman clean-shaven, wearing that syrupy cologne and sporting his best suit and tie?" For our part, we never asked, "If you really had no idea we were coming, why did you tidy up the house, bring out your best china, and reupholster all the sofas?" The lies were part of the ritual, and just because we were lying, it didn't mean we weren't sincere. We understood one another's private motivations, while making sure to keep up public appearances. These empty words were just a prelude to the main act to come, anyway. In a few minutes, the girl and the boy were to meet. Would they like each other? More important, would this audience judge them to be a good match? As it all unfolded, everyone in the room would begin to remember when they had been the object of this kind of attention.

It wasn't too long before the girl herself appeared, in her best clothes and perhaps even wearing her nicest headscarf, feeling mortified and trying to act nonchalant as she found somewhere to sit at the edge of the crowded room. There were usually so many hopeful young women of roughly the same age in the room that the mother and aunts, veterans of the field, would have to find some casual way of signaling the arrival of the shy girl we had actually come to see.

"Where were you, darling, were you doing your homework? We have guests, look."

In four or five years' worth of these visits and their disappointments, two of the five high-school girls Süleyman was interested in had used school as an excuse to reject us ("I'm afraid our daughter would like to finish her education"), so that Süleyman no longer liked hearing about girls who were supposedly "doing their homework."

When mothers feigned surprise—"Oh, I see we have guests today!"—their daughters could sometimes come out with an embarrassing reply: "Yes, Mom, we know; you've been preparing all day!" I liked these spirited, honest girls, and so did Süleyman, but from the speed with which he was later able to put them out of his mind, I figured that he must have also been a little scared of the way they might treat him.

When we had to deal with girls who flatly refused to meet suitors, we would hide our true purpose. One time, a rude and unpleasant young thing really believed that we had come by simply to bring a gift to her father (who was a waiter) and paid no attention to us at all. With another girl, we had to pretend to be friends of her mother's doctor. One day in spring, we went to an old wooden house in Edirnekapı, near the city walls. The girl we had come to see was playing dodgeball on the street with her friends and had no idea her mother was hosting a potential husband who had come to look her over. Her aunt leaned out of the window to lure her in: "Come up, darling, I've brought you some sesame-seed cookies!" She came straightaway, full of enchanting beauty. But she ignored us. She wolfed down two cookies with her eyes on the TV, and just as she was about to leave the room and go back downstairs to resume her game, her mother said, "Wait, sit down with our guests for a while."

She sat down instinctively, but with one glance at me and at Süleyman's tie, she lost her temper: "It's matchmakers again! I told you I didn't want any more men coming home, Mother!"

"Don't talk to your mother like that . . ."

"Well, that's what they're here for, isn't it? Who is this man?"

"Have some respect . . . They saw you, they liked you, and they've come all the way across the city just to talk to you. You know how bad the traffic is. Now, sit down."

"What am I supposed to say to these people? Am I supposed to marry this fatty?"

She stormed out.

It was the spring of 1989, and this was to be the last of our house visits, which were already growing more infrequent. Now and again, Süleyman would still say, "Find me a wife, Vediha Yenge," but by then we all knew about Mahinur Meryem, so I didn't think he really meant it. He was still talking about how he would have his revenge on Samiha and Ferhat, so I wasn't very happy with him anyway.

Mahinur Meryem. Some regulars at bars and nightclubs may have heard my name before, though they may not remember it. My father was a humble government clerk, an honest, hardworking, but hot-tempered man. I was a promising student at Taksim Secondary School for Girls when our team made the finals of *Milliyet*'s pop-song contest for high schools, and my name ended up in the newspapers. Celâl Salik wrote about me once in his column: "She has the silky voice of a star." It is still the highest praise I've ever received in my singing career. I would like to thank the late Mr. Salik and those who are letting me use my stage name in this book.

My real name is Melahat. Unfortunately, no matter how hard I tried, my singing career never took off after that initial success in high school. My father never understood my dreams, he often beat me, and when he saw I wouldn't make it to college, he tried to get me married off. So when I was nineteen, I ran away from home and got married to a man of my own choosing. My first husband was like me: he loved music, though his father was a janitor at the Şişli town hall. Sadly, it didn't work out, and neither did my second marriage nor any of the relationships that came after that, all ruined by my passion for singing, by poverty, and by the inability of men to keep their promises. I could write a book about all the men I've known, and then I would also end up on trial for insulting Turkishness. I haven't told Süleyman too much about it. I won't waste your time with it now.

Two years ago, I was singing in some horrible dump in the backstreets of Beyoğlu, stubbornly sticking to Turkish pop, but hardly anyone ever came, and I was always scheduled at the very end of the program. So I moved to another tiny bar, where the manager persuaded me that I could be very successful if I switched my repertoire to Turkish classical and folk songs, but again I wasn't on until the very end of the night. It was at the Paris Pavilion that I first met Süleyman—another one of those pushy guys desperately trying to chat me up between numbers. The Paris was a haunt for lovesick men not coping well with their misery but who found some consolation in traditional Turkish music, the specialty of the house, despite the name. At first, I ignored him, of course. But soon enough, he'd softened me up with his lonely presence every night, the armfuls of flowers he sent me, his persistence, and his childlike innocence.

Süleyman now pays my rent for a fourth-floor apartment in Sormagir Street in Cihangir. After a couple of glasses of *rakı* in the evenings, he'll say, "Come on, let's go, I'll take you for a drive in the van." He doesn't realize that there's nothing romantic about his ride, but I don't mind. A year ago, I stopped singing folk songs and performing in small nightclubs. If Süleyman is willing to help, I'd like to go back to singing pop. But it doesn't even matter that much.

I do love driving around in Süleyman's van at night. I'll have a couple of drinks, too, and when we're tipsy, we get along really well and can talk about anything. As soon as he's able to shake off his fear of his brother and get away from his family, Süleyman turns into a kind of lovable, charming guy.

He'll take me down a hill to the Bosphorus, swerving through narrow alleyways.

"Stop it, Süleyman, they'll pull us over!" I'll say.

"Don't worry, they're all our men," he'll say.

Sometimes, I'll tell him what he wants to hear: "Oh, please stop, Süleyman, we're going to fall off and die!" There was a period when we would have this exact exchange every evening.

"What are you scared of, Melahat, do you really think we're going to fall off the road?"

"Süleyman, they're building a new bridge over the Bosphorus, can you believe it?"

"What's not to believe? When we first came from the village, these people thought we'd never be more than just a bunch of poor yogurt sellers," he'd say, getting worked up. "Now those same guys are begging us to sell them our property and using their middlemen to try to get involved in projects. Shall I tell you why I'm so confident that there really is going to be a second bridge soon, exactly like the first?"

"Tell me, Süleyman."

"Because now that Kültepe and Duttepe are all theirs, the Vurals have started buying up all the land around where the highway to the bridge is supposed to be. The government hasn't even begun to seize land for the highway yet. But the land the Vurals bought in Ümraniye, Saray, and Çakmak is already worth ten times what they paid. We're going to fly down this hill now. Don't be scared, okay?"

I helped Süleyman forget about the yogurt seller's daughter he was in love with. When we first met, he couldn't think of anything but her. Without any trace of embarrassment, he'd tell me about how he and his sister-in-law were turning the city inside out trying to find him a wife. At first it was fine, because all my friends made fun of him anyway, and I knew that if only he could get married, I'd finally be rid of him. But now, I have to admit, I'd be sad if Süleyman were to get himself a wife. Still, I don't mind when he goes to see potential brides. One night, he was very drunk, and he confessed that he could never muster any desire for a girl in a headscarf.

"Don't worry, it's a common problem, especially among married men," I said, trying to comfort him. "It's not you, it's all those foreign women on TV and in the newspapers and magazines, so don't obsess over it."

As for *my* obsession, he never understood it. "Süleyman, I don't like it when you talk to me like you're giving me orders," I'd say sometimes.

"Oh, I thought you liked it . . . ," he would say.

"I like your gun, but I don't like you being so rough and cold with me."

"Am I a rough man? Am I really that cold, Melahat?"

"I think you do have feelings, Süleyman, but like most Turkish men, you don't know how to express them. Why do you never tell me the one thing I most want to hear?"

"Is it marriage you want? Will you start wearing a headscarf?"

"I don't want to talk about that. Tell me that other thing you never mention."

"Oh, I get it!"

"Well, if you get it, say it . . . It's no big secret, you know . . . Everyone knows about us now . . . I know how much you love me, Süleyman."

"If you already know, then why do you keep asking?"

"I'm not asking for anything. All I *want* is for you just to say it once . . . Why can't you say 'Melahat, I love you'? . . . Is it so difficult to pronounce those words? Will you lose a bet of some sort if you say it?"

"But, Melahat, when you do this it makes it even harder for me to say the words!"

12

In Tarlabaşı

The Happiest Man in the World

At night, Mevlut and Rayiha slept in the same bed as their two daughters, Fatma and Fevziye. The house was cold, but it was nice and warm under the bedcovers. Sometimes the little ones were already asleep when Mevlut went out to sell boza in the evenings. He would come back late at night to find them asleep in exactly the same position as when he'd left. Rayiha would be sitting under the covers on the edge of the bed, watching TV with the heating turned off.

The girls had their own little bed next to the window, but they were scared of being alone, and even in the same room they would start crying if they were put there. Mevlut, who had the utmost respect for their feelings on this matter, would tell Rayiha, "Isn't it incredible? They're so little, but they're already scared of loneliness." The girls quickly got used to the big bed; there, they could have slept through anything. But when they slept in their own bed, they would wake up at the tiniest sound and start crying, which in turn would wake Mevlut and Rayiha, and the girls wouldn't settle down until they could move to the big bed. Eventually Mevlut and Rayiha saw that sleeping all together in the same bed was better for everyone.

Mevlut had bought them an Arçelik gas stove, secondhand. It could turn the house into a sauna, but it used up too much gas. (Sometimes, to economize, Rayiha would warm their food up on it, too.) She bought the gas from a Kurd whose shop was three streets down in Dolapdere. As the conflict in eastern Turkey grew more violent, Mevlut watched the streets of Tarlabaşı fill up, one family at a time, with Kurdish migrants. These newcomers were tough people, nothing like easygoing Ferhat. Their villages had been evacuated and burned to the ground during the war. They were poor and never bought any boza, so Mevlut rarely went to their neighborhoods. He stopped going altogether when drug dealers and homeless, glue-sniffing young men began to frequent the area.

After Ferhat drove off in a taxi with Samiha in early 1984, Mevlut wouldn't see him again for many years. This was very strange, considering how close they'd been in their childhood and youth, and every now and then Mevlut would offer Rayiha a mumbled explanation: "They live too far away." Only rarely did he allow himself to think that the real reason for the distance between them was in all those letters Mevlut had written with Ferhat's wife, Samiha, in mind.

It was also true that Istanbul's relentless sprawl was driving them farther apart. The bus journey to and from the other's house would have taken half a day. Mevlut missed Ferhat, even as the focus of his resentment toward him kept shifting. He wondered why Ferhat never got in touch. Whatever the reason, it was clearly an admission of guilt. When he found out how happy the newlyweds were in the Ghaazi Quarter and that Ferhat was working as a waiter in a restaurant in Gaziosmanpaşa, Mevlut felt a rush of jealousy.

Some nights, after two hours of selling boza, he pushed himself to go on for just a little bit longer by dreaming there in the empty streets about the happiness awaiting him at home. Just thinking of how their home and their bed smelled, the sounds Fatma and Fevziye made under the covers, the way his body and Rayiha's touched as they slept, how their skin still burned at the contact, brought him close to tears of joy. All he ever wanted when he got home was to put on his pajamas and jump straight into the big, cozy bed. As they watched TV, he would tell Rayiha how much he'd made that night, how the streets had been, the things he'd seen in the houses where he'd made deliveries, and he wouldn't be able to sleep before he'd given her a full account of his day and surrendered himself to her bright, loving eyes.

"They said there was too much sugar in it," he'd whisper, eyes on the TV as he relayed any comments on that day's batch. "Well, I didn't have a choice, yesterday's leftovers were really sour," Rayiha would respond, defending, as always, the mixture she'd prepared. Or perhaps Mevlut might tell her how he'd spent all day worrying about a strange question someone had asked him when he'd gone all the way up to their kitchen to serve them. One night, an old lady had pointed to his apron and said, "Did you buy this yourself?" What had she meant? Was it the color of the apron? Or had she meant to imply that it was something a woman would usually wear?

At night, Mevlut watched the whole world transform into a mysterious realm of shadows, with the city's own darkness cloaking the alleyways, and faraway streets rising like rugged cliffs through the gloom. The cars that chased each other on TV were just as strange as those dark backstreets in the night; who knew where those black mountains on the left side of the TV screen were, why that dog was running, why it was on TV, and why that woman was crying, all by herself?

Rayiha. Sometimes Mevlut would get out of bed in the middle of the night, light a cigarette, and smoke it as he watched the street outside through a gap in the curtains. I could see him in the light of the lamppost outside our house, and I would wonder what he was thinking and wish he'd come back to bed. Sometimes he'd get so lost in his own thoughts, I would get up myself, have a glass of water, and make sure the girls were tucked in properly. Only then would he come back, looking ashamed of himself somehow. "It's nothing," he'd tell me. "I'm just thinking."

Mevlut loved summer evenings because he got to spend *time* with us. But let me tell you something he'll never tell you: we made even less money in the summer than in winter. Mevlut would keep the windows open all day, oblivious to the flies that came into the house, the noise ("It's quieter outside," he'd say), and all the dust from the buildings they kept knocking down for the new road up the hill, and he would watch TV all day with an eye on the girls laughing and playing in the back garden, on the street, or up in a tree, listening from upstairs in case they started fighting and he had to break it up. Some evenings he would lose his temper for no reason, and if he was angry enough, he would walk out, slamming the door behind him (the girls got used to it eventually, but it always scared them a little); he'd go to the coffeehouse to play cards or sit down for a cigarette on the three narrow steps between the entrance to our building and the pavement. Sometimes I would follow him out and sit next to him, and the girls might come, too. Their friends would soon pop out from every corner, and while they played their games on the street and in the garden, I would sit there in the light of the streetlamp sifting the rice Mevlut would later sell down in Kabataş.

It was on these steps that I got to know Reyhan, the woman who lived across the street and two doors down. She stuck her head out of her bay window one day and said, "I think your streetlamp's brighter than ours!" before picking up her embroidery and coming down to sit next to me. "I'm from Eastern Anatolia, but I'm not a Kurd," she would say, as secretive about her hometown as she was about her age. She was at least fifteen years older than me, and she would admire my hands as I sifted the rice. "Look at those hands, smooth as a baby's bottom! Look how quickly they move, like the wings of a dove," she'd say. "You should take up needlework, trust me, you'd make more money than me and that angel you've got for a husband. I earn more than mine does on his policeman's salary, and he really doesn't like it . . ."

When she was fifteen, Reyhan's father decided—without consulting anyone—to give her away to a felt merchant, so she had to go and live in Malatya with nothing but a small bundle of her possessions, never to see her parents or the rest of her family again. She was one of seven children in a desperately poor family, but she didn't think this justified their selling her off the way they did, and sometimes she still argued with them as if they were right there in front of her. "There are parents who won't let men so much as look at their daughters, never mind marrying them off to someone they don't want," she'd say, shaking her head but never taking her eyes off her needlework. She was also upset that her father had sold her to her first husband without the obligation of a civil wedding. She'd eloped with her second husband, though, and this time she'd insisted on a civil ceremony. "I wish I'd said no beatings, too." She'd laugh. "Never forget how lucky you are to have Mevlut."

Reyhan would feign disbelief that men like Mevlut—men who never hit their wives—existed, and she would argue that it must have had something to do with me. She always asked me to repeat the story of how I'd found my "angel husband"—how we'd seen and liked each other at a wedding, how Mevlut had used go-betweens to send me letters when he was away for military service. The policeman would hit her whenever he drank *rakı,* so on those evenings when the table was laid for a drinking session, she'd sit and wait for him to finish his first glass. Then, as soon as he started reminiscing about some interrogation he'd been involved in—which was usually the first sign of an imminent beating—she would get up, take her embroidery, and come over to see me. If I happened to be upstairs, I'd be alerted to her presence downstairs by the sound of her husband Necati's cajoling: "Please come home, my darling Reyhan, I won't have any more, I promise." Sometimes I took the girls with me and joined her on the steps. "Let's sit together for a while, he'll fall asleep soon enough," Reyhan would say. When Mevlut was out selling boza on winter evenings, she'd come and watch TV with me and the girls, telling them stories that made them laugh and nibbling on sunflower seeds all evening. She'd smile at Mevlut when he came home late at night and tell him, "God bless your domestic bliss!"

There were moments when Mevlut could sense that these were the happiest years of his life, but he usually kept this knowledge hidden away at the back of his mind. If he allowed himself to think about how happy he was, he might lose it all. In this life, there were plenty of things to get angry and complain about anyway, each enough to overshadow any momentary happiness: he couldn't abide the way Reyhan was always in their house until late, sticking her nose in their business. He couldn't stand it when Fatma and Fevziye started arguing while they watched TV, screaming and shouting at each other and then bursting into tears. He'd get furious when people told him to make sure to come the next day with ten glasses of boza for their guests only to pretend they weren't home the following night, refusing to let Mevlut inside the building and leaving him to ring their doorbell out in the cold. He'd get livid at the sight of a mother from Kütahya sobbing on TV over the death of her son, killed in Hakkâri when Kurdish militants ambushed his military convoy. He couldn't bear the crybabies who stopped buying cooked rice or boza from street vendors because Chernobyl had exploded and the wind had supposedly brought cancer clouds right over the city. He couldn't stand it when he took such care to reattach the arm on his daughters' plastic doll, using copper electric wires he'd carefully stripped, only for the girls to rip it back out again immediately. When the wind buffeted the TV aerial, he could tolerate the white spots that appeared on the screen like snowflakes, but he couldn't take it when the whole screen got covered in shadows and the image turned blurry. He'd get enraged when the power was cut all over the neighborhood right in the middle of a program on folk songs. When the plot to assassinate President Özal was on the news, and the footage (which Mevlut had seen at least twenty times) of the would-be killer's body writhing on the floor under a barrage of police bullets was interrupted by an advertisement for Hayat yogurt, Mevlut would lose his temper and tell Rayiha, "These bastards and their chemical yogurt have ruined street vendors."

But when Rayiha said, "Take the girls out tomorrow morning so I can give the house a good cleaning," Mevlut would forget about everything that upset him. Walking in the streets with Fevziye in his arms and Fatma's tiny hand inside his own calloused palm made him feel like the happiest man in the world. It filled him with joy to come home after a day spent selling rice and doze off to the sound of his girls talking, to wake up and play games with them (guessing whose hand was on his back or playing tag), or to be approached on the street by a new customer—"I'll have a glass, boza seller"—knowing he had all these little pleasures to look forward to.

During these years of unquestioning gratitude for all of life's blessings, Mevlut was only dimly aware of the gentle passage of time, the death of some pine trees, the way some old timber houses seemed to disappear overnight, the construction of six- or seven-story buildings on those empty plots where kids used to play football and street vendors and the unemployed used to take afternoon naps, and the growing size of the billboards and posters on the streets, just as he barely registered the passing of seasons and the way leaves dried up and fell off trees. It was just the way the end of the boza season or the football championships always caught him by surprise and how he only realized on the last Sunday evening of the 1987 season that Antalyaspor would be relegated. Or the way he noticed the number of overhead pedestrian crossings that had cropped up in the city after the military coup of 1980, and the metal barriers that had been erected along pavements in order to direct people to these crossings, only when he tried and failed one day to cross Halaskargazi Road at street level. Mevlut had heard people in the coffeehouse and on TV talking about the mayor's plans for a big new road from Taksim to Tepebaşı, which would connect Taksim and Şişhane via a route that was to run through Tarlabaşı, five streets up from theirs, but he'd never thought it might be true. Most of the news that Rayiha brought him from the neighborhood's old-timers and gossiping women Mevlut already knew from what he heard on the streets and in the coffeehouse, and through his exchanges with the elderly Greek ladies who lived in moldy, gloomy, ancient apartments around the Çiçek Arcade, the fish market, and the British consulate.

Though no one likes to think or talk about it anymore, Tarlabaşı used to be a neighborhood populated by Greeks, Armenians, Jews, and Assyrians. There used to be a stream—now covered in concrete and forgotten—that flowed from Taksim down to the Golden Horn, taking on a different name in each of the neighborhoods it crossed (Dolap Creek, Bilecik Creek, Bishop's Crossing, Kasımpaşa Creek), and on one shoulder of the valley through which it flowed were the neighborhoods of Kurtuluş and Feriköy, where sixty years ago, in the early 1920s, you could find only Greeks and Armenians. The first blow against the non-Muslim population of Beyoğlu after the birth of the Turkish republic was the 1942 property tax, through which the government, having become increasingly open to German influence during World War II, imposed levies on Tarlabaşı's Christian community that most of them would never be able to pay, and sent the Armenian, Greek, Assyrian, and Jewish men who failed to do so to labor camps in Aşkale. Mevlut had heard countless stories of pharmacists, furniture makers, and Greek families who'd lived here for generations being sent to labor camps for their failure to pay the taxes and having to turn their shops over to their Turkish apprentices or hide out at home for months on end just to escape the authorities searching for people on the street. Most of the Greek population went over to Greece after the anti-Christian uprisings of the sixth and seventh of September 1955, during the war over Cyprus, when mobs armed with sticks and carrying flags looted and vandalized churches and shops, chased priests away, and raped women. Those who didn't leave the country then had to do so overnight in 1964, by government decree.

These stories were usually traded in whispered tones by the neighborhood's long-standing residents after a few drinks at the bar or by those who felt like complaining about the new settlers who'd come to live in the empty homes left behind by the departing Greeks. Mevlut heard people say, "The Greeks were better than these Kurds," and Africans and impoverished migrants were also coming to Tarlabaşı now because the government was doing nothing to stop them; what on earth was next?

Yet when any of the Greek families who'd fled or been banished came back to Istanbul and Tarlabaşı to check on the old houses of which they were still the registered owners, they weren't exactly well received. People were reluctant to tell them the truth—"Your homes have been settled by Anatolian paupers from Bitlis and Adana!"—so even the neighborhood's most good-natured residents often shied away from meeting their old acquaintances. There were those who resented the visitors and treated them with open hostility, convinced that the Greek landlords had only come back to claim their rent; and also those who would meet with their old friends in the coffeehouse and embrace them with tears in their eyes as they remembered the good old days. But these emotional moments never lasted long. Mevlut had watched as some of the Greeks come to see their old homes were heckled and stoned by bands of children recruited by one of the many criminal gangs who operated in the area, working with the government and the police to take over the Greeks' empty homes and rent them out to the poor migrants coming in from Eastern Anatolia. On witnessing this kind of scene, Mevlut's first instinct, like everyone else's, would be to intervene: "Stop that, kids, it's not fair." But he'd start to have second thoughts immediately; the kids would never listen to him anyway, and besides, his own landlord was among the people putting them up to it, so in the end he'd just walk away without saying anything, half ashamed and half furious, thinking, Well, the Greeks seized Cyprus, anyway, or pondering some other injustice he wasn't entirely sure about.

The program of demolitions was announced as an effort to clean up and modernize the city, an approach that appealed to everyone. Criminals, Kurds, Gypsies, and thieves currently squatting in the neighborhood's vacant buildings would get kicked out; drug dens, smugglers' warehouses, brothels, bachelor dormitories, and ruined buildings that served as hubs of illegal activities would be demolished, and in their place would be a new six-lane highway taking you from Tepebaşı to Taksim in five minutes.

There was some protest from the Greek landlords, whose lawyers took the government to court over the property seizures, and from the architects' union and a handful of university students battling to save these historic buildings, but their voices went largely unheard. The mayor had the press on his side, and in one particular instance, when the court warrant for the demolition of one of these old buildings took too long to arrive, he sat at the steering wheel of a bulldozer draped with a Turkish flag and brought down the house himself, cheered on by bystanders. The dust generated by these demolitions would find its way even into Mevlut's house five streets down, seeping in through the cracks in the closed windows. The bulldozers were always surrounded by curious crowds of the unemployed, shop clerks, passersby, and children, the street vendors plying them with *ayran,* sesame rolls, and corn on the cob.

Mevlut was keen to keep his rice cart away from the dust. Throughout these demolition years, he never took his rice anywhere too noisy or crowded. What really struck him was the demolition of the big sixty- and seventy-year-old blocks at the Taksim end of the coming six-lane boulevard. When he'd first come to Istanbul, a light-skinned, fair-haired, kindhearted woman on an enormous billboard six or seven stories high had offered him Tamek tomato ketchup and Lux soap from one of these buildings facing Taksim Square. Mevlut had always liked the way she smiled at him—with silent yet insistent affection—and he made it a point to look up at her every time he came to Taksim Square.

He was very sorry to learn that the famous sandwich shop Crystal Café, which used to be housed in the same building as the woman with the fair hair, had been demolished along with the building itself. No other place in Istanbul had ever sold as much *ayran*. Mevlut had tried its signature dish twice (once on the house)—a spicy hamburger dipped in tomato sauce—and he'd also had some of their *ayran* to go with it. The Crystal got the yogurt for their *ayran* from the enormous Concrete Brothers of Cennetpınar's neighboring village of İmrenler. Concrete Abdullah and Concrete Nurullah didn't furnish yogurt only to the Crystal Café; they also did regular business with a whole host of restaurants and cafés in Taksim, Osmanbey, and Beyoğlu, all of them buying in great quantity, and up until the mid-1970s, when the big yogurt companies started to distribute their product in glass bowls and wooden barrels, the brothers made a fortune, taking over territory in Kültepe, Duttepe, and the Asian side of the city, until they were swept away in the space of two years, along with all the other yogurt vendors. Mevlut realized how much he'd envied the rich and capable Concrete Brothers—so much cleverer than he was, they didn't even need to sell boza in the evenings to make ends meet—when he realized he was interpreting the demolition of the Crystal Café as some sort of punishment of them.

Mevlut had been in Istanbul for twenty years. It was sad to see the old face of the city as he had come to know it disappear before his eyes, erased by new roads, demolitions, buildings, billboards, shops, tunnels, and flyovers, but it was also gratifying to feel that someone out there was working to improve the city for his benefit. He didn't see it as a place that had existed before his arrival and to which he'd come as an outsider. Instead, he liked to imagine that Istanbul was being built while he lived in it and to dream of how much cleaner, more beautiful, and more modern it would be in the future. He was fond of the people who lived in its historic buildings with fifty-year-old elevators, central heating, and high ceilings, built while he was still back in the village or before he'd even been born, and he never forgot that these were the people who had always treated him more kindly than anyone else. But these buildings inevitably reminded him that he was still a stranger here. Their doormen were condescending even if they didn't mean to be, which always left him scared of making a mistake. But he liked old things: the feeling of walking into one of those cemeteries he discovered while selling boza in distant neighborhoods, the sight of a mosque wall covered in moss, and the unintelligible Ottoman writing on a broken fountain with its brass taps long dried up.

Sometimes he thought of how he broke his back every day even now just to scrape by with a rice business that wasn't really profitable, while all around him everyone who'd come from somewhere else was getting rich, buying property, and building his own home on his own land, but in those moments he told himself that it would be ungrateful to want more than the happiness God had already given him. And once in a great while, he noticed the storks flying overhead and realized that the seasons were passing, another winter was over, and he was slowly getting older.

13

Süleyman Stirs Up Trouble

Isn't That What Happened?

Rayiha. I used to take Fatma and Fevziye to Duttepe (just one ticket between them) so they could spend time with their aunt Vediha and have a place where they could run around and pick mulberries, but I can't do that anymore. The last time I went, two months ago, I got cornered by Süleyman, who started asking me about Mevlut. I told him he was fine. But then, in that typical wisecracking way of his, he brought up Ferhat and Samiha.

"We haven't seen them since they ran away, Süleyman, really," I said, telling him the same old lie.

"You know, I think I believe you," said Süleyman. "I doubt Mevlut would want anything to do with Ferhat and Samiha anymore. Do you know why?"

"Why?"

"Surely you must know, Rayiha. All those letters Mevlut wrote when he was in the military were meant for Samiha."

"What?"

"I read some of them before I passed them on to Vediha to give to you. Those eyes Mevlut wrote about were not your eyes, Rayiha."

He said it all with a smirk, as if this were all in good fun. So I played along, smiling back. Thank God I then had the presence of mind to say, "If Mevlut meant the letters for Samiha, why did you bring them to me?"

Süleyman. I had no intention of upsetting poor Rayiha. But in the end, isn't the truth what matters most? She didn't say another word to me, she just said good-bye to Vediha, took her girls, and left. Occasionally, when it was time for them to go, I'd put them all in my van and drive them up to the Mecidiyeköy bus stop myself, just to make sure they got back on time and Mevlut didn't get annoyed because no one was there when he got home in the evening. The girls love the van. But that day, Rayiha didn't even bother to say good-bye to me. When Mevlut gets home, I doubt she'll ask him "Did you write those letters to Samiha?" She'll cry about it for sure. But once she's thought it over, she'll realize that everything I told her is true.

Rayiha. I sat with Fevziye on my lap and Fatma beside me on the bus ride from Mecidiyeköy to Taksim. My daughters can always tell when their mother is sad or upset, even when I don't say anything. As we walked home, I said with a frown, "Don't tell your father we went to see your aunt Vediha, okay?" It came to me that maybe the reason that Mevlut doesn't want me going to Duttepe is to keep me as far as possible from Süleyman's insinuations. As soon as I saw Mevlut's sweet, boyish face that evening, I knew Süleyman was lying. But the next morning, while the girls were out playing in the garden, I remembered the way Mevlut had looked at me in Akşehir train station the night we eloped, and I became uneasy again . . . Süleyman had been the one driving the van that day.

I took the letters out from where I kept them, and when I read through them again, I felt relieved: they sounded exactly the way Mevlut talks to me when we're alone together. I felt guilty for having paid any mind to Süleyman's lies. But then I remembered that Süleyman himself had brought me the letters, and that he'd used Vediha to convince me to run away with Mevlut, and I felt unsure. That was when I vowed never to go to Duttepe again.

Vediha. One afternoon, just after Mevlut would have left to sell his rice, I snuck out of the house and got on a bus to Tarlabaşı to see

Rayiha. My little sister greeted me with tears of joy in her eyes. She was busy frying chicken with her hair pulled back like a chef's, a huge fork in her hand and a cloud of smoke with the scent of cooking swirling around her as she yelled at the kids to stop making a mess. I gave the girls a hug and kiss before she sent them out to play in the garden. "They've both been sick, or else we would have been by," she said. "Mevlut doesn't even know about my visits."

"But Rayiha, Korkut never lets me out of the house, and certainly nowhere near Beyoğlu. How are we ever going to see each other?"

"The girls are scared of your boys, now. Do you remember what Bozkurt and Turan did that time, when they tied poor Fatma to a tree and started shooting arrows at her? They split her eyebrow wide open."

"Don't you worry, Rayiha; I gave them quite a beating over it and made them swear they'll never hurt the girls again. Anyway, Bozkurt and Turan aren't back from school until after four. Tell me the truth, Rayiha, is that really why you haven't been coming, or is it Mevlut who's told you not to?"

"Actually, if you want to know, it's not Mevlut's fault. It's Süleyman who's to blame; he's trying to cause trouble. He was saying that the letters Mevlut wrote me when he was in the army were really meant for Samiha."

"Oh, Rayiha, you can't let Süleyman get to you . . ."

Rayiha pulled out a bundle of letters from the bottom of her wicker sewing box and opened one of the yellowing envelopes at random. "'My life, my soul, my one and only doe-eyed Miss Rayiha,'" she read, and she burst into tears.

Süleyman. I really can't stand Mahinur when she starts mocking my family and saying we still belong in the village. As if she were a general's daughter or a doctor's wife or something, and not a government clerk's nightclub-hostess daughter. Give her two glasses of *rakı,* and she'll get going: "Were you some sort of shepherd, back home?" she'll say, raising her eyebrows gravely as if it were a serious question.

"You've had too much to drink again," I'll tell her.

"Who, me? You drink plenty more than I do, and then you lose control. Hit me again and I'll give you a taste of the fire iron."

I went home. My mother and Vediha were watching Gorbachev and Bush kissing each other on TV. Korkut was out, and I was just thinking I might have another drink when Vediha ambushed me in the kitchen.

"Now listen to me, Süleyman," she said. "If you cause Rayiha to stop coming to this house, I will never forgive you. She truly believes these lies and stupid jokes of yours, you've got the poor girl in tears."

"Oh, fine, Vediha, I won't say anything more to her. But why don't we get our facts straight first, if we're going to keep telling lies to spare people's feelings."

"Süleyman, let's imagine for a minute that Mevlut really *did* see Samiha and fell in love with her, but then wrote his letters to Rayiha because he thought that was her name."

"Well, that is exactly what happened . . ."

"No, what's likelier is that you tricked him on purpose . . ."

"I just helped Mevlut get married."

"Have it your way, but what good does it do to dredge it all up now? Apart from causing poor Rayiha a lot of pain?"

"Vediha, you've done your best to find me a wife. Now you have to face the truth."

"None of the things you said actually happened," said Vediha in a steely tone. "I will tell your brother, too. I'll have no more of this. Understood?"

As you see, whenever she wants to intimidate me, Vediha refers to her husband as "your brother" instead of "Korkut."

Rayiha. I can be making a warm compress to soothe Fatma's earache, when I'll drop what I'm doing and go pick out a letter from one of the bundles I keep in my sewing box and skim to find the part where Mevlut compares my eyes to "the melancholy mountains of Kars." In the evening, while I'm listening to Reyhan's chatter and to the girls wheezing and coughing in their sleep while I'm waiting for Mevlut to come home, I'll get up as if in a dream and go back to where Mevlut wrote "I need no other gaze, no other sun in my life." In the mornings, when I'm at the fish market with Fatma and Fevziye in Balıkpazarı, standing in that stench and watching Hamdi the poultry dealer plucking a chicken before he hacks it to pieces and smokes the skin, I'll remember how Mevlut once called me his "darling who smells of roses and of heaven, true to her name," and instantly feel better. When the south wind makes the city reek of sewage and seaweed, the sky looks the color of a rotten egg, and I feel a weight on my soul, I'll go back to the letter in which he told me my eyes were "as dark as fathomless night and as clear as fresh spring water."

Abdurrahman Efendi. There's no pleasure in village life anymore, now that I've married my girls off, so I go to Istanbul whenever I get the chance. As the buses rattle along and I fall in and out of sleep, I always find myself wondering bitterly if I'm even wanted there at all. In Istanbul, I stay at Vediha's and try my best to avoid grumpy Korkut and his grocer father, Hasan, who looks more like a ghost with every passing year. I'm a tired old man without a penny to my name, and I've never stayed in a hotel in my life. I think there's something undignified about having to pay for a place to sleep at night.

It is not true that I took gifts and money from Süleyman and Korkut in exchange for letting Süleyman marry my daughter Samiha, nor does the fact that Samiha eloped mean that I must have been tricking them all along. Korkut did pay for my teeth, but I saw this generosity as a gift from Vediha's husband, not as the bride price for my youngest daughter. Not to mention how insulting it is to suggest that a beauty like Samiha should be worth no more than a set of dentures.

Süleyman still won't let it go, so I always try to stay away from him whenever I'm at the Aktaş home, but one night he caught me having a bite to eat in the kitchen. We hugged like father and son, which was unusual for us. His father had already gone to sleep, so we turned with great relish to the half a bottle of *rakı* Süleyman had hidden behind the potato basket. I'm not entirely sure what happened next, but just before the call to prayer at dawn, I heard Süleyman saying the same thing over and over again. "Father, you're a straight-talking kind of man, so be honest with me now, isn't that what happened?" he repeated. "Mevlut wrote those love letters for Samiha."

"Süleyman, my son, it doesn't really matter who was in love with whom when it all began. What matters is being happy after the wedding. That's why when a girl and boy are engaged to be married, our Prophet says they shouldn't be allowed to meet before the wedding and waste all the excitement of lovemaking beforehand, and it's also why the Koran forbids women from going around with their heads uncovered . . ."

"Very true," said Süleyman. Though I don't think he really agreed with me; he just didn't dare argue against anything that had to do with the Holy Prophet or the Koran.

"In our realm," I continued, "girls and boys who are engaged don't get to know each other at all until they're married, so it doesn't matter who was meant to receive their love letters. The letter is just a token; what really counts is what is in your heart."

"So what you're saying is that it doesn't matter that Mevlut wrote letters meant for Samiha when his fate was to be with Rayiha?"

"It doesn't matter."

Süleyman frowned. "God takes note of His creatures' true intentions. The Lord favors a man who intends to fast during Ramadan over a man who fasts because he can't find food to eat anyway. Because one of them means it, while the other one doesn't."

"Mevlut and Rayiha are good people in the eyes of Allah the Merciful. Don't worry about them," I said. "They will have God's blessing. God loves happy people, who know how to make the best of the little they have. Would Mevlut and Rayiha be happy if He didn't love them? And if they're happy, then it's not our place to say any more, is it, son?"

Süleyman. If Rayiha actually believed those letters were meant for her, why didn't she tell Mevlut to ask her father for her hand? They could have been married immediately, without needing to elope. It's not like she had other suitors. But it was always assumed that Crooked-Necked Abdurrahman would ask for a lot of money in exchange for his daughter's hand . . . So Rayiha would have ended up a spinster, and her father wouldn't have been able to move on to marrying off the next daughter, Samiha—the one who's really pretty. It's that simple. (Of course he ended up making no money from his youngest daughter either, but that's beside the point.)

Abdurrahman Efendi. I left after a while and went to stay with my youngest daughter in the Ghaazi Quarter, all the way at the other end of the city. Süleyman still can't get over what happened, so I told no one I was going to stay at Samiha and Ferhat's, pretending instead that I was going back to the village. Vediha and I cried as we hugged each other good-bye, as if this time I might die when I went back to the village. I took my bag and boarded the bus from Mecidiyeköy to Taksim. Since we were not moving in the traffic at all, some of the passengers, fed up with being piled one on top of the other, yelled "Open the door, driver" every time we came to a standstill, but the driver refused: "We're not at the stop yet." I followed the ongoing argument without getting involved. We were also packed like sardines on the next bus I took, and by the time I got off at Gaziosmanpaşa, I felt I'd been completely flattened. I took a blue minibus from Gaziosmanpaşa and reached the Ghaazi Quarter at dusk.

This part of the city seemed colder and darker; the clouds here hung lower and looked more fearsome. I hurried up a hill; the whole neighborhood was really just one long slope. There was nobody around, and I could smell the forest and the lake at the edge of the city. A deep silence had descended from the mountains onto the ghostlike homes around me.

My darling daughter opened the door, and for some reason we both cried as we embraced. I knew straightaway that my Samiha was crying because she was lonely and unhappy. That evening, her husband, Ferhat, didn't make it home until around midnight and fell straight into bed. They both work so hard that, by nighttime, they have neither the energy nor the heart to be together in this house in the middle of nowhere. Ferhat showed me his certificate from the University of Anatolia; he'd finally managed to get a college degree through a correspondence course. Maybe they would be happy now. But by nightfall, I was too worried to sleep. This Ferhat can never make my beautiful, clever, darling, long-suffering Samiha happy. It's not that they eloped, you see; what bothers me is that this man is making her work as a maid.

But Samiha refuses to admit that having to clean other people's homes makes her unhappy. When her husband left for work in the morning (whatever it is that he does), Samiha acted as if she were perfectly happy with her life. She'd taken the day off to be with me. She fried two eggs for me. She took me to the window at the back and showed me her husband's plot of land marked with phosphorescent stones. We went out into the little garden of their house on top of a hill, and all around us were more hills covered with poor neighborhoods of houses that looked like white boxes. The outline of the city itself was almost invisible in the distance, half hidden like a monstrous creature lying in a pool of mud, smothered in fog and factory fumes. "Dad, do you see those hills over there?" said Samiha, pointing at the poor neighborhoods all around us. She shivered. "When we first came here five years ago, all these hills were empty." She started crying.

Rayiha. "You can tell your father that Grandpa Abdurrahman and Aunt Vediha came to see you, but you mustn't tell him that Aunt Samiha was here, understood?" "Why?" asked Fatma in her usual inquisitive way. I frowned and shook my head a little as I usually do when I'm about to run out of patience and give them a slap, and after that they both kept quiet.

As soon as my father and Samiha arrived, one of the girls climbed onto Father's chest, and the other went to sit on Samiha's lap. Father stood Fatma on his knees and engaged her in a thumb-wrestling match and a game of rock-paper-scissors, giving her riddles to solve and showing her his little pocket mirror, the watch he carried on a chain, and his lighter that didn't work. When Samiha hugged Fevziye so hard, showering her with kisses, I knew straightaway that only a big bustling home with three or four babies of her own could relieve the pain of the loneliness she carried inside. Every kiss came with an expression of wonder—"Look at that hand! And look at that mole!"—and every single time I couldn't help but lean over and examine Fevziye's hand or the mole on Fatma's neck.

Vediha. "Why don't you go take Aunt Samiha to see the talking tree in the back garden and the fairy courtyard of the Assyrian church," I said, and off they went. I was just about to tell Rayiha that there was no reason to be afraid of Süleyman anymore, that Bozkurt and Turan had started behaving themselves, and that she should start bringing the girls over again, when my father said something that made us both really angry.

Abdurrahman Efendi. I don't know why they're so angry at me. I can't think of anything more natural than a father worrying about his daughters' happiness. When Samiha went out in the garden with the girls, I told Rayiha and Vediha about their little sister's lonely misery in that crumbling one-room house out on the other side of the city with nothing but cold, grief, and ghosts for company, and how I'd had my fill of the place after five days and decided to go back to the village.

"Between you and me, what your sister needs is a real husband that can make her happy."

Rayiha. I don't know what came over me, but all of a sudden I was so furious that I said some things bound to break my poor father's heart, surprising even myself as the words came out of my mouth. "Don't you dare wreck the girl's marriage, Father," I said. WE ARE NOT FOR SALE, I said. Yet part of me knew that my father was right, and I could see that poor Samiha no longer had the strength to mask her misery. There was also something else my mind kept going back to. We'd spent our childhood and adolescence hearing things like "Samiha is the prettiest and the most enchanting of you all, she's the most beautiful girl in the world," and now here she was, penniless, childless, and full of sadness, while Mevlut and I were happy; was this God's way of testing people's devotion, or was it divine justice?

Abdurrahman Efendi. Vediha went as far as to say, WHAT KIND OF FATHER ARE YOU. "What kind of father tries to break up a marriage just so he can sell his daughter off and cash in on her bride price?" That was so hurtful I thought it might be better to pretend I hadn't heard it, but I couldn't help myself. "Shame on you," I said. "Everything I've endured, all the humiliation, it was all for the sake of finding you husbands who could provide for you, not so I could sell you off at a profit. A father who asks his daughter's suitor for money is only trying to recover some of the expenses of raising her, sending her to school, putting clothes on her back, and bringing her up to be a good mother one day. This bride price doesn't just tell us how much a man feels his future wife might be worth; it's also the only money anyone in this country ever spends on sending their daughters to school. Do you understand now? Every single father in this country, down to the most open-minded of them all, will do whatever it takes to make sure he has a son instead of a daughter—whether it be a ritual sacrifice, a magic spell, or going into every mosque he can find and begging God for a baby boy. But unlike all these mean-spirited men, did I not rejoice at the birth of each and every one of my daughters? Have I ever laid a finger on any one of you? Have I ever shouted at you or said anything to cause you pain, have I ever raised my voice or let the slightest shadow of sorrow fall upon your beautiful faces? Now you tell me you don't love your father? Well, then, I'm better off dead!"

Rayiha. Out in the garden, the girls were showing their aunt Samiha the enchanted dustbin, the train of worms that went through the broken flowerpot, and the tin palace that belonged to the weeping tin princess, who would give two shuddering cries every time you hit her. "If I really was this cruel man who kept his daughters locked in a cage, how were they able to get away with exchanging letters with some good-for-nothing scoundrel right under my nose?" said my father.

Abdurrahman Efendi. It was hard for a proud father like me to bear the weight of the awful things being said. I asked for a glass of *rakı* before it was even time for the midafternoon prayers. I got up and opened the fridge, but Rayiha stopped me. "Mevlut doesn't drink, Dad," she said. "I can go buy you a bottle of Yeni Rakı, if you want." She closed the fridge.

"You don't need to be ashamed, my dear . . . Samiha's fridge is even emptier."

"All we have in ours are the leftovers from the rice and chicken Mevlut can't sell," said Rayiha. "We've also started putting our boza in there overnight; otherwise it goes off."

I stumbled into an armchair in the corner, feeling as if some strange memory had popped into my head and darkened my vision. I must have fallen asleep, because in my dream I was riding a white horse among a flock of sheep, but just as I realized that the sheep were actually clouds, my nose began to hurt, growing as big as the horse's nostrils, at which point I woke up. Fatma was grabbing my nose, pulling on it with all her might.

"What are you doing!" yelled Rayiha.

"Dad, let's go to the shop and get you a bottle of *rakı,*" said my darling daughter Vediha.

"Fatma and Fevziye can come with us and show their grandpa the way to the shop."

Samiha. Rayiha and I watched my father, bent in half and smaller than ever under his hunched back, holding hands with the girls on the way to the shop. They'd reached the end of the narrow alley and were just about to turn the corner onto the sloping road when they turned around and waved, sensing our presence at the window. Once they were gone, Rayiha and I sat facing each other without exchanging a word, thinking that we could still understand each other perfectly just as when we were little. Back then we used to tease Vediha, and if we got in trouble, we'd just stop talking and switch to winks and gestures. But in that moment I realized we couldn't do it anymore; those days were behind us.

Rayiha. Samiha lit up a cigarette in my presence for the first time ever. She told me she'd picked up the habit from the wealthy people whose homes she cleaned, not from Ferhat. "Don't you worry about Ferhat," she said. "He's got a degree now, he has contacts at the electricity board, and he's got himself a job; soon we'll be doing all right, so don't worry about us. Don't let Father anywhere near that Süleyman. I'm fine."

"Do you know what that creep Süleyman told me the other day?" I said. I looked inside my sewing box and took out a bundle tied up with a ribbon. "You know these letters Mevlut sent me when he was in the army . . . Apparently they weren't meant for me, but for you, Samiha."

Before she could respond, I started pulling envelopes out and reciting passages at random. Back in the village, I used to read bits out for Samiha whenever Father wasn't home. It would always make us smile. But I already knew we wouldn't be smiling this time. When I read the part about my eyes, "black like melancholy suns," I almost started crying, I suddenly had trouble swallowing, and I knew that telling Samiha about the lies Süleyman was spreading had been a mistake.

"Don't be silly, Rayiha, how can that be?" she said, but at the same time she was looking at me as if what I'd said might even be true. I could sense that Samiha was flattered by the letters, as if Mevlut really had been talking about her. So I stopped reading. I missed my Mevlut. I realized just how angry Samiha was with me and with us all, far away in that distant neighborhood of hers. Mevlut would be home any minute, so I changed the subject.

Samiha. My heart sank when Rayiha mentioned her husband would be home soon, and later when Vediha looked at me and said, "Dad and I were just about to leave anyway." It all made me really upset. I'm on the bus back to Gaziosmanpaşa now, sitting by the window and feeling low. I'm wiping my eyes with the hem of my headscarf. Earlier, I had the distinct impression that they wanted me to leave before Mevlut got back. All because Mevlut wrote those letters to me! How is that my fault? I couldn't have said any of this openly, of course, since they would have just said what a pity it was that I felt this way and proceeded to voice their shared concern: "How can you even think that, Samiha, you know how much we love you!" They would have blamed my reaction on Ferhat's money troubles, my having to work as a maid, and the fact that I still don't have any children. To be honest, I don't even mind; I love them all very much. But I did wonder once or twice whether Mevlut could really have meant those letters for me. I told myself, Samiha, stop, don't think about it, it's not right. Yet I continued to wonder—more than once or twice, actually. Women have no more control over their thoughts than over their dreams; and so these thoughts ramble through my head like nervous burglars in a pitch-black house.

I lay down in my tiny maid's room in the plush home of the Şişli rich, and as the pigeons in the inner courtyard stood still on their perches and sighed in the darkness, I wondered what Ferhat would do if he ever found out. I even wondered if perhaps my sweet Rayiha had told me all this to make me feel better about my lot. One night, after a weary journey on a weary bus, I came home to find Ferhat slumped in front of the television, and I felt the urge to shake him awake before he drifted to sleep.

"Do you know what Rayiha told me the other day?" I said. "You know those letters Mevlut sent her . . . He'd meant them for me all along."

"From the very beginning?" said Ferhat, without taking his eyes off the television.

"Yes, from the very beginning."

"Mevlut didn't write those first letters to Rayiha," he said, now looking at me. "I wrote them."

"What?"

"What would Mevlut know about love letters . . . He came to me before taking off for military service, he told me he was in love, so I wrote some letters for him."

"Did you write them for me?"

"No. Mevlut asked me to write to Rayiha," said Ferhat. "He told me all about how much he loved her."

14

Mevlut Finds a New Spot

I'll Go and Pick It Up First Thing Tomorrow Morning

IN THE WINTER of 1989, seven years into his life as a cooked-rice vendor, Mevlut began to clearly observe that the younger generations were growing increasingly suspicious of his presence. "If you don't like my rice, you can have your money back," he'd tell them. But so far none of these young workers had ever asked for a refund. His poorer, angrier, more loutish customers, and the loners who didn't care what anyone thought, would often leave half their order uneaten and sometimes demand that Mevlut only charge them half the price, which request Mevlut would oblige. Then in a single, surreptitious move that he himself scarcely wanted to admit, he would put the uneaten portions of rice and chicken right back into their respective compartments in his cart and tip anything not fit to save into a box for the stray cats or to get rid of on the way home. He never told his wife about those customers who left half-eaten portions. Rayiha had been diligently cooking rice and chicken the same way for more than six years, so it couldn't have been her fault. When he tried to understand why the new generation was nowhere near as taken with his rice as those he'd served in earlier days, he came up with several possibilities.

Among the younger generations there was now a regrettable misconception, fueled by newspapers and TV, that street food was "dirty." Milk, yogurt, tomato paste, beef sausage, and canned vegetable companies kept bombarding people with advertisements about how "hygienic" their products were and how everything they sold was machine processed and "untouched by human hands," to the point that sometimes Mevlut would find himself shouting back at the screen, "Oh, come on!"—scaring Fatma and Fevziye, who thought perhaps the TV was actually alive. Before they bought his rice, some customers would check the cleanliness of his plates, cups, and cutlery. Mevlut knew that these same people, so condescending and suspicious with him, would have no problem whatsoever eating from a big plate shared among friends and relatives. They didn't care about cleanliness when they were with people they felt close to. This could only mean they didn't trust Mevlut or consider him their equal.

In the past two years, he had also noticed that filling your stomach with a quick plate of rice for lunch carried the risk of making you "look poor." Rice with chicken and chickpeas wasn't even that filling, unless you had it as a snack between meals, as you might sesame rolls or biscuits. There was also nothing particularly strange or exotic about it, unlike, say, stuffed mussels, which contained raisins and cinnamon and had once been a pricey dish served only in certain bars and restaurants until the migrant community from Mardin turned them into a cheap street snack everyone could afford. (Mevlut had never tried them, though he'd always wondered what they tasted like.) Gone were the days when offices would place bulk orders with street vendors. The golden years of Ottoman-style street food—panfried liver, lamb's head, and grilled meatballs—were all but forgotten, thanks to this new breed of office worker so fond of disposable plastic cutlery. Back then, you could start off with a street stall outside any big office building and end up with a proper grilled-meatball restaurant on the same corner, serving the same long-standing lunchtime clientele.

Every year, when it started getting colder and the boza season approached, Mevlut had gone to a wholesaler down in Sirkeci and bought a huge sack of dry chickpeas to last him until the next winter. That year, however, he didn't have enough money saved up to buy his usual sack of chickpeas. His income from the rice had stayed the same, but it was no longer enough to cover the rising costs of food and clothing for his daughters. He was spending more and more money on needless things, the treats with Western-sounding names that irritated him whenever he heard them on TV—TipiTip chewing gum, Golden chocolate bars, Super ice cream—as well as on an assortment of flower-shaped sweets, teddy bears that came with newspaper coupons, multicolored hair clips, toy watches, and pocket mirrors, which suffused him with pleasure at every purchase but left him feeling guilty, too, and somehow inadequate. If it hadn't been for the boza he sold on winter evenings, the rent from his late father's house in Kültepe, and the money Rayiha earned embroidering bedsheets for a handful of bridal trousseau shops Reyhan had told her about, Mevlut would have had trouble covering the rent on their own home and the gas he funneled into their stove on cold winter days.

The crowds in Kabataş always thinned out after lunch. Mevlut began to look for a new spot to park his cart from two to five in the afternoon. Far from reducing the distance that separated their house from İstiklal Avenue and Beyoğlu, the new Tarlabaşı Boulevard seemed to have pushed them even farther out and down the social ladder. The part of Tarlabaşı that had ended up on the other side of this road quickly filled up with nightclubs, bars, and other places where you could hear classical Turkish music while being served alcohol, so that soon all the families and the poor living there had to move out, as property prices rose, and the whole area became an extension of Istanbul's biggest entertainment district. But none of this wealth had reached the streets on Mevlut's side of the big road. Instead, the metal railings and concrete barriers running along the middle of the road and all along the sidewalks to prevent pedestrians from crossing over at street level had the effect of pushing Mevlut's neighborhood farther toward Kasımpaşa and the deprived working-class quarters that rose among the ruins of the old shipyard.

There was no way Mevlut could push his cart over the concrete barriers and metal railings that ran the length of the six-lane road, nor could he use the overhead pedestrian crossings; and so the shortcut he had always taken to get home, cutting through the crowds on İstiklal Avenue on his way from Kabataş, was no longer available, leaving him no choice but to go the long way around through Talimhane. There were plans to limit İstiklal to foot traffic (leading to endless roadwork that had littered the whole street with potholes), except for a single tramline described in the newspapers as "nostalgic" (a word Mevlut didn't like); as a result big foreign brands had opened shops lining the avenue, all of which made it harder for street vendors to come here. Beyoğlu's police patrolled in their blue uniforms and dark glasses, swooping down on those selling sesame rolls, cassettes, stuffed mussels, meatballs, and almonds, the vendors who repaired lighters, sold grilled sausages, and made sandwiches all along the main avenue and on the side streets, too. One of them, who sold Albanian-style pan-fried liver and made no secret of his contacts at the Beyoğlu police station, had told Mevlut that any street vendors who could survive around İstiklal were either undercover agents or informants who reported to the police daily.

The crowds of Beyoğlu, flowing inexorably through the streets like the tributaries of a colossal river, had once again changed course and speed, as they so often did, with people starting to congregate at different corners and crossroads. Street vendors would rush to these new meeting hubs immediately, and even though the police chased them away, they'd be replaced in time by sandwich and kebab stalls, eventually to be succeeded by actual kebab restaurants and cigarette and newspaper stands, until finally neighborhood grocers would start selling kebab wraps and ice cream in front of their shops, and fruit-and-vegetable sellers would stay open all night with a constant stream of Turkish pop songs playing somewhere in the background. All these changes, small and large, brought to light a number of interesting new spots where Mevlut thought he might try to park his cart for a while.

He found a little gap on a street in Talimhane, between a stack of timber meant for a construction site and an old abandoned Greek house. For a time, this became the place where he would await afternoon customers. The offices of the electricity board were across the road, and the people queuing up there to pay their bills, reactivate their power, and apply for a meter soon discovered the cooked-rice seller nearby. Mevlut was just starting to think that he might sell more rice if he spent lunchtimes here instead of in Kabataş when the guard at the construction site—who'd been eating for free in exchange for looking the other way—told Mevlut to get lost because his bosses didn't like having him around.

Two hundred meters down the road, he found another small gap right next to the ruins of the Gloria Theatre. This hundred-year-old wooden building, owned by an Armenian charity trust, had gone up in flames on a cold winter night in 1987. Mevlut reflected how it was only two years ago that he was out selling boza in Taksim when he'd seen the fire in the distance and stood watching it, along with the rest of the city. There had been widespread rumors of arson, as the grand old theater, known for its Western-music recitals, had staged a play that made fun of Islamists, but the allegations had never been proven. Mevlut had never heard the word "Islamist" before. A play that mocked Islamic sensibilities was, of course, not to be tolerated, but at the time he had felt that burning down an entire building was probably an overreaction. Now, as he stood there, freezing in the cold and waiting for customers that did not come, he thought about the soul of the night watchman, who'd been burned alive with the rest of the building; the oft-expressed superstition that anyone who'd ever enjoyed an evening in that theater was cursed to die young; and the fact that a long time ago this area and the whole of Taksim Square had been an Armenian cemetery. In light of all this, it seemed reasonable that no one should ever come to his hidden haven for a plate of chicken and rice. He held out for five days before deciding to look elsewhere for a place to park his white cart.

He sought a little corner for his restaurant on wheels in Talimhane, behind Elmadağ, in the alleyways that wound down in Dolapdere and around Harbiye. He still had regular nighttime boza customers in all these neighborhoods, but the daytime was a different world. Sometimes Mevlut would entrust his rice cart to the barbershop next to the burned-down theater so he could wander among the local car-parts dealers, grocery stores, cheap diners, estate agents, upholsterers, and electricians. In Kabataş, if he needed the toilet or felt like stretching his legs, he would usually leave his cart with a friend who sold stuffed mussels or with some other acquaintance, but he would always hurry back in case a customer showed up. Here, though, leaving his cart was like running away from it, a feeling straight out of a dream. Sometimes, he felt the guilty urge to abandon the cart entirely.

One day he saw Neriman walking ahead of him in Harbiye, and

he was amazed to feel his heart speed up. It was a surprising emotion, like running into your younger self on the street. When the woman stopped to look in a shopwindow, Mevlut saw that it wasn't Neriman at all. He realized that the thought of her must have been lurking somewhere in the back of his mind these past few days as he was going by Harbiye's travel agencies, and suddenly, visions from fifteen years ago, when he yet had dreams of finishing high school, started coming to him through the fog of memory: of the streets of Istanbul, which had been so much emptier back then; of the joys of masturbating at home alone; of the overwhelming isolation that had endowed everything with meaning; the leaves that fell off chestnut and plane trees in autumn, littering the streets; the kindness people used to show a sweet little boy selling yogurt . . . It had all come with a burden of loneliness and sorrow that he'd carried in his heart and in his gut, but he had no memory of those feelings now, and so he remembered his life fifteen years ago as a perfectly happy time. He felt a curious sense of regret, as if he'd lived his life for nothing. Yet he was so content with Rayiha.

When he returned to the burned-down theater, his cart had disappeared. Mevlut couldn't believe his eyes. It was a cloudy day in winter, with dusk falling earlier than usual. He went into the barbershop where the lights had already been switched on for the evening.

"The police took your cart," said the barber. "I told them you were on your way back, but they wouldn't listen."

In all his years as a street vendor, it was the first time this had ever happened to Mevlut.

Ferhat. Mevlut lost his rice cart to the municipal police over on our side of town just around the time I started working as an inspector for the electricity board, which was based in Taksim in a building shaped like a matchbox, much like the Hilton Hotel. But we never ran into each other. Had I known that he was parking nearby, would I have gone to look for him? I don't know. But this claim that Mevlut had written his love letters to *my* wife rather than his own made me realize that it was time to clarify my thoughts on the matter, both private and public.

I've always known that at Korkut's wedding Mevlut got only a fleeting look at Abdurrahman Efendi's other daughters—so what's it to me if he meant his letters for one or the other? I had no idea that he'd been dreaming of Samiha all along when he wound up eloping with Rayiha. He was too embarrassed ever to tell me. So, privately, I'm not bothered by any of it. But as a matter of appearances, what views we must take in public, it's become tough for us to be friends now: Mevlut used to write love letters to the girl who ended up being my wife . . . and I courted and married the girl Mevlut loved and could never have. Regardless of what we may feel in private, in this country it's difficult for two men in this "public" situation to refrain from immediately beating each other up when meeting by chance on the street, let alone to shake hands and be the friends they were before.

The day the local police confiscated his rice cart, Mevlut came home at the usual time. At first, Rayiha didn't even notice that the cart wasn't tied to the almond tree in the back garden. But by the look on her husband's face, she knew that there had been some sort of calamity.

"It's nothing," said Mevlut. "I'll go and pick it up first thing tomorrow morning."

He told his daughters—who never quite understood what the adults said but still caught on to all that remained unsaid—that a screw had come off one of the wheels, and he'd left the cart with a friend who did repairs in the neighborhood next to theirs. He gave them each a piece of chewing gum with a picture on the wrapper. At dinnertime, they ate their fill of the fresh rice Rayiha had cooked and the chicken she'd fried for Mevlut to sell the next day.

"Let's save the rest for your customers the day after tomorrow, then," said Rayiha, gently returning the uneaten chicken to the pot, which she put in the fridge.

That night, as Mevlut was pouring out a few glasses of boza in the kitchen of one of his oldest customers, she told him, "Mevlut Efendi, we've been having *rakı* all evening, so we hadn't really planned on buying boza. But there was so much emotion, so much melancholy, in your voice that we couldn't help ourselves."

"It's the boza seller's voice that sells his boza," said Mevlut, repeating a line he'd told his customers thousands of times before.

"How is everything with you? Which one of your daughters was meant to start school soon?"

"I'm very well, thank God. My eldest will start primary school in autumn, God willing."

"Well done. You're not letting them get married until they've finished high school, right?" said the old woman as she shut the door after him.

"I'm sending both my daughters to college," said Mevlut as the door was closing on him.

Neither this pleasant exchange, nor any conversation with his other regulars, all of whom happened to be especially kind to him that night, managed to get Mevlut's mind off the agony of losing his cart. He wondered where it might be, whether it would be mistreated if it fell into the wrong hands, how it would fare in the rain, even whether the butane stove might be stolen. He couldn't bear to think of it without him there to look after it.

The next day, a few other street vendors whose carts and stalls had been likewise confiscated were waiting inside the imposing if somewhat decrepit Ottoman-era wooden building of Beyoğlu's municipal offices. A junk dealer Mevlut had met a few times in Tarlabaşı was surprised to hear of a rice cart having been towed away. It was rare for vendors of cooked rice, meatballs, corn on the cob, or roasted chestnuts, who sold their goods from the more advanced, glass-paned rigs with built-in butane or coal stoves, to suffer a police seizure, since these vendors wouldn't have been occupying their spots in the first place without having furnished gifts and free food to the health inspectors, as Mevlut did.

Neither Mevlut nor any other street vendor managed to get his cart back that day. An elderly man who sold pizza topped with minced meat said, "They'll have destroyed them all by now," a possibility Mevlut couldn't even bear to think about.

The municipality's health and hygiene regulations did not deter street vendors, and any fines on the books had long been rendered negligible by inflation, so the local authorities would make an example of recidivist vendors by destroying their carts and taking their goods on grounds of public health. This could lead to arguments, fisticuffs, and even knife fights, and sometimes a street vendor would plant himself outside the town hall to stage a hunger strike or set himself on fire, though this was rather rare. A street vendor could usually hope to get his confiscated stall back only right before a scheduled election, when every vote counted, or else if he happened to have a contact inside the administration. After that first day at the municipal building, the seasoned minced-meat-pizza vendor told Mevlut he was going out to buy himself a new cart the next day.

Mevlut resented this man for having decided not to seek out a contact in the bureaucracy and for being realistic enough to accept that he would never get his property back. Anyway, Mevlut didn't have the money to buy a new three-wheeler and fit it with a stove. Even if he could raise the cash, he didn't believe he could make a living selling rice anymore. Yet he couldn't help but muse that if only he could get his cart back, he'd be able to return to his old life, and like those sad women who can't accept that their husbands have died in the war, he simply couldn't fathom that his white cart might really have been destroyed. There was an image in his mind, like a faded photograph, of the cart waiting for him in some municipal storeroom, on a concrete floor cordoned off by barbed wire.

The next day, he went back to Beyoğlu city hall. When one of the clerks asked him, "Where was your cart taken from?" Mevlut found out that the burned-down theater was officially in the municipal jurisdiction of Şişli, not Beyoğlu, and this filled his heart with hope. The Vurals and Korkut would help him find a contact at the Şişli Municipality. That night, in his dreams, he saw his white cart with its three wheels.

15

The Holy Guide

I Am the Victim of a Grave Injustice

Rayiha. Two weeks passed without any news about the cart. Mevlut was out long past midnight selling boza, woke up late, and ran around the house in his pajamas until noon, playing hide-and-seek and rock-paper-scissors with Fatma and Fevziye. Even at six and five the two of them could tell that something bad had happened, since there was no chickpea rice or chicken cooking in the house, and the white three-wheeled cart they loved so much was no longer tied to the almond tree every evening but had disappeared entirely. They put all their energy into playing with their father, maybe trying to suppress their worries over the fact that he was home and not working, and when their shouting got too loud, I'd yell at Mevlut:

"Take them out to get some fresh air in Kasımpaşa Park."

"Will you give Vediha a call," Mevlut would mumble. "Maybe there's some news."

Finally one night Korkut called: "Tell Mevlut to go to Şişli city hall. There's a guy from Rize who works on the second floor, he's one of Vural's guys, he'll help Mevlut out."

That night, Mevlut was too joyous to sleep. He got up early in the morning, shaved, put on his best suit, and walked all the way to Şişli. As soon as he was reunited with his white cart, he was going to give it a fresh coat of paint, add some new decorations, and never leave it unattended again.

The man from Rize who worked on the second floor of the municipal building was an important and busy person, constantly scolding the people queuing up to see him. He kept Mevlut waiting in a corner for half an hour before summoning him with a flick of his finger. He led the way down a dark stairway, through corridors that smelled of cheap floor cleanser, stuffy rooms full of clerks reading newspapers, and a canteen that gave the whole basement an aroma of cheap oil and dishwasher liquid, and finally they emerged into a courtyard.

It was a dark courtyard surrounded by dark buildings, with a number of carts piled up in a corner; Mevlut's heart leaped at the sight. As he walked toward them, he saw in a different corner two government officers hacking another cart to bits with an ax while a third man sorted the wheels, the wood from the frames, the stoves, and the glass panels into separate piles.

"So, have you picked one yet?" said the man from Rize, coming over to stand next to him.

"My cart isn't here," said Mevlut.

"Didn't you say they took your cart a month ago? We usually strip them the day after we take them. Yours would have been destroyed, too, I'm afraid. These are the ones the health inspectors impounded yesterday. Of course if they went out every day, there'd be a riot. But if we never did any roundups at all, we'd have half the country selling potatoes and tomatoes in Taksim Square tomorrow. That would be the end of Beyoğlu and any hope of nice clean streets . . . We don't usually let people claim their carts; they'd just wind up back on the square the next day. You should pick one out of this bunch before it's too late . . ."

Mevlut looked at the carts like a shopper examining the merchandise. He spotted one with a glass cabinet like his own cart had and a solid wooden frame with thick, sturdy wheels. It was missing its butane stove, which had probably been stolen. But this cart was neater and newer than his. He began to feel guilty.

"I want my own cart."

"Look, my friend, you were selling things on the street where you weren't supposed to. Your cart's been confiscated and destroyed. That is unfortunate, but you know the right people, so you can have a new cart for free. Take it and sell bread out of it, don't let your children go hungry."

"I don't want it," said Mevlut.

On the neat little cart that had caught his eye, Mevlut noticed that the previous owner had taped a picture of the famous belly dancer Seher Şeniz right next to postcards of Atatürk and the Turkish flag. He didn't like that.

"Are you sure you don't want it?" said the man from Rize.

"I'm sure," said Mevlut, backing away.

"Weird one, aren't you . . . How do you know Hadji Hamit Vural?"

"I just do," said Mevlut, trying to sound like a man of many mysteries.

"Well, if you're close enough that he's doing you favors, stop working as a street vendor and go ask him for a job. You'd make more in a month as a foreman on one of his construction sites than you do now in a year."

Outside on the square, life was ticking along in its usual humdrum way. Mevlut saw buses clattering, women shopping, men refilling lighters, guys selling lottery tickets, kids bouncing around in school blazers, a street vendor selling tea and sandwiches from his three-wheeled cart, policemen, and gentlemen in suits and ties. He felt furious at them all, like a man who has lost the woman he loves and cannot stand seeing the rest of the world go about their lives as usual. That clerk from Rize had been so disrespectful and condescending, too.

He wandered the streets just as he used to do in high school, feeling at odds with the world, and eventually he went into a coffeehouse in a part of Kurtuluş he'd never seen before and there spent three hours sheltering from the cold and looking at the television. He smoked his way through a packet of Maltepes and thought about money. Rayiha would have to step up her needlework.

He got home later than usual. When they saw Mevlut's face, Rayiha and the girls figured out that he hadn't gotten his cart back, that it had disappeared—died, in fact. Mevlut didn't have to tell them anything. The whole house went into mourning. Rayiha had cooked some rice and chicken, thinking Mevlut would be out making sales the next day;

they sat and ate it in silence. I wish I'd taken that nice cart they were offering me! thought Mevlut. The owner of that cart was probably out there somewhere thinking equally dark thoughts.

There was a weight on his soul. He felt a huge wave of inescapable darkness approach, threatening to engulf him. He picked up his pole and his jugs of boza and went out on the street earlier than usual, before it got completely dark, before that wave could reach him: walking was a relief, and it always made him feel better heading briskly into the night crying "Boozaaa."

In fact, ever since his cart had been seized, he'd taken to going out long before the evening news came on. He'd head straight down the new road toward Atatürk Bridge and onward across the Golden Horn, his quick steps full of worry, rage, or inspiration as he pressed ahead, ever on the lookout for new neighborhoods, new customers.

When he'd first arrived in Istanbul, he would come here with his father to buy boza from the Vefa Boza Shop. In those days, they hardly ever ventured off the main roads, and they never came after dark. Back then, the homes in this area had been two-story frame buildings with bay windows and unvarnished wood; people used to keep their curtains drawn tight, turn their lights off early, and never drink any boza, and after ten o'clock, the same packs of stray dogs that had ruled these streets since Ottoman times would take over again.

Mevlut crossed Atatürk Bridge and ended up in Zeyrek, powering through the backstreets on his way to Fatih, Çarşamba, and Karagümrük. The more he called out "Boo-zaaa," the better he felt. Most of the old wooden houses he remembered from twenty years ago had disappeared, replaced by four- or five-story concrete blocks like those they'd built in Feriköy, Kasımpaşa, and Dolapdere. Occasionally, somebody in one of these new buildings would part the curtains and open the windows to greet Mevlut like a strange messenger from the past.

"We've got the Vefa Boza Shop just around the corner, but it's never occurred to us to go. When we heard the emotion in your voice, we couldn't resist. How much for a glass? Where are you from, anyway?"

Mevlut could see that big apartment buildings had been constructed over what had been empty land, all the graveyards had vanished, and enormous trash cans had cropped up in even the remotest of neighborhoods, replacing the piles of trash that used to grow on street corners—and yet, stray dogs still ruled these streets at night.

What he couldn't understand was why these dogs were so hostile and even downright aggressive when he ran into them in darkened alleyways. Whenever they heard Mevlut's footsteps and his voice crying "Boza," they would get up from where they were napping, or cease rifling through people's rubbish, and assemble together like soldiers in battle formation to watch his every move, and maybe even bare their teeth in a growl. Boza sellers didn't normally come to these streets, which perhaps explained why the dogs were so intolerant of his presence.

One evening, Mevlut remembered that when he was little, his father had taken him to a house with linoleum floors somewhere in one of these neighborhoods to see an old dervish and ask him to say some special prayers to help Mevlut overcome his fear of dogs. His father had treated this visit to the spiritual sage like a doctor's appointment. He couldn't now recall where the bearded old dervish's house had been—he'd probably died years ago—but Mevlut did remember how carefully his younger self had listened to his advice and how he'd shivered as the old man breathed his incantations over him, banishing the fear of dogs from his heart.

He understood that if he wanted to cultivate the families who lived in these historic neighborhoods, who tried to haggle over the price of his boza, asked him pointless questions about its alcohol content, and generally regarded Mevlut as some sort of strange creature, he would have to devote at least one or two nights a week to walking around this side of the Golden Horn.

In his mind, he kept seeing his rice cart. It was better looking and had more character than any other he'd ever seen out on the streets. He scarcely believed that anyone could be so callous as to hack it apart with an ax. Perhaps they'd given it away to someone else, taking pity on some other rice seller who, like Mevlut, knew the right people. Maybe this scrounger was also from Rize; people from Rize always looked out for one another.

That night, no one had summoned him upstairs; no one had bought any boza yet. The city here was like a distant memory—wooden homes, coal-fire smoke hanging over the streets, crumbling walls . . . Mevlut couldn't figure out where he was or how he'd gotten there.

Finally, a young man opened a window on a three-story building. "Boza seller, boza seller . . . Come on up."

They showed him into an apartment. As he was taking his shoes off, he sensed a gathering of people inside. There was a pleasant yellow light. But the place looked like a government office. Mevlut saw about half a dozen people sitting around two tables.

They were each concentrating on something they were writing, but they seemed kind enough. They looked at Mevlut and smiled as people always did when seeing a boza seller for the first time in many years.

"Welcome, brother boza seller, we are happy to see you," said an old man with silver hair and a warm face, smiling gently at Mevlut.

The others looked like they might be his students. They were serious and respectful but also cheerful. Seated with them at the same table, the silver-haired man said, "There's seven of us. We'll each have a glass."

Someone showed Mevlut into a little kitchen. Very carefully, he poured out seven glasses. "Anyone want chickpeas and cinnamon on theirs?" he asked, calling to the people in the other room.

When one student opened the fridge, Mevlut saw that there was no alcohol inside. He also realized that there weren't any women or families here. The silver-haired man joined them in the kitchen. "How much do we owe you?" he said, and then leaned in to look into Mevlut's eyes, without waiting for a response. "There was so much sorrow in your voice, boza seller, we felt it in our hearts all the way up here."

"I am the victim of a grave injustice," said Mevlut, seized by the urge to talk. "They took my rice cart, they may have destroyed it, or maybe they've given it to someone else. A clerk from Rize who works in the municipality of Şişli was rude to me, but it's late now and I wouldn't want to bother you with my troubles."

"Tell me, tell me," said the silver-haired man, his friendly eyes saying, I feel bad for you, and I genuinely want to hear what you have to say. Mevlut explained that his poor little rice cart was out there somewhere, wasting away in the hands of strangers. He didn't mention his financial worries, but he could tell the man understood. What really bothered him, though, was how people like the clerk from Rize and other people of position (the silver-haired man referred to them ironically as "notables") tended to belittle him, never giving him the respect he deserved. Soon, he and the old man were sitting down on two small chairs in the kitchen, facing each other.

"Man is the most precious fruit of the tree of life," the silver-haired old man told a rapt Mevlut. When they spoke, other holy men always sounded as if they were saying solitary prayers; Mevlut liked how this one could look him in the eyes like a long-lost friend but still speak with all the wisdom of a scholar.

"Man is the greatest of all God's creatures. Nothing can blemish the jewel that is your heart. You shall find your cart, if it be the Lord's will . . . You shall find it, God willing."

Mevlut was flattered that such an intelligent and important man was taking the time to talk to him while his students waited in the other room, but he also suspected with some distress that this interest might be out of pity.

"Your students are waiting, sir," he said. "I shouldn't take up any more of your time."

"Let them wait," said the silver-haired man. A few further comments made a deep impression on Mevlut. The most complicated knots would come undone at the Lord's command. His might would remove all obstacles. Perhaps there were even prettier formulations to come, but Mevlut was getting visibly uncomfortable (and irritated at his own fidgeting, which betrayed his anxiety), so the man stood up, drawing some money out of his pocket.

"I can't take this, sir."

"I won't accept that; it would not be God's way."

At the door, they each insisted on giving way to the other—"After you, no, I insist"—like a pair of perfect gentlemen. "Boza seller, please take this money now," said the man. "I promise you I will not offer to pay you the next time you come around. We hold discussions here every Thursday evening."

"God bless you," said Mevlut, not knowing whether this was the right thing to say. Instinctively, he bent down to kiss the radiant old man's huge, wrinkly hand. It was covered in liver spots.

He came home late that night knowing that this was one encounter he couldn't share with Rayiha. Over the next few days, he would come close to telling her about this man whose face shone with a divine light and whose words had lodged themselves in Mevlut's mind, and how it was thanks to him that Mevlut was able to bear the bitter disappointment of losing his cart, but he always held back. Rayiha might have teased him, and that would have broken his heart.

The yellow light Mevlut had seen in the silver-haired man's house in Çarşamba had stayed with him. What else had he seen? There had been words written in a beautiful ancient script hanging up on the walls. And there was the deference of the students sitting solemnly around the table, which he liked.

Throughout the week that followed, whenever he went out to sell boza, he saw the ghost of his white cart all over Istanbul. One time he saw a man from Rize pulling a white cart uphill along a winding road in Tepebaşı, and he ran after him, only to realize his mistake before he'd even caught up: his white cart was much more elegant than this crude, stumpy contraption.

When, on Thursday night, he walked through the backstreets of Fatih and past the house in Çarşamba calling "Boo-zaa," and they invited him to come in, he hurried upstairs. In that brief visit, he found out that the students called the silver-haired old man "sir," while other visitors referred to him as "the Holy Guide"; that the students who sat at the table dipped feather quills in inkpots and wrote things down in oversize letters; and that these letters formed words in Arabic taken from the Holy Koran. There were a few other sacred-seeming old things in the house: Mevlut particularly liked an old-fashioned coffeepot; framed words written in the same script they were tracing out at the table; a turban shelf with mother-of-pearl details; a grandfather clock with an enormous case whose ticking drowned out everyone's whispers; and framed photographs of Atatürk and a few other frowning, equally serious (but bearded) figures.

At the same table in the kitchen the Holy Guide asked Mevlut about his cart, and Mevlut replied that, though he was still as determined as ever in his search, he had yet to find it and that he'd still not found a morning job (he was careful not to linger on that particular matter for long, lest he give the impression of having come looking for a job or a handout). There was only time to mention one of the things Mevlut had been thinking about over the past two weeks: his long nightly walks weren't just part of his job anymore; they were something he felt he *needed* to do. When he didn't go out wandering the streets at night, his powers of thought and imagination flagged.

The Holy Guide reminded him that in Islam labor was a form of prayer. Mevlut's visceral urge to walk until the day the world ended was surely a sign and a consequence of the ultimate truth that, in this universe, only God was on our side, and only to Him could we ever turn for help. Mevlut was unsettled by these words, which he took to mean that the strange thoughts that crossed his mind as he walked the streets were put there by God Himself.

When the Holy Guide tried to pay for the boza (there were nine students with him that Thursday evening), Mevlut reminded him of how they'd agreed that the boza would be on him this time.

"What's your name?" asked the Holy Guide in an admiring tone.

"Mevlut."

"What a blessed name!" They walked from the kitchen to the front door. "Are you a *mevlidhan*?" he asked, loud enough for his students to hear.

Mevlut made a face designed to convey that he was, unfortunately, unable to answer the question because he didn't know what that meant. His candor and humility made the students smile.

The Holy Guide explained that, as everyone knows, a *mevlit* is a long poem written to celebrate the Holy Prophet Muhammad's birthday. *Mevlidhan* is the beautiful but less-well-known name given to those who compose the music accompanying these odes. Mevlut should name his future son Mevlidhan, a name that would bring the boy good fortune. He must be sure to come by every Thursday—he needn't even announce himself by calling out "Boza" from the street anymore.

Süleyman. Vediha told me that after losing his cart and failing to get it back by using the Vurals' contacts, Mevlut now wanted to raise the rent on his one-room house in Kültepe, which was still occupied by the tenant I'd found him. Either that or he wanted a few months' rent in advance. He soon called me up to talk about it.

"Look," I said, "your tenant is some poor soul from Rize, one of the Vurals' men, one of us, basically; he'd leave the house in a minute if we told him to, no questions asked. He's afraid of Mr. Hamit. And it's not like his rent is low, he pays on time every month, cash in hand, and Vediha hands it on to you, no taxes, no excuses. What more do you want?"

"I'm sorry, Süleyman, but I don't really trust anyone from Rize these days, so he can go."

"What a ruthless landlord you are, the man's married, he's just had a kid, are we supposed to throw him out on the street?"

"Nobody took pity on me when I came to Istanbul, did they?" said Mevlut. "You know what I mean. All right, fine, don't throw anyone out on the street just yet."

"We took pity on you, we cared for you," I said carefully.

The monthly rent Vediha channeled to Mevlut had been just enough to cover a week's worth of his family's expenses. But after the phone call with Süleyman, the rent Vediha brought for the month of March, plus the rent paid in advance for April and May, was higher than usual. Mevlut didn't dwell too much on how easy it had been to raise the rent or on what part the Aktaş family, Süleyman and Korkut, might have played in accomplishing this. He used the money to buy a secondhand ice-cream cart, an ice bucket, metal vats, and a mixing machine, having decided to spend the summer of 1989 selling ice cream.

When Mevlut went to pick up the cart from a neighborhood down the hill, Fatma and Fevziye came along; as they pushed the cart back home, they were euphoric. When their neighbor Reyhan, misinterpreting the cause of all this merriment, leaned out of her window to cheer the return of Mevlut's rice cart, no one had the heart to correct her. While Mevlut and the girls repaired the cart and gave it a fresh coat of paint in the back garden, the evening news showed crowds of protesters filling up Tiananmen Square in Beijing. At the beginning of June, Mevlut was awed by the bravery of the street vendor who had stood all alone before the tanks. What had he been selling before he stepped in the way of those tanks with a plastic bag in each hand? Probably rice like me, thought Mevlut. On TV he had seen how the Chinese cooked their rice, and it wasn't with chickpeas and chicken as Rayiha did; they boiled it for a very long time. Mevlut was impressed with the protesters, though he felt it was important not to go too far protesting against the state, especially in poorer countries, where, if not for the state, there would be no one looking after poor people or street vendors. They were doing all right in China; the only problem was that Communists were, unfortunately, godless.

In the seven years that had passed since the summer Mevlut ran away with Rayiha, the major milk, chocolate, and sugar brands in the country had embarked on a fierce competition to place deep freezers in all the grocery stores, pastry shops, and sandwich and cigarette stalls in Istanbul. Starting in May every year, these shops would plant their freezers outside on the pavement so that people stopped buying ice cream from street vendors. Claiming that Mevlut was obstructing the way, the municipal police could seize and destroy his cart if he spent more than five minutes in the same spot, but they never said a word about the huge freezers from these big companies, which made it so difficult for people trying to walk by. On TV, there was a constant stream of commercials for these strange new ice-cream brands. In the narrow back alleys where Mevlut pushed his cart, children would come up to him and ask, "Do you have any Flinta, ice-cream man? Do you have a Rocket?"

If he was in a good mood, Mevlut would tell them, "This ice cream will fly farther than any of your Rockets." That joke might even be good for a few more sales. But most evenings, he'd get home early and in a bad mood, and when Rayiha came downstairs to help him with the cart as she used to do seven years ago, he would snap at her: "Why are the girls still out so late playing by themselves?" Rayiha would go looking for them, and he would just leave the ice-cream cart behind and head upstairs to stare forlornly at the TV before going to bed. In one of these moments of dejection, he saw the giant waves of an ocean of his own dark thoughts roiling on the TV screen. He worried that unless he found a real job in the autumn, he would be unable to afford schoolbooks and clothes for the girls, food for the family, and gas for the stove.

16

The Binbom Café

Let Them Know What You're Worth

TOWARD THE END of August, Rayiha told her husband that a former restaurant owner from Trabzon, a man close to the Vurals, was looking to hire someone like Mevlut. Mevlut was mortified to realize that his financial woes had once again been the subject of conversation at the Aktaş dinner table.

Rayiha. "They're looking for someone who is honest and knows how food service and restaurants work, and that's not easy to find in Istanbul these days," I told Mevlut. "When you're negotiating your salary, make sure you let them know what you're worth. You owe it to your daughters," I added, because Fatma would be starting primary school around the same time Mevlut was meant to start his new job. We both went to the ceremony they held on Fatma's first day at Piyale Paşa Primary School. They made us stand in line all along the wall surrounding the playground. The principal explained that the school building used to be the private residence of a pasha who conquered some Mediterranean islands belonging to the French and the Italians around four hundred fifty years ago. The pasha attacked an enemy warship all by himself, and when he disappeared, everyone assumed he'd been taken prisoner, but in fact he'd managed to take the ship single-handedly. As for the children, they weren't listening to the principal; they were either talking among themselves or clinging to their parents for fear of what was to come. As she walked into the school hand in hand with the other children, Fatma got scared and burst into tears. We waved to her until she disappeared into the building. It was a cool, cloudy day. On our way home up the hill, I saw tears and clouds of gloom in Mevlut's eyes. He didn't come home but went straight to the café where he was to be a "manager." That same afternoon was the only time I would need to go to Kasımpaşa to fetch Fatma from school. She couldn't stop talking about the teacher's mustache and the window in her classroom. After that day, she made her way to school and back with the other neighborhood girls.

Rayiha called Mevlut a "manager" with equal amounts of affection and ridicule, though it wasn't Mevlut who'd come up with the title but the owner of the café himself, Boss Tahsin from Trabzon. Just as he referred to his little café's three workers as "employees" ("worker" wasn't a nice word), he asked that they refrain from calling him "boss" and use "captain" instead, as would befit a true man of the Black Sea. All this achieved, however, was that his employees felt moved to call him "boss" even more often.

Mevlut soon realized that he'd been offered this job because Boss Tahsin didn't trust his employees. He would have dinner at home with his family and then come down every evening to take over the cash register from his manager. He'd handle all payments himself for the next two hours, and then he'd close the café for the day. The twenty-four-hour diners on İstiklal Avenue were always crowded and lively, but anyone who came all the way down to the Binbom Café's backstreets at night was either lost, drunk, or looking for cigarettes and alcohol.

It was Mevlut's job to open the café at ten in the morning and man the till until around eight in the evening, as well as making sure that the café ran smoothly. The Binbom Café's customers mostly worked in the surrounding backstreets—in photography studios, advertising agencies, cheap restaurants, and nightclubs featuring Turkish classical music—or just happened to be passing by. Despite being a tiny, narrow place far from the main street, the café didn't do too badly. But the suspicious boss was convinced that his employees were cheating him.

It didn't take Mevlut long to figure out that Boss Tahsin's anxiety about his workers' honesty was more than just the usual prejudice of a rich man who thinks that the poor folk he employs must all be out to get him. They were in fact up to a trick Mevlut had seen before and that the boss warned him to look out for: they used the quantities they were given of cheese, minced meat, pickles, beef sausages, and tomato paste to make more sandwiches than municipal guidelines allowed and the owner had instructed, and what they received for the extra sandwiches they pocketed. Captain Tahsin, however, had developed a countermeasure, which he proudly explained to Mevlut: every day, a man from Rize who owned the Tayfun Bakery and supplied all of Binbom's sandwich bread and hamburger buns would call the Captain to tell him exactly how many loaves he'd delivered that day, which prevented the café staff from using bits of cheese and minced meat salvaged from other portions to make extra sandwiches and burgers. But the workers could as easily work their trick with things like orange, pomegranate, or apple juice, and since there was no helpful baker to count the glasses used, it was up to Manager Mevlut to keep a watchful eye.

Mevlut's main responsibility, though, was to make sure that every single customer was issued a receipt from the cash register, that great innovation that had sprung up all over the city five years ago. The Captain believed that no matter how much they tried to scrimp on cheese, no matter how much sugary water they secretly used to top up half a glass of orange juice, there was no way his employees could cheat him if every customer received a receipt. To ensure this discipline, every now and then the Captain would send an anonymous friend of his down to the café. The undercover operative would have a bite to eat and ask for a discount on his order in exchange for forgoing a receipt, just as the rest of Istanbul seemed to be doing. If the manager at the till agreed, it meant he was pocketing the money himself, and he would be fired immediately—just like Mevlut's predecessor.

Mevlut didn't see the café's employees as opportunists waiting for a chance to cheat their boss from Trabzon but rather as the earnest crew of this boat they were all sailing. He always worked with a smile and took genuine pleasure in praising his colleagues' work—"Ah, you've toasted this sandwich to perfection" or "God, this kebab wrap looks nice and crispy!" In the evenings, Mevlut would report dutifully to his superior officer, brimming with pride in the place's smooth operation, especially on good days.

Once he'd surrendered the bridge to his captain, he'd run back home to sip a bowl of Rayiha's lentil or wheat soup, watching TV out of the corner of his eye as he did at the café all day. Since café workers were allowed as many sandwiches and kebab wraps as they liked for their own consumption, Mevlut was never hungry when he came home, nor did he expect much for dinner, and while he sipped his soup he loved to look at Fatma's school textbooks and especially at the letters, numbers, and sentences she'd written in her tiny, beautiful hand all over the white pages of her notebook (the same notebooks that in his day were of cheap yellow paper). He still went out again toward the end of the evening news and stayed out selling boza until as late as eleven thirty.

Now that he was managing the café and had another source of income, Mevlut didn't feel the pressing need to sell one more glass or to look for new customers on remote streets in the old neighborhoods across the Golden Horn, where the dogs bared their teeth and growled. One summer evening, he took his ice-cream cart and visited the Holy Guide and his students, who gave him a tray of tulip-shaped teacups to fill up with ice cream on the street, and after that day he knocked on their door whenever he felt the need to confide in someone, using boza as an excuse when winter came and the weather got cold. To make it clear that he wasn't there for business but for the depth of their conversation, he insisted that the ice cream or the boza served on every third visit would be on him, describing this on one occasion as "an offering to the school." The Holy Guide's lectures were termed "conversations."

It was almost a year after his first visit before Mevlut deduced that the apartment where the Holy Guide gave his students private instruction in the art of Ottoman calligraphy was also a secret lodge of his sect. One reason that it took Mevlut so long to catch on was that the visitors to the apartment that served as a spiritual center were all so quiet and secretive by nature—but, equally, a part of Mevlut just didn't care to know what was going on. He was so pleased to be there and know that every Thursday evening the Holy Guide would take the time to talk to him and listen to his problems—even if it was just five minutes—that he tried to avoid thinking anything that might spoil his happiness. Someone had once invited Mevlut to the Tuesday Discussions, regularly attended by twenty to thirty people and at which the Holy Guide was said to speak with anyone who came knocking at his door, but Mevlut never went.

Sometimes he worried that by going to the lodge and getting involved with the sect, he might be doing something illegal, but he would tell himself, If these are bad people doing bad things against the state, they wouldn't have a huge picture of Atatürk on the wall, would they? Soon, however, he realized that the Atatürk picture was only there for show—just like the poster of Atatürk wearing a hat that hung right at the entrance to the Communist hideout he and Ferhat used to frequent in high school—so that if the police ever raided the house, the pious students could say, "There must be some mistake, we all love Atatürk!" The only difference between the Communists and the political Islamists was that the Communists criticized Atatürk constantly (Mevlut disapproved of their foul language) even though they truly believed in him; these Islamists, on the other hand, had no use at all for Atatürk but never said a word against him. Mevlut preferred the latter approach, and so when some of the Holy Guide's more insolent and outspoken college men claimed that "Atatürk destroyed our glorious five-hundred-year-old tradition of calligraphy when he tried to imitate the West with his alphabet revolution," he pretended not to hear them.

Mevlut likewise disapproved of those conservative college guys who would use every fawning trick in the book to get the Holy Guide to notice them, only to start gossiping idly and discussing TV shows when he left the room. Mevlut saw no trace of a TV anywhere inside the Holy Guide's apartment, and this worried him because it seemed to him proof that what was going on here was something dangerous, of which the government would not have approved. Those who attended the Holy Guide's lessons could well find themselves in trouble come the next military coup when the army started rounding up all the Communists, Kurds, and Islamists. On the other hand the Holy Guide had never told Mevlut anything that could be construed as political propaganda or indoctrination.

Rayiha. With Mevlut running the café and Fatma going to primary school, I had a lot more time for my needlework. We didn't have to worry about making ends meet anymore, so I worked because I felt like it, and because I liked earning my own money, too. Sometimes they gave us a picture or a page from a magazine showing us what design to embroider on which part of the curtain . . . But sometimes all they said was "You decide." Whenever we had to decide, I could end up staring at the fabric for ages, asking myself, What shall I do, what shall I stitch on this? But I was just as likely to overflow with ideas for patterns, symbols, flowers, six-sided clouds, and deer bounding through fields, which I would apply to everything in sight—curtains, pillowcases, duvet covers, tablecloths, and napkins.

"Take a break, Rayiha, you're getting lost in the work again," Reyhan would say.

Two or three afternoons a week, Rayiha would take Fatma and Fevziye by the hand and bring them to the café. The girls didn't see much of their father outside his one hour at home every evening with his bowl of soup. Mevlut would still be asleep when Fatma went to school in the morning, and both girls were usually in bed by the time he came home at midnight. Fatma and Fevziye would have loved to go to the café more often, but their father had forbidden them from coming on their own, and he insisted that they never let go of their mother's hand while on the way. Technically, Rayiha wasn't allowed in Beyoğlu either, and especially not on İstiklal Avenue: when they ran to cross the road, she and the girls would feel as if they were fleeing Beyoğlu's crowds of men as much as dodging the traffic itself.

Rayiha. While I've got the chance, I'd like to be clear that it's not true I never fed Mevlut anything but soup for dinner in the five years he spent running the café. I also made him scrambled eggs with parsley and green peppers, french fries, pastry rolls, and kidney-bean stew with plenty of sweet peppers and carrots. As you know, Mevlut loves a roast chicken with potatoes. Now that he wasn't selling rice anymore, once a month I'd buy him and the girls chicken from Hamdi the poultry dealer; he still gave me a discount.

Although no one ever spoke about it at home, the real reason that Rayiha brought the girls to the Binbom Café was so they could eat their fill of kebab wraps and cheese-and-sausage sandwiches and drink *ayran* and orange juice to their hearts' content.

In the beginning, Rayiha had always felt the need to explain these visits somehow: "We were just passing by and thought we'd say hello!" "Good idea," one of the café workers might say. After the first few visits, the girls started to get their favorite things prepared and served up to them without even having to ask. Rayiha wouldn't eat anything, and if a kind, smiling café worker took the initiative to make her a kebab or a grilled-cheese sandwich, she always refused it, claiming she'd already eaten. Mevlut was proud of his wife's principled stance, and he never told her "It's okay, have a bite" as his coworkers expected him to.

Later, when Mevlut found out that the Binbom Café's employees were cheating Captain Tahsin, his daughters' free kebab sandwiches started to weigh on his conscience.

17

The Café Employees' Big Swindle

You Stay Out of It

At the start of 1990, Mevlut discovered the complex yet perfectly logical scheme by which the workers of the Binbom Café were circumventing the rules imposed by their boss from Trabzon to prevent them from cheating him. Every day, the café workers would draw from a common fund of their own money to buy bread and buns from a different bakery and stuff them meticulously with fillings bought from other shops, effectively preparing and selling their own food unbeknownst to the boss. Their hamburgers and kebab sandwiches were concealed like drugs in secret parcels delivered to nearby offices every day at lunchtime. Visiting every one of these offices himself with a little ledger in which he also wrote down comments people made on the food, a café worker named Vahit would collect the proceeds from these sales, bypassing Mevlut's cash register. It had taken Mevlut a long time to discover this covert well-oiled machine, and another long winter was to pass before the café employees realized that he had found them out but wasn't reporting them to the boss.

Mevlut was inclined to blame any wrongdoing at the café on the boss's youngest employee, the Weasel (whose real name no one ever used). The Weasel had just come back from military service, and his job was to manage the café's basement kitchen and storeroom, a filthy, fearsome cave measuring two by two and a half meters, where he prepared hamburger buns, tomato sauce, *ayran,* and french fries, among other things, and also perfunctorily washed—or, actually, rinsed—the café's glasses and aluminum plates, these efforts interrupted by occasional forays upstairs during the rush times to help out with anything from toasting sandwiches to serving *ayran*. Mevlut had first spotted the other bakery's bread down in the Weasel's rat- and roach-infested kitchen.

Mevlut wasn't fond of Vahit; he didn't like the way he stared indecently at any decent-looking woman he saw. Yet, somewhat to Mevlut's dismay, working together started to draw them closer over time. If there were no customers, they would while away the hours watching TV together, and at any emotional moment in whatever happened to be on-screen (there were five or six such moments a day), they would always glance toward each other with matching looks—and that, too, drew them closer. Eventually, Mevlut began to feel as if he'd known Vahit all his life. But when Mevlut realized Vahit's role in the café employees' illicit scheme, the intimacy of their shared reactions to the feelings emitting from the TV made Mevlut uneasy. Surely, he thought, genuine compassion was beyond a swindler like Vahit. As the manager, Mevlut even wondered whether this guilty employee had been using their shared responses to the TV as a way of getting into Mevlut's good books.

Around the time he first noticed the signs of fraudulent activity at the café, Mevlut also began to feel as if the one eye (not both, strangely) with which he observed Vahit and the others had somehow detached itself from his body and had, of its own accord, begun to scrutinize Mevlut himself. When he felt trapped sometimes among the people whose lives revolved around this café, the eye would be watching him; he would feel fake. But then some Binbom customers ate their kebab sandwiches never looking away from their own reflections in the mirror.

When he was still selling cooked rice on the streets, Mevlut may have endured the cold standing on his feet, and he may have struggled to find customers for his ice cream, but at least in those days he had been free. He could let his mind wander, he could turn his back on the world whenever he wanted, and his body would move as his heart might will it. Now, he may as well have been chained to the shop. During the day, in those desperate moments when he took his eyes off the television and tried to daydream instead, he would console himself with the thought that he would see his daughters later and then go out to sell boza. He had customers he loved to see every evening, and there was the rest of the city, too. By now, he knew that every time he cried out "Boo-zaaa" with a particular sentiment, the people of Istanbul felt the very same emotion in their hearts, and that was why they asked him upstairs and bought his boza.

So it was that in the years he spent managing the Binbom Café, Mevlut became a more devoted and passionate boza seller than he'd ever been before. When he shouted "Boo-zaa" into half-lit streets, he wasn't just calling out to a pair of closed curtains that concealed families going about their lives, or to some bare, unplastered wall, or to the demonic dogs whose invisible presence he could sense on darkened street corners; he was also reaching into the world inside his mind. Because every time he shouted "Boo-zaa," he could feel the paintings in his mind emerging from his mouth like speech bubbles in a comic book before dissolving into the weary streets like clouds. Every word was an object, and every object was a picture. He sensed, now, that the streets on which he sold boza in the night and the universe in his mind were one and the same. Sometimes Mevlut thought he might be the only one to have ever discovered this remarkable truth, or perhaps it was a divine light that God had elected to bestow on him alone. When he came out of the café and went home in the evening feeling uneasy, and afterward walked into the night carrying his shoulder pole, he would discover the world within his soul reflected in the shadows of the city.

He was calling out "Boo-zaa" one night after yet another day of not knowing what to do about the conspiracy at the Binbom Café, when a pleasant orange light spilled out of a window that had just opened up in the darkness. A big black shadow asked him to come upstairs.

It was an old Greek building in the backstreets of Feriköy. Mevlut remembered having delivered yogurt to this apartment with his father one afternoon soon after first arriving in Istanbul (like so many street vendors, he had the city's apartment blocks and the plaques identifying them emblazoned in his mind). The building was called the Savanora.

It still smelled of dust, moisture, and frying oil. He walked through a door on the second floor and into a wide, brightly lit room: the old apartment had been turned into a textile factory. He saw about a dozen girls each sitting at a sewing machine. Some were still children, but most were around Rayiha's age, and everything about them—from the way they tied their headscarves loose, to the serious, faraway expressions on their faces as they worked—seemed frighteningly familiar to Mevlut. The man with the kind face was the one who had appeared at the window earlier, their boss. "Boza seller, these hardworking young ladies are like daughters to me. We need to fulfill an order from England; they're soldiering on until the minibus comes to take them home in the morning," he said. "Will you be kind and give them your best boza and your freshest roasted chickpeas? Where are you from, anyway?" Mevlut looked closely at the stucco reliefs on the walls, the big mirror with a gilded frame, and the chandelier made of fake crystals—all left behind by the Greek families who'd lived here once. For many years, whenever he would think back to this room, he would become convinced that his memory was playing tricks on him, that he hadn't seen that chandelier or that mirror. It had to be, for in his recollections, the girls at the sewing machines would all look exactly like his daughters, Fatma and Fevziye.

Fatma and Fevziye would wear their matching black school uniforms, fix each other's white collar—a blend of synthetic fibers and cotton, which always looked freshly starched—to the button on the back of their aprons, put their hair up, pick up the backpacks Mevlut had bought them at a discount from a shop in Sultanhamam (a place he knew from his high-school days selling Kısmet with Ferhat), and leave for school at seven forty-five every morning, just as their father, still in his pajamas, was getting out of bed.

Once the girls left for school, Mevlut and Rayiha would make love for as long as they liked. After their second daughter, Fevziye, had grown up a bit, they'd almost never had the chance to be alone in the room as they used to be in their first year of marriage. They only had the house to themselves when the girls were with Reyhan or another neighbor or when Vediha or Samiha came by early in the morning and took them out. On a summer day, the girls could sometimes disappear for hours, at play with their friends in a neighbor's garden. When the warm weather presented Mevlut and Rayiha this opportunity, they would always exchange a pointed look the moment they were alone. "Where are they?" Mevlut would ask; Rayiha would say, "They must be busy playing in the neighbor's garden," to which Mevlut would respond, "You never know, they might come back," and that would be enough to keep them from reprising those blissful early days of their marriage.

For the past six or seven years, their embraces in their one-room house had occurred only after midnight, when the girls were in their bed in the other corner of the room, immersed in the deepest phase of their sleep. If Rayiha was up waiting for Mevlut returning late from his boza rounds, and if she received him sweetly instead of just looking at the television, Mevlut would take it as an invitation and switch all the lights off as soon as he was sure that the girls were sound asleep. Husband and wife would make cautious love under the covers, trying their best to keep it brief—for by then Mevlut was always exhausted. Sometimes they would fall asleep for a few hours only to wake up, pajamas and nightgown intertwined, and make love in hushed haste, though with deep and genuine feeling. Still, all these obstacles meant that they were enjoying their conjugal right less frequently than ever before, which they accepted as a natural feature of married life.

But now they had more time, and working at the café Mevlut wasn't as tired as he used to be. Soon enough, the enthusiasm of those early days of their marriage returned, and now they felt easier together, too, for they had come to know and trust each other, and they weren't so shy anymore. Being at home alone brought them closer, and they began once more to experience that mutual reliance that can only exist between husband and wife, and to remember how lucky they were to have found each other.

Their happiness also helped Rayiha to stop dwelling on the doubts Süleyman had cast on the intended recipient of Mevlut's letters, though she still couldn't forget them entirely. She continued to have moments of uncertainty, but on those occasions she'd read a couple of letters from her bundle and take comfort from Mevlut's beautiful words.

Mevlut was expected at the Binbom Café at ten in the morning, so once the girls left for school, husband and wife could indulge in their conjugal happiness for no more than an hour and a half, including the time they spent sipping their tea and coffee at their one and only table. (Mevlut's breakfast would always be a toasted cheese-and-tomato sandwich at Binbom.) It was during these hours of blissful companionship that Mevlut began telling Rayiha about the treachery taking place at the Binbom Café.

Rayiha. "You stay out of it," I told him. "Keep an eye on everything but pretend you've seen nothing." "But the boss put me there to find out what was going on," said Mevlut—and he was right. "The boss is Vural's man . . . Won't they think I'm a fool who can't smell a rat even when it's dangling under his nose?" "Mevlut, you know they're all in it together. If you tell the boss, they'll gang up on you and tell him you were the one cheating him all along. Then you'll be the one who loses his job. It would only make you look bad with the Vurals." I saw how Mevlut would panic every time I said this, and it made me sad.

18

Last Days at the Binbom Café

Twenty Thousand Sheep

On the night of 14 November 1991, a Lebanese merchant vessel sailing south and a ship from the Philippines carrying corn toward the Black Sea collided before the ancient fortress that stands on the narrowest stretch of the Bosphorus. The Lebanese ship sank, and five of her crew drowned. While watching TV with the others at the Binbom Café the next morning, Mevlut heard that the Lebanese ship had been carrying twenty thousand sheep.

The people of Istanbul found out about the accident when the sheep began to wash up against the piers along the Bosphorus and on the shores of Rumelihisarı, Kandilli, Bebek, Vaniköy, and Arnavutköy. Some of the poor creatures made it there alive, climbing out onto the city streets through the boathouses of old wooden mansions that hadn't burned down yet, the jetties of modern restaurants that had replaced what used to be fishermen's coffeehouses, and the gardens of homes where people had docked their boats for winter. The sheep were enraged and exhausted. Their cream-white pelts were clotted with mud and stained petrol green, their tired, spindly legs, which they could barely move, soaked in a rust-hued liquid resembling boza, and their eyes full of an ancient regret. Mevlut had been transfixed by those sheep eyes staring out from every inch of the café's TV screen, and he'd felt all the force of that regret in his own soul.

Some of the sheep were rescued by people who, having heard about the accident, sailed out straightaway in the dead of night to help, and while a few of these animals found new homes in this way, most had died before morning. The roads, private docks, parks, and teahouses lining the Bosphorus filled up with the carcasses of drowned sheep, which made Mevlut and the rest of Istanbul want to run down and help.

Mevlut heard stories of how some sheep, having managed to get out into the city streets, inexplicably attacked people only to drop dead without warning, or walked into mosque courtyards, sacred tombs, and cemeteries, or how they were, in fact, harbingers of the apocalypse that was to come in the year 2000 and proof that the prophecies of the late columnist Celâl Salik, who'd been gunned down for his views, had been right all along. Thereafter, whenever Mevlut looked at the TV at the Binbom Café, he thought of the fate of those sheep, which he saw as signs of something deeper—just as those fishermen who kept finding dead sheep entangled in their nets every day, bloated like enormous balloons, came to see them as omens of misfortune.

What made everything worse, and turned the whole matter into the stuff of the city's nightmares, were the reports that most of the twenty thousand sheep remained trapped inside the hull, still alive and waiting to be saved. Mevlut followed the interviews of divers who'd been sent down to the wreckage, but he just couldn't picture what it must be like for the sheep sitting in darkness in the bowels of that ship. Was it actually dark in there, and did it smell bad, or was it like the world of dreams? The plight of the sheep reminded him of Jonah in the belly of the whale. What sins had the sheep committed to have ended up in that dark place? Was it more like heaven or hell in there? The Almighty God had sent Abraham a sheep to spare him from sacrificing his own son. Why had He sent twenty thousand sheep to Istanbul?

Beef and lamb were rare indulgences in Mevlut's house. He stopped eating kebab sandwiches for a time. But he kept this new aversion to meat a secret from the world; it would never evolve into a serious moral stance, and it was forgotten entirely the day that the employees at the Binbom Café decided to share some crispy kebab leftovers.

Mevlut could feel how quickly time was passing; he felt himself aging every day spent trying to keep up with the treachery at the Binbom Café, until, slowly, he knew he was turning into a different person. Finally, in the winter of 1993, after three years as manager, Mevlut realized that it was too late to alert the boss to his employees' tricks. He'd tried once or twice to explain his moral quandary to the Holy Guide, but he'd never received a response that managed to ease his anxieties.

It only bewildered him all the more to see that, even when workers left the café for military service or a better job, or because they didn't get along with anyone, the duplicity continued undaunted, burdening Mevlut's conscience.

The person whom Mevlut should have denounced to the boss was the architect of the whole scheme, a man named Muharrem. Known as Chubby among the staff, he was the public face of the Binbom Café, a backstreet, poor man's version of a cartoon hero created collectively by the men of the kebab and sandwich shops lining Taksim Square and İstiklal Avenue. He was in charge of roasting the *döner* kebab in the café window (meaning that he turned it on the spit once one side was cooked, made sure it didn't burn, and when necessary cut it up for customers), and he wielded his long kebab knife the way a Maraş ice-cream vendor handled his spoon, twirling it with a flair designed to draw customers, especially tourists, off the street. Mevlut didn't care for all this show. It wasn't as if tourists ever came down this alley anyway.

Mevlut sometimes suspected that if Chubby Muharrem made all this effort for not much revenue at all, it was perhaps to hide from himself, as well as everyone else, his role as head crook. But having so rarely met anyone of genuine moral sentiment in all his days as a street vendor, he wondered whether in fact it might just be the opposite: Chubby Muharrem could have been perpetrating his expert surreptitious fraud without even considering it morally reprehensible. In the politically charged days after the bomb that killed the secular and leftist columnist Uğur Mumcu, Chubby discovered Mevlut was onto the scheme and explained that he viewed the whole arrangement as a way for the workers—underpaid and cruelly deprived of any benefits—to safeguard their own rights without bothering the boss. Mevlut was struck by the power of this leftist pronouncement, which engendered in him a new respect for Chubby. He may have been a criminal, but Mevlut could never betray him to the boss, the state, or the police.

In July, when Islamists attacked Alevis in Sivas and thirty-five people—including writers and poets—were burned alive inside the Madımak Hotel, Mevlut started missing his high-school friend again and longed to talk politics with him and to curse the villains of this world, as they used to do. Rayiha found out that Ferhat, who had been reading electric meters for the municipal government, had kept his job after the utility was privatized and was making plenty of money. Mevlut didn't really want to believe that Ferhat could be doing so well, but sometimes, when the truth was unavoidable, he would console himself by remembering that the only way to make lots of money fast was to do wrong (just as they were doing at the Binbom Café), and he would judge Ferhat accordingly. Mevlut had seen so many youthful Communists turn into capitalists once they were married. They were usually even more obnoxious than committed Communists.

When autumn came, Vahit the ledger keeper began confiding to Mevlut the details of the employees' scheme in tones somewhere between menacing and plaintive. He himself was innocent, he insisted. Mevlut must not betray him to the boss, but if he did, Vahit would have no choice but to do the same in return. Once he'd gotten that off his chest, Vahit looked at Mevlut as if to say "That's life, huh!" just as he'd been doing recently during the most poignant scenes of all those TV reports on the destruction of Mostar Bridge in Bosnia. Vahit wanted to get married, which was another reason that he needed money. It wasn't just the boss from Trabzon who was exploiting him, but Chubby and the others, too. His share of the profits from their fraud was small. In fact Chubby, "the real boss around here," was much worse than the Captain. Unless Vahit started to get his due, he would go to the boss and tell him all about Chubby's machinations.

All of this surprised Mevlut. In truth, Vahit was threatening to hit him where he was most vulnerable: his relationship with the Vurals. The extravagant praise the boss had heaped on his new manager, all to scare his other employees and make clear that Mevlut could not be bought, had backfired and might now be used against Mevlut. Some evenings, as the boss closed out the cash register, he would applaud Mevlut in front of everyone: Mevlut from Konya was an honest, ethical, and truly honorable man. He had all the innocence and sincerity of people from central Turkey. The boss spoke of heartland Turks as though he were the first to discover them in Istanbul. Once you managed to win these heartland Turks over, once they started believing in you, they would lay down their lives for you, if need be.

The Vurals cared deeply about their honor. Mevlut was one of their men, which meant that he would never cheat anybody and that he would have their backing when the time came to punish those who did cheat. From the way Vahit spoke, Mevlut got the impression that he believed the Black Sea Vurals to be the true owners of the Binbom Café, and the boss from Trabzon, like Mevlut himself, but another of their pawns. This didn't surprise Mevlut: over his years in the streets of Istanbul, he'd met thousands of people, and he'd seen how they invariably believed that behind every drama and in every battle there was always someone else pulling the strings.

One cold winter day in February, Mevlut slept through the morning after his daughters had left for school. When he got to work, twenty minutes later than usual, he found the Binbom Café shuttered. The locks had been changed, so he couldn't even get inside. The shop that sold nuts and sunflower seeds two doors down told him that there had been a big fight at the café last night, obliging the Beyoğlu police to step in. The boss from Trabzon had brought some men in to beat up the workers, and they'd all ended up at the police station. After the police more or less forced both sides to make peace, the boss had come back with a locksmith he'd found God knows where, changed the locks, and put up a sign in the window that said CLOSED FOR RENOVATIONS.

That's the official story, thought Mevlut. Meanwhile, in a part of his mind he kept thinking that he'd been fired for coming late to work that morning. Maybe the boss had discovered the workers' scheme, or maybe he hadn't. All he wanted to do was to go straight home to talk it all through with Rayiha, to share his distress at being unemployed again—if such was indeed the case—but he didn't go home.

He spent the next few mornings wandering into coffeehouses he didn't know and trying to figure out how to make ends meet. He was filled with a sense of guilt and impending doom, but there was a sort of joy there, too, which he quickly stopped trying to hide from himself. It was the same mix of freedom and fury he'd felt whenever he skipped school as a teenager. It had been a long time since he'd had the chance to walk the city aimlessly at noon, with no pressing business, and he went down to Kabataş, relishing the moment. Someone else had parked a cart for rice with chickpeas in the same spot he'd occupied for years. He saw the seller standing next to the big, ancient fountain, but he was reluctant to go any closer. He felt briefly as if he were watching his own life from a distance. Did this guy make much money? He was a slender man, just like Mevlut.

The park behind the fountain had finally been finished and opened to the public. Mevlut sat on a bench feeling the full weight of his predicament. His eyes roamed over the distant outline of Topkapı Palace in the mist, the enormous, gray ghosts of the city's mosques, big ships with metallic hues gliding noiselessly past, and the seagulls with their incessant litany of scream and squabble. He felt a melancholy coming on, advancing with the irresistible determination of those huge ocean waves he'd seen on TV. Only Rayiha could console him. Mevlut knew he couldn't live without her.

Twenty minutes later, he was at home in Tarlabaşı. Rayiha didn't even ask, "Why are you back so early?" He pretended that he'd found some excuse to leave the café and come home to make love to her. (They'd done this before.) They forgot the world—including their daughters—for the next forty minutes.

Mevlut quickly found out that he didn't need to bring the subject up at all, for Vediha had come by that morning and relayed all the news to Rayiha. She'd begun with a cutting "How can you still not have a telephone?" before recounting how one of the café's workers had told the boss that he was being cheated by his employees. So Captain Tahsin had called in his friends from Trabzon to raid the shop and take back his property. An exchange of insults had led to a tussle between Chubby and the boss, landing them both in the police station, where they'd eventually shaken hands and called a truce. This informant had also claimed that Mevlut had been aware of these scoundrels' tricks but that he'd taken money in exchange for his silence; the boss had believed this and complained to Hadji Hamit Vural about Mevlut.

Korkut and Süleyman told Hadji Hamit's sons that Mevlut was an honest man who would never sink so low, and they refuted these slanders against the family's honor. But the Aktaş family was also angry at Mevlut for causing this situation and jeopardizing their ties with the Vurals. Now Mevlut was getting angry at Rayiha for relaying all this bad news so sternly, without any hint of sympathy, almost as if she thought they had a point.

Rayiha noticed this immediately. "Don't worry, we'll find a way," she said. "There are always plenty of people who want their curtains and their linens embroidered."

What upset Mevlut most was that Fatma and Fevziye would no longer be able to have toasted cheese-and-sausage sandwiches and kebabs from the café in the afternoons. The staff had been so fond of them both, always so sweet to them. Chubby used to do funny impressions with his kebab knife to make them laugh. A week later, Mevlut heard through the grapevine that Chubby and Vahit were both very angry, calling him an opportunist who'd taken advantage of them by claiming a share of the spoils only to turn around and betray everyone to the boss. Mevlut didn't respond to any of their accusations.

He caught himself longing once again to renew his friendship with Ferhat. Whenever Mevlut asked him something, Ferhat had always had an illuminating response, even if it hurt Mevlut's feelings. Ferhat would have had the best advice on how to deal with the secret plots at the café. But Mevlut knew that this yearning amounted to an overly optimistic view about the nature of friendship. The streets had taught him that past the age of thirty a man was always a lone wolf. If he was lucky, he might have a female wolf like Rayiha beside him. Of course the only antidote to the loneliness of the streets was the streets themselves. The five years Mevlut had spent running the Binbom Café had kept him from the city, turning him into a man of sorrow.

After sending his daughters off to school in the morning, he would make love with Rayiha before going out to visit the local teahouses in search of a job. In the evenings he'd head out early to sell boza. He visited the congregation in Çarşamba twice. In five years, the Holy Guide had aged, now spending less time at the table than he did in his armchair beside the window. By the chair was the button by which he could buzz people into the building through the main entrance. A large side-view mirror from a truck had been screwed onto the wall of the three-story window so that the Holy Guide could see who was at the door without having to get up. On both of Mevlut's visits, the Holy Guide had seen him in the mirror and let him in before he'd even had a chance to cry "Boo-zaa." There were new students and new visitors now. They didn't get the chance to talk much. On both visits, no one—not even the Holy Guide—noticed that Mevlut hadn't charged for his boza, nor did he tell anyone that he no longer managed the café.

Why was it that on some nights he felt the urge to walk into a remote cemetery in some distant neighborhood and sit among the cypress trees in the moonlight? Why did a huge, black wave like the one on TV overtake him sometimes, so he found himself drowning in a swelling tide of sorrows? Even the packs of strays in Kurtuluş, Şişli, and Cihangir had started barking, growling, and baring their teeth at him, just like those other dogs in the neighborhoods across the Golden Horn. Why was Mevlut afraid of dogs again, to the degree that they noticed his fear and snarled at him? Perhaps the question was, why had all these dogs begun to growl at Mevlut, causing him to start fearing them in the first place?

It was election time again; the whole city was bedecked with political banners as swarms of cars blared folk songs and marches from loudspeakers, blocking traffic, and wearing everyone out. Back in Kültepe, people used to vote for whatever party promised new roads, electricity, water, and bus routes for the neighborhood. Hadji Hamit Vural was the one who negotiated for all these services, so he would decide what party this should be.

Mevlut had mostly ignored the elections, worried by the rumor "Once you're registered to vote, the tax office starts knocking on your door." There wasn't any party he hated anyway, and the only demand he ever had of any candidate was "They should treat street vendors right." But two elections ago, the military government had declared a curfew and sent soldiers to every home in the country, taking people's names and threatening to jail anyone who didn't vote. So this time Rayiha took their identity cards and went to have them both registered.

During the local elections in March 1994, the ballot boxes for their neighborhood were kept at Piyale Paşa Primary School, which the girls attended, so Mevlut took Rayiha, Fatma, and Fevziye and went down to vote in high spirits. There was a ballot box in Fatma's classroom, and a large crowd, too. But Fevziye's classroom was empty. They walked in and sat together in one of the rows. They laughed at Fevziye's impression of her teacher and admired a picture she'd drawn, named MY HOUSE, which the teacher had liked well enough to hang in the corner: Fevziye had added two chimneys and a Turkish flag to the red roof of the house in the picture and drawn an almond tree in the background with the lost rice cart. She'd omitted the chains that had been used to secure the cart.

The next day, the newspapers wrote that the Islamist party had won the elections in Istanbul, and Mevlut thought, If they're religious, they'll get rid of the tables of drunks eating on the pavements of Beyoğlu, and then we'll have an easier time getting through, and people will buy more boza. It was two days later that he was attacked by dogs and then robbed, losing his money and his Swiss watch; that's when he decided to give up on selling boza.

PART V

March 1994–September 2002

Every word in Heaven is a reflection of the heart's intent.

—Ibn Zerhani, *The Hidden Meaning of the Lost Mystery*

I

The Brothers-in-Law Boza Shop

Doing the Nation Proud

NOW THAT our story has again reached the night of Wednesday, 30 March 1994, I would advise my readers to reacquaint themselves with part 2 of our novel. That night, Mevlut was attacked by stray dogs and robbed of the wristwatch Hadji Hamit Vural had given him as a wedding present twelve years before—two incidents that caused him great distress. The following morning, when he talked to Rayiha about it after Fatma and Fevziye had gone to school, he remained firm in his resolve to stop selling boza. There was no way he could walk the streets at night while he carried this fear of dogs in his heart.

He also wondered whether it was a coincidence that he'd been attacked by dogs and robbed the same night. If the dogs had attacked him after he'd been robbed, he might have reasoned: The robbers scared me, and the dogs attacked smelling my fear. But actually, the dogs had attacked him first, and he'd been robbed two hours later. As he tried to find a link between the two events, Mevlut kept thinking back to an article he'd read a long time ago in the middle-school library. The article, in an old issue of *Mind and Matter,* had been about the ability of dogs to read people's minds. Realizing quickly that it would be very difficult to recall the specifics of the article, Mevlut put it out of his mind.

———

Rayiha. When Mevlut decided to stop selling boza because of the dogs, I went to see Vediha in Duttepe the first chance I got.

"They're not too pleased with Mevlut after what happened at the Binbom Café; they won't be helping him find another job anytime soon," said Vediha.

"Mevlut isn't too pleased with them either," I said. "Anyway, it's Ferhat's help I'm thinking of. I heard he's making good money at the electricity board. He could find something for Mevlut, too. But Mevlut will never go to him unless Ferhat offers."

"Why's that?"

"You know why . . ."

Vediha looked at me as if she understood.

"Please, Vediha, you'll know just what to say to Samiha and Ferhat," I said. "He and Mevlut used to be such good friends. If Ferhat's so keen to show off his money, let him give his old friend a hand."

"When we were little, you and Samiha used to gang up on me all the time," said Vediha. "Now I've got to get you two talking again?"

"I don't have any quarrel with Samiha," I said. "The problem is the men are too proud."

"They don't call it pride, though, they say it's honor," said Vediha. "That's when they get vicious."

A week later, Rayiha told her husband that on Sunday they would be taking the girls over to Samiha and Ferhat's place, where Samiha was going to make them some Beyşehir-style kebab.

"Beyşehir kebab is just a flatbread topped with walnuts as well as meat," said Mevlut. "I haven't had it in twenty years. Where's this coming from?"

"You haven't seen Ferhat in ten years, either!" said Rayiha.

Mevlut was still unemployed: ever since he'd been robbed, he'd been nursing a grudge against the world and feeling ever more vulnerable. In the mornings he wandered around the restaurants of Tarlabaşı and Beyoğlu in a bitter, halfhearted search for some job that might suit him. In the evenings, he stayed at home.

On that sunny Sunday morning they got on a bus in Taksim, the only other passengers a handful of people who were also going to see friends and relatives on the other side of the city. Rayiha relaxed when she heard Mevlut telling Fatma and Fevziye that his childhood friend, their uncle Ferhat, was a really funny man.

Thanks to the girls, the moment when Mevlut saw Samiha and Ferhat again—something he'd been dreading for ten years—passed without any awkwardness. The two old friends hugged each other, Ferhat picked Fevziye up, and they all headed out to see the plot he had marked with white stones more than fifteen years ago, as if they were there to inspect some land on which they planned to build a house.

The girls wouldn't stop running around; they were thrilled with the forest at the edge of the city, the dreamy outline of Istanbul in the hazy distance, and the gardens full of dogs, clucking hens, and little chicks. Mevlut thought of how Fatma and Fevziye, born and bred in Tarlabaşı, had never in their lives been in a field that smelled of manure, a village hut, or even an orchard. It delighted him to notice their amazement at everything they came across—a tree, a well sweep, a watering hose, and even a weathered old donkey and the metal sheets and ironwork railings that the neighborhood people had pilfered from Istanbul's historic ruins and used for the walls around their own gardens.

But Mevlut also knew that the real reason for his good mood was that he'd accomplished this friendly reunion without sacrificing his pride and come here without upsetting Rayiha. Now he regretted the silly grief of all those years over this business with the love letters. But he still made sure he was never alone with Samiha.

When Samiha came in with the Beyşehir kebab, Mevlut went to sit at the opposite end of the table. A deepening sense of inner contentment had temporarily eased his worries about work and money. Ferhat kept laughing and making jokes and topping up Mevlut's *rakı* glass, and the more Mevlut drank, the more at ease he felt. But he remained vigilant and didn't speak much for fear of saying something wrong.

When the *rakı* began to make his head swim, he started to worry and decided not to say another word. He listened to the conversation at the table but didn't join in (the talk had turned to the TV quiz show the girls had switched on), and whenever he felt the urge to speak, he would talk silently to himself instead.

Yes, my letters were meant for Samiha, and of course I would have been struck by her eyes! he thought. He wasn't looking in that direction now, but she really was exquisite, and her eyes were certainly beautiful enough to justify every single word he had written in his letters.

Still, it was a good thing Süleyman had tricked him into addressing them to Rayiha, even while thinking of Samiha all along. Mevlut knew he could have been happy only with Rayiha. God had made them for each other. He loved her so much; he would die without her. Beautiful girls like Samiha could be difficult and demanding and make you miserable in all sorts of irrational ways. Beautiful girls could only be happy if they married rich men. But a good girl like Rayiha would love her husband rich or poor. After working as a maid for all those years, Samiha was finally happy only now that Ferhat had begun to make a little money.

What would have happened if I'd put "Samiha" on my letters instead of "Rayiha"? thought Mevlut. Would Samiha ever have eloped with him?

Mevlut recognized—through a mixture of realism, jealousy, and inebriation—that she probably wouldn't have.

"Don't drink any more," Rayiha whispered in his ear.

"I'm not," he hissed. Samiha and Ferhat might get the wrong impression if they heard one of Rayiha's unnecessary comments.

"Let him drink as much as he wants, Rayiha," said Ferhat. "He's finally decided to stop selling boza, he's right to celebrate . . . "

"There are people out there who'll mug a boza vendor on the street," said Mevlut. "It's not like I want to stop." He suspected with some embarrassment that Rayiha must have explained everything already and that the point of this meal was to find him a job. "I wish I could sell boza for the rest of my life."

"All right, Mevlut, let's sell boza for the rest of our lives!" said Ferhat. "There's a little shop on İmam Adnan Street. I was thinking we should make it a kebab place. But a boza shop is a better idea. The owner didn't pay his debts, and now the shop's ours for the taking."

"Mevlut knows how to manage a café," said Rayiha. "He's got plenty of experience now."

Mevlut didn't like this pushy Rayiha who was so intent on setting up her husband with a job. But at that moment he lacked even the strength to sit there frowning at what other people were doing. He said nothing. He could sense that Rayiha, Samiha, and Ferhat had already decided everything. The truth was that he didn't even mind. He would be managing a shop again. He could tell that it was better not to ask in his drunken state how on earth Ferhat had scraped together enough money to open a shop in Beyoğlu.

Ferhat. As soon as I got my college degree, an Alevi relative from Bingöl got me a job with the municipal electricity board. Then, when power distribution was privatized in 1991, the most hardworking and enterprising among us got their break. Some of the meter readers took the retirement package and left. Those who thought they could just keep going the way they had as government employees were quickly fired. But people who showed some initiative—people like me—were treated well.

The government had been working for years to bring electricity to every corner of Istanbul, from slums at the farthest outskirts, where only the poorest lived, to lawless dumps ruled by the worst kinds of thugs. The people of Istanbul had always found ways of tapping into power lines without paying. Having failed to make the cheats pay, the government handed the problem over to private companies. I worked at one of those companies. They had also passed a law adding a significant monthly interest charge to any unpaid bills, so that the same people who used to sneer at me when I came to read their meters and demand payment were now forced to pay up, whether they liked it or not.

The man from Samsun who'd been selling newspapers, cigarettes, and sandwiches from the shop on İmam Adnan Street was smart enough, but not a particularly skilled cheat. His shop was technically the property of an elderly Greek man who'd been sent off to Athens. The man from Samsun had taken over the abandoned shop without so much as a title deed or a contract, but he'd still managed to get a meter installed through a contact at city hall. Once that was done, he'd proceeded to hook a branch line into the main line, just upstream of the meter, and this source powered his sandwich toaster and two massive electric heaters that were powerful enough to let him turn the shop into a hammam. By the time I caught him, the overdue balance plus the interest (adjusted for inflation according to the new law) was so high that he would have had to sell his apartment in Kasımpaşa to pay it all off. So instead the shopkeeper from Samsun just disappeared, leaving everything behind.

The shop wasn't half the size of the Binbom, with barely enough room inside for a single table for two. Rayiha would send the girls off to school in the morning and then, just as she had always done, she would add sugar to the boza mixture and wash the jugs at home, before heading out to buy a few things for the shop itself (a task she undertook with proprietary zeal). Mevlut would open it every morning at eleven, and since no one wanted boza so early in the day, he'd concentrate on making things neat and tidy, taking the glasses, jugs, and cinnamon shakers they'd bought and lining them up on the table that faced the street.

It was still cold when they decided to turn the place into a boza shop, and when they hastily opened five days later, there was plenty of interest. Buoyed by the initial success, Ferhat invested in the shop, refurbishing the fridge they were using as a window display, having the door and the exterior repainted (in creamy boza yellow, at Mevlut's insistence), installing a light right over the door, and bringing a mirror in from home.

They also realized that the establishment needed a name. Mevlut felt it would be enough to put up a sign saying BOZA SHOP over the door. But a clever sign maker who had worked with some of the newest shops in Beyoğlu told them that this was not a name on which to build a thriving business. He inquired about their history and got them talking, and when he found out that they were married to sisters, he knew exactly what they should call the place:

THE BROTHERS-IN-LAW BOZA SHOP

In time, this was shortened simply to "Brothers-in-Law." As they'd agreed during their long, *rakı*-soaked lunch in the Ghaazi Quarter, Ferhat would provide the overhead (a free shop in Beyoğlu, with no rent or electricity bills to pay) while Mevlut would put in the cost of daily operation (the boza he bought twice a week, sugar, roasted chickpeas, cinnamon) as well as his and Rayiha's labor. The two childhood friends were to split the profits evenly.

Samiha. After all those years I'd worked as a maid, Ferhat didn't want me toiling in Mevlut's shop. "Why bother, you can't sell boza out of a shop anyway," he'd say, leaving me heartbroken. But he was himself intrigued by the shop when it first opened, and he would go over there most evenings to help Mevlut, getting home really late. I was curious, too, so I would go there myself without telling Ferhat. No one ever wanted to buy anything from two girls in headscarves, and pretty soon our shop became just like any one of Istanbul's thousands of cafés, where the men stood at the front serving customers and handling the cash, and women in headscarves sat at the back looking after the kitchen and washing the dishes. The only difference was that we sold boza.

Ten days after the launch of Brothers-in-Law, Ferhat started renting an apartment in Çukurcuma, with central heating, and we finally moved out of the Ghaazi Quarter. All around us were junk shops, furniture repairmen, hospitals, and pharmacies. From the window I could see part of Sıraselviler Street and the crowds flowing to and from Taksim. In the afternoons, when I got bored at home, I headed over to Brothers-in-Law. Rayiha always left at five to make sure the girls weren't home alone after dark and to start making dinner, so I, too, would leave to avoid being alone with Mevlut. The few times I did stay in the shop after Rayiha had left, Mevlut always stood with his back to me, only looking in the mirror every now and then. So I looked in the other mirror on our side of the shop and never said a word to him at all. Ferhat would drop in later, knowing he'd find me there; he'd eventually gotten used to the idea of my being in the shop. It was fun being there with Ferhat, running around trying to keep up with orders. It was the first time the two of us had ever worked together. Ferhat would comment on every single person who came in for a glass of boza, like the idiot over there who blew over the top of his glass thinking boza was a hot drink. Or that other guy who was the sales manager at a shoe shop on the main street; Ferhat himself had installed its meter. One customer got a free refill just because he seemed to enjoy the first glass so much, and then Ferhat got him talking about his days in military service.

Within two months, they'd all realized that Brothers-in-Law wouldn't turn much of a profit, but no one said a thing. At best, they might sell three times as much boza as Mevlut had been able to on the street on a cold winter night back when business was good. But Mevlut and Rayiha's share of the net proceeds would barely cover half a month's living expenses for a childless couple—and even that was only due to operating rent-free and without having to budget for bribes to city hall and the tax office, thanks to Ferhat's contacts. Yet in such a lively neighborhood—just one street down from İstiklal Avenue—they could have sold anything else they put on the counter.

Mevlut never lost hope. Many people seeing the sign on the door stepped in to have a glass, most of them warmly telling Mevlut what a good idea this shop was. He could happily talk to any customer—mothers bringing their children in for a first taste of boza, drunks, proselytizing know-it-alls, and oddballs skeptical of anything and everything.

"Boza is meant to be had at night, boza seller, what are you doing here so early in the day?" "Do you make this at home?" "You charge too much, your glasses are too small, and there should be more roasted chickpeas in this." (Mevlut soon learned that if people had spared him their criticism when he'd been just a poor street vendor, they certainly weren't holding back now that he had his own shop.) "Hats off to you, you're doing the nation proud." "Boza seller, I've just had half a bottle of Club Rakı, now tell me, what happens if I drink this, and what happens if I don't?" "Excuse me, am I supposed to drink boza before dinner, or is it meant for after a meal, like a dessert?" "Did you know, brother, that the word boza comes from the English word 'booze'?" "Do you deliver?" "Aren't you that yogurt seller's son, Mustafa Efendi? I remember when you used to work with your father. Well done!" "We used to have a boza seller in our neighborhood, but he's stopped coming by." "But if you start selling boza in shops, what will happen to the boza sellers on the street?" "Boza seller, give us a shout of 'Boo-zaa' so that the kids can see and learn."

When he was in a good mood, Mevlut could never disappoint his curious clientele, especially when they brought their children along; "Boo-zaa," he'd call, smiling. Customers who told him "You are doing something very important here" and launched into lectures on the value of tradition and the Ottoman era mostly never came back. Mevlut could scarcely believe the sheer number of suspicious people who wanted to see for themselves that the glasses had been cleaned properly or who asked aggressively whether the boza was made using only natural ingredients. What didn't surprise him was the people who'd never had boza before who said "eughh" right after their first sip, or who complained that it was too sour or too sweet and didn't finish their glass. "The boza I buy at night from my street vendor is more authentic," some would say with great disdain. There were also those who said, "I thought this was meant to be a hot drink," and left their glass untouched.

A month after they'd opened, Ferhat started coming by to help out every other evening. His father's village had been among those evacuated during the army's assault on Kurdish guerrillas in the east, and his paternal grandmother, who spoke no Turkish, had come to Istanbul. Ferhat recounted his efforts to communicate with her in his broken Kurdish. The Kurds who'd moved to Istanbul after their villages were burned by the Turkish army had been settling in certain streets and setting up local gangs. It was rumored that the new mayor from the religious party was going to shut down the restaurants and bars that served alcohol and put tables out on the pavement. As summer approached, Mevlut and Ferhat began to sell ice cream, too.

Rayiha. We brought a mirror of our own to the shop, just like Ferhat and Samiha. On some afternoons, I noticed that Mevlut wasn't really looking out at the street but at our mirror next to the shopwindow. I became suspicious. I waited until he left one day, and I sat in the spot where he usually did, and looking in the mirror, I could see Samiha's face and her eyes right behind me. I had a vision of the two of them looking at each other through the mirror, hiding their glances from me, and I became jealous.

I couldn't stop thinking about it. There's no need for Samiha even to come to the shop in the afternoon when I'm there with Mevlut. Ferhat's pockets are bulging with all the cash he takes from the people who don't pay their electric bills, so why is Samiha so interested in working when they don't even need the money anymore? Late in the afternoon, when it's time for me to go home to the girls, Samiha leaves with me, but sometimes she's too busy with something: four times now she's stayed behind in the shop after I've left, alone with Mevlut.

The one thing that keeps Samiha busier than the shop, though, is their new house in Cihangir. I thought I'd take the girls over there for a visit one evening. She wasn't home, so we went to the shop—I couldn't help myself. Mevlut was there, but Samiha wasn't. "What are you doing here so late?" he said. "How many times do I have to tell you not to bring the children here?" This wasn't the kind, sweet Mevlut I used to know; this was the voice of a mean man. I was so hurt that I didn't go to the shop at all for three days. Of course this meant that Samiha couldn't go either, and soon she came to visit me. "What's wrong? I was worried!" she said. She seemed sincere. "I'm sick," I said, ashamed of my jealousy. "No, you're not. Ferhat is mean to me, too, you know," she said—not because she was trying to get me to talk, but because my smart little sister had figured out a long time ago that, for girls like us, the worst trouble always started with our husbands. I wish we didn't have this shop now; I wish it could just be me and Mevlut alone again.

Around the middle of October, they started selling boza once more. Mevlut thought it would be best to get rid of the sandwiches, biscuits, chocolates, and other summer offerings and concentrate only on the boza, cinnamon, and toasted chickpeas, but as usual he was being overly optimistic, and they didn't listen anyway. Once or twice a week, he would leave the shop to Ferhat in the evening and go out to deliver boza to his regular customers. The war in the east meant that there were explosions all over Istanbul, protest marches, and newspaper offices bombed in the night, but people still thronged to Beyoğlu.

At the end of November, a devout key cutter across the road told Mevlut that a newspaper called the *Righteous Path* had written something about their shop. Mevlut rushed to the kiosk on İstiklal Avenue. Back in the shop, he sat down with Rayiha and examined every inch of the paper.

There was a column under the heading "Three New Shops," which started off with praise for Brothers-in-Law, followed by some words on a new kebab-wrap shop in Nişantaşı and a place in Karaköy selling rosewater and milk-soaked Ramadan pastry and *aşure,* the traditional pudding of fruits and nuts: keeping our ancient traditions alive, rather than discarding them to imitate the West, was a sacred duty, like honoring our ancestors; if, as a civilization, we wanted to preserve our national character, our ideals, and our beliefs, we had to learn, first and foremost, how to remain true to our traditional food and drink.

As soon as Ferhat came in that evening, Mevlut was very excited to show him the newspaper. He claimed it had brought in loads of new customers.

"Oh, drop it," said Ferhat. "No one reading the *Righteous Path* is going to come to our shop. They haven't even included our address. I can't believe we're being used as propaganda for some disgusting Islamist rag."

Mevlut hadn't realized that the *Righteous Path* was a religious newspaper, or that the column was a piece of Islamist propaganda.

When he realized that his friend wasn't following what he was saying, Ferhat lost his patience. He picked up the newspaper. "Just look at these headlines: The Holy Hamza and the Battle of Uhud . . . Fate, Intent, and Free Will in Islam . . . Why the Hajj is a Religious Duty . . . "

So was it wrong to talk about these things? The Holy Guide spoke beautifully on all these subjects, and Mevlut had always enjoyed his talks. Thank God he'd never told Ferhat about visiting with the Holy Guide. His friend might have branded Mevlut a "disgusting Islamist," too.

Ferhat continued to rage his way through the pages of the *Righteous Path:* "'What did Fahrettin Pasha do to the spy and sexual deviant Lawrence?' 'The Freemasons, the CIA, and the Reds.' 'English human rights activist is found out to be a Jew!'"

Thank God Mevlut had never told the Holy Guide that his business partner was an Alevi. The Holy Guide thought Mevlut worked with a normal Sunni Turk, and whenever their conversations touched upon Alevis, the Shias in Iran, and the caliph Ali, Mevlut always changed the subject immediately lest he have to hear the Holy Guide say anything bad about them.

"'Full-color annotated Koran with protective dust jacket for just thirty coupons from the *Righteous Path,*'" read Ferhat. "You know, if these people take power, the first thing they'll do is ban the street vendors, just the way they did in Iran. They might even hang one or two like you."

"No way," said Mevlut. "Boza's alcoholic, but do you see anyone bothering me about it?"

"That's because there's barely any alcohol in it," said Ferhat.

"Oh, of course, boza's worthless next to your Club Rakı," said Mevlut.

"Wait, so you have a problem with *rakı* now? If it's a sin to touch alcohol, it doesn't matter how much there is in your drink. We would have to close this shop down."

Mevlut felt the hint of a threat. After all, it was thanks to Ferhat's money that they had this shop in the first place.

"I bet you even voted for these Islamists."

"No, I didn't," Mevlut lied.

"Oh, do whatever you want with your vote," said Ferhat in a condescending tone.

There followed a period of mutual resentment. For a while, Ferhat stopped coming by in the evenings. This meant Mevlut couldn't leave the shop to deliver boza to his old customers and that, during quiet spells when no one came by, he got bored. He never used to get bored when he sold boza out in the city at night, not even in the emptiest street where no one ever opened any windows or bought any boza. Walking fueled his imagination and reminded him that there was another realm within our world, hidden away behind the walls of a mosque, in a collapsing wooden mansion, or inside a cemetery.

The *Righteous Path* had published a picture of this world as it existed in Mevlut's mind. The image illustrated a series of articles entitled "The Other Realm." When he was alone in the shop at night, Mevlut would pick up the newspaper that had written about Brothers-in-Law and open it up to the page with this picture.

Why were the gravestones keeling over? Why were they all different, some of them sloped sideways in sorrow? What was that whiteness coming down from above like a divine light? Why did old things and cypress trees always make Mevlut feel so good?

2

In the Little Shop with Two Women

Other Meters and Other Families

Rayiha. Samiha is still as beautiful as ever. In the mornings, some men get disrespectful and try to touch her fingers while she's handing them their change. So now we've started putting people's money down on the glass counter rather than giving it to them directly. I'm usually the one who prepares the *ayran,* as well as the boza, but when I look after the cash register no one ever bothers me. A whole morning can go by without a single person coming in to sit down. Sometimes we get an old lady who sits as close to the electric heater as she can and asks for a tea. That's how we started serving tea, too. There was also this very beautiful lady who went out shopping in Beyoğlu every day and came in sometimes. "You two are sisters, aren't you?" she used to ask, smiling at us. "You look alike. So tell me, who's got the good husband, and who's got the bad one?"

Once, this brute with a face like a criminal came in with a cigarette in his hand, asking for boza early in the morning, and after he'd downed three glasses, he kept staring at Samiha saying, "Is there alcohol in boza, or is something else making my head spin?" It really is difficult to run the shop without a man there. But Samiha never told Ferhat, and I didn't tell Mevlut either.

Sometimes Samiha would drop everything and say, "I'm off, you'll look after that woman at the table and take care of the empty glasses, won't you?" As if she owned the place and I was just some waitress . . .

Did she even realize that she was trying to sound like one of those wealthy ladies whose homes she used to clean? Sometimes I'd go to their house in Firuzağa and find that Ferhat had already left a while ago. "Let's go to the cinema, Rayiha," Samiha would say. Or we would watch TV. Sometimes she sat at her new dressing table and did her makeup while I watched. "Come and put some on," she'd say, laughing at me in the mirror. "Don't worry, I won't tell Mevlut." What did she mean by that? Did she talk to Mevlut when I wasn't in the shop, and was it me they spoke about? I was so touchy, so jealous, and always close to tears.

Süleyman. I was walking down İmam Adnan Street one evening when a shop on the left caught my eye, and when I took a closer look, I couldn't believe what I saw.

Some evenings, Ferhat would come by the shop drunk. "What a team we used to be, eh?" he'd tell Mevlut. "All those posters we put up, all those battles we fought!" It all seemed a bit much to Mevlut, who preferred to think back on their Kısmet-selling days rather than the political battles they'd witnessed. Still, it was far more flattering to be featured in youthful memories his friend had already hallowed in myth than to be accused of voting for the Islamists, so Mevlut didn't bother to correct Ferhat.

They could spend hours chatting idly about Islamists who were heading off to join the war in Bosnia, the female prime minister Tansu Çiller, or the bomb that had gone off next to the Christmas tree in the Marmara Hotel's cake shop (the police accused the Islamists one day and the Kurds the next). Sometimes, even during what should have been the rush, they would get no customers at all for more than half an hour at a time, and they would distract themselves with long discussions on matters they knew nothing about—did TV presenters learn what they were meant to say by heart, or did they also cheat like lip-synching singers? Were the police who attacked the protesters in Taksim carrying real guns, or fakes just for show?

Mevlut had framed the article about the shop (as well as the picture of "The Other Realm" in the same edition) and put it up on the wall, copying what he'd seen in other Beyoğlu cafés. (His dream was one day to decorate the walls with framed foreign banknotes given to them by tourists, as they did in the kebab shops on the main street, but sadly not a single tourist had come in since they'd opened.) Was Ferhat upset when he saw the *Righteous Path* article on the wall, and was that why he didn't come by so much anymore? Mevlut realized that he was beginning to consider Ferhat his boss; it made him resent both his friend and his own meekness.

Sometimes Mevlut wondered whether Ferhat had only opened the shop to appease him. In moments of weakness, he told himself, He did it because he felt guilty about running away with the girl I wanted to marry. But when he was angry with Ferhat, he thought, Forget kindness! That one's nothing but a capitalist now. I'm the one who taught him that boza could be a good investment.

For two snowy, windy weeks at the end of January 1995, Ferhat didn't show up at the shop at all. When he finally came in one evening as he was passing by, Mevlut said, "Sales are strong right now," but Ferhat wasn't even listening.

"Mevlut, you know how sometimes I don't come to the shop at all? Well, don't tell Samiha about it, if you know what I mean . . ."

"What? Sit down for a minute, will you."

"I don't have time. Don't tell Rayiha anything either . . . Sisters can't ever keep secrets from each other . . ." He left, carrying the bag he used when he went to read people's meters.

"At your service!" Mevlut shouted after him, though Ferhat, who didn't even have time to sit down and catch up with his old friend anymore, missed the sarcasm. Mevlut's father used to say those words only to his wealthiest, most influential customers. But Mevlut had never told anyone "at your service" in his life. Ferhat was so busy with his philanderings and mafia friends that he probably didn't have time to reflect on such subtleties anymore.

When he went back home and saw his daughters fast asleep and Rayiha watching TV with the volume turned low, Mevlut understood the real reason that he was angry at Ferhat: he was leaving his virtuous and beautiful wife behind to go gallivanting around in the city. The Holy Guide was right; *rakı* and wine were no doubt to blame. Istanbul was crawling with Ukrainian women smuggling contraband in their suitcases, African immigrants, and shady operators who sucked people dry; the city had become a hotbed of corruption and bribery, and the government only stood by and watched.

Mevlut knew, now, why Samiha remained so melancholy even after her husband had suddenly started making so much money. He'd been secretly watching her in the mirror, and he'd seen how sad she was.

Ferhat. Mevlut reads the *Righteous Path* and may well think I'm a cruel, stupid oaf for stepping out on the clever beauty I have at home. But he's wrong. I'm no womanizer.

I've fallen in love. The woman I'm in love with has disappeared, but I will find her someday, here in Istanbul. But first, I should tell you a little bit more about the kinds of jobs and opportunities that just fell in the path of meter inspectors like me after the power grid was privatized, so you can have a better understanding of my love story and the choices I've made.

Süleyman. I still go down to Beyoğlu all the time, but for work—not to drown my sorrows the way I used to. The heartache's gone now. I got over that maid a long time ago, and I'm fine now. In fact, I'm sampling the pleasures of being in love with an artist, a singer, a mature woman.

Ferhat. When electricity bill collection went private, I made sure never to target those people who hooked up illegal connections and bypassed the meter purely because they were too poor and desperate to do otherwise. Instead, I went after the shameless rich. So I steered clear of back alleys and remote, derelict neighborhoods where unemployed men huddled for warmth with their wives and hungry children, people who either stole some power for their electric heater, or risked freezing to death on winter nights.

But when I found people living in eight-room houses right on the Bosphorus, with maids, cooks, and drivers, but still not paying their bills, I cut their power off. There was a man with an apartment in one of these eighty-year-old buildings where rich people used to live a long time ago, and he'd packed sixty poor girls in there to sew zippers until dawn; when I caught him stealing power, too, I showed no mercy. I inspected the ovens of an expensive restaurant that overlooked the whole city, the looms of a textile baron who exported record quantities of curtain fabrics, and the cranes of a contractor from the Black Sea coast who boasted of how far he'd come from the village, now that he was building fourteen-story buildings, and when I found them each bypassing a meter, I didn't hesitate. I put their lights out, and I took their money. There were lots of young idealists like me at Seven Hills Electric Ltd., ready to take from the rich and look the other way when the poor couldn't pay. I learned a lot from them.

Süleyman. I've been talking to nightclub owners who are serious about music, so the world can discover Mahinur's talent. The Sunshine Club is the best of the lot. Every now and then, though, I still can't help taking a little walk past the two boza bozos' little shop. It's not to indulge my wounded heart or anything like that; it's just for a laugh, of course . . .

Ferhat. Spoiled rich people don't pay their bills because they don't care, though sometimes the bill gets lost in the mail. Weighed down with penalties, which are adjusted for inflation, their debt grows exponentially. The quickest way to teach these people a lesson is to just cut their power off without even knocking on their door to warn them first. Back when the government still distributed electricity and sent its own inspectors to collect payments and warn delinquents they'd be cut off, the rich and powerful would just say "Oh dear, it seems I forgot to pay!" and just shrug off the threats. In the unlikely event that an honest inspector did manage to get someone's electricity turned off, those bastards would run to the electricity board's headquarters in Taksim, and instead of paying up, they'd call some politician they happened to know and have the poor inspector canned on the spot. But all those rich housewives started to fear us once it wasn't the state anymore but a gang of ruthless capitalists—kind of like their husbands—running the utility. My bosses are from Central Anatolia—Kayseri, in fact—and they couldn't care less about the sophisticated airs and crocodile tears of Istanbul's pampered class. Before, inspectors didn't even have the authority to cut someone's power off. Now, if I really want to screw them, I cut them off on a Friday evening, just before the weekend. Two days in the dark and they learn pretty quick how to keep up their payments. Last year, the Feast of the Sacrifice fell close to New Year's Eve, so with this long ten-day holiday coming up, I thought I'd take the chance to teach one of these rich delinquents a lesson.

At four o'clock, I descended into the basement of a block of expensive apartments in Gümüşsuyu. The rusty meters for all twelve apartments were churning away like old washing machines, down at the dark end of a narrow, dusty corridor. I asked the doorman, "Is anyone home in number eleven?"

"The lady is," said the doorman. "Hey, what are you doing, don't cut them off!"

I ignored him. It takes me less than two minutes to pull out the screwdriver, a pair of wire cutters, and the special key wrench from my toolbox and cut someone's power off. Number 11's meter stopped ticking.

"Go upstairs in about ten minutes or so," I told the doorman. "Tell them I'll be in the neighborhood and that you know where to find me if they want to see me. I'll be at the coffeehouse at the foot of the hill."

Fifteen minutes later, the doorman came to the coffeehouse and told me that Madam was very upset and that she was waiting for me at home. "Tell her I'm busy with other meters and other families, but I'll try to come by later," I said. I wondered if I should wait until it got dark. In winter, when night falls very early, it's easier for these people to picture what it might be like to spend ten days in the dark. Some of them go to stay in hotels. Would you care to hear the story of the guy who was too cheap to pay his bill but wound up taking his wife, her hats, and his four children to stay at the Hilton for several months while they waited stubbornly for their connections to come to their assistance?

"Sir, the lady is very concerned. She's expecting people tonight."

People always worry when their power gets cut. Wives call their husbands, some get aggressive, others take a milder approach, and while there're those who'll just cut to the chase and offer you a bribe, some people don't even know that's how to fix their problem. Most of these people still address us as government clerks, not realizing that we were all forced to give up our government jobs after privatization. But even our stupidest countrymen eventually figure out how to offer a bribe: "Perhaps I could pay the fine to you in cash now, and maybe you can switch our electricity back on?" When you reject their offer, some of them raise it; others think it will help to start threatening you: "Do you know who I am!" And then there are those who are so confused that they have no idea what to do next. I've heard people say that when an inspector goes to one of the rougher neighborhoods and threatens to turn off the power, women sometimes offer to have sex with him. It's never happened to me, though; I wouldn't believe that nonsense if I were you.

People in poor neighborhoods can recognize an inspector immediately from the bag he carries and the way he walks down the street. First they'll send out a few kids—the same ones who usually go after strangers and thieves—to throw stones at him and yell "Get out of here!" to scare him off. The neighborhood lunatic will then threaten to kill him. Some drunk may be on hand to provide a little more intimidation: "What the hell do you think you're doing here?" If the inspector looks like he's walking toward where the illegal branch connections meet the main cables high in the air, neighborhood thugs and stray dogs will try to change his mind. Gangs of political militants will harangue him with their speeches. Should he ever manage to find what he's looking for, like some poor woman who can't afford to pay her bills, there will be children playing in her garden, ready to carry word to the neighborhood coffeehouse in the blink of an eye. Any inspector who dares to walk into a house and shut the front door behind him so that he ends up alone with a woman will be lucky to get out of that neighborhood alive.

I'm telling you all this to lower your expectations now that you are about to hear my love story. Love in our parts is usually unrequited. A lady who lives in a house on the Bosphorus in Gümüşsuyu would never have noticed a meter inspector before. She will now, though—especially if he cuts her power off.

Leaving the coffeehouse, I headed back toward the building. I got into an elevator with wooden doors, a battered old golden cage, and as it groaned its way up toward number 11, I felt exhilarated.

Süleyman. One freezing afternoon toward the end of February, I finally went to the Brothers-in-Law, just like any other customer.

"Boza seller, is your boza sweet or sour?"

Mevlut recognized me immediately. "Ah, Süleyman!" he shouted. "Come on in."

"Hope you're well, ladies," I said, with all the familiarity of an old friend who just happened to be passing by. Samiha was wearing a headscarf with pink leaves.

"Welcome, Süleyman," said Rayiha, getting agitated at the prospect that I might start something.

"I hear you're married now, Samiha, congratulations and best wishes."

"Thank you, Süleyman."

"That was ten years ago," said Mevlut protectively. "It's taken you this long to wish her well?"

So, Mr. Mevlut was happy in the little shop with two women beside him. Careful now, I wanted to say, you'd better look after this place properly, you wouldn't want it to go bust like Binbom. But I held back and took a more diplomatic approach.

"Ten years ago, we were just a bunch of hot-blooded young men," I said. "At that young and turbulent age, it's easy to become obsessed with certain things, and ten years later you can't even remember why they ever seemed so important. I would have wanted to bring you a wedding gift, but Vediha never gave me your address; she just told me you lived far out in the Ghaazi Quarter."

"They've moved to Cihangir now," said that idiot Mevlut. I wanted to say Çukurcuma, the rough part of the neighborhood, not Cihangir—but I didn't. Otherwise they would have figured out that I had some men tailing Ferhat. "Thank you, your boza really is delicious," I said, taking a sip from the glass they'd given me. "I'll take some back for the others." I had them fill a bottle up with a kilo's worth. With this visit, I showed these long-lost friends—and even my fading love herself—that I was over my obsession. But my main purpose was to warn Mevlut. When he came to show me out, I gave him a hug and a message for his dear friend: "Tell him to watch himself."

"What do you mean?" said Mevlut.

"He'll know."

3

Ferhat's Electric Passion

Let's Run Away from Here

Korkut. A one-room house was all that my late uncle Mustafa ever managed to build on the land he'd fenced off with my father in Kültepe back in 1965. Mevlut came down from the village to help him out, but it didn't work, and they soon ran out of steam. We started with a two-room house on our land over in Duttepe. My father planted poplars in the garden like those he had back in the village; I bet you can see them all the way from Şişli now. When my mother left the village to join us in Duttepe, we added a nice little room one night in 1969, and then came another room, which I used when I wanted to listen to the horse races on the radio. In 1978, around the time I got married to Vediha, we added a guest room and another big room with its own toilet, and pretty soon our sprawling house was the size of a palace. Our royal gardens even had two mulberry trees and a fig tree that had started growing on their own. We made the wall around the garden taller. We also installed an iron gate.

The family business was thriving, thank God, so six years ago we decided to add a whole new floor to the house—everyone else on these hills was already doing it, and we (finally) had a title deed to fall back on. We built the flight of stairs that led to this second floor on the exterior of the house so that my mother wouldn't have to worry constantly about where Vediha was going and whether her boys had come home. In the beginning, Mother, Father, and Süleyman were very eager to move upstairs where everything was new and there was a better view. But soon my parents came back down; there were too many stairs, and it was too big, too empty, too cold, and too lonely up there. At Vediha's request, I fitted the upstairs bathroom with blue porcelain tiles as well as the latest and most expensive furniture, but still she wouldn't stop badgering me: "Let's move to the city." I kept telling her "This is part of the city now, it counts as Istanbul," but it was like talking to a brick wall. Some rich-kid bastards who went to high school in Şişli with Bozkurt and Turan had teased them about living in a *gecekondu* neighborhood. "My parents will never go to Şişli. They've got their garden with this lovely breeze, their grocery store, their chickens, and their trees," I said. "Are we supposed to leave them here on their own?"

Vediha complains about all sorts of nonsense, including how I always come home late, when I come home at all, how I take off on work trips for ten days at a time, and the cross-eyed woman with dyed-blond hair who worked in our office in Şişli.

It's true that sometimes I do disappear for ten days, or two weeks, though it has nothing to do with the construction business. Last time, it was Azerbaijan. Tarık and some other nationalist friends from our old Pan-Turkic movement were complaining, "The government has given us this sacred task, but we don't have any money." Word came from Ankara that they had to find sponsors for their coup among private businesses. How could I say no to these patriots who came to ask for my help? Russian communism is all washed up, but the Azeri president Aliyev is a member of the KGB and the Soviet Politburo. So while he's supposedly a Turk, all he wants is for the Turks to follow Russia's lead. We held secret meetings with some warlords in Baku. Abulfaz Elchibey was Azerbaijan's first democratically elected president. He had won most of the votes of the glorious Azeri people (they're all Turks, really, with some Russians and Persians thrown in), but he'd been deposed in a KGB-style coup and gone back to his village in a huff. He was sick of the traitors who'd handed victory over to the enemy in the war against Armenia; he was tired of the incompetents who surrounded him, and of the Russian spies who'd brought him down. He refused to meet us because he figured we were Russian agents, too, so Tarık and I passed the time in the bars and hotels of Baku. Before we got the chance to visit Elchibey's village to pay our respects to this great man and tell him "We've got America on our side, Azerbaijan's future lies with the West," we had news that the plans for our Turkish-style coup had fallen through. Someone in Ankara had panicked and told Aliyev that we'd come to overthrow his government. We also found out that Elchibey was under house arrest and couldn't even go out into his own back garden to feed the chickens, let alone join us to launch a coup. So we headed straight to the airport and back to Istanbul.

Here is what this adventure taught me: It's true that the whole world is against the Turks, but the biggest enemies of the Turks are Turks themselves. Also, Baku girls hated the Russians, but they'd still learned all their loose ways from them—even though, at the end of the day, they still preferred Azeri men. If that's how it is, miss, then I'm not sticking my neck out for you. Anyway, my willingness to join the cause had already strengthened my position with the government and the party. Meanwhile, Süleyman was taking my preoccupation as a chance to do whatever he wanted.

Aunt Safiye. Vediha and I couldn't find him a suitable girl, so Süleyman picked one himself. He never comes home anymore. We're very embarrassed and worried that something untoward will happen.

Rayiha. On cold winter evenings when the shop was busy, Ferhat would come by to help, and I would take the girls home with Samiha. They loved their aunt's free-flowing gossip, her vast knowledge of all the film stars who appeared on TV, the details of who had eloped with whom, her advice about clothes, how she would tell them, "Do your hair this way" or "Clip it up like that," and how she might see someone on-screen and exclaim, "Oh, I used to work in that man's house; his wife would cry all the time." When we got back home, they would practice trying to talk just like her, until one day I had enough and almost said, Don't turn into your aunt—but I stopped myself, because I didn't want to be jealous. What I really wanted to know, but couldn't bring myself to ask anyone, was "When they are alone in the shop, do

Samiha and Mevlut actually look at each other, or do they pretend their eyes have met by accident in the mirror?" Whenever I felt the poison of envy seeping into my heart, I took out my bundle of letters from Mevlut.

Yesterday, as I walked out of the boza shop, Mevlut gave me the sweetest smile, and a sneaking suspicion that he may have meant it for my sister began to eat away at my soul, so as soon as I got home I opened one of the letters: "There are no other eyes I would rather gaze upon, no face I would sooner smile at, nowhere else I would ever turn!" he'd written. There were other things, too: "Your eyes have captured me like a magnet draws metal, I am your prisoner, Rayiha, you are the only thing I see" and "Just one glance from you has made me your willing slave."

Sometimes Mevlut would ask one of us, "Clear those dirty glasses," the way a restaurant manager barks at his busboys. When he asked me, I got angry at him for giving me the dirty job instead of Samiha; but when he asked Samiha, I got annoyed that she was the one he'd thought of first.

Mevlut could tell that I was jealous. He tried to avoid being alone in the shop with Samiha or showing too much interest in her. If he's being so careful, he must be hiding something! I thought, and got jealous anyway. Samiha went to a toy store one day and brought my girls a water gun, as if she were buying a gift for a pair of boys. When Mevlut came home in the evening, he joined in their game. The next day, when the girls went to school and Mevlut went to the shop, I looked around for the gun to throw it in the trash (they'd squirted it at me plenty, too), but I couldn't find it—Fatma, I guessed, must have put it in her bag and taken it to school. That night, while she slept, I took it out and hid it away somewhere. Another time, Samiha came by with a singing doll that could blink, too. Obviously Fatma, who was almost twelve, would have no interest in playing with a doll, but I didn't say anything. The girls mostly ignored it. Someone must have stashed it away somewhere.

The most painful thing, though, was that I kept wondering, Is Samiha alone with Mevlut in the shop right now? I knew it was wrong, but I just couldn't get this thought out of my head, because Süleyman, who knew all the Beyoğlu gossip, had told Vediha how Ferhat was coming home really late at night and drowning his sorrows all over town, the way men do in films when they've had their heart broken.

Ferhat. The old elevator car, a gilded, mirrored cage, came to a halt. I still remember that day from a time that now seems as ancient as dreams, but love always feels like only yesterday. After I've cut people's power off, I find it more satisfying to rap on the door instead of ringing the bell, like some hit man from an American movie.

A maid answered and said Madam's daughter was in bed with a fever (this is everyone's favorite lie), but the lady would be with me in a minute. I sat on the chair the maid offered me and looked out at the Bosphorus. I was just thinking that the elated sense of purpose I felt in my soul must have had something to do with the swirling, mournful view before me, but then the real reason came into the room like a ray of light, wearing black jeans and a white blouse.

"Good afternoon, officer. Ercan, our doorman, told me you wished to meet."

"We are not government officers anymore," I said.

"Are you not from the electricity board?"

"It's all been privatized now, ma'am . . ."

"I see . . ."

"We wouldn't have wanted it to be this way . . . ," I said, struggling to get the words out. "I had to cut your power off. There were some unpaid bills."

"Thank you. Please do not worry. It's not your fault. You just follow your orders, whether you work for the government or for a private company."

I didn't manage any answer to the harsh truth of these poisonous words. I was falling rapidly in love and couldn't think of anything except how fast I was falling. I gathered all my remaining strength. "Unfortunately I've had to seal the meter downstairs," I lied. "Had I known your daughter was ill, I would have never cut you off."

"Never mind, officer, what's done is done," she said. She wore the strict, somber expression of those lady judges in Turkish melodramas. "Don't worry, you were just doing your job."

We were both quiet for a moment. She hadn't said any of the things I had been expecting to hear as I made my way up on the elevator, so now I couldn't remember any of the answers I'd prepared. I looked at my watch. "The ten-day national holiday will officially begin in twenty minutes."

"Mr. Officer," she said firmly, "I'm afraid I have never been able to bring myself to bribe anyone in my life, nor have I ever been able to tolerate those who do. I live to be an example to my daughter."

"Be that as it may, ma'am," I said, "it is important for people like you to understand that those officers you are so quick to look down on in fact treasure their pride more than you can imagine."

I walked back to the door seething, because I knew that the woman I loved was never going to say "Stop."

She took two steps toward me. It felt as if anything could happen between us, though I already knew, even then, that this love was hopeless.

But despair is what keeps love alive.

"Look at all these people, Mr. Officer," she said, gesturing toward the city. "You know better than I do that these ten million souls are gathered here in Istanbul to earn their daily bread, chasing after their profits, collecting their bills and interest. But there is only one thing that can keep a person going among these monstrous multitudes, and that is love."

She turned around and walked away before I had a chance to respond. In these old buildings, street vendors and meter inspectors aren't allowed to use the ancient elevators to go down. So I took the stairs as I thought things through.

I went down to the airless basement, all the way to the end of the corridor. My hands stretched out to seal the meter, which I had already disconnected. But my nimble fingers did the opposite, and the next minute, the wires I had cut were spliced together again, and number 11's meter whirred back to life.

"It was good that you gave them their power back," said the doorman Ercan.

"Why?"

"Madam is with Sami from Sürmene, who has a lot of influence in

Beyoğlu. He's got eyes and ears everywhere . . . He would have given you trouble. These Black Sea people are a mafia."

"There's no sick daughter, is there?"

"What daughter? They're not even married . . . This Sürmene man's got a wife back in the village, grown children, too. His sons know about Madam, but they don't say anything."

Rayiha. One evening after dinner, I was watching TV with the girls at their aunt Samiha's when Ferhat arrived and beamed at the sight of the four of us together. "Your daughters are getting bigger every day! Look at you, Fatma, you're a young lady now," he said. "Oh dear, it's late, we should go home," I told the girls, but he said "Don't leave, Rayiha, stay a little longer. Mevlut is capable of sitting in that shop forever, waiting for some drunk to show up for a glass of boza."

I didn't like his making fun of Mevlut in front of the girls. "You're right, Ferhat," I said. "But it seems one person's livelihood is another man's joke. Come on, girls, let's go."

We got back late, and Mevlut was angry. "You will not take a single step on İstiklal Avenue, the girls aren't allowed," he said. "And you're not to leave the house at all after dark."

"Did you know the girls get meatballs, lamb cutlets, and roast chicken at their aunt's?" I blurted out. Normally I would never have said such a thing, fearing Mevlut's rage, but God must have put the words in my mouth.

Mevlut got offended and wouldn't speak to me for three days. So I stopped taking the girls to Aunt Samiha's, and we just sat at home in the evenings. Whenever I felt the prick of jealousy, I picked up my needlework, and instead of stitching birds cut out from magazines, I decorated fabrics with things from Mevlut's letters: ruthless eyes that could capture you with a single glance, and looks that cut across your path like bandits. I had eyes dangling down from a tree like enormous fruits and jealous birds weaving in and out around them. I sprinkled the branches with hooded black eyes that looked like daffodils, embroidering an entire blanket with a tree whose hundreds of blossoming eyes peeped out from behind the leaves, like amulets guarding against bad luck. I cleared a path through the darkness in my heart. I made eyes that were like suns, with dark rays that leaped from each lash like arrows, tracing their jagged way through folds of cloth and the winding branches of a fig tree. But nothing could quench my anger!

"Mevlut won't let us come over anymore, Samiha . . . Why don't you come to us when he's at the shop," I said one day.

That's how my sister began to visit us in the evenings with bags of meatballs and crispy minced-meat flatbreads. I soon began to wonder whether Samiha just came to see my daughters, or whether she was there for Mevlut, too.

Ferhat. Back on the street, I realized I had lost my confidence up in number 11. In the space of just twenty minutes, I had fallen in love and been duped. I should have just shut the power off and left. The doorman had called her Madam, though I knew from the electric bill that her name was Selvihan.

I began to daydream that my Selvihan was being held hostage by this mafia don, and I was going to rescue her. To fall in love with a woman, a guy like Süleyman needs to see her half naked in that corner of the Sunday paper aimed at sex-starved men and then pay to sleep with her a few times until he forms an attachment. For Mevlut, it's important that he not know the girl at all, but that he catch just enough of a glimpse to fuel his fantasies. But for a guy like me, to fall in love with a woman, I need to feel as if I've squared off against her at the chessboard of life. My opening moves, I admit, were a bit amateurish. But I had a gambit in mind to capture this Selvihan. I knew a guy in our accounting and records department, an experienced, gregarious fellow who loved *rakı,* and with his help I began to comb through the most recent receipts and bank transfers for that account.

I remember spending many nights looking at my Samiha, beautiful as a rose in bloom, and thinking, Why would a man with a wife like that lose his head over some thug's mistress locked up in some room with a view? Some evenings, over a glass of *rakı,* I would remind Samiha that, after all we'd been through, we had finally made it to the heart of the city, just as we'd always wanted.

"We even have money now," I'd say. "We can do whatever we want. So what shall we do?"

"Let's run away," Samiha would say. "Let's go somewhere no one can find us, somewhere no one even knows us."

Hearing these words, I realized just how happy Samiha had been those first few months we'd spent all alone together in the Ghaazi Quarter. I'd kept in touch with some of my old friends, both from the Maoists and the pro-Soviet faction, and they were all just as sick and tired as we were of city life. If after years of suffering they'd managed to make a bit of money, they would say, "We'll save up some more and then we're leaving Istanbul and going away down south." Like me, they fantasized about olive trees and vineyards and a farmhouse in a garden down in some Mediterranean town they'd never even been to. Samiha and I both imagined that if we were living on a farm in the south, she would finally get pregnant and we would have a baby.

In the mornings, I'd say, "We've been so patient, we're making some money now, let's grit our teeth just a while longer and salt away a little more. Then we'll have enough to buy a big field in the south."

"I get bored at home in the evenings," Samiha would say. "Take me to the movies one night."

One evening I got tired of talking to Mevlut in the shop, so I downed some *rakı* and went over to the apartment in Gümüşsuyu. I rang the doorman's bell first, like a policeman who's come to make an arrest.

"What's the matter, boss? I thought it was the boza seller. Everything okay?" said Doorman Ercan when he saw me looking at the meters. "Oh, but those people in number eleven are gone now."

He was right: number 11's meter was still. For a moment, I felt as if the world had stopped turning.

I went to see the *rakı*-loving accountant at the Taksim offices: he introduced me to two ancient bookkeepers who looked after the archives and the old handwritten records of the agency that had been distributing electricity to Istanbul's neighborhoods for over eighty years. The two wise old clerks—one of them was seventy, and the other sixty-five—had taken their retirement bonuses and left, only to return to their office of forty years, now under contract with the private company and eager to teach a new generation of inspectors all the wondrously ingenious tricks that Istanbul residents had devised over eighty years to cheat the electric company and its men. Seeing that I was a young go-getter, they were especially eager to show me the ropes. They could still recall the details of every ploy, the lay of all the neighborhoods, even the women who answered the doors, and all their rumored romances. But for my purposes it wasn't enough to look in the archives alone; I'd need to check the latest records, too. It would be only a matter of time before I knocked on a door somewhere in Istanbul and found Selvihan behind it. Everyone in this city has a heart, and an electric meter.

Rayiha. I'm pregnant again, and I don't know what I'm going to do. At my age, and with two girls in the house already, it's too embarrassing.

4

A Child Is a Sacred Thing

Maybe You Would Be Happier If I Would Just Die and You Could Marry Samiha

MEVLUT WOULD NEVER forget the story Ferhat told him one night when they still had the Brothers-in-Law Boza Shop:

"During the worst days of the military dictatorship that followed the 1980 coup, with the people of Diyarbakır—a town with a large Kurdish population—cowed by the screams coming from the prison's torture chambers, a man who looked like a government inspector came down to the city from Ankara. In the taxi from the airport to his hotel, the mysterious visitor asked the Kurdish driver what life in Diyarbakır was like. The driver told him that all the Kurds were very happy with the new military government, that they only had eyes for the Turkish flag and nothing else, and that city folk were very pleased now that the Kurdish separatist terrorists had all been thrown in jail. 'I'm a lawyer,' said the visitor from Ankara. 'I'm here to defend those who've been tortured in prison and had dogs let loose on them for speaking Kurdish.' On hearing this, the driver changed tack completely. He gave a detailed account of the tortures being inflicted on Kurds in prison, of people being thrown into the sewers alive and getting beaten to death. The lawyer from Ankara couldn't help but interrupt. 'But you were telling me the opposite just now,' he said. 'You're right, Mr. Lawyer,' said the driver from Diyarbakır. 'What I told you earlier were my public views. What I'm telling you now are my private views.'"

Every time he thought about this story, Mevlut laughed as if hearing it for the first time, and he would have loved to talk more about it with his friend sometime when they were both in the shop looking after customers, but Ferhat was always busy or his mind was elsewhere. It could be that Ferhat had cut back his appearances at the shop because he found Mevlut's moralistic musings irritating. Sometimes Mevlut would let slip some crack about *rakı* or womanizing or the responsibilities of married men, and Ferhat would snap back: "Did you read that in the *Righteous Path*?" Mevlut had tried to tell him that he'd only bought that paper once because of the nice piece they'd run about the shop, but Ferhat always brushed him off. He had also mocked the picture of "The Other Realm," with its cypress trees, gravestones, and that divine light, which Mevlut had hung on the wall. Why was his friend so enamored of the kinds of things old men liked to think about, cemeteries and ancient relics?

As the Islamist parties gained more votes and followers, Mevlut saw Ferhat and many other leftists and Alevis becoming uneasy, and perhaps even starting to feel afraid. He himself had more or less seriously come to the conclusion that the first thing they would do in power would be to ban alcohol, and that would make everyone realize the importance of boza. Still, if anyone at the teahouse brought up the subject, he stayed out of it and, if pressed, offered only this prediction—which was enough to rile the anxious pro-Atatürk secularists.

Mevlut had also begun to think that another reason that Ferhat was making himself scarce must have to do with those letters Mevlut had written in the army. "If someone had written letters to my wife for three years, I wouldn't want to see him every day either," he told himself. On evenings when it became clear that Ferhat wouldn't be showing up at all, Mevlut would remind himself that his friend was barely even at home anymore. (Left by herself, Samiha had started coming over to spend time with Rayiha and the girls.) On one such evening, Mevlut got so angry and restless that he decided to close up shop early and go home. When he got home, he found out Samiha had just left. She must have started wearing some sort of perfume, or perhaps the scent drifting up to Mevlut's nose came from the new toys she'd bought for the girls.

When she saw him coming home so early, Rayiha didn't seem as delighted as Mevlut had hoped. Instead, she flared up with jealousy. Twice she asked her husband what he was doing back so soon. Mevlut himself wasn't entirely sure of the answer, but he found Rayiha's suspicion unreasonable. At Brothers-in-Law, he had always taken such pains to avoid upsetting any of them (Samiha included): he tried to avoid being left alone with Samiha, and when there was work to be done, he always spoke to Rayiha with gentle familiarity, assuming with Samiha a more distant, formal manner, as he would have done with some employee at the Binbom Café. These precautions, however, had not sufficed, and Mevlut felt himself being dragged into a vicious circle: If he acted like there was no cause to be jealous, it would look like he was hiding something, getting up to no good right under Rayiha's nose, which would only inflame her suspicion. If, however, he seemed too understanding about Rayiha's feelings, it would be like admitting to a crime he hadn't committed. Fortunately, when he got home that evening, the girls hadn't gone to sleep yet, so Rayiha held back, and the tension blew over before their argument could escalate.

Rayiha. One afternoon, while working with our neighbor Reyhan on a bridal trousseau, I sheepishly told her a little bit about my feelings. She took my side, saying any wife whose husband spent time with a woman as beautiful as Samiha was bound to feel jealous. Of course this just made my jealousy worse. According to Reyhan, I should not keep my feelings bottled up inside until I burst but rather I should talk to Mevlut and remind him to be a little more considerate. I thought I'd bring it up with Mevlut after the girls left for school. But we ended up fighting. "So what?" said Mevlut. "I can't come back to my own house at whatever time I please?"

To be honest, I take most things Reyhan tells me with a grain of salt, and I would certainly never count my dear little sister as one of those beautiful but childless women whose very existence is a threat to the natural order. The way Reyhan saw it, when Samiha played with the girls, she wasn't just nursing the pangs of her childlessness; she was also indulging in the pain and pleasures of JEALOUSY. "A woman who is barren is a woman to be feared, Rayiha, for behind her silence lies a towering rage," she said. "When she buys your daughters meatballs from the diner, she's not as innocent as you think." In my anger, I threw some of the things Reyhan had said back at Mevlut. "You shouldn't talk about your sister like that," he said.

So Samiha's got my foolish Mevlut wrapped around her finger and ready to rush to her defense, has she? Well then: "She is BARREN!" I screamed, even louder than before. "If you're going to take her side, I'll be as nasty as I want." Mevlut waved me off as if to say, You are despicable, and he curled his lip as if he were looking at some sort of bug.

He wrote all those letters to her only to marry me in the end, the freak! No, that I didn't dare say out loud. I don't know how, but as I was shouting at him I picked up a packet of Filiz tea and threw it at his head. "MAYBE YOU WOULD BE HAPPIER IF I WOULD JUST DIE AND YOU COULD MARRY SAMIHA," I screamed. I would never leave my daughters to a stepmother, though. I can see just as well as you can that Samiha is trying to charm my daughters with her gifts, her stories, her beauty, and her money, but if I dared to mention it, everybody—and especially all of you reading this—would say the same thing: "What on earth do you mean, Rayiha? Can't the girls have a little fun with their aunt?"

Mevlut tried to regain the upper hand: "ENOUGH IS ENOUGH, KNOW YOUR PLACE!"

"I know my place and I know it well, and that's why I'm not coming to the shop anymore," I said. "It stinks in there."

"What?"

"The Brothers-in-Law Boza Shop . . . IT STINKS. It makes my stomach turn."

"Boza makes you sick?"

"I've had enough of your boza . . ."

Mevlut's expression became so menacing that I got scared and cried out: "I'M PREGNANT." I hadn't planned on telling him; I was planning to go and have it scraped out of me the way Vediha does, but it was too late, I'd said it now, so I just went on.

"I have your baby in my belly, Mevlut; at this age and with Fatma and Fevziye around, it's mortifying. You should have been more careful," I said, blaming him. I already wished I hadn't told him, but at the same time I was pleased to see him mollified.

Oh yes, Mr. Mevlut, you sit in that shop fantasizing about your sister-in-law, with that smug, self-satisfied grin, but now everyone's going to know what you've been up to with your wife after the girls go to school. They're all going to say, "Mevlut doesn't waste a chance, does he!" Never mind barren Samiha, who will be even more jealous now.

Sitting next to me on the edge of the bed, Mevlut put a hand on my shoulder and pulled me close. "I wonder if it's a boy or a girl," he said. "Of course you shouldn't come to the shop in this state," he said, sweet and caring. "I won't go either. It's only making us fight. Selling boza on the street at night is better, and there's more money in it, Rayiha."

We went back and forth for a while: "You go, no really, you go, I won't go, you don't go, of course you should go," we said, and also "that's not what I meant, it's nobody's fault," and things like that.

"Samiha's the one who's in the wrong," said Mevlut. "She shouldn't come to the shop anymore. She's changed, and so has Ferhat, they're not like us anymore, just look at that perfume she wears . . ."

"What perfume?"

"Whatever it was, the whole house smelled of it when I came home last night," he said, laughing.

"So that's why you came home early yesterday, to catch a whiff of her!" I said, and started crying again.

Vediha. Poor Rayiha is pregnant again. She came to Duttepe one morning and said, "Oh, Vediha, it's so embarrassing with the girls around, you have to help me, take me to the hospital."

"Your daughters are old enough to be married, Rayiha. You're almost thirty, Mevlut is nearly forty. What's going on with you two, sweetheart? Haven't you figured out by now when to do it and when not to?"

Rayiha gave me lots of intimate details she'd never bothered to mention before, and eventually she brought up Samiha, finding some excuse to criticize her. That's how I came to the conclusion that it wasn't Mevlut's carelessness that had gotten her pregnant but Rayiha's own trick—not that I would ever say such a thing to her.

"My dear Rayiha, children are a family's delight, a woman's consolation, and life's greatest joy, so what's the problem, just pop this one out, too," I said. "I get so cross with Bozkurt and Turan sometimes; they're so disrespectful. We both know how they've always tormented your girls. I've worn myself out giving them so many smacks over the years, but they are my reason for living; they keep me going. I would die if anything happened to them, God forbid. They've got beards to shave and pimples to squeeze now; they're so grown up they won't let their mother even touch them anymore, not even for a little kiss . . . If I could make another two, I'd have the little ones to sit on my lap now, I'd kiss them and hug them and I'd be happier, I wouldn't mind so much when Korkut is awful. Now I wish I hadn't had all those abortions . . . There's plenty of women who've gone mad with regret over an abortion, but never in the history of the world has a woman ever regretted having a child. Do you regret giving birth to Fatma, Rayiha? Do you regret having Fevziye?"

Rayiha started crying. She said Mevlut wasn't earning enough, he had failed as a manager, and now they were terrified that the boza shop was going to fail, too; if not for the needlework she did for those linen shops in Beyoğlu, they would be struggling to make it to the end of the month. She'd made her mind up, she wouldn't have another child and expect God to feed it. The four of them barely had room to breathe in their one-room apartment as it was; there certainly wasn't any space for another.

"My darling Rayiha," I said, "your sister will always lend you a hand in times of trouble. But a child is a sacred thing; this is a big responsibility. Go home and think it over. I'll call Samiha, and we'll talk about it together next week."

"Don't call Samiha, I can't stand her anyway. I don't want her to know I'm carrying a baby. She's barren; she'd get jealous. I've made my decision. I don't need to think about it."

I explained to Rayiha that three years after the coup in 1980, our dictator General Kenan Evren had done a good deed by allowing unmarried women less than ten weeks into a pregnancy to go to a hospital and get an abortion. This had mostly benefited those brave city girls who had sex before marriage. For married women to be able to take advantage of this new regulation, they had to get their husbands to sign a form confirming they agreed to the termination of the pregnancy. The men of Duttepe often refused to sign, saying they might as well keep the baby, it was a sin to do otherwise, and at least they'd have someone else to look after them in their old age, and so after many drawn-out arguments with their husbands, their wives would end up with a fourth or fifth child. Some caused themselves to miscarry using primitive methods they learned from one another. "Don't you even think of doing anything like that if Mevlut doesn't sign, Rayiha, you'll regret it," I told my sister.

As I also told Rayiha, there are men like Korkut who have no qualms at all about signing those forms. They find it more convenient than taking the necessary precautions, so they go ahead and knock up their wives, thinking, She can get an abortion anyway! After Evren's law was introduced, Korkut got me pregnant three times. I had three abortions at the Etfal Hospital, though of course as soon as we started making a little more money, I wished I could take them back. But I did at least become familiar with the procedure.

"The first thing we do, Rayiha, is go to the councilman and get a certificate that confirms you're married to Mevlut, then we'll go to the hospital and get two doctors to sign the form that says you're pregnant, and finally we'll pick up a blank permission form for Mevlut to sign. Okay?"

Mevlut and Rayiha's quarrel rumbled on, heated as ever, but now it wasn't over jealousy but the more delicate question of whether Rayiha should keep the baby. They couldn't bring it up at the shop, or when the girls were around, so their only chance was in the morning after the girls left for school. Their exchanges on this subject amounted not so much to discussions as a series of gestured misunderstandings: a long face, a scowl, a sniff of annoyance, a hateful glance, and a frown carried more weight than a sentence, so they each paid more attention to the other's face than to the other's words. Mevlut was very upset when he realized soon enough that in her growing restlessness and hostility, Rayiha was interpreting his indecision as a stalling tactic.

His indecision notwithstanding, he was thrilled at the prospect of a boy and had already started daydreaming about that possibility. He would call him Mevlidhan. He thought of how Babur had conquered India thanks to his three lionhearted boys and how Genghis Khan's four loyal sons had made him the world's most fearsome emperor. He kept telling Rayiha that his own father's failures on first arriving in Istanbul had all been for want of a son beside him, and how, by the time Mevlut had come from the village to help, it had been too late. But every time Rayiha heard the words "too late," all she could think of was the ten-week limit for having a legal abortion.

Those morning hours after the girls left for school, once the time of their joyous lovemaking, now were given over to endless bickering and recrimination. Only Rayiha's tears could make Mevlut feel bad enough to relent for a moment and comfort her, to tell her "Everything is going to be fine," at which point a confused Rayiha would say that perhaps it was indeed better for her to keep the baby, only to regret her words immediately.

Mevlut himself wondered—with increasing resentment—whether Rayiha's determination to end her pregnancy was her answer to (and punishment for) his poverty and all his life's failures. He almost felt that if he could only persuade her to keep the baby, it would show the world that they had everything they needed in life after all. It would even be clear that they were happier than Korkut and Vediha, who only had two children, and certainly poor Samiha and Ferhat, who had none at all. Happy people had lots of kids. Rich and unhappy people envied the poor for their children—just like these Europeans, who kept saying that Turkey should look into family planning.

One morning, Mevlut succumbed to Rayiha's insistence and her tears and went to the local councilman for the certificate proving they were married. The councilman, who was also a real-estate broker, wasn't in his office. Reluctant to return to Rayiha empty-handed, Mevlut wandered the streets of Tarlabaşı for a while: out of old habit from his days of unemployment, his eyes roamed around looking for a street vendor's cart that was for sale, an acquaintance who might be looking for someone to work in his shop, or some furniture he could buy on the cheap. Over the past ten years, Tarlabaşı had filled with empty street vendors' carts, some of which were left chained up on a corner even during the day. Mevlut thought of how, ever since he'd stopped selling boza at night, he had felt a tightness in his chest, and he'd lost some of the old urge to feel the chemistry of the streets on his skin.

He sat down for a cup of tea and talked about religion and the new mayor for a bit with the Kurdish scrap-metal dealer who'd married him and Rayiha in a religious ceremony thirteen years ago and had also given them all that guidance about sexual contact during Ramadan. There were even more bars with sidewalk tables out on the streets of Beyoğlu now. He asked the scrap-metal dealer about abortions. "It says in the Koran that it's a big sin," said the dealer, embarking on a detailed explanation, but Mevlut didn't take him too seriously. If it really was such a horrible sin, why would so many people be having abortions all the time?

But there was something else the dealer had spoken of that stayed with Mevlut: how the souls of babies taken from their mothers' wombs before birth climbed trees in heaven, hopping from branch to branch like orphaned birds, skipping restlessly like tiny white sparrows. He never mentioned this conversation to Rayiha, fearing she wouldn't believe that the councilman hadn't been in his office.

When he went back four days later, the councilman told him that his wife's identity card had expired and that if Rayiha expected to obtain any sort of service from the government (Mevlut hadn't specified what sort of service she was seeking), she would have to get a new identity card, just like everyone else. This kind of thing always scared Mevlut. His late father's biggest lesson had been to steer clear of government records and their keepers. Mevlut had never paid the state any taxes. In return, they had taken his white rice cart and destroyed it.

Having convinced herself that her husband would eventually sign the permission form she needed for an abortion, Rayiha felt bad about having abandoned him at the shop, and so at the beginning of April, she started returning to Brothers-in-Law. One afternoon there, she threw up and tried to hide it from Mevlut, without success. Mevlut cleaned up his wife's vomit before any customers could notice. In these final days of her life, Rayiha never came back there again.

It had been decided that in the afternoon, when they were done with school, Fatma and Fevziye would stop by Brothers-in-Law to wash glasses and help tidy up. Rayiha struggled to explain to them why she herself couldn't go to help their father. But the fewer the people who knew about the baby—her daughters included—the simpler it would be to get rid of it.

Mevlut directed his daughters like cooks and nurses supporting frontline troops. Fatma would come in one day, and Fevziye the next. Mevlut made them wash the glasses and clean up, but he was too protective a father to let them serve customers and take payment, or even talk to anyone at all. They could confide in him, and they would have their usual long conversations about what they did in school, impersonators and comedians they liked on TV, their favorite scenes in some movie, or the latest episode of a show.

Fatma was smart, quiet, and sensible. She knew how much food and clothes cost and what every shop sold; she was aware of what people came to Brothers-in-Law, what condition the street was in, the doorman who sold illicit things through the beggar on the corner, her mother alone at home, and even what lay ahead for her father's business. She was full of a protective love for him, which Mevlut could feel deeply. As he often proudly told Rayiha, if his store were ever a success one day (and if Fatma were a boy), Mevlut would comfortably leave it in her twelve-year-old hands.

At almost eleven years of age, Fevziye was still a child: she hated cleaning, wiping, drying, or any other task that required effort; she always found ways to cut corners if forced to perform the duties she so readily shirked. Mevlut often felt he should tell her off, but when he tried to be stern with her, he found it so hard to keep a straight face that he knew it would be no use. Mevlut loved talking to her about the customers who came in.

Some would barely take a sip of their boza before declaring with a few unpleasant remarks that they didn't like it and then demand a partial refund. Such a tiny incident might give Mevlut and Fevziye a subject of conversation for two or three days. They would listen closely to the conversation between the two men who were going to fix the bastard who'd sent them a bad check; the pair of friends who'd just placed a bet on some horse with the bookie down the street; or that group of three who'd just come into the shop to wait out the rain after coming out of the movies. Mevlut loved to pick up a customer's forgotten or discarded newspaper and have one of his clever girls, whichever happened to be there, read aloud to their father from a page chosen at random, as if he (like their illiterate grandfather Mustafa, whom they'd never met) couldn't have read it for himself, and he would smile with satisfaction as he listened and gazed out the window. Sometimes he would interrupt them—"See what I mean?"—drawing their attention to some little lesson about life, ethics, and responsibility, which the article illustrated.

Sometimes one of the girls would give her father an embarrassed account of whatever was troubling her at that particular moment (the geography teacher who had it in for her, or how she needed new shoes because the ones she had were coming apart, or how she didn't want to wear that old overcoat anymore because the other girls were making fun of it), and when Mevlut realized that there was nothing he could do to solve the problem, he would say, "Don't worry, this too shall pass," and conclude with the following aphorism: "As long as you keep your heart pure, you will always get what you want in the end." One night he overheard them laughing over his devotion to that particular gem, but he couldn't get angry at being the butt of their jokes, such was his pleasure at yet another demonstration of their cleverness and wit.

Every evening, Mevlut was willing to leave the shop unattended for a few minutes to take his daughter by the hand—whichever one had come to help him that day—and leap with her over the immense crowds and across İstiklal Avenue to the Tarlabaşı side, tell her, "Now go straight home, no dawdling," and watch as she disappeared from view, before he hurried back to Brothers-in-Law.

One evening it was Fatma he'd dropped off, and he returned to find Ferhat inside, smoking a cigarette. "The people who've been giving us this old Greek shop have joined our enemies," said Ferhat. "Property values and rents around here are going up, my dear Mevlut. You could sell anything you like here—socks, kebabs, underwear, apples—and still make ten times what we're making."

"We don't make anything anyway . . ."

"Exactly. I'm dropping the shop."

"What do you mean?"

"We have to close it."

"What if I were to stay?" Mevlut asked timidly.

"You'll get a visit from the gang who rents out all the Greek properties. They'll charge you whatever they feel like . . . And if you don't pay it, they'll make you regret it . . ."

"Why didn't they do that to you?"

"I took care of their electricity and kept all these old abandoned houses hooked to the grid so they'd be of some use. If you clear out right away, you won't lose all this stuff. Take it all out, sell it off, do whatever you want with it."

Mevlut closed up shop right away, bought a small bottle of *rakı* from the grocer's, and went home to have dinner with Rayiha and the girls. It had been years since the four of them had last sat at the dinner table together: he cracked jokes and laughed along with them as they watched TV, and then, with the air of someone with some excellent news, he announced that he would again be selling boza on the street at night; that, after careful consideration, he and Ferhat had decided to close the shop; and that he was drinking *rakı* now because he was taking a holiday for the evening. Had Rayiha not said, "God help us all," no one would have had the feeling of having heard some bad news. His wife's words irked Mevlut.

"Don't bring God into this while I'm having *rakı*. Everything will be fine."

The next day, Fatma and Fevziye helped him carry all the kitchen utensils back home from the shop. Mevlut was outraged when a junk dealer in Çukurcuma offered him a pittance for the desk, the table, and the chairs, so he looked up a carpenter he knew, but it turned out that whatever wood could be salvaged from the battered old furniture was worth even less than what the junk dealer had offered. He took the smaller of the two mirrors home. As for the heavy one with the silver frame that Ferhat had bought, he got Fatma and Fevziye each to take one end and carry it over to their aunt's house. He took the framed clipping from the *Righteous Path* and the picture of the graveyard with the tombstones, the cypress trees, and the radiant light, and hung them side by side on the wall behind their television. Looking at the picture of "The Other Realm" comforted Mevlut.

5

Mevlut Becomes a Parking Lot Guard

Guilt and Astonishment

After his failure at the Binbom Café, Mevlut knew he couldn't ask the Aktaş family to find him another job. Though angry with Ferhat, he would have been prepared to set hard feelings aside and let Ferhat ease his conscience by helping his friend—but Rayiha wouldn't hear of it: she blamed Ferhat for closing the shop and kept saying that he was a bad person.

In the evenings, Mevlut sold boza, and in the mornings he would canvass his acquaintances in the city, looking for something. When headwaiters and restaurant managers he'd known for years offered him positions as a line manager or cashier, he acted as if he would give their proposals due consideration, but in truth he was after a job that would let him work less and earn more (like Ferhat), leaving him enough time and energy to sell boza in the evening.

One day in mid-April he heard from Mohini, who had been trying to help his friend ever since the closing of Brothers-in-Law. Mohini told Mevlut that the Groom, their old middle-school classmate, would be expecting to see him at the Pangaltı offices of his advertising agency.

When Mevlut arrived, wearing his best suit, the Groom greeted him with a formal handshake, and the two old friends didn't even exchange a hug. Nevertheless, the Groom presented him to his pretty, smiling secretary (They must be lovers, thought Mevlut) as "a very worthy and special person, and exceptionally bright," and "a great friend." The secretary giggled at the idea of her wealthy bourgeois employer being friends of any kind with this man, who was evidently poor and wholly inept. So it was not altogether surprising when it was proposed that he run the tea stall under the stairs on the fourth floor; but Mevlut instinctively wanted to be nowhere near the Groom, let alone serve his besuited underlings tea all day, so he declined immediately. He quickly agreed, however, to the alternative assignment of looking after the company parking area in the back courtyard, which the Groom pointed out from the window.

You entered the courtyard parking area by way of the street that ran behind the building; Mevlut's job was to bar unauthorized vehicles and to guard the place against those gangs commonly referred to as the "parking mafia."

In the past fifteen years, these gangs of five or six friends hailing from the same village, a mix of mafia thugs and ordinary delinquents with connections in the police force, had spread all over the city like prickly burrs. Spotting some road, street corner, or empty lot, any place in the center of Istanbul where parking wasn't forbidden, they would stake a claim of ownership—with knives and guns if need be—demanding payment from anyone who wanted to park there and punishing those who balked by smashing their quarter lights, puncturing their tires, or taking a key to the paint of the new car they'd imported from Europe at great expense. During the six weeks Mevlut spent as a parking lot guard, he witnessed a huge number of arguments, swearing matches, and fistfights involving people who refused to pay up: some thought the fee was outrageously high; others said, "Who the hell are you, where did you come from, why should I pay you for the right to park in front of the house I've been living in for forty years?" Some looked for other excuses: "If I pay, will you give me a receipt?" By dint of levelheaded diplomacy and shrewd evasion, Mevlut was able to stay out of these disputes while enforcing from the very beginning a clear border between the advertising agency's space and the street where the gang ran its racket.

In spite of their violent inclinations, their brazen, menacing ways, and their well-publicized inclination to damage people's cars, Istanbul's legions of car-park gangs provided the city's heedless rich with an invaluable service. Whenever traffic was at a complete standstill, wherever it seemed impossible to find a spot, drivers could stop on a pavement or even in the middle of the road and entrust their car to these gangs' "valets," who would park and look after it as long as needed, cleaning the windows and even washing the whole car for an additional fee. When some of the younger, more audacious gang members slipped by Mevlut to park some car in the area he was supposed to guard, he would look away, as the Groom had made clear that he didn't want "any trouble." This made the job easier. Mevlut would stop street traffic with the assurance of a cop when the Groom or one of his employees arrived in the morning and again when they left in the evening; he would offer encouraging parking counsel—"Just a little to the left now" or "You've got loads of room"—hold the car door open for VIPs (with the Groom, this was always done in a spirit of camaraderie), and provide updates for those who asked him whether so-and-so had arrived or left already. The Groom's intercession had procured Mevlut a chair, which was placed where the pavement merged into the courtyard, a point some people called the courtyard gate, though there was no gate there at all. Mevlut would spend most of his time sitting on this wooden chair to watch the traffic on the backstreet, the two doormen who stood talking to each other from outside their respective buildings, the beggar who every now and then came off the main road where he paraded his mangled leg, the industrious apprentice to that grocer from Samsun, the ordinary passersby, the windows on the surrounding buildings, and the stray cats and dogs. He would also chat with the local parking gang's most junior member (whom colleagues sneeringly called "the valet").

The extraordinary thing about Kemal, the valet from Zonguldak, was that even though he wasn't particularly clever and talked too much, Mevlut found every single thing he said interesting. The key to his appeal was his free-flowing candor about the most intimate aspects of his everyday life—including his sexual proclivities, the eggs and sausages he'd had for dinner yesterday, the way his mother did the laundry or fought with his father back in the village, and how he'd felt watching a love scene on TV the night before. These personal anecdotes often came with a side helping of unsolicited opinions on politics, business, and local goings-on: half the men who worked in that advertising agency were faggots, and half the women were dykes; the whole of Pangaltı used to belong to the Armenians, and one day, they were going to use the Americans to demand it all back; the mayor of Istanbul was secretly a stockholder in the company that built those "caterpillar" buses they imported from Hungary.

Mevlut always sensed a hint of menace in the valet's bravado: that rich bastard who'd parked his Mercedes on *their* turf without even bothering to give the poor soul there to guard it some small change for his troubles, hadn't he considered that he might just come back to find his car gone, and no one doing anything about it? Or those cheapskates who refused to pay the parking fee (which was less than a pack of Marlboros anyway) and threatened to call the police on his gang—didn't they understand that half the fee went to the police anyway? The same know-it-all jerks ready to lay into a humble valet had no inkling that in the three hours since they'd dropped it off, their new BMW had had its battery, pricey gearbox, and air-conditioning system replaced with junk. And that was nothing: a gang from the Black Sea town of Ünye, working with a shady garage down in Dolapdere, had once managed in half a day to replace the entire engine on a 1995 Mercedes with one from some old wreck, doing such a flawless job that the returning owner left the valet an especially large tip for having cleaned the car for him. But there was nothing for Mevlut to worry about; the gang had no designs on any cars under his care. In turn, Mevlut always let young Kemal park a few cars in the company lot, provided there were spots to spare, though he did keep the Groom upstairs apprised of all these arrangements.

Sometimes, the courtyard, the parking lot, the pavements, and the empty street would be suffused with a vast stillness and silence (as far as such a thing was possible in Istanbul), and Mevlut would realize that apart from being close to Rayiha and his daughters, his favorite thing in the world was watching people go by on the street, inventing stories inspired by the things he saw (just as he did when he watched television), and then talking to someone about it all. The Groom didn't pay him much, but at least he was near where there was life and not stuck in an office, so he couldn't complain. He could even go home shortly after six, once the office was closed and all the cars were gone. Then at night, when the parking lot became the gang's turf until the next morning, Mevlut had time to go out and sell boza.

One month after starting at the parking lot, Mevlut was watching a door-to-door shoeshine polishing the shoes people were sending downstairs when he suddenly remembered that the ten first weeks of Rayiha's pregnancy, during which she had the right to have an abortion, had already passed. Mevlut believed wholeheartedly that their inability to come to a decision on this matter had as much to do with his wife's mixed feelings as with his own reluctance. Even in a government hospital, an abortion was always a dangerous thing. But a baby would bring joy to the house and strengthen the bonds of their family. Rayiha still hadn't told Fatma and Fevziye that she was pregnant. When she did, she would know she had done the right thing from the pleasure of seeing her grown-up daughters welcome the new baby so tenderly.

He got lost in contemplation of his wife waiting for him back home. Thinking of how fond he was of her, how much he loved her, he nearly cried. It was only two o'clock; the girls wouldn't be back from school yet. Mevlut felt as free as he used to feel in his high-school days; he asked young Kemal from Zonguldak to look after the lot, and he practically ran back home to Tarlabaşı. He longed to be at home alone with Rayiha as in those beautiful, blissful early years of their marriage, when they never used to argue. But there was also something weighing on his conscience, as if he'd forgotten something very important. Maybe that was why he was in such a hurry.

The moment he walked in, he knew that it was God who'd made him run back home in such haste. Rayiha had done something primitive, something from the village, to try to cause a miscarriage, but it had gone wrong, and now the blood loss and pain had left her barely conscious.

He pulled her up, lifted her into his arms, and rushed out with her to find a taxi. He knew with each step that he would remember every single one of these moments until the day he died. He prayed repeatedly for their happiness to remain intact, for her pain to go away. He caressed his wife's hair soaked with sweat; he gazed in terror at her face, which was white as a sheet. On the way to the emergency room five minutes away, he saw that she was wearing the same expression of guilt and astonishment that she'd worn the night they'd run away together.

By the time they went through the hospital door, Rayiha had bled to death. She was thirty years old.

6

After Rayiha

People Can't Get Cross with You If You're Crying

Abdurrahman Efendi. We have a telephone in our village guesthouse now. "Quick, your daughter's on the line from Istanbul!" they said. I made it just in time: it was Vediha, who said that my darling Rayiha had ended up in the hospital after a miscarriage. I had two drinks on an empty stomach just before boarding the bus in Beyşehir, and that's when I knew in my heart that we were cursed, that I might drown in despair, for this was how my orphaned girls had lost their mother. Crying is some relief, at least.

Vediha. I know now that my darling angel Rayiha, may she rest in peace, gave me and Mevlut each a lie. She told me that he didn't want her to keep the baby, which wasn't true. She told Mevlut that the baby was a girl, which she couldn't have known for sure. But our grief is so great that I don't think anyone has the strength to talk about these things right now.

Süleyman. I was worried that Mevlut would think I wasn't upset enough. But in fact as soon as I saw him looking so lost and desolate, I started crying. When I did, Mevlut started crying, too, and so did my mother. Eventually I felt as if I was crying not because Rayiha had died but because everyone else was crying. When we were little, whenever he caught anyone crying, Korkut would tell him to "stop sniveling like a girl," but of course this time he had to keep quiet. He found me watching TV in the guest room on my own. "Cry all you want," he said, "but someday Mevlut will find a way to be happy again, you'll see."

Korkut. I went to the hospital with Süleyman to pick up Rayiha's body. They told us, "The best place to have her washed is at the bathhouse of the Barbaros Mosque in Beşiktaş, they have people there who specialize in handling female corpses, they'll do it with proper sponges and soap, they'll use the best shrouds and towels, and rosewater, too. You'd better tip them upfront, though." So that's where we went, smoking cigarettes in the courtyard of the mosque while we waited for Rayiha to be washed. Mevlut came with us when we went to the offices of the Cemetery of the Industrial Quarter. But he'd forgotten his identity card, so we had to go back to Tarlabaşı. At home, he couldn't find his card, and he collapsed on the bed in a crying heap, but then he got up to look for it again and finally he found it. We went back to the cemetery. You wouldn't believe the traffic.

Aunt Safiye. I was cooking halva, the special kind that's made of flour and butter after someone dies. My tears were falling into the pot, disappearing among the little clumps of flour and sugar, and with each tear that vanished, I felt like another memory was gone. Would we run out of butane gas? Should I have put a bit more meat in the vegetable stew? Whenever people got tired of crying, they came into the kitchen and lifted the lid off a pot to stare quietly at its contents. As if crying for a long time meant you could come over and see what was cooking.

Samiha. Poor Fatma and Fevziye spent the night at my place. Vediha, who was also there, said "Bring them over to ours." That's how I went back to the Aktaş family home in Duttepe for the first time since running away eleven years ago to avoid marrying Süleyman. "Watch out for Süleyman!" said Ferhat, but Süleyman wasn't even around. To think that eleven years ago, everyone—myself included—had thought I was going to marry him! I was curious to see the room where we used to stay with my father: it looked smaller now, but it still smelled of beeswax. They had added two floors to the house. This whole situation makes me really uncomfortable, but right now we're all thinking of Rayiha. I started crying again. People can't get cross with you if you're crying, or ask you any questions either.

Aunt Safiye. Mevlut's girls Fatma and Fevziye, and later Vediha, too, would come into the kitchen whenever they got tired of crying and stare into the pots and the fridge as they would at the TV. Later, Samiha arrived, too. I've always had a soft spot for that girl. I have nothing against her, even though she led Süleyman on and charmed him with her beauty only to ditch him in the end.

Vediha. Thank God women aren't allowed to attend funerals. I don't think I could take it. After the men went off to the mosque, all the women in the house, Mevlut's daughters included, started crying. The sobs would begin on one side of the room, and when they stopped, the other side would pick up. I didn't wait for the men to come back from the funeral—I didn't even wait until evening, in fact—I just went straight into the kitchen and brought out the pudding. The crying stopped for that. Fatma and Fevziye looked out the window as they ate, and we saw Turan and Bozkurt's black-and-white football in the back garden. As soon as we were done with dessert, the tears started flowing again, but there's only so much crying you can do before you're too exhausted to go on.

Hadji Hamit Vural. The young wife of Aktaş's nephew has already left this world and gone to meet her maker. The mosque courtyard was thronging with elderly yogurt sellers from Konya. Most of these people have sold me the empty land they grabbed in the 1960s and 1970s. Now they're all wishing they'd waited a little longer and made more money on it. They're complaining that Hadji Hamit took their land for next to nothing. There isn't a single one among them saying, I'm grateful to Hadji Hamit, we fenced off some public land on this godforsaken mountain one day, and even though we had no legal right to it, he still bought it off us with truckloads of money. If they'd donated even a tiny fraction of that cash to the mosque's maintenance fund, I wouldn't have to draw from my own pockets today to repair the leaking gutters, replace the lead sheets on the dome, and set up a proper classroom for Koran lessons. But never mind, I'm used to these people by now; I still smile at them with affection, and I'm happy to offer my hand to anyone who wants to kiss it with respect. The husband of the deceased was in a terrible state. I asked what this Mevlut had done after his time as a yogurt seller; what I heard saddened me. Men are as different as the fingers of a hand. Some become rich; some become wise; some go to hell; some go to heaven. Someone reminded me that I'd been to his wedding years ago and even given the groom a watch. I saw that someone had dumped empty boxes next to the steps leading up to the mosque courtyard; I said, "Is the mosque your private storeroom now?" Really, they've got to take care of that. The crowd began to gather together as the imam arrived. Our Holy Prophet Muhammad, peace be upon him, once proclaimed that "it is best to stand in the back row during a funeral prayer." I do love to watch the members of the congregation turn their faces to the right, and then again to the left, and that is why I try never to miss a funeral prayer. O Lord, I prayed, please send this woman to heaven if she was a good person, and please forgive her if she was a sinner—what was her name again? The imam said it just a moment ago. What a slight little thing this Rayiha must have been when she lived; her coffin rested on my shoulder for a moment, and it felt as light as a feather.

Süleyman. Korkut told me to keep an eye on poor Mevlut, so I never left his side. He would have almost fallen in again while shoveling earth into the grave if I hadn't grabbed him from behind. At one point he ran out of strength and he couldn't stand anymore. I helped him to another gravestone. He didn't move until Rayiha's coffin was buried and everyone had left.

If it had been up to him, Mevlut would never have left the spot where Süleyman had found him in the cemetery. He sensed that Rayiha needed his help. There had been too many people, and he'd forgotten some of the prayers he was meant to say, but he was sure that as soon as everyone was gone, the words would come rolling off his tongue, and he'd be able to give Rayiha what she needed. Mevlut knew that reciting prayers during the burial of the deceased and their soul's ascent from the graveyard was meant to comfort them. The sight of all those different gravestones, the cypresses in the background, all the other trees and weeds, and the way the light shone down from the sky reminded Mevlut of the picture he'd found in the *Righteous Path* and cut out and framed with Rayiha for the wall of Brothers-in-Law. The similarity made him feel as if he'd already lived through this moment. He'd experienced this illusion before when out selling boza at night, and he'd always welcomed it as a pleasant trick his mind played on him.

Mevlut's mind responded to Rayiha's death in three distinct ways, all of which could feel like delusions in one moment, and reality the next:

The most persistent response was to refuse to believe that Rayiha had passed away. Even though his wife had died in his arms, Mevlut's mind would often indulge in fantasies wherein no such thing had ever happened: Rayiha was in the other room, she'd just said something, in fact, though Mevlut hadn't heard; she was going to walk in now; life would go on as usual.

The second response was anger at everyone and everything. He was angry at the taxi driver who'd been too slow getting Rayiha to hospital and the government clerks who had taken such a long time to issue her a new identity card, he was angry at the neighborhood councilman, the doctors, those who had abandoned him, the people who made everything so expensive, the terrorists, and the politicians. Most of all, he was angry at Rayiha: for leaving him all alone; for not giving birth to Mevlidhan; for refusing to be a mother.

His mind's third response was to help Rayiha on her journey to the hereafter. He wanted to be of some use to her in the afterlife at least. Rayiha was so lonely now, down in that tomb. Her torment would be eased if Mevlut brought the girls to the cemetery to say a few prayers. Mevlut would start praying by Rayiha's grave, and he would get all the words mixed up (he didn't know what most of them meant anyway) or skip some altogether, but he would console himself with the thought that what really mattered was the intention behind the prayer.

In the first few months, Mevlut and his two daughters would follow their visits to Rayiha's grave with a trip to Duttepe to see the Aktaş family. Aunt Safiye and Vediha would bring out food for the orphaned girls and give them some of the chocolates and cookies that they always made sure to have on hand on those days, and all four of them would sit and watch movies on TV.

On two of these visits to Duttepe, they saw Samiha there, too. Now that she was no longer scared of Süleyman, Mevlut understood why she would come back to the house she'd escaped all those years ago to be with Ferhat: Samiha endured the strain for the sake of seeing her nieces, so that she could console them and find her own consolation in their presence.

They were in Duttepe again one day when Vediha told Mevlut that if he was planning to take the girls to the village in Beyşehir that summer, she might come along, too. The old school in Cennetpınar, she explained, had been converted into a guesthouse, and Korkut regularly sent donations to the village development association. It was the first Mevlut had ever heard of this organization, though it was to grow increasingly influential as time went by. He thought that at least if he went to the village he wouldn't spend too much money.

On the bus to Beyşehir with Fatma and Fevziye, Mevlut considered the possibility that he might never come back to Istanbul. But within three days he'd understood that the thought of staying in the village forever had been a meaningless fantasy stemming from his pain over losing Rayiha. The village was a dead end, and they could no longer be anything more than guests there. He did want to go back to the city. His life, his fury, his happiness, Rayiha—everything revolved around Istanbul.

Their grandmother and their aunts' affection distracted his girls from their grief for a while, but they quickly exhausted any amusements country life had to offer. The village was still very poor. Any boys their age soon made Fatma and Fevziye uncomfortable with their attentions and their pranks. At night, the girls would sleep in the same room as their grandmother; they would talk to her and listen to her stories about village legends, historic disagreements, and ongoing feuds and rivalries between this person and that; it was fun, but sometimes it would scare them, too, and then they would remember that they had lost their mother. During that visit to the village, Mevlut realized that deep down he had always resented his mother for not having come to Istanbul and having left him and his father alone in the city. Had his mother and his sisters joined them there, perhaps Rayiha would have never come to the point where she saw no other option but to try to get rid of the baby by herself.

But it was soothing to hear his mother say "My poor Mevlut" and to be kissed and cuddled as if he were still a child. These tender moments would always make him feel like going to hide in a corner somewhere, but then he would find one last excuse to go back to his mother. His mother's affection seemed to be laced with an anguish over not only Rayiha's death but also Mevlut's difficulties in Istanbul and his continuing dependence on his cousins for support. Unlike his father, Mevlut had never in twenty-five years been able to send any money back to his mother; that made him feel ashamed.

Throughout that summer, Mevlut found more pleasure in the companionship of his crooked-necked father-in-law—whom he went to see three times a week, walking over to Gümüşdere village with his daughters—than he did in spending time with his mother and sisters. Whenever they visited at lunchtime, Abdurrahman Efendi would slip Mevlut some *rakı* in one of those shatterproof glasses, making sure Fatma and Fevziye didn't notice, and when his granddaughters were out dawdling in one of the many gardens nearby, he would tell his son-in-law allusive, allegorical tales. They had both seen their wives die young before they could give birth to a new child (a boy). They were both going to devote the rest of their lives to their daughters. They both knew that for each of them looking at any one of his daughters was always going to be a painful reminder of her mother.

During their last days in the countryside, Mevlut took his daughters to their mother's village more frequently. When they walked along the tree-lined road over the barren hills, all three of them liked to stop every now and then to take in the view below, the outlines of little towns in the distance and the mosques with their slender minarets. They would look for long, silent minutes at smudges of green in the rocky soil, bright yellow fields lit up by the sun piercing through the clouds, the narrow line of the lake in the distance, and graveyards planted with cypress trees. Somewhere far away, there would be dogs barking. On the bus back to Istanbul, Mevlut realized that the landscapes of the village would always remind him of Rayiha.

7

A History of Electric Consumption

Süleyman Gets into a Tight Spot

Ferhat. I spent the summer of 1995 out on the streets and in the records office of Seven Hills Electric looking for traces of Selvihan, my electric lover. I've lost count of how many cigarettes and cups of tea I had sitting with those two dogged bookkeepers in that room with endless shelves of cardboard binders bound with metal rings and secured with padlocks, and all those faded envelopes and folders heaving with eighty-year-old bundles of grimy paper. Seven Hills Electric may have changed names a few times, but its dusty archives provided a full history of the production and distribution of electric power in Istanbul, starting in 1914 with the Silahtar power station. Those two elderly clerks believed that only by studying this history and learning all of the tricks people had come up with over the years to cheat the government, and only by truly understanding the ins and outs of how they used and paid for their electricity, could an inspector ever hope to get them to pay their bills.

Halfway through the summer, we realized that Seven Hills Electric's new owners, who hailed from the Anatolian heartland, might not agree. They were trying to sell the archives for scrap to dealers who bought paper by the kilo—or, failing that, to have the whole lot incinerated. "They'll have to burn us with it!" said the older of the two clerks in response to these rumors, while the other railed that if there was anything worse than capitalism, it was these new-money hicks from Anatolia. They soon resolved that they might do better getting me to appeal to our new owners from Kayseri and make them understand that the archives were a crucial and irreplaceable tool for the collection of bills; maybe that would save this vast treasure trove of human ingenuity from destruction.

We started from the oldest records, whole folders of thick, fragrant white paper predating the foundation of the Republic and the abandonment of Arabic script for the Latin alphabet in 1928, and bearing handwritten notes in Ottoman Turkish and French. We moved on to the records for the 1930s, showing which new neighborhoods had been connected to the grid and where consumption was highest, and here my pair of historians informed me that in those days Istanbul still had a very large non-Muslim population. They leafed through the yellowing sheets of one-hundred-, five-hundred-, and nine-hundred-page logbooks in which previous clerks had taken detailed notes on the far-flung households they had visited and the ingenious stratagems for thievery they had discovered, this by way of explaining to me how a new system introduced in the 1950s had given each inspector a specific set of neighborhoods to oversee, just as local Ottoman governors used to do, and how this had allowed them to maintain a surveillance of people's lives, like policemen.

These frayed and torn logs followed a color code: white for households, purple for shops, and red for factories. Purple and red were usually the worst offenders, but if "the young inspector Mr. Ferhat" took a closer look at the "elucidations" sections on each sheet and kept up with those old government inspectors' heroic efforts to record what they saw, he would notice that, after the 1970s, the city's poorer neighborhoods—Zeytinburnu, Taşlıtarla, and Duttepe and its environs—had all become fertile breeding grounds for electricity theft. The electricity board's employees had filled these "elucidation" boxes—which became the "comments" section in later versions of the logbooks—with their insights on their customers, the meters they inspected, and the various schemes of power theft they discovered, all spelled out in a variety of now-indecipherable hands, using purple pens and ballpoints that only worked if you wet the tip with your tongue. My intuition told me that all of this knowledge was bringing me closer to Selvihan.

Notes like "New fridge" or "Noted second electric stove" helped meter inspectors to estimate how many kilowatt-hours a household should have consumed in a particular period. The two clerks believed that based on these records, you could clearly deduce the date on which any given home acquired a fridge, an iron, a washing machine, an electric stove, or any other household appliance. Other remarks—"Gone back to the village," "Away at a wedding for two months," "Gone to their summerhouse," "Two people staying over from their hometown"—offered an account of movements to and from the city as they might affect energy consumption. But whenever I found any meter readings for a nightclub, a kebab restaurant, or Turkish classical-music bar owned by Sami from Sürmene, I would focus on those and ignore all the other elucidations. So the two elderly clerks would call my attention to even-more-intriguing notes: "Fix bill to nail over doorknob." "Follow wall next to neighborhood water fountain—meter behind fig tree." "Tall bespectacled man is mad. Avoid." "Beware of dog in garden. His name is Count. Will not attack if called by name." "Lights on top floor of nightclub have second set of wires running from outside the building."

Whoever had written that last comment was, in my guides' opinion, a hero, a brave soul truly dedicated to his job. If they discovered a nightclub or a secret gambling den (I'd heard that Sami from Sürmene was involved in that racket, too) artfully stealing power, most inspectors would avoid taking official note of it; that way, when they were offered money to look the other way, they wouldn't have to kick back to their superiors. Whenever I came across this kind of tip-off, I would head out for a surprise inspection of the café, restaurant, or nightclub that corresponded to that particular meter, fantasizing all the while of how close I was to taking down Sami from Sürmene and rescuing my beloved Selvihan from his clutches.

Mahinur Meryem. I was almost forty years old when I became pregnant with Süleyman's child. At that age, a woman on her own has to think about her future and how she will live for the rest of her life. We'd been together for ten years. I may have been naïve enough to believe all Süleyman's lies and excuses, but I guess my body knew what was necessary better than I did.

As I expected, Süleyman didn't take the news well. At first he accused me of making it up to force him to marry me. But as we got drunk and screamed at each other in that apartment in Cihangir, he began to realize that I really was carrying his baby, and he got scared. He got very drunk and wrecked the place, which was very upsetting, but I could also see that he was pleased. After that, we argued every time he visited, though I kept trying to appease him. His threats and his drinking only got worse, though. He even threatened to stop supporting my singing career.

"Forget the music, Süleyman, I would die for this baby," I would tell him sometimes.

Those words would soften him, and he would become gentle again. But even when he didn't, we would still have violent sex after every fight.

"How can you make love to a woman that way and then just leave?" I would say.

Süleyman would look down in embarrassment. But sometimes, on his way out, he would say that if I kept hectoring him, I would never see him again.

"Then this is our farewell, Süleyman," I would say, closing the door with tears in my eyes. He started coming by every day of the week after that, and meanwhile the baby kept growing in my womb. That didn't stop him from trying to slap me a couple of times.

"Go on, Süleyman, hit me," I said. "Maybe you'll be able to get rid of me the way you people got rid of Rayiha."

Sometimes he looked so helpless that I would feel sorry for him. He would sit there—QUIETLY and POLITELY—agonizing about his life like a merchant whose fleet has just sunk to the bottom of the Black Sea and knocking back *rakı* like it was water, and I would tell him how happy we were going to be, how looking into his soul I saw a diamond in the rough, and how rare it was to find the kind of closeness and understanding we shared.

"You've been bullied by your brother long enough, but if you could get away from him, Süleyman, you'd be a new man. We have nothing to fear from anyone."

This whole thing would get us talking about whether I would ever start wearing a headscarf. "I'll think about it," I'd say. "But there are some things I can do, and some things I just can't."

"Me too," Süleyman would say dejectedly. "So you tell me what you feel you can do."

"Sometimes women agree to have a religious wedding on top of the civil ceremony, just to spare their well-meaning husbands any headaches . . . I can do that. But first your family has to come to the house in Üsküdar and formally ask my parents for my hand."

In the autumn of 1995, Mevlut returned to Istanbul and his job at the advertising agency parking lot. The Groom—who understood entirely that Mevlut had to return to his village after the death of his wife—gave him back all his duties, which had been assigned to the doorman in his absence. Mevlut saw that in the three months he'd been away, Kemal from Zonguldak's gang had expanded its territory, shifting its borders with the help of two flowerpots and a few loose curbstones. More worrying, they had adopted an aggressive new tone toward Mevlut. But he didn't mind. After Rayiha's death, he was constantly angry at everyone and everything, but for some reason, he couldn't bring himself to feel that way about this young man from Zonguldak with his new navy blazer.

At night, he still went out to sell boza, and he devoted the rest of his energy to his daughters. But his attentions never got beyond a few very basic questions: "Have you done your homework?" "Are you hungry?" "Are you okay?" He was aware that they spent even more time at their aunt Samiha's now and that they didn't really want to talk to him about their visits. So when the doorbell rang one morning after Fatma and Fevziye had left for school, and he opened the door to find Ferhat behind it, he thought for a moment that his friend must want to talk about his girls.

"You can't live in this neighborhood anymore unless you've got a gun," said Ferhat. "Drugs, prostitutes, transvestites, all kinds of gangs . . . We've got to find you and the girls a new place somewhere . . ."

"We're happy here; this is Rayiha's home."

Ferhat said there was something very important he wanted to talk about and took Mevlut to one of the new cafés on Taksim Square. They watched the crowds pouring into Beyoğlu and talked for a long time. Eventually, Mevlut understood that his friend was offering him a job as a sort of electricity inspector's apprentice.

"But do you have any private doubts about this?"

"In this case, what I'm saying and what I feel privately are identical," said Ferhat. "This job will make you happy, it'll make the girls happy, and it'll even make Rayiha happy, worried as she must be about you all, up there in heaven. You're going to be making good money."

In fact, the salary Mevlut would draw from Seven Hills Electric wasn't very high, but working as Ferhat's so-called assistant, chasing after past-due bills, would still pay more than looking after the Groom's parking lot. But he sensed that to arrive at this "good money" would involve taking a cut from what he was able to collect from customers.

"These new owners from Kayseri know full well that their employees will take advantage where they can," said Ferhat. "Just bring your middle-school diploma, proof of address, your identity card, and six passport photos, and we can get you started within three days. We'll do a few rounds together to start, and I'll teach you everything you need to know. You're an honest, fair-minded man, Mevlut, and that's why we really want you to join us."

"May God acknowledge your good deeds," said Mevlut, and as he paced around the parking lot later, he thought of how Ferhat hadn't even noticed the sarcasm in those words. Three days later, he phoned the number Ferhat had given him.

"For the first time in your life, you've made the right decision," said Ferhat.

In two days, they met at the bus stop in Kurtuluş. Mevlut had worn his best blazer and a pair of unstained trousers. Ferhat had brought a bag that had once belonged to one of the two elderly bookkeepers. "You'll need one of these inspector's bags," he said. "They scare people."

They went into a street on the outer edges of Kurtuluş. Mevlut still came to this neighborhood to sell boza sometimes. At night, neon lamps and the light from TV sets gave this street a more modern air, but in its unassuming daytime guise, it looked just as it had twenty-five years ago when he was in middle school. They spent the whole morning in that neighborhood, inspecting almost two hundred fifty electric meters from the same logbook.

The first thing they would do upon entering a building was check the meters downstairs near the doorman's quarters. "Number seven's got a load of unpaid bills; they've had two warnings in the past five months and still haven't paid, but look: their meter is spinning away," Ferhat would say, in the tone of one trying to instill learning. He'd take the logbook from his bag, squinting every now and then as he leafed through it. "Number six filed a complaint about two supposed overcharges from around this time last year. Looks like we never cut their power off. And yet their meter's completely still. Huh. Let's have a look."

They'd climb up to the third floor, through the smell of mold, onions, and frying oil, and ring the doorbell of number 7. Before anyone could answer, Ferhat would call out "Electric company!" like an unforgiving inquisitor. An electricity inspector at the door would throw the household into a panic, and there was something about Ferhat's manner that could break into a family's private world even as he silently rebuked them for it. Mevlut had learned these nuances in his own way, during all the years he'd spent delivering yogurt door to door. Perhaps, then, it wasn't just his honesty that had led Ferhat to seek his help but also his experience navigating the intimate world of private households—in particular, his ability to talk to women without making them feel harassed.

The door to a home with an unpaid bill might open, but it could also stay shut. In that case, Mevlut would do as Ferhat showed him, checking to see whether he could hear any sounds coming from inside. If the approaching footsteps they'd heard just after they rang the bell suddenly stopped after they called out "Electric company!" it meant, of course, that there was someone inside unwilling to settle their debt. Usually, though, the door would open, and they would be faced with a housewife, a mother, a middle-aged auntie trying to tie up her head-scarf, a woman with a child in her arms, a ghostly old grandpa, an angry idler, a woman in pink dishwashing gloves, or a very old lady who could barely see.

"Electric company!" Ferhat would again say officiously through the open door. "You have unpaid bills!"

Some would reply immediately: "Come back tomorrow, inspector, I don't have any change" or "We don't have any money today!" Others would say, "What do you mean, son, we pay our bills at the bank every month." Others still would insist, "We paid it only yesterday" or "We send our doorman to the bank with the money every month."

"I don't know about that, but it says on here that you have overdue charges," Ferhat would say. "It's all automated now; the computer does everything. We're required to cut your power off if you refuse to pay."

Ferhat would glance at Mevlut, as proud to show off his authority as he was pleased to be showing Mevlut the ropes of the job and a glimpse of its vast opportunities. Sometimes he would walk away mysteriously saying nothing at all, leaving the residents to appeal to Mevlut. A few hours on the job, and he'd already learned to recognize those worried looks that said, Now what? Is he really going to cut us off?

If he decided to be lenient, Ferhat would usually deliver the news himself to the anxious customer at the door. "I'll let you off this time, but remember, it's all been privatized now, you won't get away with it again!" he'd say. Or "When I cut it off, you're going to have to pay an extra fee to have it reconnected again, so you'd best think about that, too." Sometimes his verdict would be "I won't cut you off today, seeing as there's a pregnant woman in the house, but it's the last time!" "If you're not going to pay for your electricity, you might at least try not to use so much!" he might say, to which the relieved person at the door would respond, "God bless you!" Sometimes Ferhat would point to the runny-nosed little kid in the doorway, saying, "I'll leave your lights on this time, for this one's sake. But child or no child, I won't be so generous next time."

Occasionally, a little boy would open the door and say there was no one home. Some children became extremely nervous when they were put up to this, while others were as brash as adults, having already absorbed the notion that to lie well was a form of cleverness. Having listened for sounds inside the house before ringing the doorbell, Ferhat always knew when a child was lying, but often he would play along to spare the boy's feelings.

"All right, kid," he'd say like a kindly uncle. "Tell your folks when they're back tonight that you've got electric bills to pay, all right? Now tell me, what's your name?"

"Talat!"

"Good boy, Talat! Now close the door so the devil doesn't get you."

But all this was an act Ferhat put on for Mevlut's first day, to make the job seem easier and more pleasant than it really was. They would have drunks telling them, "Our only debt is to God, inspector"; people screaming, "The government's turned to usury now, you're fleecing us, you bastards"; octogenarians in dentures saying, "Those bribes you take will land you in the pits of hell" before slamming the door in their faces; and smart-aleck layabouts asking, "How do I know you're really from the electric company?" but Ferhat never took the bait, not even batting an eyelid in that torrent of lies—"My mother's on her deathbed," "Our father's gone to do his military service!," "We've just moved in, those bills must be the previous tenants'." As they walked out of a building, he would carefully explain to Mevlut the truth behind each of the excuses they'd just heard: the man who complained "You're fleecing us!" always claimed he'd been forced to bribe a different team of inspectors every week. The old man with the dentures wasn't even religious; Ferhat had seen him plenty of times in the bar on Kurtuluş Square . . .

"We're not here to torment these people, only to make them pay for what they've used," said Ferhat in a coffeehouse later on. "There's nothing to be gained by leaving a bunch of poor men, women, and children without power if they just don't have the money. Your job is to figure out who really can't afford it, who could pay some of their bill, who could easily pay the whole thing but is just making excuses, who's a crook, and who's being sincere. The bosses have given me the power to rule on these cases like a judge; it's my job to make the necessary evaluations. Your job, too, obviously . . . Do you understand?"

"I understand," said Mevlut.

"Now, my dear Mevlut, there are two things that are strictly forbidden: If you haven't gone and checked a meter yourself, you never make up a number to write down and pretend you have. If they catch you, you're finished. The other thing—though I'm sure I don't need to tell you of all people—is that we can't even have a hint of harassing or ogling the women or anything like that. The company's got its reputation to protect; they wouldn't think twice about what to do . . . Now, how about I take you to the Springtime Club to celebrate the new job?"

"I'm going out to sell boza tonight."

"Even tonight? You're going to make loads of money now."

"I'm going to sell boza every night," said Mevlut.

Ferhat leaned forward and smiled, as if to say he understood.

8

Mevlut in the Farthest Neighborhoods

Dogs Will Bark at Anyone Who Doesn't Belong Among Us

Uncle Hasan. When I found out that Süleyman got an older woman—a singer, no less—pregnant, and now he was going to marry her, I said nothing. We were already very sad for Mevlut. When I see the calamities suffered by those around me, I tell Safiye how glad I am to have never wanted anything more than my little grocery store. Just to sit in my shop folding newspapers into pint baskets every day, that's enough to make me happy.

Vediha. Maybe this was for the best, I thought. Otherwise who knows if Süleyman would have ever managed to get married. It was just me and Korkut who went to the house in Üsküdar with him to ask Miss Melahat's father for her hand. Süleyman wore his finest. It struck me that he'd never made such an effort for any of the girls we'd gone to see together. He kissed the hand of his future father-in-law—a retired government clerk—with real deference. Süleyman must really love this Melahat. I can't say I understand why, though, and I would love to know. When she finally made her appearance, she looked dignified and stylish enough, a forty-year-old woman serving us coffee like a teenage girl meeting her suitor. I liked that she didn't treat the whole thing as a joke and that she was courteous and respectful. She got herself a cup of coffee, too. Then she passed around a pack of Samsuns. She handed one to her father—she had only just made her peace with him, Süleyman had said—and then she lit one up herself and blew smoke right out into the middle of the little room. We all went quiet. In that moment, I saw that far from feeling embarrassed to be forced into marrying this woman he'd gotten pregnant, Süleyman was proud of her. As the smoke from Miss Melahat's cigarette swirled about the room like a blue mist, Süleyman could not have looked more smug if he'd blown that smoke in Korkut's face himself, and I was confused.

Korkut. Of course they were in no position to impose any conditions. These were humble, well-intentioned people of modest means. Unfortunately, however, they were not well versed in matters of religion. The people of Duttepe love to gossip. We thought it would be best to avoid Mecidiyeköy and have the wedding somewhere farther away, so we arranged with Süleyman a small but perfectly presentable wedding hall in Aksaray. Once that was done, I said, "Let's go have an afternoon drink, just me and you, brother to brother, man to man," and we went to a restaurant in Kumkapı. "Süleyman," I said after the second round, "as your brother, I am now going to ask you a very important question. We like this lady. But a man's honor counts more than anything else. Are you absolutely certain that Miss Melahat will fit in with our way of life?"

"Don't worry," he said at first, but then he asked, "What exactly do you mean about honor?"

Ferhat. While they were busy getting Süleyman married off, I went on a reconnaissance mission to the Sunshine Club, pretending to be an ordinary customer. That's another perk of the job: you get to have a couple of drinks while you look around for evidence they might be stealing electricity, what tricks they might be using, and see the faces of those conceited club owners totally unaware they're about to get their comeuppance. All the ladies were taking up their positions in various corners of the room, and we settled down for a long night. At the table, we had Demir from Dersim, two contractors, one former left-wing militant, and another hardworking young inspector like me.

Nightclubs like these each have their own peculiar scent, a mixture of panfried meat, *rakı,* mildew, perfume, and stale breath, and over many years without a single window even cracked open, these elements ferment like wine and seep right into the carpets and the curtains. You get used to this smell eventually, until you miss it when it's not there, and if you catch a whiff of it again one night after a long time absent, your heart speeds up and it's like you've fallen in love. That night we listened dutifully to Lady Blue, the velvety voice of Turkish classical music. We watched the comedy duo Ali and Veli do impressions of the latest TV commercials and various politicians, and the belly dancer Mesrure, who is "famous in Europe, too." There were many old songs that night, a melancholy atmosphere at the Sunshine Club, and behind every lyric and every note, there was Selvihan.

I met Mevlut again somewhere in Beşiktaş two days later to continue his training. "Our first lesson today is highly theoretical," I said. "See that restaurant over there? I've been there before; let's go and have a look. Don't worry, no *rakı,* we're working after all. Nothing to upset your friends at the *Righteous Path.*"

"I don't read the *Righteous Path,*" said Mevlut once we'd sat down in the half-empty restaurant. "I just cut out that piece on Brothers-in-Law and that one picture."

"Now listen to me, Mevlut," I said, getting annoyed at his innocence. "The key to this job is reading people . . . You've always got to be alert, so no one can pull the wool over your eyes. These people who start whimpering as soon as they see me, 'Oh, it's the inspector!' It's all an act, they're testing me . . . You need to be able to spot that. You also need to know how to hold back and play the nice guy if that's what's called for. In other cases, if necessary, you need to get angry and be able cut some poor widow's wires . . . You may have to behave *as if* you were one of the Turkish government's proud civil servants, impossible to bribe. Though, of course, I'm not a civil servant, and you won't be either. The money you collect isn't a bribe, just what you and Seven Hills Electric have coming to you. I'm going to show you all the ins and outs. There are guys with millions in the bank earning interest and bundles of dollars under their mattresses, but the minute they see some poor inspector at the door, they don't know where their next meal is coming from. Eventually, they start believing their own sob stories, and, believe me, they cry harder than you ever cried even for your wife. They end up convincing you, too; they wear you down. While you're trying to read what's in their eyes and searching for the truth on their children's faces, they're watching the way you walk and talk and looking into your soul trying to figure out whether to pay up and, if so, how much and, if not, what excuse will get rid of you. These two- and three-story buildings in the backstreets are now mostly occupied by petty clerks, street vendors, waiters, cashiers, and university students, and unlike the bigger buildings, they don't have full-time doormen anymore. Usually, the owners and tenants of these places will have had serious disagreements about how to split the costs of diesel or coal and how high to turn the boiler, and because of that, their central heating tends to be turned off altogether. So they're all trying to keep warm as best they can, and most of them will try to get an illegal connection to the grid so they can run an electric heater for free. You've got to size them up and not give anything away. If they see that boyish face and realize that you're too compassionate to cut them off, they won't give up a cent. Maybe they think with inflation so high, they're better off holding out and keeping that money earning interest for a little longer. Be sure you don't let them think you're too proud to take a bit of change some old lady might offer you. On the other hand, you don't want them thinking you're so greedy you'll swoop down on any pathetic sum they propose. You follow me? Now tell me, how does the heating work here in this restaurant?"

"It works fine," said Mevlut.

"That's not what I'm asking. How is the heating being provided? Is the restaurant using stoves or radiators?"

"Radiators!"

"Let's check and see, shall we?" I said.

Mevlut touched the radiator grille right next to him and realized that it wasn't very warm. "So that means there must be a stove somewhere," he said.

"Good. Now, where's the stove? Can you see it anywhere? You can't.

That's because they've got electric stoves going. They keep them hidden because they've got them hooked up to the mains directly, bypassing the meter. They turn the radiator on a little, too, but only so no one will notice what's going on. I had a look on the way in and saw that their meters are ticking very slowly. That means there must be other rooms, ovens, and fridges in this building, all using stolen electricity."

"What are we going to do?" asked Mevlut like a wide-eyed child.

I found the restaurant's meter number in the purple logbook and showed it to Mevlut. "Read what it says in the comments."

" 'Meter next to the door . . . ,' " read Mevlut. " 'Cable for ice-cream machine is—' "

"Okay, so this place must sell ice cream in the summer. More than half the ice-cream machines in Istanbul during the summer aren't connected to any meter. It seems the honest clerk who was here last time suspected something, but the technicians never found the illegal connection. Or maybe they did, but the giant at the cash desk gave them each a ten-thousand-lira bill to keep them sweet. Some places are so clever about where they tap the line that they think they'll never get caught, so when you come in, they don't even give you a little gift to say hello. Hey, waiter, over here, the radiator's not working, and we're a little cold."

"I'll talk to my manager," said the waiter.

"He may or may not be in on it," I told Mevlut. "Put yourself in the manager's shoes. If his waiter knows they're stealing electricity, he might report it. That makes it very hard to fire him, or even tell him off for slacking or hogging all the tips. That's why the best thing to do is to call in an electrician who specializes in unmetered circuits and hand the whole place over to him one night when no one's around. These guys can disguise an illegal line so beautifully that sometimes you just have to step back and admire the genius. In the end, our job is like a game of chess with these guys. They're clever at hiding it; you have to be more clever and find it."

"I've had the heaters switched on, sorry for that," said the manager, walking into the room behind his fat belly.

"He didn't even bother to say 'radiator,' " Mevlut whispered. "What do we do now? Are we going to cut their power?"

"No, my friend. Lesson number two: you figure out what the trick is and make a mental note of it. Then you wait for the right moment to come back and take their money. We're in no rush today."

"You're as sly as a fox, aren't you, Ferhat?"

"But I still need a lamb like you, I need your gentleness and your honesty," I said to encourage Mevlut. "Your sincerity and your innocence are great assets to this company, to the world in fact."

"All right, but I don't think I can deal with all these big managers and high-level crooks," said Mevlut. "I better stick to the *gecekondu* homes, the poorer neighborhoods."

Mevlut spent that winter and the spring of 1996 combing through logbooks and neighborhoods and learning at Ferhat's side, but also venturing out on his own two or three times a week to poor quarters and backstreets in the city center, armed with only old meter readings to hunt for illegal hookups all by himself. The city center was falling apart: the broken and abandoned old buildings in which he'd lived as a waiter working in Beyoğlu nearly twenty years ago were now nests of electric thievery. Ferhat told Mevlut to stay away from that kind of place—both for his own safety and because he knew his friend would never be able to extract any money there. So Mevlut ended up in Kurtuluş, Feriköy, Beşiktaş, Şişli, Mecidiyeköy, and sometimes over on the other side of the Golden Horn, in Çarşamba, Karagümrük, and Edirnekapı—the Holy Guide's streets and neighborhoods—collecting payments from families and housewives like one of those polite government clerks who once used to come calling.

Working as a boza vendor, he'd become used to accepting little gifts on top of what he was owed—a pair of woolen socks, perhaps, or even some extra cash from people who told him "Keep the change!" and this had never troubled his conscience or wounded his pride. In a similar way, a tip for not cutting off someone's power seemed a just reward for a service he was offering, and he had no qualms at all about pocketing the money. He knew these neighborhoods and their people well. (No one recognized Mevlut, though; they could never make the connection between the boza vendor who walked down the street once a week or once every other week in the winter and the inspector who came officially knocking on their door. Perhaps it was that the good people who bought boza at night were completely different from the bad people who stole electricity.) It seemed that the street dogs were always growling at Mevlut in these neighborhoods close to the city center. He began to keep his evening boza rounds brief.

He couldn't have gone to Kültepe or Duttepe to collect money where everyone knew him, but he did take his logbooks and head over to those other hills that had followed the same course from destitution to development: Kuştepe, Harmantepe, Gültepe, and Oktepe. They could hardly be termed "poor neighborhoods" anymore. The single-story hollow-brick buildings that had once covered these hills had all been knocked down in the past twenty-five years, and now these places were all considered part of the city itself, like Zeytinburnu, Gaziosmanpaşa, and Ümraniye. Each neighborhood had its own center—usually the bus stop where one had caught the first regular service to the city some twenty-five years ago, and which would now be flanked by a mosque, a new statue of Atatürk, and a muddy little park. This would also be the spot where the neighborhood's main street began, a long road that seemed to stretch all the way to the end of the world, with five- and six-story concrete blocks on either side. The buildings brought an assortment of kebab shops, grocery stores, and banks, all on street level. Here, too, there were families, mothers, children, grandfathers, and grocers who'd set their sights on free electricity (though in fact Mevlut couldn't find that many), and their manner was no different from what you might find in any ordinary neighborhood in the center of Istanbul: the same tricks, the same lies, the same basic innocence . . . They may have been more apprehensive of Mevlut in these places, but they also showed him a lot more warmth than anywhere else.

The ancient cemeteries that would pop up in the older parts of the city, filled with strange and mysterious crumbling gravestones topped with all sorts of emblems and sculpted turbans, didn't exist in these new neighborhoods. The newer and more modern cemeteries, devoid of cypress trees or any other vegetation, were usually situated well outside the new quarters and surrounded by tall concrete walls, just like factories, military bases, and hospitals. In the absence of graveyards, the stray dogs who stalked Mevlut on his morning inspections would spend the night sleeping in the dirty little park across from the statue of Atatürk.

Mevlut always approached the city's newest and poorest neighborhoods with the best of intentions, yet he found that the most belligerent dogs of all lived here. He spent many miserable hours in these areas, most of which had only recently been assigned their own meters and logbooks. Often he hadn't even heard their names before, and getting there could involve a two-hour bus ride below the city center and away from the main highways. Once off the bus, Mevlut would exercise all of his "good intentions" to ignore the wires that people had hooked up—not even bothering to hide them—to the big cables that carried electricity between cities, and he would turn a blind eye to the clumsy circuits powering the kebab stall across from the bus stop. He could sense that each of these neighborhoods had its own leaders and chiefs, and that he was being watched. My job is just to look at the official meters, he wanted to say in his most determined, proper, and righteous tone. You have nothing to fear from me. But the dogs attacked him, and Mevlut got scared.

These new homes and gardens on the edge of the city had been built with newer and better materials than the poor neighborhoods of Mevlut's childhood. Hollow bricks had been replaced by alternatives of higher quality, plastic had been used instead of scrap metal, and gutters and pipes had all been made out of PVC. The houses were constantly growing with the addition of new rooms, just as *gecekondu* homes always had done, and this meant that the electricity meter would get swallowed up inside a room somewhere, so that if you wanted to take a reading or cut the power, you had no choice but to knock on the door. That would be the cue for the local strays to begin circling the inspector. In some new neighborhoods, a power line might have been brought in and affixed to a pole, a chunk of concrete, a wall, or even a grand old plane tree in the little local square, and sometimes this was where you found people's meters, not inside their homes. These electrical hubs, which weren't so different from those Ottoman-era fountains that used to supply a neighborhood with water, would also be under the constant supervision of small packs of two or three stray dogs.

Mevlut was standing on the porch of a house with a garden one day when he was attacked by a black dog. He checked the notes of his predecessor in the logbook and called out the dog's name, but Blackie paid him no heed. He barked at Mevlut and forced him to retreat. A month later, Mevlut only managed to get away from a raging guard dog because the dog's chain wasn't long enough. Whenever he came under attack like this, he always thought of Rayiha. These things were happening only because she wasn't there anymore.

Mevlut was in the same neighborhood again one day, looking for a spot in the park to sit down with his bag on his lap while he waited for the bus, when—*woof woof woof*—a dog approached him. A second and third dog came up behind the first. They were the color of mud. Mevlut saw a black dog in the distance, as indistinct as a distant memory. They all started barking at the same time. Would he be able to ward them off with his inspector's briefcase? He had never been so afraid of dogs in his life.

One Tuesday evening, he went to the Holy Guide's lodge in Çarşamba. He left some boza in the kitchen. The Holy Guide was much livelier than usual and free of the usual crowd of hangers-on. When he realized that he had the Guide's attention, Mevlut quickly explained how he'd first begun to fear dogs twenty-seven years ago. In 1969, around the time Mevlut had first begun to work as a street vendor, his father had taken him to see a holy man in a wooden house in the backstreets of Kasımpaşa in order to address this fear. That holy man had had a white beard and an enormous belly, and, compared with the Guide, he was old-fashioned and unsophisticated. He had given Mevlut some rock candy and told him that dogs were deaf, dumb, and blind creatures. Then he'd opened his palms up as if to pray, instructing Mevlut to do the same, and in his small stove-heated room, he had made Mevlut repeat the following words nine times: "SUMMOON, BUKMOON, OOMYOON FE HOOM LAH YARJOON."

The next time he was attacked by strays, Mevlut had to put his fear to one side and repeat that verse three times. That was the first thing that people had to do when they became afraid of dogs, demons, and the devil: they had to banish the thought from their minds. "Don't be scared, just pretend you haven't seen them," his father would say when he saw Mevlut getting agitated by the shadowy dogs on the dark streets where they sold boza together at night. "Say the verse quick, son!" he would whisper. But even when he concentrated as hard as he could, Mevlut would never remember the verse. His father would lose his temper and tell him off.

When he finished recounting these episodes from his past, Mevlut cautiously asked the Holy Guide: Can a person really banish a fear or a thought from his mind by the force of his own will alone? By now, Mevlut's experience was that trying to forget about something only made him think about it more. (In his youth, for example, the more he'd tried to get Neriman off his mind, the more he'd wanted to stalk her—but of course he didn't mention this to the Holy Guide.) Wanting to forget something, having THE INTENTION TO FORGET something, was clearly not an efficient way of forgetting at all. In fact what you intended to forget tended to stick even more firmly in your mind. These were the questions he'd never had the chance to ask the holy man in Kasımpaşa, and now, twenty-seven years later, he was pleased to find that he had the courage to put them to the Holy Guide of the spiritual retreat in Çarşamba, who was a much more modern holy man anyway.

"The ability to forget depends on the PURITY of the believer's HEART, the SINCERITY of his INTENTIONS, and the STRENGTH of his WILL," said the Holy Guide. He'd liked Mevlut's question and had graced it with a weighty response worthy of the "conversations."

Feeling encouraged, Mevlut guiltily told the story of how as a little boy, on a snowy, moonlit night when the streets shone pure and white like a cinema screen, he'd watched a pack of dogs move in a flash to trap a cat under a car. He and his late father had walked past in silence, acting as if they hadn't seen anything, pretending not to hear the cat's dying wails either. In the time that had since gone by, the city had grown perhaps tenfold. Even though he'd forgotten all the prayers and verses he was supposed to say, Mevlut hadn't been scared of dogs at all for twenty-five years. But in the last two years, he'd begun to fear them again. The dogs could tell, and that was why they barked at him and tried to corner him. What should he do?

"IT IS NOT ABOUT PRAYERS OR VERSES, BUT ABOUT YOUR HEART'S INTENT," said the Holy Guide. "Boza seller, have you been doing anything recently that may have disturbed people's lives?"

"I have not," said Mevlut. He didn't mention that he'd become embroiled in the electricity business.

"Perhaps you have and you don't realize it," said the Holy Guide. "Dogs can sense when a person doesn't belong among us. This is their God-given gift. That is why people who want to copy the Europeans are always afraid of dogs. Mahmud II butchered the Janissaries, the backbone of the Ottoman Empire, and thus allowed the West to trample upon us; he also slaughtered the street dogs of Istanbul and exiled all those he couldn't kill to Hayırsızada, the Wretched Island. The people of Istanbul organized a petition to bring the dogs back. During the armistice following World War I, when the city was under foreign occupation, the street dogs were massacred once more for the comfort of the English and the French. But again, the good people of Istanbul asked for their dogs to be returned. With this wealth of experience in their blood, all our dogs now have a very keen sense of who is their friend and who is their foe."

9

Bringing Down a Nightclub

Is It Right?

Ferhat. Don't worry about Mevlut: another six months passed, and by the winter of 1997, he'd already gotten the hang of being a meter inspector. He was earning decent money, too. How much? Even he didn't know. But every evening, he gave me a full account of what he'd collected that day, just the way he used to do with his father when they were selling yogurt together. He sold his boza at night, and generally stayed out of trouble.

The one who went looking for it was me, actually. As far as I could tell, Selvihan was still seeing Sami from Sürmene, putting any hope of being with her further and further out of reach and making me more and more desperate. I would often spend all night looking for her in the archives and around the city, but at least I always came home in the end—even if it was almost dawn.

I was at the Moonlight Club with some friends one night when one of the owners came and joined our table. These live music clubs swallow vast amounts of electricity, so the managers usually try to get in good with their local inspector. Whenever we go to these places, we can always expect nice discounts and plates of appetizers and fruit and panfried prawns on the house. Tables of assorted scroungers, bureaucrats, and gangsters are a common sight in any self-respecting nightclub, and, usually, all that's expected of these "guests" is that they sit quietly, without sending flowers to any of the girls or requesting any songs. That night, however, our table became the center of attention, because the owner's right-hand man, a certain Mr. Mustache (so named for the thin line of hair over his upper lip), kept inviting the singers to sit at our table and encouraging us to ask for whatever we wanted to hear.

Afterward, this Mr. Mustache asked if we could meet in a coffeehouse in Taksim one morning; I assumed it was to do with the usual stuff, making sure I neglected to notice some illegal wiring at the Moonlight and maybe one or two other things they were doing without a permit. Instead, he had a much bigger and more serious agenda: he wanted to "bring down" the Sunshine Club.

There was now a whole new breed of gangsters who specialized in "bringing down" bars, nightclubs, and even high-end restaurants. They exploited the havoc that privatization had brought upon the eighty-year-old game of electricity theft. With their help, a nightclub owner might conspire with electric company inspectors to plunge a rival club into darkness and have it hit with huge bills, thanks to penalties rising at twice the rate of inflation. If it all worked according to plan, the rival club would have to shut down for a couple of weeks, and if it couldn't settle its account, it would go bankrupt and disappear altogether. In the last six months, I'd heard of a number of bars and clubs in Beyoğlu, two hotels in Aksaray and Taksim (electricity theft is very common in small hotels, too), and a big kebab shop on İstiklal Avenue being brought down this way.

But bigger businesses all had contacts in the police and the district attorney's office, and they could count on the protection of mafia gangs, too. Even if some principled and meticulous inspector came along and exposed all their unmetered connections and back charges, cut their power, and put a seal on their meter, these big fish wouldn't care; they'd just reconnect the lines with their own hands and pick up where they'd left off. They might even take the trouble to arrange for the brave inspector to get beaten to a pulp in the dead of night. To bring down one of these big guys, a rival business would have to have the public prosecutor, the mafia, and maybe even the police on its side, so that once the plan went into action, it could be sure that the damage would be permanent. That day, Mr. Mustache revealed that bringing down the Sunshine Club was part of a larger scheme on the part of those Cizre Kurds who were backing the Moonlight: they were out to get Sami from Sürmene.

I asked them why they had picked me for this major operation.

"Our guys tell us that you've already got your eye on Sami from Sürmene," said Mr. Mustache. "They've seen you sniffing around at the Sunshine Club . . ."

"Cezmi from Cizre's got eyes all over the place, hasn't he?" I said. "But this is dangerous. I'll have to think about it."

"Don't worry. Politicians aren't the only ones who've become civilized these days, Beyoğlu gangs are, too. They're not shooting each other in the street over little disagreements anymore."

Samiha. "This cannot go on," I told Ferhat the other morning. "You stay out until dawn, and the only time I get to see you, you're asleep. Keep it up, and I'm going to leave you."

"You can't! I would die! You're my reason for doing it, my reason for living," he said. "We've been through hell, me and you, but we've almost made it, finally. I just have this one last big job. Let me get it done, and then I'll buy you not one but two whole farms down south."

As usual, I believed him more or less, but only up to a point; the rest of the way, I just pretended to. It's been two years since Rayiha died; how quickly the time has gone by. Now I'm a year older than she was then, and still I don't have a child, or a real husband. When I couldn't hold it in anymore, I told Vediha everything.

"First of all, Samiha, Ferhat is a good husband!" she said. "Most men are bad-tempered, pigheaded boors. Ferhat isn't like that. Most men are stingy, especially when it comes to their wives. But all over this lovely place of yours I can see money's been spent. Most men beat their wives, too. You've never mentioned anything like that. I know he loves you. You'd be insane to leave him. Ferhat is a good person, deep down. You can't just leave a house and a husband like that. Where would you go anyway? Come on now, let's go to the movies."

My sister may know everything, but she sure can't see why a person would need to stand up for herself.

When I brought it up with Ferhat again and told him I really was going to leave this time, he just scoffed: "I might be about to take down Sami from Sürmene and his empire, and that's all you've got to say?"

The most upsetting thing, though, was when I found out that apparently Mevlut had been giving his daughters a hard time about their visits: "Why are you always going over to your aunt's?" I won't tell you which one of the girls gave her father away. But I found out that he doesn't like the idea of their coming here and learning how to put makeup on, wear lipstick, and dress themselves.

"He should be ashamed of himself!" said Vediha. "He's still brooding about those stupid letters. You should tell Ferhat. Isn't he Mevlut's boss now?"

I didn't tell Ferhat a thing. Once I'd made my decision, I went over every detail in my head, again and again. And then I began to wait.

Ferhat. There are two ways to bring down a big nightclub, an expensive restaurant, or a small hotel: (1) You worm your way in and find out where all the illegal cables are, under the pretext of showing the owners even newer and smarter ways to connect to the mains. Then you make a deal with their enemies and arrange for a raid. (2) You find the expert electrician who'd rigged their illegal hookups in the first place and try to get it out of him: which walls are hiding which cables, whether this and that circuit is real or a red herring, et cetera. The second way is definitely more dangerous, because the expert in question (usually a former government clerk) might figure he can do better for himself by going straight to the owners he did the job for and telling them all about the little rat who's so interested in their wiring. Where there's a lot of money to be made, there's also a lot of blood to be spilled. You couldn't make any bricks or tiles without electricity, could you?

My two elderly clerks in the records office of Seven Hills Electric warned me about the dangers I might face. They also told me that the meter readings for the Sunshine Club, as well as most of the homes, cafés, and offices in the area, were all handled by an older inspector, a guy so strict that he'd come to be known as the Admiral. This man had flourished with all the new fines he could slap on people, and his work had caught my two clerks' eye. From the inspectors' office, we obtained the Admiral's most recent meter readings for the Sunshine Club. Using these records and all the old ones in the archives, the old clerks got busy working out the various methods by which the Sunshine Club had stolen most of its power during forty years in business. Where had they hidden the cables? How had they bypassed the meter? Could we trust the notes we'd found? I hung on their every word.

"It wouldn't take much to bring this place crashing down. Allah help us!" said one of the clerks, excitedly. They were both so energized they forgot I was even there. Nightclub wars were the worst kind of trouble: back in the day, when rival establishments and their gangs declared war on each other, they would kidnap each other's singers and belly dancers and hold them hostage, shooting them in the kneecaps eventually. Another common ploy was for a gang to go into a rival nightclub as ordinary customers, politely request a song, and start a brawl when it wasn't played. With contacts in the press, you could arrange for everyone to hear about these fights, which sometimes ended in murder, and soon enough customers would stop coming to that nightclub, leading its owners to send their own guys over to the other place to do the same to them, and on and on with more gunfire and more bloodshed. I loved those old clerks' stories.

After studying the situation for another week, I met with the owners of the Moonlight Club again. I said I could provide them with all the necessary schematics.

"Excellent. Don't give them to anyone else," said Mr. Mustache. "We've got a plan. Where do you live? I'll send our guys over to explain everything. You never know, it's always safer to talk at home."

When he said "home," my first thought was Samiha. I wanted to run back that evening and tell her how close we were to the end of our long road. I was going to burst in and say, "We're bringing down the Sunshine Club." Samiha was going to be so happy: not only would we finally be rich, but we'd be sticking it to those exploitative fat cats. But when I did eventually make it home, it was already quite late, and I fell asleep on the living room couch. When I woke up in the morning, I saw that Samiha was gone.

The Holy Guide hadn't taught Mevlut any magic words to chase the dogs away. Was there any truth to his pronouncement that they took against those who didn't belong to this land? If that was really the reason that dogs barked at people, they should never have barked at Mevlut, who even in the newest and most remote neighborhoods never once felt himself a stranger as he wandered among the city's concrete buildings, grocery stores, and laundry lines, its posters for cram schools and banks, and its bus stops, speaking to old men who always wanted to pay their bills some other day and kids with snot running from their noses. In fact, the dogs had toned down their growling somewhat since Mevlut's latest visit to the Holy Guide in February 1997. He felt there were two reasons for this welcome development.

First: the street dogs had begun to lose their grip on these outlying areas. These places didn't have any ancient cemeteries like the one in the picture Mevlut had cut out from the *Righteous Path,* and so during the day the strays had nowhere to shelter as a pack while they waited for nightfall. On top of this, the municipal authorities had equipped these neighborhoods with huge and heavy-wheeled dumpsters resembling mining trolleys. The dogs weren't strong enough to tip over these little fortresses to scavenge for food.

The other reason Mevlut was now less afraid of dogs had to do with his greater magnanimity toward the poor souls who lived in these deprived neighborhoods and couldn't pay their bills. He didn't strut around these places like some high-handed bureaucratic zealot determined to eradicate every last illicit connection. If he turned up at a house outside the city and found a few pathetic cables hooked up to a high-voltage main nearby, he would give a range of meaningful looks (perhaps even asking some pointed questions) making clear to whoever was home—be it a retired old man, a middle-aged Kurdish lady who'd fled the war, some unemployed and irascible father, or an angry mother—that he knew exactly what they were up to. But when they proceeded to deny it, affecting all the sincerity they could, he would, in turn, affect to believe every word. They would thus feel they'd outsmarted the inspector and start denying every other little misdeed Mevlut had spotted: there was no circuit bypassing the meter; nothing had been wedged under the rotor disk either; this was certainly not the sort of household where people tampered with the display dials to make the reading lower. But when confronted with these further denials, Mevlut would make it very clear that he didn't believe any of it. And so it was that he was able to infiltrate the city's roughest and most isolated parts, identify the most blatant instances of electricity theft, and come out with a decent amount of money to hand to Ferhat at the end of the day—all without angering the majority of the locals or the dogs, ever alert to the presence of a hostile intruder. "Mevlut, you've somehow managed to bridge the gulf between what people think in private and what they say in public," said Ferhat one day when Mevlut told him he'd started getting along with the stray dogs again. "You've got this whole nation figured out. I've got a favor to ask of you now, but it has to do with my private life, not my public life."

Ferhat told him that his wife had left their house and gone to stay with Vediha and the Aktaş family, refusing to come home. In fact, Mevlut knew more: their mutual father-in-law, Crooked-Necked Abdurrahman, unable to hide his glee at the news that Samiha had left her husband, had jumped on the first bus from the village to come and be near his daughter and support her in this difficult time. Of this Mevlut said nothing.

"I've made mistakes, too," said Ferhat. "But that's all going to change. I will take her to the movies. But first she has to come home. Of course, we can't have you speaking to Samiha directly. But Vediha can be the one to talk to her."

In the days that followed, Mevlut would often wonder why it would have been wrong for him to speak to Samiha himself. But at the time, he didn't object.

"Vediha is a clever woman," said Ferhat. "Out of all the Aktaş and Karataş lot, she's the smartest. She can persuade Samiha. Go tell her that . . ."

Ferhat told Mevlut about a big scheme he was part of, though, as a precaution, he didn't name any of the places, gangs, or people involved.

He wanted Mevlut to pass it all on to Vediha, so that Vediha could then tell Samiha. It really was true that he was neglecting his wife because of work.

"Oh, and Samiha was also upset about something else," said Ferhat. "She said you don't want Fatma and Fevziye coming over to our place in the afternoon to spend time with their aunt. Is that true?"

"That's a lie," lied Mevlut.

"Well, anyway, you tell Samiha that I can't live without her," said Ferhat self-importantly.

Mevlut was unconvinced, and he thought sorrowfully of how, throughout the whole conversation, they had only shared their public views. Twenty-six years ago, they had become friends while selling Kısmet owing to the hopeful belief that they could reveal all their private thoughts to each other.

Now, the two friends went their separate ways, like two inspectors who'd just concluded a routine bit of business. It was to be the last time they would ever see each other.

Vediha. With all the time and effort I've spent since marrying into this family twenty years ago—settling arguments, covering for flaws, and mending fences—is it right that I should be held responsible whenever something bad happens? After all those times I told Samiha "Whatever you do, don't leave your house and your husband," is it right that I should be blamed when my sister decides to pack her bags and come live with us in Duttepe? After I spent four years sifting through Istanbul for a nice and decent girl for Süleyman, is it my fault if he ends up marrying some old lounge singer? If my poor father decides to come to Istanbul to be with his daughters and spends more than a month living up on the third floor with Samiha, do I deserve the dirty looks from my father-in-law and husband? When Süleyman can't even be bothered to come visit his parents anymore, is it right that he should get away with saying "Samiha is there" as his excuse and put me and my poor little sister in such an awkward position? After all the times I said, "Let's move to Şişli, we've got enough money now," and Korkut ignored me, is it right for Süleyman and his wife to go and live there themselves, as if to rub it in? In fact, is it right that Süleyman and his wife haven't even invited me and Korkut to their new house yet? And what about Melahat's being so condescending about how Duttepe's roads are still not paved and we don't even have a hairdresser in the neighborhood? Or when she's telling my fortune and says, "Men have bullied you and pushed you around all your life, haven't they" as if she's so much better than I am? Should a new mother be relying so entirely on her maid that she forgets all about her baby in the other room and spends three hours prattling on with her guests, getting drunk, and trying to sing? Is it fair that my poor little sister and I shouldn't be allowed to go to the cinema in Şişli? Or that Korkut should categorically forbid me to go out, or to leave the neighborhood if he does happen to let me leave the house? Is it reasonable that I should be the one who's been taking my father-in-law's lunch over to his shop every single day for the past twenty years? That I should hurry to make sure his food doesn't get cold only for him to say "Not this again" or "What on earth is this," regardless of whether I've made his favorite meat-and-bean stew or tried something different with okra in it? Is it right for Korkut to tell Samiha what she can and can't do and order her around like his wife, just because she's living with us now? Or for Korkut to tell me off in front of his mother and father? Or talk down to his wife in front of the children? Is it right for all of them to come to me with their problems, but then always turn around and say, "You don't understand"? Does it seem fair that I should never get the remote when we're watching TV together in the evenings? Should Bozkurt and Turan be as rude to me as their father is? Or swear like sailors in front of their mother? Is it right for their father to spoil them so much? When we're watching TV together, is it right for them to say "A snack, Mom!" every five minutes without even turning to look at me? After all that their mother does for them, is it right that they never even bother to say thanks? Would it be wrong to object to how they respond "Yeah, sure, whatever you want, Mom" or "Are you insane?" to everything I say? Is it proper for them to keep those disgusting magazines in their room? Is it right for their father to come home so late every other evening? Or that he's hired some scrawny, surly blonde with too much makeup on and gives her all this attention because "She's good for business"? Should the boys turn their noses up at everything I cook? Is it fine for them to ask for fries every day even though their faces are covered in pimples? Is it okay to do their homework while they watch TV? After I've spent hours making them dumplings, just because I love them both so much, is it right that they just gobble them up with nothing to say except "Not enough meat in them"? And that they pour Coca-Cola into their grandfather's ear when he falls asleep in front of the TV? Is it right for them to copy their father and call anyone they don't like a "faggot" or a "Jew"? When I say, "Go and get some bread from your granddad's shop," is it right for them to argue every time about whether it's Turan's or Bozkurt's turn to go? Whenever I ask them to do anything, is it reasonable for them to say "I've got homework to do" even though they never really do their homework? Is it right for them to answer back "It's my room, I can do what I want!" every time I ask them to be careful with something? If once in a blue moon we decide to take the car and go somewhere together as a family, is it acceptable for them to say, "We've got a football match in the neighborhood"? Is it right for them to refer to their uncle Mevlut as "the boza seller" and be so mean to his daughters all the time, even though they're so infatuated with their cousins? How about when they take their father's tone with me and say, "You say you're on a diet, but then you stuff your face with pastries all day"? Or that they make fun of me as he does for watching my soap operas in the afternoon? Is it right for them to say, "We've got our tutoring sessions to prepare for the university entrance exams," but then go to the movies instead? When they fail the entire school year, is it appropriate for them to call the teacher a nutcase instead of admitting their own deficiencies? Should they be taking the car when they don't even have a driver's license yet? If they happen to see their aunt Samiha out on her own in Şişli, must they inform their father as soon as he comes home in the evening? Is it right for Korkut to tell me "You'll do as I say, or else!" in front of them? Or to squeeze my wrist hard enough to hurt and bruise? Is it right for them to shoot seagulls and pigeons with their air gun? That they should never help me clear the table after dinner, not even once? After all my lectures on how important it is that they do their homework, is it appropriate for their father to tell that old story yet again of how he beat up the donkey-faced chemistry teacher in front of the whole class? When they have a test, shouldn't they try studying instead of making cheat sheets? Is it right for my mother-in-law, Safiye, to say, "You're no angel yourself, Vediha!" every time I complain about any of these things? After all their pronouncements on God, the nation, and morality, is it right that all they should ever think about is how they can make more money?

IO

Mevlut at the Police Station

I've Spent All My Life on These Streets

Ferhat. Like most restaurants, cafés, and hotels that steal electricity, the Sunshine Club had a number of what might be thought of as "overt violations." These were minor connections, installed on the cheap for the sole purpose of giving the inspectors something to find on their raids (most of which were prearranged anyway) while leaving the major channels of electricity theft alone. Mr. Mustache could see I was itching to infiltrate the backstage and basement areas, where the club's singers and hostesses congregated, in order to discover the motherlode of stolen power, and he warned me to be careful: even if we did get the public prosecutor and the police on our side, it didn't take a genius to guess that Sami from Sürmene would launch a fierce counterattack to save face. Someone could easily get shot and killed in the process. I shouldn't show my face around there so much. I also needed to be careful with the Admiral. He'd been the Sunshine Club's meter inspector long enough that he had to be playing both sides.

I stopped going to the Sunshine Club. But I no longer had Samiha waiting for me at home, and I missed the smell of nightclubs, so I started going to other places instead. I ran into the Admiral one night at the Twilight. They gave us one of their private tables. The Twilight Club can be a scary place; the decor is truly sinister, the toilets always make weird noises, and all the bouncers' eyes are full of malice, but that night, the seasoned inspector Admiral was very kind and friendly with his younger colleague. He did catch me entirely off guard, however, when he started talking about what a kind and decent guy Sami from Sürmene was.

"If you got to know him personally, if you witnessed his family life and knew what he wants to achieve for Beyoğlu and for this whole country, you wouldn't believe all these lies people tell about him; in fact, you would never think ill of him again," said the Admiral.

"I don't have anything against Mr. Sami or anyone else," I said.

I had the feeling that what I'd just said would somehow get passed on to Selvihan. I was also knocking back I don't know how many drinks, since that comment about Sami from Sürmene's "family life" had really thrown me. Why had Samiha lost faith in our family life? Didn't she get the message I'd sent with Mevlut for her to come home? "A person should NEVER reveal his true intentions in life," said the Admiral. DON'T GET MIXED UP IN THESE NIGHTCLUB AND GANG WARS, DON'T GET INVOLVED IN ANY RAIDS. For some reason, this called to mind how Mevlut never gets involved in anything. I was just thinking to myself what a good friend he is, and why wouldn't Samiha come home, things in that vein, when I noticed that Inspector Admiral seemed to know all the waiters at the Twilight Club by name. They were talking in whispers. Please don't hide anything from me; that way, I won't hide anything from you either. WHAT MAKES CITY LIFE MEANINGFUL IS THE THINGS WE HIDE. I was born in this city; I've spent all my life on these streets.

I realized at some point that Inspector Admiral was gone. Had we just argued about why Fenerbahçe wouldn't win the league championship this year? There will always come an hour in the night when the club empties out, until, somewhere in the background, only music from a cassette is playing. In this city of ten million souls, you'll feel you are one of a precious few who aren't yet sleeping but are, instead, delighting in their loneliness. On your way out, you bump into someone just like you, and you think, I wouldn't mind talking some more, I've got so many stories to tell. Hey, friend, do you have a light? Here, have a cigarette. You don't smoke Samsuns? I don't like American cigarettes, they make you cough and give you cancer. Next thing you know, I'm walking through the deserted city with this man, thinking that if I were to see him again the next day, I probably wouldn't even recognize him. By morning, the pavements in front of all the shops, cafés, and diners along these streets will be full of bottles broken by people like me the night before, and all sorts of other trash and filth, and the shopkeepers who have to clean it all up will curse us as they sweep. Look, all I want is a real conversation, a friend I can be honest with, someone I can talk to about anything: Do you mind if I talk to you? I've been toiling away all my life, but the one thing I haven't done is pay enough attention to what was happening at home. What's that? I said HOME. It's important. No, let me finish . . . You're right, my friend, but we won't find anywhere that's still serving at this hour, not even around here. No, they'll all have closed already, but it's fine, let's give it a go, who am I to disappoint you. The city's more beautiful at night, you know: the people of the night always tell the truth. What? Don't be scared, the dogs won't bite. Aren't you from Istanbul? Did you just say Selvihan? No, never heard of it; it must be the last club to close before the morning prayers: Let's go in if you want, we can sing along to some of the old songs from back home. Where are you from, anyway? Oh no, even this place is closed. My whole life's gone by on these streets. Even in Cihangir, there's nowhere to get a drink at this hour. They're going to get rid of all the brothels and the transvestites soon. No, that'll also be closed now. This guy gives you some pretty nasty looks sometimes: If my friends saw him, they'd say, Ferhat, where do you find these people. Forgive me for asking, but are you married? Now, don't get me wrong . . . Everyone's got a right to his own private life . . . You say you're from the Black Sea coast, but do you have any ships? When it gets to a certain time of night, everyone tends to begin their sentences with "Forgive me" or "Don't get me wrong." But why don't they just stop saying things that could be taken wrong instead? Why would you smoke American cigarettes instead of our wonderful Samsuns? Well, here we are, my hovel's up on the second floor. My wife's left me. I'm going to sleep on the couch until she comes back home. Say, I've got some *rakı* in the fridge, let's have another glass and call it a night, I've got to be up early to meet some old bookkeepers and read all about your bygone days. Don't get me wrong; ultimately, I'm happy. I've been in this city my whole life, and I still can't let go.

Now that he was earning enough to make it comfortably to the end of the month, Mevlut had started leaving the house much later at night than he used to—well after the end of the evening news—and coming home before eleven. He was earning enough as a meter inspector that, for the first time in twenty-five years, subsistence did not feel like such a struggle. The numbers of those longtime regulars to whom he had to deliver boza two or three times a week had dwindled. Mevlut and his daughters would laugh together in front of the TV as they ate what the girls had cooked for dinner, and if he got back home before they went to sleep, he'd sit and watch TV with them some more.

Mevlut accounted to Ferhat for every last penny he collected on his rounds. Ferhat, who'd recently begun to mock his friend whenever he spoke to him, had asked one day:

"Mevlut, what would you do if you won the lottery?"

"I'd just sit at home with my daughters and watch TV, nothing more!" Mevlut had said, smiling.

Ferhat had given him a look halfway between amazement and scorn, as if to say, "How innocent can you get?" It was the way crooks and swindlers and people who thought they were smarter than him had looked at Mevlut his whole life. But Ferhat had never been one of them; he used to understand Mevlut. It had broken Mevlut's heart to see Ferhat looking at him that way after he'd been so thoroughly respectful of Mevlut's honesty for so many years.

Sometimes when he was out selling boza in distant neighborhoods, Mevlut thought how Ferhat probably agreed with all those who thought that there must be something "not quite right" with Mevlut that he should still be bothering with boza. Maybe Samiha thought that, too. But in the end she'd left Ferhat. No woman had ever left Mevlut.

He got home one night in November to find a police car parked outside, and his mind went straight to Ferhat. It didn't occur to him that the police might have come for him. When he walked into the building and saw the officer standing on the stairs, the door to his apartment thrown open, and the fear on Fatma's and Fevziye's faces, his immediate reaction was to think that it wasn't him the police were after, that this must all have to do with some scheme of Ferhat's.

"We just need to take your father's statement tonight," said the officer, trying to comfort the girls, who were crying as they watched their father go.

But Mevlut knew that in any police case, whether it involved drugs, politics, or just an ordinary murder, such reassurances were always misleading. Sometimes, people who were taken away for questioning didn't come home for years. The police station was only five minutes away; they would never have sent a car if all they'd wanted to do was take him there for a statement.

As the police car drove through the night, Mevlut told himself over and over again that he was innocent. Ferhat may have done something wrong, though. Mevlut had cooperated with him. Maybe that meant he *was* guilty—at least in his intentions. A feeling of contrition surged through him like a wave of nausea.

Once they got to the police station, it became clear that they weren't going to take his statement right away. He'd anticipated this, but he still couldn't help feeling disappointed. They threw Mevlut in a spacious cell. There was some light from an old lamp in the corridor, but the back of the cell was dark. Mevlut guessed that there were two other people in there. The first man was asleep. The second was drunk and seemed to be quietly complaining about something. Like the first man, Mevlut curled up on the cold floor in a corner of the cell and rested his ear against his shoulder so he wouldn't have to hear the second man's voice.

The thought of Fatma's and Fevziye's scared and tearful expressions as he'd left the house dampened his spirits. The best thing to do now was to wallow in his misery until he fell asleep, just as he used to do as a child. What would Rayiha say if she could see her husband right now? She'd say, "Didn't I tell you to stay away from Ferhat?" He thought about the way she used to push her hair back like a little girl, her flashes of anger, and the mischievous smile she would give him every time she found a clever way to make things simpler in the kitchen. How they used to laugh, sometimes! Had Rayiha been alive now, Mevlut would have been less apprehensive about what was going to happen. They were definitely going to beat him up when they questioned him in the morning; they might even whip his feet or give him electric shocks. Ferhat had told him so many stories about how evil the police were. Now he was at their mercy. It'll be all right! he told himself, trying to calm down. He'd been scared of getting beaten during military service, too, but it had all been fine in the end. He didn't sleep all night. When he heard the morning call to prayer, he understood what a privilege it was to be free to go out into the street and the flow of city life.

When they took him to the interrogation room, he felt sick with exhaustion and worry. What should he do if they hit him or whipped his feet to try to extract information? Mevlut's left-wing friends had told him countless stories of brave men who'd died while heroically enduring all sorts of tortures; he would have liked to emulate them, but what was the secret he was supposed to hide? Ferhat must have been using Mevlut's name in some dirty business. Getting involved in the electricity racket had been a huge mistake.

"Do you think you're at home?" said a man in plain clothes. "You don't sit down until I say so."

"I'm sorry . . . I didn't mean to do anything wrong."

"We'll decide whether you've done anything wrong, but first let's see if you know how to tell the truth."

"I will tell the truth," said Mevlut, with courage and conviction. They seemed impressed with his words.

They asked him what he'd been doing two nights ago. He said he'd gone out to sell boza, just as he did every night, and told them which streets and neighborhoods he'd been to and which apartments he'd entered at what time.

At one point, the questioning had slowed down. Mevlut looked through the open door and saw Süleyman walk past, led along by a policeman. What was he doing here? Before he could sort his thoughts out, the police told him that Ferhat had been murdered in his home two nights ago. They watched Mevlut's face closely to see how he reacted. They asked about Ferhat's work as an electricity inspector. Mevlut didn't say anything that might get either Ferhat or Süleyman in trouble. His friend was dead.

"There was some bad blood between this Süleyman Aktaş and Ferhat Yılmaz, right?" they kept saying. Mevlut explained how all that was history; Süleyman was happily married now, he'd had a child, and he would have never done anything like that. They reminded him that Ferhat's wife had left him and taken refuge in Süleyman's house. Mevlut said it wasn't Süleyman's doing, and he never went to that house anymore anyway. He'd heard about all this from Vediha. Mevlut never stopped defending both his friends' innocence. Who could have killed Ferhat? Did Mevlut suspect anyone? He didn't. Did Mevlut bear any ill will toward Ferhat? Had they ever had any disagreements over money or women? He didn't, and they hadn't. Would he have expected Ferhat to be murdered? He wouldn't.

Sometimes the police forgot he was there and started talking about other things, catching up with a colleague who'd opened the door, or teasing each other about the football results. Mevlut took all this to mean that he probably wasn't in too much trouble.

At one point he thought he heard someone say: "Three men running after the same girl!" They all laughed at that, as if none of it had anything to do with Mevlut. Could Süleyman have told the police about the letters? Mevlut began to lose hope.

When they sent him back to the cell after the interrogation, the guilt he'd been feeling turned into panic: they were going to beat him up until he told them all about the letters and how Süleyman had tricked him. For a moment, he felt so ashamed that he wanted to die. But soon he realized he was probably exaggerating. Yes, it was certainly true that all three of them had fallen in love with Samiha. Mevlut also knew that if he told the police, Those letters were actually meant for Rayiha, they would probably just laugh at him and move on.

In the afternoon, while he was busy rehearsing all these explanations, they let him go. Outside, he began to grieve over Ferhat. It felt like a major part of his life and memories had been wiped out. But the urge to go home and hug his daughters was so strong that by the time he got on the bus to Taksim, he was euphoric.

The girls weren't home, and in its empty state, the house depressed him. Fatma and Fevziye had left without doing the dishes: he felt a rising melancholy, and he was oddly even a little afraid at the sight of the same boza utensils he'd been using for thirty years, Rayiha's basil plant on the windowsill, and the big cockroaches that had gathered enough courage in just two days to start scuttling about like they owned the place. It was as if the room had turned into someplace else overnight, and everything inside it had very slightly changed shape.

He hurried outside: he was sure that his daughters would be in Duttepe with their aunts. Everyone there would blame Mevlut now because of how close he'd been with Ferhat. What should he say when he offered Samiha his condolences? He thought about all these things as he looked out the window on the bus to Mecidiyeköy.

The Aktaş family home in Duttepe was as crowded as it usually was after holiday prayers: Süleyman had been released at around the same time as Mevlut. There was a moment when Mevlut found himself sitting across from Süleyman's wife, Melahat, but they both looked at the TV and didn't say a word to each other. Mevlut mused that people were too harsh about this woman, who seemed innocuous after all. All he wanted to do was to take his girls and go back home to Tarlabaşı without anyone blaming him or telling him off for anything. Even these people's relief at Süleyman's release felt like a reproach. Thank God this house had four floors now and three TVs that were always on. Mevlut never left the ground floor; this meant he didn't get to see a tearful Samiha and express his condolences. She'd been widowed, too, now. Perhaps she knew something like this would eventually happen to Ferhat and had been smart enough to leave him.

Ferhat's Alevi relatives, his colleagues from the electric company, and a few old friends from Beyoğlu all came to his funeral, but not Samiha. Once they'd left the cemetery, Mevlut and Mohini didn't quite know what to do with themselves. An ashen sky hung over Istanbul. Neither of them particularly liked drinking. They ended up going to the movies, and afterward Mevlut went straight home to wait for his daughters.

He didn't talk to the girls about their uncle Ferhat's funeral at all. Fatma and Fevziye acted as if they believed that their jokey uncle had been murdered because he'd done something wrong, and they didn't ask any questions. What had Samiha been telling them, what sorts of things had she been teaching them? Every time he looked at his girls, Mevlut worried about their future and wanted them to think of Ferhat exactly as the Aktaş family thought of him. He knew Ferhat wouldn't have appreciated this, and he felt bad. But Mevlut's private views on the subject were irrelevant compared with the need to protect his daughters' future. Now that Ferhat was dead, the only people he could count on in the struggle to survive in Istanbul were Korkut and Süleyman.

From the very beginning, Mevlut told Korkut exactly what he'd told the police: he had no knowledge of Ferhat's high-stakes electricity machinations. In any case, the job no longer suited Mevlut; he was going to resign immediately. He had some money saved up. When he went to the big Seven Hills Electric headquarters in Taksim to hand in his notice, he found he'd already been let go. After all the depredations that had come with privatization, the company's new owners were particularly concerned with avoiding criticism and the appearance of any irregularities. Mevlut winced when he heard some inspectors he knew already talking about Ferhat as someone who had sullied the good name of all electric inspectors. If another inspector had been killed or beaten up trying to track down illicit circuits, these same men would have spoken of him as a hero who had done the profession proud.

The cause and method of Ferhat's murder remained uncertain for several months. At first, the police hinted there might be some kind of homosexual motive behind the murder. Even Korkut and Süleyman were enraged at this theory. The reasoning was that the killer hadn't forced his way inside Ferhat's apartment, so he was clearly someone Ferhat knew, and they'd apparently even had a glass of *rakı* together. They had taken Samiha's statement and seemed to believe her account of having been estranged from her husband recently, and how she'd been living with her sister and her sister's husband; she was never considered a suspect, and in fact the police took her back to the house to determine whether anything had been stolen. They arrested two burglars who habitually operated in Çukurcuma and Cihangir and roughed them up a little. The details of the investigation changed every day, and Mevlut could only keep up thanks to Korkut's political connections.

There were nine million people living in Istanbul now, and ordinary crimes of passion, drunkenness, or fury weren't considered news anymore unless there was also a half-naked woman or a celebrity involved. Ferhat's murder didn't even make the papers. The newspaper moguls who'd been enjoying a share of the profits since the electricity business had been privatized would have prevented any negative publicity. Six months later, a monthly journal to which Ferhat's old left-wing militant friends often contributed published a piece no one read on the electricity mafia, with a list of names including "Ferhat Yılmaz." According to the author, Ferhat was a well-meaning inspector who'd been caught in the crossfire of criminal gangs fighting over the spoils of the electricity racket.

Mevlut had never heard of this journal before, but two months after the issue with the piece on Ferhat was first published, Süleyman brought him a copy, watched him read the article, and never said a word about it again. He had just had a second baby boy; the construction business was doing well, and he was happy with the way his life was going.

"You know how much we all love you, right?" said Süleyman. "Fatma and Fevziye tell us you haven't been able to find the kind of job you deserve."

"I'm doing all right, thank God," said Mevlut. "I don't understand why the girls would complain."

Ferhat's property was divided over the eight months that followed his death. With the help of a lawyer the Aktaş family had hired for her, Samiha took possession of two small places around Çukurcuma and Tophane that her husband had rushed to buy on the cheap with money he'd saved during his years as a meter inspector. The tiny, ill-proportioned, and shabby apartments were refurbished and repainted by the Vurals' construction company and then rented out. Mevlut kept up with all the particulars of life in Duttepe through Fatma and Fevziye, who went to see their aunts every weekend, staying overnight on Saturdays, and told their father about everything, from the food they ate to the films they went to see, the games their aunts played, and the rows between Korkut and Vediha. After these visits, Fatma and Fevziye would come home to Tarlabaşı thrilled to show their father the new sweaters, jeans, bags, and other gifts they'd been given. Their aunt Samiha was also paying for the evening classes Fatma had already begun to take in preparation for her university entrance exams, and she was giving both her nieces some extra pocket money, too. Fatma wanted to study hospitality management. Her determination always moved Mevlut to tears.

"You know how much Korkut cares about politics," said Süleyman. "I'm convinced that one day he will be rewarded for all the good he's done for this country. We've left the village behind, but now we're creating an association to bring together all the people who've come to Istanbul from back home in Beyşehir and make sure we have their support. We've got some other wealthy people getting involved from Duttepe, Kültepe, Nohut, and Yören."

"I don't understand politics," said Mevlut.

"Mevlut, we're forty now, we can understand anything," said Süleyman. "This isn't about politics anyway. We're just going to organize some events; we've already been hosting day trips and group meals. Now there's going to be a clubhouse, too. You would just make tea all day, as if you were running a café, and chat with people from back home. We've raised some money to rent a place out in Mecidiyeköy. You'd be in charge of opening up in the mornings and closing up in the evenings. You'd make *at least* three times what some poor street vendor would make. Korkut will guarantee it. You can leave at six and still have time to sell your boza at night. See, we've thought about that, too."

"Give me a couple of days to think it over."

"No, you've got to decide right now," said Süleyman, but he relented when he saw Mevlut's pensive look.

Mevlut would have much preferred a job closer to the streets, the crowds, and Beyoğlu. Joking with his customers, ringing their doorbells, walking up and down the endless sloping streets: these were the things he knew and loved, not being cooped up somewhere. But he was painfully aware of how much he still depended on Süleyman and Korkut for support. By now he had spent all the money he'd put away as a meter inspector. His time at the electric company had also cost him a few boza customers, since he hadn't been able to do as much work in the evenings. Some nights it felt as if not a single curtain would be pulled open as he walked by, not a single customer beckoning him to come upstairs. At night, he could sense the weight of the concrete, the hardness, and the horrors of the city around him. The dogs weren't menacing anymore. Those wheeled metal dumpsters had made it all the way into the city center by now, to all the places Mevlut loved—Beyoğlu, Şişli, Cihangir, as everywhere else—followed by a new category of poor people who foraged in them. These streets—after the twenty-nine years he'd spent ambling along them—had become part of Mevlut's soul, but now they were changing again very fast. There were too many words and letters, too many people, too much noise. Mevlut could sense a growing interest in the past, but he didn't expect this would do much for boza. There was also a new class of tougher, angrier hawkers. They were always trying to cheat people, always shouting, and constantly undercutting one another . . . These newcomers were as clumsy as they were rapacious. The older generation of street vendors had been swallowed up in the tumult of the city . . .

So this was how Mevlut warmed to the idea of socializing with people from his hometown and decided to accept the job. He would even have time to sell boza at night. The clubhouse's small offices were on the ground floor. There was a roasted-chestnut vendor stationed right outside the door. In his first few months on the job, Mevlut watched him from the window and learned all the tricks of that trade and also spotted the things the man was doing wrong. Sometimes Mevlut would find an excuse to go out and talk to him ("Is the doorman in?" or "Where can I find a glazier around here?"). Occasionally, he let the man leave his roasted-chestnut stall inside the building (a practice that would soon be forbidden), and they would head off to the mosque together for Friday prayers.

11

What Our Heart Intends and What Our Words Intend

Fatma Continues Her Studies

MEVLUT SOON FOUND a pleasing balance between his rather undemanding job running the clubhouse and his boza rounds in the evenings. He often got to leave before six, handing the "venue" over to whoever was hosting that evening's event. There were several other people who also had the keys to the building. Sometimes the entire local contingent of migrants from villages like Göçük or Nohut would book the place for the whole evening, and Mevlut would hurry home (coming back the next morning to find the offices and the kitchen in a state of grubby disarray). Once he'd had an early dinner with his daughters and checked whether Fatma—now in her second year of high school—was working hard enough to make it to college (yes, she definitely wasn't pretending), he would go out to sell boza in a happy mood.

Throughout the autumn of 1998, Mevlut paid frequent visits to the Holy Guide. A new, eager, and more assertive crowd had begun to assemble at his lodge. Mevlut didn't like them much, and he could sense that the feeling was mutual and that they found his presence incongruous. Bearded believers, backstreet hicks who never wore neckties, devotees, and acolytes of various kinds thronged to the Holy Guide in growing numbers, so that Mevlut hardly ever got the chance to talk to him anymore. Plagued by a series of illnesses that left him suffering chronic exhaustion, the Holy Guide no longer gave calligraphy classes, which meant that those gossipy students who used to come had stopped showing up; at least they'd brought some vitality and good cheer to the place. Nowadays, the Holy Guide sat on his armchair by the window with people crowding around him awaiting their turn to speak, nodding gravely at some disclosure or other (about the Holy Guide's health? the latest political developments? or something Mevlut didn't know about?) in their eagerness to express heartfelt sorrow. Now, whenever Mevlut entered the Holy Guide's retreat, he, too, would put on the same sorrowful look and start talking in whispers. His first visits to this place had been very different: "Look who's here, the boza seller with the face of an angel," they'd say back then; "It's Manager Mevlut!" they'd tease him; and someone would always comment on how much emotion they'd heard in his voice as he'd walked by on the street. Today, people just drank the boza he gave them for free, without even realizing that Mevlut was a boza seller.

One evening, he finally managed to catch the Holy Guide's eye and was blessed with the chance to speak to him for a few minutes. By the time it was all over and he was walking out of the lodge, he realized that it hadn't been the happiest of conversations. Yet he'd been so intensely aware of the envy and resentment that everyone else had felt at this exchange that he was elated. That night's talk had been both the most meaningful of Mevlut's "conversations" with the Holy Guide, and the most heartbreaking.

Mevlut had just about written off this particular visit when the Holy Guide, who'd been talking quietly to those around him, turned formally toward the audience amassed inside the spacious room and asked, "Who is wearing a wristwatch with a leather strap, and who is wearing one with a plastic strap?" The Holy Guide liked to challenge his disciples with questions, riddles, and religious conundrums. As usual, they all took turns trying dutifully to answer his question, when he spotted Mevlut:

"Ah, it's our boza seller with the blessed name!" he said, praising Mevlut and summoning him to his side.

As Mevlut bent down to kiss his hand—covered in brown spots that seemed to grow in size and number with every visit—the man beside the Holy Guide rose to yield his seat to Mevlut. When Mevlut sat down, the Holy Guide looked him straight in the eyes and, leaning in much closer than Mevlut had expected, used some archaic phrases to ask him how he was doing. The words he used were as beautiful as the calligraphy he'd put up on the walls.

Mevlut immediately thought of Samiha and cursed the devil for playing tricks on his mind while everyone was looking. He had long been considering how to explain to the Holy Guide about the letters he'd written to Rayiha when he'd actually had Samiha in mind. Just how much thought he must have devoted to this problem became clear to him when he found himself suddenly able to recall years' worth of intricate reasoning. First he would invoke the notion of intent in Islam. He would then ask the Holy Guide to explain the subtle distinction between a person's private and public intentions. Here was his chance to analyze the defining strangeness of his life through the eyes of this holiest of men; perhaps what he learned that night might finally free him from all the doubts that still weighed on his soul.

But their conversation took a completely different turn. Before Mevlut could say anything at all, the Holy Guide asked another question.

"Have you been performing your daily prayers?"

This was a question he usually reserved for immodest attention seekers, people who talked too much, and newcomers. He'd never asked Mevlut before. Perhaps that was because he knew Mevlut was just a penniless boza seller.

Mevlut already knew how the question was meant to be answered because he'd heard it answered before: the chosen guest was supposed to give a truthful account of how many times he'd prayed and given alms over the past few days, while admitting with regret that he still hadn't done enough to fulfill his duties as a believer. The Holy Guide would then pardon any shortcomings and provide his supplicant with some words of comfort: "What matters is that you meant well." But the devil must have been at it again, or perhaps Mevlut simply realized that the whole truth might not go down so well; in any event, he managed only a faltering response. He said that what mattered in the eyes of God was the heart's intent, the very words Mevlut had often heard the Holy Guide himself say. But the moment they left his mouth, he knew that there was something unseemly about his repeating them like that.

"It does not matter whether your heart intends to pray; the most important thing is to truly pray," said the Holy Guide. His tone was gentle, but those who knew him recognized it straightaway as the Holy Guide's manner of scolding.

Mevlut's boyishly handsome face went red.

"It is true that any act is judged according to the intent that lies behind it," the Holy Guide went on. "THE IMPORT OF A CONTRACT LIES IN THAT WHICH IT MEANS AND INTENDS TO ACHIEVE."

Mevlut sat motionless, his eyes downcast. "THE KEY IS EMOTION, NOT MOTION," said the Holy Guide. Was he making *fun* of Mevlut for sitting so perfectly still? A couple of people laughed.

Mevlut said he'd attended midday prayers every day that week. This wasn't true. He could tell that everyone knew it.

Perhaps because of Mevlut's evident embarrassment, the Holy Guide now elevated the tone of the conversation. "Intentions come in two forms," he said: "THAT WHICH OUR HEART INTENDS and THAT WHICH OUR WORDS INTEND." Mevlut heard this very clearly and made sure to memorize it. The intentions of the heart were crucial. In fact, as the Holy Guide always said, they were fundamental to our whole understanding of Islam. (If our heart's intent is what matters most, did that mean that the most important thing about Mevlut's letters was that he'd meant them for Samiha?) But our faith taught that the intentions behind our words also had to be true. Our Holy Prophet had expressed his intentions through words as well. The Hanafi school of Sunni teaching may have considered it sufficient for the heart's intentions to be pure, but as the holy Ibn Zerhani (Mevlut wasn't sure he was remembering that name correctly now) had once declared, when it comes to city life, WHAT OUR WORDS INTEND WILL REFLECT WHAT OUR HEART INTENDS.

Or had the holy Ibn Zerhani actually said that they "should" reflect each other? Mevlut hadn't really heard that part properly, because at that moment a car had started honking out on the street. The Holy Guide stopped talking. He glanced at Mevlut, looking right into his soul: he saw Mevlut's embarrassment, his reverence for the teacher, and his wish to leave that room as soon as possible. "A MAN WHO HAS NO INTENTION OF PRAYING WILL NEVER HEAR THE CALL TO PRAYER; WE ONLY HEAR WHAT WE WANT TO HEAR, AND SEE WHAT WE WANT TO SEE," he said. He'd addressed the whole room with a placid expression, and again, a few people had laughed.

Mevlut would spend the following days dwelling dejectedly over those words. Whom did the Holy Guide mean by "a man who has no intention of praying"? Had he been talking about Mevlut, who didn't pray often enough and lied about it, too? Had he meant some rowdy rich man honking his car horn in the middle of the night? Perhaps it had been a reference to the wicked, pusillanimous multitudes who always meant one thing but then ended up doing the very opposite? And what had the people in the room been laughing at?

Thoughts about the intentions of our hearts and the intentions of our words continued to weigh on Mevlut's mind. He could see that the distinction corresponded to Ferhat's theory about the difference between private and public views, but thinking about "intentions" gave the whole matter a more humane dimension. The pairing of hearts and words seemed more meaningful to Mevlut than that of private and public opinions—perhaps because it was more serious, too.

One afternoon, Mevlut was standing outside the clubhouse watching the chestnut vendor and talking to a retired, elderly yogurt seller with some property to his name when the old man said, "We shall see what fate has in store—KISMET." That word stuck in Mevlut's mind like a billboard slogan.

He'd been hiding it away in a corner of his mind along with his memories of Ferhat, but now it was back, keeping him company on his nightly walks. The leaves on the trees twitched and spoke to him. It all made sense now: KISMET was the force that bridged the gap between what our heart intended and what our words intended. A person could wish for one thing and speak of another, and their fate, their kismet, was the thing that could bring the two together. Even the seagull over there who wanted to land on that pile of trash had started off with only the intention to do so, which it had then put into words of a sort through a series of squawks, but whether the wishes harbored in its heart and expressed in its calls could ever be realized depended on a set of factors that were governed by KISMET—things like wind speed, luck, and timing. The happiness he'd found with Rayiha had been a gift of KISMET, and he must remember to respect that. The Holy Guide's words had upset him a little; but he was glad he'd gone to see him.

For the next two years, Mevlut worried about whether his elder daughter would be able to finish high school and go to college. He couldn't help Fatma with her studies; he couldn't even keep track of whether she was doing her homework properly. Yet he followed her progress in his heart, and every time he saw Fatma fall into a sullen silence, leaf listlessly through her textbooks and scowl at her homework, march around in anger, or just sit there quietly sometimes and stare out the window, he was reminded of his own anxious high-school self. But his daughter was anchored much more firmly to the world of the city. She was, he found, both sensible and beautiful.

When her sister wasn't around, Mevlut liked to take Fatma out to buy books and school supplies, or even just to talk over a plate of shredded-chicken blancmange among the crowded tables of the famous Villa Pudding Shop. Unlike other girls, Fatma was never insolent, moody, or reckless in her relationship with her father. Mevlut very rarely told her off—not that she ever did anything deserving reprimand anyway. He could sometimes see that there was a sort of rage behind her determination and confidence. They always joked together, and Mevlut would tease her for the way she narrowed her eyes when she read, washed her hands a thousand times a day, and threw everything into her handbag haphazardly, but he never took the mocking too far. He truly respected her.

Whenever he caught a glimpse of the chaos inside his daughter's handbag, Mevlut would realize that she'd forged a much stronger and deeper connection with the city, its people, and its institutions than he'd ever had himself, and that she must talk about all sorts of things with the many different kinds of people Mevlut had only ever encountered as a street vendor. There were so many things in that handbag: identification cards, scraps of paper, hairpins, small purses, books, notepads, entry passes, parcels, chewing gum, chocolates . . . Sometimes, the bag would emit a scent Mevlut had never smelled anywhere else in his life. It wasn't the smell of her books, which he did sometimes pick up and sniff in front of her, half in earnest; yet it was a bookish smell. It reminded Mevlut of cookies, the gum his daughter chewed when her father wasn't around, and an artificial scent of vanilla he couldn't quite place: the combination made him feel as if she could easily start living a completely different life if she wanted to. Mevlut really wanted Fatma to graduate from high school and go to college, but occasionally he also caught himself wondering whom she would end up marrying. It wasn't something he liked to think about; he sensed that his daughter was going to fly away from this house, gladly leaving behind the life she'd led here.

Every now and then in those early weeks of 1999, Mevlut said to his daughter, "I can come and pick you up after cram school." The classes Fatma was taking in Şişli to prepare for the college entrance exams sometimes ended at around the same time Mevlut was done with his day's work at the clubhouse in Mecidiyeköy; but Fatma never wanted her father to come. It wasn't that she came home late; Mevlut knew her class timetable well. Fatma and Fevziye cooked his dinner every evening with the same pots and pans their mother had used for years.

That year, Fatma and Fevziye insisted that their father get a telephone installed in the house. The prices had gone down; everyone was having a phone line hooked up nowadays, and once you sent in your application, you usually got connected within three months. Mevlut kept putting it off, worried about the extra expense and the idea of his daughters spending their days glued to the phone. He was especially wary at the prospect of Samiha calling them every day and telling them what to do. When his daughters told him they were "going to Duttepe," Mevlut knew that often they just went to Şişli instead and spent the day at the cinema, in cake shops, and browsing shopping malls with their aunt Samiha. Their aunt Vediha would come along, too, sometimes, without telling Korkut.

Mevlut did not attempt to sell ice cream during the summer of 1999. A traditional ice-cream vendor with a three-wheeled cart could hardly move around Şişli and the city center anymore, let alone make decent sales. Nowadays those were only to be had in the older neighborhoods, where children played football in the street on summer afternoons, but

Mevlut's growing responsibilities at the migrants' association always kept him busy during those hours.

One evening in June, after Fatma had successfully completed her second year of high school, Süleyman came by the clubhouse on his own. He took Mevlut to a new place in Osmanbey and asked him to do something that made our hero deeply uncomfortable.

Süleyman. Bozkurt was nineteen by the time he finally managed to finish high school. That was only because Korkut forked out the cash to get him enrolled in one of those private schools at which you can basically buy your child a diploma. He hasn't done well enough on the college entrance exams this year (or last year) to earn a place at a decent university, and now he's really losing his way. Apparently he crashed his car twice and even spent a night in jail following a drunken brawl. So his father decided to send him off to do his military service at the age of twenty. The boy rebelled and became so depressed that he stopped eating properly. Bozkurt told his mother that he is in love with Fatma. But he didn't actually ask them to arrange a match or anything like that. When Fatma and Fevziye came to Duttepe this spring, they got into another argument with Bozkurt and Turan. The girls got offended, and they haven't been back to Duttepe since. (Mevlut has no idea.) Not seeing Fatma anymore was making Bozkurt heartsick. So Korkut said, "Let's get them engaged before we send him off to the army, otherwise he's going to get swallowed up by Istanbul." Korkut mentioned these plans only to Vediha; we didn't tell Samiha a thing. His father and I spoke to Bozkurt. "I'll marry her," he said, looking away. Now it's fallen to me to make the two sides meet.

"Fatma's still in school," said Mevlut. "Do we even know whether she likes him? Will she even listen to what I say?"

"I've only been beaten up by the police once in my life, Mevlut," I said. "And that was your fault." I didn't add anything more to that.

Mevlut felt it was significant that Süleyman hadn't brought up all the help the Aktaş family had given him over the years. Instead he'd focused on how the police had beaten him up after Ferhat's murder. In the time they'd both spent in jail, for some reason the police had only beaten Süleyman and left Mevlut safe and sound. He still smiled every time he thought about it. All of Korkut's influence had not been enough to protect Süleyman from that beating.

How much did he really owe the Aktaş family? There were also all those old land and property disputes to consider. He waited a long time before raising the subject with Fatma. But he did keep thinking about it, amazed that his daughter was already old enough to get married, and that Korkut and Süleyman had thought it appropriate to make this proposal. His father and his uncle had married two sisters; the next generation's cousins had done the same and married two sisters, too. If the third generation all started marrying each other now, their children were bound to be born cross-eyed, stammering idiots.

The bigger question, though, was the prospect of imminent loneliness. During those summer evenings, Mevlut would watch TV with his daughters for hours and then go out for long walks after they went to sleep. The shadows leaves cast in the light of the streetlamps, the interminable walls, the neon lights in shopwindows, and the words in billboard advertisements would all speak to him.

He was watching TV with Fatma one evening while Fevziye was at the grocery store when their conversation somehow made its way to the house in Duttepe. "Why have you stopped visiting your aunts?" asked Mevlut.

"We see them both often enough," said Fatma. "But we don't go to Duttepe much anymore. Only when Bozkurt and Turan aren't around. I can't stand them."

"What did they say to you?"

"Oh, childish things . . . Brainless Bozkurt!"

"I heard he's very upset about your argument. He's stopped eating, and he says—"

"Dad, he's nuts," said Fatma, judiciously interrupting her father so that he would drop the subject.

Mevlut saw the anger in his daughter's eyes. "Then you shouldn't bother going to Duttepe at all," he said, gladly taking his daughter's side.

They never mentioned it again. Mevlut didn't know how to deliver the news of this formal rejection without hurting anyone's feelings, so he didn't call Süleyman. But one sweltering evening in the middle of August, Süleyman came by the clubhouse while Mevlut was busy serving some factory-made ice cream he'd just bought from the grocery store to a threesome from the village of İmrenler who were trying to organize a Bosphorus cruise.

"Fatma isn't interested, she says no," Mevlut told Süleyman as soon as they were alone. "Anyway, she wants to continue her studies; I can't pull her out of school, can I? She's doing a lot better than Bozkurt ever did," he added, seized by the urge to rub it in a little.

"I told you he's going to do his military service, didn't I . . . ," said Süleyman. "Well, never mind . . . Though you could have said something. If I hadn't come by and asked, you wouldn't even have bothered to give us an answer."

"I thought I'd wait in case Fatma changed her mind."

Mevlut could see that Süleyman wasn't angry about the rejection; in fact, it seemed to make sense to him. But Süleyman was worried about what Korkut would say. Mevlut worried about it, too, for a time, but he didn't want Fatma to get married until she had graduated from college. Now, father and daughter had at least another five or six blissful years of companionship ahead of them. Whenever he had a conversation with Fatma, Mevlut always felt reassured in the knowledge that he was talking to someone he could trust to be intelligent, just as he had always trusted Rayiha.

He woke up sometime after midnight five days later to find the bed, the room, and the whole world shaking. The ground was making terrifying noises, and he could hear glasses and ashtrays shattering to pieces, the jangle of the neighbor's windows breaking, and the sound of screaming all around. His daughters leaped into his bed and huddled up with their father. The earthquake lasted much longer than Mevlut had expected. When it stopped, the power was out, and Fevziye was crying.

"Take some clothes and let's go outside," said Mevlut.

The whole world had woken up and gone out into the gloomy streets. All of Tarlabaşı seemed to be talking at once out there in the dark. The drunks were complaining, many people were crying, and some particularly angry people were shouting their displeasure. Mevlut and his girls had managed to put on some clothes, but other families had rushed out of their homes in nothing but their underwear and nightshirts, some wearing slippers, others barefoot. These people kept trying to go back inside for proper clothes, to fetch some money, and lock the door, only to run back out screaming as another aftershock hit.

The huge, raucous crowd amassing on the pavements and in the streets showed Mevlut and his daughters just how many people could squeeze into one of those small apartments in Tarlabaşı's two- and three-story blocks. Intoxicated by the shock, they walked around the neighborhood for an hour among grandfathers in pajamas, old ladies in long skirts, and children in briefs, bathing shorts, and slippers. They realized toward dawn that the aftershocks, which were already growing weaker and less frequent, were not going to destroy their building, so they went home and back to sleep. A week later, TV channels and tabloids were telling about another earthquake that was about to raze the entire city to the ground, and many people chose to spend the night in Taksim Square, out on the streets, and in the parks. Mevlut and his daughters went out to gape at these frightened thrill-seekers, but when it got late, they went home and slept peacefully through the night.

Süleyman. When the earthquake hit, we were at home in our new seventh-floor apartment in Şişli. Everything shook for a long time. The kitchen cupboard came right off the wall. I grabbed Melahat and the kids and took the stairs with only matches to guide us in the dark, and we walked through a sea of people for an hour all the way to our house in Duttepe, carrying the children in our arms.

Korkut. The house stretched and swayed like a spring. In the darkness after the quake, Bozkurt went back inside to pick up everyone's bedding and mattresses. We were just settling down in the garden, making our beds wherever we could when . . . Süleyman arrived with his wife and kids. "Your building in Şişli is brand-new and made of concrete; it must be a lot more solid than our thirty-year-old hovel. Why did you come here?" I asked. "I don't know," said Süleyman. In the morning, we saw that our house was all twisted up, with the third and fourth floors curving down toward the street like one of those old wooden houses with bay windows.

Vediha. I was serving dinner two nights later when the table started shaking and the kids yelled, "Earthquake!" I managed to fling myself out of the house and into the garden, almost taking a spill down the stairs in the process. But then I realized that there hadn't been another earthquake; it was just Bozkurt and Turan shaking the table to play a trick on me. They were watching me from the window and laughing. I had to laugh, too. I went back upstairs. "Now listen to me, you try that again and I'll give you a good slap, just like your father does, I don't care how old you are," I said. Three days later, when Bozkurt played the same prank, I fell for it again; but then I gave him the smack I'd promised. Now he won't speak to his mother anymore. My son is suffering from unrequited love, and soon he's going to go off to do his military service; I worry about him.

Samiha. When Süleyman turned up on the night of the earthquake with his wife and kids in tow, I realized just how much I hated him. I went upstairs to my room on the now-crooked third floor and didn't come down again until he and his unruly brood had gone back home. They spent two nights in the garden making a constant racket before finally returning to Şişli. They came back again a few times in September—"There's going to be another earthquake tonight!"—to sleep in the garden, and on those days I didn't even bother to come down.

The latest thing Süleyman had done to make me furious was letting Korkut talk him into asking for Fatma's hand for Bozkurt. They didn't tell me anything, figuring I'd try to stop them. Stupidity is no excuse for evil. I realized they must have done something foolish when

I noticed that Fatma and Fevziye only came to Duttepe when Bozkurt wasn't there. Vediha told me everything eventually. Of course I was proud of Fatma for saying no. I would drop the girls off at cram school every Saturday and Sunday and then take them out to the movies with Vediha in the evening.

That winter, I did everything I could to ensure Fatma did well on her university entrance exams. Vediha couldn't help but resent Fatma for having rejected her son just as he was about to leave to join the army; the more she tried to mask her feelings, the more obvious they became. So I started meeting with the girls in pudding shops, bakeries, and the McDonald's. I would take them to shopping malls: we would walk around and look in all the shops without buying anything, just staring at the windows in silence and walking under the bright lights feeling that something new was about to happen in our lives, and when we got tired, we would say, "Let's do one more floor and then go downstairs for some kebab."

Fatma and Fevziye spent New Year's Eve 2000 watching TV and waiting for their father to come back from selling boza. Mevlut came home at eleven; he watched TV with them; they ate roast chicken and potatoes. They usually never spoke to me about their father, but Fatma did tell me about that night.

Fatma took her university entrance exams at the beginning of June. I waited for her outside the door. Everyone's mothers, fathers, and brothers sat on a long, low wall across from the columns that flanked the entrance to this old building. I gazed toward Dolmabahçe Palace and smoked a cigarette. When she came out of the exam, Fatma looked just as tired as everyone else, but she seemed more optimistic, too.

Mevlut felt proud when his daughter graduated from high school without needing to take a single makeup exam and then was accepted into college to study hospitality management. Some fathers would put their children's high-school graduation pictures up on the clubhouse bulletin board. Mevlut fantasized about doing the same. But of course no father would ever display the graduation photos of an all-girls' school. Still, news of Mevlut's daughter's academic success soon spread among the former yogurt sellers and the Beyşehir people involved with the migrants' association. Süleyman dropped in especially to congratulate Mevlut; he spoke about how a man's greatest asset in this city was a child with an education.

On her first day of classes, toward the end of September, Mevlut took his daughter all the way to the front door of the university. This was the first public hotel management school in Istanbul: they concentrated as much on the management and economics of the hospitality industry as they did on the practicalities of serving guests. The school, a division of Istanbul University, was in Laleli, in a converted inn. Mevlut daydreamed about selling boza in these beautiful old neighborhoods. Once, on his way back from the Holy Guide's place, he walked for an hour all the way from Çarşamba to his daughter's school. Those parts of the city were still quiet at night.

In January 2001, four months after starting classes, Fatma told her father about a boy she was seeing. He was in the same program, but he was two years older. His intentions were serious. He was from Izmir. (Mevlut felt his heart stop for a moment.) They both wanted the same thing in life: to get a university degree and start working in the tourism industry.

Mevlut couldn't believe how quickly his daughter had reached this stage of her life. Then again, Fatma would still get married later than any other girl in the family. "You're too late now, at your age your mother and your aunts already had two children each!" said Mevlut, suffering even as he teased her.

"That's why I'm going to get married straightaway," said Fatma. In her quick rejoinder, Mevlut saw all her determination to get out of the house as soon as possible.

In February, they came from Izmir to Istanbul to ask for Fatma's hand. Mevlut found a night when the clubhouse was free and booked it for the engagement party, borrowing some extra chairs from the coffeehouse across the road. Apart from Korkut and his sons, all their acquaintances from Duttepe came to the party. Mevlut knew that none of these people, including Samiha, would go to the actual wedding, which was to take place in Izmir at the beginning of the summer. The engagement party was the first time he saw Samiha within the confines of the clubhouse: unlike all the other women there, her headscarf and overcoat weren't faded or tan colored; they were new, dark blue, and tied loose. Mevlut wondered whether perhaps she wanted not to wear a headscarf anymore. Fatma didn't always wear hers, and she had to take it off every time she went to the university. Mevlut couldn't tell if his daughter was pleased about this or not. It was mostly between Fatma and her university friends.

None of the people who'd come from Izmir wore headscarves. In the days leading up to the engagement, Mevlut saw just how much his daughter longed to become part of this family. At home, Fatma would hug him and kiss him and weep over how she was about to leave the house in which she'd spent her childhood, but a few minutes later, Mevlut would catch her deep in daydreams about all the little pleasures of her new life with her husband. That was how Mevlut discovered that his daughter and his future son-in-law had applied to transfer to the hospitality management faculty of the university in Izmir. Two months later, they found out that their application had been accepted. Thus, in the space of just three months, it was decided that after they got married at the beginning of summer, Fatma and Burhan (for that was the unappealing name of Mevlut's future son-in-law, who was stiff as a poker and always wore a perfectly blank expression) would move into an apartment in Izmir belonging to the groom's family and become residents of that city.

Of Fatma's family in Istanbul, only Mevlut and Fevziye went down to Izmir for the wedding. Mevlut liked Izmir; it was like a smaller, warmer version of Istanbul, with palm trees. All the poorer neighborhoods were right in the middle of the bay. At the wedding, he watched Fatma hold her husband close while they danced—just as in the movies—and felt embarrassed, but also somewhat moved. On the bus back to Istanbul, Mevlut and Fevziye didn't say a word to each other. The feeling of his younger daughter's head resting on his shoulder as she fell asleep during the overnight journey and the scent of her hair made Mevlut happy. In just six months, his elder daughter, the girl he'd cherished for all these years, and dreamed of keeping close to him for the rest of his life, had gone far beyond her father's reach.

12

Fevziye Runs Away

Let Them Both Kiss My Hand

On September 11, Mevlut and Fevziye spent the day watching TV footage of the planes crashing into those skyscrapers in America, and the buildings collapsing in a cloud of fire and smoke, like something out of the movies. Except for a quiet comment from Mevlut—"The Americans will want their revenge now!"—they never mentioned these events again.

They had become good friends after Fatma got married and left. Fevziye loved talking, telling jokes, and imitating other people, and she liked to make her father laugh by inventing ridiculous stories. She'd inherited her mother's talent for spotting the amusingly absurd side to everything. She could parrot the sound of their neighbor whistling through his front teeth as he spoke, or a door creaking open, or her father huffing and puffing as he clambered up the stairs, and when she slept at night, she curled up in an S shape, just as her mother used to do.

When he got home from the clubhouse one evening five days after the collapse of the Twin Towers, Mevlut found the TV switched off, no food on the dining table, and no Fevziye either. At first, it didn't occur to him that his daughter might have run away, so he just fumed at the thought that his seventeen-year-old was still out after dark, doing nothing useful. Fevziye had failed both mathematics and English in her penultimate year of high school; all summer, Mevlut hadn't once seen her sit down and study. As he looked out the window at the dark street, waiting for his daughter to come home, his anger slowly turned into worry.

He'd noticed with a pang that Fevziye's handbag and many of her clothes and other possessions weren't in their usual places. He was debating with himself whether to go over to Duttepe to inquire with the Aktaş family when the doorbell rang, giving him a brief flash of hope that it might be Fevziye.

But it was Süleyman. He told Mevlut straightaway that Fevziye had run away with someone, that the boy was "suitable" and from a good family, and that his father owned three taxis, which he rented out. The boy's father had called in the afternoon, and Süleyman had gone to see them. Perhaps they would have called Mevlut first if he'd had a telephone at home. In any case, Fevziye was fine.

"If she was fine, then why did she run away?" said Mevlut. "To embarrass her father and disgrace herself?"

"Why did you run away with Rayiha?" said Süleyman. "Crooked-Necked Abdurrahman would have said yes if you'd just asked for her."

On hearing these words, Mevlut began to suspect that Fevziye's escape might have been a form of emulation. After all, his daughter had done exactly what her mother and father had done. "Crooked-Necked Abdurrahman would have never let me marry his daughter," he said, thinking back proudly to the night he ran away with Rayiha. "I will not accept this taxi driver who's run away with my girl. Fevziye had promised me she'd finish high school and go to college."

"She missed both of her makeup exams," said Süleyman. "She has failed the year. She was probably too scared to tell you. But Vediha knows all about how you've always told the poor girl you'd never forgive her if she doesn't finish high school, and how you've been pushing her to go to college like her sister."

When he realized that what he'd thought were private matters between him and his daughter had clearly been discussed not just in the Aktaş family, but among complete strangers, too—a taxi driver and his family—and that he'd gained a reputation for being an irascible and dictatorial father, Mevlut became indignant.

"Fevziye is no daughter of mine," he sniffed, but he regretted the words immediately. Süleyman hadn't even left yet, and already Mevlut started to be overcome by the same sense of helplessness any father whose daughter has eloped is bound to feel: If he didn't forgive his daughter straightaway and pretend to like and approve of the groom (a driver? he could never have imagined it!), the news that his daughter had run off to live with a man she wasn't married to would quickly spread, and Mevlut's honor would be stained. But if he was too quick to forgive the irresponsible bastard who'd taken his daughter, then everyone would say that Mevlut himself had been in on it or that he'd taken a significant sum of money to allow his daughter to get married to the man. He knew that unless he wanted to spend the rest of his life lonely and cantankerous—much as his own father had done—he had no choice but to take the second option without delay.

"Süleyman, I can't live without my daughters. I will forgive Fevziye. But first let her come here with this man she means to marry. Let them both kiss my hand and show their respect. I may have run away with Rayiha, too, but at least afterward I went all the way to the village to Crooked-Necked Abdurrahman's doorstep to pay my respects."

"I'm sure your taxi driver son-in-law will have as much respect for you as you did for Crooked Neck," Süleyman said with a smirk.

Mevlut didn't realize that Süleyman was making fun of him. He was confused, afraid of loneliness, and in need of being comforted. "There used to be such a thing as respect, once upon a time!" he heard himself saying, and Süleyman laughed at this, too.

Mevlut's second son-in-law was called Erhan. He looked completely ordinary (short with a narrow forehead), and Mevlut couldn't understand what his beautiful flower of a daughter—the same girl he'd cherished for so many years, and for whom he'd always had such high hopes—could possibly have seen in him. He must be very sly and very clever, thought Mevlut, feeling disappointed with his daughter for failing to see through all that.

He did, however, like the way Erhan bowed all the way down to the floor and kissed his hand apologetically.

"Fevziye must finish high school, she must not drop out of school," said Mevlut. "Otherwise I will never forgive you."

"That's what we also think," said Erhan. But as they talked, it became clear that it would be impossible for Fevziye to keep going to school and hide the fact that she was married.

Mevlut knew, though, that the real cause of his anxiety wasn't the thought of his daughter not finishing high school or going to college but that he would soon be completely alone in the house and more generally in the world. His soul's real anguish wasn't his having failed to give his daughter a proper education but the sense that he was being abandoned.

In a private moment, Mevlut began to remonstrate with his daughter. "Why did you run away? Would I have said no if they'd come here and asked for your hand like civilized people?"

Mevlut could tell from the way Fevziye averted her eyes that she was thinking, Yes, of course you would have said no!

"We were so happy here, father and daughter," said Mevlut. "Now I've got no one left."

Fevziye hugged him; Mevlut struggled to hold back tears. Now, there would be no one waiting for him when he came home in the evenings from selling boza. When he had the dream of running through a dark cypress forest with dogs chasing him, and woke up in a sweat in the middle of the night, the sound of his daughters breathing in their sleep would no longer be there to comfort him.

His fear of loneliness led Mevlut to drive a hard bargain. In a moment of shared enthusiasm, he made his future son-in-law swear upon his honor that Fevziye would graduate from not only high school but college, too. Fevziye spent that night at home with Mevlut. He was glad that she had come to her senses before the whole matter could get out of hand, though he still couldn't help but mention every now and then that she'd broken his heart by running away.

"You ran away with Mom, too!" said Fevziye.

"Your mother would have never done what you did," said Mevlut.

"Yes, she would have," said Fevziye.

His daughter's willful, decisive response pleased Mevlut, but he also saw it as further proof that she'd been trying to do as her mother had done. On religious holidays, or whenever Fatma and her dithering fool of a husband came to see them from Izmir, they would all go to Rayiha's grave. If the visit ended up feeling more melancholy than usual, Mevlut would spend the whole way back home giving them an extended and embellished account of how he had run away with Rayiha, how they'd worked everything out down to the tiniest detail, how they had first met and exchanged glances at a wedding, and how he would never forget the way their mother had looked at him that night.

The next day, Erhan the taxi driver and his father—himself a retired driver—came by to return Fevziye's suitcase. As soon as Mevlut saw the groom's father, Mr. Sadullah, who was ten years older than him, he knew that he was going to like this man a lot more than he liked his son. Mr. Sadullah was a widower, too; he'd lost his wife to a heart attack three years ago. (The better to describe those events, Mr. Sadullah had sat at the only table inside Mevlut's one-room house and reenacted the way she'd dropped her spoon halfway through a bowl of soup and died with her head resting on the table.)

Mr. Sadullah was from Düzce; his father had come to Istanbul during the Second World War and worked as an apprentice to an Armenian shoemaker on Gedikpaşa Hill, who would later make him his business partner. When the place was looted during the anti-Christian uprisings of September sixth and seventh, 1955, the Armenian owner left Istanbul, handing the shop over to Mr. Sadullah's father, who had continued to run it on his own. But his "free-spirited" and "indolent" son stood his ground against his father's insistence and his beatings, and instead of learning how to make shoes, he became "the best driver in Istanbul." Mr. Sadullah would give Mevlut a knowing wink as he explained how being a driver back then, when all the cabs and shared taxis were American models, was probably the most glamorous job in the world, and from this Mevlut understood that the short, clever young man with a head shaped like an upturned bowl, the one who'd run away with his daughter, had inherited all his taste for a good time from his father.

Mevlut went to their three-story stone-built house in Kadırga to discuss the details of the wedding ceremony; he developed a close friendship with Mr. Sadullah, which would only grow stronger after the wedding, and in his forties he finally learned how to enjoy the kinds of conversations that friends normally had over dinner and a glass of *rakı*—even though he didn't drink much himself.

Mr. Sadullah had three taxis, which he rented out to six drivers working twelve-hour shifts every day. Even more than the makes and models of his cars (two Turkish Murats, one a '96 and the other '98, and a 1958 Dodge, which Mr. Sadullah himself drove from time to time just for fun, keeping it in mint condition), he liked to talk about the ever-increasing cost of obtaining a prized taxi license in Istanbul. His son Erhan looked after one of the taxis himself and kept tabs on the other taxis, too, for his father, checking their odometers and taximeters. Mr. Sadullah would smile as he explained how his son didn't really keep a close enough eye on the drivers, who were either dishonest (skimming from what they made in a day), unlucky (getting into accidents all the time), disrespectful (coming late for their shift and being rude), or downright foolish. But seeing it wasn't worth his arguing with these people over a few pennies more, Mr. Sadullah left all that unpleasantness to his son. Mevlut inspected the attic room where Erhan and Fevziye would live after they got married, checking everything from the new cupboards to the trousseau and the double bed ("Erhan never came up here that time your daughter spent the night," Mr. Sadullah had reassured him), and confirmed that he was satisfied.

Mevlut loved it when Mr. Sadullah showed him around all the places that had formed the backdrop of his life, reminiscing and telling old anecdotes in that charming way of his that only got sweeter when you let him go on uninterrupted. Mevlut soon learned where to find the Vale School (an Ottoman-era building that was much older than the Duttepe Atatürk Boys' Secondary School) in Cankurtaran, where the boarders beat and bullied the day students like Mr. Sadullah, the shoe shop that his father had brought to ruin in ten years (in its place there was now a café like the Binbom), and the adorable teahouse across from the park. He almost couldn't believe it when he found out that there had been no park there three hundred years ago, just water in which hundreds of Ottoman galleons had moored, waiting for war. (There were pictures of these vessels on the walls inside the teahouse.) Mevlut began to feel that had he spent his own childhood and youth surrounded by these broken old fountains, derelict bathhouses, and dusty, filthy, ghost- and spider-ridden religious retreats built by bearded and beturbaned Ottoman leaders—that is, if his father hadn't come from Cennetpınar to Kültepe but had gone straight to one of these neighborhoods across the Golden Horn instead, settling in old Istanbul like so many other lucky people who'd migrated to the city from the Anatolian countryside—he would have ended up a completely different person, and so would his daughters. He even felt a kind of remorse, as if going to live in Kültepe had been his own decision. But he didn't know a single person who'd come to Istanbul from Cennetpınar in the 1960s and '70s and settled in one of these neighborhoods. As he began to notice how much wealthier Istanbul was growing, he thought that he might be able to sell more boza if he tried coming to some of the backstreets in these historic quarters of the city.

Soon, Mr. Sadullah invited Mevlut to come over for dinner again. Mevlut didn't have much time to spare between his work at the clubhouse and his evening boza rounds, and so to accommodate their burgeoning friendship, Mr. Sadullah offered to come by the clubhouse in his Dodge to pick Mevlut up and load his shoulder pole and jugs into the trunk, so that once they were done with dinner, he could drop him off wherever he wanted to sell his boza that night. The fathers-in-law grew even closer after this dinner, during which they discussed all the intricacies of the upcoming wedding celebrations.

The groom's side would of course pay for the wedding, so when he found out that the party wasn't going to take place in a wedding hall but in the basement floor of a hotel in Aksaray, Mevlut had no objections. He was, however, upset to hear that there would be alcohol served. He didn't want there to be anything about this wedding that could make the people of Duttepe, and especially the Aktaş family, uncomfortable.

Mr. Sadullah set his mind at ease: guests would bring their own bottles of *rakı* and store them in the kitchen; those who wanted a drink would have to ask the waiters personally, and the requested glasses of iced *rakı* would be prepared upstairs and brought down without any fuss. Of course their own guests—his son's taxi-driver friends, the neighborhood locals, the Kadırga football team and its board of directors—wouldn't mind if there was no *rakı* served with the meal;

but if there was, they would certainly drink some, and be happier for it. Most of them supported the secular Republican People's Party anyway.

"So do I," said Mevlut in a spirit of solidarity, but without much conviction.

The hotel in Aksaray was a new building. While excavating the foundation, the contractor had found the remains of a small Byzantine church, and since such a discovery would normally have put a stop to the building works, he'd had to pay out some hefty bribes across the municipality to make sure no one noticed the ruins, and to compensate himself for the cost, he'd dug an extra basement floor. On the night of the wedding, Mevlut counted twenty-two tables in the room, which soon filled to capacity and became submerged in layers of thick blue smoke from countless cigarettes. There were six tables for men only. That part of the wedding hall was full of the groom's friends from the neighborhood and other taxi drivers. Most of these young drivers were unmarried. But even those who had wives had quite early on left them behind with the children in the part of the hall reserved for families and gone to join their friends at the bachelors' tables, which they thought would be more fun. Mevlut could tell how much those tables must already be drinking just by the sheer number of waiters needed to ferry trays for *rakı* and ice back and forth between the kitchen and that end of the hall. But guests were openly drinking even at the mixed tables, where a few, like one particularly irascible old man, lost their patience with the sluggish waiters and decided to take matters into their own hands, going to the kitchen upstairs to pour their own drinks.

Mevlut and Fevziye had considered every single permutation of Aktaş family attendance. Bozkurt was away doing his military service and wouldn't be there to make a drunken scene. Korkut, whose son had been rejected by the bride, might find an excuse not to come or bolt, saying, "There was too much drinking, it made me uncomfortable," and so ruin the party for everyone else. But Fevziye, who kept up with all the Aktaş family news through her aunt Samiha, said that the outlook in Duttepe was not quite so negative. In fact the real danger wasn't from Bozkurt or Korkut but Samiha herself, who was furious at Korkut and Süleyman.

Thank God Crooked-Necked Abdurrahman had come up from

the village, as had Fatma and her stiff-as-a-poker husband from Izmir. Fevziye had arranged for them all to share a taxi with Samiha. Mevlut spent the early part of the celebration worrying about why that taxi was taking so long, when all the other guests from Duttepe had already arrived and brought their gifts. All but one of the five big tables set aside for the bride's family were already full (their neighbor Reyhan and her husband were both looking very smart). Mevlut went upstairs to the kitchen to have a glass of *rakı* where no one would see him and lingered around the hotel entrance, waiting on tenterhooks for their arrival.

When he returned to the wedding hall, he saw that the fifth table was now completely full. When had they come in? He sat back down next to Mr. Sadullah at the groom's table and continued to stare at the Aktaş family. Süleyman had brought both his sons, aged three and five; Melahat was very elegantly dressed; in his suit and tie, Crooked-Necked Abdurrahman looked so neat and courteous he might have been mistaken for a retired government officer. Every time his eyes caught the red stain in the middle of the table, Mevlut shivered and looked away.

Samiha. My darling Fevziye, in her beautiful wedding gown, sat next to her husband in the middle of the room, and I couldn't take my eyes off her, feeling her joy and excitement in my own heart. How wonderful it is to be young and happy. I was also very pleased to hear from my dear Fatma, seated beside me, that she was happy with her own husband in Izmir, that his family was supporting them, that they were both doing very well at the hotel school, that they'd spent the summer holidays apprenticing at a hotel on Kuşadası, and that their English was improving; it was great to see them both smiling all the time. When my darling Rayiha passed away, I cried for days, not just because I'd lost my beloved sister but also because these two sweet little girls had been orphaned at such a young age. I began to keep an eye on what they ate, what they wore, who their friends were in the neighborhood, and everything else, just as if they'd been my own daughters; I became a mother to these unlucky girls, though from a distance. Cowardly

Mevlut didn't want me in his house because he was scared there might be gossip and that Ferhat would misunderstand; that hurt my feelings and dampened my enthusiasm, but I never gave up. When I turned away from Fevziye to Fatma again, she said, "You look so regal in that purple dress, Auntie!" and I thought I might start to cry. I stood up and walked in the exact opposite direction from Mevlut's table, went upstairs to the kitchen door, and after telling one of the waiters "My father's still waiting for his drink," I was immediately given a glass of *rakı* on the rocks. I retreated to the window and quickly gulped it down before hurrying back to my place at the table, between my father and Fatma.

Abdurrahman Efendi. Vediha came over to our table, told her father-in-law Hasan the grocer—who hadn't said a word all night—"You must be getting bored, Father," and took him by the arm over to his sons' table. Let me be clear: the thing that hurts me most is that even when her actual father is right there, my darling Vediha calls this dull and distant man her "dear father" just because she's married to his spiteful son. I went to sit at the table of the man who was in charge of the festivities and posed a riddle to everyone: "Do you know what Mr. Sadullah, Mr. Mevlut, and I all have in common?" They began to say that it was probably yogurt or our youth or our love of *rakı* . . . until I said, "Each of our wives died young and left us all alone in this world," and burst into tears.

Samiha. Vediha and Süleyman stood on either side of my father and walked him back to our table, but all Mevlut did was sit and watch. Couldn't he even bring himself to take his late wife's father by the arm and maybe whisper a few words of comfort in his ear? But if he were to come anywhere near my table, people might gossip; they might remember that he'd actually written those letters to me and start talking about it again . . . I bet that's what he's afraid of. Oh, Mevlut, you coward. He keeps looking at me, but then pretending he didn't. But I look right back at him, just the way I did at Korkut's wedding twenty-three years ago, just, as he wrote in his letters, as if I wanted to take him prisoner with my ensorcelled eyes. I looked at him so I could cut across his path like a bandit and steal his heart away, so that he would be struck by the force of my gaze. I looked at him so that he could see his reflection in the mirror of my heart.

"My darling Samiha, you're wasting your time staring over there," said my father, by then completely drunk. "A man who writes letters to one girl but then marries her sister is no good for anyone."

"I'm not looking that way," I said, though I stubbornly kept looking anyway and saw that, every now and then, Mevlut looked at me, too, right until the very end of the evening.

13

Mevlut Alone

You Two Are Made for Each Other

LEFT ALONE in the house where he'd spent years living elbow to elbow with his wife and daughters, Mevlut began to feel depleted, almost as if he'd fallen ill, so that even getting out of bed in the mornings seemed like a chore. In the past, even on his darkest days, he'd always been able to count on his indomitable optimism—which some thought of as "innocence"—and on his knack for finding the easiest and least distressing way through any situation. He therefore saw his current malaise as a sign of a bigger problem, and even though he was only forty-five, he began to feel afraid of death.

When he was in the clubhouse or the neighborhood coffeehouse in the morning, chatting to one or two people he knew, he was able to keep his fear of loneliness at bay. (Ever since he'd been left on his own, he had grown even kinder and more tolerant toward anyone he met.) But when he walked in the street at night, he was scared.

Now that Rayiha had died and his daughters were both married, the streets of Istanbul seemed longer than ever before, like bottomless black wells. He might find himself in some remote neighborhood late at night, ringing his bell and crying "Boza" as he made his way, when the sudden realization that he had never before been on this street or in this neighborhood induced a strange and terrifying memory or that feeling that he used to have as a child or a young man whenever he went somewhere he wasn't meant to go (and when the dogs barked): the feeling that he would be caught and punished, which he took to mean that he was, in truth, a bad person. Some nights, the city seemed transformed into a more mysterious, menacing place, and Mevlut couldn't make out whether he felt this way because there was no one waiting for him at home or because these new streets had become imbued with signs and symbols he didn't recognize: his fears were exacerbated by the silence of the new concrete walls, the insistent presence of a multitude of strange and ever-changing posters, and the way a street could suddenly twist on and on just as he thought it might be ending, almost as if to mock him. When he walked down a quiet street where no curtain twitched and no window opened, he would sometimes feel—though he knew, rationally, that it wasn't true—as if he'd been there before, in a time as old as fables, and as he reveled in the sensation of meeting the present moment as if it were a memory, he would shout "Boo-zaa" and feel that he was really calling out to his own past. Sometimes his fear of dogs would return, reignited by his own imagination or by the barking of an actual dog standing beside the wall of a mosque, and suddenly it would hit him that he was completely alone in the world. (It was comforting, in these moments, to think of Samiha and her purple dress.) Or he might see on an empty street one night a pair of tall, thin men walk past, oblivious to his presence, and get the feeling that the words he'd just heard them say (about locks and keys and responsibilities) were clues to some message meant for him—only to find that the two short, fat men in black suits walking down a narrow street of a completely different neighborhood two nights later were saying exactly the same words.

It was as if the city's old, mossy walls, its ancient fountains covered in beautiful script, and its wooden homes, twisting and rotting to the point of leaning on one another for support, had all been burned down and wrecked into nothingness, and the new streets, concrete houses, neon-lit shops, and apartment blocks taking their place had been built to seem even older, more intimidating and incomprehensible, than any place before. The city was no longer an enormous, familiar home but a faithless space in which anyone who got the chance added more concrete, more streets, courtyards, walls, pavements, and shops.

With the city growing inexorably out of his reach, and no one to come home to at the other end of each dark road, Mevlut began to feel the need for God more than ever before. He started performing midday prayers before he went to work at the clubhouse—not just on Fridays but whenever he felt the need to do so—either at the Şişli Mosque or at the Duttepe Mosque if he took a longer route or at any other mosque he happened to come across. He delighted in the silence that reigned in these places, the way the city's constant humming filtered softly inside like the light that fell in embroidered patterns along the bottom edge of the dome, and the chance to spend half an hour in communion with old men who'd cut their ties with the world or men like him who simply had nobody left; it all made him feel as if he'd found a cure for his loneliness. At night, these emotions led him to places where he would never have set foot back when he was still a happy man, like deserted mosque courtyards or cemeteries tucked away deep in the heart of a neighborhood, where he could sit on the edge of a gravestone and smoke a cigarette. He would read dedications to people who had come and gone long ago and look reverently at ancient tombstones covered in Arabic script and surmounted with turbans carved in stone. He'd started whispering the name of God to himself more often, and occasionally he would ask him for deliverance from a lifetime of loneliness.

Sometimes he thought of the other men he knew who'd also lost their wives and found themselves alone at the age of forty-five but then got married again with the help of family and friends. At the migrants' association, Mevlut had met Vahap, a man from the village of İmrenler who ran a plumbing supply shop in Şişli. When his wife and only son died in a bus accident on their way to a wedding in the village, Vahap's relatives immediately arranged for him to marry someone else from there. When his wife died giving birth to their first child, Hamdi from Gümüşdere himself almost died of sadness, but his uncle and the rest of his family found him a new wife, a gregarious, carefree woman who'd slowly brought him back to life.

But no one offered to help Mevlut in this way nor even spoke in passing of any suitable women they might know who'd been widowed at a young age (it was also important that the woman in question not already have children of her own). The reason was that Mevlut's entire family already thought that the right match for Mevlut was Samiha. "Like you, she's alone, too," Korkut had told him once. Or, perhaps, it was Mevlut himself—as he sometimes noticed—who wanted to believe that this was what everyone thought. He, too, accepted that Samiha was probably the right one for him and often got lost daydreaming about Fevziye's wedding, when Samiha in that purple dress had stared at him from the other side of the room, though for a while he'd forbidden himself from even thinking about the possibility of marrying again: Mevlut felt that wishing he could be closer to Samiha, or just trying to catch her eye as he had done at his daughter's wedding—let alone marrying her—would be enormously disrespectful to Rayiha's memory. Sometimes he sensed that other people thought the same, and maybe that was why they always found it so difficult and awkward to talk to him about Samiha.

For a time, he thought that the best thing he could do was to get Samiha out of his head (I don't think about her that often anyway, he told himself) and muse about some other woman instead. Korkut and the other founders and directors of the migrants' association had banned *rummikub* and card games from the clubhouse in the hope of sparing theirs the same fate as most other migrants' associations, which always eventually turned into ordinary coffeehouses, places where women didn't feel comfortable coming in with their husbands. One way to attract more women and families was to organize dumpling nights. The women would get together at one another's houses to prepare the dumplings and come to the event with their husbands, brothers, and children. On some of these evenings, Mevlut would be especially busy in the tea stall. A widow from Erenler came to one of these dumpling nights with her sister and her sister's husband; she was tall, with good posture, and seemed healthy. Mevlut had looked her over a few times from the tea stall. Another one who'd caught his eye was the daughter of a family from İmrenler, a girl in her thirties who'd left her husband in Germany and returned to Istanbul: her thick black hair seemed set to burst out from underneath her headscarf. While taking her cup of tea, she'd looked straight at Mevlut with her coal-black eyes. Had she learned in Germany how to stare like that? All these women seemed so much more comfortable and direct in the way they took in Mevlut's handsome, boyish face than Samiha had been all those years ago at Korkut's wedding or more recently at Fevziye's: one merry widow, a cheerful, chubby lady from Gümüşdere, had chatted playfully with him all through one of those dumpling nights and also while he'd served her tea at a picnic. Mevlut had admired her self-reliance and the way she'd just stood on the side smiling while the other guests danced at the end of the picnic.

Even though no alcohol was consumed, not even secretly, there seemed to be a state of collective intoxication by the end of these dumpling dinners and picnics, with men and women dancing together to their favorite Beyşehir folk songs. According to Süleyman, this was why Korkut didn't let Vediha attend these events. But of course if she couldn't come, neither could her inseparable companion in Duttepe, Samiha.

Certain issues had slowly begun to divide the migrants' association into supporters of the secular Republican People's Party on the one hand and the more conservative members on the other. These issues included how much women and families should be encouraged to participate in association activities; which folksinger to book for events; what to do about unemployed men playing cards in the clubhouse; whether or not to organize evening Koran readings; and the merits of offering scholarships to bright village kids admitted to college. This political back-and-forth would sometimes continue even after the adjournment of a club meeting, the end of a football match, or a day trip, and the men who relished these debates would end up going for a few drinks at a bar near the clubhouse. One night, Süleyman emerged from a group leaving the clubhouse, and putting his arm around Mevlut's shoulders, he said, "Let's go with them."

Mevlut realized that the bar they went to was the same place where Süleyman had gone for a drink with Crooked-Necked Abdurrahman many years ago while deep in the throes of unrequited passion. They ate white cheese, melon, and panfried liver, drank *rakı,* and began to discuss the association's activities as well as what all their acquaintances from the village were up to. (So-and-so had shut himself away in the house; another thought of nothing but gambling; and a third was running himself ragged going from hospital to hospital trying to care for his disabled son.)

The conversation soon moved on to politics. These *rakı* lovers might start accusing Mevlut of secretly being an Islamist sympathizer, but in truth they were equally likely to throw in some snide accusation: "We haven't seen you at Friday prayers in a long time." Mevlut would not engage with any of it. When Süleyman gleefully announced that "members of parliament and candidates standing for election will be visiting the clubhouse," Mevlut was excited but, unlike the others, didn't ask who these prospective visitors were or what party they belonged to. Somehow the discussion turned to whether all these Islamists were going to take over the country soon or whether there was nothing to worry about. There were even a few who claimed that the army would arrange a coup and bring this government down. It was all just like those debates that were constantly shown on TV.

By the end of the meal, Mevlut's mind had already begun to drift. Süleyman, who'd been sitting across from him, moved to the empty chair at Mevlut's side and started telling him about his sons, talking so softly that no one around them could hear. His elder son Hasan, who was six years old, had just begun primary school. His other son, Kâzım, was four, and since his brother had already taught him how to read at home, he was now reading the Lucky Luke comics. Süleyman's secretive manner, excluding everyone else at the table, made Mevlut uncomfortable. He may have been whispering only in the interest of shielding his family bliss from jealous attention, but there were still many who hadn't yet made their minds up about the truth surrounding Ferhat's death. It may have been five years ago already, but Mevlut knew that—even in his own heart—the matter still hadn't been laid to rest. If they saw the two cousins whispering like this, people might think Mevlut had conspired with Süleyman.

"There's something important I need to talk to you about. But you're not allowed to interrupt me," said Süleyman.

"All right."

"I've seen loads of women lose their husbands early on to street fights or car accidents and go on to marry again so they wouldn't be alone. If these women have no children, and if they're still young and attractive, they'll have plenty of suitors, too. Now there's this woman I know—I think you know her name—who's just like that: beautiful and smart and young. She knows how to stand up for herself, too, and she has real character. There's already someone she's been thinking about, and she only has eyes for him."

Mevlut liked the idea that Samiha was waiting for him—at least in Süleyman's version of the story. There was no one else left at the dinner table now. Mevlut ordered another glass of *rakı*.

"The man this woman has in mind is a young widower, too, having lost his wife to an unfortunate accident," Süleyman continued. "He is honest, trustworthy, sweet-faced, and even tempered." Mevlut was enjoying this praise. "He's got two daughters from his first marriage, but he's all alone now because they've both married and left the nest."

Mevlut wasn't sure when he was supposed to interrupt and say, I get it, you're talking about me and Samiha!, so Süleyman kept taking advantage of his indecision. "In fact, the man had once been in love with the woman. He'd written love letters to her for years . . ."

"So why didn't they get married?" asked Mevlut.

"It doesn't matter now . . . There was a misunderstanding. But now, twenty years later, they would make a great match."

"Then why aren't they getting married *now*?" said Mevlut, refusing to budge.

"That's exactly what everyone else has been wondering . . . They've known each other for years now; he wrote the girl all those love letters . . ."

"I'll tell you what really happened, and then you'll know why they're not getting married," said Mevlut. "The man didn't write all those letters to the woman you're talking about but to her elder sister. He ran away with her, they got married, and they were happy."

"Come on, Mevlut, do you have to be that way?"

"What way?"

"Our whole family and all of Duttepe, too, know by now that you meant those letters for Samiha, not Rayiha."

"Pah!" said Mevlut, almost as if he meant to spit. "You've been spreading those lies for years trying to make trouble between me and Ferhat, and you made Rayiha unhappy. She believed you, the poor thing . . ."

"So what's the truth, then?"

"The truth is . . ." For a moment, Mevlut was back in 1978, at Korkut's wedding. "The truth is: I saw this girl at the wedding. I fell in love with her eyes. I wrote her letters for three years. Every time I wrote to her, I put her name right at the top of the letter."

"Yes, you saw the girl with the beautiful eyes . . . But back then you didn't even know her name," said Süleyman, getting irritated. "So I gave you the wrong name."

"But you're my cousin, you're my friend . . . Why would you do such a horrible thing to me?"

"I never thought of it as a horrible thing. When we were young, didn't we play pranks on each other all the time?"

"So it was just a prank, then . . ."

"No," said Süleyman. "I'll be honest: I also believed that Rayiha was a better match for you, and that she would make you happier."

"They won't let anyone marry the third daughter until the second one's settled," said Mevlut. "You wanted Samiha yourself."

"Fine, I tricked you," said Süleyman. "I'm sorry. But it's been twenty years now, and I'm trying to make amends, my dear Mevlut."

"Why would I believe you, though?"

"Come on," said Süleyman, sounding like a man wronged. "No joke this time, and definitely no lies."

"But why would I trust you?"

"Why? Because when you wanted me to get you that girl, you tried to give me that piece of paper the neighborhood councilman issued for your house in Kültepe, the one that's worth as much as a title deed, and I refused to take it. Remember?"

"I remember," said Mevlut.

"Maybe you blame me . . . for what happened to Ferhat." He couldn't bring himself to say the word "dead." "But you're wrong . . . I was angry at Ferhat, very angry . . . But that was it. To wish someone the worst, to feel that in your heart, is one thing; but to actually kill him or have him killed is another."

"Which is the bigger crime, do you think?" asked Mevlut. "On doomsday, will the Lord judge us for our intentions or for our actions?"

"Both," said Süleyman, without really thinking about it. But when he saw the serious look on Mevlut's face, he added: "I may have had bad thoughts, but in practice, I've never done anything bad in my life. There are many people who start off meaning well and end up doing evil. But I hope you can see that I've come to you tonight with the best of intentions. I'm happy with Melahat. I want you to be happy with Samiha. When you're happy, you want other people to be happy, too. And there's another side to it. You two are made for each other. Anyone looking at your situation with Samiha from outside would say, 'Someone should really get those two together!' Think about it, you know two people who would be happy forever. Not helping them get together would be a sin. I'm trying to do a good deed here."

"I wrote those letters to Rayiha," said Mevlut resolutely.

"Whatever you say," said Süleyman.

14

New Quarters, Old Faces

Is It the Same as This?

After Fevziye's wedding, Mr. Sadullah had begun picking Mevlut up in his Dodge once a week and taking him to one of those remote and fast-developing new neighborhoods of Istanbul, which they both wanted to explore. Once there, Mevlut would get his shoulder pole and jugs from the trunk, taking his boza around streets where he'd never sold anything before, while Mr. Sadullah wandered the neighborhood and idly smoked cigarettes in some coffeehouse until Mevlut had finished. Sometimes he would collect Mevlut at his house in Tarlabaşı or the clubhouse in Mecidiyeköy and take him over to his place in Kadırga so that they all might have dinner together and enjoy Fevziye's cooking. (Mevlut had even started having the occasional glass of *rakı* now.) When the evening news drew to a close, Mevlut would venture with his boza out into old Istanbul, around Kadırga, Sultanahmet, Kumkapı, and Aksaray. Mr. Sadullah didn't take Mevlut just to the neighborhoods beyond the old city walls but to the historic quarters, too—like Edirnekapı, Balat, Fatih, and Karagümrük—and on three of these occasions Mevlut dropped by the spiritual retreat in Çarşamba to distribute some free boza, though as soon as he realized that he wouldn't have the chance to get any closer to the Holy Guide, he hurried back out to find Mr. Sadullah in the nearby coffeehouse, never telling him about the white-haired man and his school.

Mr. Sadullah was a seasoned *rakı* lover who had a full table of drinking snacks laid for him at least two or three times a week; he had nothing against sacred old things or against religion, but if Mevlut were to tell him that he went to a religious retreat and regularly met with a holy man, Mr. Sadullah might suspect him of Islamist sympathies and start to feel uncomfortable—or, worse, afraid. Mevlut worried Mr. Sadullah's feelings might also be hurt—just as he feared Ferhat's could have been—to see that despite their blossoming friendship, and the growing ease with which they could discuss any topic imaginable, Mevlut still felt the need to commune with this old man to open up about his inner life and his spiritual misgivings.

Mevlut could see that his friendship with Mr. Sadullah was similar to his youthful bond with Ferhat. He liked telling Mr. Sadullah about the things that happened to him in the clubhouse, what he heard on the news, and what he was watching on TV. When Mr. Sadullah brought his friend home for dinner, and afterward shuttled him in the Dodge to faraway neighborhoods, Mevlut knew that he did it out of nothing but friendship, curiosity, and a wish to be helpful.

The neighborhoods beyond the old city walls had been described as being "outside the city" when Mevlut had first come to Istanbul, and now that thirty-three years had passed, they all looked alike: they were thick with tall, ugly apartment buildings six to eight stories high, with oversize windows, as well as crooked side streets, construction sites, billboards bigger than any you saw in the city center, coffeehouses full of men watching television, and metal dumpsters built like train carriages that kept hungry strays from the trash, until every corner of the city looked identical, with overhead pedestrian crossings bound by metal railings, barren squares and cemeteries, and main thoroughfares—uniformly the same all along the way—where no one ever bought any boza. Every neighborhood had its statue of Atatürk and a mosque overlooking its main square, and every main road had a branch of the Akbank and of the İş Bank, a couple of clothes shops, an Arçelik electric-appliance store, a shop where you could buy dried seeds to snack on, a Migros supermarket, a furniture store, a cake shop, a pharmacy, a newspaper kiosk, a restaurant, and a little arcade filled with an assortment of jewelers, glaziers, stationers, hosiers, lingerie stores, currency exchanges, and photocopiers, among others. Mevlut liked discovering the idiosyncrasies of each neighborhood through the eyes of Mr. Sadullah. "That area is packed with people from Sivas and Elazığ," he'd say as they drove back home. "The ring road's razed this sad little place to the ground, let's not come here again," he'd say. "Did you see how beautiful that grand old plane tree in the back alley was, and the teahouse across from it?" he'd say. "Some young men stopped me and demanded to know who I was, so let's say one visit is enough," he'd say. "There are so many cars here that there isn't any room left for people," he'd say. "It looks like this whole area is run by some religious sect, though I don't know which one—did they buy any boza?" he'd say.

They never bought much. Even when they did, the people who lived in these new neighborhoods outside the city only ever called for Mevlut because they were amazed that there should be someone out there selling this stuff they'd only heard of in passing (if at all), because their children were curious, and because they thought there was no harm in having a taste. If he were to go back to the same street a week later, no one would ask for him again. But the city was growing so fast, spreading out and building wealth so determinedly, that even this much was enough for Mevlut, who had only himself to support now.

At Mevlut's suggestion, Mr. Sadullah drove them to the Ghaazi Quarter one evening. Mevlut went to the house where Ferhat and Samiha had spent the first ten years of their married life and which he had visited once, eight years ago, with Rayiha and his daughters. The land Ferhat had marked out with phosphorescent stones was still free. After Ferhat's death, all of this had become Samiha's property. Everything was quiet. Mevlut didn't yell, "Bo-zaa." Nobody would buy boza around here.

They were in another outlying neighborhood one evening when someone on the lower floors of a very tall building (fourteen floors high!) called out to ask him upstairs. A husband and wife and their two bespectacled sons observed Mevlut as he poured out four glasses of boza in the kitchen. They watched the toasted chickpeas and cinnamon being sprinkled over the glasses. The two kids took a sip straightaway.

Mevlut was just about to leave when the lady extracted a plastic bottle from the fridge. "Is it the same as this?" she asked.

That was the moment when Mevlut first came across bottled boza sold by a big company. Six months ago, he'd heard from an old street vendor who'd decided to retire that a biscuit manufacturer had bought out an old boza maker on the verge of bankruptcy with plans to bottle the boza and distribute it through grocery stores, but Mevlut had found this all to be utterly implausible. "No one would buy boza from a grocery store," he'd said, just as, thirty years before, his father had laughed and said, "No one would buy yogurt from a grocery," only to find himself without a job soon after. Mevlut couldn't contain his curiosity: "May I have a taste?"

The children's mother poured a little bit of the whitish bottled boza into a glass. With the whole family staring at him, Mevlut had a sip and made a face. "It's not good," he said, smiling. "It's sour already, it's gone off. You shouldn't buy this stuff."

"But this was made in a factory, by machines," said the older of the two boys with glasses. "Do you make your boza at home by hand?"

Mevlut didn't answer. He was so upset he didn't even want to talk about it with Mr. Sadullah on the way back.

"What's wrong, maestro?" said Mr. Sadullah. His "maestro" was often ironic (Mevlut could tell), but sometimes Mr. Sadullah used the word out of genuine respect for Mevlut's talent and persistence (at those times Mevlut would always pretend he didn't know).

"Never mind, these people don't know what they're doing, and anyway I heard it's going to rain tomorrow," said Mevlut, changing the subject. Mr. Sadullah could talk endearingly and instructively even about meteorological matters. Mevlut liked to listen to him and daydream as he sat in the front seat of the Dodge, watching hundreds, thousands of lights shining out of cars and windows; the depths of the dark, velvety Istanbul night; and the neon-colored minarets going past. Mevlut used to toil on foot through mud and rain, up and down these very same streets, and now here they were slipping right through with ease. Life, too, slipped by in much the same way, speeding up as it ran along the tracks laid out by time and fortune.

Mevlut knew that the hours he spent at Mr. Sadullah's house would be the happiest of his whole week. He didn't want to bring the problems and complications of his other life into the house at Kadırga.

After the wedding, he watched as the baby in Fevziye's belly grew week by week, just as he had done with the babies Rayiha had carried. He was very surprised when it turned out to be a boy; an ultrasound scan had told them it would be, but Mevlut had remained convinced that his grandchild was to be a girl, even wondering whether it would be appropriate to name her Rayiha. Throughout the summer that followed the baby's birth in May 2002, Mevlut spent many hours playing with little İbrahim (named for his paternal great-grandfather, the shoemaker), helping Fevziye change the diapers (he would look at his grandson's tiny penis with pride every time) and prepare his baby food.

He wished he could see his daughter (she looked so much like Rayiha) happy all the time. It bothered Mevlut to hear them asking her to set the table for a night of drinking when she'd only just given birth and to see her serving them without complaint while also keeping an eye on the baby in the other room. But Rayiha had always been expected to do exactly the same and somehow managed. Fevziye had left her father's home and moved into Mr. Sadullah's only to do the same things she'd done before. But at least this was Mevlut's home, too. Mr. Sadullah always said so.

They were alone one day, and as Fevziye stared pensively at the plum tree in the neighbor's garden, Mevlut said, "These are good people . . . Are you happy, dear?"

An old clock was ticking on the wall. Fevziye only smiled, as if her father had made a statement, not asked a question.

At one point during his next visit to the house in Kadırga, Mevlut felt that same sense of intimate understanding again. He wanted to ask Fevziye more about her happiness when something completely different came out of his mouth.

"I am so, so lonely," said Mevlut.

"Aunt Samiha is lonely, too," said Fevziye.

Mevlut told his daughter about Süleyman's visit and the long conversation they'd had. He'd never spoken with Fevziye about the letters (had they been meant for her mother or for her aunt?), but he was sure that Samiha had told both his girls the whole story anyway. (What must his daughters have thought to find out that their father had actually meant to court their aunt?) Mevlut was relieved when Fevziye didn't linger too long on the details of how Süleyman had tricked him all those years ago. She had to keep going back to check on İbrahim in the other room, and it took Mevlut a long time to tell her the whole story.

"So what did you say to Süleyman in the end?" asked Fevziye.

"I told him I wrote those letters to your mother," said Mevlut. "But I've been thinking about it, and I wonder if that could have upset your aunt Samiha?"

"No, Dad, my aunt would never be angry at you for telling the truth. She understands."

"Well, anyway, if you see her," said Mevlut, "tell her your father says sorry."

"I'll tell her . . . ," said Fevziye, with a look that suggested there was much more than an apology at stake.

Samiha had forgiven Fevziye for having eloped without confiding in her aunt first. Mevlut was aware that she came to Kadırga sometimes to see the baby. They didn't talk about it again that day, or on Mevlut's next visit three days later. Fevziye's warm readiness to act as go-between had filled him with hope, and he didn't want to push things too much and end up doing something wrong.

He was also happy at the migrants' association. Mevlut always enjoyed meeting the yogurt sellers and other street vendors of his generation and also his former classmates when they came to the clubhouse. Even people from poorer villages Mevlut had rarely heard of (Nohut, Yören, Çiftekavaklar) half a dozen kilometers from Cennetpınar had started coming by, eager to put up bulletin boards for their villages, with Mevlut's permission. (He would regularly have to consolidate all the coach schedules, circumcision and wedding announcements, and village photographs that got pinned up on these boards.) More people were asking to book the clubhouse for henna nights, little engagement parties (the clubhouse was too small for actual weddings), dumpling dinners, Koran readings, and fast breaking during Ramadan. Under the leadership of a few rich men from the village of Göçük, others began to get more involved in association activities and to pay their membership dues on time.

The richest of all were the legendary Concrete Brothers, Abdullah and Nurullah, from İmrenler. They didn't show up at the clubhouse too often, but they donated plenty of money. Korkut said they'd managed to send their sons to school in America. They had put most of what they'd made as the exclusive suppliers of yogurt to Beyoğlu's big restaurants and cafés into buying land, and now they were rumored to be sitting on mountains of money.

Among others who'd invested their yogurt money in land, there were two families from Çiftekavaklar who'd learned all about the construction business just by building their own homes, to which they gradually added floors, until soon they had made a fortune building houses for new migrants they knew from the village using land they'd fenced off in Duttepe, Kültepe, and all the other hill neighborhoods. People from other villages nearby came to Istanbul and started off as laborers on these construction projects, eventually becoming master bricklayers, licensed builders, doormen, and watchmen. Some of Mevlut's classmates who'd dropped out of school to take early apprenticeships were now repairmen, mechanics, and blacksmiths. They weren't exactly rich, but they were still better off than Mevlut. Their main priority was to get their children through a decent school.

More than half the people who'd populated Mevlut's childhood years had moved to neighborhoods far from Duttepe and rarely came by the clubhouse, but if they could find someone to give them a ride, they did sometimes show up for football matches and picnics. (That kid his age Mevlut used to see roaming the streets with his junk dealer father and their horse cart was, it turned out, from the village of Höyük and had remained very poor; Mevlut still didn't know his name.) Some had aged prematurely over the years, put on weight, got bloated and hunched over, lost their hair, and seen their physiognomies so transformed (the faces ever more pear shaped, with shrinking eyes, and noses and ears that seemed only to grow), that either Mevlut didn't recognize them, or they felt obliged to come up to him and humbly introduce themselves. He knew that most of these people weren't any richer than he was, but he could also sense that they were happier because their wives were still alive. If only he could get married again, he might even end up happier than they were.

On his next visit to Kadırga, Mevlut took one look at his daughter's face and knew immediately that she had news for him. Fevziye had met her aunt. Samiha hadn't known about Süleyman's visit to Mevlut three weeks ago. So when Fevziye passed on her father's apology, her aunt had no idea what she was talking about. As soon as she understood, she became annoyed at both Mevlut and Fevziye. Samiha would never have asked Süleyman for help; nor had this matter ever even crossed her mind before.

Mevlut saw the concern and anxiety on the face of his daughter the messenger. "We made a mistake," he said, sighing.

"Yes," she said.

They didn't speak of it again for a long time. As he was trying to figure out what he should do next, Mevlut also began to admit to himself that "home" was another problem he had to deal with. As well as feeling lonely in the house in Tarlabaşı, he had begun to feel like a stranger in the neighborhood. He could see now that the same streets on which he'd lived for the last twenty-four years were inexorably turning into foreign territory, and he knew the future did not lie in Tarlabaşı.

Back in the 1980s, when Tarlabaşı Avenue was being built, Mevlut had heard the neighborhood—with its crooked, narrow streets, and its crumbling, hundred-year-old brick buildings—described as a place of historic significance and of potentially enormous value, but he'd never believed any of it. At the time, there had only been a handful of left-wing architects and students saying these things in protest against the construction of the new six-lane avenue. But politicians and contractors soon began to follow suit: Tarlabaşı was a precious jewel that had to be preserved. It was rumored hotels, shopping malls, and skyscrapers were to be built in the area.

Mevlut had never truly felt that this was the right neighborhood for him, but over the past few years life on these streets had changed so much that the feeling had only intensified. After his daughters' weddings, he had been cut off from the neighborhood's female universe. The old carpenters, blacksmiths, repairmen, and shopkeepers trained by the Armenians and the Greeks had all left, as had those hardworking families ready to do any job to survive, and now the Assyrians were also gone, replaced by drug dealers, immigrants moving into abandoned apartments, homeless people, gangsters, and pimps. Every time he went to some other part of the city and people asked him how he could still be living in Tarlabaşı, Mevlut would claim that "all those people are in the upper quarters, on the Beyoğlu side." One night a well-dressed young man had stopped Mevlut and frantically asked him, "Do you have any sugar, uncle?" Everyone knew that "sugar" was code for "drugs." By now, even in the dead of night, Mevlut needed no more than a quick glance to spot the pushers who sometimes came all the way down to his street to evade the police raids, and the dealers who hid their product under the hubcaps of parked cars so as not to be caught with it, just as he could always recognize the brawny, bewigged transvestites who worked in the brothels near Beyoğlu.

In Tarlabaşı and Beyoğlu, this kind of hugely profitable vice had always been in the hands of organized crime, but now there were upstart gangs from Mardin and Diyarbakır gunning each other down in the streets for control of the market. Mevlut suspected that Ferhat had been the victim of some such struggle. He had once seen Cezmi from Cizre, the most renowned of these gangsters and thugs, passing through the neighborhood in a kind of victory procession, surrounded by private henchmen and noisy, awestruck children.

All these new people who hung their underwear and shirts out to dry between each other's buildings, turning the whole neighborhood into one big Laundromat, made Mevlut feel that he no longer belonged here. There never used to be so many street stalls in Tarlabaşı, and he didn't like these new street vendors either. He also suspected that these gangsterish types—his so-called landlords (who changed every five or six years)—might suddenly pull out and leave the house to real-estate brokers, property speculators, developers eager to build hotels, or to some other gang, as had happened elsewhere over the past two years. Either that, or he would soon find himself unable to keep up with the constant rent increases. After having been largely ignored for so many years, the whole neighborhood had suddenly become a magnet for all the misery and destructive appetite that the city could muster. There was an Iranian family who had settled into a second-floor apartment two buildings down from his; they had rented the place as somewhere to stay while they waited for the consulate to give them the visas they needed to emigrate permanently to America. When everyone had panicked and run out into the streets on the night of the earthquake three years ago, Mevlut had been astonished to discover that there were almost twenty people living in the Iranians' tiny apartment. By now, he was getting used to the idea of Tarlabaşı as just a temporary stop on so many longer journeys.

Where would he go from here? He gave this a lot of thought, by means of either logical consideration or more impressionistic day-dreaming. If he were to rent a place in Mr. Sadullah's neighborhood of Kadırga, he'd be closer to Fevziye and wouldn't feel so alone all the time. Would Samiha want to live in a place like that? Anyway, it wasn't as if anyone had asked him to come. Besides, the rents there were too high, and it was too far from his job at the clubhouse in Mecidiyeköy. He started to think about a place closer to work. The ideal solution was, of course, the house in Kültepe where he'd spent his childhood with his father. For the first time, he thought of asking Süleyman to help him evict the current tenant so he could move back in himself. Every now and then he pictured himself and Samiha living there.

It was around this time that something happened that so delighted Mevlut he felt encouraged to go looking for Samiha again.

Mevlut had never played much football as a child in the village, never having really enjoyed the game or been very good at it. When he kicked the ball, it rarely went where he intended it to go, and no one ever picked him for their team. During his early years in Istanbul, he'd never had the time, the will, or the spare shoes he would have needed in order to join those who played on the streets and in empty lots, and he would only watch the matches on TV because everyone else did. So when he went to watch the finals of the migrants' association tournament—which Korkut thought crucial in uniting all the villages—it was only because he knew that everyone else would be there, too.

There were stands for spectators on opposite sides of the wire-fenced playing field. He couldn't have felt more pleased if he'd just made it to a wedding all his friends were going to, but still he picked a corner where no one else was sitting from which to watch the game.

It was between the villages of Gümüşdere and Çiftekavaklar. Çiftekavaklar's youthful team was taking it very seriously, and even though some of the players were wearing trousers, at least they'd all pulled on matching shirts. Most of the Gümüşdere team, on the other hand, were grown men in the same clothes they usually wore to be comfortable at home. Mevlut recognized a hunchbacked, potbellied retired yogurt seller from his father's generation (every time he kicked the ball, half the crowd in the stands would laugh and clap) and his son, who seemed determined to show off his skills; Mevlut had seen them before when they'd crossed paths selling yogurt in Duttepe and at all the weddings they'd attended (Korkut's, Süleyman's, and those of many other friends and their children and grandchildren). Like Mevlut, thirty-five years ago the man's son had also come to Istanbul to sell yogurt and further his studies (he'd managed to graduate from high school); now he had two small vans that he used to distribute olives and cheese to grocery stores, as well as two sons and two daughters to applaud their father from the stands and a wife with dyed blond hair under her headscarf who kept getting up in the middle of the match to give her husband a tissue with which to wipe the sweat off his brow (and also, as Mevlut saw once the match was over, a late-model Murat, which could fit all six of them).

It didn't take Mevlut long to understand why these artificial-grass fields that lit up the night with their floodlights had mushroomed all over the city, appearing in every empty lot, car park, or unclaimed parcel of land: some of the cheer may have been a little forced, but there was no doubt that these neighborhood matchups were hugely entertaining. The crowd loved to pretend they were at an actual football match like the ones on TV. Just as on TV, whenever a player committed a foul, they would shout at the referee to "send him off!" or give the other team a penalty. The crowd would roar in approval and hug one another at every goal, while the team that had just scored engaged in prolonged celebratory theatrics, just as they had seen real teams doing. All through the game, the crowd chanted slogans and intoned the names of their favorites.

Mevlut, too, had been engrossed in the match when suddenly he was astonished to hear his own name being called: the whole crowd had seen him—their clubhouse manager and tea brewer—and started clapping and chanting, "Mevlut . . . Mevlut . . . Mevlut . . ." He stood up to acknowledge them with a few awkward gestures, giving a slight bow as he'd seen real footballers do on TV. "Yeaaah!" they screamed. Their cries of "Mevlut!" went on for a while. The applause had been deafening. He sat back down in shock, almost on the verge of tears.

15

Mevlut and Samiha

I Wrote the Letters to You

SEEING HOW POPULAR he was at the migrants' association's football match had put Mevlut in a cheerful and optimistic mood. The next time he went to see Fevziye, he pressed his daughter and showed her a new determination.

"I should go to Duttepe and talk to your aunt myself. I should apologize to her for having hurt her over Süleyman's nonsense. But I can't do that at my uncle's house. Does this aunt Samiha of yours ever go out?"

Fevziye told him that her aunt Samiha sometimes went down to the shops in Duttepe around midday.

"Are we doing the right thing?" said Mevlut. "Should I really go and speak to her? Do you want me to?"

"Yes, go, it would be a good thing."

"It wouldn't be disrespectful to your mother's memory, would it?"

"Dad, you won't survive on your own," said Fevziye.

Mevlut started going to Duttepe and performing his midday prayers at the Hadji Hamit Vural Mosque. There were very few young people there, unless it was a Friday. The mosque would usually fill up with men of his father's generation—retired street vendors, master builders, repairmen—well before the start of prayers, and afterward they would all stroll down together to the covered passage under the mosque, headed for the coffeehouse. Some of them had beards and walking sticks and wore green skullcaps. Mevlut knew deep down that the only reason he had started coming here to pray was for the chance of running into Samiha at the shops afterward, so his mind would focus on these old men's whispers, the silence inside the mosque, and the threadbare state of its carpets, and he would end up unable to inject any sincerity into his prayer. What did it mean when a believer who trusted as much as Mevlut did to the power and grace of God, and felt such a strong need to take comfort in Him, couldn't even pray sincerely in a mosque? If a person couldn't be true to himself in the presence of God, despite a purity of heart and intentions, what should he do? He thought of asking these questions of the Holy Guide; he even fantasized about what answers he might receive.

"God knows who you truly are," the Holy Guide would say while everyone listened. "Since you know that He knows, you wish to be the same, inside and out."

After prayers, he would leave the mosque and loiter in the square where Duttepe's first coffeehouses, junk shop, grocery store, and bus stop had popped up thirty years ago. The area was no different now from anywhere else in Istanbul. There was concrete everywhere, and billboards, banks, and kebab shops. By now, Mevlut had been to Duttepe three times already and still hadn't managed to run into Samiha. He was beginning to worry about how to break it to Fevziye when one day he saw Samiha standing in front of the Vurals' bakery.

He stopped and turned around, heading straight back into the passage under the mosque. He was wrong. This woman wasn't for him.

Mevlut went to the coffeehouse at the end of the passage, where everyone was watching TV; he left just as quickly as he'd come. If he went upstairs, through the back door and across the mosque courtyard, he should be able to get to the clubhouse without Samiha's seeing him.

A heavy sense of regret spread rapidly through his soul. Would he have to spend the rest of his life alone? In any case, he didn't want to go back. He went up the stairs to head out.

When he stepped into the courtyard of the Hadji Hamit Vural Mosque, he came face-to-face with Samiha. For a moment, they just looked at each other, standing two feet apart as they'd done at Korkut's wedding. These were most definitely the same eyes Mevlut had seen back then, the same dark eyes for which he'd written those letters, the reason that he'd studied all those handbooks and dictionaries. He felt close to the idea of Samiha, but as a real human being, she seemed a stranger.

"Mevlut, how come you won't even visit us when you're here, or at least let us know you're around?" said Samiha boldly.

"I'll come next time," said Mevlut. "But there's something else. Come to the Villa Pudding Shop tomorrow at noon."

"Why?"

"We shouldn't talk here, in front of everyone . . . people will gossip. Do you understand?"

"I understand."

They bade each other an awkward farewell from a respectable distance, but both their faces betrayed their satisfaction at having been able to arrange a meeting. As long as Mevlut didn't say anything he didn't mean to, or do anything to embarrass himself, the meeting at the pudding shop should go well. Mevlut had seen many married couples chatting over a shared meal at the Villa. Everyone would think they were husband and wife, too. There was nothing to worry about.

Yet he couldn't sleep that night. Samiha may have still been beautiful, even now at thirty-six, but Mevlut felt as if he didn't know her at all. He'd had very little contact with her throughout his life—save for occasional house visits, the glances they'd shared in the mirror at Brothers-in-Law (where Mevlut had always stood with his back to her), and their meetings at weddings and religious holidays—and he knew that he would never be as close to anyone as he had been to Rayiha. He and Rayiha had lived in each other's pockets for thirteen years. Even when they were separated during the day, they were still together. That kind of intimacy only came with the passionate love of youth. So what was the point of going to see Samiha tomorrow?

In the morning, he gave his cheeks a thorough shave. He wore his newest white shirt and his best jacket. He walked into the pudding shop at a quarter to twelve. The Villa was a large establishment in Şişli Square, just beyond the bus and minibus stops, along the same row of buildings as the mosque, the Şişli Municipal Hall, and the courthouse. As well as shredded-chicken blancmange, other desserts, breakfast, and fried eggs, they also served lentil soup, cheese-stuffed pastries, rice with tomatoes, and, most important, kebabs. The inhabitants of Kültepe, Duttepe, and the other hills nearby—men, women, and children—would come inside while they waited for the next minibus or ran their errands in Şişli and sit there chatting as they looked at the picture of Atatürk on the wall and their own reflections in the mirror. The lunchtime crowd hadn't arrived yet, so Mevlut managed to find a table away from prying eyes and in a quiet corner, just as he had hoped. His seat gave him a perfect view of the traffic in the pudding shop—the waiters darting back and forth, the cashier's quick-fire movements—and he began to be excited at the prospect of watching Samiha walk through the door.

All of a sudden, he saw her standing in front of him. He blushed and knocked down a plastic water bottle but managed to rescue the situation with only a few drops spilled. They both giggled and ordered some kebab over rice.

They had never sat and faced each other quite so formally. For the first time, Mevlut got to look right into Samiha's dark eyes for as long as he wanted. Samiha took out a cigarette from her handbag, lit it with a lighter, and blew the smoke to Mevlut's right. He could picture her smoking cigarettes and perhaps even drinking alone in her room, but it was something else altogether to do it in a restaurant and in the company of a man. He felt his head spin, and at the same time a thought flashed through his mind that could have poisoned their relationship: Rayiha would never have done that.

Mevlut talked about Süleyman's visit and the words he'd asked Fevziye to pass on, and he apologized for the misunderstanding. Once again, Süleyman had stuck his nose where it didn't belong and caused trouble with his nonsense . . .

"That's not exactly right," said Samiha. She spoke about Süleyman's bad intentions and his stupidity; she went on for so long that she even touched upon Ferhat's murder. Mevlut told Samiha that he sensed her hatred for Süleyman, but perhaps it was time to leave all that in the past.

That comment irritated Samiha even more. She worked through her kebab and rice and put her fork down every now and then to light up another cigarette. Mevlut had never imagined her to be so volatile and so unhappy. Then he realized that she would be happier if they framed their plans to be together as a way of getting back at Süleyman.

"Did you really not recognize me when you saw me at the end of your wedding to Rayiha, or were you pretending?" asked Samiha.

"I pretended not to recognize you so that Rayiha wouldn't get upset," said Mevlut, thinking back to the wedding twenty years ago. He couldn't tell whether Samiha believed his lie or not. They were quiet for a time, eating their food and listening to the buzz of the pudding shop getting crowded.

Samiha asked, "Did you write the letters to me or to my sister?"

"I wrote the letters to you," said Mevlut.

He thought he caught a glimmer of satisfaction on her face. They didn't speak for a long while. Samiha was still tense, but Mevlut felt that they'd done enough for their first meeting and said everything they needed to say: he began to talk vaguely about aging, loneliness, and the importance of having someone in your life.

Samiha was listening closely, but suddenly she interrupted him. "You wrote the letters to me, but for years you told everyone, 'I wrote them to Rayiha.' They all pretended to believe you even though they knew you'd meant them for me. Now they're going to pretend they believe you when you say you wrote them to me."

"I did write them to you," said Mevlut. "We saw each other at Korkut's wedding. I wrote to you about your eyes for three years. Süleyman tricked me, and that's why I wrote Rayiha's name on the letters instead of yours. But then I was happy with Rayiha; you know that. Now we can be happy, too."

"I don't care what other people think . . . But I would like to hear you say one more time, like you mean it, that you wrote the letters to me," said Samiha. "Otherwise I won't marry you."

"I wrote the letters to you, and I wrote them with love," said Mevlut. Even as he pronounced these words, he thought of how difficult it was to tell the truth and be sincere at the same time.

16

Home

We Were Doing Things Properly

Samiha. The house was an old *gecekondu* home. Mevlut hadn't done a thing to it since he'd lived there with his father as a child. He told me all about it at great length during our second meeting at the Villa Pudding Shop. Whenever he mentioned this house I had yet to see, he called it "home" in the same loving way his father had done.

It was during our second time at the Villa that we decided to get married and live in the house in Kültepe. It would have been difficult for me to get rid of the tenants in Çukurcuma, and besides, we needed the income. Suddenly everything seemed to be about the house. Mevlut would tell me something sweet every now and then, but you don't need to know about all that. We both loved Rayiha very much. We were doing things properly and moving slowly.

As long as we didn't have to pay any rent ourselves, the monthly rent from the two houses in Çukurcuma that I'd inherited from Ferhat would be more than enough to live on. Mevlut had an income, too. That was another thing we discussed, this time over a plate of rice with chicken. Mevlut was relaxed and direct, though occasionally timid. But I did not see that as a flaw; on the contrary, I appreciated it.

Fevziye was the first to find out that we'd met. Her husband and Mr. Sadullah found out before the Aktaş family did. Mr. Sadullah took me, Mevlut, and Fevziye with İbrahim on her lap on a drive along the

Bosphorus. On our way back, people thought we were a taxi cruising for fares and kept hailing us from the pavement or trying to jump in our path. Every single time, Mevlut would cheerfully shout from the front: "Can't you see the taxi's full?"

Mevlut wanted to call Süleyman immediately and ask him to kick out his own tenant in Kültepe, but I wanted to be the one to inform Duttepe of the news, so I asked him to wait. Vediha took it very well; my darling sister hugged me tight and kissed my cheeks. But she also got me angry straight after that by saying how everyone had wanted this to happen. I would have preferred to marry Mevlut because everyone was against it, not because everyone wanted it.

Mevlut would have wanted to visit the Aktaş family and give Süleyman and Korkut the news himself. But I warned him that if he made that kind of visit seem more important than it was, and turned it into something ceremonial, Süleyman and Korkut might think we were asking their permission to marry, and that would upset me.

"So what," said Mevlut to these concerns. "Let them think whatever they want. We'll just mind our own business."

Mevlut called Süleyman to tell him the news, but he'd already found out from Vediha anyway. The aging tenant from Rize who was living in Mevlut's house refused to leave immediately. Süleyman spoke to a lawyer who told them that if they tried going through the courts, it could take years to evict a tenant without a lease living in a house with no title deed to show. So the Vurals' eldest son sent one of his guys—one renowned for his ruthless thuggish ways—to speak with the tenant from Rize, and he was able to obtain the tenant's written agreement to vacate the premises within three months. On hearing that the wedding would take place three months later than planned, Mevlut showed both impatience and relief. Everything was moving so fast. He worried that it might all end in embarrassment and sometimes imagined that anyone learning that he would marry Samiha could only say "poor Rayiha" and look down on Mevlut. Of course such gossips wouldn't be satisfied merely condemning Mevlut; they were also bound to bring up that old story, nearly forgotten in the wake of Rayiha's death: "The man wrote to the younger sister, but got married to the older one instead."

When Samiha mentioned marriage straightaway, speaking to him in reasoned, decisive tones, Mevlut understood that they would not be going out to cafés, the cinema, or even for lunch at an appropriate restaurant before they married. It was only when he found himself feeling disappointed that he realized how, in some part of his mind, he had been harboring such fantasies. At the same time, all the negotiations over the wedding, the precautions they were obliged to take to avoid the notice of the gossips, and all his uncertainty over what gestures were expected of him, how much he should spend, and what lies he could get away with were so exhausting that Mevlut began to think that arranged marriages were truly a blessed convenience.

He only got to see Samiha once every two weeks when she came over to Mr. Sadullah's house in the afternoon. They wouldn't speak much. Despite Fevziye's efforts to bring her father and her aunt closer, Mevlut could see that he would never get to become friends with Samiha until they were married.

In September 2002, the tenant vacated the house in Kültepe, and Mevlut rejoiced at the pretext this gave him to improve his friendship with Samiha. Samiha took the narrow, winding road from Duttepe to Kültepe, and from there, they went to see Mevlut's childhood home together.

The one-room *gecekondu* house, which he had so lovingly described to her in their meeting at the Villa Pudding Shop, was virtually a ruin. It still had an earthen floor, just as it had had thirty years ago. The toilet beside the room was still but a hole in the ground. Through a small window in the toilet you could hear the roar of trucks along the ring road at night. There was an electric stove next to the old woodstove. Mevlut couldn't locate the illegal wiring, but he knew from experience that in a neighborhood like Kültepe, no one would buy an electric stove unless they could steal the electricity needed for it. The wobbly table with the short leg where he'd sat and studied as a child scared of demons was still there, as was the wooden bedstead. Mevlut even found the pots in which he'd made soup thirty years ago, and the coffeepot they'd always used. Just like him and his father, the tenants hadn't bought a single thing for the house in years.

Yet the world around the house had changed completely. Once half empty, the hill was now covered in three- and four-story concrete buildings. The dirt roads—some of which had been new in 1969—were now all covered in asphalt. Some former *gecekondu* homes had been converted into multistory office buildings for lawyers and accountants or architects' studios. Every rooftop was now covered with satellite dishes and billboards, transforming the view Mevlut used to see whenever he lifted his head from his middle-school homework to look out the window, though the poplars and the minarets of Hadji Hamit's mosque were exactly the same.

Mevlut used the last of his savings to pave the floor of his *gecekondu* house (he, too, had started using this term), refurbish the roof and toilet, and have the walls painted. Süleyman sent a van from his construction company a couple of times to help, but Mevlut never mentioned that to Samiha. He was desperate to get along with everyone and didn't want anyone to disapprove of his wedding.

He thought it suspicious that his daughter in Izmir had kept quiet all summer and hadn't even come to Istanbul once, but he kept trying to put it out of his mind. When they started discussing the wedding arrangements, however, Fevziye couldn't hide the truth from her father anymore: Fatma was against her father's marrying her aunt after her mother's death. She wouldn't be coming to Istanbul for the wedding. She didn't even want to speak to her father and her aunt Samiha on the phone.

As the summer grew hotter, Crooked-Necked Abdurrahman arrived in Istanbul, and Mevlut went to see him in Duttepe, where he was lodged on the third floor, which had itself gone crooked in the earthquake. Mevlut wanted to ask his permission to marry Samiha and to kiss his hand, just as he had done when he'd gone to their village to ask him for Rayiha's hand twenty years ago. Perhaps Crooked-Necked Abdurrahman and Samiha, father and daughter, might go to Izmir to persuade Fatma to come to the wedding . . . But Fatma refused even to consider receiving such a visit, and that made Mevlut feel like writing her off. After all, she had turned her back on the family.

Finally, though, Mevlut couldn't sustain any resentment against his daughter, because some part of him agreed with her. He could see that Samiha felt guilty, too. After all she had done to make sure Fatma got to go to college, and after all the care she'd lavished on her niece when Fatma's mother died, Samiha felt as wounded as Mevlut did. And yet, when Mevlut said, "Let's have the wedding far away from everyone," Samiha proposed the very opposite.

"Let's do it near Duttepe, let them all come and see for themselves . . . Let them gossip their hearts out . . . ," said Samiha. "That way, they'll get bored of talking about it sooner."

Mevlut admired Samiha's reasoning, and her brave decision to wear a white gown at the age of thirty-six. They decided to have the wedding at the clubhouse, as it was close to Duttepe and wouldn't cost them anything. The association's offices weren't very big, so all the guests came in, had their lemonades (and the glasses of *rakı* Mevlut arranged to have served on the sly), and gave their gifts, without lingering for long in the hot, humid, and overcrowded clubhouse.

Samiha had used her own money to rent the white gown, which she'd found with Vediha in a shop in Şişli. All through the wedding, Mevlut kept thinking that she looked stunning: surely any man who came face-to-face with such a beauty would write her love letters for three years.

Süleyman knew by now that he made Samiha uncomfortable: neither he nor the rest of the Aktaş family made their presence felt much at the wedding. He was drunk by the time he decided to leave, and he pulled Mevlut aside.

"Don't forget I arranged both your marriages, my friend," he said. "But I can't figure out whether it was a good thing to do."

"It was a great thing to do," said Mevlut.

After the wedding, the bride and groom, Fevziye and her husband, and Crooked-Necked Abdurrahman piled into Mr. Sadullah's Dodge and went to a restaurant in Büyükdere that served alcohol. Neither Mevlut, nor Samiha, who loved being in her wedding gown, drank anything. When they got home, they got into bed and made love with all the lights off. Mevlut had always known that sex with Samiha was never going to be awkward or difficult. They were both happier than they could have ever imagined.

In the months to follow, Mevlut would look out the window of his *gecekondu* home and, as his wife slept, stare pensively at Hadji Hamit's mosque and all the other hills covered in apartment blocks, trying not to think of Rayiha. In those early months of his marriage, there were occasional moments when he felt he'd already lived that same moment before. He wasn't sure, though, whether the illusion was on account of having just married again after so many years, or whether it had something to do with being back in his childhood home.

PART VI

Wednesday, 15 April 2009

No good will ever come of negotiating with family on a rainy day.

—Byron Pasha, *Apologies and Ironies*

The Twelve-Story Building

You Have a Right to the City's Rent

Remember, you swore, nothing less than sixty-two percent," said Samiha as she saw her husband out. "Don't let them intimidate you."

"Why would I be intimidated by them," said Mevlut.

"Don't believe any of Süleyman's nonsense either, and don't lose your temper. Have you got the title deed?"

"I've got the councilman's papers," said Mevlut as he set off down the hill. The sky was heavy with gray clouds. They were all going to meet at Uncle Hasan's grocery store in Duttepe to review the situation and go through one final round of negotiations. Vural Holdings, the Vurals' big construction company, was taking advantage of a series of recent urban renewal measures to build sixteen new high-rises in the neighborhood. They'd planned a twelve-story apartment building on the site currently occupied by the one-room house Mevlut had inherited from his father, the home he'd been sharing with Samiha for the past seven years. This meant that Mevlut, like so many others, had to arrive at terms with the Vurals. But he'd been dragging things out and digging his heels in over final points, and now Korkut and Süleyman were angry at him.

Mevlut hadn't signed the agreement yet; he continued to live with Samiha in his childhood home, even as some of the apartments soon to be built on that land had already been sold. Mevlut would go out into his garden sometimes and point at the sky overhead, marveling at the ridiculousness of those wealthy people who had paid the Vurals in advance for apartments they would one day own "up there." But Samiha didn't think there was anything funny about it. Mevlut was always impressed by his second wife's realism.

A model of the planned building was on display at the Vural Holdings marketing office on Main Street, which ran between Duttepe and Kültepe. A blond woman always in high heels would talk visitors through all the different apartment options on offer and the materials to be used in the bathrooms and kitchens before pausing to mention that all south-facing units above the sixth floor would have Bosphorus views. Even the thought that the Bosphorus could be glimpsed six floors up from the garden of his forty-year-old house was enough to make Mevlut dizzy. Before his final negotiation with the Aktaş family, he went to have one last look at the model.

When news first spread in 2006 that Duttepe and Kültepe, along with many other neighborhoods in Istanbul, had been selected for a large-scale urban redevelopment initiative, and that the government was encouraging high-rise construction in the area, local residents were thrilled. Previously, the law had only allowed three- and four-story buildings on these hills. Now you could build up to twelve floors. People felt as if they were being given bundles of cash. The decision had been handed down from Ankara, but everyone knew that behind it all was Hadji Hamit Vural's family, who had close ties to the Justice and Development Party (the AKP) and owned many acres across Duttepe and Kültepe. As a result, the governing AKP, which was already popular in the area, had gained even more votes in and around Duttepe and Kültepe. Initially, even those cynics who usually complained about everything kept quiet.

The first murmurs of protest came from the area's tenants. When it was announced that buildings as high as twelve stories would be allowed, both local rents and the value of land rose sharply, so that people who could barely make it to the end of the month as it was (like Mevlut's old tenant from Rize) began a gradual exodus from the hills. These long-standing tenants felt just as Mevlut had when he was obliged to leave Tarlabaşı: there was no future for them here, where tall, showy buildings would someday be home to the rich . . .

The new law stipulated that the site for each twelve-story building would be created by combining lots belonging to as many as sixty existing homeowners. Within a year, the municipality had designated and announced the location of these sites, which split Duttepe and Kültepe into distinct areas. Longtime neighbors, who found out overnight that they would one day be living in the same high-rise, started meeting at one another's homes, and over tea and cigarettes, they discussed the situation, choosing from among themselves a representative (there were always plenty of aspirants to this position) who could deftly manage any necessary arrangements with the government and the contractors; and soon enough they began to have their first disagreements. At Samiha's insistence, Mevlut attended three of these meetings. Along with the other men, he was quickly taught all about the concept of "land rent" in economics and how to apply it. Once, he put up his hand and told everyone about all that his late father had been through, how he'd toiled to build the house Mevlut now lived in. But he had trouble keeping up with their discussions about percentages and shares and found relief from that unease at night selling boza out on the solitary streets.

According to the new law, local landowners who wanted an apartment in one of the new high-rises first had to sell their lots to the developer. Other big Turkish concerns had tried to get involved, but Hadji Hamit Vural's company, which boasted excellent relations not only with the government in Ankara but the neighborhood as well, naturally came out on top. So the owners of the area's old *gecekondu* houses began to visit the Vural Holdings offices on Main Street to look at the model in the window, work out what they might expect of their future apartments, and negotiate with Hadji Hamit Vural's younger son.

At most of the other high-rises that had sprung up all over Istanbul, ownership was usually split fifty-fifty between the developer and the existing homeowners. If a group of locals managed to find a competent representative and act in unison, they could sometimes raise their share to fifty-five percent, or even sixty percent in some cases. This was very rare, however, and it was much likelier that the former *gecekondu* neighbors would squander their collective advantage by bickering over percentages and move-in dates. Mevlut heard from Süleyman, who always reported these things with a knowing smirk, that some neighborhood representatives were taking bribes from contractors. As both Duttepe landowners and partners in Vural Holdings, Korkut and Süleyman were always up to date with the latest gossip, squabbling, and negotiations.

Most old *gecekondu* homes had already become proper three- or four-story buildings, and their owners could drive a hard bargain with the state and the developer, as long as they possessed an official title deed. But those like Mevlut, whose only claim to their property was a forty-year-old piece of paper from the neighborhood councilman, and whose house was only a single room (more common than not in Kültepe), were likely to back down if the contractors threatened: "The government might find a way to just take it from you, you know . . ."

Another contentious issue was the expense of temporary accommodation: when they demolished old *gecekondu* homes, contractors were obliged to pay relocation costs for the displaced until their new homes were finished. Some had supposedly signed contracts specifying temporary arrangements for two years, only to end up on the street when the contractors didn't finish on time. Amid such rumors all over Istanbul, many local landowners decided that it was probably safer to come to an agreement with the contractors only after everyone else had already done so. Others kept procrastinating—single-handedly delaying major projects—simply out of a sense there would be more to gain by being the last to sign.

Korkut referred to them as "obstructors," and he loathed them. To him they were dirty profiteers hindering other people's lives and livelihoods for the sake of a better deal or more apartments than they had a right to. Mevlut had heard tales of so-called obstructors getting six—perhaps even seven—apartments in sixteen- or seventeen-story buildings while everyone else was allotted two or three. These sharp negotiators usually planned to sell off all their expensive new units as soon as they got them and move to a different city or neighborhood, as they knew it wasn't just the government and its contractors who would be furious with them for the delays but also their own friends and neighbors desperate to move into their new homes as soon as possible. Mevlut knew that in Oktepe, Zeytinburnu, and Fikirtepe these obstructors and their neighbors had come to blows, sometimes ending in stabbings. It was also rumored that contractors were secretly instigating this kind of discord. Mevlut came to know all about this business when, during their last negotiation meeting, Korkut had said, "You're no better than those obstructors, Mevlut!"

The Vural Holdings offices on Main Street were empty that day. Mevlut had attended many meetings here, whether organized by homeowners or the contractors. He'd sat there with Samiha looking at flashy models with oddly shaped balconies and tried to picture the small, northerly apartment that was his due. The office had photographs of other high-rises the Vurals had built in Istanbul, and some with Hadji Hamit holding a shovel forty years ago, working on some of his very first projects. It was around midday now, and even the curbsides, where prospective buyers from the city's better neighborhoods usually parked their cars on weekends, were empty. After wasting some time window-shopping in the arcade under the Hadji Hamit Vural Mosque, Mevlut began to climb Duttepe's twisting, narrow roads so he wouldn't be late for the meeting at Uncle Hasan's grocery store.

Just beyond the first few houses at the foot of the hill was a flat stretch of road where there once stood a row of malodorous wooden dormitories for Hadji Hamit's workers. As a child, Mevlut had looked in their open doors and glimpsed the sleeping forms of tired young workers entombed in their bunks within the dark and musty rooms. Over the past three years, the vacancy rate had risen as renters fled, expecting the whole neighborhood to be demolished soon anyway, and the now-derelict structures dotting the whole of Duttepe made the area look run-down and ugly. Mevlut looked at the darkening sky ahead and fretted. As he climbed the hill, he felt as if he were walking straight into the heavens.

Why hadn't he been able to refuse when Samiha had insisted on sixty-two percent? He didn't know how he could get the Aktaş family to agree to that. In their last round of negotiations, which took place at the clubhouse, Korkut had balked at fifty-five percent, and in frustration they'd agreed to adjourn and try one more time. But Mevlut hadn't heard from Korkut and Süleyman for weeks. It all made him very anxious, but he also liked it that Korkut considered him an obstructor; it might mean he was poised to get more than anyone else in the end. Since the clubhouse meeting, however, Duttepe and Kültepe had been designated seismic hazard zones, and Mevlut—like many others in Kültepe—had begun to suspect a trick orchestrated by the Vurals. After the 1999 earthquake it had been established by law that any building found to be structurally unsound could be demolished with the consent of at least two-thirds of its owners. Now both the government and the developers were using this measure to circumvent small-property owners who stood in the way of bigger and taller apartment buildings. With the seismic hazard law invoked in Kültepe, the lot of an obstructor was even harder, and Mevlut couldn't fathom how he was going to ask for the sixty-two percent Samiha had insisted on as he walked out the door.

It had been seven years since the wedding, and he was happy. They had become good friends. But theirs was not a friendship that revolved around all that was bright and wonderful in the world; instead, it was founded on companionable hard work, their shared struggle to overcome difficulties, and on coming to terms with the banality of everyday life. Once he got to know Samiha a bit better, Mevlut found a stubborn, decisive woman who was determined to live a good life, and he liked this side of her. But she didn't always know where to channel this inner strength, and maybe that was why she kept trying to direct Mevlut much more than he could happily bear—often going as far as to tell him what to do outright.

Mevlut would have been quite happy to settle with the Vurals for fifty-five percent: this would have given him three apartments on the lower floors of the twelve-story building, with no Bosphorus view. Since his mother and sisters in the village formally counted as his father's heirs, too, his share would have effectively come to something slightly less than one whole apartment. They would use the rents from Ferhat's apartments in Çukurcuma to make up the difference over five years (though if they managed to get sixty-two percent, this could be accomplished in three years). Either way, in the end, they would own the apartment outright between them. He had spent months going over the figures with Samiha at home. Now, after forty years in Istanbul, with a place to call his own (or half his own) never so close, Mevlut didn't want to see his hopes dashed, and so as he walked into his uncle Hasan's grocery, with its colorful assortment of vitreous boxes, newspapers, and sundry bottles, he felt almost afraid.

His eyes took some time to adjust to the semidarkness inside the shop.

"Mevlut, you try talking to my father," said Süleyman. "He's driving us mad; maybe he'll listen to you."

Uncle Hasan was sitting at the cash desk as he'd been doing for thirty-five years. He was truly old now, but he still sat up straight. Mevlut was struck by how much his uncle resembled his father; as a child, he'd never been able to see that. He hugged his uncle and kissed his cheeks, which were covered in moles and a thin beard.

The thing Süleyman was teasing his father about as Korkut laughed was Uncle Hasan's insistence on continuing to pack his customers' purchases in those little baskets he made out of old newspapers (he called them pint baskets). In the 1950s and 1960s, all Istanbul grocers used to do it, but now only Uncle Hasan still spent his spare time folding up discarded newspapers brought from home or found elsewhere, and whenever his sons protested, he would only say, "It's not hurting anyone." Mevlut did as he always did when visiting the shop: he sat down in the chair across from his uncle and started folding newspapers, too.

Süleyman told his father that the neighborhood was changing, and customers wouldn't want to come to a minimart with only dirty old newspapers in which to take home their groceries.

"Then let them stop coming," said Uncle Hasan. "This isn't a minimart anyway, it's a *grocery store*." He turned to Mevlut and winked.

Süleyman insisted that what his father was doing was pointless—profligate, in fact: plastic bags were much cheaper by the kilo than salvaged newspaper. Still worried about their inevitable discussion over the percentages, Mevlut was happy to see their argument drag on: this spontaneous division within the Aktaş camp could only help. When

Uncle Hasan said, "Money isn't all that matters in life, son!" Mevlut supported him, adding that just because there was money in something, that didn't necessarily make it a good thing.

"Come on, Dad, Mevlut's still trying to sell boza," said Süleyman. "You can't do business thinking like that."

"Mevlut is more respectful of his uncle than you are," said Uncle Hasan. "Look, he's folding newspapers and making himself useful, unlike you two."

"We'll see about respect when he tells us what he's decided. So, Mevlut? What do you say?" said Korkut

Mevlut panicked, but everyone was diverted when a boy walked into the shop and said, "Some bread, Uncle Hasan." Now well over eighty, the old grocer took a loaf out of the wooden bread cupboard and placed it on the counter. The ten-year-old kid was dissatisfied; this loaf wasn't crispy enough. "You shouldn't touch unless you're buying," said Uncle Hasan and went over to the cupboard to pick out one with a harder crust.

Meanwhile Mevlut went outside. He'd had an idea. In his pocket was a mobile phone Samiha had bought him six months ago. He carried it only so Samiha could call her husband; Mevlut himself never used it. Now, he was going to call his wife to tell her that sixty-two percent was too much, and they had to go lower, otherwise it wouldn't end well.

But Samiha didn't pick up. It began to rain, and Mevlut saw that the boy had finally gotten his bread and left the store, so he went back inside, sat across from Uncle Hasan, and resumed folding newspapers just as meticulously as before. Süleyman and Korkut were giving their father a withering account of all the obstructors who'd caused them trouble at the last minute after everything had been agreed, the schemers who'd changed their minds and demanded a new negotiation, and the scoundrels who'd secretly solicited bribes from the contractors in exchange for persuading their neighbors to sign an agreement. Mevlut knew that they would start talking about him the same way as soon as he left. He noticed with some surprise the questions Uncle Hasan was asking his sons, which suggested he must have been following all these negotiations and the various construction contracts very closely, still trying to tell his sons what to do from his base at the grocery store. Until then, Mevlut had always imagined that Uncle Hasan had no idea what went on beyond those four walls (where he spent long hours not so much for profit as for personal enjoyment).

A face on one of the newspapers he was folding up caught Mevlut's eye. The headline next to it said MASTER CALLIGRAPHER DIES. He realized with a pang that the Holy Guide had passed away, and his heart quivered with sadness. Under another photograph, this of the Holy Guide in his youth, the caption read: "The works of our last great calligrapher are displayed in museums across Europe." Mevlut had last visited the lodge six months ago. Swarmed by his legions of admirers, the man was out of reach, and it had been impossible to hear let alone understand anything he said. In the past ten years, the streets all around the house in Çarşamba had filled up with votaries of many different sects, all wearing robes of one color or another. It was the same traditional religious garb that people wore in Iran and Saudi Arabia. These people's political Islamism had begun to unnerve Mevlut, and eventually he stopped going there altogether. Now, he regretted not having seen the Holy Guide one last time before he died. Mevlut hid behind the newspaper he was holding and thought about the Guide.

"You can fold newspapers with my father some other time, Mevlut," said Korkut. "Let's get this deal worked out, as we agreed. We've got other things to do. Everyone's saying, 'Why hasn't your cousin signed yet?' Haven't we given you and Samiha everything you've asked for?"

"We don't want to stay in Hadji Hamit's dormitories after they knock our house down."

"Fine. We'll put a clause in the contract that says you'll get one thousand two hundred and fifty liras a month for three years. You can go live wherever you want."

This was a lot of money. Feeling encouraged, Mevlut just came out with it: "We also want a share of sixty-two percent."

"Sixty-two percent? Where's this coming from?" (Mevlut would have dearly liked to say, It's Samiha, she won't take no for an answer!) "Last time we spoke, we told you fifty-five is impossible!"

"This is what we feel is appropriate," said Mevlut, surprising even himself with his own assertiveness.

"That's not going to happen," said Korkut. "We have our own honor to think about, too. We won't let you rip us off in broad daylight. Shame on you! I hope you realize what you're doing. See what kind of man our Mevlut has turned out to be, Father?"

"Calm down, son," said Uncle Hasan. "Mevlut is a sensible fellow."

"Then he'll take fifty percent, and we'll close this deal right here. If Mevlut doesn't sign the contract, everyone will be talking about how the Aktaş family haven't even got their own cousin to agree yet. You know how they meet at each other's houses every night to scheme. Now our crafty Mr. Mevlut is using that to blackmail us. Is this your final decision, Mevlut?"

"It's my final decision!" said Mevlut.

"Right. Let's go, Süleyman."

"Wait," said Süleyman. "Mevlut, think about this for a minute: now that the neighborhood is officially an earthquake zone, a contractor who has two-thirds of the property owners on his side won't make excuses for anyone. They'll just kick people out of their houses. They'll only give you as much for your land as it says on the title deed or as you've declared to the tax office. You don't even have a title deed. You just have the councilman's paper. Now I'm sure you know that if you look at the bottom of that piece of paper—the one you tried to give me that night you got drunk while writing love letters to Rayiha—you'll see my father's name under your father's. If this ends up in the courts, ten years from now you won't even get half of what we're offering you today. So think about that."

"That's no way to talk to people, son," said Uncle Hasan.

"My answer is the same," said Mevlut.

"Let's go, Süleyman," said Korkut. They stormed out of the grocery store, the younger brother following the older off into the rain.

"They may be in their fifties, but my boys are still as hot-blooded as ever," said Uncle Hasan. "But this kind of arguing isn't right. They'll be back soon. Maybe then you can ask for a little less . . ."

Mevlut couldn't find it in him to say, I will. He would have been ready to settle for fifty-five percent had Korkut and Süleyman been nicer about it. Samiha was insisting on sixty-two percent out of sheer obstinacy. Even the thought of a ten-year court battle that left him empty-handed was enough to make him sick. He looked back down at the old newspaper in his hand.

The news of the Holy Guide's death had been published four months ago. Mevlut read the short piece one more time. The paper didn't even mention the lodge or his role as leader of a sect, even though these things had been as important in his life as being a master calligrapher.

What should he do now? If he were to leave, it would only make things worse, and harder for him to come back later to settle on a figure. Maybe that was what Korkut wanted: in court, they would argue "Our father's name is on the councilman's paper and he has a claim to the land, too" (making sure, of course, to ignore how they'd seized the land in Duttepe for themselves all those years ago and sold off the other plot in Kültepe) and finally leave Mevlut with nothing. He didn't know how he would tell Samiha what had happened; he sat quietly and kept folding newspapers. Women who wanted rice, soap, and cookies, and children who wanted chewing gum and chocolates were coming and going.

Uncle Hasan still kept accounts for some of his customers who paid at the end of the month. His eyesight wasn't very good, though, so he told them to write down for themselves what they'd bought. He asked Mevlut to check whether the customer who'd just walked out had written down the correct amount. When he realized that his sons weren't going to come back to smooth things over, he tried to comfort Mevlut: "Your father and I, we were such close brothers, such good friends," he said. "We fenced off the land in Kültepe and Duttepe together, we built our houses together with our own hands. We told the neighborhood councilman to put both our names down on the papers so that we would never grow apart. In those days, your father and I would sell yogurt together, we'd eat together, we'd go to Friday prayers together, we'd sit in the park smoking cigarettes together . . . Have you got the councilman's document, my boy?"

Mevlut placed the wrinkled, spongy forty-year-old piece of paper on the counter.

"We ended up growing apart anyway. Why? Because he didn't bring your mother and your sisters over to Istanbul from the village. You both worked your hearts out, you and your father, God rest his soul.

You deserve those apartments more than anyone else does. Your sisters didn't come to Istanbul to work. The right thing would be for you to have all three of the apartments the contractor is giving you. I have a few spares of those old forms. The councilman was my friend, and I have his seal, too. I've been keeping it safe for thirty-five years. I say let's tear this old thing up. Let's make a new one ourselves. We'll put your name on it, and stamp it all off. That way you and Samiha will get a whole apartment outright."

Mevlut realized that this meant increasing his own share at the expense of his mother and sisters in the village, so he said, "No."

"Don't be so quick to decide. You're the one who's been breaking his back here in Istanbul. You have a right to the city's rent."

The phone in his pocket rang, and Mevlut went outside in the rain. "I saw you called, what's the matter?" said Samiha. "It's not going well," said Mevlut. "Don't let them bully you," said Samiha.

Mevlut hung up, feeling exasperated, and went back into the shop. "I'm leaving, Uncle Hasan!" he said.

"Up to you, son," said Uncle Hasan as he folded newspapers. "Whatever happens, the Lord's purpose shall always prevail."

Mevlut would have much preferred it if his uncle had said, Stay a while longer, the boys will cool off eventually. He grew irritated at the old man, and at Samiha for having driven him to this. He was also angry at Korkut and Süleyman and at the Vurals, too, but most of all he was annoyed with himself. If he'd told Uncle Hasan yes just now, he'd have finally been able to get the home he deserved. As it was, he wasn't sure of anything anymore.

As he walked in the rain along the winding asphalt road (formerly a muddy dirt road), past the Food Stop Mart (which used to be a junk dealer's), and down the steps (which weren't there before) to the big road back to Kültepe, Mevlut thought of Rayiha, as he did so many times each day. He'd started dreaming about her more often, too. These were painful, difficult dreams. There would always be overflowing rivers, fires, and darkness between them. All of these shadowy things would then turn into a kind of wild jungle, just like the ugly apartment blocks he could see now, rising to his right. Mevlut would realize that there were dogs roaming among the trees in this jungle, but Rayiha's grave was there, too, and as he pushed through his fear of dogs and toward her, he would suddenly realize with a jolt of pleasure that his beloved was, in fact, behind him, watching him, and he would wake up happy but also strangely distressed.

Had Rayiha been the one waiting for him at home, she would have found the right words to soothe his worries. But when Samiha put her mind to something, that was all she ever saw, and this only made Mevlut more anxious. By now he felt like himself only when he was out at night selling boza.

The gardens of some empty homes were planted with signs that said PROPERTY OF VURAL HOLDINGS. The slopes along the main road that climbed up to Kültepe had been empty when Mevlut had first moved to Istanbul. His father used to send Mevlut here to collect scrap paper, wood, and dried twigs for the stove. Nowadays the road was flanked on either side by hideous *gecekondu* homes, six or seven stories high. They had once been two or three floors at most. But over the years, the owners had added so many illegal floors (burdening the already weak foundations) it would no longer have been economical to knock them all down and replace them with new high-rises. The owners had nothing to gain from the new law permitting twelve-story construction, and the contractors didn't even try to negotiate with them. Korkut had once told Mevlut that these horrible buildings, with each additional floor different from the one below, gave a bad impression of Duttepe and Kültepe, lowering the value of the new apartments to be built and ruining the image of the neighborhood; the only hope was for the next big earthquake to destroy them all.

Ever since the quake in 1999, Mevlut—like all residents of Istanbul—would sometimes catch himself thinking about "the big one," the one the experts said was imminent and would destroy the whole city. In those moments, he would realize that this city where he'd spent forty years of his life, where he'd passed through thousands and thousands of doors, getting to know the insides of people's homes, was no less an ephemeral thing than the life he'd lived there and the memories he'd made. The new tall buildings that were replacing his generation's *gecekondu* homes would also disappear one day, along with all the people who lived inside them. He would sometimes have a vision of the day when all the people and all the buildings were to vanish, and he would feel then as if it wasn't really worth doing anything at all, that he might as well give up any expectations he may have had of life.

Throughout the happy years of his marriage to Rayiha, though, he'd always thought that Istanbul would never change, that all his hard work out on the streets would gain him a place of his own someday, and that he would learn to adapt to the city. All this had happened, to an extent. But ten million other people had joined him in Istanbul over the past forty years, latching on as he had to anything they could find, and the city had emerged transformed. Istanbul's population had been only three million when Mevlut had first arrived; now, they said there were thirteen million people living there.

Raindrops were dripping down the back of his neck. Mevlut, who was fifty-two years old, looked for a place to shelter and let his heart rate slow down. He didn't have any specific worries about his heart, but he was smoking too much lately. Over on the right he saw a clearing that had often been used for weddings and circumcision parties and for the Derya Cinema's summer screenings; now they'd turned it into a football field with artificial turf surrounded by a wire fence. Mevlut had organized football tournaments there for the migrants' association. Under the dripping eaves of their office building, he lit a cigarette and watched the rain falling onto the plastic grass.

His life was still passing by in a crescendo of anxieties. Mevlut had reached the age at which he would have liked to put his feet up, but he didn't feel secure enough to do so. The deficiency and inadequacy he'd felt in his heart when he'd first moved to the city had intensified after Rayiha's death, and especially over the past five years. What would Samiha say? All he wanted was a house where he could spend the rest of his days in comfort, a place where he knew no one would ever be able to kick him out. Samiha should try to console him about his failure to get that, but Mevlut knew that as soon as he got home and broke the news to her, he would probably end up consoling her instead. He decided to tell her only the good news from the negotiation. That, at least, should be how he introduced the subject.

Kültepe's inadequate sewage system couldn't absorb all the water coursing down the neighborhood's steep slopes. Mevlut realized that Main Street must be flooded when he heard the sounds of cars honking in the resulting traffic jam.

By the time he got home, he was soaking wet. The way Samiha was looking at him made him nervous, so he went a little overboard: "Everything's fine," he said. "They're going to give us one thousand two hundred fifty liras every month so we can live wherever we want."

"I know it's all fallen through, Mevlut. Why are you lying to me?" said Samiha.

Vediha had called Samiha on her mobile phone and told her that Korkut was both deeply wounded and furious, that it was all over now, that they were cutting all ties with Mevlut.

"What did you say? Did you tell her how you made me swear on my way out that I wouldn't take any lower than sixty-two percent?"

"Are you regretting it now?" said Samiha, raising a single, contemptuous eyebrow. "Do you think Süleyman and Korkut would have been nicer to you if you'd just given in to them?"

"I've been giving in to them all my life," said Mevlut. Samiha's silence spurred him on. "If I stand up to them now, I might lose the apartment. Do you want that kind of responsibility? Call your sister back, smooth things over, tell her they scared me, and I'm sorry for what I said."

"I will not do that."

"Then I'll call Vediha myself," said Mevlut, but he didn't take his phone out of his pocket. He felt as if he were on his own. He knew he couldn't make any major decisions that day without Samiha's support. He changed out of his wet clothes, looking out at the view just as he used to do as a child when he did his homework. Right next to the old orange building of Atatürk Boys' Secondary School, in the courtyard where Mevlut had always loved running around and where they'd had gym class, there was a new building so big that he could hardly recognize his old school anymore.

Samiha picked up her ringing phone and said, "We're here," before hanging up. She looked at Mevlut. "Vediha's on her way. She said you're not to go anywhere and just wait here."

Samiha was sure that Vediha was coming to say, Mevlut made a mistake, he should ask for a little less; she urged her husband not to back down.

"Vediha is a good person. She wouldn't suggest anything that is unfair to us," said Mevlut.

"I wouldn't trust her so much," said Samiha. "She'll defend Süleyman over you. Hasn't she always?"

Was this a barbed reference to the letters? If so, it was the first time in their seven years together that Mevlut had heard Samiha make a bitter remark on the matter. They listened to the rain in silence.

There was a thunderous knock at the door. It was Vediha, who walked in complaining that she was "completely soaked," though she was carrying an enormous purple umbrella and, actually, only her feet were wet. Samiha went to get her sister fresh socks and a pair of slippers, and Vediha placed a piece of paper on the table.

"Mevlut, just sign and let's get this over with. You've asked for more than you are owed, you don't know what I had to do to calm everyone down . . ."

Mevlut had seen others with the same boilerplate contract, and he wasn't sure where to look: when he saw that it said sixty-two percent, he was delighted, but he held his emotions in check. "I won't sign it if it's not my right," he said.

"Oh, Mevlut, haven't you learned, rights don't matter in the city, only profits," said Vediha, smiling. "Give it ten years and what you've earned will become yours by rights. Now sign. You're getting everything you asked for, so don't complain."

"No signing until we've read it," said Samiha, but when she saw Mevlut pointing at the sixty-two percent, she, too, was relieved. "What happened?" she asked her sister.

Mevlut picked up the pen and signed the contract. Vediha used her mobile phone to tell Korkut. Once that was done, she gave Samiha the box of stuffed pastries she'd brought, and as they drank the tea Samiha had prepared and waited for the rain to stop, she told them the whole story, savoring every moment of her account: Korkut and Süleyman had been furious with Mevlut. In spite of Vediha's pleading, it did look like the dispute might end up in court, with Mevlut losing everything, but then the elderly Hadji Hamit Vural caught wind of what was happening, and he called Korkut up.

"Hadji Hamit's dream is to build a much taller building, a big tower in Duttepe near our old house," said Vediha. "So he told Korkut, 'Give your cousin whatever he wants.' He won't enter into any agreements for that tower until he's done with these twelve-story blocks."

"Let's hope there's no catch," said Samiha.

Later, Samiha showed the contract to a lawyer, who confirmed that there were no tricks. They moved into an apartment near Mevlut's clubhouse in Mecidiyeköy. But Mevlut's mind was still on the home they'd left behind in Kültepe. He went to check on his empty house a few times and to see whether any tramps or burglars had broken in, but there was nothing there to steal. He'd sold everything of any value, from the doorknobs to the kitchen sink.

Toward the end of that summer, Vural Holdings' earthmovers began to demolish houses in Kültepe, and every day Mevlut went down to watch. On the first day of the demolitions, there was a progovernment rally attended by journalists and solemnly addressed by the mayor. But in the hot summer days that followed, none of the people who saw their homes disappear in a cloud of dust applauded as they had done at that inaugural ceremony (not even the people who'd gotten the best deals from Vural Holdings). Mevlut saw people cry, laugh, look away, or start fights as their houses were knocked down. When the time came for his own one-room house, Mevlut felt his heart breaking. He observed his whole childhood, the food he'd eaten, the homework he'd done, the way things had smelled, the sound of his father grunting in his sleep, hundreds of thousands of memories all smashed to pieces in a single swipe of the bulldozer shovel.

PART VII

Thursday, 25 October 2012

The form of a city
Changes faster, alas! than the human heart.

—Baudelaire, "The Swan"

I can only meditate when I'm walking. When I stop,
I cease to think; my mind only works with my legs.

—Jean-Jacques Rousseau, *Confessions*

The Form of a City

I Can Only Meditate When I'm Walking

THEY NOW ALL LIVED spread out across the twelve floors and sixty-eight apartments of a single building in Kültepe. Mevlut and Samiha's first-floor apartment was the only one on the northern façade, the side without a view. Uncle Hasan and Aunt Safiye were on the ground floor; Korkut and Vediha on the ninth; while Süleyman and Melahat were on the top floor. They would run into one another sometimes, either at the entrance, where the chain-smoking doorman stood and told off the children playing football in the street, or in the elevator, where, after exchanging a few jokes and pleasantries, they would act as if it were completely normal for them to be living all together in a twelve-story building. In truth, though, they all felt uneasy with the situation.

While he was generally happy, Süleyman felt his situation to be the most abject of all. His real desire had been for an apartment with city views on an upper floor of the thirty-story skyscraper that Hadji Hamit Vural had lovingly built in Duttepe during the last years of his life—not one here in Block D. Ninety-year-old Hadji Hamit had been accommodating—"Of course, your brother and father should come and live in my tower, too!"—but after his sudden death two years ago (which drew the minister for Public Works and Housing to his funeral), Vural Holdings' board of directors had decided there was no room for Korkut and Süleyman in the building. The brothers would spend the whole of 2010 analyzing what had gone wrong, finally arriving at two explanations: The first had to do with an end-of-year staff meeting where Korkut, bemoaning the company's enormous outlay for bribes to government officials in exchange for construction permits, had imprudently asked, "Can we really not get them for less?" Hadji Hamit's sons, it was suspected, had taken offense at his implication—"You're not bribing any ministers, you're just pocketing the money yourselves"—though Korkut had meant nothing of the kind. The second explanation put the whole matter down to Korkut's hand in the failed coup attempt in Baku, an episode that had since been rehashed exhaustively, earning him the reputation of one who organized military coups. Such a reputation would have been appreciated by previous nationalist and conservative governments, but it wasn't very popular with the current Islamist regime.

In fact, as they would later find out, the reason for the exclusion was their own father's having told Vural Holdings, "I won't sign away my land unless we all get to live under the same roof." Convincing Uncle Hasan and Aunt Safiye to leave their forty-year-old four-story house for an apartment had been a challenge for Korkut and Süleyman, and they'd succeeded only by pointing out how extensively the earthquake had bent and twisted the upper floors of the old house.

On the morning of the Feast of the Sacrifice in 2012, Mevlut could find neither Süleyman nor Korkut nor their sons in the throng gathered to pray in the Hadji Hamit Vural Mosque. Back when they'd lived on separate hills and in different neighborhoods, the cousins had always made sure to find one another so that after praying they could elbow their way through the crowd and over the carpets together to kiss Hadji Hamit Vural's hand.

They all had mobile phones now, yet nobody had called Mevlut, and so even amid that ocean of men spilling out of the mosque courtyard and into the street and the square outside, he felt completely alone. He spotted some faces of Duttepe and Kültepe folk he recognized from his middle- and high-school years, as well as some of the shopkeepers and car owners who were his neighbors in Block D, but while he managed to catch their eye in greeting, the crowd was so pushy, rude, and impatient that he felt as if he'd come to pray in someone else's neighborhood. Did any of the young men gathered here know that Hadji Hamit Vural—whom the preacher had mentioned but four or five names down from Atatürk himself as one of those men "whose tireless work had made this beautiful nation and given us the chance to live as we do"—had come to Rayiha and Mevlut's wedding many years ago and presented the groom with a wristwatch?

When Mevlut came back from the mosque, Samiha wasn't home. She must have gone upstairs to see Vediha, in number 9. Crooked-Necked Abdurrahman had come to Kültepe for the holidays and had been staying up there for the past week. There were plenty of spare rooms in that apartment (all on the side without a view), and so far Korkut and his father-in-law had managed to avoid each other, while Vediha and Samiha spent most of their days watching TV with their father. Süleyman must have put his family in the car early that morning and gone to pay his own father-in-law in Üskudar a holiday visit. That was what Mevlut had assumed when he hadn't seen Süleyman's Ford Mondeo.

Mevlut's first-floor apartment looked out onto the twelve-story building's parking area, which gave him plenty of insight into the lives of the building's retired couples, raucous young strivers, married couples whose jobs he couldn't figure out, the university-educated grandchildren of old yogurt sellers, and kids of all ages endlessly playing football among the parked cars. Süleyman's sons, sixteen-year-old Hasan and fourteen-year-old Kâzım, were the rowdiest of them all. If the ball sailed out of the confines of the lot and down the hill, these lazy young things wouldn't even run after it but rather cry out "Ball! Ball! Ball!" in the hope that someone coming up the hill might pick it up; this would infuriate Mevlut, who'd walked his whole life just to make a living.

Nevertheless, in the eight months he'd already spent in this apartment, Mevlut hadn't once opened the window to scold the kids playing football for making too much noise. Six days a week, he would leave the house at ten thirty in the morning and go to the migrants' association in Mecidiyeköy. He would sell boza most evenings from mid-October through mid-April in neighborhoods like Şişli, Nişantaşı, and Gümüşsuyu, working the city's well-heeled old four- and five-story buildings. He had severed all ties with his former neighborhood of Tarlabaşı: it was now part of an urban redevelopment zone created to encourage the construction of new boutique hotels, big shopping malls, and tourist attractions; most of its century-old Greek homes had been vacated.

While his morning tea was brewing, Mevlut watched a sheep being sacrificed in the parking lot (though he couldn't see Süleyman's rams) and leafed through the Holy Guide's posthumous book *Conversations*. He'd first found out about this volume—the back cover had a lovely photograph of the Holy Guide as a young man—six months ago from an edition of the *Righteous Path* he'd spotted in a grocer's window, and thereafter he made sure not to miss a single one of the twenty coupons he would need to get it. Mevlut believed he was partly responsible for the chapter entitled "The Intentions of Our Heart and Our Words." He opened the book to those pages sometimes and studied them intently.

In the past, once the holiday prayers were over, Mevlut, his father, his uncle, and his cousins would always walk back to Duttepe together, laughing and conversing along the way, and have the breakfast of stuffed pastries and tea Aunt Safiye would have prepared for the assembled family. Now that they all lived in separate apartments, there no longer was anyplace they could all casually gather as they had done in the room beside the kitchen in the old house. Aunt Safiye had tried to keep the spirit of those days alive by inviting the whole family over for lunch, but Süleyman was going to see Melahat's family, and his kids—who, once their holiday pocket money was secured, usually tired of their grandparents—weren't there either.

When Korkut failed to show up as well that holiday morning, Aunt Safiye launched into a long rant about the greedy contractors and politicians she believed to be at the root of all these evils and who had led her darling boys astray. "I must have told them a thousand times, 'Wait until we're dead before you knock the house down, and then you can build all the towers you want,' but they wouldn't listen. They kept saying, 'This place will come down in the next earthquake, Ma, you're going to be so comfortable in the new apartments with all the conveniences,' so by the end I just gave up. You don't want to feel like you're clipping their wings. I never fell for any of it, though. 'You'll have trees and gardens in your backyard,' they swore, 'you'll be able to stick your arm out the window and pick plums and mulberries right off the branches.' Well, we've got no plums and no mulberries; no chicks or hens; no soil and no garden. We can't live without our leaves and bugs and grass, my child. That's why your uncle Hasan has fallen ill. We don't even get cats and dogs here, with all the construction work. Even on holidays like today, the only people who knock on our door are kids asking for pocket money, and that's it, no one else, not even for dinner. My beloved house on the other hill, my home for forty years, has been demolished, and in its place they've put that huge tower, and it's all I can do not to cry when I look at it, my darling Mevlut. I made your chicken. Here, have some more potatoes, I know how much you like them."

Samiha leaped at the chance to tell them all the stories she'd heard of people who'd become utterly miserable ever since moving into the tall ugly buildings that had replaced their old *gecekondu* homes. It was no doubt hugely satisfying to bad-mouth Korkut and Süleyman right to their mother's face for the way they'd thrown themselves at the Vurals and their government-backed high-rise projects. She talked about all the families who'd left behind their gardens and the homes they'd built and lived in for forty years (just like the Aktaşes), all the difficulties they were obliged to endure after having agreed to move into the new high-rises, either for the money or because they'd been pushed into it—for lack of a valid title deed or on account of their neighborhood's having been declared a seismic hazard zone. She talked about the housewives who got depressed and ended up in the hospital; the people left out on the street because the construction was running behind schedule; those who couldn't pay off their debts to the contractor; those who'd drawn a less-than-appealing flat in the lottery and now regretted ever consenting to the deal in the first place; and all the folk who missed their trees and their gardens. She railed against the way the old liquor factory, football stadium, and municipal administration buildings (formerly horse stables) had all been heartlessly demolished and all the mulberry trees cut down. But she didn't mention how she used to meet Ferhat in secret under those same mulberry trees thirty years ago.

"But, Samiha, poor people don't want to live in dirty, freezing hovels anymore, with nothing but a stove to keep them warm; they all want somewhere clean, modern, and comfortable to call home!" said Vediha, defending her husband and Süleyman. Mevlut wasn't surprised: the two sisters met up at least twice a day for idle chats in one apartment or the other, and Vediha often said how happy she was to be living in Block D. Now that she'd moved into a separate apartment with her husband, she was finally free of having to cook for the entire family every day and refill their cups of tea, no longer responsible for patching their clothes, mending their seams, and making sure they took their pills—no longer forced to be "everyone's maid," as she'd sometimes resentfully put it. (Mevlut's theory was that being relieved of these chores was why Vediha had gained so much weight in recent years.) She did get lonely from time to time, with both her sons married now and Korkut still coming home late, but she had no complaints about living in the high-rise. When she wasn't busy chewing the fat with Samiha, she went to Şişli to see her grandchildren. After much effort, extensive research, and several fruitless attempts, she'd managed to get Bozkurt married to the daughter of a plumber who'd come to Istanbul from Gümüşdere. This daughter-in-law, a middle-school graduate, was affable and charmingly loquacious, and whenever she had errands to run, she would leave the two daughters she'd borne in quick succession with their grandmother. Turan's firstborn was a year old by then, and occasionally they would all get together at his house in Şişli. When Vediha went to Şişli to see her grandchildren, Samiha would join her, too, sometimes.

Mevlut came to feel aggrieved at Crooked-Necked Abdurrahman's rapport with his two daughters. Was he jealous of their friendship and closeness? Or was it the way Samiha would laugh when she relayed to her husband some biting remark that Crooked Neck had let slip when he was drunk? ("It's a huge mystery to me how not one, but two of my daughters could find no one they liked more than Mevlut in all of Istanbul," he'd said one time.) Or was it that his eternal father-in-law, now in his eighties, had started drinking *rakı* at noon every day and was slowly getting Vediha into the same habit, having already corrupted Samiha?

Apart from the usual stuffed pastries, Aunt Safiye had also made french fries for her grandchildren, who hadn't turned up, so Vediha was eating them all herself. Mevlut was almost certain that Abdurrahman Efendi had had his midday drink upstairs at number 9 a while ago before coming downstairs for lunch, and he was beginning to wonder whether Vediha might have had a few herself. When he left for the clubhouse to wish everyone a good holiday, he pictured Samiha having another drink with her father upstairs afterward. As he exchanged holiday greetings with his fellow Beyşehir migrants and shooed the kids who came knocking on the door asking for holiday money ("This is an office!"), Mevlut thought of Samiha at home sipping her *rakı* while she waited for him.

Ever since their second year of marriage, Mevlut and Samiha had been playing a little game. It was their way of facing the question that had informed their whole life: to whom did he write the letters? In their early days together they discussed the matter so thoroughly as to come to a sort of understanding: after their first meeting at the Villa Pudding Shop, Mevlut had conceded that he had written the letters to Samiha. His private and public views on the subject conformed easily enough. He had seen Samiha at Korkut's wedding and been captivated by her eyes. But someone had tricked him, and he'd wound up marrying Rayiha instead, but he'd never regretted it, for he'd been immensely happy with Rayiha. Mevlut was never willing to spurn the joyful years he'd spent with his first wife or insult her memory, and Samiha understood his position.

What they couldn't agree on, however, emerged whenever Samiha had a glass of *rakı,* opened one of his letters, and asked him what he'd meant when he'd likened her eyes to "bandits cutting across his path" or some such phrase. Samiha believed that this kind of question did not violate the spirit of their entente, since Mevlut had admittedly been referring to her and should therefore be able to explain his meaning. That much Mevlut accepted, but he refused all the same to enter into the frame of mind he'd been in back then.

Samiha would say, "You don't have to get into that mood again, but at least tell me how you felt when you were writing those things to me."

Mevlut would sip on his *rakı* and try to explain to his wife, as truthfully as he could, the way he'd felt as a twenty-three-year-old writing that letter, but after a point he would find himself unable to continue. One day, Samiha lost her patience with Mevlut's reticence and said, "You can't even bring yourself to tell me today how you used to feel back then."

"That's because I'm not the person I was when I wrote those letters," Mevlut responded.

After a silence it quickly became clear that what had made Mevlut into a different person was not merely the passage of time and the streaks of gray in his hair, but also the love he'd felt for Rayiha. Samiha realized that she would not be able to force Mevlut into romantic declarations; and sensing his wife's resignation Mevlut began to feel guilty about it. Such had been the beginnings of the game they still played today, these humorous exchanges that had now become a convivial ritual of sorts. At a propitious moment, either one of them—not just Samiha—would read out a few sentences from one of those faded, thirty-year-old letters, and Mevlut would explain why and how he'd written what he had.

The essence of the situation was that Mevlut would never get too sentimental when he offered these explanations, that he could talk about the young man who'd written those letters like some other person altogether. In this way, they were able to explore the subject to the satisfaction of Samiha's pride—he had indeed been in love with her as a young man—without slighting the memory of Rayiha. He would read these excerpts from the letters in a spirit of good humor and of earnest inquiry, for they were, after all, mementos from his life's most intense and exhilarating years, and they helped him discover new aspects of the past he shared with Samiha.

When he came back home from the clubhouse at dusk that day, he found Samiha sipping tea at the dinner table. She had one of Mevlut's letters in front of her. He realized that she must have decided she'd had too much *rakı* and switched to tea instead, and that made him glad.

Why had Mevlut compared Samiha's eyes to a daffodil in one of the letters he'd sent from the army base in Kars? This was around the time that Turgut Pasha had taken him under his wing; Mevlut confessed that he'd gotten some help and advice from a high-school literature teacher who was also doing his military service. Daffodils had traditionally been used to represent the eye in Ottoman literature: women used to cover up even more back then, and since men could only ever see their eyes, both court and folk literature fixated on them. Mevlut got carried away telling his wife all that he'd learned from the teacher, adding as well some intricate new thoughts of his own. When you were lured in by a pair of eyes and a face as beautiful as that, you stopped being you; in fact, you no longer even knew what you were doing. "I wasn't myself back then," Mevlut allowed.

"But none of that's in the letter," said Samiha.

Caught up in the glow of these youthful memories, Mevlut recalled the importance of that letter in particular. For a moment, he wasn't just remembering the passionate young man who'd written love letters but also envisioning the beautiful girl he'd meant them for. When he'd been composing his missives, Samiha's face had only ever appeared to him in vague outline. As he thought back to the past, though, he could see the figure of a young woman, almost a child, whose gentle features appeared to him now with exceptional clarity. This girl, whose image was enough to quicken Mevlut's heart, wasn't Samiha, but Rayiha.

He worried that his wife might realize he was thinking of her sister, so he improvised a few comments on the language of the heart and the role of INTENTIONS and accidents of fate—of KISMET—in our lives. When Samiha read about the "mysterious looks" and "captivating eyes," Mevlut would sometimes remember how these words had inspired the patterns Rayiha had embroidered on the curtains she'd prepared for bridal trousseaus. Samiha knew about Mevlut's conversations with the late Holy Guide, and sometimes she would argue that her first meeting with Mevlut had been a matter not just of fate but of intent, too. This was a story Samiha often told when they played their game of the letters. As twilight began to fall on that day of the Feast of the Sacrifice, Samiha developed a convincing new finale.

According to Samiha, the first time they had ever met was not during Korkut's wedding in the summer of 1978 but a whole six years before, in the summer of 1972, after Mevlut had failed English in his last year of middle school (Mevlut had never told Samiha about Miss Nazlı) and been forced to take a makeup exam. That summer, Mevlut had walked from Cennetpınar to Gümüşdere and back every day in order to be tutored in English by the son of a man who'd emigrated to Germany with his family. As the two boys—Mevlut and the man's son—sat reading English textbooks under the plane tree on those summer afternoons, Rayiha and Samiha watched them from afar: it was strange to see anyone reading in the village. Samiha had already discovered, back then, that her older sister was interested in Mevlut, the boy who read under the plane tree. Many years later, when she found out from Vediha that Mevlut had been writing love letters addressed to her sister, she did not tell Rayiha that they were really all about Samiha's own eyes.

"Why didn't you tell Rayiha the truth?" asked Mevlut guardedly.

Every time he heard Samiha say that she had known from the start how Mevlut had actually been writing his letters to her, it made him uncomfortable. The reason was that he believed Samiha might be telling the truth. If so, it would imply that even if Mevlut had put her name on the top instead of Rayiha's, Samiha would still never have replied, because she hadn't reciprocated his feelings at all. Especially in those moments when she sensed that her husband didn't love her as much as he'd loved Rayiha, Samiha would recite this version, so painful for Mevlut to hear. It was as if to say: "You might love me less now, but back then, I was the one who loved you less." They were quiet for a long time.

"Why didn't I tell her?" said Samiha finally. "Only because I genuinely wanted my sister to marry you and be happy, as did everyone else."

"Then you did the right thing," said Mevlut. "Rayiha was happy with me."

The conversation had taken a troubling turn, and husband and wife stopped talking, though neither of them left the table. From where they sat, they could see and hear cars coming in and out of the parking lot as darkness fell, and children playing football in the empty corner near the metal dumpsters.

"It'll be better in Çukurcuma," said Samiha.

"I hope so," said Mevlut.

They had decided to leave Block D and Kültepe and move into one of the apartments in Çukurcuma that Samiha had inherited from

Ferhat, but they hadn't told anyone about it yet. For years, the rent they'd earned from those apartments had gone into paying off the flat in which they currently lived. As soon as those debts were cleared, and they had both become joint owners of the place, Samiha had expressed the wish to leave Block D. Mevlut knew that what bothered her wasn't so much the feel and the dreariness of the apartment itself; her real motivation for moving was to get farther away from the Aktaş family.

Mevlut had worked out that it wouldn't be too difficult going to live in Çukurcuma. Getting from Taksim to Mecidiyeköy was easy now thanks to the new subway system. He could also sell quite a lot of boza in Cihangir in the evenings. People who lived in the old buildings of those neighborhoods would still listen for and hail a boza seller walking past.

It was completely dark outside when Mevlut recognized the headlamps of Süleyman's car entering the parking lot. Wordlessly, they sat and watched Melahat, the two sons, and Süleyman talking and then arguing as they got out of the car with their bags and walked into the building.

"Mevlut and Samiha aren't home," said Süleyman, looking at the darkened window as they entered.

"They'll be back, don't worry," said Melahat.

Süleyman had invited the whole family upstairs for dinner. Samiha hadn't wanted to go at first, but Mevlut had persuaded his wife to come: "We're going to leave this place soon anyway, let's not hurt anyone's feelings." He was taking more care with each passing day that his wife do nothing that might sour his relations with the Aktaş family, Fevziye, and Mr. Sadullah. The older he got, the more afraid he was of being alone in the city.

Mevlut had been in Istanbul for forty-three years. For the first thirty-five, every year that went by seemed to strengthen his bond with the city. Lately, however, he'd begun to feel increasingly alienated from it. Was it because of that unstoppable, swelling flood, the millions of new people coming to Istanbul and bringing new houses, skyscrapers, and shopping malls with them? He began to see buildings that had been under construction when he'd first arrived in 1969 already being demolished, and not just ramshackle houses in poor neighborhoods, but even proper buildings in Taksim and Şişli that had stood for over forty years. It was as if the people who lived in these old buildings had run out of the time they'd been allotted in the city. As those old people disappeared along with the buildings they'd made, new people moved into new buildings—taller, more terrifying, and more concrete than ever before. Whenever he looked at these new thirty- and forty-story towers, Mevlut felt that he had nothing to do with any of the new people who lived in them.

At the same time, he liked looking at them, the tall buildings that had mushroomed all over the city, not just on the outlying hills. When he saw a new tower for the first time, he didn't automatically recoil in disgust, like his wealthy customers who sneered at anything modern, but he was filled with an appreciative fascination. What might the world look like from the top of such a tall building? That was another reason that Mevlut wanted to go to Süleyman's dinner as soon as possible: so he could enjoy the magnificent view from that apartment for a little longer.

But owing to Samiha's stubbornness, they arrived at the top floor later than everyone else. Mevlut got a seat facing not the view but only a glass-paned cabinet that a van had delivered to Melahat three months ago. The children had already eaten and left. Apart from Korkut and Vediha, and Süleyman and Melahat, the only other person at the table was Abdurrahman Efendi, who wasn't saying a word. Aunt Safiye hadn't come, blaming Uncle Hasan's illness. Korkut and Süleyman had taken their father to a number of specialists trying to figure out what was wrong with him, and he kept having more tests. By now, Uncle Hasan was sick of doctors; he didn't want to be examined or even to get out of bed or leave his room. He detested the twelve-story building he lived in; he'd never wanted it to be built in the first place, so when he did get to go outside, he didn't want to go to any hospitals, only to his grocery store, which he thought and worried about constantly. Mevlut had worked out that the empty land behind the store, which still looked exactly as it had forty years ago, could be used to build an eight-story block with five apartments on each floor. (Uncle Hasan had fenced that land off himself forty-five years ago.)

They watched the news on TV (the president had come to the Süleymaniye Mosque in Istanbul for the holiday prayers) and didn't talk to one another at all while they ate. Uncle Hasan may have been downstairs, but still the *rakı* bottle hadn't been put out on the dinner table. So Korkut and Süleyman went to the kitchen every now and then to top up their glasses.

Mevlut felt like some *rakı,* too. He wasn't like those people who prayed more and drank more as they got older; he still didn't drink too much. But the things Samiha had said earlier when they'd been sitting downstairs in the dark had broken his heart, and he knew that he'd feel better after a drink.

Ever thoughtful, Melahat followed him into the kitchen. "The *rakı*'s in the fridge," she said. Samiha came in behind them, looking slightly embarrassed. "I'd like some, too . . . ," she said with a laugh.

"Don't use that glass, here, take this, and would you like some more ice?" said Melahat, and as always, Mevlut found himself admiring her courtesy and solicitude. Right in the middle of the open fridge, Mevlut saw a green plastic bowl full of bright red hunks of meat.

"Süleyman, bless him, had two rams slaughtered," said Melahat. "We've been distributing the meat to the poor, but there is still so much left. It won't fit in our fridge. We've put a bowl into Vediha's fridge and one in my mother-in-law's, and still there's another big one out on the balcony. Would you mind if we put it in your fridge for a while?"

Süleyman had bought the two rams three weeks ago and tied them up in a corner of the parking lot close to Mevlut's window, and although initially he'd taken care of them and fed them hay, he'd soon forgotten all about them, just as Mevlut had. Sometimes a stray ball kicked by one of the children would hit one of the animals, and the brainless tethered rams would butt their heads and kick up a cloud of dust as the kids laughed. Once, before both animals had ended up in plastic washbasins to be distributed among the poor and the four refrigerators, Mevlut had gone to the parking lot and looked one of the rams straight in the eyes, remembering with sorrow the twenty thousand sheep at the bottom of the Bosphorus.

"Of course you can put it in our fridge," said Samiha. The *rakı* had mellowed her, but Mevlut could tell from her face that she didn't like this idea at all.

"Fresh meat smells awful," said Melahat. "Süleyman was going to give it away at the office, but . . . do you have any idea who might need it in the neighborhood?"

Mevlut gave the matter some serious thought: over on the opposite end of Kültepe and on the other hills all around, a new class of strange people had moved into the old *gecekondu* homes left empty when the exciting prospect of new high-rises had caused their various owners to sue one another or the state over the stipulations in the paperwork issued by the neighborhood councilman. But the newest destitute multitudes mostly lived in the farthest reaches of Istanbul, farther out than the second ring road around the city, where even Mevlut had never set foot. These people came to the city center wheeling enormous sacks along and scavenging in bins. The city had grown so big and sprawling that it was impossible to drive to and from these neighborhoods in a day, let alone walk. What amazed Mevlut even more were the strange new buildings that had begun to rise from these quarters like phantoms, so tall that you could see them from the opposite shore of the Bosphorus. Mevlut loved to watch these buildings from afar.

At first, he didn't get a chance to take in the view from the dining room as much as he would have liked, because he had to listen to the story Süleyman was telling: two months ago, the apartments in the block that had belonged to Mevlut's sisters and mother had been sold, and his sisters' respective husbands, both men in their sixties who'd rarely left the village, had come to Istanbul for the occasion and stayed for five days on the ground floor with Aunt Safiye, who was both their wives' maternal aunt and their paternal uncle's wife. Süleyman had taken them around the city in his Ford, and now he was full of stories mocking their fascination with Istanbul's skyscrapers, bridges, historic mosques, and shopping malls. The highlight of these stories was how these elderly uncles—seeking, like everyone else, to avoid paying taxes—had taken their payment for the apartments in bagfuls of dollars, rather than going through the bank, and had never let those bags out of their sight for the duration of the trip. Süleyman got up from the dinner table and did an imitation of the two old men hunched over their heavy bags of cash as they boarded the bus that would take them home. He said, "Oh, Mevlut, what would we do without you?" and when everyone turned to him and smiled, Mevlut's mood turned sour.

There was something in their smiles that suggested they found Mevlut as naïve and childish as the two elderly uncles. It wasn't that they still thought he belonged in the village; what amused them was that he'd been honest enough to refuse the opportunity to forge some paperwork and end up owning all of those apartments himself. His sisters' husbands were diligent (they'd even brought Mevlut the title deed for his share of the small village plot he'd inherited from his father); they would not let anyone cheat them too easily. Mevlut thought dejectedly that if only he had followed Uncle Hasan's suggestion three years ago and redrawn the councilman's document, he would have owned his apartment outright and could have stopped working in his fifties.

Mevlut remained pensive for a time. He tried to convince himself not to mind too much about how Samiha had hurt him: compared with everyone else's fat, blowsy old wives, his was still beautiful, bright, and full of life. They were all going to go to Kadırga tomorrow to see his grandchildren, too. He had even reconciled with Fatma. His life was better than anyone else's. He should be happy. He was, wasn't he? When Melahat brought in the pistachio baklava, he suddenly rose to his feet. "I want to have a look at this view, too," he said, turning his chair to face the other way.

"Well, if you can see anything beyond the tower," said Korkut.

"Oh no, we put you in the wrong seat," said Süleyman.

Mevlut picked his chair up and went to sit out on the balcony. He felt dizzy for a moment, both from the height and the sheer expanse of the landscape before him. The tower Korkut had mentioned was the thirty-story one Hadji Hamit Vural had built during the last five years of his life, working on it day and night as he had done on the Duttepe Mosque and sparing no expense to make it as tall as he possibly could. Sadly, it was never to become one of Istanbul's tallest buildings, as he would have wished. But like most of the city's skyscrapers, it said TOWER in English on the front in enormous letters, despite having no British or American residents to show for it.

This was the third time Mevlut had gone out on this balcony to take in the view. On his previous two visits, he hadn't noticed just how much HADJI HAMIT VURAL TOWER I blocked Süleyman's view. Vural Holdings had made sure to sell all the apartments in Kültepe's new twelve-story buildings first and only then to build Hadji Hamit's tower in Duttepe, which ruined the Kültepe apartments' views.

Mevlut realized that he was looking at the city from the same angle now as he had that time his father had taken him up the hill when he'd first arrived in Kültepe. From this spot forty years ago you would have seen factories everywhere and all the other hills fast filling up with poor neighborhoods, starting from the bottom and working their way to the top. All that Mevlut could see now was an ocean of apartment blocks of varying heights. The surrounding hills, once clearly marked out by their own transmission towers, had now been submerged, lost beneath thousands of buildings, just as the old creeks that used to run through the city had been forgotten, along with their names, as soon as they'd been asphalted over and covered in roads. Mevlut couldn't summon more than a vague sense of each hill—"That must be Oktepe over there, and those, I guess, are the minarets of the mosque in Harmantepe"—and even that only with much thought and close attention.

What faced him now was a vast wall of windows. The city—powerful, untamed, frighteningly real—still felt unbreachable, even to him. The hundreds of thousands of windows lined up along this wall were like so many eyes watching him. They started out dark in the morning and changed color throughout the day; at night, they shone with a glow that seemed to turn the night overhanging the city into a sort of daytime. As a child, he had always liked looking at the city lights from afar. There was something magical about them. But he had never seen Istanbul from so far up. It was dreadful and dazzling at once. Istanbul could still make him flinch, but even now at fifty-five years of age, he still felt the urge to leap right into this forest of staring buildings.

If you looked long enough at the landscape of the city, however, you would soon start to notice movement at the foot of each building, the signs of activity across the various hills. The pharmaceutical and lightbulb factories and other industrial works that had existed forty years ago had been razed, replaced by this assortment of frightening towers. Beyond the concrete curtain formed by all the tall new buildings, you could still make out traces of old Istanbul, just as you would have when Mevlut first came to this spot. Here and there, high gleaming towers had already cropped up, even in those neighborhoods. But what really struck him was the sea of skyscrapers and tall buildings rising even farther beyond those limits. Some were so far away that Mevlut couldn't be sure whether they were on the Asian side of the city or on this one.

Each of these buildings shone as brightly as the Süleymaniye Mosque, and at night, their radiance formed a halo over the city, honey gold or mustard yellow. On nights when the clouds gathered low, they would reflect the city's lemon-colored light, like strange lamps illuminating it from overhead. Amid this tangle of lights, it was difficult to distinguish the Bosphorus unless some ship's spotlights, like the navigation lights of faraway planes, briefly flickered in the distance. Mevlut sensed that the light and darkness inside his mind looked like the nighttime landscape of the city. Maybe this was why he'd been going out into the streets to sell boza in the evening for the past forty years, no matter how little he earned from it.

So this is how Mevlut came to understand the truth that a part of him had known all along: walking around the city at night made him feel as if he were wandering around inside his own head. That was why whenever he spoke to the walls, advertisements, shadows, and strange and mysterious shapes he couldn't see in the night, he always felt as if he were talking to himself.

"What is it, what are you staring at?" said Süleyman, coming out onto the balcony. "Are you looking for something?"

"I'm just looking."

"It's beautiful, isn't it? But I hear you're going to leave us and go to Çukurcuma."

When he went back inside, he saw that Samiha had taken her father by the arm and was walking him toward the door. Over the past few years, senility had crept up his crooked neck, and he didn't talk much anymore, instead sitting quietly with his daughters like a well-behaved child as soon as he'd had a couple of drinks. Mevlut was surprised he was still able to take the bus from the village and come to Istanbul on his own.

"My father isn't feeling too well, we should go now," said Samiha.

"I'm coming," said Mevlut.

His wife and father-in-law had already walked out.

"So, Mevlut, I hear you're abandoning us," said Korkut.

"Everyone wants boza on a cold holiday evening," said Mevlut.

"I don't mean tonight. I mean that you're going to leave this place and move to Çukurcuma." When Mevlut didn't respond, Korkut said, "You don't really have it in you to go away and leave us."

"Oh, I do," said Mevlut.

In the elevator, with music playing constantly in the background, his father-in-law's weary, quiet demeanor saddened Mevlut, but mostly he was upset with Samiha. Downstairs in their apartment, he picked up his boza gear without saying a word to her and headed out into the streets full of joy and fervor.

Half an hour later, he'd reached the backstreets of Feriköy, feeling optimistic that the streets were going to tell him wonderful things that night. Samiha had broken his heart by reminding him that there had been a time when she hadn't loved him. In moments like this, when he felt distressed, and all of his life's failures and inadequacies seemed to surge inside him like a wave of regret, Mevlut's mind would automatically turn to Rayiha.

"Boo-zaa," he cried toward the empty streets.

Whenever he dreamed of her lately, the problem he had to solve was always the same: Rayiha was waiting for him in a palatial old wooden mansion, but no matter how many turns he took and how many doors he opened, he couldn't seem to find the door to the house where she was staying, and he just kept going around in circles. He would realize that the street he had just passed had changed again, and if he wanted to find the door he was looking for, he would have to walk along the new street, too, and so he would resume his long, measureless journey. On some nights, when he found himself selling boza in some far-off street, he couldn't quite make out whether this was a scene from that dream or whether he was in fact on that street at that moment.

"Boo-zaa."

As a child and a teenager, Mevlut had already understood that the cryptic things he noticed while walking on the street were figments of his own mind. Back then, he had knowingly dreamed all these things up himself. But in later years, he began to feel that there was another power placing these thoughts and dreams inside his mind. In the past few years, Mevlut had stopped seeing any difference at all between his fantasies and the things he saw on the street at night: it seemed as if they were all cut from the same cloth. It was a pleasant sensation, intensified by the glass of *rakı* he'd just had over at Süleyman's.

The idea that Rayiha was waiting for him in a wooden mansion somewhere along these streets could be a figment of his imagination, but equally it could be true. The eye that had been watching him from above even as he walked along Istanbul's farthest streets for the past forty years might actually be there, or it might simply have been a momentary fantasy that Mevlut had ended up believing forever. It might just be his imagination that the distant skyscrapers he'd seen from Süleyman's balcony looked like the gravestones in the picture from the *Righteous Path*—just as he had been given to feel that time had started running faster ever since a man and his son had robbed him of his wristwatch eighteen years ago . . .

Mevlut knew that every time he called out "Boo-zaa," his emotions really did spread to the people inside the homes he passed, but at the same time he also realized that this was no more than a charming fantasy. It could be true that there was another realm hidden within this one and that he might be able to walk and ponder his way into it if he allowed his secret other self to emerge. For the moment, he refused to choose between the two realms. His public views were correct, and so were his private ones; the intentions of the heart and the intentions of words were equally important . . . This meant that all the words that had leaped out at him from advertisements, posters, newspapers displayed in grocery stores, and messages painted on walls may have been telling Mevlut the truth all along. The city had been sending him these symbols and signs for forty years. He felt the urge to respond to the things it had been telling him, just as he used to do as a child. It was his turn to talk now. What would he like to say to the city?

Mevlut couldn't quite work this out yet, though he had already decided to announce it like a political slogan. Perhaps this message—which he intended to write on the city walls as he had done in his youth—should relate not to his public views but to his private world. Or maybe it should be something that was faithful to both: the most essential truth of all.

"Boo-zaa . . ."

"Boza seller, boza seller, wait . . ."

A window opened, and Mevlut smiled in surprise: a basket from the old days was descending rapidly before him.

"Boza seller, do you know how to use the basket?"

"Of course."

Mevlut poured some boza into the glass bowl inside the basket, took his money, and was soon eagerly back on his way, still trying to figure out what thought he should share with the city.

In recent years, he had been fearful of old age, death, and being forgotten. He'd never hurt anyone on purpose, and he had always tried to be a good person; provided he didn't succumb to a moment of weakness between now and the day he died, he believed he should make it to heaven. Recently, though, a fear that he may have wasted his life—which he'd never felt in his youth—had begun to gnaw at his soul, despite all the years he still had ahead of him with Samiha. He wasn't sure what he could say to the city on this matter.

He walked all along the wall around the cemetery in Feriköy. In the past, the strangeness in his mind would have pushed him to go inside, even though he used to be so afraid of dead people and graveyards. Nowadays he was less scared of cemeteries and skeletons, but he was still reluctant to walk into one of these historic graveyards because they brought to mind his own death. But a childish impulse made him look over a slightly lower section of the wall and into the cemetery, where he saw a rustling that alarmed him.

A black dog, followed shortly by another, was heading deeper into the cemetery. Mevlut turned around and started walking briskly in the opposite direction. There was nothing to fear. It was a holiday, and the streets were full of well-dressed people of goodwill, smiling at him as he walked by. A man around his own age opened a window and called out to him and then came down with an empty pitcher into which Mevlut poured two kilos of boza, which cheered him up, and made him forget all about the dogs.

But ten minutes later, two streets down, the dogs cornered Mevlut. By the time he noticed them, he realized that two others from the pack were behind him, and that he wouldn't be able to back off and slip away. His heart sped up, and he could not remember the prayers his father's holy man had taught him, or the advice the Holy Guide had given him.

When Mevlut tiptoed past them, however, the dogs didn't bare their teeth or growl at him, nor was their demeanor threatening in any way. None of them came to sniff at him. Most ignored him, in fact. Mevlut was profoundly relieved; he knew this was a good omen. He felt the need for a friend he could talk to. The dogs loved him now.

Three streets, one neighborhood, and many eager, hopeful, and kindhearted customers later, Mevlut was amazed to find that he was almost out of boza, when a third-floor window opened and a man called out, "Boza seller, come on up."

Two minutes later, Mevlut was at their door with his boza jugs, on the third floor of this old building with no elevator. They showed him inside. There was that dense humidity that formed when people kept their windows mostly shut and their stoves and radiators turned low, and he detected a heavy dose of *rakı* fumes, too. Yet this was not a table of querulous drunks but a group of family and friends delighting in the festivities. He saw loving aunts, dignified fathers, gregarious mothers, grandfathers, grandmothers, and an indefinite number of children. As their parents sat at the table and talked, the children kept running around, hiding underneath and shouting at one another. These people's happiness pleased Mevlut. Human beings were made to be happy, honest, and open. He saw all this warmth in the orange light from the living room. He poured out five kilos of his best boza as a number of children observed him with interest. A gracious woman, around his own age, came into the kitchen from the living room. She was wearing lipstick and was without a headscarf, and her dark eyes were huge.

"Boza seller, how good that you came upstairs," she said. "It was good to hear your voice from the street. I felt it right inside my heart. It's a wonderful thing that you're still selling boza. I'm glad you're not just saying, 'Who'd buy it anyway?' and giving up."

Mevlut was at the door. He slowed down on his way out. "I would never say that," he said. "I sell boza because it's what I want to do."

"Don't ever give up, boza seller. Don't ever think there's no point trying among all these towers and all this concrete."

"I will sell boza until the day the world ends," said Mevlut.

The woman gave him a lot more money than what he usually charged for five kilos. She gestured as if to say that she didn't want any change, that this was a gift for the Feast of the Sacrifice. Mevlut slipped quietly through the door, went downstairs, and stopped in front of the main entrance to throw his stick across his shoulders and pick up his jugs.

"Boo-zaa," he cried when he was back out on the street. As he walked toward the Golden Horn, down a road that felt as if it were descending into oblivion, he remembered the view he'd seen from Süleyman's apartment. Now he knew what it was that he wanted to tell Istanbul and write on its walls. It was both his public and his private view; it was what his heart intended as much as what his words had always meant to say. He said it to himself:

"I have loved Rayiha more than anything in this world."

2008–2014

Index of Characters

All page numbers in **bold** refer to first-person narratives.

Chronology

1954	Migrants from the villages in the district of Beyşehir begin to arrive in Istanbul in significant numbers to find work and sell yogurt.
6–7 SEPTEMBER 1955	Non-Muslims in Istanbul are attacked; shops are looted and churches vandalized.
1957	Mevlut Karataş is born Mevlut Aktaş in the Cennetpınar village of the Beyşehir district, in the province of Konya.
27 MAY 1960	Military coup.
17 SEPTEMBER 1961	Former prime minister Adnan Menderes is executed.
1963	Brothers Hasan and Mustafa Aktaş leave their village to find work in Istanbul.
1964	In response to fighting between Turks and Greeks in Cyprus, thousands of Greeks living in Istanbul are expelled from the city by the Turkish government. Many homes in Tarlabaşı are left empty.
1965	Brothers Hasan and Mustafa move into the one-room house they have built in Kültepe, without a permit. Hasan's elder son, Korkut, joins his father and uncle in Istanbul. Aided by Korkut, Hasan and Mustafa fence off two plots of land in Duttepe and Kültepe.
1965	Construction begins on Duttepe Mosque.
1965	There are rumors of an imminent amnesty for unlawful construction work, and people scramble to

	erect more unauthorized buildings and homes. The conservative Justice Party, led by Süleyman Demirel, wins the general elections.
1966	Crooked-Necked Abdurrahman stops selling yogurt and makes a permanent return to his village of Gümüşdere.
1968	Hasan Aktaş's younger son, Süleyman, joins his father, brother, and uncle in Istanbul.
DECEMBER 1968	Hasan, Korkut, and Süleyman leave the house they have been living in with Mustafa and move into the house they have just finished building in Duttepe without a permit, on the land they fenced off in 1965. Hasan Aktaş's wife, Safiye, joins the rest of her family in Istanbul.
SUMMER 1969	Mustafa Aktaş goes to Beyşehir and changes his own and his family's surname to Karataş.
SUMMER 1969	Duttepe's first outdoor cinema, Derya, opens its doors.
LATE SUMMER 1969	When his father returns to Istanbul, Mevlut Karataş goes with him to work and continue his education.
12 MARCH 1971	The army generals' memorandum to the president and the elected parliament of the Turkish Republic pushes the government to resign.
APRIL 1971	Mevlut meets Ferhat.
1972	At the Elyazar Cinema, Mevlut watches a pornographic film for the first time.
30 OCTOBER 1973	Opening of the first bridge over the Bosphorus, also known as the Atatürk Bridge.
JANUARY 1974	Formal inauguration of the Duttepe Mosque, on the day of the Feast of the Sacrifice.
MARCH 1974	Mevlut begins to stalk a woman he calls Neriman.
20 JULY 1974	The Turkish army lands on Cyprus and occupies the northern part of the island.
MID-1970S	Big companies begin to distribute yogurt in glass and plastic bowls, which start to become increasingly common.
MARCH 1977	Mevlut puts political posters up on walls.

APRIL 1977	Duttepe and Kültepe clash in a war between right- and left-wing militants.
1 MAY 1977	Thirty-four people are killed in Taksim Square in events surrounding the commemoration of International Workers' Day.
MAY 1978	Hasan Aktaş sells the land he fenced off in 1965 with his brother, Mustafa, to Hadji Hamit Vural.
SUMMER 1978	Mevlut grows a mustache.
AUGUST 1978	Korkut and Vediha's wedding.
OCTOBER 1978	Mevlut moves out of his father's house. He goes to live in Tarlabaşı with Ferhat, and they work together as waiters in the Karlıova Restaurant.
19–26 DECEMBER 1978	One hundred and fifty Alevis are killed in the Maraş massacre organized by Sunni militants, secret government services, and ultranationalist paramilitary groups.
1979	*Milliyet* columnist Celâl Salik is murdered. Ayatollah Khomeini leads the Islamic Revolution in Iran.
LATE 1979	Korkut and Vediha's first son, Bozkurt, is born.
SPRING 1980	Mevlut leaves for twenty months of compulsory military service.
12 SEPTEMBER 1980	The army launches a coup d'état while Mevlut is with the tank brigade in the small northeastern town of Kars, on the Soviet border.
LATE 1980	Korkut and Vediha's second son, Turan, is born.
JANUARY 1981	Mevlut's father, Mustafa Karataş, dies. Mevlut comes back to Istanbul for the funeral and starts renting out his father's home in Kültepe.
17 MARCH 1982	Having completed his compulsory military service, Mevlut returns to Istanbul and moves into a rented apartment in Tarlabaşı.
2 APRIL–14 JUNE 1982	The Falklands War between the United Kingdom and Argentina.
17 JUNE 1982	Mevlut goes to Gümüşdere village and runs away with Crooked-Necked Abdurrahman's daughter Rayiha.
SUMMER 1982	Mevlut sells ice cream for the first time.

SEPTEMBER 1982	Mevlut and Rayiha's wedding.
OCTOBER 1982	Mevlut begins to sell cooked rice and chicken.
NOVEMBER 1982	The results of a referendum back the 1982 Constitution, and the leader of the 1980 coup, Kenan Evren, becomes president of the Republic.
APRIL 1983	Mevlut and Rayiha's first daughter, Fatma, is born.
APRIL 1983	The ban on abortions is lifted until ten weeks into a pregnancy. Married women seeking an abortion must provide proof of their husbands' consent.
EARLY 1984	Samiha runs away with Ferhat.
AUGUST 1984	Mevlut and Rayiha's second daughter, Fevziye, is born.
26 APRIL 1986	After the Chernobyl nuclear disaster, clouds carrying nuclear waste reach Turkey.
1986–88	The new Tarlabaşı Avenue is built.
FEBRUARY 1987	The Gloria Theatre burns down.
18 JUNE 1988	Assassination attempt on Prime Minister Turgut Özal.
3 JULY 1988	Opening of the second bridge over the Bosphorus, Fatih Sultan Mehmet Bridge, named after Ottoman sultan Mehmed the Conqueror.
EARLY 1989	Mevlut loses his rice cart to the municipal police. Around this time, he also meets the Holy Guide. Ferhat begins to work as a meter inspector for the electricity board.
4 JUNE 1989	Tiananmen Square protests in Beijing.
SEPTEMBER 1989	Mevlut starts working as manager of the Binbom Café in Taksim.
9 NOVEMBER 1989	The Berlin Wall falls.
1990–1995	The breakup of Yugoslavia introduces a period of civil war in the Balkans.
1991	The production and distribution of electricity in Turkey is privatized.
17 JANUARY–28 FEBRUARY 1991	The First Gulf War.

14 NOVEMBER 1991	In the Bosphorus, a ship from Lebanon collides with a ship from the Philippines and sinks along with the twenty thousand sheep it is carrying.
25 DECEMBER 1991	The Soviet Union is dissolved.
24 JANUARY 1993	Radical, secularist columnist and journalist Uğur Mumcu is killed by a bomb placed inside his car.
2 JULY 1993	Thirty-five leftist liberal secular intellectuals are killed when political Islamists burn down the Madımak Hotel in Sivas.
1994–95	The separatist Kurdistan Workers' Party (PKK) and the Turkish army are at war. Villages are burned down and many Kurds resettle in Istanbul.
EARLY 1994	Ferhat meets Selvihan.
FEBRUARY 1994	Mevlut loses his job at the Binbom Café.
27 MARCH 1994	Recep Tayyip Erdoğan wins the local elections and becomes mayor of Istanbul.
30 MARCH 1994	Mevlut is mugged by a man and his son while out selling boza at night.
APRIL 1994	Mevlut and Ferhat open the Brothers-in-Law Boza Shop.
FEBRUARY 1995	Rayiha becomes pregnant for the third time.
MARCH 1995	Korkut gets involved in an attempted Turkish coup against the president of the Republic of Azerbaijan, Heydar Aliyev.
12–16 MARCH 1995	Unrest in the Alevi quarters of the Ghaazi and Ümraniye neighborhoods of Istanbul results in the deaths of twelve and five people respectively.
EARLY APRIL 1995	The Brothers-in-Law Boza Shop closes down.
MID-APRIL 1995	Mevlut starts to work as a guard in a parking garage.
MAY 1995	Rayiha dies while trying to induce a miscarriage by herself.
LATE 1995	Upon Ferhat's suggestion, Mevlut begins to work as an electrical meter inspector.
EARLY 1996	Süleyman marries Mahinur Meryem. They have their first son, Hasan.

NOVEMBER 1997	Ferhat is murdered.
1998	Süleyman's second son, Kâzım, is born.
JUNE 1998	Mevlut begins to work in the Beyşehir migrants' association.
FEBRUARY 1999	Having waged a guerrilla war on the national government for fifteen years, Kurdish leader Abdullah Öcalan, who had been hiding in Syria for many years, is captured by Turkish forces.
SUMMER 1999	Süleyman asks Mevlut to allow Bozkurt to marry Fatma.
17 AUGUST 1999	An earthquake in the Sea of Marmara, close to Istanbul, kills 17,480 people.
LATE SEPTEMBER 2000	Mevlut's elder daughter, Fatma, goes to university.
JUNE 2001	Fatma meets Burhan at university. They soon get married and move to Izmir.
11 SEPTEMBER 2001	New York's Twin Towers collapse in an attack by Al Qaeda.
SEPTEMBER 2001	Mevlut's younger daughter, Fevziye, elopes with Erhan, a taxi driver from Kadırga.
LATE 2001	A hotel in Aksaray hosts Fevziye and Erhan's wedding ceremony.
2002	Mevlut encounters bottled boza for the first time.
MAY 2002	Fevziye's son and Mevlut's grandson Ibrahim is born.
AUTUMN 2002	Mevlut and Samiha get married.
3 NOVEMBER 2002	Recep Tayyip Erdoğan's Justice and Development Party (AKP) win the general elections and form a government.
MARCH 2003	A ban preventing Recep Tayyip Erdoğan from taking office is lifted, and he becomes prime minister.
20 MARCH 2003	Invasion of Iraq.
28 MARCH 2004	The AKP win local elections in Turkey.
7 JULY 2005	Fifty-six people die in London after a series of attacks on subway stations and public buses organized by Al Qaeda.

19 JANUARY 2007	The Armenian journalist Hrant Dink, outspoken about the Armenian genocide, is shot dead.
22 JULY 2007	The AKP win the general elections.
29 MARCH 2009	The AKP win the local elections again (gaining ground in Duttepe and Kültepe).
APRIL 2009	Mevlut sells his father's house to buy an apartment.
17 DECEMBER 2010	A street vendor sets himself on fire in Tunisia, leading to a series of the protests and revolutions known as the "Arab Spring."
MARCH 2011 AND THEREAFTER	Hundreds of thousands of Syrian refugees flee to Turkey.
12 JUNE 2011	The AKP win the general elections.
MARCH 2012	The Karataş and Aktaş families move into their new apartments.

A NOTE ABOUT THE AUTHOR

ORHAN PAMUK won the Nobel Prize for Literature in 2006. His novel *My Name Is Red* won the 2003 IMPAC Dublin Literary Award. His work has been translated into more than sixty languages.

A NOTE ON THE TYPE

This book was set in Garamond, a type named for the famous Parisian type cutter Claude Garamond (ca. 1480–1561). Garamond, a pupil of Geoffroy Tory, based his letter on the types of the Aldine Press in Venice.

The version of Garamond used for this book was first introduced by the Monotype Corporation of London in 1922. It is not a true copy of any of the designs of Claude Garamond, but can be attributed to Jean Jannon, a Protestant printer working in Sedan in the early seventeenth century, who had worked with Garamond's romans earlier but who was denied their use because of Catholic censorship. The italic is based on the types of Robert Granjon, a type cutter and printer active in Antwerp, Lyons, Paris, and Rome from 1523 to 1590.

Composed by North Market Street Graphics,
Lancaster, Pennsylvania

Printed and bound by Berryville Graphics,
Berryville, Virginia

Designed by Cassandra J. Pappas